REBECCA SULLIVAN AND THE BOOK OF SECRETS

To Manuel
Hope this is a good read for you.

John S. McWha.

J S MCWHA

Published by J S McWha

Cover design by Thu-Lieu Pham
Ebook Formatting by Guido Henkel

This work is fictional and all references to places, people, events, characters or anything of that nature are the product of the author's imagination. Any similarities to places, events or anyone living or dead are entirely coincidental.

I dedicate this work to my love, sweet Helene.

Without your encouragement and patience, this book would not have seen the light of day. All my love, Johnny.

CHAPTER 1

THE LIGHTS SCORCHED HER EYES FROM THE INSIDE, sounds pierced her mind with the intensity and power of a minor earthquake. Rebecca had her eyes closed now, and was pressing the fingers of her right hand against her temple in an effort to stem the flow of pain—this was the most horrid episode yet. The large older man sitting in the row of seats across from her on the old electric trolley bus leaned towards her; he came so close that the young girl felt his energy pushing on hers.

"Do you need help, my dear?" he said as his large hand caressed her knee through the flimsy material of the blue leggings under her green-tartan skirt.

Rebecca immediately smelled alcohol—it surrounded all of her senses and filled her nasal passages so intensely that she could taste it at the back of her throat.

"No…no thank you." She choked and spluttered a little, while turning her head discreetly and raising her hand to her mouth. "I am fine," she said with a half smile as she slowly pushed her pack-sack towards the window and moved away from him. Sliding her knee from under his thick fat fingers, she edged along the bench-seat towards the window, smiling and trying desperately not to hurt his feelings. The man moved away from her, satisfied, and feeling good that he had offered to help.

Rebecca hated that she had to travel so far to go to school. Thankfully, she only had two more years to go, she thought, as she looked out the window of the bus into the miserable wet darkness. The rain was being lashed against the window of the bus by a strong wind that made it difficult to see how close it was to where she was getting off. Rebecca strained and squinted as she attempted to look out the driver's large window to see where she was. The young girl frantically turned to the passenger window and wiped the condensa-tion from it, not wanting to miss her stop. She looked carefully and saw the *Shop and Go* store close to her Gran's street. She was nearing her destination, but she thought it odd that there were many flashing lights ahead, close to where she was getting off the bus.

The rain slammed against the bus driver's window as the wipers rushed back and forth, clearing a path for him to see. It looked like they were at sea in a storm, not driving down the main road navigating rush hour traffic, she thought. The stop was getting closer—she sat nervously on the edge of her seat waiting to pull on the overhead wire to let the driver know she wanted to get off. The lights were becoming brighter—she became aware of a lot of activity nearby. It was becoming clear that an accident of some kind had occurred, and most of the passengers were eagerly piled at the windows to catch a glimpse. Rebecca closed her eyes and hoped that no one was hurt. As they got closer, the bus slowed and eventually stopped, and the driver opened the doors to let people off. Rebecca moved in behind an old lady who was carrying a couple of bags in one hand and trying to open her umbrella with the other—so she reached around and held onto her bags for her.

"Let me help?" she asked with a smile as the old woman struggled.

"Thank you, dear," came the reply. "I always seem to get caught in the rain this time of year," she said, laughing.

"That's okay—my gran does too." They chuckled together, while other passengers were peering out the windows, trying to see what was going on in the road across from them.

"That looks like quite the commotion," one woman commented to a friend, "there must be a fire or something in the road around the corner. I can see a yellow and orange glow," she added excitedly. Rebecca looked up after hearing the women's comments, and then realized the problem was on her street.

"I have to go now," she said to the old woman, "I live on that street." She waved back to the woman as she hurried across the main road and turned into her street. Rebecca had no reason to believe there was anything wrong at her house, but she wanted to be with her gran as quickly as she could, just the same. As she turned into her street, there were four or five cars and trucks that lined the road in various states of disarray—with lights flashing in all directions and sirens going off indiscriminately. The rain didn't help—she tried to cover her head with the sweater she had tied around her waist. Rebecca started to get a funny feeling in her stomach the closer she got to her house. Home seemed to her to be uncomfortably close to the activity, and to where she knew her gran lived. The teenager was approximately one hundred yards from her house when she saw the firemen going into her front garden. She saw huge billows of dark-grey smoke covering most of the upper half of the house—it was spewing out from every window. Fear hit her so hard in the stomach that she felt like she wanted to throw up, right then and there. Rebecca started to run towards home, letting her sweater and pack hit the ground—her hair falling behind her as if trying to escape the trauma that was likely waiting for her.

"Gran! Gran!" Rebecca's tears mixed easily with the rain that was now pelting her in the face, and especially her eyes—so much so—that she could hardly see the front gate or who was directly ahead of her.

From out of nowhere, a force stunned her. She was pulled backwards, as she heard a man's voice speaking calmly in her ear.

"There's no use in your going in there. There is nothing left." The arms of the firefighter were powerful, and they held onto the girl, as easily as a boy would hold onto his puppy.

Before Rebecca could even speak, a woman took her from the arms of the fireman, and gently held her close. The voice whispered in a gentle yet strong tone.

"Do you live here, sweetheart? What is your name?"

Rebecca could not speak. She followed the many thoughts that seemed to tumble and fall inside her head aimlessly. The only words she kept hearing were those of the fireman telling her 'there was nothing left.' She could not process the meaning behind his words. Inside her head, she heard her own voice claiming, he must be mistaken, he must have the wrong girl. Her mind reasoned that she must've entered the wrong front gate, and that Gran would straighten it all out and tell her that it was just an honest mistake. She waited and waited, patiently, as she was being held. Her feet reached for the floor, determined to take her inside the house. Then, as if it were just another incident in the nightmare, the water stopped and the firemen began to roll up all their equipment into the two huge red and black trucks.

"Where is my gran?" Rebecca spoke, while her head rested on the woman's shoulder. There was a distinct smell of primroses coming from the woman's hair as Rebecca spoke—the craziest thing occurred to her—it was much better than the alcohol smell that had oozed from the large man on the bus. The young girl found herself having the most bizarre conversation in her mind, that she couldn't seem to stop or even interrupt.

She was eventually able to return to the present after she heard the woman's voice, once more, asking her what her name was. By this time, Rebecca found that she was in, what seemed like, the back of a large unmarked police car with blackened windows that made it difficult to see out of clearly—it was parked on the road outside her house. The door of the vehicle, however, was slightly ajar, enough that there was a one-inch-wide gap where she could see what was left of her home. Her heart sank—the sight and smell of burned wood and other chemicals stung her senses.

"Rebecca, my name is Rebecca," she spoke quietly to the woman seated next to her. "Who are you?"

"I am with the emergency services and I am here to help you," the woman reassured her. "I am sorry. I have to let you know that the old woman who lived here has died. The woman—your gran—probably died from smoke inhalation. I'm really sorry." She held onto Rebecca as the words filtered through to the young girl. "Do you have someone you can stay with while an investigation is carried out to determine what has happened here?" The woman put her hand on Rebecca's shoulder as she spoke. Rebecca thought for a moment, wondering what she'd meant by 'what happened here?'

"Yes, I can stay with my friend," she whispered. "She lives over there in the brick house." Rebecca pointed without looking—it was the only thing she could think of at the moment without raising suspicion. The officer rolled her window down and saw half a dozen people outside, watching the events. They were standing outside a red brick house across the street, about four doors down. The officer smiled at Rebecca and nodded. "Okay, you go there and I will call in on you tomorrow to figure things out." She paused for a moment. "Are you sure you are okay?" The woman seemed genuinely concerned for Rebecca. "I can easily find a safe place for you to stay, you know."

"No thanks. I will be all right. Thank you all the same." The officer helped Rebecca out of the vehicle and made sure the girl had all her things with her. She watched as Rebecca walked to her friend's house.

There was no mistaking the fact that Rebecca was not going to let child services take her into custody. She was aware enough to know that she looked older than her sixteen years, and lying about her friend's house being the place she could stay, was the only way she could think of that allowed her to remain free. The main thing she focused on was what to do—now that she had no one left, no family she could turn to. It remained to be seen if the officer would accept the lie. Rebecca swung her backpack onto her shoulder and clung to her rain soaked sweater—the one the policewoman had picked up for her off the road—as she slowly headed to the house across the way. How was she going to get through this next few minutes, she wondered. The smell of burning wood persisted in attacking her mind. She needed to think fast. The people at the house were not friends of hers or friends of her gran. She didn't have a clue why she'd chosen those particular people. She had to stop wasting time chastising herself—it was imperative that she convinces the officer that she was going to her friend's house.

The girl turned briefly to look back at the officer, and saw that she was talking into a handheld radio. She could see the small green light of the radio in the distance, flashing on and off, as she spoke. At the very instant that Rebecca saw the flashing light, she had a strong feeling that her mother was with her. She didn't understand why she was having such an undeniable feeling, but it was there nonetheless. Just as she was trying to figure out why her mother had come into her head right then, Rebecca saw an older woman standing behind two other onlookers at the gate of the red brick house. The young girl had the definite feeling that she was heading in the right direction; Rebecca had a high sensitivity to such things and was not very often mistaken. She wondered if there was a connection between her mother and the old woman as she continued to walk towards the gate. She was concerned that the officer—who was watching her might want to come over to the red brick house to talk to the people standing in front of it. The policewoman needed to establish that Rebecca was okay—once she was satisfied that she was in no danger, she could leave. The young girl had no choice but to start talking to the women at the gate. Before she could say anything to the two women, a small wrinkled hand reached between them and grabbed Rebecca's wrist, and a soft voice could be heard.

"Please, come through the gate dear girl. The officer will then be satisfied enough, and leave you alone, for sure." The tiny old woman pulled Rebecca between the younger women—who only stared at her—as she was moved through the gate and past some small hedgerows. "Be sure to wave back at the officer or we may never get rid of her." Rebecca was stunned and totally confused, but she did not resist. It was either the old woman or child services—no contest, she thought. The two younger women closed their ranks around her as Rebecca was ushered along the small pathway towards the cottage, that was situated in the middle of the property, about fifty feet away.

"I know this must all seem strange to you, my dear, but everything will be explained soon—just keep moving." The speed, at which the old woman navigated through the shrubs and trees on either side of the path, amazed Rebecca.

"I do know you—don't I? Now that I think of it, I do remember someone like you, but it was years ago. I think my gran told me you left...or...something—you look awfully familiar to me, don't you?" she was struggling to recall the events that had passed so many years before, and at the same time, trying to navigate the path and keep up with the tiny woman. As she made it into the cottage, the old lady turned and smiled.

"My name is Finnula, but you can call me Finn dear—and you're correct, you do know me. I was—I *am*—a good friend of your gran's. I did leave many years ago, but I returned today to say goodbye to my old friend, and to help her move beyond these earthly confines." She steered Rebecca to the living room near the front of the cottage. Before she knew it, Rebecca was seated near the old woman—with her belongings on her lap, she listened intently to what Finnula was telling her. There was a familiar odor in the room—like roses or lilacs—she couldn't quite tell which.

"What is that…that smell? It is so nice, so familiar." She was speaking to no one in particular as she looked around the small but cozy room. "I really know that smell," she said in a half whisper. Rebecca turned to the old lady, pausing briefly before she spoke, "What did you say about my gran? I didn't understand what you meant. I thought I heard you say you helped her move *on* to somewhere—where did she move? Only, the police lady said she died in the fire." The girl waited.

"Yes, you are correct. I did say something like that. However, this is not the time to go into the *specifics* dear." The woman's tiny hand touched Rebecca's—in a sweet but reassuring way—as she stood in front of her. Her full-length cotton dress swung delightfully as she moved. "I have something for you, dear." Finn reached into the top drawer of a dresser that stood against the wall, directly below the window. The window looked out over the front garden, where the two younger women still stood, as if guarding the entranceway to the cottage.

Rebecca felt so confused. She began to think she should leave, before she found herself in a situation she'd rather not be in, and she wasn't too thrilled being called *dear* all the time. However, she knew she needed a place to go *to* before she made any rash decisions, she reasoned.

"It's all right, dear," Finnula said, as she reached into a cedar box that had beautifully-crafted carvings on the outside, that looked to Rebecca, like nothing she had ever seen before. "I will point you in the right direction." She then turned to her holding a beautiful golden medallion and chain. "Now dear, please put this around your neck. It will help you make it through—what it is…you must do." She handed it to the girl.

"This is incredibly beautiful." Rebecca held it in her hands. The object glowed, and the chain felt like it moved in her hands as it shimmered—but that was not possible, she thought.

Rebecca was stunned at the beauty of the item Finn had given her, and in addition, it struck her that the woman had answered her concerns about having a place to go to—but that couldn't be possible either the young girl thought. Rebecca locked the clasp of the chain, as the medallion fell down, beneath her blouse.

"I really don't know if I should be accepting this from you, Finn. I hardly know you, and anyway, why did you give it to me?" she couldn't resist touching the gift around her neck. Finnula just smiled.

"Erm, how did you...?" Rebecca wasn't able to finish asking Finn how she knew what she was thinking.

"Don't worry about all that is ahead of you, Rebecca, you will have friends when the time comes." Finn sat close to her on a well-cushioned rocker. "There are many avenues, open to all of us, in this *free will* zone—many choices open up as we travel." The small woman sipped from a flowered cup—her eyes sparkling as she spoke.

"What do you mean, Finn?" she was on the edge of her seat at this point. "All this is like...like so confusing. It makes no sense. I don't know what you are saying." Rebecca took a breath, and sat back, closing her eyes. "All I know is my gran is gone, and I have no one I can go to, and nowhere to stay."

Finn swayed back and forth on her chair—sipping from the cup. "First, Rebecca, we will eat—and second, you will stay here tonight." She stopped rocking and put her drink down.

"Soon my girls will be done cooking, then we can all catch up, and I will explain things to you—things you will need to know." Rebecca opened her eyes, but before she could respond with more questions, Finn had disappeared from the room.

Rebecca was left to wonder about what the old woman had said and what it had to do with her. She couldn't fathom why they had even met. The only reason she'd spoke to the strange woman—she thought—was because it was the only avenue that had presented itself to her while the policewoman had been watching her every move. She suddenly realized what she had just thought; it was exactly how Finnula had explained that things worked, by avenues opening up for people to make choices in the *free will* zone, she exclaimed in her head. The girl immediately got to her feet and headed for the kitchen—even though she had no idea where it was. She listened for noises as she entered the hallway, and followed them. Rebecca came to the doorway of a room near the back of the cottage, and gingerly poked her face, across the threshold. She was careful not to enter fully—avoiding the bright lights that hit the walls, illuminating them.

" Hi, I've been waiting to meet you," came a voice from behind her. Rebecca jumped forward with surprise, pushing the door wide open, revealing herself to Finn and her daughter. She tried desperately to catch her breath—she wanted to yell at the girl in the doorway—.

"*Geez!*" she breathed," you scared the *crap* out of me!" Rebecca rested her hands on the large wooden table that held plates of food, cups, cutlery, breads, and jugs of fruit juice amongst other things—all the necessities for a typical family meal. As she slowly gathered her breath, the younger girl stepped towards her and rested a kind hand on her back—she rubbed the spot between Rebecca's shoulder blades with such a gentleness she had not known for a long time—while the older taller girl just leaned against the doorjamb with a big smile spread wide across her face.

"Rebecca, you're just in time to eat with us." Finn wiped her hands on a beautifully crafted, kitchen towel and sat at the table near the fire at the far end of the room. "Come, join us." Her daughters were already seated at the table and were helping themselves to the food.

The girl slowly moved towards them—she sat at the vacant chair next to the younger daughter, and in between, her and Finn. The elder of the girls—with a smile still painted across her face—offered a plate of food to Rebecca.

" I'm Rose. I helped make this for you." She lifted the plate a little higher to encourage Rebecca to take it. "You will like it very much."

"Thank you…huh…Rose." Rebecca was still annoyed at her, but she took the food, and placed it in front of her. The young girl continued to look down at the food. "Finn," she said quietly, "what do you have to tell me—because I am so overwhelmed right now and I don't know what I am doing here?" The young girl's eyes slowly began to fill.

"Everything is okay, Rebecca. I will tell you what I can after we eat, dear." Rose and her sister remained still while their mother spoke. "Now you must eat because you cannot travel on an empty stomach." Finn gave her a warm smile and motioned to them all to eat. The younger sister nudged Rebecca's arm and passed the breadbasket to her.

"Hi, Rebecca, have some bread—I made it especially for you today—you will *love* it." She reached for the jug of juice that was in the middle of the table. "Oh, and my name is Roisin. I have been looking forward to meeting you for...well...forever." Her eyes sparkled as she laughed, and that made Rebecca brighten up a little.

"Nice to meet you, Roisin. I don't remember you living here while I was growing up—but I don't remember much of that time, anyway." She looked down and began to eat—hoping that they would not sense how uncomfortable she was—even though they were very nice. Rebecca always found it difficult being with people, because she never ever, felt that she belonged or fit in with them. The sisters were right, Rebecca thought, the food did taste really good. It had been a long time since she'd eaten food that tasted that good. Her gran was not fond of cooking she remembered—and as she did—the tears wanted to flow from the teenage girl once more, but she was able to hold them back.

After the meal was over, Finn took Rebecca by the hand. "Come with me and we will discuss why you were sent to me."

Rebecca couldn't help feeling that she was being infused with the love and warmth of a great friend—as she was being led back to the cozy living room of the cottage—a friend who wanted the best for her, and wanted her to know she would never be alone, and that she would always be taken care of.

"I really want to thank you for all that you have done for me, especially with the police," Rebecca continued to talk as she walked behind Finn, "I still don't know why you appeared and began helping me?" She followed the old woman into the living room. "How come my gran never mentioned you if you were such good friends?" She wanted information and thought it is time for Finn to reveal all she knew.

Finnula gestured to the girl to sit down. "I must tell you some things, but the future must be yours alone to experience." The old woman walked to the window and watched the sun setting through the clouds—it was time for her to deliver the words to the young girl that would set in motion the beginning of something wonderful, and yet, potentially catastrophic. "At first light, you must gather your things and begin your journey. You must go to New York City and find a place to stay for a while. When the time is right, you will meet the people who are destined to become an important part of your life." Rebecca could only stare at the strange woman as she tried to process what she'd heard. It was all too nutty for her to absorb and twice as absurd.

"There is no way I want to live in NYC. Apart from the crime, and the amount of money I would need to be able to afford a place there, it is full of…of…psychopaths, sociopaths, and an assortment of egomaniacal crazies in general. I don't even know you at all Finn—so how can you expect me to do the things you suggest?" she had a point.

Finn took in a slow easy breath and prepared to explain as much as she dared. "I was with your gran when she left. We have been friends for longer than you can appreciate. Your gran asked me to set you on your way—as *safely* and as *prepared* as I could—so that is what I wish to do. I know you have questions, so ask, and I will answer as best I am allowed." The old woman rested and waited.

Rebecca thought for a moment. She struggled with the whole idea behind the conversation, to begin with. Her hand grasped the gold medallion around her neck as she thought about what she should ask the small woman who sat in the chair across from her. Unconsciously, Rebecca lifted the gold piece higher, twisting and fingering it as her thoughts deepened—suddenly, as she saw it in front of her eyes, she stopped twisting the necklace.

"I'd like to know why you gave me this medallion?" she twirled the object, spinning it on the chain—the soft lights of the small room reflected off the yellow metal, casting warm sun-colored images wherever they landed.

"The medallion you have accepted to wear belonged to a good friend, who programmed it, to protect the wearer. I know you probably wonder—protection from what? That is not relevant right now. But I will tell you this, your path will bring you truth and peace, should you choose to embrace it."

Rebecca stopped caressing the object, and let it fall inside her clothing, once more. "What did you mean when you said you were *with* my gran when she left?"

Finn knew the answer to that question would be difficult for Rebecca to accept. "When your gran decided to leave, she triggered an ancient contract that brought the onset of your journey, and everything connected to it. She cried out to the universe to allow her to return to her *light-body*, and thus, initiate the agreement. When this was set in motion, the darker forces were also notified and automatically began to search for her, and attack her light, as it moved through the transition process." Finn deliberately waited—pausing—so that Rebecca could interject if she wanted to. The tiny woman continued, "I was also summoned to fulfill my part in the agreement, which was to guide you to the first step of your journey." She looked at the girl with curiosity and compassion.

"I don't understand. I just want to know why you are helping me?" She truly had no clue as to what was going on. It all seemed too ridiculous to believe. "I want to know where my gran is—if she is dead or not?" Rebecca felt the onset of another migraine— this one was really going to hurt, she thought.

Finn left her chair and went over to the girl. "How long have the headaches been coming?" There was no answer. Rebecca only put her fingers to her temple and lowered her head "About a month—I would say—am I right?" Finn touched the young teenager's back lightly as she asked the question.

"Uh...huh." Rebecca was trying not to let the migraine take hold.

"Try to breathe slowly and deeply—it will help with the control. The migraines were the beginning of the wake-up call that would let you know a change was to come. When your gran created the *thought* of her desire to leave, the universe initiated the process that allowed her to be taken, and that was when you started getting the pains. This is irreversible—you will meet everything and everyone necessary for your journey to play out. Dear, you must not fight against it. The best way to minimize the discomfort is to embrace it at every turn. This is the only way, trust me."

"Trust you—I…I don't even know you, really." she tilted her head back and rested it on the cushioned top of the chair support. Her eyes were closed. "All I know is, my mom died when I was really small and now I don't have my gran. I…I am alone and young with no idea of how to survive without them."

Finn explained as best she dared what Rebecca must do.

"Dear, there is a wonderful time ahead for you. You need to be strong and courageous. When you awake in the morning, I will be gone, but my girls will give you my instructions and they will point you in the right direction," Finn reached behind the couch that was located under the window. "This will help you on your journey," she handed Rebecca her bag from the house.

How did you…? Where did you get this?" she was astonished at the sight of her travel bag. "This was in my closet at home."

"Yes dear, and your gran had prepared it before she left." Finn smiled a warm smile. She knew Rebecca was beginning to understand—just a little.

Rebecca opened the bag and immediately smelled her gran wafting out from it. The distinctive odor filled her nostrils and she instinctively inhaled as much of it as her lungs would allow, straining until her lungs hurt, as they pushed against her ribs. The young girl looked at the items in her bag that her gran had touched, and she gently touched each one, until her eyes could see no more. As the tears rolled down her cheek, silently, Finn gently spoke.

"This is the beginning—not the finish. You must be strong Rebecca—all is not as it seems." Finn lifted the bag from her and placed it next to the bedroll that her daughters had prepared for their guest. "Sleep now, dear. You must try to manage the grief and prepare mentally for the journey ahead. Stay focused and trust your inner voice—it is the only thing that you can trust; it will never betray you, but you must talk to it dear." With that, she kissed the girl on the cheek and left her to sleep. Rebecca was too overcome with sadness to speak. She lay down on the mattress and closed her eyes.

When she woke, light coming through the small window above her shone on her face, bringing her a sense of calm and peace. There was no sign of Finn, only the bag on the floor next to her, and the medallion around her neck were reminders of the old woman. Rebecca closed her lids a couple of times to gain her bearings and reached for her clothes; she dressed quickly. The events of the previous night flooded her brain. As she pulled her top over her head, thoughts rang around her mind, causing her stress to return. The only thing she wanted to do was go straight to the house, hoping the previous day was just a nightmare.

The front door to the little cottage was ajar, so she pushed on it a little to see if anyone was on the other side. Maybe the sisters were in the garden. She could see some sunshine through the crack in the door. As the door moved open, Rebecca leaned forward and saw there was nobody around, and she softly tiptoed up the path beside the cottage to the small wooden gate that led to the street. The young girl reached for the gate.

"Where do you think you are going at this early hour?" Rebecca's heart jumped into her throat. "You didn't even say goodbye!" Rose was right behind her with that familiar smile across her face that was really beginning to irritate the girl.

"How the hell do you manage to scare the crap out of me all the time?" she said while catching her breath.

"Ah—don't be mad" she said still grinning. "It's just the way I am—I always do things like that when I like someone," Rose said, as she looked deep into Rebecca's eyes. "I have been waiting a long time to meet you— as have a lot of people. We are just fortunate that our mother knew your gran and so we got to see you in person." As she spoke, she handed Rebecca a note. It read:

'Please embrace the path you are destined to walk, dear. Speak your mind and the truth whenever you are able, and stay as safe as you are able. Go to your gran's house and wait there for the taxicab that will come for you. The driver will honk twice and wait. Good fortune will follow you Rebecca—you can be sure of that dear'.

With that, Rebecca said goodbye to Rose and walked through the gate. Rose pushed the gate closed after Rebecca left, smiling all the while, her eyes sparkling with envy. For she knew some small details of the prophesy, and she wished she was going with the young girl.

Rebecca began to relax thinking the episode with the old woman and her daughters was at an end. The street was clear. It was always that way early in the morning. She walked across to her gran's house, not wanting to really see it, but knowing she must for her own peace of mind. She hurried through the gate, not wanting to be seen, and ran up the path to the beautiful oak door that was now warped by the heat of the flames and charred black as coal. The inside odor of the burnt material almost choked her as she held her sweater to her face. The tears began to flow as Rebecca saw a place she once knew of as her sanctuary, but that she no longer recognized.

The young girl held her head in the sweater as she rested against the staircase to get her bearings and compose her thoughts. The loud honking of the taxi pierced her mind—startling her as it pulled up outside what was left of the house. Rebecca instinctively held her breath, and pushed her back against the rail of the staircase that steadied her. There was no way she was going into child services until she was legally able to live on her own, now that all her family was gone, she thought. She was ready to go to the bus station and trust that her mom and gran would watch over her while she went to New York. She understood that she had to disappear until after her eighteenth birthday—2 years from that summer. Rebecca picked herself up, and her luggage, and left the house for the last time. She stood on the cold, smoke darkened, concrete slab that was the porch, and shivering, as a cold wind lapped at her legs through the thin blue leggings. Rebecca took one final look up at her old bedroom window as her eyes filled with tears once more, stinging as they welled up. She felt so alone, but she turned and made her way to the car, wiping her eyes so the driver would not be concerned and possibly ask too many questions—ones she knew she couldn't answer. Her journey was about to begin, and with that, hopefully, the healing that was needed for her to finally say goodbye to her family.

CHAPTER 2

THE HOSTEL ON GRANVILLE STREET—IN THE DOWNTOWN area of the city's east side—was not as welcoming as she thought it might be. There were people hurrying in every direction. Rebecca arrived at the hostel around 10:35 am, which was good, because it was relatively calm which helped her ease into the starkly different surroundings compared to what she was familiar with. She made her way to the front desk at the end of the lobby where a desk clerk was waiting to check people into the rooms. She put on the bravest smile she could muster and walked, confidently, up to the clerk.

"Hi. I need a room, please," she said. "My name is Rebecca Sullivan." He looked at her, and then he looked at her luggage, and very slowly and deliberately turned to the computer in front of him.

" Yes, there does seem to be a room available in the computer system," he mumbled without even bothering to look up. "How long would you need it, and will you be paying with cash or credit?" He waited for an answer.

Rebecca was far away inside her mind wondering what she was doing coming to such a place where the people didn't seem that nice. She missed her mom and gran desperately. She looked back toward the desk where she met his eyes glaring at her. She vaguely heard the question he had asked reverberating in the back of her mind.

" Oh, sorry. I will pay cash." she felt annoyed at the way she apologized to the clerk and vowed to stop it, but she knew that the two wonderful people whom she loved dearly had taught her to respect others, even if they didn't show the same courtesy. After she paid him, the clerk handed her a key. It was yellow and looked quite used.

"How do I get to the room?" she asked with a smile, still trying to continue to be respectful.

"Up the stairs, turn to your left, and it is on your right halfway down," the clerk answered without looking up at her.

"Thanks," she said, picking up her luggage and disappearing up the stairs.

The room was on the second floor. It was not that horrible and it didn't smell of anything bad—that was something she was concerned about—but it could have used a bit more color than the beige and brown painted walls. It had a sink that seemed clean enough to her, however the microwave looked like it had seen better days. Rebecca was determined not to let the situation cause her to spiral into a depressive episode; she'd had enough of them in the last 6 months to last a lifetime. She sat on the bed and laid back. It was not the softest bed in the world but it wasn't the worst she had slept on. She remembered the time she'd gone backpacking in the mountains with friends. Her body was battered by the time it was over.

As she lay there, she began to relax. It felt good to be peaceful and calm. However, it wasn't long before peace gave way to nervousness, and eventually, worries and anxiety. Thoughts of survival, finances, and future plans all came flooding into the peaceful space in her mind. Rebecca knew she had to get a job somewhere but what could she do, she had no experience with work of any kind, and as for future plans—she had none. By her calculations, the money she had left would last for three or four weeks at the most, and if she was really careful and did not eat too much every day, it might last a little longer. Her situation was looking very bleak, and all these thoughts racing around in her head didn't help the situation. She felt like she was spinning out of control and with no one to help her. She breathed in slowly, trying to gather calmness and peace, while trying to stabilize her thoughts and feelings. She sat on the bed looking around. The single room she was given was no bigger than the pantry at her gran's house and the bathroom was really small too. Rebecca began to feel strong emotions welling up in her again and this time they were uncontrollable. She collapsed on the bed, sobbing till she fell asleep.

She entered the dream state almost immediately, dreaming right away, but not the kind of dreams she normally had; these were lucid dreams. Rebecca was awake in the dream. She could control what she said and did. As she lay on the bed, motionless, inside her mind there was enormous activity. She was walking with other beings that were talking about various things relating to her future and past, yet they seemed to be occurring simultaneously, in what she thought was the present moment. They spoke to her about many things that were going to happen in her future. Each being that related to her did so in turn, like a well-orchestrated ballet. At some point, she remembered that she tried to speak and found she couldn't. It wasn't because her mouth wouldn't work but when she opened it to say something no sound came out—she knew they heard her thoughts. The beings with her filled her mind with information in the form of a simple knowingness that was the weirdest feeling she had ever had.

Rebecca awoke to a loud bang. She jumped up from the bed thinking the door was being forced open; however, it was only someone knocking. She held one hand to her head where she was feeling some pain and screwed her eyes closed, trying to become fully awake.

"Who is it?" she yelled. There was no reply. She dragged herself to the door. She was still connected somewhat to the dream state she was in. The door was pulled open, and in the hallway, stood a young woman about 20 years old. Her hair was the first thing Rebecca noticed—it was beautiful natural blond with long curls that hung about her shoulders and swung as she spoke. She had the most beautiful emerald green eyes that were as vibrant as the fiddlehead ferns that grew at the back of Rebecca's house in early spring. She wore a short denim skirt with a studded belt around her waist and a white lacey top that accented her figure, to say the least. "Yes, can I help you?" she asked in a sullen voice, still rubbing her head where she felt a dull ache.

The young woman smiled for what seemed like an eternity. "Hi, my name is Alison. I'm your neighbor. I live across the hall." Her eyes sparkled as she turned her head to point to the room across from Rebecca's.

Rebecca was silent for a moment, and while offering a half smile, she rubbed her left eye. "Oh, right...well, my name is Rebecca.

Nice to meet you," she said with a slow deliberate tone, indicating her uneasiness.

"I know we don't know each other," Alison said, " but I am living alone, as I think you are, right? Anyway, I thought we could get to know each other and become friends, you know, to make living in this dump bearable, and increase the girl power." At that point she threw her arm in the air, albeit, with a degree of false assuredness.

Rebecca looked at her with her head cocked to one side and lips parted, but saying nothing, as she attempted to understand what was going on.

"Want to go grab a coffee or something?" Alison's voice indicated she was feeling a little desperate and her expression pleaded with Rebecca to say yes. All the time Alison was speaking, Rebecca could only visualize the many mind-numbing episodes of school plays she endured to please her mom during the year she died. Her mom always told her that she was beautiful and she would benefit from spending time with other young girls her age.

Finally, Rebecca spoke. " Well, I suppose I could use a coffee now that I am awake," she said, with a sort of soft, gentle, compassionate tone as Alison stood in the doorway holding her hands together as if she were in pain. Rebecca sounded confident but inside she was terrified. She hardly ever had to make important decisions like going somewhere with a total stranger in a strange town. Maybe things are about to change, she thought.

"Great! Can I come in and wait?" she didn't give Rebecca a chance to answer as she walked passed her through the doorway. Alison's energy filled the room. Rebecca noticed immediately the powerful force that seemed to flow from her. Instinctively, Rebecca pulled in her own aura for protection. She had done this before while standing in line at the super market when certain people moved in close behind her.

"Would you like something to drink?" Rebecca asked, knowing full well she only had water and some old tea bags left in the room by the previous tenant.

"No thanks," she said. "Why don't you get ready and we'll go down to this little coffee shop I know and swap stories instead," she giggled.

"Okay," Rebecca replied, a little apprehensively. "Give me about ten minutes to get ready." She needed the time to pull her thoughts together and come to grips with the dream she had just come out of. Rebecca wanted to make sense of what fragments she could remember of the dream that might be responsible for her headache. But for now, she found herself beginning to like the idea of having a friend. Alison seemed to be in the same predicament as Rebecca, due to the fact that no one in their right mind would choose to live in that place if they weren't forced to. Even though Alison did seem to be a little out there, and more than a little odd, Rebecca liked the idea of spending time with someone with such high energy.

Alison looked around, made herself at home, and lit up a cigarette. There was something about Alison that didn't seem to fit. Rebecca could sense this but had no idea what it could be. She couldn't put her finger on it, so she decided to dismiss it as paranoia at being in the big city.

"Nobody smokes nowadays, Alison. Don't you know how many carcinogens are sucked into your body every time you inhale?" Rebecca made a face of utter disgust as she waited for a response.

"Yes, I do know, but I think life was meant for living on the edge." Alison grinned back at Rebecca, looking for a response. "I could walk outside this building heading to the coffee shop with you and be hit by a truck. What do you think of that?" she continued. She took a huge drag on the cigarette and blew smoke rings, while looking Rebecca straight in the eyes, without flinching.

Rebecca continued to get ready and wondered if she'd made a mistake in agreeing to go out with her. There was something about Alison that resonated with Rebecca, a kind of bad girl energy that she often wished she had. She wondered how it would feel to disregard rules, just do whatever she wanted because it felt good. She finally decided it would be good for her to make a friend, especially in these times of stress and uncertainty. She convinced herself that if things got too weird she would just stop going out with her.

"Okay, I'm ready…let's go to this café and relax for a while. It's been a rough week." She looked over at Alison.

"That's the way to look at life, Rebecca," she said with a level of confidence that didn't seem to fit with someone who was in the same boat as Rebecca.

The hallway outside the room was busy. There were a few teenage boys holding a conversation outside another of the rooms a couple of doors down. As the girls passed them, one young guy made a remark to his friends about them. The guy looked to be about 18, and he obviously had a nice up-bringing judging by his clothing and display of self-esteem that was out of place there.

"Hey, Frank, maybe we can take these two for lunch—what do you think?" He didn't take his eyes away from the two girls as his friend responded.

"Maybe—although, doesn't look like it's lunch they want." Their sick laughter echoed down the hallway. Alison didn't even miss a step as she passed them. Rebecca slid to the wall furthest away from them, using Alison as a shield.

When they reached the front desk, the lobby was packed with people. Alison skipped through the crowd, while Rebecca continually apologized when she inadvertently bumped into someone, as she made her way to the door.

"Hey, Reba! Don't worry about them, they're just New Yorkers, they like to bang into people, makes them feel alive." Alison screamed at the top of her lungs back through the door of the building. Rebecca could feel her face lighting up with sun burnt embarrassment.

"Alison, you embarrassed me in there. Those people kept looking at me all the way to the door!" she exclaimed.

"Oh, don't be so sensitive, Reba, it's only a bit of fun," Alison laughed.

"Who is this Reba person? I like to be called Rebecca, if you wouldn't mind. How would you like me to call you…err…Ally or something?" Her face was still glowing red and Alison just chuckled.

They walked down the street, sidestepping the people walking toward them. Rebecca wondered about her friend. Where did she come from? Why was she interested in making friends with someone she knew nothing about? Rebecca was not at all used to the intensity with which life in the city was lived. The energy was too harsh and the pace too fast for her liking. She was starting to miss the tranquility of the simple village she had left. They reached the café and sat at a booth near the window. Alison took off her coat and stood beside the table, leaning over to whisper something in Rebecca's ear.

"This one is my treat to celebrate the start of a great friendship." She gave her a big smile as she headed to the coffee bar.

Rebecca sat, looking out of the window at the busy street, resting her chin in her hand. She was slipping into the carefully preserved memories of her young life with her mother and grandmother. She did not want any of them to fade at all. She needed them to be as fresh in her mind as the day they were made or she feared the dark emptiness that surely would consume her without them. The young girl felt something touch her arm, something that instantly brought her back to the café.

"When we dwell on painful memories, no matter which of our loved ones call to us, we condemn ourselves to relive that pain and sorrow—better to forget and move on." Alison had returned with the coffee.

Rebecca's expression of sadness left and in its place was the sweet gentle personality of the young teenager. "Thanks, Alison." She took the coffee and put it to her lips. "How did you know what I was thinking about?" There was a quizzical look on her face.

"I've seen that look many times. Everyone with that look always ends up depressed, angry, or dead eventually. I don't think sad memories are worth feeling that bad over." She continued to pour sugar into her coffee. There was something strange about this that stuck in Rebecca's mind but she didn't have the energy to search for the meaning. They continued to get to know each other over the afternoon, swapping stories and experiences that new friends typically do.

Rebecca returned to her room at the hostel later that afternoon. She felt really uncomfortable and uneasy but she did not know why. That night she woke from a nightmare that was so disturbing it bordered on night terrors, forcing her to remain awake for fear of entering the nightmare again if she closed her eyes for even a second. As she sat on the bed, she picked up a book from the side table next to it. Half way through page one a blinding flash of light ripped across her vision. She knew what was coming, and before she could finish the thought, the flashback memories came flooding into her head. She didn't move; she could only remain stone faced as they ran through her mind. The girl was helpless as the images illuminated her consciousness. She was powerless to prevent them from being played on the screen behind her eyes no matter how hard she struggled to think of other things. After a couple of minutes, she sprang from the bed, and holding her hands tightly across her mouth, she screamed as loud as her lungs would allow. This had no effect on the images as they cascaded through her mind, one automatically linked to the other in an array of visual and psychological sensations. Rebecca was scared to death. The images had never been this bad before. She immediately thought 'brain tumor.' Was it her destiny to die a horrible cancerous death like her mom? Her heart skipped a beat as she leaned against the wall, forcing herself to breathe.

The frightening thing was that it seemed to her what was happening was originating from outside—as well as inside her head—but she could make no sense of it. She couldn't think straight. The pictures were beginning to change. She was now seeing strong and vivid colors running through the images, and something else occurred to her, she didn't recognize what she was seeing. This terrified her. How could her head be filled with memories she didn't ever experience? Eventually, the images dissipated, and after she calmed down and the episode passed, she put a comforter around herself and lay down on the bed, trying to fathom what was happening to her. She wondered whether she was losing her mind, or worse, was she possessed. Rebecca wondered about the flashes of white light that were passing through her mind when her eyes were closed. She wanted desperately to find sleep, but the fear kept her awake until she had no more strength, and then sleep eventually found her. As she slowly drifted into deep sleep, the last thing on her mind was, how was she going to survive without a job? She must spend the next day figuring things out. She pulled the comforter closer and finally slipped away. It had been a long while since Rebecca was able to sleep, uninterrupted, but that came to an abrupt end with banging on her door once more.

"Come on wake up! Hey, Rebecca, lets go! It's morning," someone yelled outside her door. Rebecca thought she was still dreaming. The voice outside sounded just like her mom. She must be dreaming. The words she was hearing were the exact words her mom used to shout from the hallway at her house when she was late for school.

"Who…who is it?" she stammered. Rebecca tried to unwrap herself from the comforter that had a hold on her as tight as a straight jacket.

The voice continued, "Hey you, don't you remember we said we would go to town this morning?" It was Alison. Rebecca had forgotten she'd said that.

"Oh…Alison, it's you."

"Yeah…it's me!" she yelled, "Get dressed. I have coffee. C'mon, open up."

"I'm still in bed, Alison…very tired…sorry." She attempted to beg out of the arrangement. She definitely decided she didn't want to have any new friends after all. Especially with all the problems she was having with the headaches and flashbacks. However, Alison was not letting her get away that easily.

"Rebecca, open the door. I am spilling the coffee—can't hold on much longer. It will spill all over the hallway carpet and I will get thrown out of my room." She made such a commotion outside the door that Rebecca had to get out of bed and let her in before other guests complained.

"Come in. I am getting in the shower." Rebecca didn't even look at her as she opened the door. She just turned around and slowly headed for the bathroom. "I will be about ten minutes."

Alison surveyed every inch of the room, comparing it to her own across the hall. "Your room looks bigger than mine." As she yelled, she took the opportunity to rifle through Rebecca's things. She was looking for something specific. It was not a random search. She had planned it.

Rebecca couldn't help thinking, as she stood in the shower, that having a friend like Alison might not be the best thing for her after all. However, she also realized that being alone right now was not a great situation either. As she stood under the shower, she noticed the energy around her building up again. There was a growing sadness swirling around her. It felt really familiar. Rebecca continued to wash her body, only much slower now. She knew this feeling. It was the onset of another episode about to begin. The headache arrived, and next, the expected flashes of light. Instinctively, she held the side of her head waiting for the searing pain that typically followed. The next thing she knew the glass shower door became a shimmering curtain of energy. The colors were incredibly vivid, blue, yellow, gold, and green.

"Alison! Come in here, quickly! Look at this!" she squealed. Rebecca leaned against the back wall of the shower stall and waited.

"What are you yelling about? Come on, let's go," Alison said as she entered the bathroom. "Look at what?" Alison turned to look at everything in the room but saw nothing out of the ordinary. "Stop playing around and let's go to town," she insisted as she left the room.

"Rebecca was amazed. She was watching the shower door acting like a lace curtain in the wind, with blazing colors changing constantly. "You don't see anything wrong with the shower door?"

"No! It's a door. Now, can we go?" Alison shouted. She decided that what she was looking for was not in the room. "I am going down to the lobby, Rebecca. Meet you down there okay?"

After Rebecca finished her shower, she dressed in her favorite top and best pair of jeans and boots and then headed to the lobby. The hallway outside her room was buzzing with people, mainly young people about her age. They were all milling around a room 3 or 4 doors down. Rebecca was curious and checked it out.

"Hi, what's going on?" she asked the guy leaning against the wall outside the room.

His eyes were a little bloodshot and he seemed out of it. "Hey, aren't you the one who lives across from Alison? Where is she man? She owes me!" He came toward her with his hand outstretched, trying to grab her coat. Rebecca backed away and quickly continued down to the lobby.

By this point, she was sure it was not a good idea to hook up with Alison. It sounded like a friendship with her would lead to trouble for sure.

"Rebecca! Over here." Alison was sitting on a fire hydrant at the entrance to the alley a few doors down, lighting up a smoke. Rebecca made her way to the alley, intent on making up some lie to get out of going to town. Before she could say anything, Alison spoke.

"I have got the best news ever, I called my brother Gary, and he's in town for the weekend." She was jumping up and down like someone possessed.

Rebecca didn't have the heart to dump her. She knew how much family means to people. "Hey, that sounds fantastic."

Alison caught her breath. "So, he wants to meet us in town and have coffee," she smiled, waiting for Rebecca's response.

"That sounds great," she said, attempting to sound enthused.

Alison straightened her skirt and belt. "There's a cab on its way. It'll be here soon."

The sun was shinning and there was a fresh crisp breeze blowing. Rebecca wished she had worn the sweater her gran bought her last Christmas. She turned her attention to Alison to prevent any memories from surfacing that would reduce her to tears as it typically did; she didn't think Alison was the type who would understand or cope with that.

"So Alison, when did you see your brother last?" she said, trying desperately to focus on something other than her family.

" Oh...must be about a year ago this December." Her tone had definitely changed. She turned to Rebecca looking her full in the eyes. "Why?"

Rebecca noticed that Alison's eyes looked really dark. There was definitely something sinister about the way she looked at her.

"No reason, just a friendly question. You seem tense. Is there anything wrong?" Rebecca hated playing these games of manipulation. They were so immature.

"No...just a bit hung over." There was an uncomfortable pause. She continued to finish her cigarette. "Gary is dying to meet you. I told him you are really something."

Rebecca didn't like the sound of that and now she was probably going to have to fight off her brother. The cab arrived and they both climbed in the back seat.

Rebecca sat as close as she could to the door without seeming obvious. She just wanted to get this over with and go back to her room.

"Where are we going to meet your brother...Gary, is it?"

"Yes—Gary," Alison was beginning to thaw a little. "He said for us to go to the downtown area at Robson and Burrard Street. There is a coffee club there with live music. We can enjoy the band, have coffee, and make new friends...you know, have a blast." She sounded more enthusiastic now, which didn't mean much to Rebecca, considering what she had witnessed so far regarding her obvious mood swings.

"Yeah, sounds great!" Rebecca said, hoping the time would go really fast. She had already made her mind up that when she returned to the hostel, she would lay low until Alison forgot about her. This was not the way she was raised to deal with uncomfortable situations or people, but by this point, she didn't care. Alison was too strong and aggressive for Rebecca. She wanted to be peaceful and walk through life doing what was required of her until she could be with her mom and gran again, however long that might take.

CHAPTER 3

THE CAB RIDE WAS NOT THAT BAD AND REBECCA SAW some sites of New York before they reached the club. She decided to make the best of the situation rather than suffer through it. Alison was very cheery during the journey and pointed out some good places to visit while in town.

"Look, Rebecca, there's the zoo. I think it is world famous, you know," she said, while fixing her top and adjusting herself, knowing full well the driver was eying her in the rear view.

"Nice." She said as she watched him ogle her. "Where are we Alison? What part of the city are we in?" Rebecca was feeling apprehensive about going all this way just for coffee. They had been in the cab for about ten minutes so far and she wanted to let Alison know she was becoming nervous.

"Almost there Rebecca. It's only a couple of blocks from here." There was an uneasiness developing between them and they both knew it. "My brother will show us a good time. He always does." Alison tried to ease the tension between them.

Rebecca's ears pricked up. "What do you mean, he always does? You said you haven't seen him in close to a year?"

There was an awkward silence for a second or two. "I meant he always did. I suppose he hasn't changed in that department. He always made sure he enjoyed himself," Alison said, laughing in an attempt to smooth things over, but Rebecca just gave a half smile. There was something going on but the young girl couldn't put her finger on it.

The cab halted at the corner of the block. Traffic was heavy but the driver didn't seem to be too concerned about his cab causing a traffic-jam. He just shouted the fare without even turning around, and put out his hand toward the back seat, waiting.

"Keep the change," Alison said.

Rebecca saw her give him almost twice the amount of the actual fare. How could she be so casual with money if she didn't have much of it? That was a question burrowing deep into Rebecca's consciousness. There was definitely more going on here than just making a new friend. The young girl was glad this was the last time she would see Alison.

Alison's brother was waiting at the door of the café. Gary was tall, slim, and dressed in black from head to foot. That made Rebecca a little uneasy. She looked at the sign above the doorway, 'The Coffee Club.' It was in blood-red neon letters. This was no café, more like a nightclub—but Alison was there to see her brother, so Rebecca went along and reasoned that it mightn't be that bad.

"Alison, it's good to see you again. It has been a while," he said quietly, while opening the door to the club.

The weird thing was, Alison didn't say anything, didn't hug him—she just walked on by, right into the club as if she had been there before. "Follow me, Rebecca," she said, as she was walking passed her brother.

There was a staircase that went down. Rebecca couldn't quite see how far down, or what was there. All she could see were vague colored lights reflecting off the walls on the way down the stairs, and she heard the sound of music playing and people talking and laughing. When they reached the bottom, Alison turned left and walked into the room where the music was coming from. She was obviously familiar with the club. Rebecca followed.

There was an empty booth with a reserved sign on the table close to the stage, where the band was playing. " This is a good spot to see the band," she said, taking a seat at the booth. Rebecca sat opposite.

She noticed that she was feeling a little lightheaded when she sat down and hoped it wasn't another episode coming on. She held her breath and didn't move. The feeling persisted. She knew what was coming next, the pain and the flashes of light and color.

"Are you okay, Rebecca?" Alison asked, as she beckoned to the waitress.

"Yeah, it's just a migraine, I think." She lied again; it was becoming a habit. She held one side of her head in her hand.

The waitress arrived with a tray. She was nicely dressed. "A carafe of your best white and…?" Alison beckoned to Rebecca.

I don't have much money, Alison. How much is this going to cost? Can we afford to stay here? Let's go to the mall? I'll bet it's a lot cheaper than this place. Besides, I have a migraine. The headache hadn't manifested but she wasn't going to admit that to Alison.

Alison looked at her, expressionless. "Don't worry about the money. We are taken care of in this place."

Rebecca decided to comply to avoid a scene. Obviously she didn't need to worry about being an underage drinker in that place. No one seemed to care. Besides, she knew she looked older than her age. If she was being taken care of, and didn't really have a choice, than she was going to enjoy herself. Last Christmas her gran gave her a drink of vodka to celebrate the holiday that made her feel good. She wanted to feel good again.

"A small vodka and orange juice please." She continued to rub her head, eyes closed.

Just as the waitress left, Gary arrived. He leaned over to Alison and whispered something in her ear that made her eyes sparkle. She gave him a nod and he left, not bothering to acknowledge Rebecca at all.

"Everything okay? We're not getting thrown out or anything?" Rebecca asked in an attempt to find out what he had told her.

Alison looked at her, cocking her head to one side. "Oh Rebecca, try not to be so suspicious. Enjoy yourself. My brother just told me that we could stay as long as we like, no problem. Right now, I have to go upstairs to talk to someone. I will be back in about ten minutes. You just relax and enjoy the music, okay?" Alison left, disappearing across the room and up the stairs.

The drinks came and Alison didn't leave any money on the table. Rebecca was afraid the waitress was going to get mad. "I'm sorry, my friend was supposed to—she was interrupted by a man's voice coming from behind her. Rebecca turned to see it was Gary, Alison's brother

"I'm paying for the drinks. Put them on my tab," he said in a quiet voice. "May I...?" He looked at Rebecca, indicating he wanted to join her.

She wasn't thrilled but how could she say no. She looked around for Alison but there was no sign of her.

"Sure...err...Alison will be back soon. I am not staying that long. I have to go search the want-ads for work." She laughed trying to hide her nervousness. Rebecca didn't get a good feeling from him, more like creepy weird-guy vibes.

He placed his drink on the table next to hers and sat. "Do you like it here, Rebecca?" His arm rested on the back of the booth seat.

Rebecca decided that was enough. She knew what he wanted as all women must. Smiling, Rebecca picked up her drink and stood up. "When your sister returns, tell her I am exploring the rest of the club. It was nice meeting you, Gary." Rebecca walked away. She could feel him watching her. It sent a cold shiver down her back.

The club was quite the place. Rebecca was curious about the type of people who came here. She walked toward the band. They were playing a really good rendition of an old rock song. The average age seemed to be early twenties, she guessed, as she made her way to the back of the large room at the far end of the dance floor. Alison was nowhere to be seen which made her angry and more nervous. Rebecca lifted the glass to her mouth, and realized she had finished her drink, and found the reason why she was feeling more relaxed. She wasn't going to waste this, she thought. The music wasn't bad and there were more than enough people there to make it fun. Rebecca spotted a nice looking guy watching her, so she decided to enjoy herself, just like Alison had suggested.

The alcohol was relieving her nervousness and anxiety and she wanted to experience some feel good energy. She stood at one of the tables that were around the columns near the dance floor. It wasn't long before the guy she saw watching her came closer. He seemed a little cautious but eventually made it to the same column by the third song.

"Hi," he said. "Would you like to dance?"

She looked into his eyes and saw a gentleness that she had missed since she had left her hometown. "Sure." The alcohol was providing the false courage she was feeling, even though she'd had only one drink. She wasn't used to its effects. They moved to the dance floor as the next song had begun to play.

Rebecca was about to step onto the dance floor when someone tapped her shoulder. "Hi, I'm back." Alison had a big smirk on her face. "I have got a job interview!" She took a big slurp of her wine. Rebecca mouthed the words of apology to her friend. He just smiled, shrugged his shoulders, and headed the other way.

"Wow, that's great!" Rebecca was genuinely happy for her. Anyone who is unemployed knows how depressing it is having no job, no money, and no prospects. "How about me? Can you ask your friend to get me one?" she begged, smiling.

Alison snickered. "Maybe, who knows what might happen after my interview but for now let's celebrate." Her energy was infectious and Rebecca hadn't had anything to celebrate in a long time. She spent the rest of the night dancing, drinking, and meeting new friends—mostly Alison's friends but they were new to Rebecca and that's all that counted.

Rebecca enjoyed herself so much that night that she no longer felt alone and thought she might be a bit hasty in dumping Alison. She decided to give their friendship another shot.

When Gary dropped them off at the hostel later that night, he mentioned to Alison that he needed her to meet him the following day at his place around lunchtime. She agreed and seemed to know what it was for.

Rebecca climbed out of the car and waited for Alison to say goodbye to her brother. "Hey Alison what kind of job are you interviewing for tomorrow?" she had a feeling the answer was going to be vague.

Alison took in a long breath and sighed. "Oh…I don't really know yet, but whatever it is, I just know it will be a good one and pay really well."

Rebecca had a feeling Alison already knew what it was but wasn't going to say. They both laughed as they walked through the entrance of the hostel.

"Wasn't that a fantastic night, Rebecca? Dancing, drinking, and guys—what a great combo." She turned the key in her door across the hall. "Well good night. See you in the morning. My interview is at nine." The door closed before Rebecca could turn from opening her door to cancel out on the interview. She was too tired to pursue Alison about it. She just wanted to sleep. She was feeling pretty tipsy and a little woozy. Rebecca leaned against the inside of the door after closing it. She took a deep breath and let out a long sigh. She wondered what good could come from the developing friendship with Alison. Although, Alison was a fun person to go out dancing with, she also showed how her moods could change in a flash. Rebecca made her way across the room to her bed. She undressed and climbed in.

When she woke up the next morning, she felt something was different. There was a heaviness that enveloped her. She took a shower, thinking it would make her feel better—it was more like she prayed it would wash the heaviness away. However, her prayers were not answered and she began to feel worse. The headaches she experienced had returned, and with them, flashes of light shot through her head like a thousand shooting stars across the night sky. Rebecca slumped to the floor of the shower. "Why me?" she groaned. "Hadn't there been enough bad things happen to me already? Rebecca put her head in her hands under the shower. Closing her eyes, she imagined her mom was with her. She needed comfort and remembered when anything bad was happening her mom always put her arms around her and held her close. Rebecca needed that warmth right now. "Mom…please come back," she sobbed. Just then, the flashes of light intensified. Rebecca could do nothing but weep uncontrollably.

The young girl crouched down in the shower hoping the event would pass and she could make her way to the bed. After about fifteen minutes, she pulled herself together and got out of the shower. Rebecca knew she had to get to a doctor about the headaches and flashing lights and with the family history of cancer she was very worried. Suddenly, she felt herself slipping away and thought she must move quickly to the bed. By now, she was freaking out in her mind, while at the same time trying to keep it together. Inside her head, at the dead center, she felt such heaviness, like a huge lead weight. It felt like it was being pulled down by something from below her feet. She heard the words "the center of the earth" in her mind. The room began to spin, faster and faster, and she felt as if she was spinning around like water disappearing down the drain in a sink. Was she still in the shower? Her eyes opened. No, she'd made it to the bed.

Her insides were trembling as if she had drunk half a dozen cups of coffee one after the other. What is happening? Am I going crazy? she thought. Crawling under the comforter, she rolled up into a ball. All she wanted was to descend into the realms of deep sleep so she could escape everything. It was useless. The headaches wouldn't allow her to sleep. Rebecca could only lie on the bed as she tried to figure out what was occurring and how she could stop it. The pain was not increasing which she thought was encouraging. She took a deep breath in, exhaled, and tried to calm her mind—she hoped it would also calm her body. This was something her mother taught her when she was growing up. She told her it was an ancient method used to absorb and neutralize the stress generated by daily living.

Rebecca's mom would sit her in the big comfy armchair in front of the fire and show her how stress and anxiety could be released, by focusing her attention on breathing in and out slowly. After a while, she would feel relaxed. She brought that memory into her mind and began to follow her breathing. Gradually, after about twenty minutes of the practice, Rebecca was able to notice a reduction in the intensity of the headaches.

After a good half hour, the pains were reduced enough where she was able to get dressed. It was 8am and she expected Alison to be banging on the door shortly. Just then, there was a bang on the door. "Hey Rebecca, it's me, Alison."

Rebecca turned the doorknob slowly. "Hi Alison," She wanted to be as polite as possible. There was no reason to hate Alison. They were just different people. "Why do you need me to go with you to your interview?" Rebecca's expression and tone did not reflect the polite manner she wanted.

"Well...I think moral support is a good reason and I would do the same for you is another good reason." Alison looked down in apparent disappointment.

After a short pause, Rebecca shrugged. "Okay...I was only asking," she said in a kinder softer voice. She was getting better at detecting Alison's manipulative games. Truth be told, she didn't want to stay in her room any longer than she had to, and if that meant going to an interview with Alison, then she could live with it.

Rebecca stepped into the hallway, locked the door, and followed Alison to the lobby. It did occur to her that she may also be offered a job if she happened to be with Alison at the time of her interview. It was beginning to turn into a potentially positive day. On the way down the stairs, Rebecca remembered the incident the previous day when the guy in the hallway made a grab for her. "Alison, a guy asked about you yesterday. He wanted to know where you were." She watched her to see the response she gave.

"Did he give his name?" she asked without turning around.

"No, only that you owed him something and he didn't say what." She waited for Alison to offer more but she got only silence. "He was drinking and seemed really out of it." Rebecca tried to illicit some information about the guy because he was in her building and knew where she lived, which made her nervous. "Alison, do you know this guy? I am really afraid because he was angry and knows where we live." Her voice was calm but strong.

By this time, they had come out of the stairwell and entered the lobby. "Yes, I think I know who you are talking about. Don't worry. I will take care of him," she said with a calm assurance that made Rebecca uneasy.

They left the hostel and headed for downtown. Alison hailed another cab at the corner. "I hope traffic is good," she said looking at Rebecca as if it were normal for them to be riding in cabs everyday.

"I have no money for a taxi, Alison, and I do not like the idea of riding along for free. It makes me really uncomfortable." Rebecca brushed her long dark hair from her face to clearly see Alison's response.

With her head to one side, and a smile on her face, Alison walked toward her.

"I can appreciate that you are uncomfortable about me paying for everything. My brother gave me some money, and told me to enjoy it, and this is how I do that by sharing it with people I like." Her eyes welled up and she gave Rebecca the biggest hug.

There was no room for Rebecca to maneuver. "That is really sweet of you, Alison, and I will repay the generosity when I find work too." She smiled as she pulled away from Alison's embrace.

The cab arrived. It was black. Rebecca had never seen a black cab before. "This is an unusual color for a taxi, isn't it sir?" she aimed the question at the young driver as she climbed in the back. He was small with kind of shriveled skin on his hands. He must have been in a fire or something.

"The park at 5th and Grand Boulevard," Alison demanded. She was determined to move this along.

Rebecca noticed the driver only had three fingers on his left hand. There was something about this guy she was drawn to. She could feel tremendous sadness coming from him; she tried to block it. Rebecca always felt things about people. She didn't do it purposefully. She was just very sensitive. This was something that only seemed to happen when there was heightened tension occurring or about to occur. She tried to stop it when it arose, simply because she thought it was invasive to the other person's privacy. It also made her feel embarrassed and she was always betrayed by the rosy red glow of her face. "We have to pick up a package from a friend of my brother's at the baseball diamond in the park on the way," Alison said. Rebecca could tell this was an inconvenience to her and she was annoyed.

"Did we meet him last night? What is his name?" she asked.

"No, he just arrived in town last night." Alison's voice was quiet. She was fixing her eyeliner in the compact mirror from her purse.

"Is everything okay? Are you still getting the job? Rebecca's voice cracked a little, revealing her concern for Alison's ability to get work for her too.

"Don't worry. I will ask him for a job for my friend too," she said in an exasperated tone. Rebecca knew she didn't mean it that way. It was just her way of trying to look like the one who controls everything, handing out miracles, effortlessly.

"I don't want to work for someone I don't know, or a job I don't know, for that matter," Rebecca said with misplaced pride.

Alison paused. "Poor people cannot choose their jobs," she said softly. Rebecca knew she was right and said nothing, just turned to look out of the window.

The cab pulled up at the edge of the playing field but there was no sign of anyone, let alone the guy she was supposed to meet. The cab driver waited for a couple of minutes before he spoke. His accent was of European origin. Rebecca knew because she remembered the friends her mother used to bring over for thanksgiving when Rebecca was a child.

"Miss," he looked at them through the rear view mirror, "What do you want to do?" There was no answer. Alison just sat there, silent.

Rebecca tried to help him. "The driver wants to know—"

"I heard him," Alison spoke while she twisted the ring on her finger, staring into space. "Take us to the mall at 14th and Pine, downtown."

The cab moved swiftly through the traffic, swerving and navigating the roads with incredible precision for someone with reduced hand mobility. They were driving through downtown traffic within minutes, obviously the cabby wanted to get this fare over with and pick up a more lucrative one.

"Thanks, that will be $20 please" he didn't look up just continued to write down the details of the fare.

Alison handed him $30 and just kept walking hurriedly toward the mall entrance. "Rebecca, we have to go." Her hair flew in the wind; the blond curls glistened as she swung from side to side when she walked. "My boss is waiting."

"Okay, I'm there. Slow down—my legs aren't as long as yours." It was true. Rebecca's stride could not match Alison's; she had to be five-eight. Rebecca really needed a job and she was prepared to suffer through anything Alison wanted for the chance to work.

"Where are you meeting your boss?" she said, catching up to her inside the entrance to the mall.

"The coffee shop on the second floor." She turned to Rebecca. "You must stay outside and after the interview I will introduce you to him." She made it very clear to Rebecca she must stay out of sight. They took the elevator and remained silent until it reached the second floor. "Remember, stay out of sight until I call for you. I will step out of the café and wave." Alison disappeared into the café while Rebecca remained nearby.

The mall was full of shoppers, all wanting to consume something they probably didn't need. Rebecca prided herself on the fact, that her restraint regarding shopping just to be cool was immoveable. Although she did concede that she rarely had the opportunity, financially speaking, to exercise such restraint. She browsed through the second floor at all the stores for teenagers. Rebecca had window-shopping down to an art form and her quizzical expression was perfect whenever someone inside the store caught her eye.

Alison finally emerged from the café and gave her a wave. She didn't seem overly enthused but Rebecca knew her well enough to know that didn't mean anything. She waved back and headed in the direction of the café. Alison had gone back inside to her table, and when Rebecca came in, she held her hand up beckoning for her to join her.

"Where's the guy…your boss?" she inquired softly, not wanting anyone to hear her.

"He left just after we finished business," she said casually. We have to go and meet my brother Gary. He has something for me that my boss needs." Alison continued as if she were talking to an employee, not a friend. "When we get the package, we are to meet my boss at the Coffee Club, where we will both be given some money and instructions for our next job." She talked, while handing Rebecca a cell phone.

"Wait just one minute!" Rebecca was not amused. "Who do you think you are?" she demanded. Her voice was becoming louder than the restaurant could handle.

Alison looked around, not wanting to cause a scene. She moved closer to Rebecca. "Let's go out into the mall and talk?" she half-smiled and put her hand under Rebecca's arm while walking her out. "What are you talking about?" Alison was genuinely perturbed.

"You assume too much, Alison. You think I will go along with this wild goose chase just because you say so!" she said staring into her eyes. Alison knew she had gone too far this time.

"Sorry Rebecca. I did make an assumption but I thought you wanted to work no matter what. I can be insensitive sometimes and I apologize." She bent her head and fingered the cell phone for a few moments.

This was all too much for Rebecca. She wasn't used to mind games. This friendship was really hard work and the effort was taking its toll, even with the promise of a job. She began to calm down and realized she did need the work. Rebecca reached hesitantly for the phone. "Apology accepted." Her tone was somewhat subdued as she turned to Alison, "but you have to consider other people's feelings before you make decisions that concern them, Alison." Saying this, Rebecca knew her words fell on deaf ears. "One cannot change the personality of another, one can only influence them positively or negatively." She realized she was quoting her mother's words and at that moment her memories came flooding back to her. Rebecca wished she could see her mother and gran again. She dismissed the thoughts as pure wishes of the heart and focused on Alison.

"Okay, Rebecca, I promise. Can we go now? There is not much time to get the package from Gary and get it to my boss by 6pm." She waited for her response. "We are working girls now, you know," she quipped, hoping to lighten the situation.

"I'm ready," Rebecca said without much conviction. "Where are we meeting him?" she continued as they walked out of the mall.

"Remember the baseball diamond at the park we went by? That's where Gary will meet us and give us the package. It shouldn't take long," she said.

Rebecca looked down at the phone in her hand. "Why do I need this?" she held it up in front of Alison as they stood outside the mall, waiting for yet another cab. "I don't want this guy keeping tabs on me. What's it for?"

"Don't worry, the phone is for you and me to communicate when we are on the job only, Rebecca." Alison moved away to light a smoke. "Anyway, don't you feel cool having your own cell? I do. Everyone has them." She took a huge drag on the cigarette and held it in for ages, closing her eyes as if in ecstasy. "Ah, I've been waiting for that for an hour," she said happily.

Rebecca was twisting the phone around and wondering what she was getting herself into. Her gran would have a fit, and her mom would sit her down and talk to her about what decisions were good and what ones were not. Rebecca missed those talks. Sadness started to prey upon her thoughts. She fought back the tears and made a promise to her self, right there, sitting at the curb outside the mall entrance. No matter what happened, she was not going to live in poverty, and she was definitely not going to marry someone for money—*she* was going to marry for love. She believed in love and trusted in the universe to bring her soul mate to her.

The cab arrived. "Rebecca! Lets go." Alison climbed inside, waiting impatiently. "Fifth and Grand Boulevard," she said coldly.

Rebecca got in, putting the phone in her pocket. There was a distinct nagging feeling that was growing in the back of her mind about what they were to do. Instinctively, she was sensing trouble of some kind ahead but she couldn't put her finger on what it was. It was like the time her gran was taking her to see a movie one afternoon, and while they were getting ready, she'd had the same feeling. Rebecca told her gran about it and her gran explained that she must always listen to those feelings, no matter what anyone says. They didn't get to see a movie that day. Gran convinced her they should go shopping instead. A news report on TV that night revealed the bridge across the river on the bypass road to town had collapsed, one of the bridge pylons had disappeared because of a huge sinkhole beneath it. Rebecca and gran would have been on the bus that was carried away in the river.

The cab pulled up to the curb at the park, where the only activity was someone walking her dog. It was quite windy but the clouds were not heavy with moisture. Rebecca watched as the animal ran and jumped for the ball after it was hurled speedily through the playing area.

Alison looked out of the window with obvious concern. "Where is he? There isn't time for this." She sounded really frustrated.

"Could that be him? Rebecca wiped the condensation from the window, pointing to the far side of the park. "Alison, whoever that is they are carrying a package." She was pleased with herself at having such great observation skills.

There was an outline of a dark figure in the distance running toward them. The door of the cab swung open. Alison stepped out. She put her hand to her forehead, squinting. "He is not alone," she said, jumping back into the car. There seemed to be other dark figures running in the same direction and they were closing the gap between themselves and Alison's brother. "Drive toward him," she demanded, looking at the cabby.

The cab driver refused. "Are you crazy! Those guys are not going to thank me for interfering with their business." He made a grab for his radio. "I can radio for help though. They will never know who called. That's the best I can do for that poor fool."

"Wait!" Alison shouted. "No need. I'll use my cell." She turned to Rebecca. "Lets go meet him. It'll be okay…and they will back off when they see witnesses coming." Alison turned to the driver. "Stay here. We will be back in a moment."

"If it looks like trouble, I'm out of here," he said with conviction.

Rebecca, by this time, was standing next to Alison watching the figures in the distance. "What do you think is going on? Why are they chasing him?" There was no reply.

They both watched, hoping her brother could reach them before the others reached him. It did not look good. The dark figures were gaining ground.

"Alison, maybe you should call 911. I think your brother is in big trouble here." Rebecca couldn't understand why Alison insisted on delaying.

The leading figure was close enough now to be positively identified as Gary and he was definitely carrying something. The pursuers had caught up with him and were surrounding him. It looked like they had various crude weapons.

Alison started to run toward them, yelling and shouting. "Hey! Police! Police!" She held her cell phone high so they could see and then put it to her ear letting them know she was calling 911. Rebecca followed in support, although there would not be much two young girls could do against them. They prayed the perpetrators would fear the threat of the police more than anything.

The two girls were close enough to see what was going on and they were concerned. Two of them jumped on Gary, taking the package and hitting him with a few blows to the body and head, knocking him over. They wrestled the package from his grasp and fled.

By the time Alison reached him, they were out of sight. Rebecca caught up with Alison. She was glad the guys had gone.

"Are you alright?" Rebecca asked with genuine concern even though he gave her the creeps.

"Did they get it?" Alison inquired with a total lack of concern for his wellbeing.

"No, I have it hidden." He writhed in pain. "I think they broke my rib," he cried, spitting blood from his mouth. Rebecca tried to help him up with absolutely no help from Alison.

The cab drove closer to them after seeing the gang disappear. "Hurry, I will take him to the hospital," he shouted from the car. Alison was further away talking to someone on her phone.

Rebecca turned and yelled in her direction. "Alison, hurry we are taking him to emergency."

There was no reply but Alison did make her way to the cab. She climbed in the back. "Rebecca, would you mind sitting up front?" she asked, knowing that her words conveyed there was no choice; she was just being polite.

"Sure." Rebecca closed the rear door, after making sure Gary was comfortable and stepped to the front. "Hi, thanks for waiting." She really meant it. The cabby was under no real obligation to wait for them, especially, when there was potential danger for him. He just nodded and smiled. The vehicle began to move.

"The Coffee Club, please driver," Alison said while staring out the window.

There was silence until Rebecca reached back and tapped her knee. "What are you doing, Alison? Your brother is hurt or hadn't you noticed? He needs to go to the emergency."

"We have everything he needs at the club. I phoned my boss and he told me to bring him there. They have a medical room and a registered nurse on duty." She seemed very confident.

"Alison, that is a coffee house slash night club. Why would they have a nurse on duty?" Rebecca didn't get it.

"Because it is a night club. If anything happened to a customer or an employee, lets say an accident while in the club, the owner, our boss, would want to make sure they had medical facilities and staff available on the premises." Alison sounded like she was part of an organization. She spoke as if she had been with the Coffee Club for years. "It makes good sense to me. Anyway, he is offering those facilities to Gary since he is an employee, even though he screwed up." She shot him a glare that a sister would not have given to a brother who had suffered such a traumatic event.

This made Rebecca sit silent for a while. What was Alison getting her into? Alison was a selfish egomaniac, that was the truth, but Rebecca could not believe she was ruthless. If she was, why befriend some homeless teenager like herself? What did she want? The thoughts running through Rebecca's head were ringing. There was something not right here.

When the cab neared the downtown area, Alison turned to Rebecca and explained that they were going to patch Gary up which would take awhile. "Do you mind if I drop you at the mall and pick you up later, Rebecca? I will call you first and meet you at the mall, okay?"

"Sure, whatever," she said. Rebecca welcomed the idea. It would give her time to think things through. Even though she was desperate for work, and Alison was her friend, there was no way she was going to join her until she was sure the job was legitimate.

Rebecca watched as the cab drove away. She walked around the mall for a while, trying to think of what she should do. The mall was too busy, too noisy; she couldn't think. The more she thought about her present situation the more anxious she became. She needed to find a nice quiet place to be calm and peaceful so she could sort things out; Rebecca did her best thinking in such a place. Whenever there was a problem that needed to be solved, she always seemed to find the answer in the peace and quiet of her local library. It was old, quiet, and had a certain type of feeling to it as if it embraced her when she was there.

That's it, she thought. There must be an old library or bookstore nearby where she could sit and think. She left the mall and walked toward town. A couple of blocks down and across the main street there was a small side street that looked promising. Rebecca headed for it being cautious of the traffic. Drivers in this place were not like those back home, she thought, as she watched the cars and trucks whiz by her. When the lights had eventually changed, Rebecca took off like a gazelle. As she maneuvered through traffic, she moved with grace and awareness. The truckers honked as she leapt to safety. She saw the smiles as they leered at her form. She came across an old bookstore about halfway down the block but it looked like it was going to be too small to be of any help. Rebecca pushed open the door and walked inside. She was pleasantly surprised. The lobby was quite big and the store encompassed the building to the left and right of it, with entrances from inside the original bookstore itself. She saw a staircase that began at the right-hand corner, near the front of the store, winding its way up to a beautiful balcony of pine and oak indicating more than one floor of books for her to explore.

Rebecca smiled as she walked toward the woman who was busy fixing a display. "Hi, I am looking for a place to sit and relax while I enjoy a good book and a coffee?"

The woman pointed to the far side of the store. "There is a coffee area over there, near the travel section, through to the other side of the store. We have an excellent stock of books for all types of readers. When you are ready to find the book you want, just give me a wave. I will be glad to assist." She offered a smile that welcomed Rebecca with the warmth of a genuinely, goodhearted person.

She navigated the aisles of books, following the wonderful aroma of great coffee. Rebecca was becoming totally reliant on coffee. She had developed the desire for a specific blend. "I'd like a cappuccino, skimmed milk, three shots, and a quarter foam please."

The girl, taking her order smiled. She was about the same age as Rebecca. "That's an interesting combination. Can I suggest a shot of syrup with that? How about caramel?"

"Sure, that sounds good." Rebecca took her coffee and headed to the great room of books. Her anticipation of settling down with a nice book was heightened by the shear size of the store and by the volume of books it held within its walls. The store was very deceptive from the outside. It looked like a small ma and pa venture when looking at it from the sidewalk, but the moment you step inside, there is the wonder of the huge selection available.

Rebecca strolled through the aisles for a few minutes, trying to decide which section was most interesting. She loved to read about ancient philosophical ideas, especially those that involved anything to do with the workings of the universe. She moved toward the rear of the store, inquisitively drawn there by a strange feeling that made her energy tingle. She was always able to sense different energies ever since she could remember and she had learned to trust the indicators when they appeared. Rebecca came upon an aisle of books that were in a section marked '*Independent Lost Philosophy*.' She had never seen a section like this before and wandered between the aisles hoping to be guided to a specific book.

Rebecca was just about to move on to another section of the bookstore, when a single flash of indigo light that she thought she saw coming from the bookshelf struck her peripheral vision, attracting her attention. She investigated the bookshelf and came across a strange looking blue leather-bound book at the end of a row of books towards the rear of the aisle. Rebecca touched the book with her right hand and stroked the cover with the intention to pick it up. As she did so, she was aware of a light electrical sensation that was not static, more like the tingle from a slight electric current. The beautiful blue leather looked ancient, and as she brought the book closer to her face trying to read the inscription on the side, she became aware of a pleasant odor emanating from it.

Rebecca held the book in both hands, and by now, the electrical sensation had stopped. This must be a hundred years old by the looks of it. What a beautiful blue leather book, she thought.

"Well, that's because in those days, many thousands of years ago, books were respected and treasured as the guardians of the knowledge of the universe."

A mans voice spoke to Rebecca as clear as if he were standing next to her. She quickly looked around the rows of books but could see no one. She wondered who could have spoken, and more importantly, how could they answer her when she had only made the comment in her mind. The young girl remained silent, still holding the book and looking for the owner of the voice. She thought it had come from the direction toward the back of the bookstore. The closer Rebecca got to the rear of the store, the more she sensed something, an energy that seemed familiar to her. She saw an opening in the old stonewall at the back and slowly headed for it. She was sure the voice came from there. When she got there, she saw it wasn't a door, but an archway leading to another room that was full of books. In the far corner was a figure, sitting in what looked to be, an old leather armchair. Rebecca walked closer very cautiously.

She looked back over her shoulder frequently as she navigated the bookshelves. She didn't know what she would find when she finally stepped out from the row of narrow pine shelving. When she did, she felt a strong sensation of energy coming from above her that flowed through the top of her head, down through the souls of her feet, and into the ground. Some kind of soft, gentle warmth filled every cell in her body and the closer she went to the figure in the chair, the stronger it got. Rebecca stood still, closing her eyes, allowing the energy to run through her body. It felt so good. It was the same feeling she used to get when her mom held her hand as she walked her to school, and when she hugged her mom's neck kissing her cheeks at night before bedtime. She wanted so much to have that feeling again. She began to sway under the weight of the memories and emotions. It felt like light, but not sunlight—other light—pure white light, and it had a sound as well. How could the light feel like it was hugging me? She thought this very strange. Rebecca could not make any logical sense of what she was experiencing but she also couldn't stop herself from drawing even closer to the man in the armchair.

He wore a red, gold, and orange colored garb that seemed to vibrate ever so subtly.

"Yes, you are not mistaken dear one. You are sensing the energy around me," he whispered. "It is not that common for anyone to feel the energy with such an intensity as you. You are extremely sensitive." His eyes were soft and clear.

Rebecca said nothing. She only stared at him with her mouth slightly open, still walking toward the chair. It felt so natural to want to get close to the man. There was something about him that encouraged her.

"My name is Shaulmarhime, Shaulmar for short." He smiled. "What might your name be, dear one?" There was a pause—then she spoke.

"Rebec...Rebecca Sullivan." She stumbled through her name as if it were the first time she'd uttered the words. She couldn't take her eyes away from his smile. It had a warmth and peace about it that was nurturing to her. She could see a golden hue emanating from around him; it shimmered and moved, permeating through the air. Rebecca had seen people's auras ever since she was a child but none ever came close to the beauty of what she was seeing with him.

Shaulmar beckoned gently to her with his hand. "Come, sit in the chair next to me Rebecca and I will tell you all about that wonderful book you feel so drawn to."

She had completely forgotten that she had the book. "Oh, yes the book." She moved to the chair at his side. Rebecca thought there was only one armchair in the room when she entered but she probably just hadn't registered the second one in her mind. She looked at him and wondered who he might be...what he was doing at the back of an old bookstore sitting in a worn red leather armchair, as if he were sitting in his own living room, sipping hot tea? These thoughts ran through her mind in what seemed to her to be a split second.

Shaulmar picked up his cup of jasmine tea and held it to his lips, sipping slowly. "I am an old man who doesn't get out much," he said. "Sometimes I come here at the request of the owner. I help out when he is short-staffed during the busy times."

Rebecca was stunned. She didn't know what to think. Did he just answer her questioning thoughts—again? She knew that was not possible. So, what was possible? "Oh, I see...and are you paid... or just get to read the books?" she asked rather sarcastically, in an attempt to seem unruffled by the whole experience, while projecting a calm demeanor, despite the thoughts that were bouncing around inside her head.

"I am paid a specific amount for every person I am able to help," he said with a smile. Rebecca thought she saw a definite gleam in his eye while he spoke to her. He was being evasive toward her questions, as if deliberately avoiding the truth but not lying per se. Being paid for every person he was able to help had definite meanings other than the obvious one. The help he referred to did not necessarily mean he found a specific book for them, or interpreted difficult text, or explained certain nuances in a book. Rebecca intuitively sensed there was a deeper more profound meaning behind his words. She also sensed that their meeting was not coincidental, there was a deeper meaning to that too.

"How long have you been helping out here at the bookstore, if you don't mind me asking?" she said sweetly, trying not to seem overly invasive.

"Oh, off and on for a time," he replied with the warmest smile that seemed to imply so much more but she just couldn't quite put her finger on what it was. One thing she was sure of, though, Shaulmar was not who he seemed to be. He definitely was much more than a bookstore temp. Rebecca talked with him for about an hour but to her it seemed more like only a moment.

Shaulmar described how the blue leather-bound book came to be in the possession of the small family-run bookstore and where its origins lay. "Fifty years ago, a shipment of books was sent to this area for sale to many stores. In this shipment, there was a very special book hidden within the cargo for safe keeping," he said with a noticeable softness in his voice.

"Where did the books come from?" Rebecca asked with genuine interest. She was still holding the blue leather book in one hand, letting it rest against her chest, and sipping the coffee with the other hand, totally enthralled with the man in the chair. "What is that wonderful smell?" she looked down at her coffee cup. "It is not coffee, that's for sure," she said, pushing her nose into the air in an attempt to capture the scent again.

"That is the tea I am drinking. It is an ancient blend of herbs and the leaves of a tea plant from my home. I always carry some with me. It keeps me connected to the ones I love." Shaulmar paused to drink the tea.

The aroma was very different than anything Rebecca had ever known before, certainly not anything she ever enjoyed in her home. It smelt flowery and sweet, yet not syrupy, and strong like sandalwood.

"The shipment of this particular cargo of books came from Tuscany, a northern province of Italy. Many Italian estates were forced to sell some of their possessions, family heirlooms, in order to sustain their vineyards." Shaulmar enjoyed talking about the history of the book with Rebecca.

"Why?" What happened to the vineyards?" Rebecca loved listening to a good story, always hoping for a happy ending. "Well," he continued, "quite often, heavy rains during the growing season would cause bad crops, and with no grapes to sell, sadly, there was no money to live on," Shaulmar explained. He continued with his story after drinking more tea. "That is why the families decided to sacrifice their possessions. The book's journey begins much further back in history, at least 2000 years earlier. It made its way to Europe carried by Persian travelers who handed it over to a pagan Druid order of monks living in the Tuscan province."

Rebecca was deeply intrigued. "What happened then?" she asked, becoming more and more relaxed, sipping her drink, and squirming a little while adjusting her body position in the chair. By this time, she had lost all track of time and had forgotten about her own situation.

"The Druids welcomed the travelers, and over a period of time, they became like family to the Persians," Shaulmar explained with an emotional tone in his voice. His face lit up as he continued with the story of the book, especially as he described the coming together of two such beautiful cultures of the world. The beauty of the Persian culture, all the philosophy of the ages, as well as the love of the earth, plants, animals, and the universe was combined with the spirit of the Druid religion. Just then, Shaulmar fell silent and looked toward Rebecca as if he were in a trance or staring off into space. Whatever it was he was occupied with, it seemed more important than the story of the book.

After a few moments, Rebecca motioned toward him with her hands. "Hello…hey there…are you okay?" she couldn't remember his name so she just kept waving her hands in front of him and repeating the words softly to try and get his attention.

Shaulmar didn't move he remained sitting, staring with a peaceful serene expression on his face.

Rebecca looked around but no one was close to them. In fact, she realized that since she had been in the room of books with him, she couldn't recall any other customer coming in there. She gave up trying to get his attention and sat back in the chair thumbing through the blue leather-bound book. She had only just began to read the inscription on the inside front cover when the man in the chair spoke.

"Sorry for leaving you so abruptly, it was rude of me. Again, please accept my humble apology Rebecca?" His voice was soft and humble. "I was conversing with an old friend. He always comes to me when I recount our story from ancient times.

Rebecca looked around. She already knew there had been no one there at all. "Sorry…who came?" she returned her gaze to the man in the chair.

"Please, do not be concerned. I will explain later," he said cheerfully.

Rebecca became aware of an uneasy feeling in the pit of her stomach. She pulled back from him instinctively and inhaled a very large breath. "So, it was nice meeting you. I hope you help many people and thank you for the wonderful story of the book and the ancient times and druids and…and so on." It was the only thing she could think of to say as she gently closed the book. Rebecca smiled an uneasy smile and laid the blue book down on the chair as she got up, intending to leave.

"Until we meet again, dear one." It was all Shaulmar said as Rebecca made her way around the bookshelves and headed towards the entrance she had come in through. As she passed the aisles of dusty old books, she was engulfed by the same warm, peaceful energy as before. She slowed down a little, enjoying the embrace, then passed through the archway and back into the front part of the store. Immediately after stepping through the archway, she felt a cold chill that made her shiver from head to foot, as if she had just walked out of a warm and cozy home filled with the love and caring of family and friends, and into a cold, dark, lonely, wind swept street. It made her think of the family that had been so cruelly taken from her.

Rebecca stood in the doorway of the old bookstore, pausing to gather her thoughts, while she prepared to enter the icy reality that was her life. Her cell phone rang surprising the hell out of her. She had forgotten all about Alison and the job she was praying for. "Hello," she yelled, "this is Rebecca speaking."

A voice at the other end answered. "Rebecca, I know it's you. I gave you the phone," Alison quipped sarcastically, "why are you yelling? Please, don't yell down the phone. I can hear you just fine. You don't have to yell, okay?" she pleaded.

"Sorry, Alison. I am not used to using things like this. I won't yell anymore alright?" she giggled.

"Okay, thanks. I just wanted to call to let you know that I cannot make it back today. I have to take Gary to hospital. He is having his ribs taped. I will meet you at the Club in the morning, okay? Try and be there by 10am. We have to do a job."

"A job? Do you mean I have a job? Rebecca was overjoyed. She immediately thought of the money and how she could pay the rent at the hostel, and after awhile, maybe she could get a real apartment. She spun off into a whole world of possibilities.

"Yeah, you have a job," Alison was not as taken by the event as Rebecca. She always assumed she would work somewhere and so was not feeling like a life changing event had just occurred. "So, can I count on you for tomorrow?" she asked.

"Yes, of course. I will be at the club at 10am. Thank you Alison," Rebecca said gratefully.

On her way back to the hostel, Rebecca sat on the subway train replaying the events of the day, especially the encounter with the man in the old bookstore. The image of him in the leather armchair holding a cup of tea in his lap, while spacing out totally, was firmly embedded in her memory. A slight grin graced her mouth as she sat there and recalled him looking across the room with that glazed expression. Rebecca took a deep breath and exhaled. The only thing she wanted to do was to go back to her room and have a nice, long, hot shower and get some take-out. Now that she had a job she could afford to splash out a little.

CHAPTER 4

THE NEXT MORNING REBECCA WOKE WITH A SPLITTING headache. She was getting really tired having to endure the pains in her head and not knowing why they were happening. She tried to ignore the pain by focusing on something else to keep herself occupied so she could make some breakfast. Toast made of stale bread and chocolate syrup are good company for microwave coffee. Rebecca sat on the edge of the bed munching toast. She was attempting to feel quite upbeat while thinking about her new job. She wondered what kind of job Alison had accepted for her. It was funny for her to think that, when she didn't have the job, any job would have done. Now that she was employed, she didn't think she was being picky by wondering if the job was legal or not, especially since it involved Alison and the people she knew at that nightclub. Another thought occurred to her as she swilled the coffee down. What if she and Alison had a fight? Would she loose her job? Suddenly Rebecca wasn't hungry anymore and slowly stopped eating and reached down to put her toast in the garbage. Thoughts like that began to mingle with other ones and quite soon she was no longer feeling so upbeat.

She leaned her shoulder against the wall next to the bathroom and looked out of the small window overlooking the alleyway and feeling a little dejected. Almost immediately she sensed a warm, gentle, and very subtle energy moving toward her. Rebecca was engulfed in the sensation. She knew intuitively it was not going to harm her, so she relaxed and allowed it to move through her, embracing it fully. She moved to the end of the bed and relaxed and accepted the energy as it washed over her like a mother putting a soft blanket over her child. After a few minutes, the energy left as quickly as it had arrived, leaving Rebecca feeling refreshed, not as refreshed as if she had slept but refreshed none-the-less, and the headache was reduced to a slight throbbing.

"That's it. I will walk to the club to meet Alison," she whispered to herself while she picked up her coat, "This place is like a jail cell. I can't take it any longer. I need some fresh air." Rebecca stepped into the hallway, locked her door, and headed down to the street. It was only an hour before she was to meet Alison but she thought walking briskly should get her there on time.

Rebecca had walked for some time, and in that time she entertained thoughts that were sad in nature regarding her future. Why she had to suffer the loss of her family—struggle to find work just to make enough to survive—draw people to her that seemed somewhat odd to say the least? All these thoughts ran around in her head while she walked to the club for her first day at her new job. She moved quickly through the streets toward town. She knew she was getting close to the outskirts because of the increase in foot traffic. She passed a sports arena and remembered how she used to love to skate. Rebecca's mom taught her how to ice skate when she was about 5 years old. She relived the wonderful feelings and memories that filled her with happiness as she continued to make her way. Her legs were beginning to feel tired. She hadn't walked this long in some time but she knew it was doing her good. She thanked her gran, in her mind, for caving in when she asked for the hiking boots she was wearing. They had probably saved her the pain and discomfort of pretty sore feet after walking this far.

The rain started to fall quickly, developing into a downpour. Rebecca was only wearing a windbreaker that was not very rainproof so she ducked into the nearest store. As she removed her coat and wiped her face with the sleeve of her sweater, she looked around and thought the place was familiar. She had inadvertently walked into the little bookstore where she had seen the man in the chair. She checked again, searching for the woman who spoke to her, telling her where the coffee booth was. Sure enough, there she was working behind the cashier's desk. The Coffee Club was only a couple of blocks from here, she thought, there was just enough time to meet Alison. Rebecca waited for a few minutes till the downpour eased, and putting her coat on again, she left the store.

The building where the club was located was in the middle of most of the downtown activity. Constant traffic flowed noisily in both directions, bumper-to-bumper most of the time. Rebecca was forced to run between cars and trucks again to navigate to the big black and red door that defined the front of the club where she was to meet Alison. When she got to the building the doors were closed. She looked around, peeking in the window but saw only her reflection. The windows were stained with a black tint, probably to dissuade any unwanted eyes. Rebecca was trying to decide what she should do next. She inspected the door one more time, hoping someone would come but she thought it was unlikely since the place seemed so desolate. She noticed there was an inscription embedded in the dark black door near the top. She tried to make out what it was and that's when she peered right into the security camera in the corner that she hadn't been aware of. Rebecca stepped back quickly in an attempt to give the impression of innocence to the eyes that undoubtedly were looking back at her. She prepared herself for what she knew was coming. A few seconds later, the inevitable occurred, the door opened and a guy came out carrying a white envelope. "Are you Rebecca? Alison's friend?" He looked like the hulk, only black and much bigger.

Rebecca stepped back a little, afraid, but trying not to show it. "Ye...yes I am. I think I work here," she said, not very sure at all.

"Here," the monster of a man held out his huge hand that was gripping the envelope. "She told me to give you this and a message. She wants you to meet her here at the club, tonight, at 7:00 pm."

Rebecca took the envelope slowly. "H...how do I get in?" she asked, not wanting to seem stupid.

He looked her up and down...smiling slowly. "Just tell the doorman you are a friend of Cahn." He laughed as he turned to walk back into the building.

"Wait," she shouted, "what's this for?"

Cahn gave her a confused look. "Payment for your first job. Well done." He smiled.

"But I haven't done any jobs yet," she answered.

"Didn't you go to the park and help Alison get the package to us the other day? He frowned, moving closer to her. His voice became deeper, more threatening, obviously, ready to investigate any misdeed he might have uncovered.

"Y...yes, yes that's right, I did. Thanks. Thanks, Mr. Cahn. I...I appreciate the money. Thanks." Rebecca backed away, waving. She visualized a horrible ending to her life at the hands of someone that huge and mean.

After the episode with Cahn, Rebecca calmed down and opened the envelope. Her eyes widened when she saw all the money. "Oh my God," she whispered to herself, "I'm rich." She pulled the money out and began to count. She stopped almost immediately, pulling the money close to her, and looked around as she imagined there were hundreds of eyes watching her. There wasn't, but can't be too careful, she thought. People were walking in every direction all around her. She would need to find a place to count the money, a safe place. Rebecca was new to town so there weren't many safe places she knew of or could think of. Suddenly it hit her, the coffee booth at the bookstore. It was just a couple of blocks from where she was. She put the envelope in her jacket pocket and zipped it shut. Now the money is safe, she thought. Rebecca couldn't believe it. The traffic had not subsided at all. She would have to traverse her way back down the block, sandwiched between the New Yorkers and their cars and trucks. She thought of the annual event of the running of the bulls in Spain as she constantly sidestepped the onslaught of bulls coming at her. Navigating through traffic was like playing Russian roulette with an oozy, timing had to be perfect, and if they sensed hesitation or fear it was all over.

Rebecca made it across the main road running between cars, trucks, and busses, and headed down to the side street where the bookstore was located. When she reached the building, she noticed a sign outside above the main display window. It read, Ancient Arabic Books. She had not remembered seeing it the first time she was there. Rebecca went inside, waving to the girl she'd met earlier, who was serving customers; she got a wave back. It felt nice to connect with people, especially when circumstances sometimes bring loneliness and despair. A friendly smile can be like a strong wind blowing the dark clouds away and making room for the sun to shine; it was very uplifting for her. She made her way to the coffee area and sat at one of the tables. She took off her damp coat and placed it on the back of a chair. There was a small line at the coffee counter, so she joined it, smiling at the older lady ahead of her.

"Hi. The coffee is nice here," she said, making small talk.

"Yes, it is. I often come here on my way to work I call it my reward for working all day in that mess we call the city." Her eyes were tired but she still managed a smile at the end of her comment.

Rebecca smiled back. "Well, you're right. We all need to do nice things for ourselves, no matter how small." The woman nodded in agreement and turned back to the counter.

The girl's voice from behind the counter came loud and clear. "Next." The older woman stepped up.

Rebecca turned to her table to be sure her coat was still there, concerned about the wad of cash hidden in the pocket. She began to think about Alison, and for some reason, she wondered why the phone hadn't been ringing. If Alison wanted to give her a message, why wouldn't she use the phone?

A voice came thundering into her ears "Next!"

Rebecca stammered as she stepped up to the coffee counter. "I would like...I mean can I have...do you have a..." She stopped, closed her eyes, and took in a large breath to collect herself. "Would you please make me a half-sweet, non-fat, triple shot, twenty ounce cappuccino?"

The girl nodded. "For here or to go?"

Rebecca thought for a moment, blurting out the first thing that came into her mind, usually was not what she wanted to say. Her gran used to tell her to understand what she was being asked before she answered. Staying calm in stressful situations was one thing gran was good at. "To go, please," she said gently but in a strong voice. Rebecca returned to her table and prepared to count her money. She was quite apprehensive about the amount. What if it was too much? What if Alison wanted more from her, regarding the job, than she was prepared to give? It was all becoming too scary. Rebecca opened the envelope, making sure no one was watching. There were quite a few $20 bills at first glance. When she had finished counting, she had $420 in her possession. She had never seen so much money in her hands before.

Her first thought was she could pay for the room at the hostel and buy some clothes and...she stopped herself from running away with thoughts of spending the money. Reality arose in her mind. What was she expected to be doing for this kind of money? She tried to think of what could have been in the package that was hidden by Gary's friend and delivered to the club? What scared her even more was the fact that the guys that attacked him and took the decoy package were going to be out looking for the real package. All these thoughts took the shine off the fact that she had a job that obviously paid well. She couldn't get a regular job because of her age, and then, social services were probably looking for her. She would undoubtedly be put in foster care if they found her till she was old enough to live and work legally. That was something she was never going to submit to.

Rebecca picked up her jacket and her coffee and moved toward the bookshelves while sipping her cappuccino. She wasn't feeling upbeat anymore. A nagging sensation was eating at her. She wandered through the book aisles, thinking. She wondered if she should make her way to the rear of the store and see if the blue leather book was back on the shelf where she had found it last time? Rebecca had a growing curiosity about the contents of the book since she'd held it in her hands and felt the energy surge through them. Without seeming conspicuous, she systematically searched the bookshelves in the aisles at the rear of the store, pretending to be someone looking for a book to buy. She hoped beyond hope that she would come across the old leather-bound volume. As she walked amongst the aisles, she noticed a young boy searching the shelves in the aisle marked 'Religion'. Rebecca avoided that aisle like the plague—she didn't want any adolescent boy on her case. She headed for the back of the store and what she saw when she got there was very strange. There were three stone steps leading to the room where she thought she was when she'd encountered the old man. Each step had an indentation, deeper in the middle, then shallower toward the outer edges. It was obvious to Rebecca that the steps were worn due to many years of foot traffic but how could that be?

She dismissed the oddity not bothering to expend the energy needed to rationalize it and stepped down into the room. The word 'Philosophy' was inscribed in the oak panel above the door. Two symbols she had never seen before were also carved into the wood, one either side of the word. This was where Rebecca had found the book and met the nice but weird man. The room was smaller than the main store area but it held three aisles of bookshelves full of some very interesting books. She couldn't see the old blue leather book she was drawn to. As she moved through the room around the shelves she was actually relieved to find the room empty. The two chairs that were in the room last time were gone and it seemed a lot darker and colder. Rebecca searched the shelves in the room to no avail.

"Didn't think the book would be here," she mused out loud, "but it doesn't cost anything to look."

Just at that precise moment, the young lad she had spotted earlier stepped down into the room.

"Smells pretty musty in here," he said.

Rebecca only grunted. She didn't fancy trying to make small talk with some adolescent boy, with raging hormones, in the back of a small bookstore. She picked up a book from one of the shelves, not even bothering to read the title, and made a beeline for the door. She was a little disappointed in not locating the book but that only served to increase her desire to come back and try again. If she were to be really honest with herself, she would concede to being just as disappointed at not seeing the man who had been sitting in the worn leather chair the last time she'd been in this room. She really enjoyed his company, even if she thought he was a little eccentric looking, but he spoke with a gentleness that she missed, and she thought he was very interesting in the things that he said. Rebecca considered him to be knowledgeable and she thought she would like to have him as a friend. In order to do that, she knew she must return to the bookstore.

She wandered toward the front of the store, drinking what was left of her coffee. She placed the book she'd picked up on the cart near the door on her way out. Rebecca braced herself for the cold, wet, windy weather outside. The traffic was as strong as ever. The sounds of cars and trucks speeding down the street in both directions, was something she thought she could never get used to. The rain made things worse; as the traffic rushed by her, she felt the cold wet spray in her face and she shivered like a pup out in the cold.

Her coat was zipped up as high as it would go but still it wasn't enough. She mumbled that when she had the time, she would buy a heavy coat with thick lining for warmth.

When she finally arrived back at the hostel, she was annoyed at herself for not thinking to hail a cab but she'd forgotten about the money. Now she was soaked to the skin and only had one thought and that was to shower and change. However, when she reached the lobby, the hostel manager had other ideas.

"Miss Sullivan," he waved her over with his hand while looking down at his ledger, " can I have a word?" He oozed arrogance and insufferable airs of superiority. "It's important. It's about your next week's rent." His voice echoed in the lobby.

"Can't it wait, Mr. Holden? I am soaking wet and need to go to my room to change," Rebecca shouted back, hoping the others in the lobby would take notice at how much of a jerk he was being.

"Sorry, I need you to sign the register now for next week. Those are the rules Miss Sullivan. I don't make the rules. I need you to pay me for next week or your room will no longer be your room." He shouted the words even though Rebecca had walked right up to his desk.

She gripped her coat in her hand, while trying to remain calm, squeezing it, wanting it to be Mr. Holden's neck. He was organizing the guest register and looked up to see Rebecca with a burning look in her eyes.

"Sorry, but you must appreciate I have to run a tight ship here or the whole place would go to the dogs," he insisted with a tone of total indifference.

"Of course, Mr. Holden, it must take all your time, energy, and initiative to keep a place like this running as smoothly as you do," she snapped sarcastically.

After the weekly register was signed, Rebecca asked if she could give him half the rent then and bring the rest down the following morning. Mr. Holden didn't really have a choice since she had given him all she had. Rebecca didn't want to use the money she'd got from Alison until she was sure the job was going to work out. He had a look of resignation on his face.

"Okay, but be sure to bring the balance to this desk first thing tomorrow, Miss Sullivan." She started walking away. "No later than 10am Miss Sullivan." He was trying to sound adamant but she had already turned the corner to the stairwell.

Rebecca walked slowly upstairs and took a nice warm shower. She had to meet Alison at the club later so she needed to relax and maybe even nap a little. Soon after her shower, Rebecca lay down on her bed intending to sleep for a while, but as soon as she closed her eyes, the room began to change. She wasn't imagining it. A swirling energy began at the foot of her bed. This time it was visible to her in her minds eye. Rebecca quickly sat up, pushing her back against the wall, her eyes moved from side to side as she followed the swirling energy. She didn't know what to do. Panic was beginning to manifest, and her thoughts were frantically racing across her mind, trying to gather whatever options were available. The energy hadn't moved—it was stagnant, just swirling slowly around the foot of her bed. It was starting to manifest into something physical. A light mist was forming within the swirling vortex, and by this time, Rebecca had gathered herself and jumped from the bed and moved to the bathroom doorway. She was scared to death. She didn't think this could be real. Maybe she was having a nervous breakdown? One thing was clear, she was looking at a swirling mist in her room at a hostel; so it must be real or she was losing her mind, she thought.

Why wasn't it doing something? What did it want? Rebecca was stunned. It just spun and grew larger and the mass was now touching the ceiling and the floor. There was no sound, only a visible misty fog, hanging between the floor and ceiling of her room. She was about to try and make a dash for the door when a sudden heavy thud sensation hit her in the head. It was so powerful that she collapsed where she was and saw different colored bright lights that seemed to be floating above her. That was all she remembered, until the phone in her jacket pocket rang, waking her up. She raised her head slowly, holding it in her hand, and got off her bed to reach for the phone.

"Hello, this is Rebecca." She spoke slowly and deliberately due to the fact that she was not fully back yet.

"Rebecca! It's Alison. Where are you? You are supposed to be meeting me at the club." The voice on the end of the phone sounded irate and loud.

Rebecca held the phone away from her ear for a couple of seconds. "Alison what time is it? I just woke up." She held her hand to her forehead. "Something weird happened." Her voice was slow and kind of erratic sounding.

"Whatever, just get down here as quick as you can. We have a job waiting." Alison hung up the phone before Rebecca could reply.

Rebecca was in no condition to work but she felt obligated to Alison for getting her the job. She put the phone back in her coat and stumbled to the bathroom. There was a strange glow in the room that convinced Rebecca she hadn't dreamed the event. She was relieved she wasn't crazy but she was just as frightened that it was obviously so real. She swilled her face in the tiny sink and then rubbed it in an attempt to wake up but it was no use, she was still very groggy. She left the bathroom and sat at the end of the bed looking at the semi transparent shimmering light; it glowed with a purple haze on the floor and ceiling. The light was not reflecting off anything. She thought that was strange. It should have reflected off the walls or the night table or something. The light just shimmered like the residue left by a very powerful rainbow and it seemed to be diminishing by the minute. Eventually it disappeared, leaving the dull beige color of the wall the only thing visible.

Rebecca didn't know what to make of the whole experience but she did know that she couldn't meet with Alison that night. She was too out of it. She pushed the buttons on her phone and waited. She was asked to leave a message.

"Hi Alison. This is Rebecca. I have to stay home tonight. I am sick. I will see you tomorrow. I hope I haven't let you down but I just cannot handle coming tonight, sorry, must be the flu." She hung up and was thankful Alison wasn't available.

Just as she hung up, there was a knock at the door. She looked through the security peephole but didn't see anyone. Rebecca went to the bathroom to look for aspirin but there was another knock at the door. She hurried to look through the window again but there was no one. She opened the door and went into the hallway, looking both ways, but again she saw no one. Returning to her room, Rebecca closed the door and engaged the safety latch. She turned to the room while resting her back on the door.

Her head was throbbing. She wanted to teach the pest a lesson. She waited behind the door, intent on scaring the little monster enough so that no other unsuspecting soul would be a victim of this stupid and annoying prank. She waited and waited but the knock didn't come again. Never had Rebecca felt so alone and so helpless as she did at that moment. She pushed herself off the door and made her way to the bed, falling onto it. She felt so depressed. The helplessness she was experiencing was the kind that originated from the very fiber of her being. Every cell of her body cried out in pain. She sat up on the edge of the bed holding onto the comforter. The heaviness she felt before had returned falling on her from above like some horrible, cold, damp blanket. The only thing she could think to do was to return to the practice of concentrating on her breathing to bring calm and peace back to her mind and body.

Even though Rebecca was suffering with the painful headaches, she had found a way to be at peace with them through detaching from the pain as best she could. Gradually, she felt herself slipping downward as if being pulled by a very strong force. She lay back on her bed and decided that whatever was going on must be 'meant to be' and so she allowed herself to release any desires she had to fight it. Eventually, Rebecca felt herself descending into a shadowy darkness that gave her no indication whether she was going to come back okay, or at all, but she really didn't care anymore—considering what her life consisted of.

CHAPTER 5

WHILE SHE SLEPT THAT NIGHT, A NOTE WAS SLIPPED under her door. After pushing it under the door, the messenger walked down the hallway and disappeared downstairs. The morning light came in through the alley window. Rebecca regained consciousness. She could tell she had slept late by the sounds coming up from the street. There were many questions in her mind as she lay there trying to make sense of what had occurred. She wasn't sensing anything bad had happened, and she couldn't exactly remember what had actually happened, but she was all right it seemed. The young girl knew that she had experienced something out of the ordinary while she'd slept, and that there were things given to her that had something to do with what she was to do in the future. What those things were she couldn't remember but they had left a profound impression on her mind. She was left with the feeling that she was supposed to accomplish something very important and not just for her own benefit.

Rebecca was still a little drowsy but she felt good enough to go outside and get some fresh air, knowing that would make her feel better. She took a shower and got dressed then headed for the door. That is when she came across the note that had landed on the carpet there. Rebecca bent down and slowly reached for it. The note was on a white piece of paper and it was open-faced with the words, 'Do not be afraid. All will turn out well. Your path is set in stone by the forces of the universe, forces that cannot be stopped,' It was hand written. There was no indication of who wrote it or whom the messenger was who had delivered it. She opened the door quickly, looking up and down the hallway, but she saw no one so she retreated back inside the room.

"What the hell is this?" she whispered. She was at a loss to know what to do. Should she disregard the note as some nut's idea of a joke? Or was it more sinister? She was really scared. Rebecca thought of the weird guy that tried to grab her in the hallway, and wondered if this was going to be her future…being preyed on by crazy psychos for the rest of her life? This was not anything she imagined could be her destiny. She was a young person with no home or family so she wouldn't be missed. She began to imagine all kinds of scary scenarios. What if there was a cult that looked for girls in situations like hers and tried to kidnap them? Rebecca was avoiding the authorities due to her circumstances and maybe they knew about it, somehow? She had to stop thinking about it because the images that surfaced were too disturbing for her to contemplate. She started to wonder that a foster home might not be as bad as she'd thought.

Eventually, Rebecca stuffed the note in the garbage can at the foot of her bed and left the room. She stopped at the reception desk on her way out. "Mr. Holden, Mr. Holden," she repeated.

The awkward little man raised his balding head from under the counter where he was searching for something and muttering to himself. "Yes, yes, what is it?"

His annoyed tone didn't affect Rebecca. She was already in too much of a bad mood. "Mr. Holden, I have been the object of someone's idea of a prank."

"Prank?" he became less annoyed at the thought of a guest complaining and put on his pleasant hat. "What kind of prank?" he asked her, while making himself ready to repel any serious claims for refunds or the likes.

"Someone has been knocking on my door and then running away, Mr. Holden. It has to stop!" she demanded.

A look of relief appeared on his face. "Of course, Miss Sullivan I will look into it right away." He had no such intention. "While we are talking Miss Sullivan, do you have the outstanding balance of the week's rent for me?"

She had forgotten about that. Mr. Holden's tone had changed to one of distain and it was obvious that he was not someone she should spend anymore time with than necessary. So she decided to hand him the money from the envelope she'd gotten from Cahn. But before he could grab it with his eager little fingers, she reminded him to make out a receipt for the full amount.

The little man climbed onto his pedestal and stretched his waistcoat down over his tiny, rounded belly. "Miss Sullivan, when you arrived to pay me this morning you will have undoubtedly noticed that I was preoccupied. I was attempting to recover my official receipt book. Unfortunately, I was not successful," he said apologetically.

Rebecca said nothing. She only continued looking at him—squarely in the eyes—waiting for the horrid little man to come up with a solution.

"So, you do understand why I am unable to give you a receipt right now, Miss Sullivan?" he said, cocking his head to one side slightly, while he cracked a half smile in an attempt to entice her into letting the matter drop.

"Well," she said, "you do understand, Mr. Holden, that if a receipt is not put under my door by the time I return, I will be forced to lodge a complaint to your superior." Rebecca made sure their eyes met so he would know she meant business. Although she really didn't know who Mr. Holden's superior was to lodge a complaint to or where she should lodge one.

He only smiled and tried to fake a humbled look but he knew he had the upper hand. Rebecca could see his insincerity as clearly as she could see his idiotic multicolored bow tie. On her way out of the building, Rebecca felt lightheaded again but this time an image was flashed on the dark screen behind her eyes as she closed them to rub her head. She didn't want Mr. Holden to see her stagger against the wall, so she used all the strength she could muster to remain composed until she was able to disappear from view. When she reached the street, there was a pillar near the entrance that supported her for a few minutes.

As she leaned against the pillar, she was shown images of planets and stars with other celestial objects she couldn't recognize shooting past them. Rebecca was astounded. The experience continued while she kept her eyes closed, and she wasn't sure that she should open them. The colors were absolutely amazing. The images were so vivid. She saw Jupiter, Saturn, and a most beautiful blue Earth displayed in its entire splendor as the frames of light and color passed before her eyes. This was obviously another of the episodes that she had endured over the past week. She now realized that they were probably not going to stop anytime soon, so she tried to live with them, not necessarily in an attempt to understand them, but to avoid struggling to escape from them because that only made the effects worse. This particular episode, however, was very different from the others in that it was explicit in nature and spectacularly beautiful. The feelings that came with the experience left Rebecca excited, as if she had received a shot of adrenaline that caused a rush of energy like a quickening of sorts.

The episode eventually passed but she was at a loss, as usual, in figuring out what it meant or why it was occurring. However, the only thing on her mind at that point was figuring out a solution to the continuing problem of her inability to keep paying Mr. Holden the rent. Even though she had the job with Alison, she didn't have much faith in its working out. Rebecca was starting to feel anxious again about her future. How was she to survive alone? She was missing her mom and gran desperately. Her imagination ran riot regarding her troubling situation. Was she destined to live on the streets? How was she going to buy food with no money? She had heard about people who preyed on vulnerable girls like her; what if she was kidnapped by one of them? Social services persisted in entering her mind as the only logical solution but she refused to entertain the idea of living with some strange family till she was legal.

How could this be happening, she thought? Why couldn't God just help her? She was a good person. She had even prayed for divine help; other people claimed they got it. As she made her way from the front of the hostel to Main Street around the corner, there was a shout from behind her. She turned to see who it was. "Oh no—Alison—please go away." She hissed to herself as she turned back, pretending she hadn't seen her.

"Hey, Rebecca! Hey. Stop. Wait for me!" Alison yelled.

Rebecca put on her best fake smile as Alison caught up to her. "Hey Alison, how was it last night? Sorry, I was just too sick to show up."

"I was on my way to see you," Alison said. "No harm done. There is another job for us tomorrow, so everything is okay."

Rebecca didn't say much of anything. She was trying to think of what to do but she knew she couldn't ignore her. "Sounds good," she said trying to sound upbeat. It was very obvious to her that Alison wanted to continue their friendship and she didn't have the heart to tell her different. So it was off for a walk with Alison in tow. They headed in the direction of the city again. The conversation turned to the job Rebecca was given. She wanted to know what it entailed. It was about time she knew what she was getting herself into.

"What exactly do we do when we are working for your boss?" Rebecca asked as inconspicuously as possible. "I mean it's nothing illegal, right, Alison?"

Alison turned and gave her a look of disgust. "How could you possibly even think I would be involved in anything like that?"

She quickly turned the disgust into the most convincing look of hurt feelings Rebecca had ever seen. "Sorry Alison, but we have to be very careful when we are working for people like your boss and being paid under the table."

"I agree but I can assure you the jobs are legit," she claimed with authority. After a short silence, Alison pulled a small brown bottle from her coat pocket and put it to her lips. Rebecca watched, curiously.

"What's that?" she asked.

Alison let the hand with the bottle drop to her side. "Just a small tonic." She put her hand to her lips letting out a small burp. "Sorry Rebecca, that always happens when I drink—want to try?"

Rebecca's first thought was to refuse, clinging to her moral upbringing, but she stopped herself and reached a hand out to Alison, beckoning for the bottle. "Why not, things haven't been great lately and I don't see a way out."

Alison had a huge grin on her face. "All right, Rebecca. Prepare to see far and wide." She handed her the bottle. "This will take all that nasty pain and anxiety away. Now, lets rock!" She giggled while twirling around, almost losing her footing. It had the desired effect. Rebecca instinctively reached out to save her from falling over, giving Alison the information she needed. Rebecca had indicated to Alison, unknowingly, that she cared enough to reach out to the helpless, and therefore, had revealed her weakness.

"You're insane," she moaned as she helped Alison stay on her feet. "Give me that bottle." Rebecca took a swig, closing her eyes. When the liquid ran down her throat, she gagged a little. After battling to compose herself, she handed the bottle back and turned away, not wanting Alison to judge her as inexperienced. "Okay... let's rock," she responded—almost in a whisper.

"Come on Rebecca. Lets go have some fun." Alison bent down to fix her shoe.

Rebecca stopped and turned to her with a questioning look. "What about work?" she said in a half panicked tone.

Without straightening up, Alison spoke. "Don't worry. I took care of it. I knew you needed some time to get used to your situation, so I spoke to the boss, and he told me to give you a welcome to New York night."

"What does that mean?" she asked, not really wanting to know but she had a good idea what it meant judging by the bottle in Alison's pocket.

"Oh, just show you a good time so you are in the right frame of mind to start your new job. I have to say my boss really likes you. He thinks you carry yourself well." Alison poured on the sweetener.

Rebecca was starting to feel a little better. The fire in the bottle had fulfilled its purpose. Alison put her phone to her ear and called a taxi while lighting up a smoke. The question still loomed large in Rebecca's mind regarding the description of the job she was being hired for. She was concerned that Alison hadn't offered any information about it, and to her that was not a good sign. She looked over at Alison, watching her trying to light the cigarette and hold her phone at the same time. She was sensing something more than someone just trying to make friends with her. There was something more than that. There was something darker. Rebecca continued to observe Alison, unnoticed. She had learned to trust her intuition from an early age.

Alison suddenly jumped off the curb onto the street and was waving her arms in the air hysterically. She was hailing a cab that had just turned the corner.

Rebecca objected as strongly as she could. "Alison, be careful, these roads are dangerous." she had an uneasy feeling in the pit of her stomach that was not going away, it was getting stronger. The young girl could feel her self-control weakening as the good feeling provided by the alcohol was becoming stronger. The cab slowed and the two girls got in the back.

Alison put her hand on the back of the driver's seat, "The Coffee Club." She didn't show much respect for people in general. She turned back to Rebecca. "The club officially opens at five but I can get us in a little earlier. So I thought we could go to the sports bar on the corner for an hour or so, have a bite to eat, and then hit the club. It's going to be packed tonight. There is a great band playing." she waited for Rebecca to respond.

Alison's eyes were sparkling and there was an excitement about her that Rebecca didn't understand. "Are you okay? You seem excited about something. Is there anything I should know, Alison?"

"No, no. I am just happy that we are going out together and are hitting the town," she said while putting her arm around Rebecca and passing the brown bottle again.

"I still have a job, right?" Rebecca needed a little reassurance before she could relax and let her hair down. She was concerned that by not helping Alison with the job the night before, she might be getting the sack before she'd even put in an hour's work.

"Of course you do," Alison said as she took another gulp of the booze. "Now, stop worrying and relax. Take another swallow. I told you our boss likes you." She handed her the bottle again. "Tonight we party. Tomorrow we worry about work. Its all been arranged. I am under orders to show you a good time and that is what I am going to do," she said, taking the bottle back and raising it in the air. "To tonight. May everything go as planned." Alison's head bent backwards as she emptied the bottle.

The cab pulled up outside the club and the two girls got out. Alison paid the cabby and stopped to straighten her clothes. Rebecca turned to the club, looked at the huge black and red door, and wondered if it was such a good idea to work in a place like that. She still had the uneasy feelings in her stomach but she was sick of the way her life was going. Even though Rebecca didn't like some things about Alison, she did know how to have a good time, and that was what Rebecca wanted right now. She needed to have a distraction, to take her mind away from her troubles, and a night out with Alison fit the bill.

The afternoon went quickly at the sports bar, and before she knew it, Rebecca was at the entrance to the club. A line was forming with mostly girls just a little older than Rebecca, and some guys too, but they looked older. Alison walked to the front of the line and banged on the door. There were some funny looks directed her way by people in the crowd but she didn't seem to care. The big door swung open and there stood Cahn, dressed in a dark black tuxedo with purple silk lapels and a black shirt. This man was huge. He looked at them, smiling.

"Hey, Alison, good to see you." His voice was deep and strong. He turned to Rebecca. "Rebecca, I was looking forward to seeing you last night. I hope you're feeling better."

Rebecca felt the power coming from his voice. It was weird. It felt like she was hit by a force of some kind, not powerful enough to move her or stop her, but she did know something had impacted her energy. With everything that had been happening to her lately, Rebecca just took it on board as another weird experience to add to the others and walked in behind Alison. When they went down the big staircase and reached the door of the room where the band was playing, Alison stopped and turned to Rebecca.

"Tonight is your night, Rebecca," she spoke in a quiet voice. "You must spread your wings and embrace your destiny. I will make certain everything is as it should be." Smiling, Alison turned to the door and opened it. The full force of the music hit them all at once. Rebecca visibly winced at the impact of the volume of the music as it hit her ears.

Alison led the way to the same table in the corner, close to the music and dance floor, that they'd used the last time they were there.

"What a loud band these guys are." Rebecca shouted in Alison's ear as they moved to the music.

"Yeah. It's great!" Alison yelled back while taking hold of a guys arm and leading him away across the dance floor between pillars that were situated all around the dance area.

The room was filling rapidly with people all intent on having a good time. Most of them were dancing as if possessed, and making Rebecca a little nervous, but she reminded herself she was going to have a great time. She sat at the table looking around, imagining that she was going to meet a guy, and maybe he would be special, maybe even really, really sweet too. At that point, Alison showed up and sat down next to her, breathless.

"Really great music, eh Rebecca? Want a drink?" Without waiting for a reply, Alison made her way to the huge bar that ran the full circumference of the room and ordered their drinks.

Rebecca sat, swaying slightly to the music. She was slowly beginning to feel relaxed and was actually seriously thinking of having a good time.

"It's time to let go," she heard a voice say in her ear. She turned around and saw Alison standing with a tray full of drinks. There must have been a combination of at least six or eight drinks, including what looked like vodka orange, shots, and beers. She knew it was not a good idea to let go to that extreme. If she did, who would take care of her if something went wrong? Rebecca thought of Social Services and what they would make her do if she got in trouble and they caught her. All these thoughts ran across her mind within a split second as the drinks were held in front of her. She didn't really know Alison that well, nor did she know the place they were in. What she did know was that all her rational and logical reasoning was on its way out of the nearest window. All she wanted at that point in time was to become numb to the stress and anxiety she was suffering with, and the constant headaches, and strange visions she was experiencing.

Rebecca reached across and took a vodka drink from the tray. "Thanks, Alison." She paused as she sipped the drink. Rebecca had made her mind up. " What the hell! Time to let go," she smiled. "This is going to be a real blowout."

Alison smiled the kind of smile that indicated her plan had succeeded. She saw that Rebecca was slowly succumbing to the power of desperation.

They drank, sang, and danced for what seemed like hours to Rebecca. Periodically, the teenager would sit, and then pass out for a while, and she wasn't sure, but she might have thrown up once or twice as well. It was really clear at such a young age, as well as not being used to drinking alcohol, that after three or four drinks, Rebecca was getting pretty drunk. Alison was providing all the drinks and friends for Rebecca to enjoy. Yet, everything was not as it seemed.

Alison was not the person she portrayed herself to be. The only reason she was living at the same hostel as Rebecca was to get close to her, to become her friend in order that she could gain her trust. The events about to unfold would define the rest of Rebecca's life and she was oblivious to everything. She was like a helpless insect about to meet the owner of the web she was entangled in. The night held a possible start of a downward spiraling, disastrous, life-threatening course for Rebecca and she was helpless to protect her self. Alison had put in motion events designed to introduce Rebecca to the underworld of abuse, addiction, and eventual self-destruction.

The reason Rebecca was targeted for this nightmare had its origins embedded deep in ancient history. For millennia, various secret societies were formed to fight the strongholds of the religious groups of the period. These societies became enemies across the centuries and the feuds that developed continue to the present day. Alison was a member of one of the sects that embraced the power of the darker forces of the universe. Rebecca, unknowingly, was affiliated with an opposing secret society through birthright, so as things stood, Alison had the element of surprise over Rebecca and her plan was to lead her over a metaphorical cliff and into the abyss below.

Alison was trained from birth for this very task. She displayed an exceptional aptitude regarding the ability to develop a hate and hunger for the total destruction of members of other secret societies. She displayed a rare talent for guiding her victims into a situation where they had a false sense of security and she enjoyed watching them slowly descend into various stages of self-destruction. She had a reputation amongst her colleagues for never missing any of the last throws of her dying victim. It was a tradition with her and some even used it as Alison's signature when referring to her in conversation. The inevitable and eventual, apparent suicide of her victim always became a ritual with her. Alison took pleasure from every stage of the experience from the initial friendly contact to the desperate pleas for help near the end. Rebecca was totally unaware of the nature of the beast that was Alison, and she had no idea of the severity of what was in store for her.

Alison eyed Rebecca from across the table, unnoticed. She had been waiting for this for an eternity. She stood up, putting her shot glass to her mouth, and emptied it. "Okay Rebecca, finish that drink. There's a couple of guys over there with our names on them."

"Wait. I don't think I can dance in this state. I feel sick." Rebecca slumped back in the chair.

Alison stood and looked at her for a few seconds without saying anything, just staring. Eventually, she spoke. "Come with me." Alison walked around the table and grabbed Rebecca's arm. "I'm taking you to the ladies room to fix you up. I know just what you need." She helped her to her feet.

Rebecca was drunk and could hardly remain stable as they made there way out of the dance hall. The restroom was half full. There were three girls sharing a joint, a couple making out, and three or four laughing and smoking in the corner.

Alison brought Rebecca over to the end cubicle and kicked open the door. "Right, sit there and rest. I will be back soon." She disappeared.

The other girls in the room were making jokes and laughing about the poor slob drunk in the cubicle. A tall girl commented to her friends, sarcastically, regarding how unhealthy it was to mix booze and drugs.

Alison returned and knocked on the cubicle door. "Rebecca, are you okay? I have something that will make you feel so much better,

I promise," she said, grinning, as she strummed the small black and red wooden container with her fingers.

One of the girls smoking a joint in the corner yelled to Alison. "Hey, blond bitch, what you got there? Something nice I bet?" Alison slowly turned to her. The girl continued. "How about you give it to me. I am feeling sick too." They all laughed.

Alison wanted to engage the girls in the rest room but she had her heart set on destroying Rebecca. The dark sorceress comforted herself in the knowledge that there would always be opportunities to deal with girls like these at a later time.

"I'm okay, Alison, just give me a minute," came the voice on the other side of the cubicle door. Rebecca was definitely feeling the effects of all the alcohol Alison had given her. She was feeling very odd and very faint. "I think I should leave now and go back to my room, Alison. I am not feeling good at all."

Alison turned her attention to the voice behind the door. "I know you are not feeling well Rebecca. That is why I have brought you something to make you feel better. Just trust me. Open the door." There was a pause while Rebecca tried to gather herself. Alison held her head up when the door latch slid back. "Here, this will take all the nausea and lightheaded feelings away. Drink it back in one shot. It has the most potency that way."

Rebecca remained seated and lifted her head from her hands. "More drinking. I don't know if I can put anymore liquid in my stomach and expect it to stay put." Her face was white and her eyes red. She eventually reached for the vile of dark blue liquid that Alison had taken from the container and was holding it in her outstretched hand as she beckoned Rebecca to take it.

Rebecca put it to her lips and with her eyes screwed shut she gulped the liquid down in one shot. "Ugh! That was vile Alison. You poisoned me." She massaged her throat as the fluid went past.

"You will be feeling better in a few minutes. Trust me." Alison put the black box in her pocket and helped Rebecca to her feet.

They both headed for the dance hall. When they got there the place was rocking. The two girls made their way back to their table close to the band. Rebecca sat for a few minutes while she caught her second wind. Alison looked around the room as if she was expecting someone.

"You were right, Alison, I do feel much better. What was that poison you gave me?" Rebecca couldn't believe how much better she was after just a few minutes. "That stuff is amazing. Where did you get it?" she asked while they finished the drinks on the table. "I feel like I could party all night," Rebecca laughed.

Alison ignored what she was saying and continued to order more drinks from the waitress. "Hey, Rebecca, do you see those two guys over there?" she pointed discretely across the floor to a couple of guys who were leaning against one of the pillars, talking and drinking beers.

Rebecca turned to look over at them as Alison passed her a drink. "Yeah, the one in the blue shirt looks nice," she said. "Do you know them? Maybe we could dance with them?" Rebecca didn't hear a response so she turned back to the table and noticed Alison was no longer there. She looked around between the people standing at the dance floor and beside the pillars. She finally spotted her. She was standing at the bar talking to Cahn, and from what it looked like to Rebecca, the hulk of a man standing with Alison seemed to be getting handed his head. She watched in amazement as Alison looked like she was tearing a strip off of him. Alison finished with Cahn. Then she walked around the pillars, alongside the dance floor, towards the two guys she pointed out earlier. Rebecca watched Cahn scurry out of sight up the stairway to another floor.

As the young girl sipped on her vodka, she continued to watch what developed between Alison and the two guys. She remained with the guys for what seemed like ages. She was laughing and drinking. Then, without warning, Alison turned and pointed at Rebecca all in one motion. If that wasn't embarrassing enough she had the guy in the blue shirt wave and smile at her. Rebecca wanted to shrink and die. If there had been a hole in the floor that had no bottom she would have gladly dived in at that moment. Instead, she lifted her drink and emptied it in one go, then sank in the chair, trying desperately to disappear from sight. At the same time, Rebecca did get a kick out of the fact that the cute guy in the blue shirt obviously fancied her.

Alison eventually returned to the table, her curly blond hair bouncing as she walked between the pillars and tables. "Rebecca, the guys want to join us and maybe spend the rest of the night with us dancing and having some fun. What do you say?" Alison was not smiling like an excited schoolgirl at a local dance, more like someone who was up to something. Rebecca couldn't think straight at that point, so she gave up the concern, ignoring the alarm bells going off in both ears, and took another sip of her drink. "Sure, whatever you think. I am having a good time and feeling no pain right now, so why not?" she said leaning back in her chair. She was obviously too drunk to care, and more importantly, unaware she was nearing the point where her ability to help herself if something bad were to happen, was in serious jeopardy.

Alison turned to the guys across the room and waved them over. "Great, this is going to be so much fun," she said leaning toward Rebecca, "The guy in the blue shirt really likes you. He said he could really show you a good time." By this time Alison was becoming more and more excited. Rebecca began to sense there was something not right with the whole thing. Even in her state of inebriation, she felt Alison was up to something.

Rebecca sat up straight and took a large breath in, trying to gather her wits before whatever was going to happen, did. "Sounds fantastic, I just have to go to the ladies room. I will be back as quickly as possible, okay?" she tried to seem as unperturbed as possible under the circumstances.

Alison was silent for a moment then she spoke. "Don't you leave me here with them after all the work I did to get them for us." She had the same look of cold darkness in her eyes that Rebecca kept seeing, indicating she might be capable of anything.

Rebecca stood up composing herself and headed for the door. She was forced to navigate through a hall full of young people having a great time and most of them were hammered too. She spent some time in the toilet cubicle in a frantic attempt to sober up. However, it was quite useless. It seemed the stuff Alison gave her was a very powerful substance. It made her feel better but Rebecca was sure it had other purposes too, since she recalled Alison practically forced her to drink it. Rebecca knew she couldn't stay in the restroom for long or Alison would be in there to get her. She resigned herself to the fact that she had to see this through but that in the morning she was saying goodbye to Alison, even if it meant loosing her job. She decided she'd had enough of Alison for sure.

Rebecca pulled herself together as best she could and opened the cubicle door. The other girls in the rest room were all frantically making themselves as desirable as possible for the guys outside, something that made her recognize that she wasn't like them, and shouldn't be in a place like this. She tripped as she stepped into the hallway outside the restroom and almost pushed a guy over as he was walking by.

"Sorry, I didn't mean to fall on you. I tripped on something." Rebecca slowly pushed her long dark hair back across her face as he supported her in his arms.

"That's okay." The young guy held her in his arms until she had steadied herself. "Are you all right?" he asked pulling his arms away.

Rebecca could tell he was genuinely concerned, and as far as her condition allowed, she thought he looked really nice and didn't seem drunk either.

"I'm Robbie—nice to meet you. What is your name?" he asked in a low gentle voice that resonated with her immediately. He had blue eyes that sparkled and thick blond hair.

"Rebecca," she half slurred. "Thanks for not letting me fall. I have had a bit too much to drink as you probably noticed. I don't usually go to clubs drinking but...." She realized he was staring at her and that she should shut up quickly if she wanted to leave what was left of an attempt at a good impression.

She saw that he was really looking at her in a way that meant something. Rebecca was not used to this kind of attention. It was different than the leering looks she got from the truck drivers when she crossed busy streets. She never had the time for boyfriends growing up because she was always too busy with one thing or another.

He had a slight smile when he realized she was embarrassed at being a little drunk. "Are you here with anyone, Rebecca?"

She tipped her head up towards his face and hesitated. "Not really I…I mean I have a girl friend—we came together." She didn't know what to say, she really liked him and she sensed they had a connection, somehow.

"Okay, can I walk back with you to the dance hall?" he asked, hoping. Robbie also felt something. The connection was strong with him too but he didn't exactly know what he had felt. He just knew he liked her.

Rebecca knew she was drunk but she was determined that it was not going to be enough to put Robbie off talking to her. "Yes, I would like that," she replied in the best voice she could muster, trying her best not to slur her words.

They entered the dance hall and walked toward the floor, where she hoped he would ask her to dance, preferably to a slow song. Just as he looked likely to ask, Alison showed up.

"Rebecca, where have you been? The guys are waiting for us." Alison had seen her come into the hall with Robbie and didn't want anything to come between the plans she had arranged for her. She knew the guy with her would be put off when he realized Rebecca was already with a guy. Alison was right. Robbie quickly made an excuse and left.

"Alison, why did you do that?" Rebecca was upset. She really liked Robbie.

"What do you mean? Do what? We are expected back at the table." Alison had guided Rebecca to the pillar nearby. "Look, Rebecca! Understand this, I have gone to a lot of trouble to get those guys over to our table, and if you hadn't noticed, we are outnumbered by girls three to one in this place. So when a couple of guys are interested, you do not let them get away…understand?"

Rebecca saw the look in her eyes. There was a cold darkness behind them and there was no way she was going to piss her off enough to see what Alison was capable of. "Okay, Alison, lets go back to the table," she said with a half smile.

"Good. You go back to the guys and keep them occupied. I have something else to deal with. I will see you in about ten minutes." Alison left and walked in the direction of the stairway to the upper floors.

The young girl was saddened and was on her way over to the table where the guys were when someone held on to her arm. She spun around to see who it was. Rebecca's face lit up. "Oh, hi Robbie." She felt her face glow. "I thought you would never speak to me again."

"I would like to call you sometime, Rebecca, if it is okay?" He gazed right into her eyes, looking for a sign, something that told him she was interested.

Before she could think, the words were already free. "Sorry Robbie, I don't have a phone." She knew as soon as she spoke that it was not going to sound good.

His expression was one of total disappointment. "Oh. Okay." He stammered something awkward and turned to leave.

Rebecca stopped him before he got fully turned around and pulled his arm back. "What I meant to say was that I am…in between places right now and would like to see you again but I am staying at the hostel at Granville and Main and there's only a desk phone. You can leave a message at the desk, though, and I will get it." She held her hands together hoping Robbie would be okay with it and not think she was a total flake.

His eyes glistened as he smiled. "I'd like that." There was a slight pause. "I have to go now but I will call you tomorrow. Maybe we could go out sometime for a walk or pizza or something," he decided to stop talking and quit while he was ahead.

"Okay, sounds good. I will look forward to that." Rebecca was feeling tired. "I have to go back to my table, so I will see you later Robbie, okay?

"Sure, I will call you. My friend is waiting upstairs for me. I have to go" Robbie started to leave, walking backwards up the stairway toward the exit in order to see as much of Rebecca as he could before she disappeared back into the dance hall.

The young girl was happy for the first time in a while. She had just met a guy that she really liked and he seemed to like her too. It was great. The smile left her face when she spotted Alison coming down the stairs toward her. The expression on her face betrayed her. She did not look happy. But Rebecca didn't care. There was nothing she could do to take away her good feeling.

"I saw you with that guy, Rebecca. Who was he?"

"Just someone I met in the hallway. He is really nice and I like him," she said not caring what Alison thought.

"Where are the other guys I left you with?" Alison demanded, looking over at the empty table. The guys must have got bored waiting for them to return. "Rebecca, they are gone. I told you to keep them there till I got back."

She was not listening because she was still reliving the meeting with Robbie in her mind. Alison became more insistent and drew closer to Rebecca, so close that Rebecca could smell the stench of alcohol evident on her breath. She knew she should not have been able to identify such a strong odor because she also had alcohol on her breath. This alarmed her and she was also starting to feel her energy was being drained from her. Rebecca assumed it was because of all the people mixing in a small place but it was gaining in strength and intensity, that ruled out the dancehall full of people. It was difficult to understand how her energy could be drained, or by whom, but it was unmistakable, and it felt to her like all the air was being sucked out of the room.

Alison became progressively more aggressive. "Don't think for one minute you are going to ditch me for some guy who smiled at you more than once. You and I are here to hit the heights, understand!" There was a significant change in her tone of voice that was definitely of a threatening nature but simultaneously veiled enough so as not to freak Rebecca out, causing her to leave.

However, Rebecca was cleaver enough to recognize when someone was not who they presented themselves to be. She was convinced, after spending the day and evening with Alison, that something dark and disturbing lurked behind the shroud she covered herself with. Rebecca's intuition kicked in again, warning her to get away from her. She listened, and reinforced within her mind, that this would be the last night she would spend with Alison. Still, Rebecca didn't anticipate any danger in finishing out the night dancing and having fun, and she considered it foolish to leave prematurely and miss out on a good time. She made it clear to Alison that she didn't appreciate being told who to be with and whom she couldn't.

Once the two settled their differences and the air had been cleared, Alison brought a typical grin to her face.

"Here Rebecca, a peace offering. Lets both go to the dance floor and dance with the first guys we see and enjoy the rest of the night. We've earned it. I am sorry. I can be a little overbearing sometimes." She held out a glass of vodka to her.

"Okay, let's just take it easy and enjoy what is left of the night." Rebecca reached for the drink.

As she put her drink on the table, Alison tapped her shoulder. "Hey, I see someone I know at the bar. I will be back in a minute. Don't go anywhere"

"Okay." The young girl didn't care if she ever came back. Rebecca was in heaven thinking about Robbie, and wondering if he was the one, and if he called the hostel she would have his number forever. The music had a great beat, and she closed her eyes, allowing the sound to transport her into an imaginary world where she and Robbie danced and held each other close. Rebecca fantasized about their first kiss and how that would feel. Her head was slowly swaying back and forth to the music. She was feeling really peaceful for the first time in a long while.

Alison walked up to the bar and spoke with two guys. She turned around to face Rebecca every so often. They had dark short haircuts and wore jeans and long dark coats, like something out of the Wild West.

Rebecca opened her eyes suddenly; she was aware of something nagging at her senses. Automatically, she wanted to know where Alison was and she looked around, eventually looking in the direction of the bar. She saw Alison and the guys, there, talking and looking at her. They were drinking and laughing. Rebecca didn't understand what was going on but she just shrugged it off as just another part of Alison's persona. She was enjoying the music by herself anyway and preferred it that way now she had met Robbie. Before she leaned back in the chair to recapture the peaceful state she had found, Rebecca noticed something about the two guys sitting with Alison. The coats they were wearing seemed to float and move while they were seated on the bar stools but that wasn't possible, there was no wind machine going or anything like that to cause their coats to do that. Rebecca was baffled and decided it was the effects of too much alcohol in her system making her hallucinate.

Alison handed the two guys a gold locket. It had a small inscription on the back that read, 'If you should ever need me you need only think it'.

"This is the key to all we have been promised. It has fallen into my hands after all these years." She held the locket in her hand so they could see. "The job I asked you here to do is delicate but can be accomplished with some arrangement. I will prepare the target and you two will finish her off." Alison stared directly at them; her eyes were like death. They knew what she meant.

"When can we do this for you, my friend?" the taller one of them asked her.

Alison took another mouthful of beer. "Soon, my friends…very soon."

Rebecca was watching Alison and her two friends. She noticed she handed something to the two guys but could not make out what it was, and she thought no more about it.

Alison stepped between the two men, and faced the bar, turning her back to Rebecca. "Okay, I think we need to do this fast. She is getting very suspicious. This has to be done right—I don't want a repeat of the fiasco that happened last time you performed the service, understand?" Alison was trying to keep the conversation quiet.

"We understand, and our promise is to remain loyal, no matter what threat comes forth." The two remained sitting at the bar, drinking, while Alison returned to the table carrying the drinks.

Alison stood next to Rebecca, where she was sitting with her eyes still closed and listening to the music.

"Hey Rebecca, my friends have offered to come join us for drinks, and to get things started, they sent these over. Isn't that cool?" she held up two glasses full.

Rebecca opened an eye and saw Alison holding the glasses. Her first urge was to refuse but she didn't. Instead, she reached for the nearest glass and put it to her mouth.

"Thanks," she slurped the first mouthful because the glass was really full. "Where do you know those guys from?" she asked.

Alison looked away for a second, thinking. "I've known those guys since junior high. We used to skip class to go smoke a joint in the pit," she said, laughing.

Rebecca didn't pursue it; she didn't have the energy. All she wanted to do was enjoy the rest of what was left of the night and think of her time to come with Robbie.

"Sounds like you had fun in school, Alison." Rebecca meant it—but not in the normal sense.

Alison watched her drink the potion she had slipped, unnoticed, into her drink. Rebecca was totally unaware of what was happening. Alison enjoyed watching her consume the drug. "I'll go back and let them know it's good to join us, okay?"

"Sure Alison, that's fine," she said. "I wouldn't mind dancing for a while."

Alison walked back to the bar making her way through the crowd of dancers where her two friends waited for her to give them the go ahead.

"Okay, you must somehow get her to the back of the hall, to the recovery room, without her causing a fuss, and place her on one of the couches in the corner. Be very discrete!" Alison was extremely insistent. "I will be there, waiting."

It was called the recovery room, because often, people would be taken there when they had too much to drink, and they could sober up enough to start drinking again, which was good for business. The room was set up to be dark and cozy, with soft music playing, so people could recuperate without being interrupted—which was why it was perfect for what Alison had in mind for Rebecca.

The men decided only one of them should go to Rebecca and ask her to dance, then while slowly making there way across the dance floor, he would set about getting Rebecca to the recovery room without her suspecting anything.

"I will go to her," the smaller of the two men insisted. "When I bring her close to the edge of the dance floor, you will call to me from near the entrance to the recovery room, beckoning for us to join you. Then you must quickly disappear into the room so she cannot have the opportunity to refuse," he said, handing his friend his long black coat.

The men left the bar, one heading to the back of the room, the other towards where Rebecca was sitting.

"Hi Rebecca. I'm Raul. Alison mentioned that you would be willing to let me join your table to enjoy maybe a little dancing and some good conversation?" he said, smiling.

Rebecca sat cross-legged at the table, sipping her vodka. "Hi. Yes. Nice to meet you." She saw that he was quite nice and seemed to be no threat at all. "Actually, I feel like dancing too, but before we do, I need to explain that I am not looking for anything more than dancing." She gave him a polite smile and waited for his response.

"Oh, I understand, Rebecca, and I am only looking for a dance partner too. I love to dance but not the complications that usually come with meeting people at a night club," he reassured her.

Rebecca put her drink on the table and stood up.

"Shall we try this one?" Raul asked, turning to watch her expression as they listened to the music, evaluating it to determine if it was a song they could handle.

"Okay," she said. Rebecca leaned on his shoulder, speaking into his ear as they moved closer to the dance floor and the loud music. "But lets start off slow, agreed?"

Raul looked back at her, smiling and nodding, in agreement. "Yeah, great idea."

The two danced for a couple of songs before Raul's partner began the sequence of events designed to bring Rebecca to her end. Raul manipulated their dancing to bring Rebecca close to the edge of the floor, knowing she would be able to clearly see the frantic beckoning of his accomplice.

Rebecca, seeing this, tapped Raul on his arm. "Hey, isn't that your friend waving to us from over there?" she pointed to the back of the hall while they continue dancing.

Raul, playing along, gave a look of quizzical surprise and waved back, pretending not to know anything. "Yes, it's Stavros. I think he wants us to go over there." He turned to face Rebecca with an expression on his face that intimated he thought they should. "Rebecca, do you mind if we go to see what he wants?"

After dancing for a while, Rebecca didn't feel at all well but she didn't let him know because she didn't want to spoil the good time he was obviously having dancing. However, she did realize going over there would provide an opportunity to rest. "Sure, Raul, I could use a break. I feel a little woozy"

The two of them left the dance floor and headed in the direction of the recovery room at the rear. It was a struggle to move through the crowds who were using the break in the music to get more drinks. When they entered the room, it was quite dark compared to the hall. Raul saw Alison and Stavros seated at one of the many booths placed around the room. He led Rebecca to the furthest corner of the quiet area where Alison was waiting.

"Hi Rebecca. Look at this place isn't it fantastic? I love how they made it so private, don't you?" Alison kept her gaze centered on Rebecca's face until she sat at the booth. She waited for Rebecca to notice the gold locket Stavros was swinging around his fingers. Alison was determined to enjoy every morsel of what was to follow. The two men closed in on Rebecca as she sat next to Alison.

Rebecca saw her gold locket and automatically reached for her neck to affirm it was not there. She didn't answer Alison because something made her sink into the booth holding the side of her head. The lightheaded feelings she suffered with had returned. She had no idea what was going on and she thought she was about to have another of the episodes she been experiencing the last few weeks. Rebecca hoped the large amount of alcohol she had consumed that day would help prevent the headaches and visions from returning.

Alison rested her elbow on the table in the booth and then slowly placed her chin in the palm of her hand.

" Rebecca, you don't look okay, is your head hurting again?" At that moment, she looked deep into Rebecca's eyes. Rebecca moved back instinctively as she felt a sharp, stinging, surge of energy strike her, making her eyes water as if she had been poked with something.

" What was that?" she quickly covered her eyes with her hands and fell back into the booth. At that moment, the band started to play their next set. Rebecca lay down on the bench seat, her eyes watering and stinging. Soon after that, the waitress arrived.

" Yes, I will have a carafe of the white wine and my friend here will have a vodka tonic." At this point, Rebecca still had not surfaced from the booth seat. The waitress took the order and quickly disappeared.

Alison tossed her long blond curls back off her face. " Why don't you sit up—the pain will go away soon," she said with a coldness that sent shivers across Rebecca's body. "I have something for you, Rebecca." Alison played with another vile of colored liquid between her fingers.

Rebecca pulled herself up off the seat. Her head was heavy with the increasing pain. "What is happening to me? Alison, what did you do?"

Alison continued, with her elbow on the table and her chin resting in her hand, she smiled and leaned forward toward Rebecca. " Whatever do you mean? You are my friend. I wouldn't do anything to hurt you." The waitress came back with the drinks.

Alison brought her attention right to her. "Put them down and leave," she said curtly. She poured some wine into her glass and sipped it slowly. "You do not know how long we have been planning this evening, Rebecca. Years have passed since we last met, and I just know you are not going to enjoy this at all, but I will explain anyway."

Rebecca struggled with the heaviness she felt in her head as she tried to remain sitting upright on the booth seat. "What are you talking about? Have you drugged me? I feel as if the floor keeps falling away from me, as if I were falling down a dark hole." She pushed her back against the seatback with her legs, and tried to keep her head as still as possible, which made her feel not as bad.

Alison licked the side of her wine glass to catch a drop that rolled down. " Please, Rebecca, have a drink. You will feel better. It will ease the pain, I promise." She slid the vodka tonic across the table to Rebecca.

Rebecca rested her head on the back of the booth seat and looked at Alison " You know I'm only sixteen, right? I'm too young to drink." Rebecca was voicing the first thoughts that came into her head to buy time, while she tried to sort out what was happening, and who the hell Alison was.

Alison just stared while she sipped her wine. "Don't worry, no one will bother us in here," she said quietly.

Alison was right. The music was playing loud and the place was full of people who were drinking and only interested in having a good time.

" Who are you? What do you mean, you know me? How did you know about the pain in my head? Rebecca was very scared. "I don't feel so good," she whispered and began to lose consciousness. She tried to find her feet but the two men put a hand on each of her arms forcing her back down on the seat. At that point, she slowly closed her eyes. Everything began to go dark for Rebecca. Although she could still hear the music, it was faint; clearly she was starting to pass out.

Alison and the two men left Rebecca in the booth to die, after covering her with one of the long black coats, to discourage anyone from disturbing her. Raul wanted desperately to finish her off with his blade.

"Master, we should use this opportunity to give her as an offering to the Dark One. You know how much pleasure it would give him, and I could use the blade?" His hand clutched the knife, showing his desire and eagerness.

Alison gripped his arm with amazing strength, causing Raul to wince. "Don't ever forget who your allegiance is with. Have you forgotten so soon the pain you were forced to endure after the last fiasco?" Alison's eyes glowed with a green hue.

Raul's face showed signs of pain and tiny blood vessels surfaced on his arm while his mouth betrayed his suffering. "No, master," he hissed in a way that told her he had enough. Alison released his arm and immediately Raul clutched it. Little droplets of blood ran down to his wrist. Alison's nails had easily penetrated his skin.

"I have the key to the past and I have the Prophesied One. Her soul will be mine soon, something Lord Bastian will never have, do you two understand?" Alison took the golden locket from his hand, and turned back to the booth, watching Rebecca sink deeper into her coma. She swung the golden locket around her hand and whispered to the young girl. "Never trust anyone, Rebecca. That was your downfall. Didn't your mom tell you that before she was taken from you?" she laughed softly.

The young girl was barely moving, only the motion of the coat covering her indicated as much, while she struggled to breathe. Alison's words squealed through Rebecca's brain like a red-hot ice pick. She only had moments left before she slipped into the artificially induced coma caused by the drug cocktail given to her by Alison. How could she have been so stupid? What did Alison mean when she said her mom was taken? Mom died of brain cancer. Her gran's voice rang through her head. All the thoughts shot through her brain in an electrical storm of activity, indicating the last throws of life for someone on the verge of death.

Alison walked toward the exit with Raul and Stavros following behind. They left the room, navigating the dance hall through the hundreds of revelers still partying as if it was their last night on earth.

Rebecca could not move now; the poison had reached her nervous system and was beginning to asphyxiate her. There was panic in her heart as she lay dying on the couch in the seedy nightclub. All of a sudden, a blinding flash of golden, white, light streaked across the dark screen in front of her eyes. She thought this was the end, her breath was very short and her heart was close to stopping. Just at that moment of shear fright, she felt someone touch her hand, and as her awareness focused on the physical presence, an overwhelming sense of peace and warmth surged through her. The presence sat with her holding her in the booth. Rebecca felt her head being tilted upward; a cool wet sensation brushed passed her lips. Her mouth opened and she could feel the liquid running down her tongue to the back of her mouth and into her throat. She began to breathe easier. After a bout of coughing and some tears, she sat up, taking in a deep breath and filling her lungs with life-giving oxygen. The presence held her close with tenderness and love. She slowly opened her eyes and was astonished to see who was sitting on the couch next to her, holding her hand.

"Thank you. I thought I was going to die. I can not feel my arm or legs." Her voice was very weak.

"Please, try not to speak. The liquid will bring all the life back to your body in a few moments. Please, breathe deeply, your blood needs the oxygen, it is what makes the antidote work."

"What are you doing here…? How did you know what was being done to me?" she managed to force the words out of her mouth before she coughed and spluttered, spewing a mixture of bodily fluids on the floor of the booth.

Alison suddenly stopped at the bottom of the staircase outside the dancehall and turned to the two men. "Raul, Stavros, do you not sense him? Go back. She is not dead. He has revived her. Kill him! Kill them both! Before it is too late for me to claim her." Alison continued up the stairway to the exit where a cab was waiting. "Take me to the Apostle building downtown." She hurriedly climbed into the back of the cab.

The color and warmth had not fully returned to Rebecca's face yet but she had revived well enough for the danger to pass. The potion she was given to combat the poison worked as it was designed to.

She rested her hand on his. "Thank you again, you saved my life." Rebecca still had trouble moving, especially her arm and one of her legs. "That is what friends are for," he said with the warmth of the morning sun. "You are not clear of danger yet, we must hurry Rebecca."

Shaulmar stood with his back to the booth. He held the long black coat at arms length. The coat moved as if struggling to free itself from his grip, and Rebecca thought she heard a high pitched whine, as if the coat were alive.

She stood gingerly and leaned on the backrest of the booth. "What was that they put on top of me? I distinctly felt an electrical charge as if all the electrons in my body were being sucked from every atom by a giant magnet." She moved to the front side of the booth, hobbling a little, as the potion Shaulmar had given her began to take hold and the re-oxygenated blood began to flow freely throughout her body. "I can remember as everything went dark, my mind began to shrink and my body became rigid, as if frozen." Her voice was getting noticeably stronger.

Shaulmar threw the garment on the table in the booth. "Yes, this coat, or Shroud of Pain, as it is known in their world has the power to devour the life force of anyone not aligned with the dark forces of the universe." His voice was quiet as he looked around, suspiciously, for something. "There are many shrouds within the four dimensions of this reality. This particular shroud is worn by specific tormenters and servants of Lord Draco Bastian, the leader of dark forces at work here."

At that moment, as if from nowhere, the two dark figures appeared to intervene in the rescue of Rebecca. They stood ominously in front of the two of them, blocking their path. Stavros retrieved his shroud while Raul engaged the man at Rebecca's side.

"You will not be so fortunate this time, Bedouin," Raul said as he slowly moved his hand to his belt, revealing the huge blade he had wanted to use on Rebecca earlier as she laid vulnerable and dying. Raul and Shaulmar were not strangers; they had met many lifetimes ago when the battle of good and evil raged across the earth. There was a score to settle between them; however, the being holding Rebecca's hand had other ideas.

Rebecca was scared and she squeezed Shaulmar's hand. "What are they talking about? Do you know them?" the girl asked, becoming even more confused as she turned to Shaulmar. "They are friends of Alison, the one who poisoned me," she whispered.

Raul moved closer. "So, you think you are going to interfere with our plans for young Rebecca here? Do you really imagine you can save her? Her destiny is to die here tonight." Raul's eyes were the color of coal. "This time it will not go your way, Bedouin! We aim to see to it."

There were still many scores of people in the club, still dancing, and quite a few had come to the recovery room to rest. It would be a mistake for the two assassins to try to kill them now and Shaulmar knew this.

"If you persist with your intentions, I will stop you. Rebecca Sullivan is not to die tonight according to our laws of light and harmony. The authorities will arrive before you can finish and remove any trace of your atrocities, I promise you." Shaulmar had moved his body between the two men, standing sideways to them, revealing his own weapon beneath the cloak he wore. "You know your master will not be thrilled at being implicated in such a messy affair, especially with so many witnesses."

Shaulmar was correct and Raul knew as much. The one thing Raul's master would not allow, was for him or his foundation to be uncovered and exposed to the world, under any circumstances.

Stavros leaned toward his partner and whispered something in his ear. Raul was at an impasse and he knew it. They could not afford to anger the dark lord. It would mean the end of their life. "Bedouin, do not assume this is ended. We will be seeing each other soon." Raul sheathed his blade and touched Stavros on the arm indicating their exit from the confrontation.

Shaulmar watched them leave, and as they finally disappeared amongst the partiers, he turned his attention to his friend and helped her to her feet. Rebecca was gaining momentum in her fight to regain some semblance of normalcy; her muscles were returning to normal and she was breathing easier now.

"I am sorry to admit this but I do not remember your name. I am so sorry." She was genuinely embarrassed.

He smiled and touched her hand. "Shaulmarhime, but you can call me Shaulmar. Rebecca, I know this must have been very traumatic for you, and there are probably many questions you would like answered but for now we must leave this place. There are many Dark Ones here unseen, darker than the ones you know." His eyes watched everything, while he helped Rebecca out of the recovery room. He knew it was essential he get her to a safe place, and soon, before Alison had another opportunity to strike.

"We must leave now. I will take you to a place where you will be safe," Shaulmar said with an undoubted concern etched deep into his half smile.

Rebecca did as he asked and gathered herself together well enough to make the journey upstairs to the street. Shaulmar led her out of the dance hall and up to the street where he hailed a cab, carefully looking in every direction, before he allowed Rebecca to emerge from the doorway. He helped her into the rear of the vehicle and sat next to her, his arm around her shoulder, protecting and comforting her.

Shaulmar sensed the dark forces were close at hand. They were attracted to the building that housed the nightclub. He was troubled at what he was sensing. There seemed to be a stronghold for the lower vibrational energies at that place. He felt a surge of energy as the cab pulled away from the curb that tried to stop them from leaving, and in his minds eye, he was shown a powerful vortex of darkness emanating deep from below the building. Shaulmar was aware there was a balance that had to be maintained in the universe, and when that was threatened, a natural process came into effect for that very purpose. He knew this confrontation was just the beginning but he didn't want Rebecca to be fearful, unnecessarily. The wizard also knew he would have to answer all of Rebecca's questions, that she was undoubtedly storing up for him, and would ask when she felt well enough.

The cab stopped at an old stone and brick building that stood alone on a large piece of land at the corner of a quiet avenue. The many trees that lined the driveway up to the house where Shaulmar lived swayed in the wind as if to welcome the master wizard home. Shaulmar paid the driver and held onto Rebecca as they made their way into the house.

Rebecca was relieved to be in the care of her friend, even though she didn't know much about him, at all. However, her intuition that she valued so much was telling her that she was safe and that she was where she should be.

The great wizard led her to the rear of the house where the extra rooms were located. "This way. You can stay in the room across from the conference room. It's quite nice and especially quiet and peaceful." He helped her to the bed. "I will return in a moment, Rebecca. Will you be okay by yourself?" she nodded as she steadied herself on the end of the bed. She was still very sick but was getting better steadily.

Shaulmar was gone for a few minutes, and when he returned, he was carrying a mug of warm sweet-smelling liquid. "Rebecca before you sleep, please be sure to drink all of this; it is very important for your recovery." He handed her the mug.

She looked at it and then at him. "What is it? It smells really delicious." Her voice was still weak and it cracked when she spoke.

Shaulmar gave a look of reassurance. "Something to help remove the poison from your system and clear your head a little. By the morning, after a restful sleep, you should be feeling much better." He left the room and closed the door.

CHAPTER 6

THE SUN SHONE THROUGH THE WINDOW IN REBECCA'S room the golden rays gently warming her face, coaxing her to wakefulness. She awoke, letting out a moan that indicated she had slept well. She snuggled beneath the comforter and yawned. The rush of fresh air filling her lungs felt really good to her. She climbed out of bed and put on the robe that hung on the back of the door. Rebecca remembered being brought there by Shaulmar but she was having difficulty recalling much of anything prior to that. She opened the door to see if she knew where she was and stepped into the hallway where she caught the aroma of coffee and French toast in the air. It had been so long since she'd smelled toast as good as that, it reminded her of home, and the memories that flooded her head were overwhelming. She followed the aroma all the way to the source.

"Hi Rebecca, how are you feeling this morning?" Shaulmar asked. His smile was infectious. He stood over a stove brimming with all kinds of foods being cooked.

Rebecca smiled back at him. "Thank you for bringing me here last night. I slept well and feel better. She sat at the table on a seat next to the window. "I don't know what would have happened to me if you hadn't found me?

Shaulmar beckoned to her from the stove. "Please, Rebecca, say no more. It was my responsibility to keep you safe after we had successfully made the connection once more at the old bookstore." His voice indicated an air of honest and genuine truth.

Rebecca fell silent. It was another strange and confusing piece of information that caused her to wrestle inside her mind as she tried to unravel what was happening to her, and more importantly, what was yet to come.

"Yes—the bookstore…you looked a lot…older then." She couldn't quite fathom that piece of information. "How come?" The wizard just continued to prepare the breakfast. Rebecca sat at the table and reached for some coffee. She was surprised, and thankful at how much better she was feeling; it was as if her mind and body had been completely cleansed of all poisons and toxins.

"Shaulmar, what was it you gave me last night before bed? I feel so different than normal, so clear, I don't really know how to explain it in words," she asked.

He continued to prepare the breakfast table. "It is a mix of various juices and herbal flora that encourage rapid energy repair along with an infusion of elements and minerals to speed recovery. It is an ancient medicinal concoction that has been handed down through my ancestral tribe for eons." Shaulmar came to the oak table nestled in the nook at the window of the kitchen carrying plates of food and utensils. He wanted to deliberately trigger her curiosity about various things he was to teach her. Shaulmar knew her curiosity would be peaked about the herbal rapid infusion, it sounded so cool.

Rebecca helped him display the food around the table. "Well, it is a fantastic...uh...medicine," she said, not knowing what to call it specifically, but with a true conviction, trying to impress upon him how grateful she really was.

The wizard wanted to set the mood for Rebecca concerning different things he was to reveal to her. He knew a strong foundation of trust and honesty was necessary for the relationship to progress, and he also knew that Rebecca's knowledge and understanding of the larger universe had to be developed for each of them to remain safe. Shaulmar trusted that the path he was on was destined but what he didn't know yet was if Rebecca was willing to tread the same path.

They were both enjoying the breakfast he had made when suddenly Rebecca stopped eating and looked at her friend. "What did you mean exactly by rapid energy...what was that last part?" she looked confused.

"Infusion," he said with a mouth full of breakfast, " rapid energy infusion." He tried to say it more clearly after he'd eaten half the food in his mouth, then apologized for doing so.

"Yes...right, rapid energy infusion, what is that anyway? Never heard of it, is that some kind of scientific thing?" she asked with the energy of a teenager her age. Her energy and alertness, coupled with her appetite was the confirmation Shaulmar was looking for. It provided evidence to him that the herbal potion he gave her the night before had absorbed all of the poisons in her system and neutralized them effectively.

"Actually, it is an ancient art of healing that I learned from the tribal healer where I was born. What you were given was an ancient remedy that promotes toxic release and neutralization that includes multi-dimensional intervention." His explanation and description of the process only served to heighten her curiosity and confusion. "I know you must have some questions you would like to ask me, and there are things I wish to explain in full to you, but for now, this must wait till I return later today. In the mean time, would you please remain here in my home and rest? Your recovery is not complete yet. I promise, when I return we will spend time discussing everything. In the mean time, you will not be troubled here and all you will need is here. Please treat my home as your own." Shaulmar bowed low and left the house.

Rebecca watched from the window as he walked down the path to the street and disappeared along the tree-lined avenue. She began to process the events of the last few weeks—the information contained in images, conversation, and recollections gradually filtered down through her synapses and trickled into her conscious mind for processing. The teenager was feeling the onset of one of her headaches, probably due to the intense thought processes, so she decided to explore the house in an attempt to discover who her friend was for real.

Shaulmar needed to go to the old bookstore downtown. There was something there he had to have if he was going to convince Rebecca of her ancestry and heritage.

The bookstore was busier than normal when Shaulmar arrived, so he knew he had to be very cautious while retrieving what he had come for. While he was able to secure the object he needed, he made a call to a longtime friend, asking for an immediate meeting. Shaulmar was sure his friend would be able to assist him in what he had to do regarding the situation with Rebecca. He walked through the narrow aisle at the bookstore in the direction of the small room at the rear. As he entered the ancient stone archway, he felt the usual surge of power, and as he walked into the center of the room, a flash of pure white light enveloped him. Shaulmar was down on one knee while the energy surrounded him, penetrating every part of his being. With his head bowed, the intensity of the white light diminished, and he stood rigid raising his arms and arching his back looking to the heavens. He chanted a sacred mantra handed down to him through ancient tribal ceremonies. After he finished chanting, he walked to the leather armchair and sat silently waiting with his eyes closed while letting out a long breath of relaxation. A few minutes had passed when there was another huge flash of pure golden-white light. Shaulmar did not stir from his meditative state where he remained silent and still. Eventually, the flashes stopped and a woman appeared in the center of the stone room.

"Good to see you again, my friend," he said as she walked toward him.

They were old friends who belonged to the same ancient secret society and both were protectors of those who walked with the light on earth. The evolution of the human spirit was cradled in the hands of those ones who dedicated their existence to be of service to those incarnates who chose to progress through earthly experiences.

"Yes, and you my friend," she stood tall and straight, resting one hand on her hip and the other on the velvet pouch that hung from a beautifully carved leather belt around her waist. "It will be good working with you again, Shaulmarhime. What is it this time? Her voice hinted at the trouble she knew must be near.

Shaulmar stood up from the chair and they embraced. There was an instant glow produced as soon as they each entered the other's auras.

"I will explain everything tonight at the house. There is someone I want you to meet." His tone was troubling and she knew it but she knew him enough to know that he would tell her everything when the time was right. The two friends left the stone room and walked between the narrow book aisles to the front of the store where they exited to the street.

While they were in the room at the back of the bookstore, there was a pair of eyes watching everything they did and a pair of ears listening to all they spoke of. Those eyes belonged to a young boy, brash and daring, one who could not resist adventure, who looked for it everywhere. This lad was in the store that afternoon, as he was every afternoon, in the comic aisle seeking the elusive Knights of Orban comic book series. Most of the time, this kid was living on the streets. He could take care of himself very well. He was a survivor. He loved the bookstore for the chance to rifle through the comics, and he loved to daydream about being a detective from the future coming back to the past to solve crimes.

One of his dreams was that he would be reading a few comics and stumble across the lost articles of pulp fiction chronicling the guardians of light from Orban. The young lad spent most of his time on the streets but what he witnessed in the back of the store that day frightened him to death. He thought he was having some kind of hallucination or maybe he was having a reaction to the pills his friends had given him the day before, he didn't know? What he did know was that he wanted to know more and see more, so he followed them through the store and to the street. When he reached, the street the two mysterious persons were gone. The lad really wanted to know more about them and discover how they could make the stone room light up the way they did; but as he looked around the neighboring streets and stores, he realized they were nowhere to be seen and that he had to face facts, he may never get another chance to see them.

***

Rebecca was becoming more uncomfortable by the minute; she had been left in Shaulmar's house alone long enough. She began to weigh up her situation and she realized the bottom line was that she had no idea who the guy was, why he helped her, or what he wanted with her. She snooped around the house but to no avail. She saw nothing weird nor out of the ordinary, except maybe the collection of what looked like ancient carvings and scrolls on the walls in his study. Outside she could hear the sound of a car pulling up so she walked to the window and saw a yellow cab stopped in front of the house. She saw Shaulmar step from the front and watched him pay the driver then she saw another figure step out from the rear of the cab. It was a woman and she was slender, tall, and very assured looking. As Rebecca watched the two figures, she felt a sense of familiarity sweep over her that made her reach for the wall beside the window, and as she leaned against it she saw the woman outside look straight at her and smile. Rebecca instinctively moved back from the window as if she had been busted for doing something she shouldn't. She quickly went down the hallway passing the pictures on the wall and native carvings standing at either side of the staircase and hopped and jumped the stairs two and three at a time to the bottom. When the door opened and the two entered, Rebecca was in the lounge taking a seat on the indigo velvet couch and picking up a book, doing her very best to make it look to them as if she had been there for a while reading.

Rebecca heard the lounge door open and quickly looked down at the book. Shaulmarhime came into the lounge carrying a package, and as Rebecca lifted her eyes from the book, she saw a beautiful crystal on a gold chain around the neck of the woman who entered the room behind him.

"Hi Rebecca, was everything okay while I was gone?" he asked.

Rebecca gave the impression she was engrossed in the book "Yes, I drank coffee, listened to the radio for a few hours, and then decided to read." It was her way of making it known she didn't appreciate being left for so long.

Shaulmar turned to the woman next to him and held out his hand gently. "This is Morghanz, my very close friend," he looked at the woman as he introduced her. "This is Rebecca, the girl I was telling you about." He moved his arm slowly back toward Rebecca who was standing by this time. "Why don't we all make ourselves comfortable because there is much to discuss and a long night to do it in?" He looked at both women and motioned for them to sit on the couch.

Shaulmar began by pacing up and down on the beautiful Persian carpet, explaining to Rebecca as best he could who he was and what was happening to her, while trying to minimize any anxiousness that might result from the information.

"As you know, Rebecca, my name is Shaulmarhime but what you do not know is that I am a member of a secret society that is many thousands of years old. My friend Morghanz," he gestured to her, "is also a member of the same society. As members of this society, we are bound by universal and spiritual laws to protect humankind from any force in our universe that wishes them harm."

Rebecca looked at the both of them as if she thought they had lost their minds. However, one thing Rebecca could not dismiss was the fact that Shaulmar had saved her life the night before. So, even though she wanted to just get up and leave before they got even weirder, her intuition made her stay.

"Your gran gave you that gold locket the day your mother died, didn't she? Morghanz had decided to take control of the situation because she was sensing that Rebecca was withdrawing and would eventually make her excuses and leave. So Morghanz knew she had to be very careful in what she said and in how she said it. It was like trying to coax someone off a bridge before they jumped.

"How did you know that? No one knew that. I didn't tell anyone that." Rebecca's voice was filled with anxiety and confusion. Shaulmar stepped toward her and held up his hands half way to his chest in an attempt to calm Rebecca.

"Rebecca, it's okay to feel confused and frightened. Morghanz knows about the locket because we are protectors of the chosen ones, of which you are one."

Morghanz slowly walked toward Rebecca and touched her shoulder. "Please, calm yourself, we mean you no harm. However, there are others who are here to do just that," she said with a calm finality.

"What do you mean there are people here to harm me? I don't know any people!" her face was red and flustered.

"Rebecca, they know of you. Do you not recall the things that have happened since your gran was taken?" Morghanz stared at her waiting for her to make the connection. "Have you forgotten about Alison and what she tried to do to you? Her voice was deliberate and insistent.

Rebecca was silent as the words filtered through her mind. There was a period of dead air that bordered on panic for Rebecca, and Shaulmar seemed to take a back seat to the proceedings. Morghanz decided to seize the opportunity before Rebecca came back to the realization of the danger she was in to offer her an ancient method of bringing calm to the body in the face of anxiety or panic. She knew this would distract her and also help ease the sense of panic she was obviously feeling.

"Try to bring into your mind thoughts of peace." Rebecca closed her eyes and tried to imagine what she thought was peaceful. "Breathe in slowly and focus on the air as it enters your body through the nose and into your lungs. I find it helpful to bring my awareness to the breath, which eventually calms it, and if the breath is calm then ultimately this will allow the body to become more calm." She motioned to Rebecca with her arms and encouraged her to stand next to her while she showed her the exercise. Rebecca was reluctant but Morghanz patiently waited for her to join in. They stood in the middle of the huge room, both willing to show the other that they were not afraid of what may happen.

"Please, bring your arms above your head while filling your lungs with air." Morghanz turned to Rebecca and looked her squarely in the face while trying to read her, energetically. "Now drop your arms as you exhale." Her tone was gentle, soft, but strong.

Shaulmar had, at this point, moved quietly to the edge of the room and was edging his way to the door. He realized that Morghanz was in control and had moved to take Rebecca under her wing. He thought it best to leave her to it as he knew and trusted Morghanz with his life and with that of his friend's.

The sun was getting low in the sky as the two women began to forge their bond, and rays of burning orange and red light entered the square windows of the lounge falling on them as they moved together in harmony. Rebecca became aware of her own body as she struggled to follow Morghanz's instruction. "I cannot do this much longer, my arms feel like they are going to fall off," she cried, as her twisted form complained vigorously.

"Breathe." Morghanz's voice seemed devoid of concern for her pupil's pain. "Your pain will not remain, follow the breath, and so your pain will also follow the breath, and so the body will realize the pain is no longer connected to it."

By this time, Shaulmar had made himself scarce. He did not wish to involve himself in the training of the young novice. His task was to prepare her for the onslaught that he knew was coming. He knew the darker forces were capable of many unimaginable terrors and he had witnessed first hand exactly how powerful they were and what could happen to Rebecca if they found her. He reached the kitchen and filled the copper kettle with water from the sink. Thoughts were racing around inside his head; this was possibly the most dangerous assignment he had been given, he thought. He placed the ancient vessel on the stove and reached into the cupboard above for his favorite loose-leaf tea.

***

Rebecca held her head in her hands while Morghanz massaged her back and stroked her hair. They had just completed their first meditation session and it looked like they were quite comfortable with each other.

Rebecca moved her head so she could see her friend. "Morghanz, you seem to know more about what is happening to me than I do, so please tell me how all this began?" There was a protracted pause and Morghanz only continued to stretch her long slender legs while sitting on the carpet. Rebecca continued, "I am sixteen years old. I just lost my gran. The next thing I know I am staying at some lame hostel and worried sick about how the hell I will take care of myself without money or help from anyone." Her voice cracked and tears began to fill her eyes. "I meet someone who lived in the room across the hall from me, she claims to be my friend, and turns out to be the *psycho bitch* from hell…"

Before she could finish, Morghanz took her hand and sat next to her on the couch. She knew she had made a strong connection with the young girl. "Do not fill your heart with worry and anxiety, those emotions are extremely toxic to the system. Please Rebecca, try to understand that everyone has a destiny, including you," Morghanz put her other arm around Rebecca's shoulder. "We must embrace what is put on our path. If we fail to experience what we came here for, the universe will find a way to bring the opportunity to us over and over again until we recognize that it is our destiny to experience what we must." The beautiful sorceress put her hand under Rebecca's chin and lifted it gently, "I know you are strong enough to embrace those experiences so please allow me to stand with you on your path and I promise that I will never leave your side?" Their eyes met, the bond was forged.

Rebecca was overwhelmed and wiped the tears from her eyes but she couldn't hold back any longer. "Thank you, Morghanz. I would like it if you would consider me a friend too." She hugged Morghanz around her neck and didn't let go for a few minutes. The teenager realized that Shaulmar and Morghanz were genuinely concerned for her and that she should trust them when they tell her they want to help.

Shaulmar knocked on the door, not knowing what to expect. "May I come in?" He peaked around the door as he opened it. "Is everything okay?" Shaulmar waited for a response before entering fully.

"It's okay my friend," Morghanz answered. "We are finished with the first exercise." She kissed the top of Rebecca's head and smiled.

Shaulmar walked across the room to where Rebecca was sitting and touched her hand in the most gentle and compassionate manner. "Now, Rebecca, if you want I will explain as best I can, and within the boundaries of my authority as governed by the laws that restrict the imparting of knowledge to souls, what you must accomplish during this incarnation." The great and ancient wizard waited for her agreement while looking deeply into her eyes. That made her smile, slowly, as if he was telling her something in his mind.

"I would like that, Shaulmar, please tell me what you can." Rebecca was calm and peaceful now.

He looked over at Morghanz and nodded. She left the room quietly, not even looking at Rebecca on her way out. Rebecca was curious, but after all that had gone on, she was not surprised. Shaulmar returned his attention to Rebecca and took in a large breath.

"What I can tell you for the moment is that your lineage goes back for more than five millennia, and so, I am permitted to offer you certain knowledge that you have earned the right to hear." Rebecca remained silent, not because she didn't know what to say but because she was so serene in his presence that she found it unnecessary to speak. Shaulmar continued, "Such information is not common or in the public domain, and as such, the receiver of the knowledge must be prepared to assume responsibility for the safe keeping of it." He looked at Rebecca, and she instinctively nodded in acceptance of the conditions offered. "The knowledge that is rightly yours must be treated with right intention." His explanation was not going over as well as he thought and he noticed that Rebecca was looking confused so he thought it would be a good idea to offer her a piece of information that might bring comfort to her. "Your mother and gran reside on another plane of existence; they are not together but they are not dead in the sense that they do exist still." He spoke with a smile that he hoped would provide some measure of comfort for Rebecca and ease her mind a little to help her to relax.

"I don't understand," she said with the confused look still in place. She did seem to be less agitated but there was sullenness in her voice and a deep sadness in her eyes when she heard her mom and gran being spoken of. "Do you mean they are not dead?" she said with a soft and quiet voice as she sat on the couch like a small child who didn't know what was going on or what she was supposed to do.

Shaulmar saw this in her and moved closer to her. "Not dead in the traditional sense but not alive here with us. He was not really sure how to proceed with the explanation but he knew she needed to understand what he meant so he continued being cautious not to cause her any pain. "When we die we make a transition from here to another realm, some call it another dimension. I know our essence, the energy of who we are continues to grow and learn, and that is where your family have gone." Shaulmar hoped that would end that particular topic of conversation.

Rebecca had other ideas. "If they are not here, then where do they live? I mean, where does their essence live?" she felt silly having this sort of conversation but she was trying to seem grown up by talking to Shaulmar about death and essences. However, talking about her mom and gran only made her feel sad and lonely. By this time, Morghanz returned. She had been busy in the kitchen making refreshments. She was carrying a large tray full of different items, like tea, juice, and various cakes and pastries.

Shaulmar sat forward and pulled the small oak coffee table toward the couch. "There are many alternate dimensions in our universe where many different beings exist. They all aspire to evolve to the one level of vibration where all beings are seen as one. The vibration I speak of is known in my home as the golden thread that permeates and connects all life through all dimensions but here on earth you call it 'Love'. His hand automatically went to his heart, and with tears welling up in his eyes he looked gently at Rebecca. "Your family loved you very much and held you close and dear to their hearts, as they do to this day."

Rebecca could not stop the flow of tears as they streamed down her face, spilling on.to her hands that were resting in her lap. "I miss them so much, I feel so lonely without them," she sobbed uncontrollably, "I just want to die!" she cried. Her heartbreak was obvious from the explosion of pain, despair, and anger. "Why did they have to die? They were supposed to take care of me but they didn't." Her serenity was obliterated at this point. "I'm only young. Who will take care of me and love me now?" By this time, Rebecca was yelling almost incoherently and Shaulmar knew she was close to breaking down. Morghanz glanced over at Shaulmar for some indication of what was to be done. He held up his hand as if to say wait a little longer and that was when Morghanz knew what he meant. He wanted Rebecca to expel all the toxins in her body from the poisoning she'd endured the night before. This was a perfect opportunity for that to happen. It seemed a bit mercenary and callous but Morghanz also knew it was necessary before any healing could take place. So, the two friends stood by Rebecca, comforting, encouraging, and nurturing her as she fumbled through the severe pain and anguish associated with the loss and grief she was reliving. It was clear to both of them that there would be no exploration or planning that night.

Rebecca was worn out by the time she had released all the pent up emotional and physical energy. Morghanz turned to Shaulmar and saw his eyes close, momentarily, and he nodded slightly indicating they were thinking the same thing. "Rebecca, let me help you stand." Morghanz moved to her and held out her strong hand. The youngster complied as if she were in some kind of trance, Morghanz led her out to the hall and up the wide, dark wooden stairway to the top, where her room was. She was hoping she would sleep through the night without any interruption. It was clear that Morghanz was becoming emotionally attached to her young prodigy.

Shaulmar stayed in the lounge running various scenarios through his mind that might come about as a result of his intervention with Rebecca. He was well aware of the things Alison was capable of and the inevitable confrontation she would be planning. Shaulmar must ensure Rebecca's safety and he was starting to put a few things together that had looked out of place from the beginning of his assignment. The council sent him to earth on what he thought was a routine mission but it was turning into something much more than that, he thought, as he lit the large indigo candle on the oak table in the lounge.

During the rest of the evening, Shaulmar and Morghanz deliberated on ways to combat the attacks that would inevitably come from Alison and her soldiers.

"Do you think Rebecca will be okay through all that must come?" she spoke in a low voice. The wizard didn't reply right away. "Shaulmarhime of the Ancients, do you think she has what is required to survive this? You know of what I speak." Her tone was laced with impatience, at his silence.

He finally spoke. "I have full and total faith, my friend, in the decisions of the council. They sent us here to help Rebecca, so I believe she will come through this just fine. The council knows far more than you or I, they have authority to foresee much concerning souls on this plane of existence." His explanation was an irritation to her because of how she felt toward the council but the great wizard continued. "With unconditional faith and trust, there is nothing a soul cannot accomplish. That young girl upstairs has, according to the council, a destiny that is set in motion by the creator of all things seen and unseen. This cannot be prevented from materializing here in the physical dimension of earth; that is why we must assist in any way we are commanded for our own evolution as well as Rebecca's." There was a long silence in the room. Morghanz recognized the power surging from Shaulmar when he spoke of things of truth. He had a strong presence when energy was running through him from the universe through his crown chakra.

Morghanz decided to break the silence. "Okay, who and what are we dealing with here? Am I going to need to bring across the heavy guns again or are we counting on the council prophecy to manifest at the last moment and save us all? She was not as strong in the trust and faith department as her friend. She had enough courage and strength to match anyone but putting her trust and faith in the words and opinions of others, for her, was not something that came easy, even if those words came from the 'Sacred High Council.'

"No, I don't think we will need any reinforcements for this particular situation," Shaulmar sounded very sure of what he was saying, "The main objective for the immediate future is to teach Rebecca what is necessary for her to become a productive member of the society, and of course, to ensure her safety and survival." He said it with such a self-conviction that it sent chills down Morghanz's spine.

Morghanz reached for the drink she made for herself which sat on the tray. "Do you think Rebecca will believe you when you eventually explain things to her? Because she doesn't come across, to me, as someone who has experienced much during her short life so far," she whispered through the sipping of her tea.

He knew what she was getting at and he had to agree with his friend. "I know what you mean and I do see your point Morghanz. I am hopeful—with the love she has for her family and with our help—that she will become the one who is, as claimed by the council, destined to fulfill the prophecy. I think after some evaluations and training from you, we will know better whether Rebecca has what it will take to embrace the truth." He walked over to the large oval window and took another sip of the tea Morghanz had made for him. "I think if you teach her some energy work and sight she may feel a lot more receptive towards the more demanding aspects of the work she needs to do." There was a pause as they both digested the ramifications of the situation. "What do you think my friend?" He hoped she would concur because at that point he was fresh out of ideas on how to begin working with Rebecca.

Shaulmar was always given male charges by the council to mold and form into society members, and they were always born in places like the Far East, Middle East, or Africa. He would guide them with a natural instinct that many thought to border on absolute knowing; this was considered to be an ability bestowed on only the most venerated persons. It was obvious to him that the Sacred High Council was using this assignment of taking charge of Rebecca in western society as the opportunity for his soul evolution also.

Morghanz sensed that her friend was a little uncomfortable with the situation. "Well…I will do my best, you know that—and you should also know me enough by now to be sure that if I cannot help her through this, then no one can." She laughed softly as she took another mouthful of tea but they both knew what she had said was true. "Please, Shaulmarhime, just do not let that council mess things up again?"

He knew what she was referring to and trusted his own strength enough to reassure her that he would see to it. "You know me by now too, Morghanz, I would never allow that nightmare to gain power over any other developing member of our Sacred Order. As long as I wield the powers of Orban, the dark forces will not succeed, I swear to you my friend." Shaulmar meant every word and she knew it. "Morghanz, I must leave early in the morning. I must return to the bookstore. Would you stay with Rebecca and make sure she is safe?" He was certain that if he could persuade Rebecca that other dimensions existed there would be less resistance from her when the time came for her to learn about the Book of Secrets.

CHAPTER 7

REBECCA CAME DOWNSTAIRS TO THE SOUND OF CRYSTAL bowls resonating from the lounge. Morghanz was in the throws, of what looked to Rebecca, like yoga or something. "Hi, Glad to see you this morning," she said. "I was wondering if I had been dreaming last night and that maybe you and Shaulmar were part of that dream." Rebecca looked around the room. There was incense burning in a star shaped wooden holder and music playing but no sign of Shaulmar. There was no response from Morghanz; it looked to Rebecca like she was meditating. Actually, she was in an altered state and wasn't ready to come out of it yet.

Rebecca felt odd standing there. "Sorry," she said softly, "I didn't know you were busy." She bit her bottom lip and stepped gingerly backwards out of the room. She was feeling really hungry which was unusual for her so she tiptoed to the kitchen to see what there was to eat for breakfast. There was plenty of good wholesome food in the cupboards, but no junk, so she made toast with honey sprinkled on and poured some juice from the container in the fridge. She sat at the table in the nook by the window overlooking the back garden. The toast she'd made tasted good but her mind was elsewhere. She was stirred by what Shaulmar had said the night before about energy, planes of existence, and other dimensions. The most important thing she remembered him saying was that her mom and gran were still alive somewhere but she didn't fully understand where. She tried hard to get her mind around the different dimension thing, and she thought that if she said it enough times to herself then she would understand and believe it. However, the more Rebecca repeated the words in her mind, the more ridiculous it sounded to her, until eventually she just dropped the toast onto the plate and got up from the table. She walked to the sink where she leaned for a while starring out at the garden in the back.

"What the hell am I doing? I don't know these people and they don't know me," she said as her head hung down on her arms over the sink. "All this crap about beings in other dimensions and other planes of existence…" She stretched her arms out while holding onto the edge of the porcelain sink, with her head down and the slim lines of her upper back pointing skyward, she looked like a feline streching. Rebecca was developing into the beauty her mom knew she would become. "I must be losing my mind, getting mixed up with strange people in strange places." She stood and pushed her long thick strands of hair away from her alabaster toned features. "Why did I ever go into that stupid bookstore?" she whispered, as she brushed her hands across her face chasing away imaginary cobwebs.

"Don't feel bad, Rebecca." A voice came from the doorway. Morghanz was standing there holding a small clay bowl with grey smoke billowing from it. "Please, come with me to the lounge, I would like to show you some thing." She stood in the hall, just outside the doorway, and motioned for Rebecca to make her way to the other room. They entered the lounge where Morghanz had been practicing. The music was still playing and the white crystal that Morghanz had worn around her neck was placed on the altar in the furthest corner of the room.

"Do you know anything about energy or how it changes its state?" Morghanz asked softly.

"No, not really," Rebecca replied sternly.

Morghanz moved to where the altar was and put the bowl down on a gold and white cloth that looked as old as any museum artifact Rebecca had ever seen. "Energy flows from the universe…to us and through us. Some people are more sensitive to this energy than others, and as a result, are better able to channel the power through their own energy body." She looked up at her, using only her eyes so as not to be noticed, and waited to see Rebecca's response before deciding to continue. Rebecca remained silent, trying very hard to look like she was aware. "If we are sensitive to the energy, then we have an obligation to work with it." Morghanz paused to give Rebecca the opportunity to speak.

"What do you mean, work with it?" Rebecca asked.

That was all Morghanz needed to hear, according to the laws of universal energy transportation, Morghanz was required to have the subject request more knowledge willingly, and that is exactly what Rebecca did. Now she could be given all the teachings of the ancients as far as she has authority to receive that is dictated by the evolution of her soul signature.

"Working with universal energy requires that we train our mind and body to receive and channel the energy in ways that are helpful to others. So, let me offer you the beginning teachings concerning the connection we must forge with the energy. Our bodies have energy centers at various points, some are major centers, and others are minor. These centers are considered to be transformers that accept incoming energy and slow it down to a level that our sluggish physical bodies can cope with successfully."

Rebecca was becoming intrigued the more she cared to listen. "What happens if the energy doesn't slow down enough?" she made a face that showed Morghanz that she felt her question was silly and kind of adolescent in nature.

"That's a good question." She desperately wanted to keep her interested. The outcome of the battle with the dark forces depended on how she felt toward the knowledge offered to her. "Various things can happen but for now let's just say the energy is slowed down adequately, okay?" Morghanz was very tactful and coaxed Rebecca away from the question and toward the necessary knowledge she needed to begin the process of entering into the membership of souls.

"Okay." Rebecca said surrendering reluctantly.

Morghanz smiled gently and continued. "When the energy is slowed, it is able to be absorbed by specific glands in the physical body, for example, the pineal and pituitary glands located in the brain. The spiritual names given to these glands are the third eye and crown chakras, respectively. You may have heard of them?" she stepped over Rebecca's legs, and moving to the altar, she picked up the White crystal holding it in front of her.

"Ah," Rebecca responded, in an attempt to infer that she understood.

Morghanz continued. "Anyway, when we can sense this energy, we can often connect with other beings or loved ones that have moved to other dimensions."

"How can we learn to sense these energies of our loved ones?" Rebecca became very interested at the possibility of being able to be with her mom and gran again in some way. She remembered watching TV shows of people claiming to do exactly what she was hearing Morghanz describe. Although she thought they were phonies and didn't pay much attention to them. Like her friends at school, Rebecca made fun of the ones who claimed to speak to or get messages from dead people.

"It takes time and patience to develop the sensitivity needed to connect to the energy, some people are able to do this quicker that others, mostly because they are innately more sensitive to begin with but anyone can encourage the ability to various degrees. If you are serious about developing the ability, I will teach you what I know." Morghanz knew that by offering to teach her, she could stay close enough to her, and that was a high priority.

Rebecca's eyes lit up. "I would love it if you would teach me," she said, with a self-conviction that brought a smile from Morghanz. Rebecca wondered if they could become close friends. It would be really nice to have someone to talk to about things in general, she thought.

★★★

Shaulmar arrived at the old bookstore with wet clothing. New York seemed to have more than its fair share of rain for that time of year. There were a number of people browsing the aisles in the store, some of them were only waiting for the rain to ease, but most of them were legitimately looking for books to buy. The wizard had to wait for an opportunity to go through the archway at the back of the store, so he perused the bookshelves while making mental notes of how many shoppers were in the vicinity of the portal. All his attention was focused on making his move through the archway at the right time when no one was around, and because of this, he didn't notice he was the focus of someone else's attention.

"I'm sure that's the guy, it must be, same height, approximate weight, and that look of mistrust...definitely up to no good." The boy whispered to himself as he followed the stranger around the store in and out of the book aisles.

Joaquim was a lad in his very early teens, although he would never admit to being younger than sixteen. He had sandy coloured hair, deep brown eyes, and a wiry physique that would impress girls of his age. Following Shaulmar around the store was a game to him. He often imagined himself as a small time detective who was hired to follow various people around making notes of where they went and who they met, just like a real detective. He prided himself on his ability to predict their behaviors then follow them to see how right on he was.

Shaulmar was still unaware of his little admirer and was heading to the archway in the grey stonewall. He had seen an opportunity opening up as a young couple left the aisle leading to it. Shaulmar timed his movements to perfection as he had done many times before. The couple moved around one side of the book aisle in the direction of the front of the store and sales counter and Shaulmar walked around the opposite side of the aisle and through the archway, unseen. "Made it, that was a bit close, even for me," he remarked to himself. However, what he failed to notice was that his little stalker had entered the room immediately behind him. The boy had challenged his own abilities to gain access to the room as close to his mark as possible without being detected. This was what he wanted to develop as his calling card or trademark as an operative. The young boy's dream was to become an international spy, loved by many, feared by all.

Joaquim was about to introduce himself to the stranger and explain how he had followed him without his knowing through stealth and cunning. He thought he might pretend to be a store detective in training; that might explain his age. At that very moment, he saw the stranger fall down on one knee and heard him speak the sacred mantra that opened the inter-dimensional portal. Immediately flashes of golden white light surged from the space directly in front of him.

"Shit!" Joaquim hissed, as he remained hidden behind one of the bookcases. The energy in the room swirled and surged, as the portal opened, the stranger stopped chanting. Joaquim saw a beautiful golden light shine through the swirling energy and directly onto the old man, he seemed to go into a trance. After a few minutes, the light disappeared and the man seemed to awaken.

Shaulmar stood and moved to the leather armchair in the corner of the room. He was now in contact with the Sacred High Council telling them of his plans for protecting Rebecca from the darker forces that were intent on killing her. Shaulmar's conference was interrupted by a sudden and loud thud from behind one of the bookshelves. Joaquim had inadvertently knocked a big leather atlas off of the shelf onto the floor. He tried to stop it before it hit the floor but only succeeded in causing more books to fall along with a very old bottle of ink that spilled all over everything. "Sorry, I didn't mean to make such a noise," he clamored trying desperately to fix it, "I will go and see if I can find something to clean up the mess." He made a dash for the archway only to realize it was nowhere to be found. Joaquim knew it must have been there when he entered, but now he couldn't—for the life of him—find that hole in the wall.

"Remain still, my little intruder." Shaulmar spoke without having to look in the direction of the noise. He ended the connection he had made with the council and turned his attention to the boy. "What is your purpose here?" He asked in a tone that put fear into the young boy.

Joaquim stopped dead. "I am sorry for messing up your…phone call," he shouted from the back of the room, not knowing what else to say. He began to feel panic rising in his legs, and his chest was heaving a little as the adrenaline surged to his vital organs, ready for the fight or flight situation to commence, he leaned more to the flight option. "I was just wandering around and don't know how I came to be in here." Joaquim attempted to play dumb in the hope he could be excused for being an idiot but there was only silence, so he tried again. "I think I have lost my dad, have you seen him? He is really big, you can't miss him." He tried to convince the old man his dad was in the store, he was desperate, and Joaquim could tell it wasn't working by the silence.

Shaulmar stood and motioned to the boy to come into the center of the room. "Come here little one. Do not be afraid. I mean you no harm." He was mystified at how the intruder was able to gain access to the room. Only those chosen ones who have an energy signature recognized by the seven meridian lines of light, emanating from the universe that pass through the earth, are granted access. This was the only means of protection the portal has from the dark forces.

There was no response from Joaquim—he was rooted to the spot with fear. Shaulmar walked around the book aisle. "What is your name?" His voice was calm and gentle, he sensed the boy was scared and that was not good. Shaulmar looked down the aisle and saw Joaquim stooped behind a corner of the bookcase that only concealed three quarters of him, his rear end stuck out plain as day. Joaquim was looking for the old man, but chose the wrong side of the aisle to look down. "I am not scared, I have a gun so you better not try anything, and now tell me how to get out of here before I get really mad." He thought that would do the trick, and waited for the response.

Shaulmar stood behind Joaquim and cleared his throat. The boy leapt out of his skin, and with his eyes wide open he scurried backwards leaning on his hands and using his feet as propulsion, hitting the stonewall with a thud. He waved his hands ferociously in the air directly in front of the old man. "Stay away from me. I know kung Fu." Joaquim was clear out of ideas, and he thought this was it, the end of his pathetic little life.

"What is wrong with you?" Shaulmar asked in a tone that inferred his impatience with the boy. "I told you I was not intending to harm you. I only want to know who you are and how you got in here?" He held out a hand to Joaquim wanting to help him up.

Joaquim, feeling a bit silly, stopped waving his hands about and grabbed hold of Shaulmar's hand, pulling himself up. The old man was stronger than he looked, he thought. "My name is Joaquim," he said while dusting himself off. "I am a store detective working with the bookstore to help stop book theft. It's on the rise you know." Joaquim tried to sound really confident and in control. Shaulmar knew different.

"How did you manage to gain entry to this room?" Shaulmar asked with genuine disbelief.

"I just walked in behind you," Joaquim sensed that he had accomplished something he was not supposed to be able to, and quickly impressed this on the wizard "That is why they call me the phantom," he remembered the name from the comics he read as a kid. "I can go places others cannot. I can do things others cannot." He tried to sound like it was a common occurrence. Shaulmar turned away from him, shaking his head.

"Come, follow me," Shaulmar waved his arm beckoning to Joaquim, "Come sit next to me." He pointed to the small chair that had appeared next to the leather armchair. "I must figure out what is going on. The universe is at work here," he whispered to himself as he made his way to the chair.

Joaquim followed with caution, he still didn't know if the old man could be trusted enough for him to relax and let his guard down. "How old are you, anyway?" the words came out before he could stop them. "I…I didn't mean anything by it. I always say stuff. Just ignore that, okay?" The desperation in Joaquim's voice made Shaulmar chuckle.

"What did you say your name was again, my friend?" he asked with gentleness in his voice that made Joaquim feel much less anxious inside, although he continued to put on the tough exterior. "Joaquim is my name, and I am from Montenegro, near Siberia." He threw his head back proudly even though the truth was that he had no idea where he was from. Joaquim had watched a documentary on TV in one of the department stores downtown on Montenegro and Siberia. He liked it so much he adopted them as his home, although he was not aware they were in different countries.

"Oh, I see, Montenegro, Siberia, is it?" Shaulmar chuckled again but disguised it enough so as not to hurt Joaquim's feelings. "So, how is it you came to be a store detective in New York, then?"

There was a profound silence. Joaquim was toying with a couple of beautiful crystals that were sitting on a small altar next to the armchair. "How come this room feels much different than the rest of the store? Why don't any people come in here to look at books? You don't look like you are hiding from anyone like you were before you came in to this room. Why?" Joaquim's developing curiosity was on fire, he blasted Shaulmar with questions that were both relevant and insightful.

"They are all good questions, Joaquim," Shaulmar said while he rubbed his chin. "However, I am not at liberty to answer them at this time. I would like you to do something for me though, my friend, if you would be so kind?" he said warmly.

"What?" Joaquim replied with a natural curiosity and willingness to be of help.

"Well, do you see those two crystals sitting on the altar beside you?" Would you mind taking them in your hands and holding them lightly? One in each hand, please?" Shaulmar held his hands out palms up, "like so."

Joaquim agreed and smiled widely, showing strong, white teeth. "Okay." He reached across the altar picking up the crystals. "What should I do after I hold them?" he quizzed. Right at the moment he finished what he was saying, he felt sure the crystals had moved in his hands. "Wow! Hey! They moved!" Joaquim exclaimed excitedly. "It feels like they are trembling in my hands. It tickles," he giggled. "How did you do that?"

Shaulmar rested his chin in his hand, leaning his elbow on the arm of the chair. "Hmm, I thought that might happen." His voice was quiet and he seemed far away, deep in thought, mumbling to himself. After a few moments he realized what Joaquim had said. "They aren't trembling," he laughed, "they are vibrating." He paused as the meaning of what he had said began to filter through. His expression changed. "If they are doing that in your hands then I have the answer as to why you were allowed to enter this room," he said worriedly.

"What do you mean?" Joaquim said quietly, while playing with the crystals, tossing them around in his hands, and sporting the biggest grin ever.

"I will explain later, my young friend." His worry became solidified. "For now, I will take you home to your folks. Where do you live?" He moved off the chair and beckoned for Joaquim to follow him.

There was no answer, only the disappearance of the huge smile from Joaquim's face. Finally, he spoke, "I live around." He tried to project self-confidence. Joaquim was homeless but he didn't want pity from anyone. He wanted respect and practical help from those willing to offer it. Joaquim had the added pain of being an orphan. His parents were killed in a car wreck when he was a child. "Hey, nice star of David, how did you get it to light up like that?" Joaquim pointed to the object.

Shaulmar looked at him with genuine surprise. "You can see that?" he asked.

"Yeah, don't you?" Joaquim thought it was a weird thing for the old man to ask, when it was obviously right there in the middle of the ancient stone floor, in front of both of them.

"Let's go," Shaulmar said hurriedly. "We can go to my place. I will treat you to dinner. My family will be happy to meet you," he said nonchalantly, like it was a common occurrence for him to bring home strangers for dinner.

"I don't know..." the boy paused, "I...I got stuff to do...people are expecting to see me, you know how it is." He tried his best to sound truthful. Joaquim was still unsure about the old man, even though he sensed there was something he liked about him, something warm and kind like the protection of family.

"Maybe you could give them a call and let them know you'll be late, okay?" Shaulmar knew what the boy was doing and allowed him to remain in control of the conversation.

"Okay, maybe they could do without me for once. There is a call box outside I will need a minute."

"The time is right to leave the room. Follow me," Shaulmar said as he put his arm around the young lad and ushered him through the archway.

"Wow!" Was all the youngster could muster when the archway appeared out of nowhere. Then, after a few seconds, the inevitable questions flowed. "How'd you do that? Can you teach me? Can you do that anyplace? Maybe we could go to the mall after they close and go in and get stuff?" Joaquim's imagination ran off the rails.

Shaulmar just kept his arm around the young lad's shoulder letting his energy seep to the boy as he guided him out of the hidden room. The bookstore was not busy when they entered from the ancient stone room. Shaulmar made for the exit at the other end. When they were outside, Joaquim pretended to use the phone that was on the wall next to a sculpture of a man holding a small black crystal. Shaulmar waited at the curb until the boy was done—he knew he didn't have a quarter to be phoning anyone. When he decided the boy had wasted enough of their time he waved down a cab.

"Okay, Joaquim, let's go. The cab is waiting."

Joaquim was thankful there was a cab because he didn't want to keep the phone near his mouth any longer—it had an awful smell, even for a thirteen-year-old teenager. "Be right there," he shouted and hung up the phone.

Shaulmar knew the boy was orphaned and alone, but what he also knew, and what turned out to be the most important revelation about his young friend, was the fact that the meridian lines guarding the ancient portal at the back of the old bookstore had recognized him. This told Shaulmar the boy was connected to the sacred society in some way and he intended to find out how at some point in the future.

They both got into the back of the cab. "Seventh Street and Wood Grove, please driver, and would you mind taking the scenic route. I am in need of some peaceful time before I reach home?" Shaulmar spoke to the cabby with such respect that it made Joaquim sit up and take notice. The driver looked at them through the rear-view mirror. He had a confused expression. "Okay, sure, if that's what you want but it will cost more."

Joaquim leaned across the seat to whisper in the wizard's ear. "He will probably stiff you good." Shaulmar didn't answer, "Do you want me to take his number?" The kid waited for the response.

"That will not be necessary my young friend. People are here to survive the best they can, and if that means he asks for more than he should, then I will give it. Money is what we need to stay alive on the earth but I know it is regulated by the universal laws of what is owed and what is given." He stroked his chin, thinking.

"I hope you know what you are doing," the boy whispered as he turned back to watch the driver.

They eventually reached the house and Shaulmar was satisfied they were not followed. He paid the driver, who was still astounded that he'd made triple the fare with no trouble at all. "Thanks man, please call again, and be sure to ask for Anton. I will be glad to drive you around peacefully again." The cabby laughed as he pulled away from the drive.

Joaquim shook his head. "Man you really got burnt. That guy saw you coming for sure."

Shaulmar only smiled as he led the way up the drive to the house. Joaquim followed the old man onto the driveway. As he did so, he was hit with a strong energy, a force that was very similar to the one he'd experienced as he had walked through the archway at the entrance to the portal in the bookstore. "Hey, what was that? It felt like the electric shock I got at the room back there." Joaquim jumped forward, and looked back as if he expected to see what had hit him. "I'm starting to get freaked here."

Shaulmar's shoulders heaved up and down under his leather cloak as he tried to conceal the laughter that wanted to burst free. "Do not be concerned, young Joaquim. I am certain there are no ghosts here." The lad stayed close to the old man watching everything he could as they walked up the long winding drive. "Are you sure? Because I think others want to visit this place." He knew them to be unfriendly at best. Shaulmar said nothing.

Morghanz had stepped out onto the driveway and Rebecca stood in the doorway.

"So, you made it back in one piece?" Morghanz welcomed her friend and his guest.

Shaulmar just smiled. "Can we go inside and I will introduce you to this young lad? You will be amazed at how we met." They all went inside the house.

"I think it is best if we have tea in the lounge and get to know each other. We have a lot of work to do and I am sure the two of you have many questions for us to answer." Shaulmar made his way to the lounge. "Please, will you make yourselves comfortable while

Morghanz and I prepare some refreshments for us all?" Shaulmar bowed as he retired from the room.

The two teenagers looked at each other. Joaquim was the only one with a huge stupid grin on his face. "Hi, my name is Joaquim." His eyes were leaping from their sockets as he ogled every inch of her. Morghanz stood at the door of the lounge and hallway. "Please, enjoy getting to know each other. I think you two are destined to become family." Her sincerity and assuredness made Rebecca wonder.

When Morghanz reached the kitchen, Shaulmar had already made some of his favorite Persian tea. "How did you come across the young lad?" she asked with a whisper. "He seems like a nice boy." Morghanz pulled some rye bread from the cupboard.

"I don't think he is as strong as he wants us to think," Shaulmar was concerned for the safety of the youngster. "We must begin at the beginning with both of them. I hope the council knows what they are doing."

"Don't you mean the power of the Universe?" Morghanz was making her statement again of what she thought of the council. Shaulmar ignored the statement. He was aware of why she thought that way and he understood the pain associated with it.

"Morghanz, my friend, you must forgive those who have done you wrong." Shaulmar was careful to select his words where the council and Morghanz were concerned. "The only energy in the universe that can heal the pain of the soul, as you well know, is the vibration of what is known here as *love*" His words caressed her softly as she cut the bread slowly into pieces, ready to serve the guests.

"I know, but I swear to the powers that be, if the council members ever reveal to me the identity of the ones responsible for the death of my family, I don't know if forgiveness would be possible." Shaulmar knew her voice was that of a darkness lurking deep inside of her. He sensed that the anger she harbored towards the council was bubbling close to the surface, so he tried to pull her away from the connection to it.

"Morghanz," she didn't respond. Shaulmar repeated but with more energy, "Morghanz! Do you think Joaquim is connected to the Fahquar? The light beings of Orban?"

Awareness returned to Morghanz's face. "Oh, I don't know. I would have to spend some time with him to determine that." She thought for a moment. "Where did you two meet? He is a really nice boy, when you get past the tough outer shell, don't you think?" she gave him a familiar stare.

"Yes, I think you're right." Shaulmar continued to place the cups and bowls on the tray he was preparing. He knew what she was getting at. Joaquim reminded her of someone else she once knew, a young soul with the courage of a lion and a heart of gold. "Joaquim followed me into the bookstore portal. He was hiding, pretending to be a bookstore detective. He saw me open the portal and was witness to the sacred chant. So, what do you make of that?" he said half smiling.

"Obviously, he was not destroyed. Why didn't the safety protocols activate? Isn't that supposed to happen when the portal identity is compromised?" she sounded very annoyed. She took a deep breath and closed her eyes as if there was something she was hearing. After a few seconds she spoke, "Was he carrying anything when he entered? Maybe a scroll, crystal, or even a neck band, something that could contain a signature?" she waited for his answer.

"Nothing." He leaned back against the counter top. "I scanned him as soon as I found he was inside the room with me." Shaulmar waited for his friend to connect the dots.

"Oh, of course, his signature…" Morghanz reached for the copper kettle and filled it with water, then searched her pouch for some herbs to infuse into the tea.

Rebecca appeared from the hallway, looking a little frazzled.

"I know this is your house and everything, and I realize you have given me a place to stay but you left me in the other room with some strange teenage boy, who I don't know and who thinks he is much older than he really is—if you know what I mean?" she glanced at Morghanz when she said that part because it was too embarrassing for her to look at Shaulmar. He was confused at what she was saying and turned to look at Morghanz who only starred back at him, knowing full well he would get it momentarily.

"Yes, sorry Rebecca. We are coming now to talk with you both," his voice was a little subdued. We want to explain as best we can about who we are, and why we are here, as well as try to answer any questions you might have."

Shaulmar and Morghanz knew it was going to be a very long night—first they had to figure out how to deal with the threat to Rebecca's life, and then they had to convince her just how real that threat was. They also needed to explain how Rebecca's ancestry and lineage had played out in all of this, and how these aspects would inflence her future. If that wasn't a high enough mountain to climb, there was the unexpected addition to the equation, Joaquim....he was an enigma for the moment, but he would need to be unraveled in quick time, if all was to go well. When they appeared in the living room, Joaquim was inspecting the display of ancient paintings hanging on the wall opposite the huge fireplace.

Shaulmar was the first to speak.

"Okay—Morghanz and I will try to explain, as best we can, everything that needs explaining at this time." What he said smacked of a disclaimer Rebecca thought but she said nothing, she didn't want to interrupt the flow of information from him. "Firstly, we are travelers of sorts. The kind of traveling I speak of involves portals, planes of existence, energy flow, and inter-dimensional connections." Shaulmar's voice was a little shaky but that was understandable considering that his audience consisted of a 16-year-old girl and a 13-year-old boy who thought he was a 1930's gumshoe.

"Is that what you were doing in the back room of the bookstore...the one that looked like an ancient stone cave or something?" Joaquim said excitedly.

"Well yes and no...." Shaulmar thought for a moment trying to decide how to best explain. "When you followed me into that room, I was in the middle of opening the portal to contact my superiors. You see I am given directives from the Sacred High Council. I was not there to travel between dimensions which is how we came to be here at this time," he pointed to himself and Morghanz. He was speaking with more ease now, "I traveled to earth because

Rebecca needed help, even if she didn't know it. When called upon, members of our society offer their services for the highest good of all concerned. We all have an individual destiny and some are changeable as seen by the use of free will. However, there are souls who have reached a specific evolutional level, a plateau if you like, and cannot continue to grow, spiritually, they become stagnant. At some point it occurs to them, either by profound dreams or intuitive episodes, that there might be more to life than what they are experiencing. When they connect with the feeling, it is difficult if not impossible for them to shake it, and so they accept it, but for the soul to move to a higher level of existence it has to take a solemn oath of truth. This oath of truth is in fact a sacred contract between the soul and the universe, whereby it is declared that the soul will incarnate with a specific destiny that is set in stone and authorized by the highest laws in existence. This destiny is unstoppable and cannot be changed; however, the soul is not indestructible and there are a couple of ways it can be destroyed. The first occurs if the soul decides the incarnation is too difficult and commits suicide. The second manner in which the soul can succumb to destruction, which is more common, happens when the darker forces of the universe use every means at their disposal to attack and ultimately force a soul off its path. If the soul is successful in completing its destined path, it can then ascend to a higher level of existence to continue its spiritual evolution."

The room remained silent as Shaulmar looked around at each of the young souls and wondered what they were thinking. Rebecca was just starring at him with no specific facial expression and obviously she was processing the information. Joaquim glanced around at everyone else as if he understood nothing or he totally believed everything—the wizard couldn't tell which.

"This is why we are here. Rebecca is such an incarnated soul and we need to protect her from the forces of evil that wish to prevent her from completing her destined path." Shaulmar had an intensity in his eyes that was evident and they knew he spoke the truth. "Now if you have any questions, I would be happy to answer them as best I can." His voice was peaceful and calm as if he were infused with the love of the universe. "Do not be afraid…please begin." There was silence in the room; Morghanz remained focused on the two youngsters, almost willing them to open up to their natural curiosity.

Suddenly the silence was broken. "How come when I followed you into the room at the bookstore, the moment I stepped into the room across the doorway I felt all warm and nice and stuff?" Joaquim spoke first.

"That was because of the difference in energy from this earthly dimension, and the other dimensions of the universe, such as the one I opened in the ancient stone room. When I crossed the threshold of the room, my soul signature resonated naturally and set in motion an identification sequencing that allowed the portal to be activated. When anyone enters the bookstore and comes near the stone wall at the back, the vortex of light that runs through the earth, into the area around the room, and up into the universe automatically permeates their physical bodies and touches their soul body. If they are recognized as having a soul vibration high enough, giving them spiritual authority, then the portal is opened. When it opens, the portal triggers an immediate shift from one dimension to another." Shaulmar explained to Joaquim as best he could without losing him in the translation.

Joaquim continued before anyone else could speak. "Why did you have me hold the crystals while we were in the room? Why did they trem...vibrate? he corrected himself.

"Those crystals are ancient and have a memory, and as they come in contact with people, either by them being carried in their pocket or bag close to them or holding them in their hands, they acquire the specific soul signature of the person. This signature is their sacred vibration that is manifested at the very instant they were created many eons ago, even before what your scientists call the big bang. The crystals record this vibration forever in their memory. When and if they are held by the same person again, no matter how long the span of time, the crystals vibrate and sometimes illuminate as they reconnect with the sacred soul signature that lays within," Shaulmar explained.

"So, what you are saying is that these crystals remember me? But how could that be? How could they remember me when I have only held them once? For them to remember me I would have had to hold them more than once, right? Joaquim didn't get it yet and the others waited patiently. Rebecca glanced at Morghanz but she only mouthed the word "wait" to her. Shaulmar gave Joaquim an encouraging smile and continued to wait for him to connect with his intuition. Joaquim looked at the others and wondered why they were waiting—he began to replay the conversation in his mind and eventually, he, to the delight of the others, finally got it.

"Wow, do you mean I have met them before in another place?"

"Not exactly," Shaulmar sat next to him on the couch.

"Think about the time portion of the answer to your question," Rebecca suggested in a non-condescending way. She had begun to like him and realized that he might be as much an innocent victim as herself in some ways. Joaquim paused and you could visibly see he was trying to rewind the tape in his head to hear the explanation of the crystals given to him by Shaulmarhime; it was quite amusing in a childlike kind of way.

"Ooh, yeah! Now I get it," he exclaimed, "but if that is true then you're saying I have met those crystals before…before now, I mean before…I was born," he said the last few words really slowly as the implication hit home, and as soon as it did, he sat back in silence like someone had walked over to him and switched him off. Joaquim looked confused and scared. He looked at Shaulmarhime and Morghanz in a different light. He sat back on the sofa eating a piece of bread while he wrestled with the thoughts and images that raced around in his head.

After a prolonged silence there was an air of tension that had manifested in the room, it was building, and everyone was sensing it.

"Okay, shall we try to figure out what we should do about the situation concerning any threats that will undoubtedly come our way when the dark forces attack?" Morghanz said enthusiastically. No one answered they just kept eating, except for Rebecca.

"What about the book?" she said quietly as she looked straight at Shaulmarhime.

"The book," he repeated. He knew what she meant but he didn't know if it was the right time to tell her what it was, or what it really meant to her path of growth.

"Yes, the beautiful dark blue leather-bound incredibly crafted book, the one at the book store that I was drawn to," she explained. "You said I was drawn to it for a reason, you said it held secrets…secrets that I may be able to understand one day," she insisted.

"Ah…the ancient Book of Secrets," he pretended to only just recall the book—which was a manipulation to buy more time while he allowed his intuitive energy to focus on the situation concerning Rebecca and the book. As she waited for a reply, Shaulmarhime was given a feeling in the pit of his stomach, a feeling that was neither excited nor queasy, and to him, this was information from the universal energy source sending an answer to the question. His energy center or solar plexus chakra received the energy and transformed it into a feeling or emotion that could be interpreted in the physical body through the gland associated with the chakra. "Yes," he said "that book was sent to this particular place at this particular time, not through coincidence, but as part of the divine plan that is your contract of destiny. You are to know this book and it is to know you," he said with assurance.

"What do you mean 'Book of Secrets' and how will a book know me?" she wanted to know more, however, Shaulmarhime had other plans.

"Morghanz, will you share with Rebecca your intensions concerning personal protection and earth grounding that will help her defend herself against adversarial attack?" he asked.

Morghanz had been silent throughout all the discussion and debate, now she was going to share with them the benefit of many centuries of knowledge through the sacred teachings of masters from ancient times. Rebecca looked disappointed but she knew intuitively that these friends were exactly that, friends. She could sense they came from their hearts in everything they did and said. She didn't know if what they claimed was real or what, but one thing she did know for sure, was that she preferred them to the Alison's of this world, and since she had no one else, it felt good to have people show her love and caring.

"First, if you are willing Rebecca, we will begin with an easy flowing regime of physical and energetic practices that will benefit the body and mind in preparation for more intensive work," she said with an intensity that almost caused Rebecca to step back, and as she did, the thought of the intense body and mind work didn't sound that appealing.

"Okay," Rebecca replied timidly, "when shall we begin?"

"How about this evening?" There was a look of fear on Rebecca's face that made Morghanz continue, "or...in the morning—early," she said concretely.

"If I am to stay here," Rebecca began, "I must go to the hostel and get my things—okay?" she looked around at Shaulmarhime and back to Morghanz for their response. You could tell by their expressions and body language that they thought it might be dangerous. "I won't be long and I will make sure the manager escorts me to the room and waits while I pack okay?" she said confidently and smiled at them both.

"Okay, but please be careful and don't stop the cab in front of the hostel; get out a block away," Shaulmar said. "Maybe Joaquim would go with you to make sure there are no suspicious people hanging around the lobby or the building in general? What do you think Joaquim?" Shaulmar said.

"Sure," he said. He looked over at Rebecca. "Don't worry, Rebecca. I am really good at undercover work—trust me?" she smiled but inside she was a little concerned that while getting her stuff, Alison might be waiting. Rebecca still was unable to be convinced of the things that Shaulmar and Morghanz were trying to tell her, although as she sat in the chair finishing the food in front of her, it suddenly occurred to her that since she had been at Shaulmar's house...two days...her headaches and the flashes of light had stopped. She stopped eating and swallowed hard.

"It has just occurred to me, ever since gran died, and on a daily basis, I have been experiencing headaches and blinding flashes of light. There is no warning before they come, only that there seems to be a connection to the earth, because I feel like I fall towards the center of it every time," she said as she looked at both Morghanz and her friend, Shaulmar.

"Now, it seems, ever since—" Shaulmar interrupted, "ever since you have been staying at this house, about two days, they have stopped," he said.

"Yes—they've completely vanished," said Rebecca with an excited and confused look. Shaulmar and Morghanz looked at each other and smiled. They knew that the information they had given her was finding its way to Rebecca's mind and rational thoughts, through the heart vibration of these words of truth, and they were pleased.

"I am so happy," said Morghanz, "that I accepted the call of service from Shaulmar. Moments like this make it worth while."

"What do you mean?" Rebecca asked. "Do you think there is something happening to me while I am here at this house?" she queried, almost worriedly.

"Don't worry," Shaulmar said, "we are not brainwashing you. What is happening with you is something that is controlled by you, your soul energy, and the energy of—and contained within—everything in the universe. The reason that you no longer suffer with head pains and blinding lights, I would guess, is something to do with your proximity to the meridian lines of light, vortex of light, and...I definitely think it is due in large part to the Book of Secrets and your proximity to it," Shaulmar explained with a passion and warmth that made Joaquim sit still, his eyes fixed on the old man and his mouth agape as bits of pizza fell onto the floor.

"Joaquim, your pizza is falling on the floor," Rebecca shouted.

"Sorry," he said, apologetically, while trying to scoop up as much of it from his knee and the floor as he could.

The rain was falling in torrents and the wonderful sounds it made as it hit the roof and gutters provided a sense of safety and comfort to those inside. As Rebecca looked out at the rain-soaked windows and into the night, she decided right there and then that Shaulmar and Morghanz were of the truth and that she now considered them friends and would relax around them. Of course, she included Joaquim in the friend part, as he was beginning to grow on her, as she turned and looked at everyone as they connected with each other in the living room of this wonderful old house.

"I think we should go and get my things. It's only 6 o'clock and I figure we could be back by 8:00. What do you think Joaquim?" Rebecca sounded very upbeat and positive, something she had not felt for the longest time.

"Sure, let's go and get everything and then come back and set up our stuff here," Joaquim sounded like someone in charge. He came across like Rebecca's big brother and protector. She thought it was really sweet and endearing.

"Remember, don't go straight to the hostel. Leave the cab a block away and walk the rest of the way," Shaulmar restated.

"Don't worry, I will take care of her. No one will get near her as long as I'm around," insisted Joaquim, as he put on his tattered old windbreaker and laced up his runners, being careful not to pull on the laces to vigorously, in case they snapped.

Shaulmar and Morghanz set up the living room for meditation and reflection with soft music, incense, and candles. "Would you like to join us while you're waiting for the cab?" he asked, "or you could just watch and listen if you prefer." Rebecca and Joaquim opted for the latter. Neither of them knew the first thing about meditation but they were curious enough to sit by and watch.

After a while, the cabby arrived and honked to let them know he was there. They said their goodbyes and headed out the door.

"See you later," they heard as the door closed.

CHAPTER 8

THE TAXI DISAPPEARED DOWN THE STREET, TURNED THE corner, and headed for the hostel on Granville and Main. As soon as it turned the corner another cab pulled up in front of the old house.

"No, I didn't think you were going to let them do this alone," Morghanz said with some relief. "Please, don't make me go through that again without letting me know what you are planning. I almost slammed the door before they could walk through."

"Yes, sorry. I needed to let them do this but I didn't realize it was going to happen this way until the last minute," he said apologetically.

"Sometimes our guidance is given to test us also. Even though we are travelers, and function on many levels of existence, the information we get is not forthcoming when we want it." Shaulmar sounded stressed out.

They put on their coats and stepped outside to the waiting taxicab. "Granville and Main please," he said to the driver.

"Are you expecting any trouble at the hostel?" Morghanz asked. She was placing crystals in her leather pouch in a specific way and programming them to assist in focusing energy, should it become necessary to do so.

"I have a feeling that the dark forces of the universe are aware of how important it is for another soul to progress through their 'pinnacle sojourn' here on earth, as much as we are," he said. "Souls are extremely vulnerable at this juncture in their evolution. If, as you know, they are prevented from completing 'pinnacle lifetimes' then they are forced to return to the spirit dimensions to convalesce until they are deemed well enough to attempt completion again. If the dark forces are allowed to successfully prevent enough souls from completing their lifetimes, then the soul balance will be upset and disharmony will reign, and that is why we are here as sacred protectors of these souls. So, in answer to your question, yes, I think there will be something or someone waiting for Rebecca and Joaquim when they arrive at her room at the hostel because if I were Alison—or who ever she is– I would be waiting there."

Rebecca and Joaquim got out of the cab half a block from the hostel. They could still see the front entrance of the hostel even though the rain was heavy. The building looked quiet, with only a few people coming and going, as they both made their way to the entrance.

"Wait! I've got a better idea. Why don't I go to the front desk and ask…what's the guy's name?" Joaquim asked Rebecca.

"Mr. Holden," she said with a wisp of indignation.

"Yeah, Mr. Holden, and ask him if you are in your room because I want to speak to you—right?" He said with a very 'proud of myself look' on his face.

"That's a very good idea," she said.

"Well, don't sound so surprised. I told you I was good at this," Joaquim replied. He made his way towards the front entrance. The lobby was empty apart from the guy at the desk—Joaquim assumed it was Mr. Holden. "Excuse me, do you know if Rebecca Sullivan is in her room? I'd like to speak with her," he said to the man behind the desk. The man looked at Joaquim and asked if he knew what her room number was.

"Sorry, she never told me that. She never tells me much. She tells all her friends that her little brother is a worm." Joaquim looked as hurt as he possibly could.

"Well, I suppose you could be her brother. Such as it is, I will tell you what I know. Miss Sullivan has not been here for a couple of days, and why she would pay rent and not make use of her room, is beyond me. Teenagers have far too much money these days," he ranted on and on so Joaquim backed away and left before the guy had time to resurface from beneath the counter.

"No one is here as far as I could tell and that Mr. Holden doesn't seem to like you much. What did you do to him?" Joaquim laughed. "Oh…and he doesn't like your little brother either," he added, while pointing both thumbs back at himself with a huge grin of satisfaction across his face. "He believed every word I fed him."

"Oh, boy, now I have a brother," she rolled her eyes and walked back towards the entrance. "You stay hidden," she yelled back at him.

Rebecca walked into the hostel lobby with the confidence that said she owned the place. It was a totally false confidence though, inside, she was terrified that she might bump into Alison.

"Hello, Mr. Holden," she waved at him as she passed through. He just stared at her until she disappeared up the staircase. She reached the second floor and was making her way down the hallway to her room but the closer she got to her room the more she felt an uneasiness creeping up to her stomach. There was no one around so she continued on. "Don't be so silly Rebecca," she whispered. "There's no such thing as ghosts, goblins or dark forces, only nasty mean people,"

Rebecca took out her key and opened the door to her room. She walked inside and closed the door. She was about to find out just how wrong she really was. While she gathered her belongings, what little there was of them, she began to feel sick. Rebecca shrugged it off as being the result of a bad slice of pizza and returned to her packing. After a couple of minutes, she had to sit for fear of falling down. The nausea increased to painful stomach cramps, and now she really was scared.

"Oh God—what's happening to me?" she cried as she fell on to her bed in pain.

With malicious intent Alison had in fact gained access to Rebecca's room earlier that day. She had placed three crystals in the room, one dark green, one blood red, and the other smoky black. She placed them in such a way as to form a triangle within the room that encompassed 90 percent of its totality. The crystals had been programmed by Alison, who was indeed a member of an ancient order of the darker forces of the universe. She was very adept and powerful and she possessed a deep knowledge of such malevolent powers. Rebecca had fallen pray to these powerful energies that were programmed within the crystals. They were attacking her life force systematically as she lay there, helpless. She was surely going to die.

A cab pulled up outside the hostel. Shaulmar and Morghanz stepped out. They made their way to the entrance and stepped inside. Joaquim saw them but could not let them know where he was—he had been jabbed with a needle full of tranquilizers by two men who had grabbed him and put him in the back seat of their long black car.

"Won't be long now, they'll feel the power of the dark forces and suffer the fate of many travelers who have gone before them," the tall stranger in the seat in front of the boy said. His companion only grunted, probably because he was so big he was forced to keep his head bent forward because the roof was in the way, Joaquim thought. At the same time Joaquim felt that his eyes were spinning in different directions but he did think it was kind of cool that he felt as light as a feather.

"Morghanz, prepare yourself. I sense much power here and its origins are not from the higher planes of existence. We may have underestimated this 'Alison' person. Obviously she is well versed in the ancient arts," he said with a sense of urgency.

"Yes, I sense it now my friend. We may be in for a battle here," she replied as she reached for her crystals.

The travelers cautiously made their way into the lobby of the hostel but as soon as they appeared, they were hit with a field of energy that had a frequency that was designed to immobilize them. Thankfully Morghanz's crystals transmuted the energy surge, making it ineffective.

"Looks like you were right, Morghanz, there will be a battle this night," Shaulmar said. "We must find Rebecca before anything happens to her." Shaulmar tuned into Rebecca's soul signature and followed its direction up the stairs to her room. They opened the door and saw the energy field as it was in the process of devouring her.

"Step back, Morghanz," Shaulmar commanded as he reached upward with his left hand and downward with his right hand. With his head bent down and his eyes closed he spoke, "Creator, grant me the power to help your child in this room. Her soul cries out for help. She wishes to remain and fulfill her destiny as commanded by divine will." Shaulmar spoke these words in an ancient verse of a language that even Morghanz did not recognize.

Rebecca was struggling for her life as she lay on the bed. Her skin was the color of stone and her hair was streaked with white. Shaulmar composed himself, and trusting in the power of the universe and the power of destiny, he walked across the threshold of the room and into the energy field generated by the three deadly crystals. He felt the power of the crystals—it was the most powerful negative energy he had ever encountered during his time as a traveler on earth. The crystals became aware of him as he slowly walked towards the bed and they began to divert some of their energies to attack him. The intensity of the attack increased, it was almost as if the owner of the crystals was in the room commanding them. Shaulmar called upon the energy of the universe to flow through him and protect him, as he attempted to save Rebecca, if that was in accordance with her destiny. He felt a surge of power course through his mental and emotional bodies. He was being surrounded with a sort of insulation from the attacking forces. Shaulmar noticed, as he was able to move closer to Rebecca, that the attack increased and the crystals focused on him rather than his friend. He began to train his mind on the energy coming from them rather than on getting to Rebecca. As he did this, the crystals turned all their power to Shaulmar. As they did this, they released their grip on Rebecca's dying life force, enabling her to begin to come back to life. It was now a battle between whoever was controlling the crystals and the ancient skill and sacred knowledge of the old man.

Morghanz seized the chance to remove Rebecca from the room. She summoned her own crystal power for protection and called forth the masters of the universe for help before she stepped into the room. Her first steps into the room across the threshold made her feel ill. She felt the room vibrate at a frequency that hit her energy body with the force, of what felt like, being struck by a bolt of lightening. For the first time ever, Morghanz felt fear run through her mind. She was experienced enough to compose herself and to use the power and strength of her mind to detach from the fear projected on her by the deadly crystals. She steadied herself and made her way to Rebecca. Shaulmar took all the focus of the three crystals on himself, and this allowed Morghanz to pull Rebecca off the bed, onto the floor, and then to drag her to safety. When she got Rebecca out into the hallway, the girl immediately began to recover. Morghanz sent Rebecca healing energy from the universe, as she stepped aside and allowed it to flow through her, unimpeded, to her friend. Rebecca's skin color returned as she regained consciousness. "Where am I?" she asked. "I feel awful. What happened?" Her voice was weak.

"Try to conserve your energy, Rebecca. I have to get you out of here. They're trying to kill you," Morghanz told her as she helped her down the hallway and into the stairwell.

"Please, Morghanz. I must sit and rest on the stair. I think I am going to faint," Rebecca said as she slumped against the wall. Morghanz placed a crystal in each of Rebecca's hands, an amethyst in the left and a rose quartz in the right. All she could do was hold her in her arms as they both sat on the stairs. "Divine Creator, please help this child. The forces of evil are strong here and wish to drown out her light. I know she has a destiny that does not include being dragged into the darkness that is devoid of all light." Morghanz spoke from her heart, as she felt the love growing stronger and flowing from her to Rebecca. She noticed Rebecca moved slightly and heard a rush of air fill her lungs. "Come on my friend, up you get, we have to make it down the stairs and out to the street before we can be totally free of the dark force in your room," she said. They both stood and began the descent to the main floor and lobby. Rebecca was moving more steadily now as her breathing became rhythmic and stable.

Neither one of them could guess what was taking place in Rebecca's room, of who was winning the battle of strength and power, between the forces of good and evil. Morghanz could only pray that her friend would survive his battle with the dark forces in that room.

Shaulmar stood in the middle of the crystal triangle. He was glowing the color of yellow-gold. The power surging through the room was so incredible that it produced a vortex of energy strong enough to open a hole into another dimension. When this happened, there was a blinding bolt of lightening, and thick black smoke filled the room. After it cleared, somewhat, Shaulmar saw the one who was responsible for the attack on Rebecca. The thing he saw was distorted by the vortex of energy created by the triangle of crystals—they were becoming out of control as the power that was being generated was getting too strong for them to contain, and this was how the tear in the fabric that separates the dimensions was created. Shaulmar was powerful enough to protect himself from the effects of the tear, and so was the owner of the crystals. Her energetic signature was fixed in the memory of the crystals. Eventually, there was enough buildup of power in the room that sent the crystals and their dark force back to its origin, leaving Shaulmar unharmed. The room returned to its former state as Shaulmar slumped to his knees, exhausted. When he was sufficiently recovered, he collected himself and tried to leave the room as quickly as possible, even as he knew the conflict was not yet finished. Whoever was in that room and had activated those crystals was very powerful indeed. Shaulmar realized he was going to have to train Rebecca as best he could, including everything he knew about the ancient and sacred arts.

Morghanz and Rebecca made their way through the lobby. Mr. Holden was still at his post behind the check-in desk. Even though there had been such a battle going on up in Rebecca's room, where powerful energies were thrown about by Shaulmar and his foe, it seemed that no one on the earth plane had been affected at all.

"Goodnight, Mr. Holden," Rebecca managed to shout across the lobby as she and Morghanz left the building. "I don't think we will be meeting again. You can rent my room to some other unfortunate and you can also discard all my stuff!" she was well rid of that place and it felt good.

Shaulmar joined them out on the street. He was none-the-worse for wear thanks to his own sacred training from many millennia past. "Thank heaven you two are all right," he said hugging both of them.

"We were worried about you. The power in that room was heightening as we left and we didn't know if you could handle it or not," Morghanz said calmly. "Rebecca is okay but she will need to rest for a while." There was concern in her voice.

"I'm all right," Rebecca claimed, "just a bit worn out." She sat down on the step outside the hostel while Shaulmar hailed a cab

"Wait a minute," Morghanz said, "where is Joaquim?"

"Oh yes, I forgot, I told him to stay hidden, while I went into the hostel for my things, before all this began," she said with mounting concern.

"It's okay," Shaulmar said calming everyone. "I will go back for him. You two please wait here for me. Sit in the cab if it comes." Rebecca said, "I told him to wait down there—down the block." Shaulmar ran down the street towards the next block where he hoped he would find Joaquim.

There was no sign of Joaquim when Shaulmar arrived. He stopped outside a bar and looked around. He decided to go inside and see if anyone knew anything about, or had seen anything, of the boy.

Rebecca and Morghanz were sitting outside the hostel when they heard sirens. They hoped nothing bad had happened to Shaulmar and Joaquim. Just then, Mr. Holden came outside.

"Miss Sullivan you had a visitor yesterday. The young man wanted to speak with you. He left when there was no answer from your room," he said with a look of contempt.

"Did he say anything or leave a message for me?" she asked eagerly. She thought it might be the cute guy she had met at the Coffee Club.

"Yes he did," Mr. Holden handed Rebecca an envelope that had her name on it. After everything that had been happening to Rebecca, she didn't think anything could make her feel good again. This small envelope had that effect on her. It made her smile and gave her a sense of expectation. She refused, however, to let her imagination run wild and explore of the possibilities of romance just because she really liked him. Although she never spoke of him, she thought of him often, especially throughout all the stressful and anxious times she had been experiencing recently. The mind will try to protect us from stress and anxiety by presenting nice thoughts for our consciousness to feed off. However, the heart is another story. It doesn't concern itself with anything but love, and when two people connect an energy exchange takes place, and that connection will bring those people together again and again if it is their destiny, no matter what.

"I am going to open this when we get home," she said to Morghanz while she held the envelope close to her. Rebecca realized, after she'd said it, that she had just referred to Shaulmar's place as 'home.' This made her feel a little sad because it made her think of her mom and gran and she could feel the tears building. However, after the emotion passed she did think that making friends with Shaulmar, Morghanz, and Joaquim was a good thing. Obviously, the bonds between them were getting stronger and they felt like family to her. Rebecca decided she would tell Morghanz about Robbie once her emotions settled down a bit. Just then the taxi arrived and Rebecca and Morghanz climbed in the back.

"Please, wait for a few minutes we are waiting for two more people." She asked the driver. He made it quite clear that they would pay extra for waiting time and that he was 'not in the business of charity.' Morghanz wondered how long it would be before Shaulmar returned. She was feeling uneasy, so she asked the cab driver to move half way down the block in the direction Shaulmar had gone for safety.

Shaulmar looked around the bar. There were more empty seats than occupied ones.

"I'm looking for my young nephew. He was waiting outside for me about half an hour ago. Do you know where he might be?" He said to the young bartender

"No, I don't think I do but let me ask in the back. I'll just be a minute," he said with genuine concern. Shaulmar sat on a stool. He closed his eyes and took in a slow, deliberate, deep breath. He held the breath in his lungs for a few moments then slowly released it in a gentle exhalation. The effect was calming and gave him the opportunity to connect with the universal energy that unites every living being on the planet. Then, he created a specific question in his mind, "Is my friend and brother, Joaquim, alive on this plane?"

What he sensed was fear and helplessness. These were not his emotions but those of someone close to him.

The bartender returned to the bar and Shaulmar opened his eyes in anticipation of what information he might have about Joaquim.

"I spoke to my staff, and my dishwasher said he saw a black saloon parked in the alley half a block away with two big guys sitting in the front and a young lad slumped on the back seat. He said the lad was waving his arms in a very peculiar manner when he was passing," the bartender explained with a hopeful expression on his face.

"Thank you my friend," Shaulmar said. He left the bar in a hurry and headed towards the alley in the middle of the block. Shaulmar hoped with all his heart that his young friend was unhurt and safe from the clutches of the dark forces.

There were no black saloon cars in the alley when Shaulmar arrived, only garbage cans, various types of debris, and broken drainpipes leaking water all over the place. He was drawn to the very end of the alley where the lighting was extremely poor. Only one bulb hung over the back door of a restaurant near the end that cast a dim light over the small area. Shaulmar stood in the alley waiting for something, anything, to let him know why he was drawn to the alley's end. He trusted in the universal energy and put all his senses on high alert to be certain not to miss any signs. There was a huge dumpster in the corner. Shaulmar went over to check it out. He thought it wouldn't be so simple as to find Joaquim lying behind it. He was right; it wasn't going to be that simple.

"Why am I in this alley?" he asked of himself. "Trust and faith, trust and faith," he whispered to himself, more as a mantra, than wistfulness. There was an illuminated window on the second floor above the small restaurant with the single light bulb that hung above the back door. At the window, he caught sight of a wrinkled old face looking back at him. The tiny old lady was dressed in black with a white shawl wrapped around her shoulders that matched her hair.

"Hello, young man," she said. Shaulmar smiled at her but said nothing. "Are you missing something?" The kindly soft-spoken woman asked.

"Yes, as a matter of fact I am. Do you know anything of a young lad in trouble around here in the last couple of hours?" Shaulmar asked hoping. The old lady threw down a key and asked him to enter through the small door at the back, and then gestured for him to come up to the second floor. "Joaquim, you are alright," he sighed with huge relief.

The old lady was sitting in an old rocking chair in the corner of the room. She smiled at Joaquim as he lay on the sofa. "Now, don't you go getting into anymore trouble or I might not be around to save your hide next time," she said laughingly, "and you leave those big fellas alone. They don't take kindly to smart remarks aimed at them by young lads like yourself." She pointed her bent finger at him accusingly then laughed like a small hyena.

"Thank you for helping him, ma'am," Shaulmar said, "and May the universe repay you in kind." Joaquim hobbled over to her and kissed her cheek. At the same time, Shaulmar bowed low in front of her and then he helped Joaquim down the stairs, into the alley, and out onto the street.

Morghanz and Rebecca were waiting in the taxi on the street. When they saw Shaulmar and Joaquim, big smiles flashed across their faces.

"Well," Rebecca said, "looks like you were in the wars after all." Joaquim could only manage a small grimace due to the bumps and bruises he had suffered at the hands of Alison's henchmen.

"Well, lets all go back home and nurse our wounds," Morghanz said as she put her arm around Rebecca. She tried to lighten the mood but she knew they were going to have to work hard to protect themselves. The dark forces wanted Rebecca dead.

When they arrived at the house not one of them was in a talkative mood. They were too preoccupied with reliving the events of the night in their minds, although, no one dared to speak their thoughts out loud for fear of alarming the others. It was plainly obvious because of what had happened in the hostel, that Rebecca was in great danger, and that the danger would eventually find its way to Shaulmar's house. This concern had to be addressed without delay.

"I'd like to take a bath please if that is okay? I feel a little drained," Rebecca said quietly. Morghanz nodded and smiled. Shaulmar was busy helping poor Joaquim to the sofa.

"There are clean towels in the hall closet," he said while turning his head to acknowledge her, and while still holding Joaquim's leg up as he sat him on the cushions.

"My leg feels like it has been pushed and pulled all over the place," he said with a look of pain on his face.

"We will have a family meeting when everyone is able to." Shaulmar glanced over at Morghanz who was standing by the window peering out.

"Who was the owner of those damn crystals?" she snapped. "One thing is for damn sure, it wasn't someone by the name of 'Alison'."

"Hey, I just realized something. You called us a family, didn't you?" Joaquim said looking straight at Shaulmar.

"Yes, I did," came the reply, "and I meant it with all my heart," he added. "As long as we are here, you will always have a family. That is my promise to you, Joaquim." Shaulmar wanted him to hear these words. He knew Joaquim was suffering from deep and traumatic issues of abandonment along with the effects of post-traumatic stress that so often accompanied situations like his.

While Rebecca was taking her bath, Morghanz went up to speak with her and to be sure she was okay. Morghanz understood that traumas, no matter how great or small, could cause detrimental effects to the individual. She wanted to be sure that Rebecca was not suffering from any delayed reactions due to her overly stressful day.

"Hi Rebecca. Are you okay? Can I come in for a moment?" she shouted through the door.

"Yeah, sure, Morghanz," Rebecca shouted back. She could sense the concern in Morghanz's voice and she appreciated it. After what had transpired that night, Rebecca considered Morghanz more then just a friend.

"Hey," Morghanz said, "I thought I would come up and see if you were alright...you know...to see if you needed anything."

"Thanks. You know, Morghanz, if it wasn't for you dragging me out of that room, I don't know if I would be taking this bath right now." She locked eyes with Morghanz. "I will never forget what you did." Tears were rolling down Rebecca's face.

"Rebecca, you know Shaulmar and I are travelers. We are not from this dimension but from the love vibration that permeates all dimensions, and that is how we feel about you and Joaquim—we care about you, and just like your biological family, we will do everything we can for you," she said lovingly.

"So, do you think I am going to be killed by this dark force" Rebecca asked frankly, "because if they are going to try again, you will have to teach me what to do to defend myself."

"Don't worry. We will begin first thing in the morning. I think, from what Shaulmar has explained, you will have no problem aligning yourself with the ways of the sacred ancient arts," Morghanz told her. "I will see you downstairs after your bath, okay?" Rebecca nodded and sank back into the tub. She was thankful for the warmth of the salt water as it caressed her body and wounds just as a mother comforts her baby.

Downstairs, Shaulmar was attending to Joaquim's cuts and bruises. When Morghanz arrived in the living room they were laughing loudly and rolling back and forth on the sofa.

"What are you two laughing about?" she asked with a broad smile.

"Joaquim was just explaining to me what happened to him, how he ended up in the back of the black sedan, and how the old lady found him. It was very scary at the time but looking back now, it seems it has its funny side," he said looking at Joaquim and laughing. Morghanz made Joaquim repeat every detail of the story for her. It did have its funny side.

"What's everyone laughing at?" Rebecca had entered the room. After her bath, she showed no signs of depression or sadness, and displayed no other side effects of her traumatic adventures that day. She sat down next to Morghanz who was seated in a wicker loveseat with beautiful deep purple cushions on it.

Shaulmar knew it was time to discuss, with Rebecca, some very important and necessary things that she needed to understand. She had to know why she was here in incarnation on the planet this time around and what was necessary to keep her safe. He also wanted to share information to help guide her along the path that would take her through this life. Shaulmar wanted to be sure that Rebecca was ready to integrate the knowledge necessary to help her on her path. That is why he requested Morghanz as his partner for this particular assignment. He trusted her intuitive skills when it came to teaching Rebecca the ancient ways.

"I must begin by telling you both that there are no coincidences, and that everything that happens to us here on earth is predestined. Granted, the practice of 'free will' plays a part in the development of the soul's path here but ultimately there are only two outcomes of any lifetime. The first one concerns the consciousness of the soul that is guided through its sojourns and then accepts the resulting guidance and lessons, learning the easy ones as well as embracing the more difficult ones. This process allows for soul growth to occur. The second outcome is quite the opposite, whereas the soul energy or consciousness avoids guidance from spirit entities that have agreed to play the parts of guides for the incarnate soul, thus choosing other paths through life that prevent soul growth. This choice ensures the soul's repetition of incarnations until such a soul decides to accept the path necessary for soul evolution." Shaulmar spoke with the kind of gentle authority that encourages independent opinions and positive debate, the kind that comes from the imparting of valuable knowledge, and that also fosters acceptance and understanding.

"I don't understand all this stuff about what you said," Joaquim said with a long tone of confusion, "I don't want to be left out, though, so I try my best to listen," he added, sounding a little desperate because he didn't want to miss out on all the serious adult stuff.

"Joaquim, don't worry, you will understand in time—and in the meantime, we will never abandon you. You must trust us. We love you, all of us," Morghanz told him with a firm tone that left no doubt in the young lad's mind that she meant what she said.

"Morghanz and I were asked to come here to help Rebecca fulfill her destiny...or at least to guide her to the path that will lead her to her destiny," Shaulmar began, as he looked over at Rebecca. "Our guidance will begin in the morning with the training and energy work that Morghanz will pass on to her. For my part, I will teach Rebecca about the 'Book of Secrets,' what it contains, and how to use it," he said with an air of conviction. "All this will take time and effort on all of our parts, including yours, Joaquim," he said, looking over at him with a smile.

"Me!" came the reply. "I don't know how to do anything but follow people around and get into places that are hard to reach." He said looking at the other two as he spoke. "That's because I'm very wiry for my age as mom used to say," Joaquim joked.

"Well, let me assure you, Joaquim, you were guided to that bookstore where you were able to see me open the portal to other worlds. Your destiny is connected to all of ours," Shaulmar told him.

Now that Shaulmar had said he was going to teach Rebecca about the 'Book of Secrets,' he wanted to connect with the Sacred High Council to inform them of the events that had occurred thus far. To do this, he would have to make another trip to the old bookstore in the city. For now, Shaulmar wanted to ensure that all his friends were comfortable, and he wanted to reassure the young ones that while they were in the house, no dark forces could hurt them. He knew explanations would be required as to why the home defenses were impenetrable, especially where Rebecca was concerned. She was strong, intelligent, focused, and highly sensitive to the energies that were around her. She had probably already picked up on the meridian lines of light that flowed through the property the house was sitting on. Shaulmar intended on explaining how such meridian lines provided energy for many things, one of them being the force of protection that surrounded the house.

"Rebecca, I heard you received a letter from a friend today. Was it good news?" Shaulmar asked interestedly. She was taken by surprise with his question—it put her off guard. Her mind raced through a variety of possibilities for an answer but by the time she decided on one, Morghanz jumped in and interrupted her thoughts.

"Yes, the manager at the hostel, Mr. Holden, gave it to her. Apparently, a young man had handed it to him earlier the day before with specific instructions to give it only to Rebecca Sullivan," she said proudly. "His name is Robbie," Morghanz added.

"Thanks, Morghanz, if you don't mind, I think I can tell the rest of the story." Rebecca gave her a cynical smile, but truth be told, there was no malice intended. She was glad Morghanz had brought up the subject because that gave her the chance to feel good about sharing the fact that a boy was interested in her.

"Where did you meet him?" Shaulmar asked. He was interested but he also wanted details so he could meditate on them to learn more about the boy. He wanted to shield Rebecca from all potential harm, no matter what the source. By tuning into the energy of his name later that night, Shaulmar would be able to open himself up to an information network used by travelers throughout the universe. In this manner, the meditator is able to connect with the universal energy that shares information and is referred to as the 'Divine Eye.'

"We met at a place called the Coffee Club. He asked me to dance, and I said yes, then he had to leave."

"So, are you going to meet up with him again?" he asked.

"Well, as a matter of fact, I have a date with him the day after tomorrow. I called him earlier," Rebecca said excitedly. She felt very proud of herself.

Morghanz, who sat across from Rebecca, had the most wonderful smile on her face. The promise of love and the happiness she felt for Rebecca was reflected in her eyes. "Tell us more about him, Rebecca, what is he like?" Morghanz asked.

"Well he is handsome with blond hair and blue eyes, and when he smiles, I feel wonderful," she sighed. "Other than that, we have only spoken to each other for maybe half an hour, so I don't really know that much more about him."

Shaulmar continued to smile while Morghanz and Rebecca discussed Robbie but he was thinking of other things. As long as they remained in the house, he knew they would be protected by the meridian lines and the powers of the high council, but once they were outside the boundaries of the house they would be susceptible to the powers of the dark forces. He wondered how he was going to protect Rebecca when she was outside, and at the same time, not infringe on her privacy. There was more to learn about the dark force that was intent on harming Rebecca. Shaulmar had to find out what that was. He was determined to provide Rebecca with everything she would need to embark upon her journey. Shaulmar was going to the old bookstore the very next morning. If there was to be a struggle for dominion over good and evil, the wizard wanted access to all the knowledge and ancient wisdom the Sacred High Council could offer him. Shaulmar excused himself from the conversation and went up to his room. There was something there he wanted to give Rebecca before she went on her date.

"Hi you guys," Shaulmar said, as he returned from upstairs. He was looking quite tentative as he walked over to Rebecca. "Here, Rebecca, would you consider wearing this while you are outside of this house? It will play a part in keeping you safe when you are not with either Morghanz or myself," he said while glancing over at his partner.

"What is it?" Rebecca asked, holding out her hand.

"This is known as the 'Orban Crystal.' It has many qualities to fight against the dark forces and anyone else or thing that embraces such harmful forces," he said with pure admiration for the object. "When worn by a member of our society it offers us a major advantage of soul signature identification. If a soul who works for the forces of darkness comes within 100 feet of the crystal, or the wearer, it notifies the wearer through a soft glow of illumination. I would insist that you wear this Rebecca. My insistence is out of love and concern for your wellbeing," he added.

Rebecca took the crystal in her hands. It was tiny and beautiful and was set in a golden octagon-shaped chamber. "I would be honored to wear this beautiful crystal," she said.

"The golden chain that carries the crystal, when placed around your neck, will keep it close to your heart," Shaulmar said.

Morghanz stood up and walked over to Shaulmar. "We must conduct the ceremony this night. I will go and prepare everything," she said.

"What did she mean—everything?" Rebecca looked at Shaulmar.

"You will see," he said, "but first we must wake our young friend, Joaquim. We wouldn't want him to miss out on such an auspicious ceremony." He laughed as he put his hand on the lad's head and moved it from side to side.

"Ooh, sorry," Joaquim moaned, "did I sleep long? What did I miss…? Nothing good I hope?" he murmured. Everyone began to feel much better after the ordeals of the day and they all looked forward to the ceremony.

"I am going to perform a sacred rights ceremony for Rebecca where she will be initiated into the sacred ancient order, and then she can use the 'Orban Crystal' for protection against the dark forces that wish to do her harm," Shaulmar said.

"The Orban Crystal—what is the Orban Crystal?" the lad asked inquisitively.

"It will all be explained after the ceremony," Shaulmar replied with a smile.

Morghanz returned to the room carrying a small alter covered with a purple cloth that was embossed with gold embroidery and edging—she put her sacred alter in the middle of the room. Next she produced a purple cloth bag that was tied with a gold rope, and then she began to remove its contents with the care and attention that the sacred ceremony warranted. Joaquim walked over to her, feeling a bit better and more energetic after his nap. He began to fondle the contents, as all thirteen-year-old boys will do, while Morghanz was placing the ceremonial items on the altar.

"Joaquim, what you are holding in your hand right now is something that is held very dear to all members of the secret society we belong to.

"What do you mean 'we' Shaulmar?" he said with more than a tone of curiosity.

"I mean all four of us, and that includes you, Joaquim. When you entered the room at the back of the bookstore that was an indicator that your soul was, at some time, a member of our society. "Cool," whispered Joaquim. That fact can never be changed, no matter how many lifetimes you have reincarnated into since you were first initiated," Shaulmar told him with a big smile on his face.

"Okay, I've made the preparations, Shaulmar. Shall we get ready to begin?" Morghanz looked over at him for his response. Shaulmar looked at Rebecca and then at Joaquim. He saw the young lad's excitement, and the sparkle in his eyes showed Shaulmar that his spirit body was feeling the passion of anticipation. Joaquim would not know it was a soul passion brought forward into this lifetime from the past lives he had lived. He would only know the excitement of seeing something really 'cool' happening. However, when Shaulmar cast his eyes to Rebecca, he saw something altogether different. There was a distinct apprehension in her expression. She was probably wondering about the ceremony but he thought there might be something else bothering her.

"Alright, let's begin. I will explain how the ceremony will proceed and I want everyone to feel comfortable and to enjoy the whole experience—nothing we do can be construed as wrong," he said. "Remember that everything is predestined." Shaulmar took hold of Rebecca's hand and whispered in her ear, "I will direct you every step of the way. Don't worry, Rebecca." His words were comforting to her.

"Thank you. I am a little nervous," she said.

Shaulmar stood at the altar in the middle of the room. "Please, we must place these crystals in an octagonal formation," he said. With that, he laid out eight quartz crystals. Four clear quartzes embossed with male energy and four cloudy quartzes contained female energy. They were placed, alternately, around the room to represent the eight points of the octagon. When this task was completed, Shaulmar began to recite a sacred chant that was completely incomprehensible to both Rebecca and Joaquim. After his recital, Shaulmar lit a white candle that was placed on one side of the altar and a purple one for the opposite side. He then produced an abalone shell containing a mix of sacred herbs and other ingredients that he lit with a match until the herbs caught flame and burned. The aroma drifted across the room—it was intoxicating. Rebecca became a little less apprehensive as the ceremony commenced. As the sacred chanting continued, the energy in the room changed slowly but noticeably. At the same time the eight crystals were increasing their vibratory rate, and as a result, were becoming visibly brighter. The cloudy white female crystals reflected light like that of the silvery moon and the crisp clear male crystals shone with an electric light, that when combined with the others, produced a luminescence that glowed with an electric beauty within the octagon. At this time, Shaulmar motioned to Rebecca to come to the center of the room where the altar stood. While she stood waiting to do what was asked of her, Shaulmar produced a package from beneath the altar. It was wrapped in a purple and gold shroud. There were embroidered symbols and what looked like words of a language that was unknown to her. She looked on expectantly, and when Shaulmar unveiled the object, her heart skipped a beat. The beautiful blue leather-bound book sat on the altar before her. Shaulmar looked directly at her. "Please, Rebecca, place your dominant hand, the one you use most often, on the cover of the book."

Rebecca placed her left hand on the cover of the book. Shaulmar spoke more sacred words, and as he said them, a surge of energy began to build within the octagon that was felt by every one in the room. The eight quartz crystals placed around the room resonated in harmony, and while Rebecca's hand was on the book, she felt moved emotionally within her heart. The energy that now filled the room, emanating from the crystals as well as from the book, had moved her to feel the love of all things in the universe. Rebecca had never before experienced anything like this in her life. The book was speaking to her through emotions and energies that seemed to connect her to everything that was good within the universe. Joaquim was feeling the energy all throughout his body also. He smiled as he held his hands out in front of him, fully expecting them to be glowing as the energies moved through him. Although he couldn't see them glowing on this physical plane, they were shining brightly on a higher plane of existence. Shaulmar moved to Rebecca's side. Holding her left hand out in front of her, he placed the Orban Crystal in the center of her palm.

"Do you, Rebecca Sullivan, swear to uphold the laws and ideals of the Sacred High Council and to put your life in the hands of the universe while you are in service to the highest good of all beings?" he asked.

"I do," came the response. Shaulmar then took the Orban crystal and placed it over Rebecca's head and then laid it around her neck. The small crystal glowed as it hung there on her chest directly in front of her heart chakra. She knew that what had transpired was destined and that it symbolized the beginning of something very powerful. Shaulmar the great wizard concluded the ceremony by reciting more powerful and sacred incantations. Then he offered a closing prayer of protection and thanks to the Divine Universal Energy. Finally, he extinguished the candles on the altar along with the sacred herbs that were burning in the abalone shell.

"Well Rebecca, how do you feel now that the ceremony is finished?" he asked.

"Amazing," she replied. "That was absolutely amazing. I feel wonderful." She fingered the crystal that Shaulmar had put around her neck as she spoke. Morghanz took care of repacking the sacred items from the altar while Shaulmar continued to assess the effects of the ceremony on Rebecca.

Joaquim carried on playing with the energy he was still sensing all around him. "This is so weird. I can feel prickles and jolts of electricity in my hands, head, and legs," he said to no one in particular.

Morghanz looked over at the boy. "That's because you are a very sensitive being and the energy that was generated in the room by the performing of the sacred ceremony is powerful indeed. Plus the meridian lines of light that run through this house are very strong, especially when the vortex is amplified by the quartz crystals as they are positioned in a sacred geometric configuration. All those things contributed to the wonderful event that took place and to your ability to receive and sense the vibrations," Morghanz explained as she was dismantling the sacred altar and removing the eight crystals from the room.

Shaulmar knew that the powerful energies that were manifested during the ceremony had occurred for the reasons stated by Morghanz but he also knew that other powerful contributing factors were at play as well. The soul signature of Rebecca was one of the main reasons for the surge of energies, and her ancestors from the spirit realms who connected with her had added their momentum also. When these already powerful forces combined with the ceremonial energy, it acted as a catalyst that kicked things into high gear. Shaulmar was even more convinced, now, that he must get back to the bookstore as soon as possible to speak with the Sacred High Council. There was something that he sensed had been triggered by the sacred ceremony as he was speaking the sacred words but he did not know what it was just yet.

"Okay, goodnight everyone," Rebecca said gently, "I have to be up early in the morning. I am meeting Robbie at 9am."

They all wished her a good night, in turn, and then said their goodnights to one another. Shaulmar retired to the sanctity and privacy of his own room. There was something he wanted to do but before he could do it, there were certain preparations that were required. He intended to enter into a meditative state through breath work and mental focus. The room was filled with the aroma of a blend of sacred herbs and flora, that included sage, sweet grass, and tobacco, with lavender oil sprinkled over top of the mix. His ancestors, who performed the sacred ritual when they needed to access the higher planes of existence where all the records of every soul are kept, had handed down this particular blend to him. Only souls authorized by universal laws are granted access to this information.

Shaulmar lay down on his bed after placing the bowl of sacred mixed herbs and flora on a bedside table. He inhaled slowly and deeply and allowed his breath to fill his lower abdomen and lungs. The energy in the room slowly changed—it increased in intensity as the smoke billowed around the bed. Shaulmar's breath-work heightened his awareness and allowed him to move into an altered state of consciousness. The meridian lines that passed through the house intersected in his room and permitted an energy focal point to exist. It was this focus point of the vortex of light that was created that facilitated his ability to enter into an altered state. Shaulmar's consciousness left his physical body and moved to the center of the room exactly at the point of intersection of the meridian lines. As soon as his energy came into contact with the vortex of light, a whoosh of sound and a flash of light appeared, as his energy body disappeared from the room.

The energy that was Shaulmar emerged at the Hall of Records in a higher dimension of existence. He was met by the 'keeper of the gate' a being who was charged with the protection of all that was held beyond the gate, and who never manifested as the same apparition more than once. The manifestation this time was that of an archangel, a figure whose wings spanned the distance from Shaulmar and back again, as she greeted him. Her wings shone with a brilliant white light and each individual feather was laced with the deepest darkest midnight blue.

The two figures communicated through telepathic means, as was the norm for that particular place.

"What do you wish to know, Shaulmar, my good friend?" the archangel asked.

"I have a charge, Rebecca Sullivan, a soul on earth who is in great peril. To protect her, I must know better the soul called Robbie Cavanaugh to determine if he poses a threat or danger to her," Shaulmar transmitted telepathically to the archangel. The keeper of the gate held out her hand and beckoned to Shaulmar to enter the hall of records where he could retrieve his answer.

After Shaulmar had recovered his answer, he returned to the earth plane. As he entered back into his physical consciousness within his own room, he noticed there had been a shift in the energetic field of the house. He felt more of the surge he had felt during the ceremony with Rebecca. A definite change in the strength and direction of energy in the area had occurred. For now, Shaulmar had other tests to complete that carried more priority; yet he maintained an awareness on the energy shifts that might still occur, until he could find a better time to investigate them more fully. The information he had secured from the hall of records was favorable for Rebecca. Robbie Cavanaugh was a pure soul of the family of light known as the Rainbow Energies. These beings were sent forth into the universe from the breath of the Creator of all things in the known and unknown universe. This was good news for Shaulmar, also, because it meant there was one less potential threat to occupy his concern.

CHAPTER 9

THE FOLLOWING MORNING, SHAULMAR MADE SURE HE WAS awake to check with Rebecca before she left to meet with Robbie.

"Morning Rebecca," he said as he greeted her in the kitchen.

"Morning Shaulmar," came her reply. "Thank you for the ceremony and the crystal last night—it was so wonderful and it made me feel so good." She thanked him again. "I will be back soon to join Morghanz. She is teaching me uh…stuff."

"Did you put the crystal around your neck this morning?" Shaulmar wanted to be sure Rebecca would be protected.

"Yes I did." She pulled the crystal from inside her t-shirt and showed it to him. Shaulmar smiled and poured himself a cup of coffee.

"By the way, Robbie is a good guy, you can take my word for it. He is a pure soul," he said with a lot of assurance. Rebecca laughed and left the house through the front door. She didn't really know what Shaulmar meant, or if he was telling her something she could be certain of, but she did know that she really liked Robbie as much as she could remember him anyhow. That night at the club where they had first met, Rebecca had felt some kind of special connection between the two of them. She didn't think much of it at the time, but after everything that had happened since, she understood there was more to this physical world than she could see or touch. Rebecca had agreed to meet Robbie in the city at a soccer game. Her anticipation was building. She didn't know if he remembered that she was quite inebriated when they'd first met, and she didn't know if that state had painted the wrong picture of her. Rebecca's concerns led her mind to replay the events of that particular night, and she was reminded of Alison and her obvious plans to cause her harm. She grasped the Orban Crystal that hung around her neck and twisted it around her fingers as she rode the bus into the city.

★★★

Shaulmar welcomed Joaquim when he finally came down to the kitchen from his room. The boy looked much better after a full night's sleep.

"Morning my friend," Shaulmar said smiling. "You look well rested. How are your bruises?"

"Morning. I feel great. That drink you gave me last night made me feel good and helped me to sleep. Thank you," he said.

"Well, the potion is an ancient remedy from my homeland. It is designed to heal and remove toxins from the system while you sleep," he explained.

"Hi everyone." Morghanz had come in from outside. She was just returning from a walk in the garden after completing her morning meditation practices. Now she was ready for a healthy breakfast. "So, where is Rebecca? Did she go to meet with her friend?" she asked while popping some bread in the toaster.

"Yes, she said she would be home soon to begin her training sessions with you," Shaulmar told her."

"Good, the sooner we begin the better I will feel, and the better equipped she will be to deal with any threats that might come to her from the dark forces," she said with a strong assertion.

They sat and enjoyed breakfast together just like a real family. Joaquim was especially happy because he had found people who really cared for him. He did get a little carried away with the idea, as he was planning an outing where they would all go out for the day and have a great time—maybe to a parade or something—like a real family. However, Shaulmar and Morghanz had other ideas.

"Well, I must go now. I shall not be too long if all goes well for me at the bookstore," Shaulmar told them.

"Yes, may the universe bless your travels and keep you safe my friend," Morghanz said with a note of genuine love and concern in her voice.

"Wait!" Joaquim shouted, "what about me? I don't have anything to do or anywhere to go. What shall I do?" He was completely unsure of what it was that he could contribute to the group.

"Joaquim, I would be honored if you would consider joining my training group," Morghanz told him. "When Rebecca returns, I think it would be most beneficial if we all began to practice together. The addition of your male energy will add the perfect balance to the task of preparing for the confrontation with the dark forces that awaits us," she continued.

"Wow, that would be fantastic! Do I get to know secrets, too, and special things only the Sacred Order can do or know?" He pleaded with big brown eyes that sparkled with excitement.

"Of course," she replied. Joaquim jumped up in the air about two feet and landed on the corner of a chair before falling to the floor.

"Sorry, I was only trying out some moves before training begins," he said in an attempt to disguise his mishap.

Shaulmar shouted, "Good luck!" as he left for the bookstore

Morghanz laughed as she put the dishes into the sink and then she took Joaquim into the garden to show him some techniques of energy work while they both waited for Rebecca to return.

The soccer game where Rebecca was to meet Robbie had already started when she arrived. There were a few hundred spectators settled around the pitch. She thought Robbie might meet her at the entrance gate, but he was nowhere to be seen, so she paid her entrance fee and went inside.

"I hope this is the right game," she whispered. Just then, she heard her name being called.

"Hey Rebecca," Robbie shouted," over here in the bleachers." He was sitting with some friends. Rebecca went over and sat next to him. "Good to see you, Rebecca," he said smiling.

"Hi, good to see you again," she smiled back. Rebecca was beginning to feel she was a part of a normal life again after having been left alone to fend for herself over the last six months.

***

Shaulmar arrived at the old bookstore and made his way through the crowded store and towards the back room. He was passing the section of books on Satanism and devil worship when he was gripped with a strange familiarity as if he were with an old friend, one who's energy signature he hadn't felt for many centuries. The wizard stopped and looked around fully expecting to see a good friend. However, although he saw nothing, he felt a deep dank darkness that sank into his bones and made him feel nauseous. Shaulmar called in the protection of the Archangels and moved to the back of the store as fast as he could without looking too suspicious. He was careful to traverse through the aisles, somewhat, as a precaution against any unwanted eyes. When the coast was clear, he crossed the threshold of the hidden room and activated the portal. He traveled through the portal, then through the gateway that sheltered the planet Orban, before he arrived at the halls of the High Council where the council members were gathered.

"Welcome Shaulmar," the gatekeeper said, "the council welcomes you and asks if you would submit to the genetic isolation control scan before you speak with them?" the gatekeeper asked him out of protocol.

"Not this time my friend!" he said, as he just about knocked him down on his way past. "I need to see the council immediately!" he shouted as he picked up speed.

"They will not be very happy that you refused to move through the isolation chamber," came the fading reply from the distant figure that was busy steadying himself. Shaulmar eventually reached the hall of the sacred council. Meanwhile, the members were discussing amongst themselves the many problems of traveling through the dimensions and how researchers were getting no closer to finding a solution to the extensive illegal traveling done by criminals who were assisted by the forces of darkness.

"We must encourage the council members to increase the attention and intellectual focus of the researchers to find a way to protect our gateways from unwanted travelers to our world," one member was saying just as Shaulmar entered the hall.

"May I address the council, please, your honor?" he stated calmly and strongly to the chairman and other council members.

"Shaulmar, you were supposed to go through the isolation control chamber—what happened?" the council chair declared with some conviction and a hint of venom.

"I will explain that your honor. Please, your lordship, may we convene right away?" Shaulmar asked with rising urgency. The council was called to session, and after some dignitary insistence, the chair opened the meeting.

"Mr. Chairman, I have returned from Earth on a quest for information concerning the protection of the reincarnated soul you assigned to my care. The forces of darkness assigned to her demise are stronger and more powerful than was first estimated. In addition, while I was at the eastern portal on Earth I sensed energy connected to the dark force that was familiar to me. It was that of the dark master, Draco Bastian. This traveler is of the darkest evil to come from the dark forces, as you well know, and if he is now trying to prevent Rebecca Sullivan from fulfilling her destiny...well, that is why we need to come up with a stronger, much stronger, game plan." When Shaulmar had finished his presentation, the council members were already whispering quite frantically amongst themselves, so much so that the presiding chairman was forced to call order.

"What do you suggest we do?" the chairman asked.

"The first thing I will need is the Archangel's ring," Shaulmar stated in an almost demanding tone that caused more than a few eyebrows to be raised across the bench.

"You do realize the ring is not something the council offers freely every time the dark forces raise an ugly head," one of the council members blasted down to the wizard.

"That is something I understand completely, sir, and I know that when the council is fully aware of the power associated with this dark master, they will understand the urgency of my request. If this situation is allowed to move forward without the necessary protection, the ramifications will become far reaching and quite unstoppable," he reinforced his words with a look that ended all comments from the bench.

"The council will hold an emergency meeting. I need someone to second the motion," the chair asked.

"Seconded," came the response even before the chair had finished his sentence.

Time was passing quickly. Shaulmar began to feel edgy as a sense of anxiousness crept into his energy. Even though he was a master of energy manipulation and conduction, Shaulmar was a little susceptible to emotions of the heart. The love vibration ran strong within him.

"The High Council is in session. Please return to your seats," the gatekeeper bellowed from the doorway.

"We have come to our decision concerning the matter brought before us by the eminent wizard, Shaulmarhime of the Ancients. The Archangel's Ring will be sanctioned as a deterrent against the dark forces and Shaulmar will be the guardian of the ring while it remains away from the sanctuary of this council," the council chairman decreed. All the council members gave their seal to consecrate the act thereby attaching an energy vibration to the ring that would allow it to pass freely and unrestricted through the portal while in Shaulmar's possession. The keeper of the gate entered into the hall carrying a simple yet elegant crystal dome. Underneath the dome was the ancient and sacred artifact. The Archangel Ring was transferred to Shaulmar and as he pushed it onto the index finger of his right hand his soul signature connected with the ring's energy. Now, until the ring was returned to the council it could not be removed from Shaulmar's hand. He ran back to the portal gate and initiated the dimensional activation sequence that triggered the opening of the portal doorway.

★★★

Rebecca and Robbie were leaving the soccer game and walking through the crowds toward the exit gate. "I am having such a great time Robbie," she said.

"So am I. My friends really think you are alright," he said nervously.

"Oh and I really like them too," her heart was racing in anticipation of his next move. There just has to be another date she insisted within her mind. "I moved to a place outside the city you know,"

Rebecca told him. "It's not far, maybe 20 minutes by bus." She looked at Robbie for some sign of a reaction that would tell her if he was thinking about the possibility of another date.

"Maybe, I could come out for a visit...you know check out the area. I've never been to the suburbs before...might be interesting. What do you think Rebecca?" he asked, hoping that Rebecca wanted him to visit her. She probably saw right through his lame attempt at nonchalance—promoting his desire to see some place outside the city, anyplace, rather than admit to her just how he wanted and needed to see her again.

"Yeah...Okay. I can call you about a time. Is that okay with you Robbie?" she said, smiling slightly while avoiding full eye contact with him—she was almost bursting with shear joy.

"Yes that is great," he caught himself before he turned into the ten-year-old who had been told that his father had just bought seasons tickets to the Nicks—in the front row. "Please, call as soon as you can and okay it with your folks," he insisted. He walked Rebecca to the bus stop. Not every 17-year-old owned a car, although Rebecca kind of wished he did.

The whole time she was sitting on the bus that drove her home she thought of Robbie—how his smile was so beautiful and natural, how cute his haircut was, and how it accentuated the fullness of his ears. She giggled to herself as she daydreamed about the next time they would be together.

***

Morghanz and Joaquim were in the back garden of the house practicing energy work. Joaquim was having difficulty standing in the positions Morghanz was showing him for more than a few seconds at a time.

"Joaquim, try to set your mind in motion before ever setting the exercises in motion," she suggested with a nurturing tone that told him he was not being seen as a 'Numpty'!

"Do you mean go through the whole thing inside my mind first just to see what it is like?" He asked.

"Well yes…and no. Go through the process in your mind but do it as if you are actually really doing it right then," she told him.

"But what's the point of that?" Joaquim looked like he thought he was being laughed at. Morghanz saw the expression on his face.

"It's okay to trust me, Joaquim, I am your friend and not someone you have to be on guard with. Can you not see the difference between me and those others you have come into contact with in your life thus far?" she asked softly. Joaquim was silent while he obviously processed the information Morghanz had put to him.

"Here is a perfect opportunity to show you what I am trying to teach through energy work. Please follow me through the explanation, Joaquim. First, you must focus your mind-power on the problem. Then concentrate on a memory you have of someone you met who turned out to be a disappointment to you in some way. Now, use your mind-power to focus on every part of that memory to map every nanosecond of it. Use what you know about the experience to compare it with what you know and have experienced with us—Shaulmar, Rebecca, me. When you have made the distinctions you will understand how our mind-power and use of energy focus can bring clarity to our lives." Morghanz had made an impression on her young student. He was convinced that she genuinely cared for him—really cared for him—and not because she wanted something from him—this was a very different and unique experience for Joaquim.

Rebecca came walking up the pathway to the house where she heard voices coming from the rear of the house and made a detour towards them. "Hi you guys," she said.

"Hey, how did it go with Robbie?" Morghanz asked before anyone else could say anything.

"Great! He's a wonderful sweet guy and I could really fall for him for sure," she said, as she held both her hands on her heart and flaunted a dreamy expression on her face. She walked over to where they were sitting and sat next to Morghanz. "I was wondering could I invite him to dinner one night?" she asked hoping.

"I think that would be a lovely idea. I'm sure Shaulmar would agree. It would give us a chance to meet him and see what he is like," Morghanz said as she leaned over to hug Rebecca. They continued to talk about the date she had with Robbie and the idea of inviting him for dinner while Joaquim continued practicing the moves Morghanz had shown to him in training.

Shaulmar arrived at the house and went straight to his study where he intended to research some historic events that had occurred a few centuries in the past. He was sure Draco Bastian had manifested through inter-dimensional travel in order to complete the murder of Rebecca Sullivan that he had previously failed to accomplish. Shaulmar had to be sure that his suspicions about Draco Bastian were correct. He picked up a book volume from one of the shelves in his study. There was one way that Shaulmar could be certain that Draco Bastian was really here in this present incarnation but he needed to find a specific historical event. During the 16th century, Shaulmar was known as an alchemist—or to some folk—a wizard but he was a traveler then as he was this day. He recalled a period of time, long ago, when the darkness was strong and the people were tormented, as if the biblical apocalypse had already come to pass. There was one place on earth where evil was particularly rampant, in a village in England, where life was nothing more than the training ground for dark forces to grow and evil to be nurtured. To this day, this place still holds the energy of those who practiced evil, and any written reference alluding to such atrocities also holds the same energy. Shaulmar needed only to hold and read such writings, original writings by an original hand, to recognize the energy of that accursed reaper, Draco Bastian. The volume he held in his hands from the collection spoke of such a time and place. He could only withstand to read just a few lines before his memories betrayed him. This entity and those under his command tore the souls who incarnated in that place to pieces, both psychologically and spiritually.

As Shaulmar closed his eyes and slowed his breathing, and as best he could, released all his 'beingness,' the darkness flooded through the words on the pages directly through his mental-energy body and filled his mind. He shuddered as he struggled to mentally force the darkness back, back through his being, and back into the book—as he did so the Archangel Ring on his hand glowed strongly. Shaulmar could feel the power of the light surge through him. As the ring became a pinnacle of light, the dark energy emanating through the book quickly receded. This surely was the dark master, Draco Bastian's work," he thought to himself. "I recognize his soul signature from our first meeting centuries ago." He knew he must defeat the dark master, or Rebecca would be slaughtered spiritually, as all the other targeted souls had been so defeated. Shaulmar slammed the book shut—his ring dimmed, and the heavy, lower vibrational energy of the dark force subsided.

He took a large breath that traveled fully down to the bottom of his lungs and into his stomach. It felt similar to the satisfaction he normally experienced when he returned to consciousness after a meditation and opened his eyes. He knew now that Draco Bastion was here in this dimension to prevent Rebecca from fulfilling her contract, her destiny. Shaulmar sat back in his armchair and contemplated the events to come. As he twisted the ring back and forth on his finger, the blue sapphire in the center of the silver band glistened in the light. What plan could Draco Bastion have in mind for the demise of Rebecca Sullivan? he wondered. Shaulmar needed to meditate on the question, to try and connect with the energy of the dark forces summoned for this task.

Powerful masters can tap into the universal energy that permeates all things and are able to receive messages from other beings, whether they come in the form of images or audible links, as they connect with them through the unified energy of the universe. We only need to believe and reach out with thoughts to make a connection. Shaulmar knew this but also knew that Draco Bastion had access to the same knowledge and power. There was a knock at the study door that brought him back to the present moment. Morghanz was standing in the hallway on the other side of the door.

"Come in," he shouted. "Hi Morghanz. How are you managing and how is everything going with the training?"

"Fine for now," he heard a little concern in her voice. "Rebecca is still a little skeptical but young Joaquim is very enthusiastic—he is a natural," she beamed.

Shaulmar explained to Morghanz what had happened at the bookstore, and that he had verified the presence of the dark master at this present time in history. He also shared his overwhelming suspicion that Draco Bastion was probably here to locate and kill Rebecca. Morghanz's smile slowly left her face and was replaced by a look of tormented anguish. She also knew of Draco Bastion. Centuries ago, she had incarnated as the niece of a wealthy catholic bishop who was murdered by the followers of the dark forces. All the stories that were told about the murder were of a hideous dark master intent upon upsetting the balance of dark souls and souls of the light in the universe. Travelers were made aware of the existence of this dark master through the energy signature that was left at the scenes of his atrocities. His signature was embedded in the earth as a vortex of darkness that reached deep into the planet and far out into the blackness of space.

Draco Bastion had been master of the dark forces for eons and he could take human form at will when he chose to walk upon the earth. The only reason he was present was likely to rectify the failed attempts by the dark sorceress, Alison, to get rid of Rebecca, and it was a forgone certainty that his intended target would not be walking the earth for much longer after he accepted the assignment from the forces of darkness.

"What did the council have to say about this?" Morghanz wanted to know. She didn't have much faith in anything that involved the council procedures. Usually, by the time they had debated, discussed, brainstormed, and voted, the problem had either solved itself or the situation had become ten times worse.

"They gave me this," Shaulmar held up his hand and wiggled his index finger at her.

"Well, you must have impressed them to no end," there was a little smack of jealousy in her voice. "The Archangel Ring is not offered lightly," she said as she came closer to inspect it while trying not to appear overeager. "Boy! It sure feels powerful. The surge of latent energy is very apparent as you come closer to it," she said.

"Yes, my own soul signature is aligned with the signature of the ring—we are one," Shaulmar said ominously. "We do not know his plans, nor when he intends to strike, but we do know where Rebecca is and we can protect her as best we can," he added.

"As best we can…? What do you mean as best we can? We have to protect her no matter what!" Morghanz demanded. "We cannot allow her to fall prey to this evil. We must preserve the balance in the universe. Bastion has eliminated many souls and even turned some to the darkness," she concluded with a painful intensity that surprised Shaulmar.

"Yes…yes. I know. Don't you think I am aware of the precariousness of the situation? Trust me, I know what this dark being is capable of. No human soul has ever been immune to the will of Draco Bastion. He is evil to the core and that is where we must seek him—weakness, my dear Morghanz, we must find his weakness," Shaulmar whispered.

"If there is such a thing," she retorted as she left the study, highly charged, and as she entered into the garden again.

"Hey, where did you go? I've been practicing like crazy. I think I've managed to get it down," Joaquim insisted.

Rebecca looked on as Morghanz watched Joaquim complete the exercises set out by her that afternoon. His movements were incredible. He flowed with every turn. His wiry frame made it possible for him to remain supple, and yet strong enough, to sail through the routine almost effortlessly. When he finished his exercises, there was an audible silence in the garden. Then, an almighty applause from both Morghanz and Rebecca that was so loud it brought Shaulmar running from the house and into the garden to see what was going on.

"Well done! Well done!" he heard Morghanz shouting enthusiastically.

Shaulmar walked up beside her and whispered in her ear, "What's going on?" There, in front of him, was Joaquim smiling and bowing very low to the sounds of applause while waving his arms in the air with an exaggerated air of grandiosity.

Morghanz turned to Shaulmar while she continued to applaud the young lad. "You won't believe this." She turned back to the youngster. "Please, Joaquim would you mind showing Shaulmar what you have learned today?" she shouted to him in a serious and professional tone that indicated her admiration. The attention made Joaquim feel very grown up and very accomplished. Rebecca stood beside the others and watched Joaquim prepare to perform the exercises while holding her hands over her mouth. Joaquim steadied himself and closed his eyes. He centered himself and focused his mind on each step in his head before making the first movement. Then, suddenly, he moved and with such precision, swift and sure, he executed each exercise in turn.

The expression on Shaulmar's face revealed much. "Joaquim, you are very adept at the practice of energy work. Did you know this before you began today, or even before you met us for that matter?" he asked curiously.

Joaquim inhaled a breath with the control of a practitioner who was more than an initiate. "No, I had no idea I was good at this stuff. I didn't think I could be good at anything much really, if the truth be told," he said while displaying his best grownup serious look.

"It is obvious to me that energy work is to be part of your destined path this time around. When souls reincarnate, they bring with them certain gifts they have earned through previous lifetimes. The gifts are mastered in past incarnations and remain with the soul as characteristics they can take into their future lives. The gifts are needed in order for the soul to progress successfully through the next life as it will always be more challenging than the previous one," he explained as best he could without going into too much detail.

Joaquim tried his best to look like he was following everything Shaulmar was saying. I'm just a kid, I don't get it, he thought.

Shaulmar looked straight at him and smiled. "Don't worry, you will," he whispered as he turned to go back into the house, "you will." Joaquim just stood with his mouth wide open and with a look of total wonderment on his face, as a thirteen-year-old would. "Okay, Rebecca, your turn, before the light has disappeared out of sight," Morghanz said enthusiastically.

"Remember, go through the whole sequence in your mind first. Focus all your energy on performing each move within the exercise perfectly, then when you feel the time is right you can execute the moves," she explained. Rebecca was motionless for what seemed like the longest time. The intensity of the expression on her face showed that she was trying to focus her mind on the task ahead. Morghanz was becoming concerned at the amount of mind-power

Rebecca was conjuring up. She was about to intervene when at the same moment the student moved. Morghanz could see the flow of blue healing energy coming from Rebecca's hands as she moved—she finished the exercise—she was as graceful as a swan. Morghanz was visibly moved. "That was beautiful, Rebecca."

"Thank you." Rebecca replied.

"You're really something," Joaquim said. Rebecca smiled as she caught her breath.

"That felt really good and really…weird," she said. "It felt as if I was part of everything, as if I was moving—not physically—something else." She looked at Morghanz with a confused expression on her face.

"I could see clairvoyantly the energy of 'everything' around you and when you began to focus your mind the surrounding energy was being drawn to you."

"Oh." Rebecca said with a blank look on her face.

"It shows us that on a soul level you are very well connected to the universe and all things in it. Every being on earth, and of course the universe, is connected energetically but unfortunately very few souls are aware of this wonderful gift that is offered freely to us."

Morghanz talked about this very wistfully. She had been traveling the earth plane for many thousands of years as other masters had but there were times when she just felt so tired in the physical body. Living on the earth plane is the most draining experience for the soul because physical reality is made possible by the lowest vibrational frequency of energy in the universe. This low vibration manifests as our physical reality when we encounter energy outside of ourselves. Our various energy bodies outside of our physical one come into contact with it. Then, through our chakra system the energy is slowed down so we can gather information from within the energy. Some souls come into lives with the ability to sense this energy, and through this, they are strongly connected to everything else in existence. Rebecca was one of these souls, and Joaquim was also, but to a lesser degree. They all went inside the house as darkness began to fall. Morghanz was the last to go inside. She looked back outside toward the garden, then up to the hills beyond. Before she slowly closed the door, Morghanz paused for one last look around to be sure there was no threat building up anywhere. Joaquim went straight to the kitchen. He wanted microwave popcorn, the kind with double butter—he loved that. Everyone else went into the living room.

"Shaulmar…I was wanting to ask you something," Rebecca said, looking a little nervous as she turned to Morghanz who gave her an encouraging gesture.

"What is it?" he asked, giving her his full attention.

"I was…uh…wondering—" after what seemed like the longest pause, she just came right out with it. "I would like to invite Robbie Cavanaugh to dinner, and of course everyone else…and it's okay if you don't want to have dinner with us…or anyone…I mean…you can but you don't have to…and you can say no too…we can go somewhere else…I mean…" she stammered.

"I would love that," Shaulmar interrupted in an emphatic tone that he knew would put Rebecca at ease. She took a huge breath of relief and sat down on the sofa thinking she had made a hash of it all. Morghanz sat next to her and put her arm around her lovingly.

"Well…he's a really nice guy and I really like him," Rebecca whispered slowly.

"Rebecca," Shaulmar moved to the sofa and knelt in front of them putting his hand in hers. "We are your family if you accept us. We love you and want to see you succeed in all things. Please know," he looked at Morghanz and back to Rebecca, "you can talk to me or Morghanz about anything…anything at all—no exceptions. So realize you are an equal and integral part of this family group, as are Joaquim, Morghanz, and myself. We all are as important as the other in our quest for soul evolvement," he was visibly moved. As he spoke from his heart, the love vibration was strong with him. He had walked the earth plane for many millennia and through many experiences. The knowledge gained through these incarnations had equipped with him the gift of love. Shaulmar knew through his own soul growth that the love vibration was the most powerful energy in the universe, even though the dark powers of the universe would disagree.

This is how the soul is able to progress, by the recognition that the power of love is infinite, and it is the only way for souls to move to the higher planes of existence. When the soul finally makes the conscious recognition that the love vibration fuels the universe, then that is when the soul's signature is changed forever. Until that time, however, souls reincarnate continuously to learn and evolve, unknowingly aspiring to reach higher dimensions within the universe. The great and ancient wizard knew that soul evolution was as simple and beautiful as this. However, he also understood that there were many obstacles, hurdles, and restrictions that are placed before the soul to provide an understanding of the lessons we must learn and what characteristics we must nurture to be successful. If we are to move forward with soul growth we must first master the lowest vibrational plane that is the physical, and including mental, emotional, and psychological mastery.

The next morning Rebecca awoke to a resounding headache. She held the side of her head in her hand. "Why are these blasted head pains returning?" she voiced out loud even though she was alone in the room. "I thought Shaulmar said they were just the results of my being drawn to the bookstore." She sat up straight and laid her head against the pillow trying to use the meditative mind focusing that Morghanz had taught her to help reduce the pain. The technique was working, slowly but surely, when she suddenly had a flash of an image shoot across her mind. She was frightened of what she saw and the feelings that accompanied the images. It was enough for her to jump out of bed, put on her housecoat, and scurry downstairs where she hoped to find Morghanz and Shaulmar in the kitchen.

"What is wrong?" Morghanz asked. "You look terrified." Shaulmar was meditating in the other room.

"I woke up with a blinding headache. I tried meditation to ease the intensity of the pain when…these images kept flashing through my head." At this point she was shaking and began to sob as Morghanz reached out to comfort her. Shaulmar entered to see what had happened. When he saw the two of them hugging, he remained silent, waiting patiently to find out what was upsetting Rebecca.

Morghanz looked up at Shaulmar who was now standing at the table. "There has been a development," she said in a calm voice, but her eyes told Shaulmar it was indeed a serious development. "I think it is time for us to reveal to Rebecca what we can. Maybe, she could gain some peace of mind if she at least knew what was really going on."

"What do you mean—really going on?" Rebecca said in between sobs. Shaulmar sighed. "If you think that will help," he said. "Okay, I will make some coffee if you wouldn't mind taking Rebecca to the living room." Shaulmar looked into the tear-filled eyes of Rebecca. The compassion he felt for her showed in his face. She has chosen a very difficult path this time around, he thought.

Morghanz helped Rebecca down the narrow hallway to the living room where they both sat on the beautifully crafted wooden sofa. "Don't worry, everything will be as it was planned to be, and whatever that is, we must embrace it or be consumed by our own fears." she whispered to Rebecca as she dried her tears. Shaulmar stood by the fireplace with his arm resting on the oak mantle. He was silent and motionless as if he was communing with someone or something unseen.

Then he spoke. "Yesterday I went to the bookstore to activate the portal to other dimensions. Do you remember when we first met in that back room?" he asked.

Precisely at that moment Joaquim entered into the room. "Why is everyone in here? I woke up sweating. Is anyone going to make breakfast…? Is everything…okay?" he said slowly. There was no reply. Morghanz was still consoling Rebecca and Shaulmar had moved to the armchair in the corner of the room.

"Please come in and sit down, Joaquim." Shaulmar gestured toward the other chair next to the window." We are in the middle of a discussion that is very difficult to talk about. It involves Rebecca's future—and come to think of it, your future too," he told him.

"No one is leaving are they? We are a family aren't we?" Joaquim needed reassurance from the others before they could begin the discussion again. Even though he didn't speak those words, it was plainly understood by the panicked look on his face.

"No one is going to leave," Shaulmar said, looking around at everyone. "There will be no abandonment in this family by anyone." His mentor delivered the assurance that Joaquim needed to remove his panic and anxiety, emphatically. Joaquim sighed with relief and sat back to listen to what was being said.

"As I was saying, I traveled back through the portal to speak with the high council. I informed them of the dark force that I was sure was close to us, and I explained that I thought it was the dark master, Draco Bastion.

"Draco...who?" Rebecca asked.

"Bastion," Morghanz whispered. He is very powerful and very dangerous," she said.

"Yes he is but we will be safe as long as we remain vigilant and smart," Shaulmar insisted. "I was given this ring to help protect and combat these dark forces, especially Draco Bastion." Joaquim couldn't keep his eyes off the ring. He moved as close as he could towards the armchair so he could see it better. Rebecca was also curious about the ring.

"What does it do?" she asked.

"That depends on what is attacking it or attacking its wearer," Shaulmar said. "The ring-bearer must activate a strong sense of trust and faith in the ring and its power," he said while he looked at it. Shaulmar wondered if indeed he did have a strong enough trust and faith in the power of the Archangel's ring.

There were stories told by travelers down through the ages about how the ring would not offer any protection, or the use of its power, to some beings who wore it. Only until such time as they looked evil in the face, giving themselves over to the will of the universe, and resigning themselves to the inevitable and gruesome death that awaited them. Then, at the very last possible moment before the dark force claimed them, the humble gesture of acceptance by the bearer would activate the ring. These are stories passed on through the oral tradition, and by all accounts, are the truth.

"Whom did the ring belong to?" Rebecca asked. She wanted to know because she could swear that she had been with the ring before, or at the very least, she felt coming somewhere from the depths of her mind, that she had prior knowledge of it. "It feels really familiar to me but I don't recall ever seeing a ring this beautiful ever before," she insisted.

"The ring is known as the Archangel's ring. It was St. Michael's ring that he wore when in battle with the dark forces," Shaulmar stated. "After the dark forces were banished from the highest levels of existence in the universe, the Archangel lovingly bequeathed his powerful ring to the Sacred High Council as a force for good that would assist in maintaining the balance of the forces of good and evil in the universe," Shaulmar explained as he held out his hand proudly displaying the sacred artifact. Rebecca sat calmly thinking and after a few moments, she stood.

"I had a very disturbing dream last night, actually it was more like early morning. It took place in, what looked to me, like a tunnel or a cave or something," she made a facial expression that said she had no idea if it was a cave or a tunnel—just something dark, damp, and spooky.

"Go on," Morghanz said.

"Well, I was walking down this...uh...place, looking for something in particular. At first, I thought I was just trying to find my way out, but that was not true. I began to feel like I was looking for something special, or sacred, like a religious object, I think." She started to realize she was sharing an intimate, if not, a very weird dream with three other people. Her nerves began to get the better of her and so she said, "Oh, it was nothing really," and promptly sat back down. Morghanz almost giggled but managed to stifle it before it was halfway out of her mouth. Rebecca gave her a look of being totally put off. Morghanz transformed the giggle into a throaty cough.

"Sorry...sorry, tickle in my throat." She wasn't fooling anyone.

Joaquim just laughed out load. "What was that all about?" He looked straight at Rebecca.

"Rebecca, please continue with your dream. It may contain precognitive information that could offer us insight into what Draco Bastion and the dark forces have in store for us, for you in particular." Shaulmar coaxed her with soft words until she eventually stood up again.

"Okay, there was more but I was so scared when I woke up that it may not be as clear to me now as it was then. I remember being urged to look deeper into the place, toward the end of it. I don't know who or what was telling me to do this. The feeling was a mix of someone being kind to me, you know like a kind of stranger giving directions, and then I would have the impression that someone really nasty was there, whispering things—I don't even want to try to remember what those things were. It just felt really…really bad like…really bad," she said in a voice that was almost in a whisper, as if she was afraid the entity was in the room right there beside her. Morghanz saw her fear and immediately took her hand and gave it an encouraging squeeze. Rebecca had a subdued look on her face as if she were reliving the nightmare again.

"Rebecca," Shaulmar snapped. "Rebecca, come to focus again!"

"Yes…yes, sorry," she said apologetically. "Anyway, as I was looking for this object. I had a sense of people being in the place with me. Well, I don't know if they were people because they felt different than if you were with a person, really. I'm not making any sense, am I?" she asked as she sat down and buried her head in her hands.

Morghanz pushed Rebecca's hair away from her face and looked her square in the eyes. "You are making perfect sense as far as dreams do make sense," she said confidently. "Just you stay seated and tell us as much more as you can and as slowly as you want to. We are behind you Rebecca—you are with friends now," she said lovingly.

Rebecca smiled and continued, "As I continued down the dirty, smelly, walkway, I just somehow knew I was being protected from those bad energies by that person whom I thought was walking with me but I couldn't see anyone. At some point, the walkway or path turned to the right and I followed it. When it straightened out again there was a huge building at the end in the distance. Shaulmar thought that was significant.

"Can you try and describe this structure for us Rebecca, as best you can? Don't feel that you are under any pressure, okay?" he reassured her.

Rebecca composed herself and tried her best to recall the image. "The building looked like it was made of that marble or stone on buildings downtown in the business district. It had huge doors on the front, with something written on the stone above it, and there were also some symbols too on the stone above the big doors. The next thing I know is that I am being flashed by these small narrow beams of light crisscrossing all around me...but the funny thing was—maybe this is why such things are called dreams—there were jet black beings of...uh...well, I still want to say lights because that is what they felt like to me in my dream. I know I am describing an oxymoron when I say jet black beams of light but there you are," she insisted. Rebecca was proud to have recalled so much of her dream and also that she knew what an oxymoron was—only because she remembered looking it up in school 'cause it sounded so cool—and had applied it correctly.

Shaulmar disappeared hurriedly. Rebecca looked over at Morghanz who held up her hands and shrugged her shoulders. She was just as bewildered at his disappearance.

"Oxy...what?" Joaquim asked.

"Oxymoron. It's a word used to describe things that fly in the face of logical sense," Rebecca explained, although she didn't really know if her definition was all that correct but it was being explained to a thirteen-year-old boy so what the heck, she thought. Shaulmar returned to the room carrying the Book of Secrets in his hands. This time, when Rebecca came close to it, a visible exchange of energy was transferred between the book and herself. It felt as if an electric charge had been sent to her from the book...the others thought so too.

"Are you alright?" They all rushed to her.

"Yes, I'm okay," she whispered. "What happened? Did the book just bite me?" she asked.

"No, I think the necessary connection to the book was just made," Shaulmar explained. The book had reached out to her and an energy transfer was initiated and the respective energy signatures were then firmly established.

"This book has now claimed its owner for this lifetime, and judging by the ease with which the connection was made, the binding time will undoubtedly be short...and it does indicate that you two have been companions through many reincarnations," he continued. Shaulmar placed the leather-bound book on the altar in the corner of the room.

"Wherever you may be Rebecca, the Book of Secrets will always be available to you. No matter where you are on earth you will always be able to go to the book and commune with it—that is why the initiation of the connection and binding process was established just now," Shaulmar assured her with a smile.

"For now, we will reveal to you, Rebecca, the purpose of the Book of Secrets and tonight we will conduct the binding ceremony of the sacred order to cement the union for this lifetime," he said.

They all went into the kitchen to have breakfast, as Rebecca was feeling much better after she had shared her dream.

In the kitchen, Shaulmar continued to tell Rebecca all about the book. "The Book of Secrets is here to serve you while you travel through this life. The dream you shared with us indicates to me that one of the primary purposes of the book is to provide you with clues. These clues are to provide guidance for you to locate places where sacred ancient artifacts and relics can be found. The reason for your search for these objects is unknown to me at this time but it is ordained by the highest levels of spiritual energy, this you can be assured of," he explained in the most concrete yet loving manner. She could tell he was feeling honored and moved to be part of her experience in this lifetime. Joaquim had made some herbal tea and brought it in to Rebecca. He carried it across the kitchen to the breakfast table without spilling a drop for which he felt very proud and eternally thankful. Although everyone else in the room had to watch where he was going because his eyes never left the cup for a moment—from beginning to end.

"Here you are, Sis," he said as he carefully set the cup and saucer down on the table.

Rebecca looked up. "What did you say?" she quizzed him with half a smile.

"I know, I said Sis," he snorted, "and I know I didn't ask but can I please call you Sis?" he begged.

"Of course you can," she replied. "I would love that. You are going to make a great brother. After all, we are all family here, aren't we?" she said, looking around at the others. Rebecca stood and gave Joaquim the biggest hug he had ever had. That didn't impress him, in fact it made him squirm a little, but he thought it was a small sacrifice for having a big Sister.

"Are you up to some more training this morning you guys?" Morghanz asked. They both looked at each other and gave a positive nod. "Okay, after we eat we will continue but make sure you don't overdo breakfast," she continued.

"I will be in the study if anyone needs me," Shaulmar told them. Rebecca sipped the cup of warm fruity tea Joaquim had made for her while she looked through the window that overlooked the garden and beyond. She began to daydream about what her life had been like before both her Mom and Gran had died, compared to what it was now. The people in her life now were like family and she thought about how they had all ended up together. "What events had taken place for that to happen?" she wondered. Rebecca started to replay the movie in her head that showed vignettes of the moments leading up to the present...the sadness and pain she felt around the deaths in her family...the stress and anxiety and desperation she'd experienced while trying to survive in New York City.

Morghanz put the dishes in the sink. "Joaquim, it is not a good idea to 'work out' with your stomach so full of food," she said as she watched him reach for his third slice of toast and jam. He sheepishly returned the food to the plate and chugged down the milk that sat in front of him. Morghanz went out to the back garden. The weather was not too bad for the middle of October. It was a little brisk but she knew they would warm up fast while doing the exercises. Rebecca and Joaquim followed her out into the garden.

"Hey, there's a bald eagle," Joaquim shouted impulsively. They all looked up into the grey sky and marveled at the grace of the raptor as it glided through the air effortlessly navigating the high winds as if knowing they were provided for its use only.

"The beauty of the universe is reflected in miracles of nature such as that eagle," Morghanz said softly. They all enjoyed the moment, each in their own way.

CHAPTER 10

THERE WAS DARKNESS OVER NEW YORK CITY THAT DAY, yet millions of souls went about their business too busy to even notice. Draco Bastion had descended into the city streets—he was looking for his 'mark.' He scoured the streets with his army of dark followers. He had given them orders to find the particular soul who walked with the Light.

Bastion had already arranged a meeting with Alison, so he left his minions to complete the task of locating the girl. The Dark Angel looked forward to his meeting with the sorceress, the excitement of delivering the inevitable scathing attack on the witch before final retribution was to be handed down, was one of the few delights the Dark One treasured.

***

"You will learn what it means to be out of favor with me before much longer," he said to Alison as the dark master held up his hand and conjured the powerful forces of evil within his black heart. The room was filled with shadows moving across the ceiling like an infestation of black, snarling, and soul devouring entities. Alison was overcome. The energy was too much for her apparently feeble powers to combat. She could hardly breathe and her throat began to tighten as it squeezed the life force from her body.

"Please…stop, she gargled. Bastion only cocked his head to one side slowly as he continued to observe his prowess in the torturing of others. He watched intently as the shadow creatures enveloped the entity's feet and legs all the way up to her knees. Alison gradually fell to the floor. She was writhing in such severe pain that it caused her body to twist about so unnaturally that it forced some of her bones to crack. Bastion waved his hand across his body and the shadow creatures responded immediately. His victim was permitted to gasp for life-saving air, just enough to remain conscious while the dark master slowly walked to where the heap on the floor was.

"I am here only because of your inept attempt at removing one simple soul from its destined path," he said in a quiet controlled voice as he watched her fighting to stay alive. Alison was, by now, completely enveloped by the creatures of darkness, except for her face. The shadows were slowly draining the life from her vital organs and inflicting terrible pain throughout her entire body. Her skin began to change—its coloring became darker, much darker, until her veins and arteries protruded from beneath her skin. The heap on the floor before him was no longer Alison. She was…something else. Her voice became audibly deeper as she groaned throughout the tortuous ordeal. This hideous process of murder at the hands of the notoriously evil Draco Bastion was known throughout the universe.

"What have you to say for yourself before I end your miserable existence?" He held up his hand once more to quell the shadow creatures before they could finish her off. The thing on the floor was at the brink of death, closer than any other he had witnessed who had gone to the other side before her. Bastion held her at the edge of death, just enough so that she could feel the torment and terror of being both earthbound and dead at the same time. As he watched her squirm, he enjoyed a sinister pleasure as she suffered excruciating pain that ran through every cell of her body. Her features were no longer those of Alison. Her face was contorted in pain—her eyes were black as coal—her skin looked unnatural, like burnt wood.

"Master," the thing spoke, "please, let me live…please?" it begged.

Bastion paused, allowing it to experience still more pain "For what purpose would it serve me to let you live?" he inquired, toying with the abomination on the floor in front of him. It tried to move across the floor closer to him.

"I can serve you, help find Rebecca for you. I was friends with her up to the day I had arranged for her to be taken," the thing pleaded.

Bastion continued to hold up his hand, at any moment, ready to give the order to his Dark Ones to end its existence.

"I'm curious," he said playfully, "before I kill you, why did you fail to take this one? You had never failed before. After thousands of years of successful assignments, why this one? His voice echoed with feigned curiosity. He was intentionally twisting the proverbial knife in the wound. The thing on the floor choked and spluttered. It was obviously dying. There was not long left. Even Bastion could not torture it indefinitely.

"The light soul was taken by a member of the sacred order before my followers could complete the assignment," he was told. The dark master stepped backwards then slowly turned and returned to his dark high-backed chair. Thoughts ran through his head as he processed the information. Suddenly, he snapped his fingers. Instantly the dark shadow creatures released the thing on the floor. Bastion looked down at it through black piercing eyes.

"Sacred order, you say?" he said with a deep low voice. Tell me as much as you know of them. Drag yourself to that place...and speak," he demanded, while he raised his arm towards a corner of the large room—his long thin, finger stuck out from his outstretched hand like an ominous pointer of death. The heap on the floor began to move very slowly, grunting in pain as it did so. It reached the corner and began to speak as best it could.

"After Rebecca was taken from the Coffee Club by the one known to be a traveler, I tracked them using her soul signature that I was able to possess from the locket given to her by her mother." There was a pause as the thing struggled to remain conscious. The pain was almost unbearable. "Please, master, forgive me. Let me serve you once more? The pain is too great...pl-please...help me... I cannot bear it." It writhed in agony. The Dark One waited...then, in a flash, the pain was stopped. "Thank you, master." The life force began to return to the entity on the floor until very gradually she was transformed back to her previous self.

"I am not entirely convinced of your sincerity. Do not be fooled. I will destroy you as I have destroyed many souls of the dark force before you—as well as those of the light forces. You must have realized that dark forces beyond your comprehension give me my powers. So, if you fail again, you will die! Now, continue with your account," Bastion leered at her.

She steadily regained control of her mental and bodily functions as she continued to speak. "The traces of light energy I found connected to her locket originated from an old bookstore in the area. There was a powerful vortex of energy there that somehow anchored the light of the universe. I was unable to enter the bookstore because of this." Her voice was getting stronger.

"I know the bookstore of which you speak and the vortex of light is not the only energy source there. There is another vortex that flows through the earth and through that location. The universe exists because of harmony and balance and that is why there is a vortex of darkness that exists to complement the light. Such dark forces of energy that permeate the earth utilizing the meridian lines also protect me. You, however, are not even close to being powerful enough to protect and sustain your life force while moving through such places," he declared with an air of superiority in his voice. "The one you call the traveler, does he visit the bookstore?" Bastian asked, while he proceeded to light two black candles, one at each side of his chair.

"Yes, I think so," came the reply. At that instant, a surge of energy flew from the dark lord hitting its mark with ferocious precision. Alison let out a bone-curdling scream of pain. He looked over at her while admiring his power.

"If you are to serve me, you must learn quickly. I tolerate no one, especially those who think of themselves as being my equal. When you come to me, it will be at my invitation only—unless there is an emergency—and the only reason I will summon you is for information. Make no mistake. I do not hold your life in any way valuable. I will destroy you at the first display of non-compliance. You will be sure that the information you bring to me is accurate or you will forfeit your miserable existence, understood?" he glared at her.

"Yes master," came the humble reply.

"Now, leave before you feel the power of the darkness once more," he shouted, as Alison struggled to reach the door of escape. The physical reminders of the ordeal, however, remained—but these concerns were not important to Alyson in that moment. The act of staying alive consumed her focus as she disappeared out of the room and down the ally that ran alongside the building.

***

Shaulmar emerged from the study in time to see Rebecca sitting at the window in the living room—she was staring outside. Joaquim was thoroughly engrossed in practicing his energy work.

"Hi you two," he said kindly, "what are you doing?" They both turned to him and shrugged their shoulders, and then laughed because they had done it at the exact same time. Rebecca had been thinking of Robbie. She wanted to see him again. "So when can I call Robbie and invite him to dinner?" she asked out of the blue.

Shaulmar looked back at her. "Well, I think tonight is a special occasion," he said calmly. Rebecca's heart was racing at the thought of having Robbie over for dinner. Then she saw a look of disapproval on his face that made her heart sink and she let her face fall downward to stare at her hands as they lay on her knee. Shaulmar looked back at her. "So, I think you should ask him to be here well before seven," he said letting out a small snicker.

Rebecca had the biggest smile on her face. "Oh, you made me feel so disappointed for a second," she said looking back, as she ran to the door.

It felt so good to see joy and happiness in the face of someone who had been through so many painful experiences during the course of her short life thus far. The fact that Shaulmar knew that more pain and suffering were heading in Rebecca's direction in the near future made him want to bring as much joy to her as possible at this time. It was her destined path to gain powerful knowledge and soul strength in this lifetime so that she could gain the wisdom needed to evolve to the higher planes. Joaquim was still laughing even after Rebecca had left the room—he laughed so hard that he almost choked on the juice he had just gulped down.

"You will most likely be in Robbie's shoes one day so I wouldn't laugh too hard if I were you. The universe has a way of bringing things back to bite you," Shaulmar laughed. Joaquim took a large drink of juice to send the coughing and sputtering on its way.

Just as he did so, Morghanz appeared—she was looking for something. "Has anyone seen the bag with the eight crystals?" she asked, while peering under the altar.

"I think they are in the study," Shaulmar said. "Would you like me to get them?" He asked, as he got up from the sofa.

"Please…if you wouldn't mind. We have so much to do before the binding ceremony." Morghanz was a little unnerved at the prospect of having the ceremony not go well if something were to go awry.

Joaquim watched as she reorganized the room for the occasion. "Does everyone get to have a secret book or secret ring, or maybe a secret bike and have a ceremony and stuff?" His imagination was getting the better of him.

Morghanz continued to work as she spoke. "That depends on many things."

He was silent for a moment. "Like what kinds of things?" he asked.

"Well, your destiny, for one thing—if it is not predestined for you to experience those things, then they will not manifest in the physical plane," she said while placing the altar on a small table in the center of the room.

"How does destiny know what I am to do…? I mean, who deals out the destiny?" He said proudly as he listened to his own logic.

Morghanz snickered under her breath. "We all negotiate our personal destiny concerning reincarnation. Our soul energy controls what we wish to experience in any particular incarnation. However, there are rules as to what the soul can actually choose to experience. We must earn the right to choose our experiences and the level of soul growth achieved at the time in question dictates this. If we have the authority to experience what we want to, we can request these desires before we incarnate onto the earth plane," she said simply.

Joaquim stood with his mouth open a little. He looked as if he had just been involved in a political debate—or something like it—

that was totally beyond him. He rubbed his forehead. He felt the beginnings of an ice cream headache, a brain-freeze that promised to make him forget about asking too many questions in the future.

Morghanz saw the expression on his face and realized that he needed to be comforted. "Don't worry, Joaquim, you have a good destiny this lifetime. We all do, and I bet yours will be a great adventure," she smiled reassuringly. Her eyes sparkled like some mischievous leprechaun.

The room was finally ready for the binding ceremony. The crystals were placed around the room in an octagonal configuration; exactly like the ceremony they'd performed to initiate the connection with, and subsequent protection from, the Orban Crystal for Rebecca. The three of them were gathered in the living room in preparation for the event. Rebecca was quite nervous. She was about to become the main attraction in a ceremony whose purpose it was to bind her to an ancient leather-bound book, whatever that meant. At the same time, she had been having some weird experiences lately that would make most people think she was a little crazy. She was finally starting to accept there might be other possibilities for living life on earth, other than the ones described in every day living. Things could be happening in the world, and in the universe, that were beyond her comprehension, she thought. Rebecca, who had been sitting in her usual spot at the window, was brought back into the present moment abruptly.

"Hi, Rebecca." It was Robbie. He must have taken the bus across town at night, she thought.

"Hi," she said softly. This was a good sign, he must like her a lot to take the bus that far in the dark just to be with her and to meet her family. Although she didn't know, Rebecca's face was beaming with happiness.

"Hi, you must be Robbie," Morghanz said, "nice to finally meet you. She casually looked him over and she winked at Rebecca as Robbie walked by on his way towards Rebecca. Shaulmar smiled as they both sat on the sofa. He was looking at the point just about two inches above Robbie's head. He was reading his energy and assessing his aura for a glimpse of the boy's soul. A master of the light forces can observe the energy of some one and locate the soul clairvoyantly while sensing its vibration. As Robbie greeted Shaulmar, there was a pause before he responded in kind. Shaulmar closed his eyes for a moment and then opened them. He had seen enough to know that the soul of Robbie Cavanaugh was of the light realm and posed no threat to Rebecca. In fact, the young man shone with a love that burned in his heart as it had done for many lifetimes. Rebecca had a soul mate but this was something Shaulmar would not reveal to her unless he was forced. Finally, with a look of relief on his face, he sighed. Joaquim stood behind Robbie, looking him over, from what seemed like every angle. He was silently impressed by Robbie's strong build; however, he was confused by the way Rebecca was acting around him. She smiled constantly, and accommodated his every wish, or so it seemed to him. Joaquim recalled that whenever he did anything at all to annoy her, whether it was when he left dishes in the sink, or neglected to close the OJ container before putting it back in the refrigerator, she'd always let him know about it, and hardly ever smiled at him so much for no reason.

"Shaulmar," Joaquim whispered in his ear, "what is wrong with her? Shouldn't you do something to protect her? She is acting really weird…maybe the black forces people are attacking her? He looked at Shaulmar for an answer.

"What do you mean," he said looking over at the two of them, "they look just fine to me, like two doves cooing at one another." Shaulmar knew quite well what he was being asked but decided that Joaquim might benefit from the whole process of surrogate brotherhood. The previous heart connections Joaquim and Rebecca had experienced in past lives, physical and hormonal changes brought about by the onset of teenage male adolescence, and good old human male cluelessness were at work here.

"She's just acting weird…is all," he said, stomping off to the kitchen. Morghanz put some really gentle peaceful music on the player. "Okay everyone," she said softly, "let's come together and open the ceremony with a prayer." She paused. "Where is Joaquim?"

There was a noise coming from the kitchen. "Sorry…." Joaquim returned with something in his mouth, trying desperately to swallow it.

Morghanz continued, "Please, can we all join hands in a circle around the altar and I will open with a sacred prayer of protection and love." She initiated the circle by reaching out to Rebecca on her right and Shaulmar to her left. Robbie held up his hands with Rebecca and Joaquim. He was quite nervous but if he was to be with Rebecca there would have to be some sacrifices made, he guessed. For example, holding hands with a kid who was looking at him as if he was about to pounce at the first opportunity or finding himself in a prayer circle of a sacred ceremony that was meant to bind his girlfriend to an ancient leather book. If he told his family or friends they would have thought he'd joined a cult…or worse. The strange thing was that he somehow understood what was going on in the ceremony—and what's more, he felt good at being part of it—it felt natural to him.

Morghanz explained that the sacred words spoken to open the circle and the ceremony would be in a language they wouldn't understand, and that they should just feel the energy of the words as the vibration struck each of them, and that they should embrace the resonation that would fill their bodies. She was right. Energy flooded the circle, passing through everyone like cosmic dust from a super nova. Gradually, the room was transformed and the crystals that formed the octagonal shape within the room began to raise the vibration of all those present. Everyone felt the energy. It could not be ignored, as Robbie found out when he tried—the power of the crystals was too strong. Rebecca looked around as the opening prayer was being delivered. She was concerned that Robbie would be put off and not want to be part of her weird little family. He didn't seem unnerved by the whole thing at all though. Rebecca gave his hand a gentle squeeze. Morghanz had finished the prayer and lowered her hands and that gesture gave the others the motivation to do the same. Shaulmar moved to the center of the circle where the altar was positioned and where the book was sitting—he turned to Rebecca.

"Rebecca Sullivan, please come to the altar," he waved his hand in the air motioning her to move toward the Altar. Rebecca walked to the center of the circle, anticipating a nice warm embrace, and maybe a small ritual of her reciting some ancient poem or ceremonial words of acceptance. She calmly took a deep breath, smiled appropriately, and thought that would be the end. She placed her hand on the blue leather book and Shaulmar placed his hand on top of hers. There was a momentary pause and the event became ingrained in everyone's memories. As Rebecca turned to give Robbie a smile, there was a surge of energy and light that came from below them—the energy vortex sent a beam of white light that pierced the book, dead center, and then through the hands of both Shaulmar and Rebecca. Ripples of energy cascaded outwards from them until its cocoon enveloped Shaulmar, Rebecca, and the book. They were transported to a place unknown to the others—who all looked at each other in total disbelief—as Shaulmar and Rebecca disappeared inside the vortex of light. Joaquim was the first to react. He ran to the place where he'd seen them last.

"What's happening? Where are they? Please, Morghanz, do something," he pleaded with her. His eyes were filled with terror. Robbie only looked at the center of the circle as if waiting for Rebecca to magically reappear. Morghanz had never witnessed anything like it before. She was sitting on the sofa, deep in thought, not speaking at all. Her eyes were closed as she attempted to connect with Shaulmar and Rebecca through an energy link—she was using the crystals as amplifiers to strengthen her energy signature.

Shaulmar Rebecca and the book had rematerialized far below the house inside the power vortex of light. They appeared to be in a cave that surrounded the origin of light that they were standing in. The cave looked to be very old—there were artifacts there that indicated the presence of others who had been there before them. As they reentered the physical plane, the book dropped to the floor from beneath their hands, and both Shaulmar and Rebecca tumbled to the ground of the cavern.

"Shaulmar, where are we? I am scared. Is this how I am going to die?" her voice was trembling with fear.

"No! This is not how you are going to die Rebecca," Shaulmar insisted, knowing full well that was not something he knew for certain. "There is no danger here. I can sense it far off when it is there, and besides, the Orban crystal is not activated." His intention was to sound confident and strong to keep Rebecca from being afraid. They stood still while examining the cavern. Crystals, embedded in the walls, refelected the light coming from the vortex.

"This place is a haven for souls of the higher dimensions," he said quietly as he continued surveying the immediate area.

"You mean aliens, right?" she said, not totally believing what she was asking. There was no response from Shaulmar. He had walked further down the passageway and was almost out of sight. Rebecca ran hurriedly after him. It was amazing how the previous inhabitants had figured out how to provide enough light so they could see in this darkness. The quartz crystals were embedded in the cave's walls, that were selectively cleared of rocks and other debris, so the crystals could provide maximum light. However, there was something else going on with the crystals, Shaulmar noticed.

"Rebecca, do you see this?" He pointed to something chiseled into the cavern wall just about a foot from one of the illuminated crystals. Rebecca moved closer to Shaulmar. She was still unnerved by the whole experience. She wasn't fully certain she wasn't in some wild dream world that she was about to awaken from, with her heart beating a mile a minute, and with sweat-soaked bed clothes wrapped around her like some psycho's straight jacket.

"What is it?" she asked, while looking at the symbol on the cavern wall with great curiosity. Shaulmar, who was still examining the marking on the wall and tracing it with his index finger, paused for a moment.

"Templar priests were here. The stories told about them must be true after all," he said out loud, still caressing the wall with his hand. "Now I think I understand. Let's go back to the vortex. We can pick up the book and figure out how to get back to the others." Rebecca walked beside him but she kept looking back down the passageway where they had been. She had a strange feeling about the place.

"What did you mean when you said you understood?" she asked, as they hurried toward where the vortex was anchored into the earth.

"I will explain in good time my friend," he said as he bent down to collect the book. His hand reached to within six inches of the cover but was able to go any further. Shaulmar was perplexed. He stood there looking at the book, then over to Rebecca, and then back to the book. Finally, with a huge grin on his face, he looked back at Rebecca once again.

"So, the binding ceremony was successful after all."

"What do you mean by that?" she asked. Rebecca walked over to where he was standing and looked down at the blue leather-covered book.

"Well, the book only recognizes one soul now," he told her, as he continued to seek out the source of the power vortex.

"Oh, I see." Rebecca knelt down to the book slowly as if she thought it were a small kitten or puppy. She reached for the book with one hand as if to gently stroke it. Suddenly, its pages flew open like a Chinese fan on automatic, then, it stopped abruptly at a particular page. Rebecca jumped back, startled. She pulled her hand away as fast as she could. "What's it doing, Shaulmar? Look! The book is moving," she cried. He quickly came over to where the book had rested. He saw the page the book had opened to. It showed them a drawing of a Templar knight who was standing in the archway of, what looked like, an ancient monastery. Just as Shaulmar cast his eyes toward the book, the image disappeared.

"That appears to be a blank page, Rebecca. There is nothing to see," he said. Shaulmar looked totally perplexed. He wiped his forehead with his sleeve. Then he looked at Rebecca and smiled, "Don't worry. I won't let anything happen to you."

"What's the problem? Rebecca was becoming a little annoyed. "Don't you see the guy in the white robe holding that huge sword? Looking very confused, she continued, "What about the huge red cross right in the middle of his chest?" she insisted. She was looking at Shaulmar as if he'd lost his mind.

"No, I don't see anything but blank paper," Shaulmar rubbed his jaw with his hand. Thinking deeply, he wagged a finger in the air in front of them both. There was something—he was getting something in his mind but he just couldn't grasp it yet—the answer was on the tip of his tongue. "Wait! The book! It is bound to you now and that means..." The information was nearing completion within his mind, just like a slow download on a cheap computer. "Only you are permitted to retrieve its contents, Rebecca." That was it. Rebecca and the book were one, so to speak. "Okay, let's find the way back. Then we can interpret what the book is trying to tell you." Shaulmar walked around the base of the wall of the cavern until he had completed a circle. The power vortex was strong and it was running energy continuously. "The vortex of light is right here," he said quietly, as he pointed towards the center of the circle. "It feeds the meridian lines that flow around the earth. We must repeat, exactly, what we did during the binding ceremony. We must walk into the center of the vortex."

Rebecca was not pleased with the plan. She was not aware of the energy he was speaking about, and so, she didn't fully believe what he was saying. However, because her rational mind told her to, she looked around to see where she was. One thing was for sure—it was not the living room of Shaulmar's house. Rebecca held the book in her hands, one hand on the bottom and the other one on top. Shaulmar placed his right hand on Rebecca's and they looked at each other, Shaulmar, with a look of encouragement that she knew was for her benefit. They proceeded to walk to the center of the circle and into the vortex. An energy surge enveloped them both. It felt to them like they were swimming in an ocean of pure light. The very next thing that Rebecca remembered seeing was Robbie standing in front of her. He was holding a white candle and the distinct odor of burning sage and lavender swept through her nostrils.

"Thank God you're alright," Robbie rushed to Rebecca. He wanted more than anything to hold her in his arms.

Morghanz smiled at Shaulmar, uncomfortably, and blew out her candle. "Are you okay?" she asked as she retrieved the purple candle from Joaquim's hand. "We were a bit concerned that the dark forces had something to do with your disappearance but we also knew the archangels were with you."

"Yes, thank you Morghanz," he said, "the book connected with the vortex and transported us deep beneath the house where we were able to walk through a cavern previously used by Templar priests about a thousand years ago. The purpose, I think, was purely for the benefit of Rebecca." Shaulmar paused and gazed over to where she was still being embraced by Robbie. "The vortex of light that is anchored beneath us recognized the power of the book, and of Rebecca, as they connected during the ceremony. It remembered them from the times of the Templar priests and it wanted to be reunited with old friends. That is my best explanation for the reason we were transported to the cavern of the Templars.

Joaquim was looking a little lost and stood silently beside Morghanz "What happened? Why did the book take you guys away?" he asked. He was feeling a little confused and fearful.

Shaulmar sensed the youngster was feeling anxious and a bit panicky. He understood that the fear of abandonment and uncertainty was one of the lessons Joaquim would wrestle with in this lifetime. "The book did what it was destined to do. It gave Rebecca knowledge of her path and the information she needed to take the first steps toward fulfilling her own destiny." Joaquim tried to understand but the meaning of what he was being told to him was just too difficult to register in his mind. He was too young to grasp the deeper meaning within Shaulmar's words.

"What does all this mean? I am not sure what I'm supposed to do. I don't know if I want the responsibility of doing what is expected of me." Rebecca was feeling the pressure and weight of all the implications that seemed to be attached to the book. "The book has secrets deep within its pages, that is obvious, and I am supposed to know what they are and what I am to do with them—right?" she looked around at everyone. "This is all too much for me. I am afraid," Rebecca said, tearfully. She hurried out of the room and ran upstairs.

Morghanz looked at Robbie and indicated that he should go after her. "Robbie, please go and try to console her. She needs someone to be with her, someone she can hold on to. Shaulmar was more concerned that Rebecca might not be up to the tasks that lay ahead of her. She would need to commune with the book and learn its secrets in order to successfully navigate through the maze that was to become a large part of her future life. However, there seemed to be a positive aspect that had emerged from the union between the book and Rebecca, and that was the indisputable fact that the book had chosen her. This was very unusual in that the book was normally guided by higher universal powers that picked the soul the book was supposed to bind with. Shaulmar didn't know what all this meant but he was sure it was a good thing. Even if Rebecca rejected the idea of being bound to the book, she had certainly signed a contract before incarnating, as we all do. She would eventually accept the union.

Having realized this, Shaulmar pondered the possible phases Rebecca would be guided through. The phases began as they all do, with parents chosen by the soul to facilitate the incarnation. After the date and time of the projected incarnation into the present earth existence, the path is then solidified, astrologically, with the physical place of birth chosen to anchor the soul's signature into the earth to provide a baseline to work from. Of the entities that had agreed to guide Rebecca, one of them included the Book of Secrets. The manner in which the book provided the guidance was through its pages of knowledge. The information was given to Rebecca so she might understand and interpret it as best she could, using her physical brain, and also her soul energy.

"What should we do next, Shaulmar?" Morghanz asked quietly but with genuine concern. Joaquim, who sat on the edge of the sofa, was listening keenly to the conversation and eagerly awaiting Shaulmar's response.

There was a heavy silence that seemed to go on forever, until finally, Shaulmar raised his head. "The book has offered its first suggested course for Rebecca to take. I think we must prepare her for the arduous task she must undertake." Joaquim moved his head back and forth from Shaulmar to Morghanz like a trained dog waiting for his master's commands. "Joaquim, please go to Rebecca's room and ask her and Robbie to join us in the kitchen. We will all have supper together and discuss what must be done next." Shaulmar's enthusiasm galvanized Joaquim into action, and with the quickness of a gazelle, he disappeared from the room.

Rebecca was sitting on the edge of her bed with her head in her hands. She was mumbling something about her mom, her gran, and her life in general. Robbie moved closer to her, and just as he put a comforting arm around her, the door opened and in walked Joaquim speaking as he entered, "Rebecca I…" He stopped as soon as he saw Robbie with his arm around Rebecca's shoulders. He was whispering to her gently.

"Please don't cry, Rebecca, my heart breaks for you when you are in so much pain. We have only been together for such a short time but I feel a deep connection with you. I don't even have such feelings for my own family, my mom, dad, or brother," he continued. "I can't explain it but I would go anywhere with you if you wanted me to."

By this time, Rebecca had stopped crying but she continued to sob periodically as she gradually composed herself. "I feel so stressed out. I don't think I believe what happened downstairs." She looked up, while wiping her eyes with her blanket, and saw Joaquim standing by the door. By this time, he had found a place to lean against while he waited for her to stop crying. Rebecca gave him a semi-smile just to acknowledge he was there because she knew he was concerned. "Disappearing from the room and then reappearing some place deep beneath the earth in some ancient cave once used by a religious secret society—I would think I was crazy if Shaulmar hadn't been there too." She needed a friendly ear and Robbie was happy to provide it for her. He was a kind and unassuming person with a gentle personality, always considerate of others. He held Rebecca in his arms while she sobbed.

"It's going to be alright. Your friends will support you through this while things are being sorted out and they seem to know what they are doing. I think we can trust them to look after us," he explained softly.

Rebecca lifted her face away from his chest and looked him in the eyes. "You really mean that don't you? When you say 'us' do you mean what I think you mean?" A smile returned to her face.

"Yes…I…I think so," he sort of stammered, "do you?" he held his breath, waiting.

She looked down sheepishly. "Yes, I think so too." Her voice was soft and sweet. Rebecca was convinced that she and Robbie were meant to be together and she'd had the feeling ever since they'd first met. She always believed in the concept of 'soul mates,' where two people were fated to be together, and she always wondered if she would be fortunate enough to find hers. What Rebecca didn't know was that soul mates resonate, on an energetic level, at the same rate and frequency. When she was close to Robbie, she felt strong and unmistakable energy recognition deep within her heart. The intensity was overwhelming sometimes, and it was difficult for her to figure it all out. All she really knew was that Robbie was the 'one.'

"Hey you guys, Shaulmar would like us to have dinner and talk about stuff down in the kitchen," Joaquim said, as he moved off the wall and opened the door for them to pass through.

CHAPTER 11

DRACO BASTION WAS ADAMANT THAT HE WAS GOING TO deny Rebecca Sullivan the opportunity for soul evolution. He was intent on taking her soul—not just to disrupt the balance of souls on earth—but also to contaminate her soul enough so that her vibratory rate would be lowered, so he could eventually bring her over to the darker side of the universe. It was not a common thing for masters of the darker powers to take a personal interest in a particular soul, other than as an assignment given to them by the powers of the dark side of the universe. However, while Bastion was researching the soul, Rebecca Sullivan, some interesting pieces of information about her had surfaced. Bastion realized, that when he was a younger man, he had tried to take the soul of Rebecca's mother. She was a very strong soul, indeed, with a tenacious personality that did not succumb. There were others within the circle of dark masters who had witnessed how the young Draco Bastion had struggled to overcome the woman's spirit and energy. The struggle had not looked good for Bastion in the eyes of the more powerful of his kind. At the time, the dark masters who were his mentors were evaluating Draco's potential for advancement to master level, and he knew this soul assignment was ruining his chances. Word of the struggle between Draco Bastion and the soul of Rebecca's mother had spread like wildfire throughout the darker realms during that time. It appeared that the soul, 'Alexandra Shievchyenko,' was proving to be too much for the young aspirant. Draco Bastion was starting to accept the fact that he was not as powerful as he had originally thought. One night, while he sat alone, he had desperately searched a way to capture his assignment. He thought he might attempt an invasion of her energy and mental-body, through astral travel, while she slept. However, the young Draco was paid a visit by one of the dark masters in secret. The particular Dark One knew Draco Bastion was the key to the future of the dark powers of the universe, and this particular dark master was prepared to mentor and safeguard the young apprentice's progression until he reached master status. Thus, it followed that the dark master gave Bastion the sacred mantra and related secret black art knowledge that was usually only conferred to exceptional practitioners of the dark arts. This new information helped the young initiate to overcome and claim the soul of Alexandra Shievchyenko centuries later. With this, Draco swore his allegiance to the Dark One. He promised to claim as many souls as he could, and to transport them across the chasm to align them with the darker universe, until the night of his descent to the depths of hell where he could join with the ancient dark practitioners forever more.

Although Bastion had, since that time, lived through centuries as a practitioner of the dark arts, he was also bound to follow the laws of the universe regarding reincarnation, the very same laws the followers of light had to obey.

★★★

Draco Bastion was, after all, grateful to Alison for failing to secure her assignment once he realized exactly how important this soul assignment was to him. The satisfaction of sending Rebecca Sullivan into death's limbo was so great an incentive that he was prepared to break a few rules of his own unholy order to accomplish the task.

The dark master was seated in a huge throne-like armchair in the office building that housed his penthouse apartment downtown. The apartment was filled with many ancient African fertility statues, Jamaican voodoo paraphernalia, and ancient Mesopotamian religious icons. As he sat contemplating his plan of attack, Bastion's thoughts drifted into the past. He remembered the many years of turmoil he suffered when he was just an initiate as he struggled to secure his place within the ranks of the Sacred Dark order. He recalled the numerous indignities he underwent at the hands of the various dark masters who were hell-bent on his destruction, for one reason or another. After he had gained his master status, Bastion maintained only visions of greatness for himself that eventually helped him attain his inevitable and coveted position within the

Sacred Dark order. With this status, he also secured immortality and power that he used to wield on earth in whatever way he felt inspired. Bastion remembered feeling, deep within himself, an unwavering pull towards his goal.

However, all that changed when the assignment came up again to try to capture the soul 'Alexandra Shievchyenko' and steal her for the domain of the dark powers of the universe. He hated her with such fervor because she had made him look like such a weak fool. When he finally captured her soul and forced her to succumb to the dark powers, he wished there was more he could do to increase that one's pain and suffering. He was eventually forced to accept that there was no more he could do to her since the Sacred Dark order decided to relocate her to the prison of suffering souls that would foster her eventual transformation.

Now that he had uncovered the information that led him to the daughter of Alexandra Shievchyenko, he eagerly awaited the intensities of pain and suffering that he would inflict upon her. Bastion reveled in the idea of increasing her torment as she spent eternity locked away in her own private purgatory. He smiled to himself as he leaned to one side of the enormous silver-trimmed dark walnut desk. As he pushed a concealed button under the lip of the desktop, he watched the huge oak doors to his penthouse swing gracefully open to reveal the dimly lit hallway. Almost immediately, two large men stepped inside the room and stood facing him. "I want you both to go to the old bookstore I showed you earlier. Stake it out for a few days and let me know if any travelers show themselves." Bastion flicked his fingers and the men left the room. He got up from the desk and walked over to the huge mirror above the mantle. Where are you little Miss Sullivan? he demanded. You cannot escape the dark forces and you most certainly cannot escape me! His eyes were as black as coal. The door to his office suddenly opened again revealing a tall dark figure that stepped quickly into the room.

"Master, there is someone wishing to speak with you." He waited patiently for the response. Bastion said nothing. His eyes were cold and treacherous as he stared out through the full length, floor-to-ceiling window that overlooked New York City. He was deep in thought—he must know where they were hiding her.

"Send it in," his tone expressed his present annoyance because he knew what was on the other side of the great doors.

"Master, may the dark powers of the universe flow freely through you for all eternity." The voice crackled as it spoke the words as humbly and submissively as it could within the limited physical mechanism.

"What do you have for us? And it had better be something substantial for your own sake," he barked menacingly, not even bothering to throw a glance in Alison's direction.

"Master, I have learned something of the whereabouts of the soul you search for, and possibly the travelers that attempt to watch over her, to protect her," she claimed, in full awareness that the information she offered him gave her a degree of protection against the wrath of Draco Bastion.

"Do not attempt to bargain with me. Do you so easily forget what transpired the last time we met?" He looked at her with hands poised to deliver another deadly salvo.

Alison fell to the floor, cowering like the lowest member of a wolf pack, in submission to the Alpha Male. "Please, Master, I will give freely the information I have and serve you in any manner you desire—just do not harm me again," she pleaded with her face bent down and touching the floor.

Bastion rose from his throne and walked calmly around the desk over to where the poor wretch was whimpering and spoke to her more kindly than she had been expecting. "Now, tell me everything. Leave nothing remaining in that brain of yours."

Alison could not help but notice that Bastion was wearing the Ring of Dread given to him by the ancient ones. She was trying slowly to rise to her feet but the injuries she had sustained the last time they met were proving difficult to overcome. However, Alison was healing fairly quickly due to the help of her own ancient family healing remedies that were handed down through generations by her ancestors. "Master, the one known as Shaulmar the Bedouin protects them, and his assistant Morghanz, stands with him." She offered the information in the hopes that it would be enough to appease the dark lord.

Bastion was toying with his prey. There was one distinct difference between the powers of the dark and of the light realms of the universe, and that was the overwhelming desire of the darkness to inflict as much pain and suffering on as many souls as possible. The intoxication generated by such practices by the Dark Ones was so intense that it gave them the ultimate 'high,' both psychologically and physically. To witness another being experience soul wrenching pain was, and continues to be, their main objective without exception. For souls such as Draco Bastion, who resided in more realms than one, it meant even more than that. The sensation he felt when he knew he was responsible for such atrocities sent him into soul raptures that resonated through his being on many levels throughout his physical and astral bodies. It was generally known around the universe that this 'Being' was one of the darkest and most sinister souls in the universe.

"And where are these travelers to be found?" Bastion had an idea, but in order to control the events of the future, he must have knowledge of how powerful these travelers were and what kind of an adversary this Shaulmar being might turn out to be.

Alison needed to think fast—it was not very wise of her to have come to Draco Bastion with only partial knowledge. "Well, my minions are very close to locating them and I expect to hear from them in the next few hours," she said, while squirming and avoiding his eyes as best she could. There was no response. Draco had returned to his beautifully crafted blood-red armchair. He lean back, resting, while continuing to watch her squirm. He so much enjoyed this feeling. Bastion was twirling a short handled knife between his fingers with the skill of a surgeon; then, without warning, he released it with the speed of a bullet. The weapon sliced through its mark with ease. Blood dripped to the floor, making a sickeningly dark pattern on the marbled tile floor.

"Well, now that is what I call a sharp knife, almost as sharp as a scalpel," he commented, while observing the scene at the other end of the room. Alison tried her damnedest to remain calm and still but the sight of the bird almost split in two, skewered to the back wall of its cage by the blade, left her in no doubt of the intended message. Bastion searched her eyes, reading them for confirmation of her understanding. He found it indelibly etched on her retina and then stamped in the occipital lobe of her brain forever reminding her of the terror that is 'Draco Bastion.'

Alison became aware of the soft, gentle, trickle of what she realized was her own blood as it dripped onto her hand. Bastion had deliberately nicked her ear lobe with the blade as it shot passed her on its way to the poor bird. "Thank you, Master. May the Darkness honor your name for all eternity," she said without showing any sign of having been hit by his blade.

"Good, make sure you understand. This assignment is one I will not allow to slip through my clutches. I want you to locate the place where the travelers are staying and when you are successful come to me with a report. Is that clear?" His expression was one of pure evil, and Alison knew this as fact, when she felt the surge of energy he sent through her. There was no doubt in her mind that she was nowhere close enough or powerful enough to challenge Draco Bastion for domination over the dark forces.

"Yes Master." She didn't dare meet his eyes with her own. Alison made her way towards the great doors that would remove her from his presence but she made sure he saw how much of a struggle it was for her to move across the room. She made her injuries seem just as fresh as the day Bastion had inflicted them on her as she slipped from the room. Alison harbored a deep hatred for the one who left her almost totally crippled, physically. Through his methods of torture, she feared he had changed her likeness forever. She had a discussion within herself that had become more frequent since Draco Bastion had damaged her. One voice in her head wanted her to exact revenge against the dark master, but another more intelligent energy, that whispered in her ear proved the most convincing. It insisted that Alison burrow into Bastion's world so that she might eventually gain a position where she could do whatever she wanted to him while simultaneously becoming more powerful than any other master within the Sacred Dark order. Alison found herself in the alley outside the building and stepped into the car that was waiting for her arrival. The two figures in the front seat did not move or speak as she climbed inside; they were obviously her minions. "Drive," she commanded. The car sped down the alley and into the darkness beyond.

***

There was excitement in Shaulmar's kitchen. Morghanz and Joaquim were setting the table for five people and Shaulmar was at the stove bringing something to the boil. The heavenly odors reached up the stairs to Rebecca's room where she and Robbie were discussing things.

"That smells good," Robbie, said more in an attempt to ease any traces of newness he might project as being the latest member of the group. He was particularly sensitive to the feelings of Joaquim because he knew that he was quite young and might be feeling a little animosity towards him. Joaquim was obviously threatened by another male having made his way into the group, particularly one who was paying special attention to Rebecca. Joaquim considered her to be his Sister, and as such, displayed protective characteristics probably related to the onset of his early adolescence.

"Hi Joaquim, how is the training going?" Robbie offered with a smile. He was trying to bond with the youngster, and to impress upon him that he posed no threat to him, or more importantly, to Rebecca, and that he only wanted to be friends.

Joaquim paused a moment before answering—this was his attempt to appear adult-like. "It's going okay." He put his best serious frown look forward, and the deepest throatiest voice he could muster, even though his own voice hadn't broken yet. Robbie was disappointed and turned away. He was about to chalk the attempt up as a miss when Joaquim continued. "Hey Robbie, do you know how to fix skate boards? Only…one of the brackets holding my wheel on is broken."

Joaquim glanced at Shaulmar who was giving him the thumbs up. "There are some tools out back. Maybe you guys can look at it after dinner?" Shaulmar knew they would be okay together and that it would make Rebecca happy also because she considered Joaquim a brother and would not want his feelings to be hurt in any way. The food was now being set on the big oak kitchen table where everyone chose a place to sit and prepared to eat.

"Please, will everyone be patient while I say a blessing before we serve?" There was silence while Morghanz closed her eyes and spoke. "Divine Universal Light shine on all of us at this gathering today. Please, give your blessing to each one of us as we try our best to walk the path of destiny, and please, let the Light protect us on our journey." She asked for the blessing as she had many times before but Shaulmar detected an uncertainty in her voice that the others did not notice. "We must all find our own personal way to connect to the universal energy and cultivate a deep sense of trust and faith in the highest power of the universe because I fear the future is going to bring some very tumultuous times for us all." She sounded very serious. As the others at the table began to eat, they remained silent still, waiting for Shaulmar to speak.

"Morghanz and I are travelers. We are called upon to come to various places in the universe, such as earth, to help souls continue on their predestined path. We act as protectors of these souls against many foes and we call upon the power of the light within the universe to work through us for the highest good of all. Rebecca is such a soul of which I speak and she has a contract with the universal energy of light to successfully walk her destined path no matter how difficult it might become. As we are protectors of souls within this universe, we understand that harmony and balance must be maintained in order for it to continue to exist. So the universe must contain both polarities of good and evil, or opposites, for harmony and balance to remain in place. Having said that, the reason for the existence of the dark forces is to provide the balance that is needed. The darker side of the universe has its own aides that do its bidding, and that is why we are allowed also to protect souls who are aligned with the light on their journey.

I know and I understand that it is difficult to accept things that seem to be of an otherworldly nature, such as the event experienced by Rebecca and myself when we were transported to the cavern deep beneath the house. Morghanz and I have experienced things on our journeys that continue to cause us to doubt our own physical senses. However, let me assure you all, that there are many more facets of our universe that are not accessible to the physical plane of existence. Such things can only be experienced from a higher plane or dimension to be understood, and to experience them and understand them, you all must develop a deep and strong connection with them." Shaulmar lowered his head and was silent for a moment before continuing.

"I realize this may be too much for you all to absorb but we are nearing a confrontation with the dark master, Draco Bastion. So, we must try to speed things along in the interest of survival." He looked slowly at each person at the table. "However, we must also eat if we are to survive, so please begin." Slowly, they all began to move, reaching for food from the table, and gradually the sound of voices and cutlery were becoming louder and more relaxed.

Robbie did not fully trust what had been said but he was prepared to pay the price for acceptance within the group so long as he could remain close to Rebecca. Although he had witnessed Rebecca's disappearance during the binding ceremony, Robbie had blocked the event from his memory. Joaquim didn't understand much of what was said either but he felt a lot of excitement at the thought of battling the dark forces, and to him it sounded like the perfect adventure to be part of.

Rebecca was the one who completely understood what it all meant and she had been experiencing many of the things Shaulmar was alluding to. She thought about her headaches and the flashes of bright light, and all the strange energies she had felt, and especially the transportation down to the cavern.

"I trust you both," she said looking at Shaulmar and Morghanz. "Please, tell me the truth about what you are saying and what exactly it all means? What kind of plan do you have?" Her voice was solemn but there was definite strength and conviction there too. She meant to see this thing through to the end.

Morghanz had grown very close to Rebecca over the preceding weeks, something that the Sacred High Council frowned upon. Both she and Rebecca were aware of the connection that had developed between them and both were happy to be reunited in what appeared to be a deep and lasting friendship.

"Rebecca, you know we will assist you all we can through any situation that arises or that you may choose to experience. This time around you are to experience those life-events that permit your soul energy to increase its rate of vibration, thus allowing transformation to the higher realms of existence within this universe possible.

These realms are known to some evolved souls who walk the earth as ascended masters. Shaulmar and I function from the angelic realms and gather our power from there but we are able to access the realms of the ascended masters for assistance if necessary." Morghanz glanced at Shaulmar to make sure he wanted to continue with offering the information and he gave a discrete nod to affirm his intentions. Robbie was eating more slowly now as he attempted to process all the information he was hearing.

"We do not know exactly what your future will be Rebecca. We are not allowed access to that information at this time. We can only attempt to help you as you face each adversity during your time here. However, one thing we do know is that the dark powers of the universe are trying to prevent you from continuing on your path. So, this in of itself is a very strong indicator that your path is of great importance to your soul growth. When dark masters such as Draco Bastion show a strong interest in a soul's path, as he obviously has with yours, there can be only one reason for it. Your path must be significant in maintaining the balance of souls on the earth plane."

The others at the table were eating but in a curious and staggered manner. They seemed to be a little overwhelmed by all that was being discussed and dinner was being enjoyed on autopilot, so to speak.

Joaquim was the first to leave the table. "Does anyone else want a glass of water?" he asked with his back to everyone while he filled a glass from the sink.

There was no answer. However, Rebecca had a question of her own for Shaulmar that resonated throughout the room. "Why did the Book of Secrets open at that specific page in the cave?" The tone of her voice indicated to him that she needed an answer and not a sugarcoated one at that. Shaulmar felt the power of the universe flow through Rebecca's voice. It was true—she must indeed be strongly connected to the power of the forces of light, he thought, as he looked her squarely in the eyes.

"The book was attempting to tell you what you must do to begin the journey that you must take. The Book of Secrets will be a guardian of sorts, and if you meditate on its secrets, you will gain much knowledge from its pages. It was offering itself to you—unconditionally—search your inner guidance Rebecca and you will find your answers." She was silent, and he could see the information-process at work in her eyes. Shaulmar knew that he must continue. "What the book showed you was the place where the Templar priests made their sanctuary centuries ago, even before any westerners had ever arrived here. The stone archways were very significant for the times and were a design specific to the Templars. Try to recall the design during your meditations. There may be some significance the book wishes you to know and even some indication as to what you are to do next."

Shaulmar tried to be as impartial as he possibly could, even though he did actually know how the book functioned, and what the soul bound to it was required to do. However, it was for the book to interpret the promptings of the pages within. It is during the first part of the initiate's training that they must learn to use their intuitive abilities to connect with the Book of Secrets and decipher what instructions and knowledge that is being offered. Rebecca looked as if she were struggling to grasp what was expected of her as an initiate, and thus, Shaulmar made the decision to explain the process of initiation to her in more depth.

"You know Rebecca, you have been chosen to be the guardian of the Book of Secrets and the recipient of its knowledge—as such, you are also an initiate into the Sacred Order of Light. You must try to comprehend what an initiate is and the duties associated with initiation into such an ancient order. Do you begin to understand what is required of you?" Shaulmar's tone was not very soothing.

Rebecca's face was becoming very flushed and she knew her rose-colored cheeks could be seen by everyone in the room. All eyes were focused on her waiting for her response. She didn't like how she felt when she was the center of attention and there was an uncomfortable sense of self-consciousness that accompanied the experience as well. The most painful and overwhelming sense of fear rushed through her very being. The fear of failure was an extremely strong and debilitating experience. Early childhood memories flooded into her head. She felt she had no control over her destiny. After all, she wasn't strong enough to save her mother or her gran. So, how could she possibly be relied upon to fulfill some important and momentous task that she didn't really understand how to accomplish.

" 'Ehm...no...no I don't have any idea...of anything, she said trying her best to appear strong and confident. However, her trembling voice gave her away. Robbie sensed this and his automatic response was to comfort her, so he reached out and grasped her hand. This had the opposite effect, and as she turned immediately to him, he realized he had just cemented all the feelings she was experiencing at that moment and his heart sank.

"I'm so sorry, Rebecca," he whispered the words in her ear. There was no response. Rebecca only looked down at the floor as the many thoughts cascaded through her mind, crisscrossing back and forth, like miniature piranha chomping at her consciousness.

Shaulmar saw what was happening and decided it was time to bring the real Rebecca Sullivan to the surface. "If you do not object, Rebecca, we can enter into a meditation session together where I will be able to teach you more about the functions of the initiate, okay?" His voice and tone were extremely soothing and gentle.

Rebecca turned to Morghanz and saw an encouraging smile appear on her face. "Okay—I really want to do what I am supposed to. If you teach me, will I be able to understand what the book is trying to show me? Will I understand what I am supposed to do with my life?" she asked, as if it was the only way she could know how to live.

Shaulmar held one of her hands in his—then he looked into her eyes and held her hand close to his heart. "Rebecca, your destiny is set in stone. The energy of the Light is strong with you. You may not feel as if you know what to do. It may seem like the world is a cold and empty place for you, but know this, there are many beings sending you light and love through time and space. They assist you from the higher planes of light vibration. You must go inside yourself to find the courage and strength to embrace all the experiences that await you in this life." There was a pure golden silence that was felt around the room.

Joaquim had taken a back seat to all the talking but he was still feeling really hungry. "Can I have that rice stuff please, Robbie?"

His voice sounded really out of place in the serenity of the room but it was the only thing the moment needed.

Morghanz went to the stove where an herbal mixture was brewing. "Does anyone want to try some of my herbal tea? It is very good for the digestion and immune system." She brought out a container full of the rose-colored liquid.

"I would like some, please," over the last few weeks Rebecca had begun to enjoy the herbal teas Morghanz had made her and was developing a taste for them. Joaquim just made an awful facial expression to Robbie leaving him in no doubt of his opinion.

Robbie laughed and was glad the tension had been broken. "No thanks, Morghanz, I think I will stay with the coffee," he said in a very respectful tone. Morghanz moved toward Joaquim.

With both hands in front of his face he mumbled. " Erm…no thanks, Morghanz, that stuff makes me go. Can I just have some juice instead?" Morghanz smiled and moved on toward Shaulmar. She lifted the pot towards his cup.

"Yes please." Shaulmar sipped the tea as he looked across at Rebecca and Robbie as they came together again after such a stressful discussion. "They really are meant to be together, aren't they?" he said softly and sipped again.

Morghanz put the clay pot on a macramé coaster at one end of the big oak table. "Yes, that is very true. The way they look at each other, and how naturally and beautifully their auras connect and run from one to the other when they are close, is a wonderful thing to witness," she whispered, trying not to intrude on them with her words. "When will you begin the meditation sessions with her?" Morghanz wanted to know but at the same time she didn't want to seem pushy.

Shaulmar thought for a moment. "I think we must start right away. Rebecca must connect with the universal energy as well as the book for her own good," he said. "I feel there is a shakeup coming."

Morghanz gave him a puzzled stare. "What do you mean, a shake up? Is there something you haven't told me? You know how I like to be forewarned." She offered him a napkin. It was not like

Shaulmar to be this guarded. She thought there must be something big coming. She could even sense it.

"I will reveal all that I can later tonight when everything I think will have transpired, has. The universe dictates all events as you well know Morghanz, and even you my closest friend and ally, may not be privy to what I must do during this sojourn." His eyes betrayed himself to her. There was much danger ahead and Morghanz knew him well enough to know the truth

Robbie stood in the hallway with Rebecca and he reached for his coat. "I have to go now. My folks are always worrying about me and I promised them I would be home early tonight." Rebecca went with him to the door as the others all said their goodbyes to him.

"When can I see you again?" Rebecca asked while they were locked in an embrace.

Robbie kissed her tenderly on the lips. "I will come by tomorrow around noon after I do some chores for my mom," he explained.

"Okay," Rebecca left him with a kiss and a smile. See you around noon."

Shaulmar was in the process of setting up the room for their first meditation session. He had placed cushions on the floor, with yoga mats all around to lie on, and placed candles and crystals strategically around the room. The only thing left to do was to locate and place the Book of Secrets near to where Rebecca would be meditating.

Morghanz entered the living room. "This looks wonderful. The vibration in here is high and I can feel the intensity of the energy increasing. It's very powerful, Shaulmar. There must be an active energetic connection building for the meditation session with the two of you. Will you be able to control it?" she whispered tentatively.

"I think so. I have a feeling Rebecca is going to experience a breakthrough concerning the book. I am here only to facilitate something that Rebecca must realize is second nature to her." His expectations for the meditation session were quite specific, and to Morghanz, they appeared to be a little optimistic. She knew him well, and if he said Rebecca was a natural, and the meditation sessions would convince Rebecca of the reality of other dimensions and realms of existence other than earth, she would not dispute his wisdom.

CHAPTER 12

IT WAS THE MIDDLE OF THE NIGHT AND THE BLACK SALOON was parked at the end of the block, it looked like a ghost car. The neighborhood was upscale, with surveillance cameras at every house that were connected to a central control station downtown. Alison sat in the back of the car waiting for something, anything that might reveal to her, the identity of Draco Bastion's ancestral base. Alison knew that if she uncovered this base, she would ultimately uncover the origins of his power, and thus could figure out his weakness. All souls, including dark souls, must have a foundation origin, a place where they can anchor their connection to the universe and that allows them to function in the physical plane. This foundation is where the soul enters into this world and is imprinted with the physical soul recognition, its soul signature, more commonly known as its birthplace. Alison needed to be very cautious—any adept caught attempting to locate the origin of a dark master's ancestral power would risk being sentenced to an eternity in oblivion.

"Just drive around the complex. We are not going to find anything tonight," she ordered.

"Yes, Master." This was the only response from the dark figure in the front seat.

Alison knew that if she was to regain her power then Draco Bastion had to be destroyed. There had to be a weakness in his power, and she thought the source of his power was a good place to begin searching. She knew she would have to bide her time and plan her attack. It was going to take a large amount of skill, and a degree of luck, to successfully overcome Bastion.

"Take me home and be damn sure you are not seen returning to the dark zone." There was a streak of hatred and evil within her that surfaced every time she spoke of the one who'd taken everything from her. Alison was going to make him pay with his life and his ancestral power source. She hadn't figured out how she would accomplish it but she was determined enough. The black car pulled up to the building, silently, and a dark figure stepped out of the front and into the entrance. Alison turned and watched the car pull away. She knew there was a certain satisfaction in thinking ahead to formulate a plan that was going to remove Draco Bastion from this world. He had caused her more pain than even some of her most feared enemies ever had. There were even stronger feelings of satisfaction growing within her at the prospect of witnessing the disintegration of his ancestral lineage and having his power source transferred to her.

First, Alison had to bring Bastion the information concerning the whereabouts of Rebecca Sullivan or he would remove her from existence without a second thought. Then, he'd just use the next willing aspirant to gain information or one who was unwittingly indebted to him. Alison walked into the apartment building. The doorman was motionless when she passed him, except to acknowledge her entrance with his eyes. She had on a dark purple cloak with a hood that hid most of her face. She was self-conscious about the disfigurements inflicted on her by the Dark Angel. The doorman watched her with as much discretion as possible but he did watch her all the way to the elevator. Alison knew that he wanted to get a glimpse of Bastion's work and that was not going to happen, she assured herself. The elevator door closed sealing her off from prying eyes and she thought about removing the hood from her face. She was so hot underneath it and the lights in the small space intensified her discomfort. She was just about to get some relief from the heat when she looked up and saw that in the top right-hand corner of the elevator car she was being watched. There was a discrete camera looking back at her.

"Damn, why is there such a need for surveillance in this building? It's not as if most of the tenants are vulnerable to the criminal element—as if anyone could possibly do any thing to us," she whispered, just within the earshot of the surveillance engineer who must be watching and listening to her. Alison opened the door to her apartment very cautiously. There's no telling whom Bastion may have sent to visit me, she thought. She held out her hand when she stepped inside the entrance. Her apartment was as dark as the deepest nightmare and it was what she preferred for décor. Alison held a smoky quartz crystal in her hand—she whispered a few words of an ancient ancestral incantation into the crystal to ascertain whether there had been an uninvited visitor to her apartment while she'd been away.

"Good," she said out loud. "Now, where is that drink? Let's make it a triple." Alison had always tried to raise her spirits by talking to herself out loud—it had a calming effect on her energy. Ever since the confrontation with Bastion, she needed to have a few drinks in order to be able to look at herself in the mirror, without wanting to slice open her wrists. Alison lit her apartment mostly with candles, because of the soft and warm light they created, and because the light made her reflection a little more palatable. Just because I am a follower of the dark powers, it doesn't mean I am not able to feel soft and warm when the moment presents itself, she thought, as she tried to convince herself she was a good person. Although, she knew being a good person was not something she generally gravitated towards.

Alison pushed a button on the wall in her bathroom and the sound of rushing water could be heard filling the huge sunken hot tub that was situated in the far corner. The walls that surrounded the tub had huge windows that allowed her to view most of the city outside as she relaxed in her bathtub. Before getting into the tub she pushed a disc into the CD player, grabbed her drink, and dropped all her clothes to the floor. This was the only time she got naked. There was the slightest noise as she slid into the water; the powered water jets were turned on full. Alison sipped her drink while her mind traced through the moments of her day. There had to be some sort of weakness in his operation, she mused to herself. She was, of course, speaking about Draco Bastion and the methods he used to remain at the top of the list of the most feared and successful dark masters. Thoughts began to form in her mind as to how he was able to attain the level of evil that he had. She'd heard about the mysterious backer who had given him the Ring of Dread so many years past—she wondered who it might be. Alison became more and more relaxed as the alcohol produced the desired effect, flowing through her blood stream and across the blood-brain-barrier to the reward center, offering her the feeling of comfort.

Then, the answer just seemed to appear—it hit her mind with the force of a hurricane. "The ring! That's it! The ring!" She almost dropped her whiskey in the tub trying to get out. "Where is it? Where…where is that damn book?" Alison dragged her body from room to room, she searched one bookcase after another. She was looking for her books on ancient ring designs. Her desk was littered with books open at various pages that displayed all kinds of ancient cultures and their many designs of ceremonial rings. Hours had passed and yet she had not found any reference to the Ring of Dread.

Alison was becoming very discouraged. "Maybe there is no record of the ring's origin? Maybe it was so secret that only inside members of the most dark and secret satanic sect knew of its existence and its power?" Her voice was getting louder as her disappointment gradually manifest as anger. "This has to be the weakness in his system. I must find the origins of the ring!" By this point, Alison was yelling into her hands. Fortunately for her, the CD was still playing quite loudly and it provided a buffer for the noise she was making as she succumbed to the anger, and then, the eventual and inevitable rage that exploded from her. Alison was still somewhat disabled as a result of the Bastion confrontation, and so, there was a limit to her mobility. However, as the rage spewed from her she became more animated—it was fueled by the power of the anger and hatred that flowed through her every cell, with her rational mind offering very little in the way of resistance. The power of the dark forces of the universe shot through her with frightening ease, and it was painfully obvious that she would be a very powerful entity if she were ever allowed to walk through the doors of mayhem, and join the dark circle of masters that resided within its realms. However, if Draco Bastion ever got wind of what she was attempting, or how much potential she had, it would not be long before he sent her to the realms of the dark shadows.

Any dark master has the power and authority to regulate the aspirants within the realms that they control. This meant that if an aspirant or apprentice committed any kind of offence against a master, or a sacred practice they had sworn allegiance to; the offender could be sent to the realm of shadows. This realm was a sort of reprogramming and reconditioning limbo station that weeded the weak from the strong. More than 70% of offenders sent to the realm of shadows were returned to the earth plane in a comatose or vegetative state.

When individuals arrive at the realm of shadows, they are forced into an altered state of consciousness that compels the soul body to travel to other dimensions, while their physical body remains immobile, usually enhanced by a drug-induced coma brought on by black-magic spells and potions. Only the strong-willed aspirants survived to make their way back to rejoin their physical bodies, unassisted. If that happened, the particular individual was given a reprieve or even offered Dark Master status—depending on the level of power they were at before they were sent into the realm of shadows.

Finally, Alison was spent. She lay limp on her bed. She breathed heavily to recoup her energy and to clear her head of the pain and anguish she'd suffered at the hands of the Dark One, Draco Bastion.

Eventually, a sense of calm flowed over her body and then through her mind. Alison continued to breathe slowly and deeply. She inhaled the refreshing and ambient air around her, holding it in her lungs as long as she could, to gain the maximum amount of oxygen into her bloodstream. She didn't exhale for at least thirty seconds, letting all the calmness of the re-oxygenated blood fill every cell, and then with some force, she let the air escape. Alison moaned slightly. She was now able to think more clearly, more rationally. I must find the one who escaped my wrath. Rebecca Sullivan is the key to my eventual return to power. I must locate her before Draco Bastion finds her and takes her from me, she thought. There was a sense of purpose in her inner voice again and the feelings of hopelessness and despair had all but vanished amidst the cleansing ritual of her anger and hatred. The problem Alison was dealing with was that she had no idea where to look for Rebecca. It was as though she had disappeared from the face of the planet. She knew the travelers were responsible for her sanctuary and that meant Rebecca would be shrouded in the power of the light. "There had to be a way to identify the travelers by means of the power of the dark forces or at least by using some black magic spells," she spoke the words out loud, trying to create a sounding board for her own mind.

It is well documented that a substantial portion of the members of the dark order suffered from various kinds of psychological disorders of one kind or another. Because of this, they dwell in an altered state during their dreamtime—a trait that is exactly what the dark masters look for when recruiting souls into the Sacred Dark order. The Sacred Order of Light identified this last piece of information as the *killing time*—if there was a need for confrontation, this was the hour when the Sacred Dark Masters tried to orchestrate it.

Alison felt revitalized by the ideas that were formulating in her mind and she wanted to continue looking for any testimony of the Ring of Dread that might have been recorded throughout ancient history. If she were lucky enough to find a description of the ring, and maybe even a drawing that displayed the crest design, she would be able to identify Draco Bastion's ancestry. If Alison was to be successful, she must learn the location of the power source of Draco Bastion's particular lineage and family lines. It was getting late and Alison was still determined to search more for the ring through the archives. She was like a wolverine tracking her prey—relentless.

There was a knock on the door that catapulted Alison to consciousness. She'd fallen asleep with her head resting on the desk in her study. "Who is it?" she yelled.

"Master, it is time to go…." the voice trembled beyond the doors as it tried to explain.

"Go? Go where? I have things to do here you mindless puc!" Alison spewed. Puc was the name of the most vial creature to ever wander her home planet of Orban and it was the name she gave to anyone who made her angry.

"Master, the Dark One has summoned you to him immediately," came the brave response. The anxiety of the Puc heightened. He didn't wish to anger his master but neither did he want to incur the wrath of the dark master—Draco Bastian— if the summons were ignored. A protracted silence ensued.

"Okay, damn it, I will be ready shortly." There was anger in her that spilled out every time she was involved with Bastian. Alison made her way to the shower hoping to regain some of the calm she'd experienced before being so rudely awakened by the summons. During the shower an idea came to her. What if I could get a closer glimpse of the ring on Bastion's hand, she thought, as the soapsuds washed over her body and ran down the length of her scarred torso? "Maybe the ring would reveal its crest design if I could get close enough to it," she continued her conversation out loud, "maybe a potion would trick the ring into thinking the master had prompted it to see the family crest?" Alison became more excited as the plan began to manifest. Her energy level elevated substantially. Alison quickly started to concoct the potion in her mind, one that would be potent enough and powerful enough to convince the ring of the deception, but not too powerful as to alert Bastion of the trickery.

Alison's depression was totally gone. It had been lifted by the prospect of gaining the knowledge of the ring. However, as she dressed, it occurred to her that she was to stand before the Dark One soon, and that he would be expecting information concerning the whereabouts of Rebecca Sullivan. Panic crept into her mind then full-blown anxiety took its hold.

"Stop! Stop!" she whispered like some tormented snake. "Stop! Alison, control your fears. You are a powerful being in your own right," she hissed, while grabbing a handful of hair and twisting it around in her fingers. She was trying to create pain severe enough to take her focus from the anxiety. Alison had used the creation of pain in the past as a distraction for her own survival through many terrifying experiences. There was nothing else for her to do—she knew what must be done. Alison was backed into a corner and the mongoose was moving in for the kill.

She must contact the Rhostos, the beings that inhabited the energy between dimensions. Alison had done favors for them during her time traveling through the dimensions. The Rhostos are polar opposites of the Archangels and just as powerful. They don't align with any particular planetary beings or species of any kind. However, they do pride themselves in repaying all favors they consider to have been of value. Alison knew that if she asked for their help in trying to locate Rebecca Sullivan, they would seize the opportunity to rid themselves of their indebtedness to her. The Rhostos were the only ones, not aligned with the light, who could penetrate the angelic shroud that protected Rebecca and shielded her whereabouts. It was the only option left open to her that she could see, and it was time to fight back, she thought. To contact the Rhostos was easy enough. All she had to do was program the quartz crystal, given to her by the Rhostos, to vibrate at a particular frequency—before too long they would answer her by materializing in the physical plane, eager to make restitution. Before Alison left for Bastion's office, she programmed the quartz crystal and placed it in the middle of the floor, being sure to leave enough room for the Rhostos to manifest without wrecking the place. Then, she went down to the awaiting car.

"Tell me, where do your loyalties lie?" she confronted the two men in the car. They answered emphatically and in unison. "With you Master."

"Then we have much work to do, but if I am betrayed by either of you, my wrath will ensure that you will both need to reincarnate a thousand times before you arrive at the place you are now—understand me?" Her tone was striking and they each knew that she could do what she claimed. They had witnessed the power of her black artistry before but they did truly want to serve her, and even without the threat, they both would have stood by her side unto death. They greatly admired her power and her potential to move up the ranks within the Sacred Dark order.

"Yes, we understand Master." The man in the driver's seat made it very clear that he spoke for them both. Their allegiance gave Alison the added conviction that was needed for her meeting with Draco Bastion that day. The dark saloon pulled up beside the huge business tower downtown. The alley was not the place she wanted—or deserved—to be in, she thought to herself.

"I ought to be walking in through the front entrance and using the penthouse elevator, not Draco Bastion," she steamed.

"Yes, Master. Shall we remain in the alley, Master?" the driver asked softly, not wanting to annoy her further.

"Yes, this shouldn't take too long."

The doorman at the building entrance was very indignant towards her as she informed him of her summons to his boss's office. "Take the service elevator and make sure you keep that face covered," he snapped.

"Do not think for one moment that I am finished. You would be wise to treat me well my large friend." Alison looked him square in the eyes—her eyes pierced through his mind like a white-hot needle through flesh. The huge man stepped aside saying nothing more. He knew he had walked into a very precarious position, indeed. If she survived the wrath of Draco Bastion, the doorman expected her to pay him one final visit.

Alison arrived at the penthouse office where two guardians occupied the space in front of the huge petrified-wood oak doors. They were charged with ensuring the safety of their master, Draco Bastion. As she stepped from the service elevator, she made her way slowly towards them. "Alison, the Master is waiting. Do not make him wait any longer," one of them said angrily.

"Please, my body is not yet fully healed. I move as quickly as it will carry me." She embellished the severity of her injuries to cloud their perception and enlist the element of surprise. If she was seen to be suffering pain and debilitating agony, it could be helpful to her at the right time.

"Master, I am here," Alison kneeled before him, not daring to move until Bastion commanded her to do so.

" I have been waiting for information. Do you have something to offer me?" Bastion was sitting in his throne-like armchair behind the black oak desk. He could sense she had nothing to offer, yet there was something she was withholding from him, of this he was sure.

"Master, I will know where this Rebecca Sullivan hides by tomorrow, I am certain. My sources are very close to locating the signature of the travelers and are closing in on them as we speak. Alison hated how she was forced to do his bidding, and the memory of the physical pain he had inflicted on her came flooding back into her mind like a hot poker that seared the experience into every cell of her brain. Inside her mind she screamed with such venom that she almost lost control and narrowly averted disaster. The only thing she could think of doing, to restrain the rage that threatened to explode from her, was to repeat 'Draco Bastian will suffer a thousand deaths at my hand' within her mind. She clung to these words as if she were clinging to her very existence.

Bastian poked a finger in the air as if he were testing it then glanced over to his prey. He slowly wiggled the index finger as if he were shaking it loose from its reigns then spun it deliberately in the air. Round and round he moved it in an anti-clockwise direction, eventually a dark cloud began to manifest before him, becoming greyer and then darker as the intensity grew. Bastian had conjured to him a torture cloud he intended to use on her. The dense black cloud and shards of lightning and claps of thunder that emanated from the dark sphere spun menacingly in the air in front of Draco Bastian. He continued to manipulate the object until it threw out bolts of deadly energy two feet in all directions. Alison winced as the energy came closer to her head but she dared not move a muscle.

Bastian grinned with delight. "Do you see the power within the sphere?" he asked rhetorically, while caressing the space around the sphere.

"Yes, Master," she answered. Her head was spinning almost as fast as the object that wanted to kill her. Her mind was full of thoughts of death, and what if anything, she could do to stop him from killing her now.

"This is my baby—my pet," Bastian spoke to the thing in the air without looking at her at all. His voice sounded playful but contained a very ominous warning, and for the life of her, she couldn't sense if he meant to kill her or keep her alive until she found Rebecca. The fear and panic that enveloped her mind was like a vice, squeezing and tightening, very quickly.

Think! Think! You must think you idiot. This is not how you want to go—is it? She heard her mind scream. The sphere came so close that time that the heat from the laser-like energy singed her hair as it spun by her head. Alison was rooted to the floor. She was trying with all her strength to avoid the death sphere but she knew only too well that he was using a strong and powerful incantation to guide it. How could you have been so naïve as to walk right into his den and allow him to get his hands on you so easily without even so much as a whimper. The voices continued as she hung her head low. It would all be over too soon and she knew it. Alison continued to run thoughts through her mind, chastising her for acting like a rookie and for losing everything so easily to the one dark soul she hated the most, Draco Bastian.

Alison finally gave in—she let go of all the resistance to the sphere. She knew that the next pass it made towards her would be the last thing she would see of anything on this earth. She closed her eyes, took a deep breath, and waited for death to claim her. There was a sense of relief within her consciousness as she wondered what it was going to feel like—she bent her head forward, anticipating the final blow. There was nothing, for what seemed like an eternity, only the noise and odor of charred molecules of air, as the sphere move closer.

"Do not think you will so easily leave this reality my evil little demon," she heard him say softly. She thought she must have been dreaming. Alison remained silent. She was trying to think.

Suddenly, the huge doors swung open again. Alison opened her eyes as a man walked in. He was smaller than Bastian. He was dressed in a blood-red suit with a black shirt and shiny black shoes. Alison was still unable to break free of Bastian's powerful spell, but she directed her focus to what they were saying, just in case it was not the day Draco Bastian was going to take her soul.

"Master, you look good," the man said, "the years have been kind. May the dark power run through your heart for eternity." Bastian smiled and opened his arms to welcome him.

"Drandos! My brother. You have finally returned from the darker realms." They were held in an embrace for a few moments and Alison sensed a strong wave of energy pass between them as if the dark side of the universe was rejoicing. "So, the stories running through the circle about you having recognition as a feared dark warrior—are they true?" Draco's eye's sparkled in the presence of his younger brother.

"Yes, of course. My name strikes fear in the hearts of all beings as does yours my brother." They both enjoyed their own laughter for some time.

The sphere had disappeared by this time. Drandos looked over at the pathetic heap on the floor and then back at his brother. "Ah…s-till tormenting the lesser beings I see. You haven't changed at all, have you Draco?" Drandos gave him a look that said either kill it or let it go so we can enjoy our reunion over a good meal.

Bastian waved his hand over Alison then walked over to his brother. He put his arm around Drandos' shoulder and they both marched toward the door that exited the office. "Get out of here and bring me the information I desire tomorrow!" he shouted, as the brothers walked away without glancing in her direction at all.

"Yes, Master. Thank you, Masters" she found herself saying. Alison crawled to the nearest wall for support. She pushed her back against the wall as she slowly eased herself to her knees and into a standing position. To escape the wrath of Draco Bastian was a miracle in itself, she thought as she left the room, but to escape him a second time was pure destiny. This realization was the only thing that kept her sane while she scurried down the back stairway of the office tower to the waiting car in the alley. Alison pushed the door of the stairwell open on the ground floor and walked across the lobby as best she could without attracting too much attention from the security officers and the doorman. As she left the building by the side exit, she couldn't help wondering about the fact that Draco Bastian having a brother had escaped her notice. The lights of the black saloon illuminated the alley as the vehicle pulled up close to her side. As the door swung open, she climbed inside.

"Take me home and make it fast," she ordered.

"Yes, Master." The driver replied in a slow and docile tone. Alison had much work to do if she was going to remain alive to fulfill her promise. Rebecca Sullivan held the key to her plans for destroying Bastian and she must get her hands on the light bearer before anyone else did.

Draco Bastian was happy to see his younger brother again. He felt a sense of responsibility towards him—after all, Bastian was the one who had initiated Drandos into the Sacred Dark Order many years previous.

"So, tell me everything about your conquests during your time-traveling in the dark realms and do not spare me any of the juicy details," he insisted, as he put a hand on Drandos' cheek and gave it a brotherly rub.

"Well, since you insist, I was able to perfect the ability to manipulate energy, just like you taught me, but I reached a level of control that I'd never dreamed possible. I owe it all to you Draco. No brother could ever hope to compare with you, and if you hadn't brought me to see the darkness as all powerful, I would be living an ordinary life filled with depression and mediocrity like everyone else." He clasped Draco's hand between his with sincere affection. "Thank you. You are a true brother and friend."

"Alright, that's enough heartwarming words for one night. Let's go and have a great dinner and catch up. I know the perfect place." Bastian grabbed his brother by the neck, playfully. All the brotherly emotional energy he was experiencing was making him feel very uncomfortable. The many years Bastian had spent working with the dark powers of the lower universe, perfecting his black arts, had taken its toll on his soul. Bastian was unable to respond positively to the outward display of heartfelt goodness and affection shown to him or to anyone else. He was only interested in gaining more and more power over others. Draco Bastian had only one goal and that was to control the power within the house of the dark masters of the universe.

CHAPTER 13

REBECCA RETURNED TO THE LIVING ROOM AFTER watching her boyfriend leave the house. "Shaulmar, can you see the future?" she looked at him hopefully.

"See the future? Maybe. There are many possible futures for everyone and it depends on the choices made in every instance. His words were meant to help Rebecca realize that there were more experiences to explore than those put forward by tradition and social expectations. "Why do you ask?"

Rebecca was silent for a moment. "Well, I really love Robbie," she explained softly, "and I know that I am supposed to be too young to say that. I want to be with him always, but that is why I wanted to know if you could see into my future, so you could tell me if Robbie and I will be together...for always." Rebecca was very serious about this subject and Shaulmar could see it in her eyes.

"Whenever seers or magicians look into the future they are only connecting with one of many possibilities. There are multiple, and even infinite, possible futures for every being in the universe." He was telling her the truth. "If you really love Robbie, you must try to connect with your inner self, that part of you that we consider the core being or soul. When you are able to touch that part of your being, you can then really get a sense of how that feels, how that makes your heart feel. If you are able to embrace that feeling honestly, unconditionally, and without manipulation, then you will know more than you would ever imagine. This is true for more than just love between two people. There is a far greater love that embraces everything and everyone in the universe. It is that way for everything that has ever existed." The great wizard was trying to teach the young aspirant to open her heart and soul to recognize and embrace love for all beings under all circumstances. This was the first and one of the most important steps that was required on the path to mastery. Shaulmar observed her reaction and let her sit silently until he decided she had wrestled long enough with what he had said.

"Rebecca, we must now focus on the matter at hand and you must try to remove all thoughts of Robbie from your mind. We must remember that emotions are extremely powerful, and within that power, they have the potential to make or break us." Shaulmar did not want any strong emotional attachments to interfere with Rebecca's training. He knew the meditation sessions could mean the difference between success and failure when it came down to battles with the darker forces.

The room was lit by candlelight. Morghanz gave Shaulmar an incense concoction to burn, and the Book of Secrets was placed equidistance between them. Both Rebecca and Shaulmar were seated in straight-backed chairs to help minimize sleepiness during the meditation ceremony. Shaulmar pushed a button on the music center console and beautiful crystal bowl musical tones began to flood the room.

"Now, please Rebecca, hear the sounds of the crystal bowls, mixed with the sound of my voice, and allow them to penetrate your consciousness like the soft and gentle rays of a warm sun as it comes up over the horizon on a beautiful midsummer morning. Inhale a slow full breath, allowing it to travel from your nostrils down to the bottom of your lungs, filling them both. Then, hold the breath there gently, comfortably—don't try to force it to remain in your body." Rebecca did as she was asked. The air traveled down and felt like a warm summer breeze as it entered into her lungs. She felt surprisingly calm and peaceful.

"As you exhale," Shaulmar continued, "think of all the negative thoughts that have passed through your consciousness and have embedded themselves in various parts of the body. Try to connect with those parts of your body that were affected by the negative energies. Try to get a sense of where they might be. Your body knows and will tell you if you listen carefully. Just try to feel those places and only observe how the body feels, as you are made aware of the aches and pains. Enter their space with the help of the meditation and experience them as best you can. Now, try to remain detached from the emotions that may be triggered as you are reminded of the memories of the experiences or situations that originally created those emotions."

Rebecca remained silent but she was amazed at how peaceful and calm she felt within her body and her mind. The crystal bowl music playing in the background was so soft and gentle, yet it pierced her mind, and particularly her head where the blinding headaches and flashes of light occurred. The various sounds of the individual crystal bowls seemed to find their way into her body, but through some way other than the physical, she thought. Each note seemed to unlock a part of her being as it connected with her. She tried desperately to concentrate on the inhaling and exhaling of her breath. This focusing made her feel a little anxious about getting it right, not being able to follow the instructions, while at the same time, trying to remain calm and peaceful.

Shaulmar sensed what was happening. "Rebecca," he spoke softly but firmly, "please, do not try to control the meditation. It is not possible to be the teacher and the student. The brain is a wonderful mechanism. The left hemisphere houses the logical side of our consciousness and the right half houses the creative aspect of our consciousness."

Rebecca struggled with the confusing yin/yang aspects of her energy. "This is so irritating and confusing," she said out loud.

"Just focus on entering a state of what you would imagine to be total peace or bliss." He could sense her struggle, but he knew it was necessary if Rebecca was to gain the knowledge that was accessible through the process of meditation. He was resolute in helping her break through the social and human conditioning which prevented her from realizing her true potential. Rebecca resumed her posture and continued to inhale long slow breaths. She felt her mind wander away to other places and then caught herself and brought her focus back to the task of meditation.

"Shaulmar, I am having difficulty concentrating on what I am supposed to do, and the more my mind wanders, the more disappointed I become with my failure," she complained bitterly. Shaulmar just remained still, sitting across from her in total silence, with his eyes closed. She waited for his response. There was nothing, but she kept looking at him, patiently waiting. She knew that he had heard her and that made her even more frustrated, along with the additional and annoying irritation of the chair making her bum cheeks numb. Then, all of a sudden as if a light bulb was turned on in her head, she gasped. "This is what I am supposed to do, isn't it?" No response came. "You are not answering me so that...I might realize...in time...that meditation is used to concentrate the power of the mind on the task of focusing...on stilling the mind?" Rebecca smiled generously, and gave herself a round of applause in her mind. Shaulmar also smiled but he did not move his lips or open his eyes. He only continued with the meditation practice. They both sat in a meditative position for about half an hour before they returned their attention back to their bodies and to the chairs they were sitting in. Rebecca enjoyed the experience, and Shaulmar expressed admiration for her ability to stay with the process. He rang a small Tibetan brass bell, and after a few moments Morghanz appeared, carrying two glasses of water.

"Please, both of you, refresh your bodies with this water before you continue with the session." She stood with the tray in front of her.

"What do you mean? Is there more to do?" Rebecca asked partly with interest but mostly with a tone of disappointment. She was feeling bored, and after all, nothing had happened during the session that she thought should have happened.

"You sound disappointed. Did you not like the meditation session?" Shaulmar knew perfectly well not enough excitement was going on to occupy the mind of a 16-year-old to the extent of keeping her interested in the training. "Do not underestimate the power of meditation practice. The stilling of the mind is an exercise that has been practiced for thousands of years with great benefit for the practitioners," he explained

"How long does it take to feel something happen?" Rebecca was feeling more irritation now than at any other time she could remember. "Why am I feeling so irritated, Shaulmar? Usually, things don't get to me so easily. I never feel this irritated at something. Usually I have more control over myself," she said.

Shaulmar had remained sitting in the meditative position—he used the breath to inhale and exhale in perfect rhythm, peace, and harmony. "The mind does not like to be controlled. When you force it to remain focused on one thing, and deny it any connection to the many stimuli it is normally subjected to, then it attempts to regain control by using such instruments as irritation, discomfort, and recollection of pleasant or unpleasant memories." His words were clear, direct, and absolutely true.

"So how should I do it? Is there some special magical potion or sacred mantra you use to stop all these irritations and things?" Rebecca was experiencing a sense of loss of power over her own feelings and emotions. She was not used to feeling this way. She was always in control of her emotions. Even when her mom died, she only allowed herself to cry because she knew she was missing her mom and that she was sad. However, the emotions she was experiencing during the meditation session were of an uncontrolled nature. There were irritabilities, anxiousness, and a sense of hyper activity in the brain. All these things were due to her mind being under siege from stimuli outside as well as inside of her body. Rebecca's mind was sensing all of these things, but it was unable control, or initiate a response to them due to Rebecca's will power and desire to perform the exercise properly and to remain in the meditative state.

"How long do I have to keep this up?" she blurted out. "My mind is running all over the place and I am getting aches and pains in my legs and back." There was only silence. Shaulmar knew that when all of her words were spent, and there was no response to them, that she would have no choice but to settle down into an altered state of consciousness or to get up and leave.

Teaching meditative practices to the novice requires a teacher with a heightened sense of awareness and a good deal of skill in areas such as human behavior, he reasoned. Shaulmar was a master and knew how to guide Rebecca into the practice with a fair amount of ease. He counted on her strong will and honesty. He knew she would follow through with her promise to adhere to the practice, and that it would help her on her destined path.

He eventually opened his eyes to see how she was doing. " You are progressing very well, Rebecca." His voice was soothing to the girl. "I want you, now, to let go of all the distractions that are present inside of your head. Watch them. Observe how each thought enters your mind. Eexperience it fully, wthout reacting to it, except for your awareness of its presence. Then after a time, you will be surprised to observe how the distractions dissipate and fade away, taking their irritations with them, and leaving no impact on your consciousness." Shaulmar offered this training with such authority and assurance that Rebecca began to feel a bit more confident.

"Okay, Shaulmar, I will try as you've said to observe the feelings and emotions while offering them no response or resistance." Her tone gave him the impression that she was determined to be successful with the practice. They both returned to the meditative exercise. Rebecca was more at ease now, and found that the advice Shaulmar had given her was working a little—after some time, she found she was feeling quite calm and peaceful, even though, the various irritations continued to invade her mind throughout the remainder of the session.

Not much time had passed before things did actually begin to develop. Rebecca sensed a change in the energy close to her. She had always been sensitive to the energy around her ever since she could remember. It felt to her like a very gentle charge of electricity was being passed through her body, but she was feeling it before it actually reached her physical body, something she thought was very weird. This change was not fleeting but would prove to be the catalyst that would trigger a significant development in Rebecca's life. It would be an experience involving the power of the light forces contained within the universe that many before her had also experienced.

"Shaulmar, I am feeling something weird around me, it's like prickly and…erm…moving really fast." She sounded a little unnerved.

"Yes, I know. Do not be afraid. Remember, you must embrace all aspects of your path, both good and bad, comfortable or unnerving." He sensed what she was feeling was of the highest vibration and not in any way dark, so he did nothing to interfere. He connected with the energy signature and delved deeper to discover that it was emanating from the angelic realms.

"I...I think—it seems like it is...Shaulmar! It's coming from the book!" Rebecca shut her eyes tightly and tried to shake the feeling by shunting her shoulders up and down rapidly, and at the same time, twisting her torso from side to side. There was only one response from the wizard. "Stop shaking so much. The energy cannot be affected that way and besides you are making me carsick. The energy is of a high vibration. There is nothing to be concerned about." The wizard took in a large breath, more of exacerbation than anything else. "Just try to allow your mind to connect to everything, to all that is." The great wizard rested against the chair back with his eyes remaining closed.

Rebecca became still again, although she was feeling a little childish and a little embarrassed, and she was thankful that Shaulmar was the only person in the room with her. After a while, she was quite happy that something seemed to be occurring as a result of her persistence with staying in the meditative state. She basked in the warm, soft, gentle energy that seemed to be coming from the Book of Secrets. For a fraction of an instant, she thought there was a golden chord coming from the center of the ancient book cover that was trying to connect with her but she put it down to the wild imagination her Mom always claimed she had. However, there was a distinct tickling sensation that she felt at the back of her neck that told her there was more going on than just her imagination.

"Shaulmar, I think there is something touching me," she reached around with her hand to feel for it. "It's tickling me...whatever it is...it wants to connect with me inside my head." She was snickering nervously and she desperately wanted him to respond this time.

"You are protected by the powers of the Light, Rebecca. This is a sanctuary. No dark energies can enter this place and there is nothing here that can harm you."

Shaulmar spoke without opening his eyes and his voice seemed to be a little different, she thought. "What shall I do? The book is talking to me through the electric thing." She laughed out of nervousness, something she did whenever she didn't know what to do in any given situation.

"What do you wish to do?" the wizard spoke with an irritating indifference. "Try to allow your inner guidance, your inner voice, to point the way—remember? And stop laughing. You will block the link from the book." He knew what the book was doing and was thankful it had finally decided to fully accept Rebecca. Rebecca had calmed down somewhat—she'd been sitting silently for a few minutes trying to decipher what her inner voice wanted her to know as suggested by her friend. Her logical mind took over. It suggested that she should determine, first, what her inner voice sounded like—then, she wondered, where was she supposed to go in order to hear it.

Shaulmar inhaled deeply. The sound he made echoed and vibrated around the room. "You must decide, Rebecca. You must decide to join with the Book of Secrets completely or you must leave and live your life following another path. It is your free will to decide this. However, when you make the choice, when you decide, it must be with your heart and soul, and not with your head or any conditioning you have been exposed to during your young life. This is what I say to you as the wizard, Shaulmarhime of the Ancient Ones."

Rebecca was stunned and scared. She had no idea what was happening. Her friend didn't sound like anyone she knew. When he spoke, Rebecca felt his voice, not in any hearing way, but in a vibration way, as if she had drunk too much coffee that had made her all jittery.

"Shaulmar…is everything okay? You are making me nervous. Are you alright?" Rebecca waited in silence for the wizard to answer her.

"Do not encourage your fear, dear one. Embrace the intuitive sense that runs through your heart. Return to the sanctuary of the stillness and peacefulness of the meditation and continue to 'observe'."

Shaulmar was absolutely certain there was a change coming. He needed to prevent Rebecca from losing her connection with the energy in the room. He was sure the book was actively searching for her soul signature to perform the final stage of the binding. When the final stage of the binding was completed, it would signify to the rest of the universe that a new traveler had been chosen. It also meant something even the great wizard was not aware of. The book would never again leave Rebecca Sullivan—not ever!

The essences of both beings would be interwoven for all eternity. A new direction for the evolution of the soul was about to take place. It was the desire of the *awakening* within the Essence of the book. After many eons of making connections with different souls, it wanted to unite with this one soul, Rebecca Sullivan. The book chose many different beings and vibrational entities to bind with and a seed of gratitude and thanks was left by the Essence of the book with every entity it had bonded with. On completion of its tasks throughout time, the Essence of the book now desired to progress its soul by uniting with another entity, completely. The time had now come for the book to bind with the soul it had chosen to remain with for the rest of eternity, and that soul lived inside, Rebecca Sullivan. The book shone with a gold light that emanated from its center of it—it was a soft light that sparkled and was cloud-like in appearance. Rebecca had moved from the stiff-backed chair to a cushion on the floor after the pains of discomfort became too great. A soft cloud of gold light moved towards her—it stopped at her feet then it began to circle her body in a clockwise direction. It followed the original path of the energy that flowed through the golden chord coming from the book and it touched Rebecca's neck. The cloud was the actual essence of the book, everything it was, everything it had come in contact with, and every experience it had was embedded as a memory within the golden cloud that was about to become a part of Rebecca. The Essence swirled about her as she sat quietly, with her legs crossed, back straight, and with both hands resting on her knees.

Shaulmar sat with his eyes closed. His focus was fixed on the event. Although he did not understand the full extent of what was happening, he did know that the highest powers of the universe were overseeing and guiding the process. The incense was sending up a white-grey smoke that was being drawn to the golden Essence of the book as it swirled about Rebecca. As the smoke from the sacred herbs joined with it, the Essence quickened, and the room took on a gold and indigo hue that made the walls vibrate softly. At this point, the Essence had reached Rebecca's chest. It was spinning faster and faster around her heart chakra, at both the front and back of her body. She shifted and moaned slightly on her cushion, as the burning concoction drifted up her nasal passages to the pleasure-center of her brain, where it had an immediate calming affect and eased the slight nervous tension Rebecca had been experiencing. She was completely unaware of the Essence around her. All she felt was the slight tingling of the electrical energy that was generated by the golden chord coming from the book. At that moment, the Essence reached the exact frequency needed for the final stage of binding, then, with the help of the three crystal bowls, the Essence initiated the final binding sequence. Shaulmar suddenly held both arms above his head, palms facing upward as if he were about to accept something, some energy or blessing coming from above. He had raised his vibration using the incense and crystal sound vibrations. He was almost in his light body. As a master wizard, this was a fairly normal occurrence during such ceremonies, especially one as sacred as this. Shaulmar was, however, still oblivious to the higher significance of what was transpiring between Rebecca and the Book of Secrets.

The time was almost right—the Essence was ready. The room was vibrating softly under the influence of the cloud. The master wizard was now standing and ready to deliver the sacred incantation. Shaulmar had wondered if something unusual might happen within the meditation session, and he was right to a degree, but he was not aware of the true intensions of the Book of Secrets and the degree to which its plans were extending. Suddenly, with a strong surge of power, the cloud completely covered Rebecca. The soft golden glow gradually slowed and vibrated in rhythm with Rebecca's breathing and with her heart chakra. The Book of Secrets glowed brightly now as it merged with Rebecca's energy, and the Orban Crystal around her neck, shone with an intensity that would have harmed her if she were not protected by the binding stage and the book's golden-indigo power that had already enveloped her energetic aura.

"Shaulmar, I feel really hot inside my head. It's getting very uncomfortable." The great wizard, finally, opened his eyes as his concern for her was awakened. When he saw what was going on, his mind raced—he had never been witness to anything like this during a binding ceremony. He tried to sound as calm and as matter-of-fact as he could.

"Don't be concerned, Rebecca. There is nothing here that can harm you. Are you in any pain?" He frantically tried to understand what the book was doing while he attempted to prevent Rebecca from seeing what was going on. "Stay in the meditation dear one. Remain still and let the energy of peace and love flow through and around you while your eyes remain closed. Visualize a beautiful mountain top above a meadow, full of flowers and animals, that is canopied by a vibrant rainbow." Shaulmar, who had moved out of his chair by this point was observing the golden chord, that had by now, fastened itself to the back of Rebecca's skull. An intense sense of panic shot through Shaulmar's brain, and the only thing he could think of to do, was to try to make contact with the book. He used silent mental telepathy to ask the book what it was doing. As soon as the great wizard initiated the thought processes, and sent the thought to the Book of Secrets, he felt a jolt of power that was strong enough to force him to catch his breath as he struggled to channel it through his body and into the earth. Shaulmar could not identify the vibratory signature. He turned to the girl.

"Rebecca, how are you feeling now? Are you still in some discomfort?" His questions of concern were his way of maintaining some degree of control by trying to keep the girl calm.

"Wow! It's a bit prickly back there—not too bad though—actually it feels kind of nice and gentle. It's like reconnecting with an old friend who's been gone for a long time, but then you have the excitement of discovering how different they may have become during their time away...do you know what I mean?" she said with a big smile and with a kind of irritated excited kind of energy, as she tried to convey her feeling sense to the great wizard.

"That's...that's good...very good." He cautiously moved closer to where she was sitting, while still attempting to identify the power surge that he felt coming from the book. "Erm...do you feel anything other than the electric prickly feeling on your head and neck?" Rebecca didn't answer right away.

"Erm—nope...should I?" Her voice told him that concern was rising up in her mind, and that if he was going to keep her from opening her eyes and becoming aware of what was really going on between her and the book, then he had better think of something fast.

The cloud continued to swirl about her and the indigo energy danced ferociously within it. Shaulmar had no clue as to what he should do at this point. All he knew was that the book was of the light—it had been for eons—and so he assumed that if any danger was present that he would be aware of it. He didn't sense any real danger. He felt so helpless, and so useless because he couldn't help Rebecca, the charge given into his care by the Sacred High Council. He was about to do the only thing he could think of which would be suicide for him, that fact he knew without any shred of doubt, but he was prepared to do it for Rebecca and the highest good of all. He turned to her once more.

"Rebecca, listen to me very carefully. I want you to—but he wasn't able to finish his thought.

"Shaulmar of the Ancients, do not be alarmed." Rebecca was speaking but the words were not hers. "Please, my friend, trust what you hear and from whom you hear it." Shaulmar stood in silence, but his mind was in a whirlwind. Rebecca faced him holding up her left hand. She was vibrating softly and she did not appear to be in any kind of danger. She seemed actually to be channeling the energy of the Book of Secrets. That energy or essence had fully bound itself to the soul signature of Rebecca and it was using her vocal chords as a means to connect with the great wizard.

"This is the one I have been seeking. Many eons have passed since I have become what I am in this moment…and as I evolved, so did my need for a traveler and power source of sufficient energy to form this symbiotic relationship." The explanation was simple enough. However, Shaulmar had many questions of importance for the Essence…before he could be comfortable with the situation.

"Does Rebecca know of this, and if so, did she give her permission for this to occur?" He watched for any indication of the Essence in Rebecca's eyes, the only exposed part of her brain.

"The entity known in this sphere of existence known as, Rebecca Sullivan, has consented fully to the binding of her soul's consciousness. This agreement took place before she incarnated into this realm. Although, I had no idea when or where this was to occur in this realm, my only wish was to evolve into higher plains and higher vibrations of existence. This energy, you call Rebecca, can provide me with this opportunity and in return I will offer any assistance I can, that might help her realize her own innate desire to evolve towards the higher states of being." Shaulmar still could not identify the Essence's power origin but he was sure that the Orban Crystal would sound the alarm if the girl were in any kind of danger. Not even the power within the book could override the power of the crystal to alert her to danger. The universe had programmed the crystal for that specific task.

"So, what happens next?" he asked the Essence.

"Next? Now we are one. We commune through channels of higher consciousness and our energy vibrates as one." The Essence had claimed the right to the terms of the contract entered into prior to their existence within this realm, a contract sanctioned by universal law. They were now, bound souls...forever.

What of the Sacred High Council? Do they know the full extent of what has occurred here today?" Shaulmar was searching for a way to identify the book's signature. He was playing for time. He knew the council was a club of which the members had formed into an elite group. The real problem was, that they allowed their own thoughts to dictate how the universe would be best served, rather than listening to the universe with their hearts and doing what they knew intuitively would be of the most benefit to all beings of the universe. The Essence spoke only once more before it returned to the book that sat on the sacred alter—it then released the girl from the connection.

"The council of whom you speak knows nothing of the true workings of the earth and the universe. It is as Morghanz has said, the council is not to be trusted to think and make decisions for the betterment of all beings in the universe." Rebecca remained still and Shaulmar was unsure if the Essence remained with the girl or if it was gone. He remained still and did nothing for the moment. The cloud seemed to slow down a little and the swirling, intensity of the gold-indigo energy began to dim.

"Shaulmar, where are you?" Rebecca had indeed returned to the delight and relief of the great wizard.

"I am here. Do not worry, dear one, I would never abandon you." He tried to reassure her.

"Where did I go? There was a space somewhere that just appeared. I was thinking about a friend I used to know, but for the life of me, I couldn't recall the name. It was on the tip of my mind, but I wasn't able to grasp it, no matter how hard I tried." She sounded so confused. Shaulmar watched the cloud gently recede back into the book.

"It's okay now. You are back," he said

"Yes…back…but from where, Shaulmar? Oh God…I'm so confused. The book talked to me…not talk-talk but more like mind-talk, am I making any sense?" Rebecca was talking faster as she looked into his eyes, pleading with him to straighten it all out, and tell her that he understood what had occurred.

Shaulmar put his arms around the girl. "It's okay, he said. I know. I know."

"I…I felt the book was inside my head, Shaulmar…not just thoughts like before…but really with me in my head…you know…physically in there…with me." She stared into his eyes with such burning intensity that he felt the awakening strength of her soul. Rebecca was no longer the misguided, troubled young girl who was so alone in the world, even if she wasn't aware of that fact quite yet. They held on to each other for what seemed like the longest time, until finally, the wizard spoke once more.

"Maybe you and I should clean this room to within an inch of its life? Let's put all the candles and crystals back and we'd best not reveal any of this to the others, okay? It's not necessary to alarm them when we don't even know if there is actually really anything to be alarmed about, yes?" While Shaulmar was speaking to Rebecca, he was gathering and putting away the crystals, in an attempt to impress upon the girl a feeling of calm and serenity, and to dispel any notions of fear or discomfort that she was likely experiencing. She didn't seem to realize or understand that she had channeled the Essence of the Book of Secrets. Best to keep that from her for now, he thought. There would be a time and place to share that information with her, he reassured himself.

"Shaulmar, I feel okay, you know. I mean there is nothing wrong with me—is there?" He knew exactly what she was asking him. She wondered if she was going crazy or not.

"If you feel okay, then you must be okay, that's what I always say. You are the only one who knows how you are inside your own head and you must trust that you know this." He smiled warmly, but he knew what he had said was no longer true. Rebecca and the Book of Secrets knew whatever was going on inside the other. Joaquim appeared at the door, eating something. It was a sight that seemed to be happening more frequently than not.

"Hey, how'd it go Sis?" He always loved to call Rebecca 'Sis.' It made him feel great! Rebecca slowly wrapped the book in its cloth cover before returning it to its original place. She was seemingly oblivious to what the boy was saying. Joaquim looked over at Shaulmar with a puzzled expression.

"Hi Joaquim. How are you? We are just finished here and everything is good. You look like you are enjoying yourself." Again Shaulmar wanted to preserve the harmony and balance while Rebecca was continuing to process the event.

"Yes, I am having a little snack before supper," he said in a subdued tone. He decided to go along with Shaulmar. He realized that Rebecca was somewhere a million miles away. "Do you guys want some? I can easily get more from the kitchen." Joaquim knew something out of the ordinary must have occurred and he played along as best he could. Rebecca remained totally preoccupied. She was starring blankly at the Book of Secrets. She desperately wanted to understand what was going on but it all seemed so foggy and confusing.

"Rebecca, would you please go to the kitchen with Joaquim and help make some nice tea for us all?" Shaulmar said strongly, but his tone was laced with loving-kindness and he had a warm smile on his face. He looked directly into her eyes in an attempt to make an impact that was designed to snap her back into the present moment and away from the Book of Secrets and any questions that might be emerging from deep within her consciousness.

"Sure." Rebecca stood still as she held the book in her hands. The wizard intercepted her as she made her way to the door.

"I can put that away for you," he said, taking the book from her grip before she could register that he had done so. Joaquim and Rebecca left for the kitchen for a nightcap.

CHAPTER 14

THE BLACK LIMOUSINE PULLED TO THE CURB OUTSIDE OF A very prestigious restaurant in New York City. Bastian and his brother Drandos stepped out of the car and walked to the restaurant entrance. When they entered, they were given the most sought after table in the room.

"Well, Draco, my friend, it has been a while since your presence has graced one of my tables." The voice belonged to a tall well-built man who stood at the entrance to the dining room that over-flowed with the most powerful and privileged clientele in New York.

"Do you count the hours Mandrake?" he retorted. Drandos looked at the large man and wondered how his brother could command such respect. "This is my brother Drandos." The owner of the restaurant offered his hand to Drandos.

"I am pleased to meet the brother of such an honored and re-spected citizen of our city." Mandrake released his hand. "I will have Fiona serve you tonight, Mr. Bastian." He was well aware of the desire of Draco Bastian to indulge in the raw beauty of his fa-vored waitress.

"That will be appreciated, my friend." Bastian looked around the room for the waitress without bothering to disguise his intentions. Mandrake showed the two men to their table. It was located at the furthest and most private position within the expansive and crowded room. There was a large window-lined wall surrounding the table that possessed a spectacular view of the city's lights.

"This is absolutely fantastic brother." Drandos was very im-pressed as he looked out across the city. He could barely contain his adoration for his elder brother and the power he wielded. This place was a haven for the privileged and the powerful. Everything that occurred, or began as a thought, that materialized within this city, was first discussed within the confines of this room.

"Ah, this looks like the work of Fiona." Draco Bastian sipped the wine that was placed in front of him by the young wine waiter. "I know she is here somewhere," he whispered while looking around. This was the only place that the Dark One was comfortable enough to relax in, and Fiona was the only one he trusted for any degree of human contact that he might enjoy. She was able to connect with the only aspect of Bastian that was still marginally human. "There she is," his eyes sparkled a little as he beckoned for her to join them.

"Hi Draco," she leaned over his shoulder from behind. Her long dark hair fell across his face as she kissed him passionately. "Who is this?" Fiona smiled at the younger brother.

"This is my brother, Drandos." His hand rested on hers, something that did not escape his younger brother's notice.

"Hi Fiona," he said with a smile and slight nod of his head, "pleased to meet you." Fiona just smiled generously. She stood about five foot ten inches, with olive-toned skin, and a well-proportioned figure that didn't escape the eyes of the young aspirant, nor of any of the other men in the room for that matter.

"Fiona, would you bring us the best steaks in the kitchen and make sure they are prepared correctly. You know how I like them and you know how I don't." She laughed and turned away from the table. "I will be back soon," she whispered. The waitress wore a dress that left no mistake as to what was beneath and Draco Bastian loved the way she flaunted her beauty. He saw his little brother was in agreement as he was smiling to himself.

"Very nice eh, Drandos?" Bastian made the comment while keeping his eyes on the waitress.

"Yes brother, exceptional." There was an uncomfortable pause before the Dark One spoke again.

"Okay, Drandos, tell me of your escapades and do not leave out any details, and remember there is not much information concerning the dark forces of the universe that manages to escape my detection.

"Yes I know. When your name is mentioned around the dark realms, fear is the only response I see. My first mission was to go to Orban, and with the help of my instructor, I was to capture my first soul there. It was to be my first experience with the powers of the darkness. I was so nervous, but thankfully, my instructor guided me and it all turned out well.

"Well, Drandos, I am proud of you. The family tradition continues as I always thought it would." Bastion placed a hand on his younger brother's shoulder. As they sat in the dimly lit room, all eyes were on them. Many of the entities in that room wanted desperately to see the great Draco Bastian fall from power, but they were not courageous or powerful enough to persue it personally. Bastian knew of their desires and who they were, and he made sure they felt the power of his steely glare whenever he saw them at the restaurant. More drinks arrived before too long.

"Here you are, gentlemen." Fiona had the most intoxicating smile and her hazel eyes sparkled whenever she spoke. "Please enjoy your evening and don't hesitate to call me at any time if there is anything more you need." Drandos watched her face during everything she said, paying close attention to her lips as she spoke. He was unaware of the slightly boyish smile that had appeared on his face and became more obvious the longer she remained at the table. It was an unconscious act on his part but it was very apparent that he was taken with her beauty and sweetness. His eyes followed her as she walked away as they traced every line of her body.

"Wow, Draco, she is fantastic. Who is she? Can you get her to sit with us?" Drandos was very young in this respect, the dark master thought.

"You really like her, don't you?" Bastian sounded very warm and interested "do you think she would like you?" He waited for his brother's response; the words leaving his lips had become very slow and deliberate as he finished the sentence.

"Yes, I think she liked me. She looked right at me the whole time. It was obvious she wanted me." Drandos had convinced himself of something that turned out to be imagined fantasy. Unfortunately for him, his bloated ego and immaturity triggered a response from his brother that immediately brought repressed memories of Drandos' childhood cascading into his consciousness, and that forced him to rediscover who his big brother really was.

"Well, my little brother, I will put this as gently as I can. However, I must tell you that the last person who was as free with his expressions of desire for that waitress at this wonderful restaurant suffered a terrible and unforeseen accident almost immediately afterward".

"What...do...you...mean?" Drandos spoke slowly and carefully. Then it hit him like a bad dream. He began to remember the feeling he used to get in his stomach right before his big brother did something mean to him when they were youngsters—it was the same feeling he was experiencing at that very moment. He felt himself slip ever so slightly downward in his chair in anticipation of what was to come. Drandos thought he might avoid the full extent of his brother's anger if he tried to appear genuinely confused. However, he recalled that it had not worked in the past and was probably not going to work now.

"They found the poor man a few blocks away from here. He was in terrible shape."

"Terrible...shape? What are you trying to tell me brother?" Drandos tried desperately to cling to the façade but he was about to have his naïve question emphatically answered and he knew it. Drandos braced for impact. He hated that this was still happening to him so many years after he and his brother had gone their separate ways.

"It wasn't a pretty sight, let me tell you," the Dark One cast his eyes from his brother, and nonchalantly rested his arms on the studded leather arm rests of his chair while his napkin dangled ominously from the finger tips of his left hand. "The poor man's arms looked like they had been blown clean off just below the elbows, his face was torn from his head and his innards were found everywhere." Draco Bastian sounded very clinical, his rendition was very disturbing, and something in what he was saying resounded in the dark recesses of Drandos' mind. "Apparently," he continued, "according to by-standers there was also an alarming amount of blood at the scene due to the fact that the victim was impaled with a steel lance that pined his carcass to a wooden telegraph pole for all to see."

Drandos struggled to keep the Dark Angel from invading his mind but the vivid imagery of the account was making it difficult. Bastian enjoyed immensely the very obvious strain that had appeared on Drandos' face. The younger man was very naïve for a dark wizard's apprentice.

"Brother, why would you go to all that trouble for this waitress?" Drandos had a look of genuine disbelief on his face.

There was a long intense pause as the Dark One locked eyes with his young brother. "Be…cause…it…pissed…me…off! Bastian's eyes turned blood red, and the expression on his face put the fear of all hell into Drandos.

"I…erm…I'm so sorry brother. Please, accept my humble apologizes. I didn't know…uhm…I didn't realize…well…err…please forgive my mistake brother?" Drandos was visibly shaken and all the attention in the room was on the two men. Draco's menacing stare loosened from his brother to direct its mark at various places around the room, forcing the other diners to resume their conversations or face the consequences they knew would come from the dark master. Their voices gradually returned, and eventually, the heated conversations in the room resumed.

"Draco, why didn't you tell me about Fiona? I would love to hear all about it—every detail, dear brother." Drandos was a much more sensitive soul than his older brother, even though like Bastian, he too was a practitioner of the dark arts. However, Drandos' soul journey didn't allow him to totally embrace the ways of the darker realms of the secret order, no matter how hard he tried to be like his brother.

"I don't like to talk of such things, besides, I have not made my full intentions known to her. Such things are of no consequence to me when I consider the true meaning of our existence here." He made it very clear that to continue along the same road in the conversation would not be very healthy for anyone, especially not his brother.

"Okay, maybe now is not a good time to pursue this so, how about we enjoy our meal? Then if you feel like it we can go to that night club you took me to when I was here last—I think it was called the Apollo? We can let off some steam like we did then.

What do you say, Draco?" Drandos attempted to alleviate the stress of the situation. He remembered when he was a child when time after time his brother would turn on him, for no reason whatsoever. Drandos had to develop the ability to think fast on his feet to appease his brother and snap him back to the present or suffer his wrath. Drandos had always thought that his brother was quite unstable, almost as if he was on the edge of a cliff not knowing whether he should jump or remain where he was.

"Maybe brother, maybe." Draco looked impatient. The food arrived, and although Fiona knew what had transpired between them, she did not give any indication of her awareness. That would be unprofessional, something she did not consider herself to be.

"So, who had the chicken?" she looked at Drandos who quickly averted his eyes.

"I think, Draco, you ordered the steak, yes?" he said softly while keeping his eyes firmly rooted on his brother for safety reasons of his own.

"Okay, here you are, sir, a beautiful meal prepared by the best chef in New York City." Fiona's eyes sparkled with delight. She loved to serve people and watch their faces light up with joy when she brought their perfect meals to them.

"Thanks." Bastian didn't even look at her. He was not happy. His mood was dark. He still had not returned from the heavy anger that had previously enveloped him and had been brought on by the situation with his younger sibling.

"That looks delicious." He made very little eye contact with the waitress. "Inform the chef it is a beautiful presentation. Thank you." He smiled without looking at her and made sure his brother witnessed his casual indifference.

"You're welcome, and please call me if you need anything." Fiona tried to look at both men and thought it a little strange that they both avoided her attention. As she turned and walked away, Drandos instinctively began to turn his head to watch her walk away, as he would for any woman as beautiful as she was while allowing his desires to flow freely through his mind. However, although he was young and a little naïve, he wasn't an idiot. He caught himself just in time, making his movement look like he had turned to pick up a napkin. He hoped Draco had not realized his mistake so he might avoid another unwanted confrontation.

"Boy, these things are difficult to keep on your knee aren't they?" His comment went unanswered. The conversations around the room heightened until the two men blended into the environment once again—just a couple of exclusive members of the elite club who were dining out for the evening. Draco became still for a moment. The chewing of the food in his mouth came to a halt. He sat motionless and his eyes widened.

"What is it brother?" Drandos became concerned. Was his brother going to lash out at him again? Or was he going to apologize for the attack on him earlier. "Are you all right? Can I get you some water or something else?" he said. Drandos automatically laid down his utensils while he focused on the man opposite him. He was about to get up to help his brother when Bastian swallowed, hard.

"No! Remain where you are…there is…something…can you feel a change? A subtle ripple in the energy matrix of this room has occurred." Bastian carefully turned toward the rest of the diners in the room to assess the event. There was nothing to indicate that danger was near.

"Draco, what are you thinking? Are we in danger?" His voice was soft, almost a whisper.

"Danger? Do you really think I could possibly be in any kind of danger?" The Dark Angel was disgusted with the implication made by his brother.

"No! No! What I meant was…uh, what I wanted to say…erm was, do you know what it is or who it is creating the disturbance brother?" Drandos trod very carefully.

"Do not concern yourself little brother. You are in no danger, not as long as I am close by." Draco was confident that there was no cause for concern. However, he did not recognize the soul signature that caused the disturbance in the energy of the immediate area and that did concern him. Who or whatever was responsible had to be very powerful to cause such a ripple as they, or it, moved through the energy field of the earth. The dark master looked around once more to reassure himself there was no change in the room. There was nothing. Everyone had remained the same as far as he could ascertain.

"Brother, what do you think caused the ripple?" Drandos was unsure of how to appease him and did not want to anger him by saying the wrong thing. Drandos was reminded once more of his childhood years. He knew his brother could become extremely dangerous if he thought he was being challenged in any way by anyone.

"Don't worry. It was probably an underground event."

"What—like an earthquake?" Drandos automatically looked around.

"Probably not, dear brother," he said with some condescension. "You can be so naïve but that's all right because you are still only an apprentice. I should remind myself of that when you prove to be a source of irritation. In answer to your question, no, I think the disturbance was caused by the construction down the block. They are digging a huge foundation for the office tower going in there. It was more likely the aftershock of the blasting that I felt." Bastian was becoming weary of his brother and was looking forward to the end of the evening when he could return to the peace and quiet of his penthouse apartment where he could ponder the whereabouts of the Prophesied One and fantasize about the great pleasure he would enjoy as he captured her soul.

"Draco, do you remember when we were young and we made a promise to each other that no matter what happened we'd always take care of one another?" Drandos had been hurt by what his brother had said and wanted Draco to be reminded that he was a kind person who loved his brother. Even though they were both aligned with the dark forces, Drandos wanted the closeness and love of his brother. He desperately wanted to experience the connections of family and not feel so alone in the universe. Draco thought for a while. He continued to eat his steak and sip his wine.

"Yes, brother, I remember it well. I remember it was also a long time ago and we were only kids then. Drandos, things change. However, since we did make the pact and you are my brother I do feel a certain degree of responsibility for you and I will take good care of you, don't worry. I will do this only until you reach master status then you must take the responsibility for your own wellbeing." There was a deathly coldness in his voice. Drandos felt it in his heart. "Now, enough of this brotherly bonding. I think we understand one another. We both know enough, that it is clear, that in order to survive in this reality it becomes necessary to disconnect from others in order to become strong enough to accomplish what we need to without having to rely on anyone else, including family!" Draco was cold and distant with his words and Drandos realized that he would be tossed aside by his brother if it were necessary for his own survival.

"Yes, Draco, I agree! We must each secure our respective survival—that is the most important thing we can do." Drandos was so hurt and so disappointed with his brother and how he could feel that way about his own flesh and blood. However, Drandos knew better than to express his real thoughts and feelings for fear of incurring the wrath and anger of his brother. Drandos continued to eat his meal while trying not to let his brother see what he was really feeling.

"So, brother, tell me more of the experience of taking your first soul. I want to hear all about it as we savor this time together, dear Drandos." Draco paid more attention to the steak in front of him than he did to his brother.

"Well, it was not entirely what I expected." His thoughts of pain and disappointment evaporated. That was evident in his enthusiasm for the retelling of his accomplishment of the whole soul-capturing experience. "There was a mix-up to begin with. The soul that was prepared for me by the priests of Orban accidentally died, leaving the body before I even arrived in the immediate vicinity. Supposedly, the one who prepared the soul for capture got it wrong. They had totally destroyed the soul and accidentally sent it into the cosmos through the portal of Ramos. So, anyway..." Drandos didn't sense the same feelings of enthusiasm from his brother as he recounted the event, but that didn't deter him from finishing the story he was so proud of, "another potential soul was located and the head priest came to me and explained that because of the spontaneity of the capture it would be much more dangerous. So, because of the nature of the situation he told me the replacement soul would not be subdued as was customary to safeguard the aspirants, that it would be necessary for me to use excessive force to take her." Drandos witnessed his brother's curiosity peak when there was mention of greater danger. Draco continued to slice away at the steak with the ease and skill of a surgeon.

"So what happened next? Did you go and claim the soul as directed by your instructor priest?" He took another mouthful of the red meat and chewed it with vigor.

"Yes brother, you would have been proud of me." He smiled as he sipped his wine. "I had to go to the planes of Bourdon where the soul lived. She was the daughter of a herdsman, a nomad family, who considered themselves blessed after the mother had given birth to a healer, a mystic, who was able to cure the ills of all those in the tribe." Drandos was deadly serious as he continued with the account of the soul capture. "I was escorted to the portal and given instructions on how I was to proceed. The soul was to be taken intact and brought back through the portal for the success of my first capture to be legally registered with the counsel of voices."

"Were you given specific knowledge of how best to accomplish this?" Draco interrupted. He looked at his younger brother with a little more interest, and even a sliver of surprise, as he sipped his drink comfortably. Draco seemed more interested in the story than the waitress now and that pleased Drandos.

"Yes, my advisor told me the best way to snag this soul was to conjure the whirling demon to subdue the soul, while chanting the sacred incantation of separation to remove the spiritual essence from the physical body, then to trap it between layers of poison for the journey back through the portal." Drandos was feeling very proud of his expertise as he described the account. Draco was quite impressed with the obvious and unexpected abilities of his brother as he showed more and more interest.

"Go on brother, continue, I wish to know the outcome of the assignment, continue…continue." Drandos was overcome with the attention and emotion he felt inside, and in a swirl of happiness and excitement, he reached across the table and put a heartfelt hand on his brother's arm, then he returned to recount the events of his first soul capture.

"So, having made the journey to the plains of Bourdon through the portal, I was left to my own devices as to how to locate the soul. The terrain was very treacherous and the portal placed me within five hundred yards of the tribal encampment and my target. But, it was still quite difficult to locate the targeted soul through the blizzard that had been raging since before I arrived." Drandos was less aware of his brother at this point. The young aspirant was so engrossed in the memory of the event and the emotions triggered by the adventure that he was reliving right there in the restaurant.

"Well, Drandos, I am really proud of you. Thus far, you seem to have conducted yourself admirably under the circumstances. Bravo brother." Draco expressed his genuine feelings of respect for his brother. At that very moment, Fiona appeared with more of the delicious wine—she poured it into each of their glasses, while leaning over the shoulder of the Draco as she guided the subtle hint of desire from her heart straight into his.

"There! That should taste even better than the last—it was an earlier vintage where the weather was more beneficial and kinder to the grape." She directed a long stare at the older brother. "Enjoy gentlemen." She left the bottle wrapped in a beautiful linen cloth and disappeared as silently as she had arrived.

"Continue, Drandos. "Draco was impatient to hear the details of the capture. It was his favorite part of his work, so much so, that he didn't even notice his favorite waitress as she was coming or going.

"Okay brother, now where was I? Ah yes, I was trying to navigate through the blizzard to find the tribal enclosure. The sandstorm was thick. I couldn't see ten feet in front of me. I was getting desperate, and I don't mind telling you, I was a little afraid." He was serious about being afraid. He had good reason to be. There were many predators within the whirling sandstorm. Drandos only knew of these predators from the classes he had attended during his first year on Orban with the priests of the Sacred Dark order. He hadn't actually seen any, although, he had the ability to sense when they were close by and he usually managed to steer clear of them.

"Being afraid is all part of the experience." Draco moved his glass around as he sat back in the comfortable chair. "When you can see past the fear and into the future then you have truly mastered the physical realm." The two men were actually bonding to a degree as they were talking about their lives. Draco Bastian found himself giving advice to his younger sibling as if it was the natural order of things.

"Do you think I will ever progress to become a master like you, brother? I sometimes think I lack the killer instinct to become the deadly force of darkness that is required to fight against the powers of the light." He looked to Bastian for the reassurance he craved, and that was his downfall. His brother hated the weakness that oozed from the low self-belief his young brother displayed.

"Do not look to others for your own self worth. Only you can discover that it is either innate, and rages forth like the lava of a volcano, or has dried up like the sand on a pretty beach. If you insist on searching for it outside of yourself brother, you will surely meet a dismal and torturous end. Draco's tone was devoid of the compassion that typically exists between blood relatives—he only projected distain and disappointment towards his brother.

"Yes brother." Drandos felt the icy coldness of the dagger that ran through his heart.

"Now, tell me the rest of the story. Obviously you were victorious but with that lack of self belief it is a wonder you are here tonight to enjoy my hospitality." The Dark One had no time for his brother after that and Drandos lost all enthusiasm for the remainder of the account.

" I located the tribal village compound and used the energy of the universe to pinpoint where the healer was as I made my way to her. I moved quickly and when I sensed I was close I began to recite the sacred incantation of separation, and simultaneously, I summoned the whirling demon." Drandos took a drink of the wine to compose his thoughts. He didn't want to make a mess of the story and risk further disrespect and disconnection from his brother. "The storm raged as I made my way towards the target. By the time I reached the compound barrier, the whirling demon had formed. There were two guards at the entrance that I had to disable while I continued to recite the incantation, being careful not to break the rhythm of the sacred words."

"Yes...yes. Carry on little brother.

Draco wanted to hear in great detail how the soul was subjected to the pain and torture of soul separation, and as the words impacted the basal ganglia of the reptilian brain in his head he dissected every move his brother described, feeling pleasure through the vicarious imagery that was generated. At the same time, he was cognizant of the potential for any flawed moves that would allow him to torment his younger sibling further so he could keep reinforcing the hierarchy that existed between them that he enjoyed so much.

"That is when I saw the target. She was covered from head to foot in some typical nomadic clothing. My senses did not deceive me—it was the village shaman I was contracted to take. The initial confrontation did not manifest quite as I expected. The soul became aware of me through the intuitive senses, regarded by some as clairsentience abilities, and she refused to separate even though the spell had been cast. I waited for a brief moment. I made sure I recited the incantation correctly and that the swirling demon had a good hold on the soul's physical body." Drandos sounded very sure of himself at this point and he felt good about the way he had conducted himself during the capturing process that was reflected in his words and demeanor.

"Yes, Drandos, I would have done the same thing so far. Rechecking all the steps leading up to that point indicates a good foundation in the discipline, especially during such adverse conditions. This will only increase your ability to capture souls and allow you to grow and progress as a practitioner of the dark arts, brother. Bravo again." Draco was not as sure now of the weakness in his little brother. The only attribute Draco Bastian admired in anyone, especially his brother, was the ability to seize his desires with lightening speed and unbridled ferocity. "Continue brother...finish the account."

"Well Draco, at this point, I was at a loss as to why the soul refused to comply and how she was able to fight the powers of the incantation. According to the teachings, once all the items are in place, there is no other alternative for the soul but to submit fully to the capture. However, I realized there was an unusual glow surrounding the girl as the demon secured her. She seemed to stop struggling, and at that moment, her light shone bright through the storm, giving the body a light green aura. It was as if she was enlisting help from outside of her own soul, from something else out in the universe."

"Yes...yes Drandos, you were to capture a healing soul, one who was sent to ease the suffering of other souls within the tribe." Through his brother's words, Bastian was vicariously living the wonderful challenge sent by the universe to Drandos. He was remembering how it had felt during his first soul-capture, and the personal challenges that were set before for him also, as he progressed through the rigorous training of the dark order.

Drandos continued, infused by the energy of his brother's encouragement. "Yes, so I didn't know what I should do, and it was very clear to me that if the capture didn't happen soon, my time through the portal would expire and so would I. The demon continued to subdue the healer's physical body, but no matter how I tried or what energy I could muster and fire at the soul, the green aura protected it." Drandos paused to take a drink. His throat was feeling sore.

"Did you feel like you were about to die? Did anyone come to the aid of the healer? Bastian was more intrigued than ever. He loved danger, especially if it held the potential for death. Drandos sensed his brother's lust for the thought of death and wondered if he wanted that more than he wanted the story to have a happy ending for himself.

"Yes brother," Drandos responded, "during the ordeal, I sensed that others were attempting to navigate through the sandstorm to help their friend. However, the instant the demon made physical contact with the healer's body, it was dragged deeper into the storm—and as you well know—the first thing the demon instinctively does is move the target to a place that makes it more vulnerable and inaccessible to rescue attempts. I was still unable to accomplish the capture and I thought it was the end for me. There was very little time left at the portal and the healer was strong. She must have incarnated throughout the universe many thousands of times to have that kind of resistance built up. Suddenly, just as I thought my time was up, something occurred to me regarding your training experiences. I recalled those times when we used to talk at night, when your classes were finished for the day." Drandos held his hands out as if appearing to have an epiphany.

"What are you talking about? We never talked about my work." Draco looked disgusted at the thought of such a thing. However, it occurred to him that if he accepted the idea of including his brother in his adventures and progress through the Sacred Dark order, then he also must have been responsible for saving his young brother's life on the plains of Bourdon. Draco Bastian smiled. "Oh…wait…now I remember…yes we did have some heart-to-hearts years ago."

Drandos' smile faded. "Not exactly…more like the insight you provided during the recounting of your experiences while learning the black arts." He began to realize as the evening wore on that his hope of rekindling the brotherly bond between them was not going to be that easy.

"Oh yes." Draco paused looking upward as he recalled the memory. "I remember those little talks brother. I was bored to hell during the training. The others' abilities were so much more inferior to my own and their natural desire to do well was limited at best." Draco basked in the recollection.

"Anyway, would you like to know how I was able to eventually capture the soul and return through the portal from Orban?" The tone of Drandos' voice betrayed him, and he knew from the stone-cold expression that fell across his brother's face that trouble was near. "Sorry brother. I meant no disrespect," he said, lowering his head in submission and hoping the trouble had been averted.

There was only a long silence—then Draco spoke, "Continue."

"Well, it hit me," Drandos breathed a sigh of relief, "that during the training process on how to capture your first soul that it included two apprentices joining forces to seize the soul. One apprentice was needed to control the swirling demon and the other to recite the sacred incantation that initiates the actual separation in order for the subdued soul to be taken. However, you gave me a tip regarding the process of capture concerning the incantation. You told me that just before you were about to deliver the sacred spell, the apprentice that was with you somehow lost control of the demon therefore rendering both of you in danger of being destroyed by it. To escape death, you hit the demon with every microbe of power you could summon and you hit it full force. The screams were so loud, and of such a high pitch and frequency, that the physical body housing the soul you were to capture actually exploded. The soul was distracted enough by the event that you were able to enclose it between the layers of poisonous energy thus capturing it forever." Drandos lifted his eyebrows in sheer delight and excitement. Bastian followed his brother's reasoning, however, he was having difficulty recalling the exact memory his brother was referring to, besides it had happened many years ago. "Brother, you don't remember telling me, do you?" Again Drandos realized a little too late that his tone was inflammatory and before too long if he was not careful, Draco was going to let him have it. Once more Drandos was forced to hold up his hands and lower his head while he apologized profusely to his elder brother. "Sorry…sorry…I know I did it again brother…I didn't mean to…I'm sorry."

"Do not make a habit of this little brother—beware. Have you so easily forgotten the catacombs beneath the house and the many occasions you spent there? Do you so easily forget the things you experienced there my brother? Draco laughed. "I can send you back there if you wish? It would be so easy and the amusement it would give me would be appreciated."

Drandos swallowed hard. "No…no…it's fine Draco. I don't need a reminder of that time in my life. I meant no disrespect, and of course, I will be most careful in the future concerning my tone, brother…trust me, please." He remembered all too clearly the catacombs beneath the childhood home where he had vivid recollection of going to sleep at night with his brother close by. The next thing he remembered was that he was waking up in the catacombs where there were many night crawlers and vermin scurrying all throughout the tunnels as well as other entities that wanted to feed off of his life-force energy. It turned out that Draco was putting a hex on him before he went to sleep that made him sleepwalk so that he ended up in the tunnels every night for a week. If it weren't for the intervention of his dear mother Drandos would still be there. " Shall I continue brother?" He desperately wanted to bring the focus back to the present situation before Bastian had time to think about how delightful it might be to send him back into the tunnels.

"You may," he replied.

"As I was saying, the storm was raging and I was struggling to capture the soul and the time remaining at the portal had reached a critical point." Drandos leaned into the table and rested both arms on the edge, and then he began to whisper. "Is it safe to speak of these things here in such a public place?" He looked to his left then to his right.

"You are paranoid, Drandos. If you were to let any great and dangerous secret loose here for all to hear," Draco increased his volume and deliberately cast a gaze around the room, "it would fall on deaf ears. I can guarantee it. Please relax…you can be somewhat of an irritation at times."

"Sorry, I was only thinking of you. Anyway, it occurred to me as I fought to capture the soul that if I destroyed the demon, the screams would be enough to disrupt the soul of the healer, enabling me to capture it. I summoned as much destructive power as I could and fired it at the demon."

Draco listened with more curiosity but with less enthusiasm.

"It worked. As soon as the demon felt the full impact of the power, it began to physically disintegrate, and with a scream that would have woke the dead." Drandos almost leapt from his seat with excitement. At that motion, his brother reached for his wine glass and pushed himself a few inches away from the table.

"Control yourself, Drandos. Now tell me what happened next."

"Okay. As soon as the demon let out the torturous scream, the soul's physical body exploded, causing the distraction that allowed me to move in for the capture.

I remembered to strike the soul with the force of the Sacred Dark order as I concluded the separation incantation, and as I did so, the soul energy was trapped between the two layers of poison where I could attach the chord and bring the soul back with me through the portal. It happened so quickly that I was hardly able to compose myself. Before I knew it, I was back in the temple training school standing before the priests with the soul I had captured floating next to me encased in the layers of poisonous energy." With that, Drandos sat back in his chair. With quickened breath, he briefly and nervously glanced around the room.

"So brother, you seem to have been quite successful and I suppose your teachers were impressed with you also?" He waited for the response.

"Yes, you could say that. They were very pleased with my ability to capture souls and to think on my feet in high-pressure situations. In fact, one of them commented that I was a natural." There was the trace of a satisfied grin on his face but Drandos quickly suppressed it before it fully manifested. He had finally learned that his brother was not interested in sharing any good feelings between the two of them.

"So, during all the attention and admiration from all your teacher priests and peers, did you happen to inform them that I—your elder brother Draco Bastian—was in fact the master whom you owed everything. I was the one responsible for saving your life and capturing the soul of the healer?" Draco had managed to twist everything around that his brother had accomplished into something where he deserved all the credit. The smile of satisfaction left Drandos' face and was replaced with the disappointment of a young boy who had looked up to his brother with hero worship, only to again witness the reality of his brother's deep hatred and dislike for him.

"Don't look so glum brother," Bastian said, "if it wasn't for my desire to have the family crest be honored and admired by all the powers within the Sacred Dark order, you would not be enjoying your meal right now." Draco sat back, sipped his wine, and stared directly into his brother's eyes. He was toying with the young apprentice.

"What do you mean?" Drandos said slowly.

"Do you think I coached you on the dark arts and insights on how to progress within your training for no reason? Maybe you thought I was seeking your friendship and admiration little brother? Draco Bastian smiled. Drandos was thoroughly confused and deeply hurt by the words of his brother. "That was not my intention, and your friendship was certainly not the reason I guided the training you so eagerly poured yourself into." Bastian was feeding his brother veiled information that was difficult for Drandos to process. "Wait, I am not following you Draco—are you saying that the last two years of training that I dedicated my life to and followed with total conviction has been orchestrated and directed by you?" Drandos expressed all the range of emotions that were riffling through his mind. There was no response from his brother, just the cold stare that Drandos was accustomed to. He watched as his brother continued to consume the very fine wine the restaurant had procured for him. Eventually, Draco spoke.

"The only thing you should understand brother is that this life, here, and everything I have accomplished thus far is concerned with power and how to wield it effectively. Power is what allows me to control the forces that are available in this reality. Did you know that our house was once considered to be the most powerful of all the houses within the Sacred Dark order? This is what drives me brother. It is not about love or family, only power and conquest." Drandos was speechless. He had witnessed for the first time how ruthless and devastatingly evil his brother could be towards anyone, even family.

"I am grateful for all of your guidance brother. Drandos was careful not to cross the line with his brother again but he was now certain that he did not mean that much to Draco and that revelation hurt him deeply. He continued, "So, I am required to return to Orban tomorrow. So, if you don't mind, I think will go back to the hotel and prepare. I will call you before I leave, Draco." He threw back the rest of the wine and made a gesture for his wallet.

"That's okay, Drandos, I will take care of the bill. I still possess a modicum of responsibility towards assumed family duties." His tone was like a chilled night air during the coldest of winters. Drandos fumbled with his jacket, hoping his brother would offer him a kind word before he left. Just as Drandos attempted to rise from the table, Draco held up his hand motioning for him to remain seated.

"Wait! Do you sense that brother?"

"Sense what?" he replied.

"The ripple of disturbance that is traveling through this area once more." Draco starred into space as if he was consciously searching his mind for the origin of the energetic disturbance.

"No…no…I don't feel anything brother. Are you sure of what you sense?" The moment the words left his lips, Drandos knew he had once more challenged his brother's abilities and he waited for the anger and rebuking words that were sure to follow. "Sorry." Drandos lowered his eyes again, "I meant no...." Before he could finish, Draco held up one finger in silence and closed his eyes.

"Remain seated brother. I do not know what is causing the shift but it is getting stronger—or closer—or maybe even both." He was resting his hands on the tabletop at this point, breathing slowly and deliberately. Drandos was about to see his brother, the Dark Angel, at work for the first time. Draco Bastian was considered to be one of the most powerful wizards of the current time. Drandos looked around, tentatively, and realized that others were also observing the dark wizard discretely. He noticed that Fiona was heading for their table, carrying more wine. When she was close enough, he held up a hand and mouthed the words for her to stop. In turn, she stood still, smiled, and mouthed back affirmatively before going off in another direction. Drandos remained convinced that Fiona was into him regardless of what danger his brother posed which was easily dealt with because his brother had his eyes closed. As Drandos savored the idea of Fiona and himself together, he was snapped back into reality. Draco, being the dark wizard he was acutely aware of his surroundings even without his sense of sight. Drandos lost the inner smile and the good feelings he was enjoying as a film of moisture began to develop across his brow.

"Drandos! Do you not sense the power rippling towards this place from the etheric realm?"

"I will try, brother." He inhaled heavily and closed his eyes. He recalled what the priests had told him as an aspirant regarding connecting to the universal energy that permeated all things both animate and inanimate, seen and unseen. If anyone wanted to connect to the universal energy, they must focus, and create the desire to link to the power of creation. Drandos had developed his own way of connecting that felt right for him and he was careful not to reveal it to any of his cohorts for fear of them stealing it and becoming more adept than himself. As he closed his eyes, he imagined that he was walking in nature through a thunderstorm. The clouds were black and filled the sky completely. He saw himself alone in the countryside, with only the deep clapping of thunder surrounding him, as shards of blue-white light streaked across the dark clouds above. Drandos imagined walking out of a wooded area and into a meadow that was flanked with hills. As he reached the top of the highest mound, he stood in the cold windy darkness of night, hardly able to see his own hand in front of his face. He reached inside his cloak and pulled forth a huge sword. Its steel blade reflected the lightning as it flashed above him. Drandos held the black-handled weapon in both hands. He pointed it in front of him, and with one mighty heave, hoisted it high above his head towards the darkness. At that very moment, a thick bolt of searing energy grasped the blade, ran down the sword through Drandos and into the earth below. Drandos was fully connected to the universal energy now and he sensed the pulse of moving energy that his brother was referring to. It was different than the energy he felt when they entered the restaurant—the energy then was cold and hard like the floor they stood on. The ripple he felt now was simple, fluid, and very strong. He could sense the power within it.

"I sense it now, brother, but I cannot identify its source or origins."

"That does not concern me now." Draco spoke. "The energy is strong and is not diminishing. We must wait...be alert...and cautious." He remained motionless and kept his eyes closed.

"I still don't understand. The ripple we are sensing could be anything. It is not necessarily a threat to us, right?" He spoke more in hope of his brother's reassurance.

"Do not be so *naïve* and *weak*, Drandos. If we are about to experience danger, then we must embrace the experience with strength and courage, and if we are to meet our death then we must inflict as much pain and suffering on the perpetrator as possible with all the powers we can muster." The Dark One finally opened his eyes—they were the color of a tiger's—black and gold. "Remain where you are, brother." Draco got up from the table and turned toward the door of the foyer.

"But...where are you..." Drandos wasn't able to finish his sentence before his brother was out of sight. Drandos looked around at the other people in the room. They were exceptional at staying out of other people's business. However, he recognized fear in the eyes of the older couple eating at the next table over. They seemed desperate to know if they were in any kind of danger. Drandos offered them a half-smile and then turned to face his meal. Draco Bastian had reached the foyer by this time and Drandos was at a loss as to what he should do. Drandos again tried to identify the disturbance in the etheric realm that his brother had gone to investigate but it was beyond his ability now. He was desperate to do something, so he tried to connect to the only energy he knew, the energy that belonged to his brother. Drandos held his head in his hands and focused his consciousness on the energy signature of his brother as he sat as quietly and unobtrusively at the table as possible.

"Hi again," the shapely Fiona stood in front of him at the table."

"Oh…hello." Drandos sheepishly let his hands drop from his head and onto the table, effectively breaking the connection with his brother's energy signature.

"Would you like anything else from the bar, sir?" she knew she was being admired, something for her, that was not an uncommon occurrence.

"Oh, …uh. No thank you, Fiona." Drandos couldn't take his gaze from her eyes. He fell headfirst into her mesmerizing gaze.

"Are you alone now?" she was interested, and she knew exactly how to convey the message. Fiona moved to the side of the young apprentice and leaned across the table as she collected the plates. Her eyes met his before he drew his gaze back.

"No, my brother went to the foyer for a moment. He will return soon, I imagine." Drandos wanted to ask her out but was afraid of what his brother would do to him. The waitress fumbled clumsily with her hair, and as she stretched to tie it back behind her head, her lips parted ever so slightly—just enough for him to fantasize about the possibility of kissing her. " Okay, if there is anything else you would like then get my attention and I will see what can be arranged…sir." Drandos had enough awareness to regain his composure.

"Please, call me Drandos." His eyes sparkled when he saw her smile. She walked away from the table and turned back almost immediately to see if his attention was still captivated. Drandos had lost all focus relating to where his brother was. Instead, he watched the shapely waitress as she went about her business with the other customers. He watched other men, as she touched them with her beauty and charisma, smile and fumble about.

CHAPTER 15

BY THIS TIME, BASTIAN HAD ENTERED THE LOBBY OF THE hotel. He searched cautiously for the source of the energetic disturbance he was sensing. The lobby was filled with guests coming and going. He made his way toward the main check-in desk, intending to speak to an acquaintance that worked behind it. The friend was also a follower of the dark arts and considered the Dark One to be his hero, and he would open the guest register without a second thought, making it easier for Bastian to stay informed of any strangers that might arrive and pose a threat to him.

"Crespo, do me a favor," Bastian leaned his arms on the huge desk, "pass the register to me." The clerk didn't hesitate.

"Sure…anything for you, Draco. What's going down? Anything I should be aware of?" He looked around as if he were involved in the biggest undercover operation ever undertaken.

"No, nothing of any importance yet." He flipped through the pages quickly. "Nothing here," he said aloud to himself. "Let me know if you see anyone out of place or anyone at all who doesn't fit-in, okay?" Bastian liked the guy for reasons he didn't quite understand. There was just something about him. He was funny, harmless, and he was very, very loyal. There was probably a connection to a past-life they had shared together, because Bastian felt so comfortable in Crespo's energy. In order to be that comfortable right off the bat, there was a strong posibility a past-life sojourn had occurred. "See you later, Crespo," Bastian turned and watched the people milling about in the lobby for a moment before he returned to tracking the source of the ripple he'd felt in the etheric realms.

Suddenly, he felt the ripple again, but this time the energy was stronger, much stronger. He closed his eyes for a brief moment and when he opened them again there was the energy source he had been tracking. Bastian paused for a moment, checking to be sure of what he was sensing. He opened his mind using his powerful third-eye to pierce the aura of the entity but he was surprised when he was blocked with a similar powerful intention from the entity near him. It was very unusual for the master Dark Angel to be prevented from entering into the aura of another while in search of their soul signature. As Bastian attempted to ascertain the identity of the entity, he became aware of a resonation in his hand. The Dark One instinctively pulled up his hand as he realized the Ring of Dread had been activated and had automatically created an energy-field of safety around the wearer.

The Dark Angel allowed the protective field to surround him and thanked the ring telepathically. When the Ring of Dread activates in this way it means only one thing, it has detected a threat—it immediatelly alerts the wearer of the ring. Bastian now knew that the ripple he had detected was a threat but he still wasn't sure if the threat was aimed at him. There were many entities that moved freely through the 3rd dimension, where most were malevolent and typically at war with others. Bastian was a master of the sacred dark arts, and as such, he had developed a particularly high sensitivity to such subtle energy shifts that allowed him to pick up on a disturbance very quickly. The entity moved toward him. Bastian observed him closely. As he crossed the busy foyer, he noticed the green hue that surrounded him. The being came nearer. He wore a beige-colored cloak that moved closely about him as he walked and a deep purple tunic that looked Persian in nature. The stranger's hair was graying, cropped short in the front, and was progressively longer toward the rear. The Dark One looked him square-in-the-eyes.

"Well, so you are the traveler who protects my target." His voice resonated with a highly charged frequency intended to unnerve the receiver with its power. Shaulmar only looked back at him with a strong gentleness.

"Draco Bastian, you would do well to heed my words. The one who is chosen cannot be taken. Forces you could barely comprehend protect her, and as for me, I am merely a facilitator who is here with you out of compassion for your soul evolution. If you persist in this attempt at gaining and accumulating power through upsetting the balance of souls in the universe, I am authorized to stop you." Shaulmar was very powerful. His aura shone with light green and pink light that represented the universal divine healing energy. The two wizards faced each other with only seven feet between them as the hotel guests and visitors moved about them oblivious of the magnitude of the encounter.

"Threats from the Order of Light do not worry me, wizard. Bastian moved cautiously away from the wizard towards the end of the check-in desk. "As long as Miss Sullivan walks the earth, I will remain here until I have her soul. That is an inevitable fact traveler." Shaulmar matched his movements as he held the Archangel Ring close to his chest, fully aware the Dark One could sense its presence. "You have been warned, Bastian." Shaulmar began to slowly ease away from the dark wizard, never taking his eyes from his face.

"We shall meet again and you would do well to heed my words, traveler. Protect yourself with that pathetic bauble on your hand, if you can, for I will surely destroy you when next we meet. Do not think you can prevent me from taking the soul I hunt. My destiny is also foretold and by forces not possible for you to understand. I will have Miss Sullivan's essence. That is my promise to you, Bedouin." Bastian's voice trailed off as Shaulmar disappeared from sight. The Dark One looked concerned for the moment. He remained in the hotel lobby. He seated himself by a beautifully sculptured marble statue of a gladiator that was taken from the Roman Coliseum. He knew all too well that the traveler possessed the power of the light and he was also sure he would prove to be a formidable opponent. Bastian sat with eyes closed, trying to close off the noise and bustle of the busy hotel lobby. He desperately wanted to send his mind and thought energy to track the traveler. If Bastian could follow him back to his place of rest, his hidden origin, he would surely locate the soul he so badly wanted to capture. Gradually Bastian surrounded himself in the energy of the dark forces, releasing himself from the confines of the physical realm. When he had firmly connected his physical body to the darkness deep within the earth, he sent out a stream of his essence through his power center, the solar center of his etheric body. A beam of energy emanating from his abdomen shot straight up toward the ceiling of the lobby and out high above the city. Bastian's mind controlled the direction where his essence would go to look for the traveler. Through the city park, down toward the lake, moving between the trees, into tunnels, and out over the hills searching for anything that would lead him to the white wizard's hiding place. There was no sign of Shaulmar anywhere. Bastian directed his essence toward the docks in an effort to uncover the resting place of the travelers, but there was nothing, no sign of any vibration familiar to him.

The Dark Angel recalled his essence into his physical body. He would not waste any more time with this futility. His seemingly disconnected presence in the hotel lobby was drawing the curiosity and attention of other people in the large foyer. The danger of psychosis is very real for astral travelers, and even the Dark Angel was not immune, so he came back and re-connected with the mass in the chair in the lobby. Bastian surged forward, then settled back to regain his normal state of consciousness before moving. After resting for a moment, he left the chair a little disgruntled and headed back to the restaurant where his brother sat waiting as he was ordered. Drandos was still sitting at the table and when he saw his brother walk through from the lobby he stood up immediately.

"What happened, Draco? You were gone so long, I thought something had harmed you." Bastian looked around the room to reassure himself there was no longer any threat directed toward him or his brother.

"I located the source of the disturbance in the energy field, and as I suspected, it was the traveller, Shaulmar of the Ancients," he said as he reached for his unfinished wine glass from the table. Drandos took his seat.

"Shaulmar of the Ancients. The name sounds familiar but I cannot place it. What did he look like, brother? Bastian swallowed his drink and gave his brother a look of superiority. He really had no respect for anyone whom he thought was his inferior, especially his younger brother.

"Hurry and finish your drink. We are leaving," he said in an awkward tone. Drandos said nothing. He eventually reached for his wine and gulped it down. He hated the treatment he was receiving from his brother but he was not yet aware that his consciousness was coming closer to severing all ties with Draco Bastian. Feelings of deep hurt and pain began to surface and these feelings were gradually developing into a real hatred for his older brother. As they both left the table and headed for the exit, Drandos looked around for the waitress, Fiona. She was serving a table in the far corner of the room. He tried to walk as slowly as he could just in case she turned around, but all too soon the two brothers walked out of the restaurant.

★★★

A black saloon car pulled up outside the apartment building. It was clear to Alison that much was to be accomplished before she'd be ready to seek revenge from the dark master.

"The two of you must protect me until I have regained my strength. If I do not succeed, you do not succeed. Remember that when you find that your eyelids are too heavy to hold up." Alison spoke quietly. She didn't waste any more time explaining things to the minions. The tired and drained body of the dark priestess took its toll on her energy and she wished only for the rejuvenating comforts of sleep. The ride up in the elevator seemed to take forever. When she opened the door to her apartment, she was in for a rude awakening. "What the hell!" She stepped inside the suite and was immediately forced back against the inside of the door. "Wait! Wait!" Alison held up her medallion given to her by the Rhostos. "It's me! It's okay. It's me!" she spluttered, as she held up her hands with the medallion in their clasp. The hand that forced her throat to close released her immediately. Alison coughed as she gulped air into her lungs once more—she held one hand to her throat to ease the pain. "I called you here to give you the opportunity to repay me and to rid yourself of the indebtedness you rock stars hate so much, not to kill me and increase the debt—you fools!" She coughed again, hanging her head and leaning against the door.

"Sorry, but we could not be seen to have come through the portal to the planet that is outside of our authorization zone. We had no way of knowing whose place this was when we arrived. We only had your message to rely on. It could have been a trap. There are many who would like to see the Rhostos brought before the Sacred Council." The Rhostos were large and very powerful beings that looked like they should fear no one.

"Well, next time you could scan the portal destinations for my soul signature before you travel through—that might be an idea, hey?" Alison was still massaging her throat as she picked up the crystal from the center of the room. She placed it back in the dark wooden box in her bedroom. There was an uncomfortable pause as the huge men stood in the center of the room waiting to hear her request.

"Maybe you are right. We owe you a debt of thanks for giving us the opportunity to erase the huge debt we are held by."

"That's more like it. Now, please, sit down…anywhere. I do not have much time to explain what I want from you." Alison walked as best she could over to the large windows that overlooked the New York City skyline. "Do you recall the time on Orban when there was a conflict, a war between the archangels and the Rhostos?" she turned to face the men and tried to read their thoughts.

"We do…." The larger of the two took a step toward her. "What has that to do with why you summoned us?"

"I will explain." Alison had difficulty connecting with their minds. They were blocking her somehow. The Rhostos were neutral in every sense of the word, physically mentally, and emotionally. Although, there were many conflicts occurring across the universe, the Rhostos were immune to the demands of the more powerful beings of the universe and to the cries for help of the less powerful and weaker beings who were under attack. They functioned with total neutrality and remained that way to stay free of debt from others.

Alison looked at them again. "Do you recall why the war began?" she looked at the two mountainous beings standing in her living room, casting darkness over most of the room. The two looked at each other as they tried to remember the reason. The war was some time ago and the Rhostos were not known to dwell on past events, especially events that were not fruitful to their culture.

"Not really, the war was a war like many that have taken place with the Rhostos. We do not focus on the past. Why do you dance around the reason why you summoned us? Is it something that you wish to use as a method to trick the Rhostos?" They became tense and moved slowly toward her. She could see the stiffening in their bodies in anticipation of the threat they imagined might happen.

"No—no my friends. I will explain all that is on my mind. Please, sit." Alison waved her hand and beckoned for the two beings to join her in the study in the next room. "Please relax here and I will have some refreshments brought in." She summoned one of the guards from the entranceway. "Bring me wine," she said. Alison turned back towards the two monstrous beings.

"Now, why are we here, Allison Warrior?" The Rhostos were not known for possessing any degree of patience. They considered time to be extremely precious.

"I will refresh your memory concerning the war with the archangels where many Rhostos were eventually destroyed. The reason was clear. Does the name Draco Bastian mean anything to the Rhostos? Alison looked at both of them. She utilized the maximum effect of the pause she left, allowing the two beings to digest what she had said, and to prepare them for what she was about to say. The two warriors looked at each other bemusedly. Neither of them recognized the name, Draco Bastian. Alison waited for the right moment. She knew the two beings were getting closer to what she was implying and she waited for their anger to arise. She realized within herself that her timing must be perfect for fear of incurring the wrath of the huge beings.

The Younger Rhostos was becoming very agitated and was fingering the handle of the short sword on his belt. Alison knew that the time was now—she stood before them and spoke.

"The one you know of as the Dark Angel is the one I speak of," she said strongly. She could not hide the anger she held towards him in her voice. "He is the one the Rhostos are sworn to destroy should the opportunity ever arise." The larger of the two Rhostos leapt onto to his feet.

"Where! Where is this abomination?" He frantically moved about the place, sure that he was going to find this dark entity that was responsible for damaging his people so deeply.

"He is not here, my friends," Alison was breathing heavily. She hated Bastian as much as they did and she reveled in their hatred for the Dark One. The Rhostos were very confused at the whole situation. They still didn't have any idea why they were summoned to this place, through the singing crystal portal, and how they were to repay the debt they owed to the human called Alison.

"We want to know what all this is about and why you have summoned the Rhostos." The older warrior moved towards her with deathly intentions and she could feel his power.

"Please, calm yourselves. The Rhostos are my friends and I am their friend." She spoke the words with a soothing tone, the way she was taught to speak with the Rhostos, to help lessen any threat they might hold. The mind and the soul of the dark practitioner merged, while producing a vibration through the vocal cords that had a very soothing and disarming effect on the hearts of the Rhostos. That was their weakness although it lasted only for a few moments—not many knew about this trick.

"I will explain to you both how you can repay the debt the Rhostos owe to me, how the Rhostos can help prevent the Dark Angel from gaining a soul he really wants to collect." Allison smiled and waited for the information to sink into their brains.

"How do we repay the debt to you? This is the only thing we want from you at this time." There was a pause then the young warrior turned to his partner.

"Why can't we have both? You know what this black soul did to us, to our families, both yours and mine. We must take this opportunity for revenge." His anger was intense and the pain was evident on his face.

"No! We must remain cautious." The Rhostos warrior knew there was more information to be had before he would allow any rash decisions to be made through the emotions of anger and inexperience. He gave a look towards his young accomplice.

"As you wish, my friend," the younger warrior replied.

Alison was patient. "Erm...well, I do know how you can prevent him from gaining the soul he prizes above all others." She turned with an air of aloofness that she knew would infuriate the Rhostos.

"Okay, what is it you want from the Rhostos that would remove any debts owed to you?" The old warrior was no idiot and Alison knew she would need to tread very carefully with him.

"I want you to find a specific soul here on earth. I have a particular soul in mind that has a destiny that is pivotal in the fight for harmony and balance in the universe. That is all I will say about the matter. You will accept the request?" Alison was strong and clear with what she said and there was little room for the Rhostos warrior to maneuver. After a long deliberation, the warrior spoke.

"If we do as you ask, the debt will be erased, and there will be no more you will require from the Rhostos?" He passed his hand over the leathery cloak of his winged appendages that identified him as a Rhostos warrior. "The Rhostos must be allowed to ally with the Allison warrior." Alison bowed slowly to the Rhostos. She knew it might come to this, but she knew having the Rhostos warriors as allies was worth the price to see Bastian go down in flames. The message was clear. Either she share in the secrets that surrounded the soul in question, or as soon as the debt was repaid, the Rhostos would become yet another interested party where Rebecca Sullivan was concerned.

"It will be as you wish," she said.

"Now, you will give the Rhostos all the information you have concerning the soul." The elder Rhostos was no fool and the younger warrior was obviously very eager to learn the ways of the Rhostos warrior clan.

"The Rhostos do not allow themselves to be aligned with any other beings, master," the young warrior whispered in his master's ear with his back turned away from Alison. "Why are we striking a bargain with this one? We Rhostos will only be in her debt once more." His concern came from the imprinting of thousands of years of neutrality that was the foundation of the Rhostos society and culture.

"I will explain later my young friend. All will be made clear. Trust the wisdom of your master." He rested his hand on the shoulder of the young warrior as reassurance that he would not lead them down the road of shame and cause them to forfeit their Rhostos heritage. The elder warrior turned to Alison. He met her eyes with his. He meant to impress upon her that further danger would befall her should she decide to deceive the Rhostos in any manner.

"Does the Allison Warrior understand the wrath of the Rhostos? Does she know what results from attempting to trick the Rhostos?" He waited for the mind process that he used to register upon her iris. This was the method the Rhostos used to detect emotional or psychological movements within the boundaries of the brain.

"I am aware of the Rhostos's strengths in that regard." Alison eyed the warrior with equal intensity and conviction. "I am also aware of the weaknesses that plague the Rhostos." This was a very dangerous game she was playing with the Rhostos warrior. With one movement, the warrior could easily remove her head from the rest of her body. "However, my only desire is to gain the trust and respect of the Rhostos people and of the Rhostos warrior. If an allegiance is the only way to gain this trust then I accept the terms of our contract." Alison had got what she wanted from them and was fully prepared to deal with the Rhostos warrior when the time suited her. She had no intention of remaining tied to a contract that was created by what she considered to be an inferior species.

"We, the Rhostos also accept the terms of the contract and we expect to discuss the partnership and all the benefits that go along with that contract." The old warrior was speaking of the financial gains and the power that would accompany it.

"But, of course, we will determine the stakes of any monetary gains that result from the successful capture of the soul in question." Alison was only going through the motions of the terms of the contractual obligations. She had no intentions of ever handing over any money, or power for that matter, once she figured out why Rebecca Sullivan had become such a significant soul to Draco Bastian. "Rest easily, my Rhostos warrior, you will have your prize. I can promise you that." She smiled at them both and offered them more wine that the young warrior accepted gladly. The old warrior slowly grasped the wine glass, pausing before removing it from Alison's hand, where their eyes met yet again as the Rhostos warrior tried to read her thoughts and emotions once more. The warrior took the glass when he was satisfied that Alison was not hiding anything from him.

"To our partnership." He raised his glass. "May we all be the recipients of great and good fortune?" The elder was still very tentative but he was prepared to continue until the new path he was forging for the Rhostos culture was created. His desire was for the Rhostos to reside in their own dimension rather than be seen as inferior beings occupying the space between dimensions—he wanted his species to be respected and recognized by all other societies in the universe as equal and prosperous.

Alison bowed low and sat in the chair closest to the huge window that overlooked the city below. "I will give you the information you need to track the soul, Rebecca Sullivan, and I ask that you use any and all means at your disposal to locate her."

The young apprentice spoke quickly. "Yes, that is acceptable to the Rhostos." He was trying to create a position for himself as a Rhostos warrior even though he would not be recognized as such until his wing appendages grew out from his spine. The black leathery material only formed when the young Rhostos warriors reached a time and place of great importance in their lives. This stage in the young warrior's life is seen as the right of passage of the Rhostos culture. Some warriors do not reach this position while other warriors reach the position but are unable to move through the difficult demands of the rites of passage.

"That is for me to say," the elder Rhostos warrior put the young warrior in his place easily. "I will guide you through the passage safely but you must remember there is no place for unsupported or unsupervised acts of aggression." The young warrior realized his mistake and immediately bowed his head and apologized.

"Forgive me, master. I have much to learn."

Alison waited for the Rhostos warriors to regain the positions of their hierarchical structure. During this time, she used the opportunity to observe any established weaknesses that could be exploited later. The elder finally regained power and quickly turned to Alison. He knew what she was attempting to do. He would have done the same in her position.

"So, what information are you willing to give the Rhostos to locate the soul, Rebecca Sullivan." He tried to regain his position of strength in her eyes but it was gone and they both knew it.

"What I have is her soul signature," she handed him a crystal, "and I am sure that is enough for a seasoned Rhostos warrior such as yourself." There was a deliberate pause before she continued. "That is, if no unauthorized interruption impedes the progress," she smiled. The warrior knew she meant his control over the younger warrior was in question.

"The location of the soul you desire will be delivered to you soon. Be sure you remember your agreement with the Rhostos, warrior Alison, you would not want to incur our wrath." She knew he meant he would love nothing more than to kill her, and keep all the rewards.

"Our contract is binding, Rhostos," She wanted him to know that she did not fear him…or death. After all, Bastian wished that for her anyway and he was very close to making that desire a reality.

"We shall return soon. Be ready. The Rhostos cannot remain in this dimension for long periods as you well know, and as we are now partners in this venture, it remains the Rhostos way to inform you of any surveillance used to remain connected to our allies. We must let you know that we can now track you wherever you may choose to move or travel to. The Rhostos have the ability to recognize the soul signature of any species that choose to enter into contracts with us. The Rhostos can find the Allison Warrior anywhere she may be, for the rest of eternity if that is warranted." The warrior was smiling. He knew Alison had not counted on the cunning of the Rhostos warrior's abilities. The elder warrior read her iris and smiled.

"The Rhostos are true adversaries and worthy opponents." She conceded the fact that she had underestimated the Rhostos warrior. However, the contract had not changed. She would concede everything just to witness the demise of Draco Bastian. "Come!" the elder Rhostos warrior snapped at the young apprentice. "We must cement our new contract by finding the soul, Rebecca Sullivan." The two Rhostos warriors left through a portal that appeared, with the conjuring of one hand, by the elder warrior. The portal sparkled with a light energy understood only by the Rhostos. The light brightened as if it recognized them as they moved toward and through it and disappeared into the realms between dimensions.

Alison sat in the chair next to the large picture window. She felt her time was drawing closer and nearing the point where she would no longer be alive in the 3rd dimension. This thought saddened her. There was a deep-rooted sense of imminent danger lurking within her soul that was telling her to make different choices that would not steer her towards her own destruction. Alison was beyond the point of no return. She was unable to respond to the quiet feelings that stirred deep within her soul. Even if she wanted to veer off in another direction, she was unable to find the strength to do so. All she wanted in this moment was complete revenge, the kind that could only be satisfied by the total destruction of the Dark Angel, Draco Bastian, the one being in the universe she hated most. She sat quietly and drank the wine that had been brought to her for the Rhostos' enjoyment. She was never going to reach the bottom of the dark pit that consumed her. She was prepared to burn in hell for the many things that she had done to others this time around. Alison knew she would have to pay for all her acts of terror and darkness. This was something she knew she could not escape. If she were permitted to look Bastian in the eyes, as he suffered his destruction, she thought it would be worth every moment of time spent in hell. The city lights, as the waters of the harbor reflected them, were mesmerizing to her. She sipped her wine and wondered where Rebecca Sullivan could be. Was she warm and cozy, wrapped in the embrace of the travellers who were sent to protect her?

There was a heaviness surrounding Alison. She liked Rebecca, and at the same time, she hated her and everything she represented. Why was someone like Rebecca offered the path to all good things while Alison only had darkness to walk through, she wondered. As Alison became more and more drunk, and the hate and anger of her own miserable existence became stronger and more powerful, it became obvious to her that to enjoy the total destruction of the Dark Angel, he must be denied the pleasure of capturing the soul he wanted so much, and therefore Alison must destroy Rebecca Sullivan, preferably in full view of the dark master.

CHAPTER 16

SHAULMAR RETURNED TO THE HOUSE UNSCATHED FROM his meeting with Bastian. Morghanz was the first to greet him as he arrived.

"Shaulmar, Did you see Draco Bastian?" she looked at him closely as he walked into the house, making sure not to miss any injuries, blood stains, or any other signs that he had been hurt.

"Don't worry so much, Morghanz, it wasn't that kind of a meeting. It was more of an information-swapping encounter. He was trying to establish who he was and show me the extent of his power. Shaulmar hung his cloak on the rack in the hallway as he'd always done and continued down the hall towards his study. "I am a little concerned for the safety of our young disciple. Draco Bastian has become quite a powerful being. We both have heard the stories, and after standing in front of him, I would say they are more likely to be accurate than fictitious."

Morghanz lifted an eyebrow. "Do you mean 'powerful' as in he could light a candle at forty feet or 'powerful' as in avoid at all costs?" Morghanz's voice contained a strong hint of sarcasm, but Shaulmar knew it was designed to let him know that she was not going to run from anyone, not even Draco Bastian. She really wanted to know, in Shaulmar's opinion, how difficult it would be for this wizard to kill her.

"You are never going to find out how powerful this being is, Morghanz," Shaulmar told her. In these few words spoken by Shaulmar, the power of Draco Bastian was conveyed to Morghanz. Shaulmar was never going to allow Draco Bastian anywhere near Morghanz or Rebecca—he was far too powerful. "Where is Rebecca anyway?" Shaulmar enquired, as they both entered the study. The wizard proceeded to rifle through his bookshelves—he was looking for something—whatever it was he knew he needed. However, he had no clue as to its identity but he thought it would come to him eventually.

"She is in her room practicing the yoga exercises I taught her. She doesn't seem to want to sleep. She has been practicing for a couple of hours now. I convinced her that she must bring her mind into a state of peace and balance. I showed her some yoga positions that will address that. They are designed to calm and bring peace to the mind." Morghanz stood in front of Shaulmar. Their eyes met. There was more on her mind, but she didn't think the time was right, so she offered some tea to her friend. Morghanz was a little annoyed and hurt at the fact that Shaulmar thought she could not handle herself if Draco Bastian were to attack. She knew he only had her wellbeing in mind and that thought comforted her somewhat. Although, she thought, he does not know me, nor is he aware of the true depth of my power. At the same time, she did not want to face a confrontation with Draco Bastian until she was sure that she would survive the ordeal. So, for the moment, she decided to detach herself from the topic. "What are you going to do?" she asked.

Shaulmar thought for a moment and then spoke softly—he was unsure of what was coming himself. "I have no idea." He sat down and relaxed in his favorite high-back leather chair while he stared at the painting of the cosmos that hung on the wall behind his desk. "I must wait for answers to come to me, and I hope for all our sakes, they come soon," his voice trailed off to a whisper. Morghanz did not say anything for a while and then she walked over to him and nestled a comforting hand on his shoulder.

"I'm sure your answers will come soon. They have never let us down before, and as long as we have the trust and faith in the light that drives the universe, they will not let us fall now." Morghanz was able to bring comfort to him by saying such things and he was grateful for having such a dear friend during times of fear and darkness.

"Thank you, Morghanz. You never fail to help me realize the beauty of all that is. You are a true friend." He put his right hand on her cheek as she bent down and then he kissed her gently on the lips. Morghanz also felt better after the kiss. She hugged him with all the love she felt for him, and that had grown, from all the years they had spent together as travellers.

"So, was he as powerful as you thought he would be?" she was very serious and she wanted the real facts from Shaulmar with none of the sugarcoating that he normally used to soften bad news.

"Yes, I'm afraid so, he may even be more powerful than I thought. When I met him in the crowded foyer at the restaurant, I felt his mind actively searching for me before I even saw him. When we eventually saw each other, his energy was holding me back as I tried to move in his direction. It felt like I was walking through thick clay up to my thighs with a ship's anchor tied to my back. I did not let him see how difficult it was for me to move against his power, but in effect, it took a large amount of my resources to project to him that his energy was having no effect on me."

Morghanz listened closely. After all the years they had worked together and through their many battles with the darker forces, she had learned how to help Shaulmar find the answers he was searching for. "Go on…" She encouraged him to display all his thoughts and ideas in plain view so they could both see them in all their various forms.

"Well, he seemed to me to be as comfortable as I must have seemed to him. However, I have to believe in my own power and my own heart, and I must believe that he was affected by my power also—no matter how powerful he appeared to be. Shaulmar was beginning to gain his clarity and his equilibrium back. Through the process of rationalization and logical reasoning, he was able balance his thoughts, and to reaffirm that indeed he was a very powerful wizard in his own right.

"Was there anything about him that you saw that could assist us somehow later?" Morghanz was trying to provide the catalyst that would trigger the answers to help them better understand their enemy. Shaulmar didn't answer right away.

He was trying to recall the event as clearly as he could within his mind's eye, and as the scenes were being recreated, he suddenly spoke.

"He was being protected by something...Draco Bastian was being protected by something," the wizard became excited. "He possesses a talisman that is very ancient and extremely powerful." Shaulmar closed his eyes and slowed his breathing. He desperately wanted to replay what his subconscious mind had recorded during the encounter. "I think he wore a ring, a gold ring on his left hand, that was what was shrouding him in the powerful energy." Morghanz touched his hand gently. "What else can you sense about the ring? Does it possess the wearer or does the one who wears the ring have the control? Does it have a name?" she was desperately trying to help Shaulmar to retrieve more information.

"I...I think the ring has a consciousness but it does not control. It does not dictate to the.... Wait! Wait...it seems to...." There was a long pause before Shaulmar began speaking. "Oh, God!" he said somberly. "I know why I felt so drained and like I was being pulled downward as if walking through quicksand." Shaulmar's face looked like the face of someone who had witnessed something so atrocious and heinous that it was almost impossible to believe. "The ring he wore was somehow making me feel that way. It is able to project feelings of anguish and suffering onto others. That ring has torn and ripped the energy from the souls of thousands of beings throughout the universe. It is sworn to defend only one, the Dark Angel, Draco Bastian. Now I realize why I felt familiar energy in the old bookstore that day. I felt it was an old friend that was calling to me but I couldn't figure out who it was until this moment right now." Morghanz held onto his arm tightly.

"What do you mean? What are you saying?"

"Morghanz, I'm saying that Draco Bastian is protected by the Ring of Dread!"

"What? Uh...no—that ring was destroyed on Orban centuries ago," she said, "I'm sure of it." Her face betrayed hints of doubt.

"No...no...I saw the ring on his hand. I am not mistaken. It is the very same ring that took my old friend so many years ago." At that moment, Shaulmar felt such a heavy sadness had engulfed him. "We must stop Draco Bastian and destroy the ring before it gains the opportunity to capture Rebecca." Shaulmar was shaken by the very realization that Bastian and the Ring of Dread' was the force that was trying to upset the balance of souls in the universe. He thought the Ring of Dread' and its wearer were a myth. Shaulmar was just a boy—his grandfather told him the stories of how souls were tortured for days before they were captured. Shaulmar thought they were just stories, stories to scare young boys out of their ego-tisticle tendencies, so they could focus more diligently on their trainings for a life of service in the Sacred Order of Light. "Morghanz, I think the Ring of Dread and Draco Bastian tried to capture me today when I met them in the hotel lobby. I think the only thing that saved me was the Archangel Ring." He was experiencing a sudden and disturbing realization as he spoke.

"Oh, Shaulmar, if anything happened to you, I couldn't bear it." Morghanz blurted out the words before she could stop herself, and when she realized what she had said; she looked away, as if that act would erase the words.

Shaulmar did not want to embarrass her further, so he continued. "There is some good that has come of this," he said. He stood up and walked over to the library shelves that were full of books. He started to search through the volumes of books. He was searching for information about the *Ring of Dread* and its history. "If they were intending on capturing me, they must think of me as a threat to their successful capture of Rebecca's soul." Shaulmar's logic was sound. "I must inform the Sacred High Council of what I have discovered concerning the Ring and the Dark Angel, Draco Bastian. I will leave for the bookstore in the morning." Shaulmar had regained his energy and was feeling rejuvenated and purposeful. He now had a sense of what he must do. The answers did in fact come, finally. "First, I must speak with Rebecca about her future, and most importantly, my fears about her safety. She must be prepared!"

"Wait, Shaulmar, are you sure Rebecca is ready for that information? "I do not think she is the same person as she was, even from yesterday." Morghanz looked at him seriously.

"What do you mean?" Shaulmar thought that was a strange thing for her to say.

"I'm not really sure," she continued, "all I know is that she seems to be different almost with each passing day. I tried to connect with her today through the oneness that is our universal force but I was not permitted to connect with her on a deep and meaningful level." Morghanz waited for Shaulmar to process what she was telling him. She knew she was out of her depth now concerning what was going on with Rebecca.

"I don't really understand it either. I think the changes I felt some time ago are manifesting or are drawing closer anyway." Shaulmar removed his robe and hung it behind the door. "There are many choices that are presented to me at this time. However, the best choice has not revealed itself as of yet and I think it is because I need to connect with Rebecca." Morghanz agreed.

"I think she is still awake. Shall I go see if she is up to spending some time with you?"

"Sure, and Morghanz please surround yourself in white light and activate your crystal amulet." He knew the last thing he said would evoke more questions from his friend.

"Shaulmar, do you know what you are saying?" He knew the question was rhetorical but he still wanted to provide Morghanz with as much information as he could...without saying more than he dare.

"You are telling me to be aware of our good friend, the one we are sworn to protect." She could not believe what she heard. "Shaulmar, you must tell to me what you know. I must insist." The wizard hung his head in his hands. He was just so overwhelmed with the way things were escalating.

"Morghanz, we have been together for eons, haven't we?" he said. He still held his head in his hands and his face was covered. "I believe now is the time for the two of us to share our true feelings with one another, don't you." He waited, knowing full well that the time had come for him to make his feelings known to her. The great wizard stood silent. He was sincerely praying that Morghanz would tell him what he wanted to hear.

"Shaulmar, I love you and I have loved you from the beginning...my love." Her heart pounded inside of her chest. She couldn't say anymore. Her thoughts were loose and he had heard her every word—that alone scared her to death. If he had not meant what she thought then she would never be the same. Their friendship would not be the same. Morghanz realized that her words might change everything between them forever. She was feeling panicked. She desperately wanted to put the genie back in the bottle. She knew that was impossible, so she hoped in favor of her love for him and his for her. Morghanz held her breath tightly and stopped breathing so he would not notice how incredibly nerve-wracking this was for her.

Finally, he spoke. "Morghanz, our hearts share the same beat." was all he said—it was the only thing needed. They came together in an embrace, and for the next few moments, nothing else mattered. Shaulmar pulled away from her slowly and gently. "I must speak with Rebecca before she goes to sleep. Could you see if she will talk with me my love?"

Morghanz breathed a sigh of relief. "Of course I will, Shaulmar. Give me a few moments and I will return." Morghanz was no longer smiling. She felt a heaviness descend over her as she walked up the stairs. Halfway up the stairs, she had to hold onto the oak handrail to prevent her self from falling. The energy was so strong around her. The white sorceress' only thought was to get to Rebecca, ask her to go down and speak with Shaulmar, then go to her own room and lie down on her bed. She reached Rebecca's room and knocked on the door quietly. She whispered through the door.

"Rebecca would go downstairs and speak with Shaulmar? He has something important he wants to talk to you about."

"There was no answer, so Morghanz slipped the door open and stepped inside.

"Oh hello, Morghanz. I was just finishing the yoga exercises that you taught me. Do you know I am able to perform more exercises now than I could last week?" Rebecca was sitting in the lotus position and that was highly unusual. This position was not supposed to be obtainable to the beginning practitioner, at least, not until they had developed a strong inner discipline and had dedicated a significant amount of time to the practice.

"Rebecca, that's extraordinary." Morghanz was genuinely surprised.

"Does Shaulmar want to speak with me right now, because I am feeling really tired, and I was going to take a nap after the yoga."

"Sorry…yes he does…if that's okay with you." Morghanz was leaning against the door jam at this point. She still did not know or understand why she was feeling the way she was, heavy and lethargic. Maybe it was just the stress of everything she'd heard today, she thought.

"Anyway Rebecca, I have to lie down for a bit myself right now, so I will see you in the morning, alright?"

"Okay, Morghanz, good night." Rebecca hugged her hard and then went downstairs.

Morghanz remained in Rebecca's room for a few moments where she sat on the end of the bed. She began to understand finally what was happening. She closed her eyes and tried to relax. She focused her concentration on her energy body because she was feeling there was an entity that had attached itself to her energy. The entity had made a connection with her. It had connected itself to her left shoulder just a couple of inches below her neck. The only thing she could do was to try to remain calm and try to identify the entity by its vibration and frequency. She hoped it was of a higher vibration because entities of a lower vibration tended to be more difficult to dislodge and disconnect from. She knew the process of removing an invading entity was sometimes lengthy, so she walked down the hall and entered her room locking the door behind her. She didn't want to burden the others with something like this. She considered it to be a stressful yet minor concern that she did not want to share with her friends. Morghanz figured she would be rid of this entity, or possibly, psychic parasite by morning and it would be sent to the light or to hell to burn by dawn.

★★★

When Rebecca walked into the study, her power was strong. Shaulmar could sense her energy even before she arrived.

"Hi Rebecca. How are you?"

"I'm fine, Shaulmar, and you?"

"Morghanz says you have been focusing…on your studies…"

"That's right. I've been practicing my yoga and I'm getting good at it, too. Did you find what you went looking for today?" she was feeling more comfortable with her new life and family.

Shaulmar wanted to shout to her to pack up her most prized possessions and run for her life. However, he managed to allow the strength of the emotion to dissipate before he answered her. He continued to stoke the fire in the hearth to keep the room warm.

"Somewhat, but I have more to do. Incidentally, that is what I wanted to speak to you about. Please, come and sit with me Rebecca. I will make some tea and we can talk about it, okay?" Shaulmar had never been in a position like this one. He wondered how he could even begin to tell Rebecca what he had learned about the developments so far, and most importantly, what was about to manifest in the near future—her future, specifically.

Rebecca sat in the leather armchair beside Shaulmar's desk. "So, Shaulmar, what is it you wish to talk to me about?"

"Rebecca, to be honest, I don't really know where to begin." He rubbed his eyes and took a deep breath. "You know the things that have happened so far, and the things you have seen, the strange things you've seen?" Shaulmar paused. "Do you believe they were real?"

Rebecca thought for a moment. "I think they were. I mean it was strange at first when I was with Alison and things started to happen, weird things, like the headaches and the flashes of light. The heavy energies that tried to smother me in my room were terrifying, and yes, they were all weird, but maybe, kind of explainable. However, it was when the book transported you and I into the Templars' cavern that scared me most. Then, for sure, I had no doubt there were things happening in the world that were unseen and misunderstood by us. So, I decided to develop an open mind... I mean...how else could a person deal with something like that?" she sounded really together, he thought.

"Yes, I am glad you were able to open your mind enough to see the possibilities of other things...unknowns...in the universe. The universe has many wonderful things in it and countless beings of many origins to experience them." He was finding it difficult to bring the conversation around to the present situation. He knew he must tell Rebecca the truth and forewarn her about the dangers and challenges that lie ahead of her.

"So, what was so important that you wanted to talk to me about right away, Shaulmar?" she smiled politely and waited. Rebecca was tired and she just wanted to go back upstairs and go to sleep.

"Sorry Rebecca, to be honest..." he paced around the room, all the time, looking at her, "I am at a loss as to how to proceed with the conversation. I don't know how to say what I must." He ran his hand through his hair and leaned on the mantle above the huge fireplace where the painting of one of the sacred masters from Orban was displayed.

"Maybe you could just say it and you'd feel better. Really Shaulmar, that's how I get through things like this." She put a friendly hand on his shoulder. "Shaulmar, I am no longer the naïve little girl you rescued and took into your home. You must realize that by now. You must have noticed the changes that have occurred in me." She waited patiently for the wizard to respond.

"Yes, yes of course," he said softly while turning to face her, "I have to tell you that you have become the very strong and kind person that I always knew you would become." She stood tall in front of her friend and she looked him straight in the eyes.

"Then, my friend, please treat me as that person and tell me what you must. You are the one who made me realize that even though we have free will to do whatever we want, our path is very solid and guided by wonderful caring beings, like you, who help us to stay close to our life's purpose." Shaulmar had tears in his eyes. He wanted to protect her but he was not sure that he could and this awareness was breaking his heart.

"Rebecca, the situation is grave. Dark beings are coming closer to us. I will do what I can to protect us but there may be too many, and one in particular, who is very powerful." He held her hand in his. There was a silence that was heartbreaking. Rebecca lowered her head as if she realized the severity of the situation.

"So, you are saying that Draco Bastian is coming to kill me and that he will probably succeed." Her voice was soft and deliberate but there was no trace of fear, panic, or anxiety in it.

"I will do all I can, you know that Rebecca? However, I must be as honest and truthful as I can. He is very powerful, more so than I originally suspected, this angel of the sacred dark arts. I went to see him earlier today and I found out how powerful he really is." The wizard began to pace the room once more. He was running his hand through his hair. This habit always helped him to think more clearly.

"Rebecca, I'm going to the bookstore in the morning to speak with the Sacred High Council. I will stand before them and find a way out of this situation." He continued to pace back and forth. "Maybe they can come up with a solution to stop Bastian from capturing you, and taking your soul, and killing the rest of us in the process." He stopped pacing and leaned against the mantle again.

"Okay Shaulmar. Now, I'm really tired and I think I need to go to bed. I will talk with you again when you get back from the bookstore after your meeting with the sacred...high...uh...council." She moved slowly toward the door. "Shaulmar," she turned back to look at him.

"Yes," he said solemnly. He felt like he was failing her along with the rest of his friends.

"Please, don't feel bad. I know you're going to do the best you can." She paused to fight back her tears. "If it was not for your intervention that night at the nightclub, Alison would have killed me anyway. You have been a good friend to me and I am truly grateful for that." She opened the door to the study and turned to look at him once more. "There's always a silver lining to all situations, and in this situation, I would get to see my mom and my grandmother again, just sooner than I expected to." She smiled wryly and left.

Shaulmar was still running energy, still running every bit of information he knew about the Dark Angel and the dark arts, through his mind. How could wizards such as him protect loved ones against such a hostile force? The fire glowed as Shaulmar spent the rest of the night in the study pouring through the books in his library. However, he could not find anything that could help them fight against the Dark Angel. He knew he needed to search for any weaknesses that could be exploited but he was running out of time and he knew it. It finally occurred to him that he could do some lucid dreaming to try to find a solution. Eventually, he allowed his head to rest on his arms as he gave in to the pressure behind his eyes and slowly closed them. Shaulmar floated off into a deep sleep where he was no longer plagued by the torments of his troubled incarnation. He began to dream right away, and automatically he made himself recognize that he was in the dream state, as he slowly became more and more lucid or consciously aware that he was in charge of his dreams. This was an ability all master wizards were able to accomplish with well-practiced ease. Shaulmar did not believe that it was Rebecca's destiny to die at the hands of Draco Bastian, even though, he knew Bastion was powerful enough to take her life. He knew that the dark wizard had to have a weakness, an Achilles heel, just like all beings within the universe. Everything in existence required harmony and balance, with one another, and within the universe. This meant that to have strengths one had to have weaknesses also.

Morghanz lay on her bed. Her head was aching. There was something that was not right with her. She was beginning to suspect that someone who wanted to do her harm had guided the entity that attached itself to her energy body, to her. The thought did not occur to her that the intended target had been missed, and that she was just an innocent, in the wrong place at the wrong time. However, she did know the ways of the healer and she set upon the task of removing the invader. First, she knew she must identify the entity. In order to accomplish this task, she needed to relax and enter into the meditative state once more. She focused her attention inward, then, by using the breath and her Buddhist meditation practices, Morghanz allowed her physical, mental, and psychological states to merge. What she saw with her intuition scared her to death. The entity had attached to her aura just below the shoulder and had embedded itself within her astral body. The astral energy field surrounding the white sorceress at the seventh layer of her aura was where the dark entity had embedded itself. By vibrating at a frequency that disrupted the energy flow in Morghanz's aura, much like a parasitic worm burrowing its way into its prey, it started to break down the energetic field that sustained her life in this incarnation. Morghanz knew she was in trouble. She needed help to fight this entity—she feared that it was powerful enough to kill her if she didn't do something to stop it now. She slowly returned her mind to the present moment and opened her eyes before she attempted to raise herself up from the bed. Before long, Morghanz realized that she was physically unable to lift her body from the bed. The dark killer had already drained so much energy from her that her body felt as if it was ten times heavier than it actually was. She just could not overcome the thing, no matter how hard she tried. Morghanz could feel it in her energy body—it was slowly infecting her—little by little. The more she tried to put up a fight, the more powerful it seemed to become. The thing had grown long, thin, black hooks at the ends of its arms and had plunged them deep into her etheric body. The black entity was burrowing it hooks deeper and deeper—it was moving towards her heart. She was very weak and she knew her life was slowly being devoured. If Morghanz didn't get help soon, she knew she would not last through the night.

Rebecca walked solemnly up the stairway towards her bedroom. She could only think of how typical it was of her life that she was going to die soon, just when things were getting better for her. She had found a new family that she had grown to love very much, and she had finally met someone that she could spend the rest of her life with and be happy. But now, all she could think of, was that everything she loved was being taken away from her once more, just like her mother, her grandmother, and now Shaulmar, Morghanz, and Joaquim. She decided she was cursed, and that the laws of karma that Morghanz had talked about, had made it their mission in life to plague and hound her until she was dead. Rebecca reached the top of the stairs and walked along the landing. She arrived at Joaquim's room and thought she might go in and speak with her adopted brother. She rested a hand on his door but then decided she wouldn't be able to talk to him about anything that was happening because he wouldn't understand. She thought he was too young to offer any helpful contribution to finding a way out for them. She didn't want to place all the troubles and probable outcomes of the near future on his shoulders. Anyway, it would only cause him pain and suffering with no practical usefulness. There was music coming from beyond the closed door, so Rebecca left him alone. She continued along the first-floor landing and stood outside Morghanz's bedroom. She felt a strong sense of sadness. She closed her eyes and tried to ask Morghanz, in her mind, to come and talk with her. Soon after, she felt silly for trying to connect with her friend telepathically. Although, she knew Morghanz had instilled in her it was a perfectly normal thing to do and we all have the ability to do such things if we only knew how to tap into it. Rebecca sat on the floor and rested her head against Morghanz's door. The hallway was dark and it reminded her of the room she'd had at the hostel, downtown, before she'd met Alison. She sat on the carpet outside Morghanz's room and let the tears fall from her eyes, down her cheeks, and onto her lap. She sobbed quietly and thought about all the heartbreaks she had suffered throughout her short life and that only brought on more tears. Eventually, she pulled herself together and stood up once more. She walked down the landing to her room, crawled into bed, and slept. She felt like she didn't ever want to wake up again.

★★★

Bastian glanced over the black oak desk to where his brother lay sleeping, he tried to search his heart for the kinds of feelings that are supposed to exist between biological siblings but it was difficult and eventually became boring. The only feeling he recognized was of stale emptiness, like a huge and bottomless chasm of infinite space. How could he be so devoid of any good feeling, of a heartfelt love, for his only brother? The thought lingered within his mind for a second or two then it was replaced by a steely, concrete, brute strength that yearned only for power and domination. He turned his leather chair towards the city and towards the wealth and power he sought out there.

"You are not like me brother," he muttered, "I am on the cusp of greatness." Bastian twisted the ring on his finger back and forth. The glow from the morning sun was reflected in the ring he wore on his finger, before the ring absorbed its brightness into the black crystal at its center. "I think you would crumble under the weight of the power I am about to join with dear Drandos. But, do not worry, I will remain true to my responsibilities as an older brother and take care of you—besides, you may be useful to me yet." The Dark One looked over the city wondering how long it would be before he was sitting in the Hall of Demons at the head of the Sacred Dark order. Bastian had a vision for the future of the power structure within the sacred order that included his reign over all the dark beings that existed within the universe. The only thing that stood between him and his vision was the one who was prophesied to be the soul mate of the ancient Book of Secrets. He must capture that one's soul and claim the book as his own before could attempt to take control of the Sacred Dark order.

"Morning, Draco, did you sleep well?" His brother walked around until his senses began to adjust to the surroundings.

"I have no need of sleep, Drandos." The voice that traveled across the room was as cold as ice. "Make yourself ready. I have a job for you."

"A job. What do you mean a job? I am visiting. I am on vacation brother from my schooling with the Sacred Dark order." Drandos was getting tired of feeling like a dog that was constantly being kicked around by its master.

"Do not attempt to elevate your position any higher than it is. In reality, brother, you are nothing more than an apprentice, a dishwasher within the dark order. You will do as you are asked, without question, if you wish to remain in your position. I am your guardian even if you think you are on vacation. You are misguided enough to assume you have free will. You are not free to do as you please until you have passed the final test of the council of black sorcerers, of which I am one." Bastian, at this point, hovered dark and menacingly, over his brother. Drandos swallowed slowly and cowered on the couch where he sat. He remained silent. He prayed his brother would not do anything rash like hurl a bolt of lightning in his general direction. All who knew Draco Bastian, and those who heard the stories about him, feared his wrath. Many stories circulated throughout the dark realms that described his great power, and the anger and rage that fuelled it, in great detail. When Drandos was in training at the place of darkness, he enjoyed some popularity from those who wished to be considered for a position with the Dark Angel when they graduated. He, of course, knew it was for this reason alone that he received their attention and their favors. Drandos did not mind this fact one bit. He loved that his brother, Draco Bastian, was known as the Dark Angel, the most feared sorcerer within the Sacred Dark order of souls.

"I will gladly do as you ask brother. Forgive me…if there was any sign of disrespect, it was not intended," Drandos hurriedly dressed himself then disappeared into the bathroom to give Bastian some time to cool down. Bastian walked to the balcony of the penthouse and leaned on the chrome-plated rail.

"My father was weak when he lay with Drandos' mother. He was old and had lost his passion for power and wealth." He calmly spoke the words into the morning mist. Drandos had just returned to the room when he heard his brother's words.

"My brother is also weak, too weak to walk next to me as I claim my destiny." The words stung Drandos like a knife thrust through the heart.

"Don't worry mother. All that you wish for me—your only true son—will I take from those who destroyed you," Bastian hissed the words with the venom of 1000 cobras.

Drandos had decided to pretend he didn't witness the event. He appeared at the balcony and accepted his fate for the present.

"Brother, what do you demand of me, your servant and apprentice?" Bastian didn't even bother to turn around.

"Get ready to move, Brother, it would serve you well to remember all you have learned of the dark arts." Drandos turned back into the penthouse without a word. His own thoughts and emotions simmered within. He wondered what his future would hold. He was only an apprentice. Even though he had captured the soul of the healer on Orban, that powerful one act might not be enough to save him from death. What did Draco have in mind for him? What did he want him to do? he wondered. Could he somehow run or escape from this place without incurring the wrath of his brother or the disgrace of the dark order of wizards. All these things ran through his mind as he readied himself and as he waited for his orders in the huge penthouse lounge. The day had arrived and the morning sun warmed the depths of the huge building. Rays of golden light entered through the full-length lounge windows and lightened the walls and silver surfaces occupied by his brother's space.

"Drandos, I will tell you what I think you need to know about this day that lies ahead of us. You must give me your full and most focused attention. Can you do that?" He eyeballed his brother like the eagle eyes a jackrabbit.

"Yes brother." The young wizard's apprentice did everything in his power to give the impression of total compliance with the will of the Dark One. Drandos had made up his mind. He no longer had a brother. No matter how brokenhearted it made him feel, he knew it was how he truly felt. He finally realized Draco would always just be the Dark Angel and would never see Drandos as his true younger brother. The fact was, although they shared the same father, their mothers were different and they were only half brothers. Drandos had never acknowledged that difference before now—he had always seen Draco as his big brother. However, this idea had to be changed now that he had spent more time with his brother and had witnessed the same abuse from Draco as he had as a child. The only thought in Drandos's mind, at present, was to get back to Orban, finish his training, and then continue his life there. He had no desire to return to Earth or to his half brother. "What do you want me to do, Master?" Drandos knew his brother would see his compliance as a weakness, and hopefully, he would be happy to be rid of him. Drandos hoped he could leave and return to Orban once Bastian realized he was no longer useful. Bastian collected his favorite ring and a few other items from the mantle in his secret hideaway that was located behind the bookcase in the library of the penthouse.

"Prepare yourself young apprentice. You are about to find out why the Dark Angel is feared by all. We are going into battle today, and you would do well to understand that if you fall in battle you will be remembered, by the Sacred Dark order of souls as the one who walked alongside me, but that is all. I will not sacrifice my own interests to save you my brother." His heart was truly black, Drandos thought.

"Yes Master." Drandos lowered his head and pulled his cloak together in readiness.

"Good, now let's embark on to greatness. This day is destined to put me at the top of the mountain, my friend, my brother." Bastian was covered from head to toe in black leather and other precious hand-woven materials. Drandos eyed his brother with both awe and fear at the same moment. The Dark Angel was tall, slim, muscular, and his power oozed from him effortlessly.

"Draco, you look invincible—almost godlike." The young apprentice was truly overwhelmed by the vision of his elder brother as he stood in the doorway. The morning light captured the menacing figure as if he were a black hole swirling within the darkness of the universe.

"Come! Let us take charge of our destiny!" Bastian had spoken.

CHAPTER 17

THERE WAS A QUICK FLASH OF PIERCINGLY BRIGHT LIGHT as the Rhostos manifested through the crystal portal in the space provided by Alison. The elder warrior was alone. His wings folded back automatically as he materialized into the room.

"Rhostos, you have returned. Do you have news of the soul of Rebecca Sullivan?" Alison moved towards the window—she did not want to be any closer than necessary to the open portal.

"Yes. I have located the soul signature. I placed my protégé close to its source to advise me of any changes that might occur." The Rhostos warrior shook himself just as a dog would shake itself after emerging from the water. He carefully brushed his wings to remove any excess debris that had accumulated from his travels through the spaces between dimensions.

"So, where is she?" Alison took a couple of steps closer to the warrior as she spoke to convey to the Rhostos warrior the urgency of the matter. The warrior casually lifted his head and eyed her questioningly. She stopped her aggressive stance and took a deep breath as she slowly retraced her steps back to the window. She was made painfully aware of the potential backlash of her actions. "I must ask for your patience. The Rhostos do not know of my desire for a speedy end to this matter. I offer my sincerest and deepest apology for my rash actions just now." Alison hoped that would be enough groveling to quell any thoughts of anger that might be swelling in the mind of the Rhostos warrior. If it was not, she was prepared to kill the warrior before she was through. The Rhostos only paused as he looked down at the tips of his long leather membranes between the frames of his wings. He continued to stroke them slowly and deliberately. Finally, he spoke.

"The Allison Warrior does not understand the Rhostos—not many do. It is a common mistake for the Rhostos to be underestimated concerning our power, strength, and most importantly, the resolve of the Rhostos." The large being raised his face slowly so she could clearly see into his eyes—they were blood red. Then he whispered in a deep guttural tone, "Do not make the same mistake that others have made regarding the Rhostos. I would like to continue our partnership. The rewards are very enticing for both of us." His voice hurt her body. Her aura was impacted by a strong force, similar to that of a large wave that is pounded onto a sandy beach.

"Thank you. The Rhostos are truly a forgiving people." She took in a deep breath as she tried to hide the fact from the Rhostos warrior that her lungs were expanding and contracting in pain. Alison used her knowledge of the dark arts to deflect his power as she attempted to regain her composure. The experience was not enjoyable, however, she was afforded an unforeseen yet a very important insight as a result. The force of the Rhostos power was nowhere close to being that of the Dark Angel, she assumed. This experience gave her knowledge of how a fight to the death might go between her and the Rhostos warrior. She avoided his gaze. "Rhostos warrior, can you reveal to me the soul known as Rebecca Sullivan?" she had turned away from him this time so as not to give him the opportunity to read her irises.

"No...I cannot." The warrior paused for effect, trying to keep her off-guard and unfocused. "However, I am able to show you." The warrior waited for her response. He knew his words must have activated many thought processes within her mind but he could not read her thoughts because she was turned away from his gaze.

"Why can you not give me the address where the travelers keep her. You are the Rhostos and your word is your bond." Alison was trying to bide time as she formulated a counter attack to the information he had shared. Well, if he could not tell her where Rebecca was hiding, then that was an indicator of the weakness within the Rhostos. Why was the Rhostos unable or unwilling to give the address she had asked for, she wondered?

"So, Allison Warrior, are you prepared to come with me or shall the Rhostos take the soul for themselves and sell it to the highest bidder?" He was testing her to the fullest now. She could feel the anger and hatred that were building within her emotions. Her voice was steaming under the pressure and her desire to yell and scream obscenities at the Rhostos bastard was about to overcome her resistance.

"The Rhostos warrior is under contract. Do you wish to return to the position we were before our agreement? If so, you will find that being indebted to me once more will prove much more difficult to repay." She thought quickly and cast out magical energies with her words. She conjured a spell that created a field of energy around her to help repel anything the Rhostos warrior could project at her, whether it were mental or physical. The Rhostos paced the room slowly. His size made it easy for him to move from one side to the other. The Rhostos were between 6 and 7 feet tall and weighed somewhere between 300 to 400 Pounds. His huge frame struck fear into the hearts of mortal men, and Alison was under immense pressure to remain calm and in control, as she watched him pace the room without saying anything at all. "What are we to do Rhostos? Have you a plan for me yet?" she decided to force his hand and find out what he had in store for her. Better to know now—not when he was cleaving her head from her body. The warrior reached into a pouch that hung from the silver and black leather-braided belt that hung around his waist. From the pouch, he retrieved the most beautiful crystal she had ever laid eyes upon. As soon as the sunlight that was streaming through the windows behind her struck the faceted crystal, it threw out a beam of light that was reflected on the far wall.

"If you wish to know where the mark that you seem so desperately intent on capturing is located, then you must do as I suggest." The warrior was being deliberately confusing. Alison was unable to contain her displeasure any long.

"What the hell do you think you can accomplish by playing such childish games, warrior? Are you so caught up in the notion that you're all powerful and in control of everything around you, huh?" she was on the verge of exploding into a rage that would consume her mind and emotions and would probably initiate the end of her life. However, the warrior had other plans. In one swift movement, he released his huge wings, spreading them out to almost touch each wall on either side of the large room—simultaneously he waved both arms out in front of him.

"You may now begin." As he spoke the words, Alison could no longer speak. Her muscles seized and she found herself rooted to the very spot she was in. The Rhostos calmly folded his huge wings and looked about the room as he moved in closer to his prey. When he reached the spot where Alison was contained, he circled around her body and inspected his work. He leaned closely toward one of her ears and whispered, "Now, Allison Warrior, I will begin to explain what you must do to come face-to-face with your mark, and also and maybe more importantly, to remain breathing on this planet where you stand." The Rhostos was indeed more powerful than she had first thought. Alison was very thankful that she was still able to think these thoughts at this moment. "The power of the 'immobilizer' is not fatal nor is it a permanent state. I have restricted your ability to process the energy all beings need to function on, at every level of existence in the universe." He looked her up and down as he walked around her statue-like form and as he touched various parts of her physical anatomy. "The Rhostos were given this unique ability for reasons we do not fully understand." He continued to twist and prod various parts of her body. She could feel all that he was doing but could do nothing to stop him. "What we do know about this gift is that we are able to immobilize any being if it is written within the destiny of that being's soul signature." "Also," the warrior held a crystal close to her eyes, "if we wanted to kill the being that is immobilized, we could not. The universe would not allow it—not even if the being were the Dark Angel." His hands were touching her more and more and there was something strange and different about his touch.

Alison was still able to sense energy and she sensed there was something very subtle going on within her body. "Ah, how very curious." The Rhostos had a smile on his face, as he looked her in the eyes. "There has been some trauma to your physical body, recent trauma." He was touching her lower back and shoulders. Then he rested one of his large hands over her stomach and the other across her heart. "Well...well...well...hmmm." His eyes were closed now and a calm peace seemed to emanate from him. "Allison Warrior, the Rhostos function through harmonics, in line with universal law, whereas you seem to function with only personal desire, such as power, greed, and in your case, hatred and revenge." The

Rhostos was speaking while his eyes remained closed. He was now standing in front of her, and to her awareness, he seemed elevated but she couldn't tell for sure. The crystal he was holding was no longer glowing. Although it was still sending a pulse of energy through the warrior, she could sense it was less potent than when he first began to touch her. "When we are called upon to perform this service for others, we maintain a state of gratitude to the Source of all that is. When we perform the service, Allison Warrior, many things are made possible." She could hear every word he said but not with her ears. There was a sense of some sound, but it felt like the color yellow and that was strange—how could she feel the color yellow? Alison had knowledge of the dark arts but she did not know anything of this magic. "There, we are finished." The Rhostos warrior put the crystal back into his pouch and spread his wings once more. He waved his arms as he had before, but this time, he seemed to yell something. His mouth was wide open and his face was contorted in three different ways—to Alison, it looked extremely painful. Almost immediately, the Rhostos slumped to his knees and Alison was free to move again.

"Ooh," she moaned as she crumpled to the floor. The warrior stood close to her. His huge mass threatened to crush her.

"Do you understand what has just transpired, Allison Warrior?" He held out his huge arm, beckoning her to stand. She hated being on the floor beneath him. She felt so vulnerable and betrayed. It had always been difficult for her to bring her damaged frame into an upright position ever since the Dark Angel had taken her body and broken it. There was nothing for it—she had to drag her body to her feet while the Rhostos warrior watched the pathetic sideshow play out in front of him. It was going to be embarrassing and she knew it but she could not remain on the floor forever. The Rhostos wasn't leaving any time soon.

"Watch if you must, Rhostos. I hope you're disgusted by what you are about to see." Alison took a large breath in, filling her lungs in anticipation of the pain that she knew was coming, as she attempted to lift her bulk from the floor.

"Grasp onto my arm, Allison Warrior." The Rhostos stood in front of her offering his hand. She reached up, anticipating a sharp stab of pain—she winced in anticipation. To her astonishment, there was no pain.

"I don't feel pain, Rhostos." She touched his hand with venom. "What have you done? Why do I not feel pain?" Not only was she pain-free but she could also rest all of her weight on the one leg that had been damaged so badly by the deadly force of Draco Bastian's power.

"You have accepted the healing power of the universe, my small friend." The warrior smiled as Alison eased herself to her feet and stood tall before him.

"I feel no pain at all. I can stand straight with my full weight bearing down on my legs and hips." She adjusted her legs and her upper body.

"The Rhostos are not surprised. We have witnessed many times the healing power of the universe as it restores the soul of a being. Indeed, we revel in the happiness and joy their loved ones express as they also witness the magic of the healing powers of the universe." Alison stood in amazement as the Rhostos again looked tentatively around the room as if watching for something.

"We must continue with our mission. There is only so much time the Rhostos have before they must return to the space between dimensions." He was looking nervously at Alison. The warrior needed some indication that she understood what he was telling her.

"Yes, yes, I hear you. We must go." She spoke as she continued to inspect her body and especially her legs as they moved around the room effortlessly devoid of any pain. "What did you do to me?" she asked as she watched him play with some other crystal, a dark Crystal, in the center of the room.

"The Rhostos did nothing to you." He paused while setting the crystal on the flat of its base and the Rhostos again closed his eyes. "Please, do not interrupt me. If I program the crystal incorrectly, you will not have to be so concerned with walking at all." She closed her mouth and thought about what he was saying. The Rhostos warrior spread his wings once again. Alison automatically and instinctively took a couple of steps backwards, just in case. The misty crystal began to vibrate as the warrior stood over it, with his arms held outward, pointed toward the heavens. Alison looked at him then she looked at the crystal—thin shards of golden light shot through it from the base to the top. The crystal sprayed small beams of golden light in all directions, creating a force field all around it, of about 3 meters in diameter and 3 meters in height. Alison observed the crystal vibrate and resonate while it gathered momentum—as its speed increased so did the beams of golden light. When it seemed to reach the desired vibration, and thus the desired result was attained, the Rhostos open his eyes and lowered his hands. "Do not be afraid, the portal is very safe," he spoke slowly and softly. As she looked into his eyes, she thought they were not quite as reassuring as his words.

"Wait one lousy minute. You don't expect me to go in there with you?" she was not about to trust the Rhostos warrior, especially one who had entered into an alliance with her, even if he did do something to heal her badly deformed body.

"You must," he said, "it is the only way I can take you to the soul you seek." He looked at her with bemusement.

"I thought you meant we would go by car or something, something normal like that, when you said we must go." She took another couple of steps backwards towards the sofa that leaned against the far wall.

"I have no more time for this." His voice was hurting her aura again. "You come with me now or our alliance is dead and the Rhostos will be free of any indebtedness." The Warrior was a force to be reckoned with and she knew this very well…now. Alison could not allow Rebecca to be captured by Draco Bastian or anyone else for that matter. The Rhostos warrior stood by impatiently—he was very nervous which made Alison suspicious. There was a nagging feeling in the back of her brain that told her there must be a reason for the Rhostos warrior to be nervous. She wondered why he was alone when he came back through the portal. The voice in her head was constantly nagging at her as to why a Rhostos warrior would be nervous. They are not known to be a nervous species. Her intuition was speaking to her within her mind. It was telling Alison to survey her surroundings and so she did. She looked around to see if anyone or anything else was in the room with them but everything seemed to be normal. Alison considered her knowledge of the dark arts and sorcery to be powerful enough to protect her from the warrior in the eventuality that she needed to do so. Thus, she dismissed the lunatic voice inside her head.

"I have never travelled through a portal with anyone but the members of the Sacred Dark order. How can I be sure it is not a trick and that you don't plan to kill me?" she decided to put the question directly to him and she was prepared for a fight.

"We have a common interest. I wish Rhostos to take a new direction in the evolution of our species and I have picked you, Allison Warrior, to help me. It is your choice to come with me or to lose your target. That is all I will say." He beckoned for her to come to the crystal portal. Alison knew he was correct. She had a choice to make and the decision was hers alone. Alison definitely did not want to lose Rebecca.

"Okay, I will come. But know this, Rhostos Warrior—I will use all the powers of the dark arts and its forces if this plan is a deception. You can mark my words, Rhostos." The warrior said nothing. He only continued to prepare the crystal portal. "What must I do," she asked him eventually.

"You must break the force-field before I do or you will be lost in the space between worlds for all eternity. The portal knows my signature and is programmed to connect with it automatically. So, I will stand behind you with my hand on your shoulder, and when you reach into the force field, the crystal will recognize my signature as it travels through yours. This will allow the portal to create and execute an exit portal at the destination I decide." The Rhostos warrior looked indifferent in his neutrality.

"Okay, I see that I have no choice but to trust your judgment." Alison moved in front of the force field; she gave him one more glance as the Rhostos rested a large heavy hand on her shoulder.

"Now, reach into the crystal portal," he said calmly. Alison's arm stretched and her fingers stiffened as they edged forward into the beam of light coming from the crystal. She felt an immediate tingle in her hand as her fingers entered into the force field.

"Oh, that tingles all the way up my arm," she spoke out loud without really wanting to.

The Rhostos warrior said nothing. He only leaned on her shoulder, urging her into the pulsating light of the crystal portal. There was a bright flash as the crystal portal engulfed them both—the room they'd exited from became dull again with only the crystal remaining behind.

CHAPTER 18

IT WAS RAINING SUDDENLY, AND THE WIND PICKED UP, whipping the wet dampness in every direction. The traveller had turned the corner to the bookstore. His cloak offered some protection from the dismal weather. It was too early for the store to be open, so he slipped down the alleyway of the large building. The great wizard Shaulmar was preoccupied with many thoughts that were running through his mind. He was desperately trying to figure out how he was going to convince the council of what he knew concerning Draco Bastian and the Ring of Dread. As he walked down the alleyway, he failed to notice the wet heap on the cobblestone floor until he was almost upon it. He knelt down beside the bundle and stroked the only half-covered small head that protruded from the debris. An old pain-soaked face looked up at him with cold eyes that were empty of hope.

"Please, take this humble offering my friend. Do not despair. Whatever has brought you to this place has done so through love and to honor your highest good. Trust me." Shaulmar put what money he had into the old man's hand then he continued on his way down the alley. The building extended to the end of the alley where Shaulmar knew the approximate location where the portal existed. He stopped just behind a huge garbage receptacle, and then looked around, making sure no eyes were watching him. However, it would not matter if there were, he was going through the portal opening either way, he thought. The wizard ran his hands along the old sandstone wall, feeling for the vibration of the vortex of light that fed the portal. His feet shuffled through the muddy debris that had gathered along the cobblestone floor. The moment his energy connected with the vortex, he disappeared through the stone archway that made its appearance in front of him. Shaulmar was glad to be inside the ancient building and out of the rain. He looked around the bookstore and saw that he was alone. Thus, he moved along, lightly, between the aisles of old books. He made his way to the back of the bookstore and into the small room where he prepared to open another portal that would take him straight to the Sacred High Council. He was nervous and concerned about leaving his friends alone during this time of danger. The Wizard found the stream of energy near the center of the vortex and lowered himself to one knee as he raised both of his arms with the palms facing upwards. He bowed his head, closed his eyes, and recited the incantation that would open the gateway to the other world. The vortex was amazingly powerful, and without any hesitation, there was a quickening of vibration. Shaulmar immediately felt the change in energy all around him.

The wizard was transported through the portal at the speed of light. The sensation of traveling had always been one of the most enjoyable experiences of his life. As his energy was being ushered to the exit, he let all negativity flow out from him. Shaulmar often used the portal energy or gateway energy as a cleansing method to filter out unwanted thoughts that might have hindered his negotiations with the sacred council. He must be clearheaded if he was going to convince the council of the dangers that threatened his friends, and maybe even the Sacred High Council, themselves, if Draco Bastian was allowed to move forward. Shaulmar exited the portal. He had arrived in the room below the main hall of the Sacred High Council. He brushed himself off, removing any particles that he had collected during the transportation, and rearranged his clothing. The traveling aspect of his work was always enjoyable. But sometimes the residue left on his body and clothing irritated him and it didn't always smell that great either. The room was brightly lit and the custodian of the portal came forward to greet him.

"Shaulmarhime of the Ancients, you are looking well. How are things in the life of a traveler?" The old man had been custodian of the portal at the Sacred High Council for centuries and had witnessed many changes in the way the council ran the organization.

"Things are as they should be, I suppose." Shaulmar forced a smile on his face for the custodian, and tried to make it as kind as possible as he moved through the isolation control chamber. He rested his hand warmly on the old man's shoulders as he walked past him. Once inside, Shaulmar wondered if there was going to be any high council left to consult, if the Dark Angel was not stopped in time and was allowed free reign throughout the universe.

"The council is gathered in the Great Hall. They are expecting you, Shaulmar." The custodian spoke as if he knew what was coming and that did not surprise the traveler.

"Thanks old friend. This will not take long." Shaulmar walked into the hallway of the huge building. His footsteps echoed throughout the immense place and resounded off the ancient marble and granite walls. Shaulmar pushed the huge wooden doors open and stepped comfortably inside. He knew there was going to be a room full of eager members of the sacred order, as well as a full quota of council appointees, sitting in the high benches above everyone. The room was noisy, buzzing with all the latest gossip and speculation stories, the kind that circulated within any institution of sentient beings.

"Ah, Shaulmarhime of the Ancients. You grace us with another visit so soon. What can be so important as to bring you before us again, especially as we all know, you do not have the greatest confidence in your Sacred High Council?" The chairman of the Sacred High Council spoke. At the same time, he appeared to be scribbling furiously on a pad in front of him, not giving the wizard his full attention. The disrespectful action did not go unnoticed.

"Yes. Thank you for your glowing and warm welcome, chairman." Shaulmar walked confidently and assertively towards the high council seats.

"Chairman…council members," he bowed low making sure he made eye contact with each of the council members. This custom of respect was an integral part of Shaulmar's nature as it had been passed down from his people and his culture, "I have news and I must warn you it may not be of the best."

"Pray, what news do you want to share, traveller?" One of the youngest council members spoke from the far left of the grand concave bench above the wizard. Shaulmar shifted his body to address the member who had spoken.

"Currently, I am assigned to the soul, Rebecca Sullivan, as she navigates her destined path. However, there are beings that intend her harm. They intend to capture her soul." The chairman quickly interrupted him.

"Is that not why we sent you there? Did this council not send the most respected and powerful sorcerer to earth to prevent the capture of such an important soul? Please ancient wizard, you have not come before this council to explain to us that you cannot fulfill your responsibilities concerning the protection of the soul you have sworn to keep safe, have you?" The Chairman was standing high above Shaulmar at this point, as he leaned over the edge of the bench. His voice stung deep into the heart and soul of the great wizard. Shaulmar was shaken, and it took a few moments for him to regain his composure, even though the chairman was only voicing his obvious displeasure at seeing him. Shaulmar was ashamed to say that the chairman was closer to the truth than he was actually aware of.

"I need assistance with the task of protecting the soul of Rebecca Sullivan. There are many dark forces intending to do her harm, and namely to capture her. The main threat I am facing is from the dark entity, Draco Bastion, as many of the council members are already aware." Shaulmar knew quite well there were three or four of the council members seated in front of him who sat up straighter and paid attention when he mentioned the name of the Dark One, "The Dark One who goes by the name of Draco Bastian is the same powerful wizard also known by many who fear him as, the Dark Angel. I don't think you are aware that Bastion's powers have evolved and are far greater than I had originally anticipated" He looked quickly along the bench height above him, scanning the faces for those who were familiar with Bastion's great powers, and who were betrayed by their expressions.

"Ridiculous! That entity is no greater than you. Surely, your powers are more than a match for his?" The chairman was almost yelling down at the wizard as he eyeballed him. The redness of his face showed how intense his emotions were concerning the man before him. There was a definite history between the two wizards, and it ran deep, if one was to make a guess.

"Hear! Hear!" Another of the council members shouted from further down the bench. He was a small man of maybe 35 to 40 years old with most of the hair missing from the front of his head making him look like a weasel. Shaulmar gave him a perceptive stare and the man promptly disappeared behind a white folder.

"You may be correct in what you say, Mr. Chairman." Shaulmar eyeballed him right back. Shaulmar knew the time was fast approaching for another major war between the darkness and the forces of light. It was part of the evolutionary process and was necessary in order for harmony to exist between the two sides. "However, there are new developments that you cannot possibly be aware of." He waited for the predictable response from the chairman.

"If there are any new developments, the Sacred High Council should have been informed before all the travelers were, don't you think?" The chairman cast an accusatory glance at the young assistant who was hiding his face in the piles of files on the desk where he was working beside where Shaulmar was standing. "Now traveler! Stop stalling and let the high Council know what you know, if it is that important." The chairman used a tone that hinted somewhat of dismissal. Shaulmar didn't quite know what to say, exactly, but he was sure he was running out of time.

"Draco Bastian is on the earth plane and is determined to capture the soul, Rebecca Sullivan, and I am afraid that he may succeed. He wields an immense power that is formidable, indeed!" Shaulmar was emphatic. He decided that it was pointless to give the moron sitting at the center of the council bench the respect the title of chairman should command. He reached into the small pocket inside his cloak. He looked up at the council while holding an amethyst crystal in the palm of his hand so that all could see. Shaulmar looked straight at the chairman. The Amethyst he held was a deep purple color and it shimmered gently in his hand.

"This memory crystal has recorded the encounter I had with the Dark Angel." The purple crystal shimmered in the center of his palm. Shaulmar handed it to the council assistant.

"This dark entity, Draco Bastian, is a powerful threat, much more powerful than this council is aware." His voice almost begged them to listen to what he was trying to tell them.

"This is now a matter for the council to attend to wizard," the chairman spoke with such disdain for him.

"I have more for you to ponder." Shaulmar had pretty much decided to severe all ties with the Sacred High Council at this point. "Bastion's power is joined with the power summoned by the Ring of Dread." He was certain his words would cause uproar amongst the council benches, but he didn't care. All he wanted was to protect his family on earth at this point.

"Wizard, you're trying the patience of this High Council. It is well documented that the ring of which you speak was destroyed centuries ago." The chairman had what he needed to finally retire the traveler for good. "This Council will retire to consider the issues brought before it. We will present our findings to the audience within a few days." All in one movement, the chairman stood up and slammed his gavel on the bench—his ceremonial gowns of indigo and green flowed out all around him with the momentum. He made it very clear that it was his intention to conclude the meeting.

"Stop!" Shaulmar threw a hand in the air, ferociously. It seemed for a fraction of a second that time stood still—an eerie silence filled the chamber halls. Until, suddenly, the chairman slammed his gavel down on the bench, once more, splintering it into thousand pieces.

"Wizard! You have just sealed your own fate. There have to be leaders even within the Sacred Order of Light. Order must prevail. Your childish insistence will not be tolerated. It is highly disrespectful and disregards everything we stand for. It also sets a bad example for others to witness. The chairman whispered into the ears of the council members seated on either side of him, then he spoke. "Shaulmarhime of the Ancients, you are suspended as a member of the Sacred Order of Light and as a practicing wizard of light. You will not practice the secrets of the arts until a review board of your peers has conducted a full investigation and can determine what your punishment will be." The chairman took great pleasure in delivering the order, effectively putting Shaulmar on suspension. The great wizard did nothing but look straight back at them. He glanced briefly at each one seated on the high bench in front of him.

"I will save this council the trouble." He walked slowly towards the center of the bench directly below the chairman who occupied the most coveted position in the Sacred High Council. "I, Shaulmarhime of the Ancients, offer all of you my heartfelt thanks and good wishes. I leave this institution regretting only one thing, that I have failed myself as a wizard of the light and a compassionate being in service to the universe. I return to planet Earth to do what I can, and what I must, to save my friends. Consider this my termination of this Sacred Order of Light." Shaulmar turned around slowly, and wrapping the auld beige-hooded-robe around him, he walked away from the eyes of the council. As the wizard reached the wooden doors of the Grand Hall a voice reverberated off every wall and pillar.

"Stop!" Shaulmar did so, and his first thought was, that the members of the High Council had come to their senses. The wizard turned back around…slowly and deliberately.

"What is it that compels you to prevent me from leaving?" Shaulmar was preparing to be welcomed back into the fold. The chairman stood up.

"You! …Shaulmarhime of the Ancients have made your choice but you will not leave this room until you have returned that which was pledged to you by this council when you were one of us." The chairman waited purposefully. He wanted his words to burrow into the mind of the wizard until the meaning slammed deep into his awareness like a meteorite plummeting to Earth. Shaulmar eventually made the connection. He was unable to prevent the awareness from becoming evident in the expression that flooded across his face and eyes.

"You cannot be serious! You mean to deny me the protection of the Archangel Ring?" He looked down at the beautifully crafted talisman on his finger. A faint glow emanated from within the stone. Its power was evident as he touched and caressed its smoothness. He was desperately trying to think of a way out, a way to keep the ring. He needed the ring so desperately if he was, in any way, to save Rebecca and the rest of his family.

"Please, do not embarrass yourself further. Show some dignity and respect for the order that has allowed you to serve its highest directives over the centuries." The chairman was enjoying every morsel of pain Shaulmar was being subjected to, even if some of the other council members were visibly uncomfortable—however, they had neither the power nor stomach to intervene. After a brief moment, Shaulmar lifted his head and walked the 50 meters back to the figure standing at the pinnacle of the bench. He gathered momentum along the way—his energy was increasing with every step.

"Here is your precious ring, chairman Tachov." Shaulmar flipped it up to him and watched as the feeble attempts of the man reaching out to snag the ring failed. He was forced to grovel on the floor behind the bench between the feet of other members of the council as he desperately tried to retrieve the ring.

"Do not attempt to come back to this council sniveling for your reinstatement wizard." He began to wipe the ring clean as he yelled down from the bench and across the Great Hall after the wizard. "You are not welcome here." The chairman held the ring up to the light to make sure it wasn't damaged. He even had the audacity to slip it onto his own finger when no one was looking. It felt good, he thought.

"You will be seeing me again, Tachov." Shaulmar walked away with a powerful confidence. His cloak rippled in the wake of the wind generated by his power and movement. He reached the great doors of the hall pushing them apart effortlessly and disappeared around the hallway. It was but a short distance to the portal entrance that was located one floor below. Shaulmar had calmed down enough to realize the depths of his situation. Shaulmar had gone to the Sacred High Council for help and had inexplicably returned with no help and no Archangel Ring to protect his friends from the forces of darkness that were so intent upon their destruction. At this point, he lowered his head into his hands. For the first time in his long career as a traveller, he began to doubt the teachings that governed the highest good of all beings. Shaulmar desperately needed to reconnect with his trust and faith—was the destiny of earth as a vehicle for souls to evolve to the higher planes of existence still in place? He wondered how the situation he found himself in could possibly be for the highest good of all.

Shaulmar suddenly snapped out of the fear and anger he was feeling. He hurried down the hallway of the large marble building and made his way to the portal entrance as if his life depended on it. Back in the Great Hall, the bewildered members of the sacred council whispered amongst themselves about the dismissal of

Shaulmar of the Ancients from the Sacred Order. However, the chairman maintained his stance.

"I believe the Bedouin will cause unnecessary friction between the forces of darkness and our own desires for harmony." It was obvious for those with eyes to see that the chairman was only interested in retaining his position of power within the forces of the universe, no matter the cost. "We must detain him and prevent him from returning to the Earth. Ancient and beloved members of this council interpreted the prophecy regarding the girl and I believe they interpreted it correctly. It clearly states that the soul in question must not be helped in the quest for her evolution. This means that the Bedouin must not reach that portal." He waved his arms and a couple of monks dressed in war apparel appeared before him. "You two are charged with preventing Shaulmarhime of the Ancients from assisting the soul, Rebecca Sullivan. Now, go and retrieve him and bring him back here at once." The monks left quickly. The first challenge was to prevent Shaulmar from activating the portal in the basement of the sacred building.

When Shaulmar reached the basement, the custodian of the gateway greeted him, and as always, Shaulmar stopped to return the greeting. He never refused to have a conversation with another. It was not the way of the Bedouin culture.

"Good evening, my friend." Shaulmar bowed low and brought his hands together. He touched his heart, his lips, and his forehead with his left hand while motioning with his right hand as if paving the way to peace and prosperity.

"You are to travel once more then, Master Wizard." The custodian had watched Shaulmar come and go on many occasions and he held the utmost respect for him. He knew Shaulmar fought for the time when peace would reign within all domains of the universe.

"Yes, I am to return to Earth to stop the forces of darkness from claiming another soul in their desire to upset the balance of souls in the universe." Shaulmar rarely informed others of his plans and he was at a loss as to why he spoke so freely with the custodial of the gateway now. The old man smiled and grunted as he raised himself off the seat of wood.

"Do not worry, Shaulmar. The forces of evil do not have power over a heart that beats as strong as yours does." Shaulmar had not noticed how strong and vibrant the custodian appeared for his age.

"Thank you my friend," he said

"Please proceed to the gateway. It is ready for you to begin the activation process." The custodian spoke while walking back toward the hallways where Shaulmar had just come from. Shaulmar was disturbed, somewhat, at the actions of the old man.

"Do you not want to witness the portal opening and sealing after I have gone? That is the protocol of the Sacred Order, is it not?"

"Do not be concerned Master Wizard. The universe knows you, and if you do not already understand, the universe watches over you and your kind." He turned his head as he walked towards the grand staircase of the first floor. "Please, activate the portal as soon as you can. I may not be at liberty to stall the monks that are sent to stop you for very long." He disappeared up the stairway and only his voice could be heard. Shaulmar understood immediately what had happened. The chairman of the Sacred High Council could only have sent the monks. No one else had authority to do so. As he began the activation sequence, Shaulmar started to put things together in his mind concerning the actions of the Council. On various occasions in the past, such actions seemed to him quite inappropriate at the time but were not challenged or questioned by anyone. The vortex of light that surged through the center of the building throbbed as Shaulmar approached it. He knelt before the crystal doorway that stood between him and the entrance to the gateway. The great wizard raised his left arm with the palm of his hand facing up and stretched towards the heavens. His right hand was poised in front of him at right angles to his wrist, with his palm facing out, as if he were pushing on something. Shaulmar suddenly grimaced in pain because of something terribly wrong with the activation sequencing.

"Lord of Light…Power of the Universe…assist me in my desire to unlock the portal gateway." He was caught within the energy of the gateway vortex and the magic of the activation incantation that authorized him on many occasions to move through the portals of the universe, unhindered. The pain in his body increased, and he knew at some point that he would be torn to pieces, if he weren't helped soon. There was definitely something that was interfering with his progress through the portal gateway. Throughout the ordeal, many thoughts entered Shaulmar's mind, just like an explosion forces shards of steel through everything in its path without conscience or reason. He realized how strongly he and Morghanz felt for one another and he regretted lost opportunities where they could have expressed and shared their love.

The intensity of the pain was doubled now and Shaulmar began to succumb to the powerful energy that the vortex emitted. He was beginning to lose consciousness. When Shaulmar was a child, he remembered climbing the rocks to the tribal encampment in his homeland where he had grown up. He could feel the sharp jagged points of rocks under his feet as he grasped them to help keep his balance while he scaled the small outcroppings. It felt so real. It felt like he was really there but he knew he must be reliving the experience from memory because he knew he was only nine at the time. A light appeared within his mind. The illumination came from within him, and simultaneously, from outside of himself. Shaulmar fully understood now that everything in existence in the universe was connected, energetically, to everything else. Pain could be felt between all beings throughout the universe. He didn't want to leave his friends. He, especially, didn't want Rebecca to become a prisoner of the Dark Angel as her mother had before her. Everything he wanted to know about the universe was accessible to his mind at this point. Shaulmar truly understood that knowledge was energy, vibration, and it was connected to everything that existed. He felt humbled by the power and the simplicity that he came to understand as the Love of the Creator for all things in existence. Shaulmar made a decision—the thought was created by his soul—that he would remain in this incarnation to fight for his friends. He visualized all the people, places, and things that he loved. All wizards who worked with the power of light knew this method of regaining the life force. Gradually, his life force began to return to him. The power of the vortex holding him was his means of escape. As an apprentice, Shaulmar was taught that if the power of any vortex were embraced, then through energy recognition, the power would flow through his energy body and become aware of the life force that was his. When such recognition was initiated, then the soul signature of Shaulmar would be identified and the destiny of his soul would be determined. Only then would Shaulmar be released or destroyed in accordance with the knowledge acquired by the energy vortex through the records of eternity.

The great wizard relaxed under the power and strength of the light as he released any thoughts of fighting against the vortex from within his mind. Any force he could muster, even as a Master Wizard of the Sacred Arts would not be enough to affect the stream of light that coursed through the fortress that enclosed the Great Hall of the Sacred Order of Light. He focused his mind and visualized himself moving through the gateway without any ill effects coming to him. When the vortex had retrieved the record of Shaulmar's soul signature, the wizard was ushered through the portal where he landed back in the old bookstore on earth. He fell to his knees as he entered the room at the back of the store and inhaled the air to fill his lungs as if he had just taken his first breath. As his back heaved up and down, and his hands rested on his legs, Shaulmar's thoughts came rushing back into his head. He must get to the house as quickly as possible. With what he had just experienced in the sacred halls himself, he knew his friends must be in desperate trouble. He pulled himself up into his leather armchair and closed his eyes for a few moments. He wanted to make damn sure that he was clear-headed before he set off for the house. He had always called upon the power of the light within the universe whenever he needed to bring his thoughts, emotions, and strengths into alignment. He removed a crystal from the pouch that hung on his belt. He held the crystal in his left hand, while he turned with his right palm facing up, and laid it on the arm of the chair. He could immediately feel the energy pulse through the crystal and into the wheel of light at the center of his palm. He sensed the presence of the Archangels. They are masters themselves and are always aware of the struggles that those of the light must experience when they are courageous enough to incarnate into the physical realms such as those on Earth. His strength had returned and his head had cleared enough so he could consider returning to his house where his friends were probably waiting for his help. He was still a little shaken, though. He'd never before experienced the full force of the vortex of light, that allowed travellers to move through the universe, as it held him in stasis for the whole time he was immobilized and vulnerable to its power. He had travelled through the vortex gateway many times before. He could only assume, this last time, there had been a deliberate sabotage attempt designed to prevent him moving through the portal.

Once Shaulmar had regained enough strength and composure, he pulled on his cloak and his wizard's belt. On the belt was his pouch that contained crystals, potions, and amulets that were programmed to respond to the energy of the wizard as well as the energy of the universe. Shaulmar remained still. He was sitting motionless on the armchair that faced the center of the room where the vortex of light passed through into the earth and up and out into the universe. A great sadness spilled over him as he pondered strategies to help prevent the Dark Angel from taking Rebecca as he had done previously with her mother. Shaulmar was considered one of the most powerful and knowledgeable wizards in existence. That was the reason the Sacred High Council trusted him with all the most difficult assignments, typically soul-protection and neutralization of dark forces when necessary. As the great wizard sat with his head in his hands, he thought he should just go to the house and do what he could to help his friends. Shaulmar desperately wanted to prevent the dark forces from capturing Rebecca, but he realized it was going to be a futile attempt, at best, considering he no longer had the protection of the Sacred High Council nor the power of the Archangel Ring to protect them. All he knew in his heart was that he had to try to do something. He could not sit by and allow his friends to be taken. Suddenly, a light went on inside his head. It occurred to Shaulmar that Draco Bastian and any others who embraced the forces of evil always avoided any kind of ceremonial or sacred grounds.

"Of course! That's it!" He jumped out of the chair and rushed over to the pile of books on ancient magic and lore that were handed down through the ages by wizards and other members of the Sacred Order of Light. Shaulmar ran his hands and fingers along the rows of books desperately seeking one in particular. "Aha!" He grabbed hold of the red hardcover book. On the book's cover near the top was a green circle inside of a yellow triangle—underneath the symbol was a silver and gold spiral that was braided in such a way that it looked like the tale of a comet. "This will do nicely," he whispered, as he made his way back to the space in front of the vortex of light. His confidence was increasing by the moment. Shaulmar slipped through the first few pages with a scowl on his face, indicating that he may have selected the wrong book after all. Then, as quickly as it appeared, the scowl changed to the most satisfying of smiles. "There it is," he said quietly. "You are going to help my friends avoid the most painful of experiences and I wish to thank you now, dear book, and all of the ancient ones who carried you forward into this moment. Shaulmar kissed the pages, as if they were the most beautiful women in the world. He put the book on the altar and stood back from it a couple of feet. A humming sound that was created around the book was coming up from the vortex—it was aligned with the raw power that continually surged through the Earth and up and out into the universe. The great wizard had to be sure of his spell. The power was too great for him to be wrong. It was too unstable for a do-over. It had to be exactly right the first time or it was over for good. He closed his eyes and thought only of peace, and of the love he held for all beings of the Earth. After a few moments, he lifted his arms from his sides and held them upwards in front of his body. Still with his eyes closed, he drew in a large breath, held it for a few seconds, and allowed it to fill his lungs, completely.

The exhaled breath was released with some force, so as Shaulmar followed his breath, his energy centers became charged. This energy gave him the impetus he needed to deliver the spell. The incantation would allow him time to get to the house, at the very least, before the forces of darkness took his friends. This type of spell was one of the most difficult and hardest to control and direct. When Shaulmar felt there was enough energy and charge available to him, he threw his arms up to the heavens, arched his head back, and with eyes still closed, he recanted the sacred spell.

"To all who will see, to all who will know, the power of the Creator and the Vortex of Light will flow. Through darkness and pain, through desire and expectation, a love of all beings will continue to grow." He turned and faced the opposite direction, and put his left hand to his forehead and his right hand to his heart. "I ask for the magic of all that has gone before me, come to me now and assist in this greatest of needs. When heaven calls down the names of my friends, they shall hear the call from inside the cathedral." Shaulmar reached into the pillar of light that was the vortex that held him, as he put his full trust and faith in the magic he knew came from the universe. The energy shimmered and moved like a wave on a vast ocean. Shaulmar felt more power than he had ever felt in his whole life as a sorcerer of the light. The pillar of pure white universal light engulfed him up to his shoulders and he pulled his face back for fear of harm from it. He felt as if the vortex was pulling him further into the column of light. There was a panic that swept over him, and he was about to tighten his body in anticipation of danger, when he felt the grip loosen, and he was allowed to remove his arms at last. "Thank you, Creator, I ask that you guide my steps to the ones who need my services this day." Shaulmar was finished. Now, he must get to the house as fast as he could to begin the battle that he knew he must fight with the Dark Angel. He knew that he must always be prepared to embrace his destiny wherever and whenever that might be.

CHAPTER 19

REBECCA DIDN'T KNOW WHAT TO DO AS SHE STOOD nervously outside of Morghanz's bedroom door. Something had disturbed her sleep—it was a feeling, a sense that something wasn't right. She stood with her hand raised to knock on the door but then she reneged at the last minute. She began to pace up and down the hallway, not knowing whether she should disturb her friend or not.

"Stop being such a wuss!" she said out loud. "What could she do but make us eat more homemade date loaf." It was then that she summoned the courage to knock on the door. There was no response. This was a sure sign that something was not right. Morghanz always answered the door, no matter what, even if it was only to explain that she was sleeping. "Morghanz, are you awake?" There was still no answer. Rebecca put an ear to the door. There was a slight murmur coming from beyond the door. It was time to cross the line and enter the room. She could not believe what she was seeing as she entered the room. Morghanz was fully clothed and sprawled across the bed as if she had fallen on it in a drunken state the night before. She looked like she was still passed out only…Rebecca had never seen Morghanz drunk before and she didn't believe she was drunk now. Rebecca began to cry as she rushed to the side of Morghanz's bed. "What is happening, Morghanz? Are you okay?" she sobbed. There was nothing—no movement, no speech, no lucidity of any kind—no signs of life. Rebecca feared the worst as she knelt down beside her friend. Rebecca rested her head on her friend's arm. She didn't know what to do. All she could do was cry as she reached across Morghanz's chest to hold her. As she held Morghanz, Rebecca's tears fell on her hand. She could feel them—they were cold. Rebecca realized her hand was close enough to her friend's airway, that her faint breath ran across the tears, making them seem cold on her hand. She looked up and wiped her face, and moved her cheek close to Morghanz's mouth and nose. "Oh

God, you're not dead. Morghanz, can you hear me? What is wrong? Tell me what to do." She was panicking at this point. The figure on the bed still did not move. Her skin was grey and she had black veins protruding all over her face. "I have to get you out of here." Rebecca continued to speak so that she could gather enough courage to take charge of the situation. Morghanz was too heavy to lift. She tried to get behind her friend and slip her arms under her shoulders to pull her up from the bed. It was no use. Rebecca began to cry out in desperation. She was alone with her friend and felt helpless to do anything. "Joaquim! Joaquim! Help us!" She rested her head on her friend's shoulder, as she lay on the bed, motionless. The dark veins had spread to her neck. They were the color of blackstrap molasses. "Wake up, Morghanz, wake up! Joaquim!" Rebecca yelled at the top of her lungs. The door to Rebecca's room burst open. "In here! We're in here—in Morghanz's room," Rebecca screamed. The door burst open and there stood the young boy—his hair in his face and everything else. He could only open one eye and had difficulty focusing that one on the images before him.

"What...what's wrong? Why are you all yelling?"

"Joaquim, Morghanz is sick. I think she is dying. I cannot wake her and she is too heavy for me to lift off the bed." Rebecca was still sobbing, which made the young boy swallow with difficulty, because of the huge lump in his throat. He could feel tears wanting to fill his eyes. His heart began to race like a herd of mustangs running across the plains of New Mexico. He was rooted to the floor. He couldn't believe what his eyes were trying to tell him. His good friend was dying. She had black streaks across her face, neck and hands, and her skin was now as white as snow. "Joaquim, you have to help me get her up off the bed and downstairs to the study." Rebecca pulled herself together enough to snap him out of his fixed stare.

"Err...oh...okay Sis." He jumped back into the present. "I can carry her top half if you can get her legs." Joaquim was strong. He had been since he was forced to live on the streets where he had to climb over walls and fences on a daily basis.

"Okay," Rebecca said, relieved. The two of them struggled to carry Morghanz from her bed, out into the hall, and down to the study. They put her on the big leather couch near the open window for light and air. They thought it might help to wake her.

"What happened to her?" Joaquim touched her face to see if the black things moved.

"I don't know. I found her like this when I went to speak with her just 10 minutes ago. Morghanz was all right last night—I was talking with her before she went to her room." Rebecca stood over her friend, and looked down at her, feeling totally helpless.

"Where is Shaulmar? I have no idea what we should do here. Do you, Sis?" Joaquim looked on, happily passing responsibility on to Rebecca. After all, she was the eldest, ergo, the one in charge, he thought to himself.

"I don't know," she said shakily. "One thing is for sure. Morghanz is not going to survive if we do nothing." Rebecca wiped her eyes and took a deep breath, as if trying to summon some internal strength to inspire a solution to the dilemma. The two of them made Morghanz comfortable on the couch, as comfortable as possible under the circumstances. Joaquim placed his hand on her forehead. He was very curious, in a morbid 13-year-old kind of way, about the black veins that protruded from all over her face.

"I wonder what could have caused this?" he said out loud, not realizing it. Rebecca turned to him with a look of annoyance on her face.

"How would I know? If I knew, then I would do something to help, wouldn't I?" The words became louder and more irritated the longer she spoke. "Why don't you do something useful for a change? Go and find Shaulmar. He is probably the only one who can help, if you think you can handle something that important." Joaquim was astonished at the words that were coming out of his friend's mouth.

"Why are you 'pissed' at me? I didn't do this to her."

"Well, you're not exactly helping are you?" Rebecca was really mad and she didn't know why, but she did know that Joaquim did not deserve to be yelled at. "What is wrong with me?" she put her hand to her head, as she winced with pain, then it happened. The blinding headaches and flashing intense bright lights and the feeling that she was losing consciousness had returned to haunt her again. "Joaquim," Rebecca sat on the end of couch at Morghanz's feet, "I'm having the pain and those flashing lights again." She closed her eyes lightly again as if waiting to absorb the impact of another head pain or flash of light.

"What should I do? Shall I get you some water or juice?" Joaquim had no idea of how to deal with things like this. The only thing he really knew was how to survive on the streets, stealing food, or stealing money, or stealing things to sell for money to buy food. "Where is Shaulmar?" Joaquim felt panic rising up from his legs. "He would know what to do."

At this point, Morghanz began to moan slightly. She was becoming conscious again, but as she moved, the dark veins all across her face seemed to move in unison with her. The black invaders had covered about 90 percent of her neck by now, and whatever black substance was inside the veins was also moving. Rebecca was afraid for her friend but she was also concerned about her own problems. The pain in her head was getting worse, and the lights were getting brighter and were the worst she had experienced yet.

"Joaquim, would you make some tea, that kind that Morghanz usually makes us before we go to bed, please?" she tried to sound as together as possible so as not to alarm him too much.

"You mean that smelly stuff? The stuff that was supposed to help relax us so we could sleep better?"

"Yes, that's it," she said, trying not to get mad again. "Maybe it will help alleviate the pain that she is in." Joaquim disappeared in a flash and was thankful that he could help, that he could be of use in this time of stress, but also thankful that he didn't have to look at his friend dying in front of him. When he left the room, Rebecca slumped on the chair—she was holding her head in her hands and groaning slightly—the pain and flashes of light behind the eyes were intensifying to the point were she was sure she was going to pass out. She heard Morghanz moving—it seemed to her that her friend was in excruciating pain. Rebecca was really scared that Morghanz might be dying. There was nothing the young girl could do—her own pain had continued to increase and she felt like her head was going to explode. She reached over to her friend with one hand, while using the other to keep her own head steady—any slight movements seem to make the pain worse. The tears were streaming down Rebecca's face as she leaned toward her friend.

"Morghanz can you hear me. I don't know what to do to help you, I'm sorry, I just don't know. Please don't die. Tell me what to do!" Rebecca was sobbing while she laid her head in her friend's lap. Morghanz was semi-conscious—the intense pain, coupled with the trauma of the poison that was cursing through her veins and making its way slowly to her heart, prevented her from hugging her friend and consoling her.

"Rebecca," she spoke in a whisper, gasping for air to fill her lungs so she could say the words that were forming in her mind. "I know I am dying…the entity has poisoned me…there is no hope for me…." She drew in an enormous breath. She'd lost consciousness. She was surviving only because of her autonomic nervous system at that point.

"Oh God, no!" Rebecca hissed. She knelt down beside the couch and clutched at Morghanz wrist, feeling for a pulse.

"I can't find the tea, Sis. I can't find the stuff she puts in the teapot." Joaquim looked around the room and caught a glimpse of Rebecca with her head on Morghanz's chest. He held his breath, waiting to hear her say their friend was gone. Morghanz's arm was hanging beside the couch and Joaquim could see that the black poisonous veins had spread past her elbows and halfway to her wrists. "Oh shit!" he said. "Rebecca, look!" He pointed to Morghanz's arms. "That stuff is moving down her arms—what do we do?" Joaquim was scared now, and he didn't care who knew it. He shook as he waited for Rebecca to answer, but all she could do, was begin to sob again.

"I don't know…I wish Shaulmar was here," she said in a voice of desperation and hopelessness. Rebecca was giving up and she knew it. The pain in her head and the searing blinding light were just too much to bear. "I can't help Morghanz! I can't help us Joaquim. You don't know the pain I am in—it's the worst it's ever been." She squinted up at him. "I'm sorry, Joaquim." At that precise moment, Rebecca lost consciousness. Joaquim quickly went to her side and lifted her up onto the leather armchair.

"It's okay, Sis. I will take care of you." Those were the only words he could think of to say, but they fell on deaf ears, because Rebecca was no longer conscious. "Why is this happening?" he said out loud, as if somebody were there to hear him. "All my life it's been this way," he said, as he tried to comfort his friends. He pulled a blanket from the cupboard and covered Rebecca with it, then he looked over at the couch where Morghanz lay, dying. "I wish I knew what to do? What would Shaulmar do?" The young boy began to think. Shaulmar would conjure a spell or something, he thought. "It wouldn't do any harm," he said out loud. He walked into the center of the room, and raised his arms to the ceiling, whilst looking at both of them. "Wait!" he whispered to himself, quickly, as he ran to the hallway. Then, after a few moments and a lot of noise, he returned wearing one of Shaulmar's beige hooded-cloaks and leather pouch tied around his waist that pulled the garment closed. "This should do it." Once again he stood in the middle of the room between his friends and began the ritual. "Oh God...Universe...Creator of all that is..." As he spoke the words, he tried to recall anything he'd heard Shaulmar say when he was in the old bookstore hiding behind the shelves. "Let the power of the light be with me at this time to help my friends not be sick." He thought that last part was pretty lame, so he was about to begin again—he held his arms high above his head, letting the sleeves of the cloak fall down to his boyish elbows.

"And what exactly do you hope to accomplish with all that mumbo-jumbo, little one?" The voice came out of nowhere. Joaquim turned to where it came from, tripping on the bottom of the robe as he did so. He fell to the floor with the hood of the cloak covering both his head and face.

"Who's there?" he said, pushing the hood off his face. There was no answer. Joaquim hurriedly scrambled to his feet, trying to look respectable. He pushed the hood from his face and frantically looked around the room. He saw no one, except his unconscious friends. "I must be going insane—out of my mind," he uttered. He crept lightly to the doorway and looked down the hallway in case it was those Dark Ones that were after Rebecca.

"Do not worry—you and I are the only ones here." There was the voice again, deep and manly, but at the same time, gentle and kind of peaceful. Joaquim turned quickly and saw Rebecca was standing over Morghanz. She was whispering something he just could not make out. Her hands were placed together as if she was praying.

"Rebecca, so glad you're okay. I thought you were a goner there for a minute." The young lad shuffled closer to her, almost tripping over the hem of Shaulmar's cloak again.

"Please, if you wouldn't mind removing the wizard's cloak before you cause yourself an injury." The voice said, coming forth from his friend. Joaquim froze in his tracks.

"You're…you're not Rebecca! How can that be? What have you done to her?" Joaquim struggled to understand what had occurred.

"My host, the one chosen, who was named in the sacred prophecy of the ancients, the one you know as Rebecca Sullivan is the channel for my essence. This is what is speaking with you at this time. The physical body of Rebecca Sullivan moved very differently than what Joaquim was used to seeing. Usually, Rebecca glided effortlessly around any room she was in, barely touching the ground. "We must hurry if we are to avoid the imminent danger that is almost upon us. First, we must once more perform the ceremony that enabled the binding of the soul with my essence." The voice coming from Rebecca sounded as calm and peaceful as any voice Joaquim had ever heard before. Under the circumstances, there should have been some anxiety or nervousness or something like that he should be feeling, but he wasn't, he thought.

"Shaulmar did the ceremony. I have no idea of how to perform any kind of ceremony," Joaquim said, while removing the wizard's cloak. He felt kind of stupid talking to Rebecca and hearing a man's voice coming from her mouth. He kept an eye on Morghanz periodically as the events unfolded—he was sure she was going to die at some point. "What about Morghanz, Rebecca?" He looked at her and waited.

"I am the Essence. The one you refer to as Rebecca is only here, physically." Rebecca's body moved to the other end of the room beyond the couch that held Morghanz. "We must move, quickly. No more questions please. Do exactly as I say and we will survive the danger." The Essence seemed to know, somehow, that if they did what was asked of them the danger it spoke of would not succeed in doing whatever it was intending to do to them, the boy thought.

"Okay, what do you want me to do?" Joaquim stood ready, expecting to face the worst.

"Joaquim, you must help me to place the poisoned one on the table in the center of the room. That small long table will suffice." The Essence used Rebecca's body to indicate to Joaquim to bring the rectangular coffee table to the center of the room. When the table was in place, correctly, the Essence spoke again. "Now, you must help me to place the poisoned one exactly in the right position on the table, so that I may conduct the healing ceremony successfully." Rebecca stood at the foot of the couch and beckoned to Joaquim to take a position at Morghanz's head. "Lift her at the shoulders so as not to hasten the demise of the one you call, Morghanz. The Essence directed the operation with speed, accuracy, and determination. Joaquim could not keep his eyes off Rebecca as they conducted the proceedings together. He had never seen anything like this…ever. Although, once he had insisted to his friends on the street, that he had witnessed the abduction of an old street-person, by aliens. However, this was way cooler because he was actually talking to a book that was speaking to him through his friend, Rebecca.

"There is one more thing to do before I begin the binding ceremony…" Rebecca finished placing the candles beside Morghanz and then she—or it—lit the incense in the abalone shell, "I need the Book of Secrets in order for the ancient legend to draw strength and power from the vortex of light energy that pulses through the heart of this place." Joaquim stood silent for a few moments with his mouth wide open. The book was given to Shaulmar after the last ceremony and he didn't know what he'd done with it. "The Book of Secrets is the key to our survival, young warrior, we must have it in the ceremony." The essence that channeled through Rebecca slowly moved towards Joaquim. "Please try to remember where the wizard might have placed the ancient book?" Joaquim felt good at being called a young warrior even though the words were coming from Rebecca's mouth—the fact that it was the Essence telling him this wasn't so bad. Joaquim scratched his head and spun around trying to replay the event in his own mind. I remember seeing the wizard...he took the book from Rebecca and put it in his study! Joaquim yelled, as he ran down the hallway to Shaulmar's private room. It wasn't long before the young warrior returned, very excitedly, holding the indigo cloth-covered book in his hands.

"I knew I could find it!" He handed the book to Rebecca. "They don't call me the next Sherlock Holmes for nothing, you know!" He was beaming as he watched Rebecca remove the book from beneath the cloth and place it on Morghanz's abdomen, at her solar plexus chakra. As they prepared the necessary items for the ceremony, the black poison spreading through the veins of Morghanz's body began to push forward to her stomach, as if it was aware of the book's presence. As the ancient blue-leather manuscript rested on Morghanz's stomach, black fingers of poison came out from her naval and wrapped themselves around the book—there were two, then six, and before it could be realized, only the sacred symbol on the cover could be seen.

"Joaquim, we must perform the ceremony at once," the Essence shouted from across the room. "Place this crystal at her feet." Rebecca tossed the rose quartz crystal across Morghanz's body. Joaquim reached up and snagged the crystal one-handed and placed it carefully at her feet.

"What the hell are these things?" He was looking at the black puss oozing from the fingers that were wrapped around the book.

"Don't worry about them. The book is in no danger—trust me. However, if we don't help your friend soon, it may be too late." The Essence moved Rebecca's body towards the head of her friend, Morghanz, as she was laid out on the table.

"Light of the Universe, allow us to assist the soul of this one known as Morghanz. We are beings in service to all who are in need. We are all one from the source of all that is." Rebecca held her arms outstretched over the body on the table. Her eyes remained closed, and in one swift movement, her arms were raised high into the air, and she looked like a kind of vessel. At that very moment, Rebecca began to glow, and soft white-light energy filled and surrounded her body. Joaquim just stood still and starred in awe at the sight of his friend's light. It was obvious, there was a connection being made between Rebecca, the Essence, and the natural vortex of light that ran through Shaulmar's house. While the light had encompassed Rebecca, completely, Joaquim glanced at the book—he saw the dark poisonous energy was increasing rapidly. Worry entered his mind and fear was quick to follow. He looked up at Rebecca, and saw that she'd begun to shimmer gently, like the haze rising up from a hot blacktopped road in the summer. The next thing he knew, Rebecca was talking to him…but it was funny because he knew he wasn't hearing her voice…her thoughts were somehow inside his head. She told him not to be concerned at all, and that she was safe. She also told him that whatever happened he must remain calm.

"Okay Sis," he said instinctively, out loud. Almost immediately, Joaquim saw what she was talking about—the book started to glow, lighter and lighter. It began slowly at first, changing from the beautiful midnight blue to a lighter blue, as its vibration quickened. The poisonous entity within Morghanz's body didn't seem to do anything—it just continued to expand and feed off her energy. Joaquim stood at her feet—he was at the point of wanting to do something to help her—anything. He thought of grabbing for the book, and the tentacles wrapped around it, and dragging it from the house where he could beat the black poison to death. He knew where the huge machete was that Shaulmar kept at the end of the garden and he was prepared to use it. The impulse reached a critical mass—that was the point when he heard Rebecca again in his mind, telling him to remain calm, and that all was 'as it was supposed to be.' She insisted that he trust her and have faith in the protection of the vortex of light. In the very next moment, unbeknownst to him, Joaquim was going to witness the most amazing thing he had ever seen. He returned to the foot of the table and assumed his position.

"Sorry Sis, I lost my head there for a moment. I promise I won't do *that* again." There were no more thoughts sent into his mind from Rebecca. The book had quickened by this time and was vibrating so fast that the poison tentacles could no longer hold onto it—they began to lose their grip. Then, one after the other, as the book quickened, even more of the black fingers just began snapping into pieces. The book was now surging with power that was being fed into it by the universal vortex of light. Then, in an instant, the book broke apart into billions of points of light that swirled around the body of Morghanz, as if the book were free to be what it was truly meant to be.

The points of light had life and began to connect with the main body of light-molecules gravitating to the position directly above the heart chakra of Morghanz. The remainder were still quickening into what seemed like a random pattern close by, as if waiting for the main body to establish its form. Joaquim was having a hard time absorbing what was happening but he had always been blessed with the ability to have an open mind, and more importantly, an open heart. Rebecca was still standing with her eyes closed and with her arms outstretched high above her head—she was accepting the energy from the earth and the universe, undisturbed by the transformation of the Book of Secrets. Suddenly, as if by some unseen command, the remainder of the energy swirling around the column of light above Morghanz's heart chakra swiftly took its position. Like the wings of a great golden phoenix, the energy settled a third of the way down. It was an amazing sight to behold—the manifestation of the apparition from blue leather book to the flight of some mystical bird—that left Joaquim stunned. The manifested object vibrated so fast that it seemed to emit sound, like a musical beauty, that made his heart beat faster. Before Joaquim could do or say anything, there was an enormous flash of brilliant blue-white light, the kind that occurs during the largest and most ferocious of lightning storms. He saw the apparition speed toward Rebecca as if on a collision course. The next thing he knew, they were all in what looked like the cavern described by Shaulmar and Rebecca.

"What happened? Where are we?" Rebecca was back but unaware of the events that had brought her back to the cavern beneath the house.

"What do you mean, Sis? Don't you remember the flashes of light, the poisonous veins, or the book exploding into light?" Joaquim couldn't believe she didn't remember anything as cool as what just occurred. "You were talking to me in my mind and we had another ceremony and everything!" He began to get overexcited as he recounted the events that had played out in the room above them.

"Wha…what? Do you mean it happened again? The book spoke through me again? Where is Shaulmar? We need to do something to help Morghanz." Rebecca walked around the table were Morghanz was lying and bent down to see if she was still breathing.

"Wow! Sis, your neck! How did that happen?" Joaquim put his hand on Rebecca's neck as she bent forward to inspect Morghanz.

"Ouch! What did you do?" she snapped angrily.

"Nothing! Nothing!" He pulled his hand back quickly. "I just wanted to touch your tattoo. It looks so cool." Joaquim had a hurt look on his face.

"Tattoo? What tattoo? I don't have a tattoo!" Rebecca instinctively reached behind her head and touched her neck…she pulled back her hand as she winced in pain once more. "How the hell did this happen? Oh God! Am I blacking out and injuring myself now?" she said out loud, not really expecting an answer from anyone. It was said more in desperation and fear than anything else. Rebecca sat down on a sandy-colored rock near a wall of the cavern and began to cry.

"Don't cry. Don't cry, Sis. I can't handle it when you cry." Joaquim went over to her and knelt down beside her. He put his arm around her, being very careful not to touch her neck in the process. "You know," he said, looking over at Morghanz, "when we were up in Shaulmar's study doing the ceremony thing—Joaquim was interrupted before he could utter another word.

"What do you mean, ceremony? What ceremony?" Rebecca was not as agitated as before, but just very subdued by the total confusion and the lack of memory recall.

"Well, it started out with you finding Morghanz on her bed unconscious and all these black veins sticking out of her face. Then we took her down to the study to try to find something in Shaulmar's cupboard that could help. We placed Morghanz on the couch and then the next thing I know you're holding your head complaining of headaches and blinding flashes of light." Joaquim was very proud of the way he could recall the events precisely for her.

"Oh, then what?" Rebecca wanted to know everything.

"Then what? Then you were not you any more. The book was you—and you were not Rebecca—that's what!" Joaquim began to sound a little angry—his experience was fully processed by now and the delayed reaction was kicking in.

"So, how did we get here?" she pointed a finger erratically around at various places in the cavern. "Down here in the Templar's cavern?"

"I don't know—all I do know is there was a lot of bright lights, black poison things grabbing at the book, and you saying all kinds of things about the universe and the vortex, etcetera, and then we were down here." He was quite upset at this point. "Then the tiny yellow lights shot through you just before we disappeared and ended up down here." By this time Joaquim was reliving the full trauma of the experience. He wasn't sure whether to be angry, scared, or okay with the whole thing and he couldn't stop his lower lip from quivering or the tears from welling up in his eyes, which was not a comfortable feeling for him at all.

"It's okay Joaquim. I'm sorry. Nothing was your fault. It's just that I feel a bit funny right now and we still need to help Morghanz." Rebecca went to him and gave him a hug that seemed to calm him down. "I have to see how Morghanz is. There has to be something I can give her to stop the poison. Maybe she has some concoction in her pouch—she's always claiming she has healing herbs in it." Rebecca walked back to where her friend was laid out and knelt down beside her—she reached across her for the pouch. The way Morghanz was laying made it difficult to get to the pouch, so she grabbed Morghanz's hand to lift it off the table, thus freeing the pouch. At the exact moment she did that, she felt a surge of energy passing through the crown of her head, moving down her left side, then exploding from her left hand. Instinctively, Rebecca dropped Morghanz's hand and jumped back away from her. She had no idea what it was…whatever it was had made her feel a stabbing pain that hurt from the base of her skull, down her spine, across her shoulders, and down through her arms. "Oh shit." Rebecca began to shake her hands and arms, while spinning around, trying to get rid of the sensations.

"What's the matter? You okay?" Joaquin was beginning to freak out. He couldn't handle all the weird stuff that was going on.

"No…it's alright. I think I just got a shock, you know, static electricity—it can really hurt sometimes, right?" she was lying through her teeth but what else could she do? She couldn't tell Joaquim what she really felt—it would freak him out worse than he already was.

"Yeah,—I've had them. They can sting pretty badly. You can get a wicked jolt from rubbing your feet on the carpet with your socks on…ha ha…." Joaquim was relaxing much more now that his mind was on something that he could relate to. Rebecca had to pull herself together and figure out what to do—there was no Shaulmar to rely on and Morghanz was no use to her in the condition she was in.

"Hey, Joaquim," she spoke softly, almost in a whisper.

"Yeah." He dropped the box he'd picked up

"Do you think you could reach down next to Morghanz and fetch me her pouch— there might be something in it that could help her."

"Sure," he said, hesitating. He was not really happy about the request but he didn't want to be seen as being afraid. After all, it wasn't like she was bad or anything, he thought reassuringly. As Rebecca watched him make his way slowly to the table where Morghanz lay, she distinctly heard a voice tell her, "There is nothing in the pouch that would be of any help to your friend. All your friend needs is for you to go to her and speak with her."

"Joaquim—did you just say something?" she looked at him intently.

"N…no" He said nervously.

"Well someone just did, and it sounded like it was right here, right with us." Rebecca looked around expecting to see someone and secretly hoping it would turn out to be Shaulmar who had come to help them. She walked away down the pathway and lifted a torch from its holder on the wall. "Joaquim, do you have any matches or lighter I can use to light the torch?" she held it up for him to see.

"Why? Where are you going? Don't leave us here. I won't know what to do. You know I'm not good at any logic stuff. I function on instinct alone and that might not be the best thing in this situation." He looked very nervous.

"Don't worry. I won't go far. I just want to see if there are any clues of how to get out of here." She lit the torch—it came to life immediately. "Anyway, what could happen to you down here?" she headed down the passageway that she and Shaulmar went down the first time they were transported down to the cavern. The yellow flame of the torch was large and warm—it made the passageway seem so inviting to her. As Rebecca shone the torch from side-to-side, she noticed signs on the cavern wall and she moved closer to inspect them. She studied them for a few moments and decided they had no value to her because she didn't understand them. "So much for a sign from the sacred brotherhood of whatever," she scoffed out loud.

"There is no such organization, at least not on this earth plane, but there might be such a group further afar, within an orbiting planet in the galaxy to the left of the seventh dimension of light." There was that voice again.

Rebecca fell against the cavern wall, while frantically waving the fiery torch back and forth. She had no idea who or what produced the voice, but she wasn't about to let it kill her without a fight, that much she had learned from her grandmother.

"What do you mean, kill you? Do you really think I am here to do harm, Rebecca?" The Essence had surfaced again, however, it had its own voice now and so Rebecca did not have to be subdued.

"Who are you? Where are you? Come out and show yourself, Coward!" She was scared stiff and the only thing she could think of was to appear courageous and brave.

"Rebecca, if I reveal myself, do you promise to put down the flame torch?" she still could not figure out where the voice had originated.

"Sure…now…reveal yourself." Her heart was pounding so much that she could hear the blood rushing through her arteries as clearly as if her heart was on the outside of her body. Rebecca waited. She gripped the flame torch with both hands—her knuckles were white as she held onto the torch with such force. A few minutes passed. Rebecca had decided she'd had just about enough of this nonsense, and she decided to make a run for it, back the way she'd come from. Suddenly, she became rigid. She felt a burning sensation at the base of her skull, and it felt like a ball of fire spinning around about the size of a golf ball. Rebecca dropped the torch—luckily it fell against the wall of the cavern and remained upright, so that it continued to burn steadily and keep the cavern alight. "Oh, God, what is happening to me? Why am I being attacked all the time? I haven't done anything bad enough to have all these things thrown at me," she was blubbering at this point, with tears falling down her cheeks and onto the floor.

"Do not fear me, Rebecca, trust what you see and hear." Just as the voice spoke, the beautiful green light appeared in front of her that seemed to come from above and behind her. The energy shimmered in front of her—as she looked at it through her tears, she felt a very strong sense of love coming to her from the vision. "Do you recognize me now, Rebecca? Search your inner being, your soul self." The voice was gentle and powerful at the same time.

"I…I don't know, I think so, but how? You are the book, but how can this be?" she was suddenly drained and couldn't think any more. Rebecca fell against the wall and sat on the sandstone and gravel floor. A dark puddle appeared in the sandstone were her tears had fallen. She held her head in her hands.

"Rebecca, please look at me. I am the Essence." The green entity shimmered against the rose-red sandstone wall. "You and I have been drawn together ever since you incarnated here. I felt your presence and jostled signature the moment you enter into the world." The Essence floated closer to her, very slowly, not wanting to alarm her. "We were destined to become twin souls, to be as one—it was written eons ago—the prophecy foretells our union as being the original of the first-bound souls."

"What you do mean, bound souls?" Rebecca still had her hands covering her head as she bent toward the ground. "That sounds not really a good thing to me." She looked at the vision through the gap in her fingers that covered her face, trying to figure it out. It was a beautiful green color, the kind of green she had never seen before. A vibrant, yet smooth color, not neon green to stun the eyes or anything. As the Essence spoke, she thought it was so precious.

"Do you remember the original binding ceremony that was performed by the ancient wizard, Shaulmar?"

"Yes, I remember it clearly. You kidnapped us and brought us here." Rebecca lifted her face towards the Essence. "That really freaked me out, by the way." The Essence shimmered once more.

"That transportation was necessary, trust me." The energy shimmered and spun once, making a full revolution in a fraction of a second. "The ceremony didn't really mean anything. I allowed it to happen so as not to raise any suspicion on the part of the travellers." Rebecca couldn't keep herself from drinking in all the beauty, love, and peace that was emanating from the Essence. "I needed to get you down to the Templars cavern where your soul signature, your essence, could be joined with mine. The energy vortex contains the designated binding power that was destined to forge our essences together." The green entity spun again making one full revolution, then it hovered for a while, waiting.

"I still don't get it…are we separate? Or tied together? …Because I see you across from me, floating…." She hesitated, as if trying to locate a better descriptive word. "While I am sitting here and…not floating." The Essence stabilized in front of her.

"We are one, but we are not captives, we are able to connect and disconnect at will. That is the most appropriate word. We have free will in all things Rebecca. We both exercise free will. This occurred when we made binding contracts before we both entered this earthly existence." The Essence glowed with such beauty and grace that Rebecca could not help but feel special that something as magical as the Essence would pick her to *bind* with. "Yes, Rebecca, and I feel just as special knowing you chose me." The green Essence spun with the energy of the earth. Rebecca thought she heard *laughing* as the orb spun and sparkled against the backdrop of the rose-colored cavern.

"You heard my thoughts?" she said, as if she had been violated in some way.

"Don't worry. You will hear my thoughts too, any time you wish when you learn to listen to the vibration we share. Please, do not feel violated. We are bound souls. I could never hurt you and you could never hurt me. That is the wonder of universal law created by the natural order of things." Rebecca held her head again, feeling totally confused, and no closer to understanding the *binding*.

"What about Morghanz? I think she is really sick. I have to get back to her." Rebecca pushed herself off the cavern wall and stood, a little shaken, but really no worse for the experience.

"Morghanz has been invaded by the dark forces that wish to dislodge the balance of souls here on earth." The Essence spun, then shimmered slowly, like the northern lights over the mountains of Alaska.

"She is my friend, and I won't leave her to die, without trying to do something to help her. If you hadn't brought us down here, again, I could have at least tried to get her to the hospital." She hurried back down the passageway, clutching the burning torch. It took a few minutes before she made it back to where she'd left her friends. "Sorry to have taken so long to get back." She handed the torch to Joaquim.

"You were gone for hours, Sis…and…whoa…" Joaquim stumbled back at the site of the Essence following behind Rebecca "What the hell is that there now?" He frantically pointed to the shimmering green light, not realizing he had used the hand with the burning torch, nearly losing the whole thing, but catching it again before it reached the floor.

"That's the book in its true form. Do you remember the book changing into the blue energy and tiny blue lights when it was on Morghanz's stomach during the ceremony?"

"Ah huh." He grunted while pushing against the cavern wall with his back—trying not to appear scared.

"Well now, it's…well…that." Rebecca pointed over to the Essence without even looking. She knelt down beside her friend, Morghanz, who didn't look good at all. The dark fingers full of poison were over most of her body, including above her skin, and the black substance began to ooze from many breaks in her skin. "I'm so sorry, Morghanz." Rebecca put her hands on her friend's forehead and arm, stroking her gently, "I don't know what to do and Shaulmar isn't here. He probably doesn't know where we are. I don't know if you can hear me, but...." Rebecca couldn't hold back her tears any longer—she couldn't stand to see Morghanz this way. She sobbed as she let her head fall onto Morghanz's chest, even though the poison was oozing out of cracks in the skin onto her neck. Joaquim's eyes filled and he couldn't prevent the tears from falling down his cheeks. He tried to look away, pretending to hold the torch up toward the cavern wall while looking for signs, anything that could help them, while using his sleeve to wipe the tears away, unnoticed.

"Rebecca, you know what to do!" The Essence hovered close to her, whispering gently in her ear. "The pain and suffering in your heart is great. What does it tell you to do?" The Essence was provoking her—it knew what was possible and wanted her to know that too. However, part of the agreement made between the two souls was for each to only allow the other to discover their own gifts. Both beings must guide the other towards knowledge, but they are forbidden to just hand over solutions to problems on a silver platter.

"I want to take away Morghanz's pain. I want to have her pain rather than see her in such pain." Her heart was breaking. Her vision was blurred because of the tears. She nestled her cheek on Morghanz's chest. The Essence slowly backed away, shimmering and floating steadily. The veins on Morghanz's neck throbbed with the dark poison that was flowing through them. The poisonous entity that had attached to her was almost finished, but it sensed another close by, and it naturally gravitated towards Rebecca's soft rosy-colored cheek. The vibration and disturbance caused by her heartfelt sobbing guided the poisonous veins toward her like a laser-guided abomination. Joaquim still preferred to take his attention elsewhere, for fear of breaking down in an emotional heap, and he definitely didn't want to see his friend pass away in such a disgusting manner. The Essence continued to hover further and further away from the two, one near death, and the other wanting desperately to bring her back. The dark entity had almost reached Rebecca's face—it would not be long now before it would claim both of them for the dark forces of the universe. Finally, the poison reached its mark, oozing its black death onto her white skin. "Oh my God, that stings" She pulled away but the poison was faster—it went deep. "Oh no! Please dear God, help me." She tried to pull the tentacle from her cheek to no avail. It had sunk its hooks in deep and Rebecca fell to the floor.

"Sis, what's wrong?" Joaquim ran to her.

"Stay back! Stay back!" She held up her arms stopping the boy from touching her or getting too close, "The poison is in me. Please, don't touch me." Joaquim panicked. He ran towards the passageway then stopped. He ran back and fell in a heap close to Rebecca, feeling horrified and helpless, not knowing what to do, if anything.

"You!" He turned to the Essence. His face was racked with pain and anger. "Do-oh something!" he demanded. The Essence did nothing, just hovered close by, glowing, and spinning. Joaquim picked up a rock and threw it at the Essence. The red stone passed right through the beautiful green energy. Joaquim broke. He cried like a man, a man who was watching his first love die a horrible death. Still, the Essence floated near the cavern wall, shimmering, but doing nothing. Rebecca rolled over onto her back. The poison had covered half her face.

"No! You will not win." She could only whisper the words through the pain. "I will not let you win." Her voice became clearer and stronger. The Essence spun closer, its glow became brighter, more intense, it shimmered, it quickened. Joaquim sniffled and wiped his face of the tear—mixed with mucus—that had flowed from him.

"Sis!" he called out, almost gagging on the fluid that had built up in his throat. Rebecca was trying to move up off the floor—she lifted up to her knees, and placed her hands on the gravel, to steady herself.

"Ugh, you will regret attacking me…you piece of crap!" She took a deep breath and forced her way to the cavern wall, pushing herself up, until she was standing her legs apart with her fist-clenched hand against the ancient wall. The Essence came even closer, spinning faster now. Joaquim rushed towards her and stopped abruptly—he remembered she didn't want him to touch her.

Something inside Rebecca had come alive, a spark of something, she didn't know what, but in the instant her life was threatened, something was ignited within her. She clawed at the wall, pushing her fingers into any crevice she could find that could help her remain standing. As soon as she was able to stand strong again, she punched the air above her head and claimed her power. "With the power of the universe I command this entity banished from me! Leave my body now!" As she spoke the words, the Essence glowed the most deep-vibrant-green Joaquim had ever seen. Rebecca's power grew, the vortex of light knew who she was and responded to her command, as if being called upon by its master. The dark mass infecting Rebecca's face began to recede. The fingers of dark poison fell away from her neck and face. The power within was truly strong, and when all the poison was gone, the Essence spun around in a circle until a slight hum could be heard.

"Sis, you're all right." Joaquim stood close to her.

"Yes, Joaquim now let me be with Morghanz." She touched the woman on her forehead and her hand—immediately the healing energy and the power of the light that was inside Rebecca began its work. "Morghanz is not going to die. The darkness that runs through her now will transform into light." As she spoke the words, the green energy of the Essence returned to her and merged with her once more. Moments passed, and the poison was removed, all the tentacles broke away and disappeared. Morghanz started to breathe easier and more regular—deep breaths—eventually, she opened her eyes and spoke.

"What happened? I dreamt I was fighting, struggling, with something—struggling against the darkness—the forces of evil were close to me. Morghanz lifted her hand to her chest.

"You're okay now...you're safe with us." Rebecca kissed her friend's cheek and smiled.

"Thank God, you didn't die. Those black veins were really killing you." Joaquim stood next to Rebecca, looking down at Morghanz.

"I don't think it is necessary to tell her all the details, Joaquim."

"Okay, sorry." He hung his head. Morghanz regained her strength and managed to stand on her own.

"Where are we?"

"The book transported us all down to the cavern, like it did before," Rebecca knew what was coming next.

"Where's Shaulmar? Why did the book bring us here?" Morghanz regained her awareness as the seconds past.

"Shaulmar went to the bookstore to confer with the Sacred High Council. He is probably on his way back to the house by now."

"Rebecca, why are we down in the cavern?" Morghanz had a feeling there was something Rebecca was holding back.

"There was another binding ceremony that included me, the book, Joaquim and you, while you were fighting the poisonous entity that had attacked you. The book spoke through me again and told us what to do." Rebecca turned away from Morghanz a little, and pulled her sweater down slightly across her shoulders, just enough so that Morghanz could see a small point of the green tattoo appearing from her neck and shoulders.

"Oh, my God, what happened? How did you get that?" Rebecca quickly covered it up. She was kind of a little embarrassed and a little afraid of what Morghanz might say if she saw all of it.

"It's a long story. The book and I are bound soul to soul." she looked at Morghanz, as if to say, the situation is not that great. "I don't know if it's such a good idea, a good thing, but there was nothing I could do to change it."

"I know one thing, Rebecca. If you are truly bound to the book as you say, then you can take my word for it, it is a great thing," Morghanz smiled and kissed her on the cheek. "Bless you, Rebecca. I owe you my life," she whispered, as she held her in a warm embrace.

"What are we going to do now?" Joaquim said, struggling to keep the torch going…this thing isn't going to last much longer."

"I have no idea what we're going to do. The only thing I was told by the Essence was that there was some kind of danger coming to the house." Rebecca turned to Morghanz as she spoke.

"The Essence? What is the Essence?" asked Morghanz.

"It's the book. It transformed into pure energy and transported all off us down here, and it lives inside me, as the tattoo on my back." Rebecca touched her neck symbolically, reminding herself of its presence.

"Oh, I see." Morghanz was trying to piece together the events that had brought them all down into the cavern and into the present moment. "Okay, so let's try to put things in order, and figure out some kind of priority, so we can get a feel of what we are to do."

"Okay Morghanz, and so glad to have you back to normal. I missed you and we didn't want you to die." Joaquim gave her the biggest hug, more for his own peace of mind.

"Thank you, Joaquim. Now tell me of this danger coming to the house, Rebecca. What did it mean?"

"That's just it. I don't know what it means. The Essence didn't explain or give details—it just transported us down here during the ceremony." Rebecca felt useless and wondered why she was gifted the ability to bind with the book if it was no use to her or anybody else when needed. Morghanz saw the despair settling into her friend's face and moved to quell it, immediately.

"Rebecca, this is the beginning of your destiny. The Essence and you are embarking on a journey, so trust that everything is in its place, and that place is where everything should be." Morghanz stroked Rebecca's long silky-soft-hair and looked her in the eyes with such compassion and strength. "Courage is what you need to develop. Search inside for the courage you will need to embrace your journey." She smiled while resting her hand on Rebecca's shoulder, love and excitement flowed between the two friends and Rebecca felt uplifted.

"You're right as usual, Morghanz. I can embrace what I came here to do. All the things that I have seen in the last six months were real, maybe not in this physical dimension, but certainly real on some level. I can draw upon all the power of those things and look to the strength within me to help me move forward." When she heard her own voice and knew what she had said, she was still a little skeptical, but she was determined enough to let the energy of the moment carry her with it.

"Then, what are we going to do about the danger coming? The book brought us down here to avoid it." Joaquim looked at them both very seriously. "If what the book said is true, then when Shaulmar returns to the house, he will be walking right into the danger too." Joaquim was absolutely correct and he seemed to have developed a knack of bringing focus to the importance of the present moment.

"He's right. What are we going to do?" Rebecca said calmly.

"Well, first we must determine what the danger is and when it is going to arrive," Morghanz thought for a moment. She seemed to have fully regained all of her faculties since the dark entity had been removed. "How did the book speak to you, Rebecca?"

"I lost consciousness after thoughts came to me, then Joaquim said I just started speaking." Rebecca looked over to Joaquim for some sign of confirmation that what she was saying was in fact what happened.

"Yeah, that's right. That's how it went," Joaquim said, nodding his head and raising his eyebrows high.

Morghanz walked up and down the passageway deep in thought. After a moment or two, she turned to them.

"Okay Rebecca, can you have the book speak through you now?" she didn't say anything. She had never thought to do that before. Any connection was always initiated by, or to be more correct, the initiation came from the essence of the book.

"I...I don't know. The book always connected with me, never the other way around." She looked at both of them nervously.

"Well, do you think it's possible?" Morghanz asked in a friendly voice designed to keep a peaceful tone that would in no way raise the stress or anxiety of the situation. She was very adept at calming people and bringing forth the best from them. Rebecca thought for a moment and then moved the red sand all around with her feet.

"I guess it's possible, although, I really don't know how I would go about it," she said sheepishly. Joaquim was still holding onto the old metal torch holder but the light was fading—all he could do was stuff it with bits and pieces of an ancient clothe lying all around the cavern floor.

"Joaquim, don't stray too far looking for material to keep the light going. It's not safe." Morghanz's voice echoed off the cavern walls.

"Sure Morghanz, I will stay close, don't worry." Morghanz went to Rebecca's side and put her arm around her.

"Do you remember when we used to meditate together and I would guide you through the visualizations?"

"Yes…yes. I like that it worked well. What has that got to do with now?" she asked.

"Well, I can do the same for you now in this situation. I can guide you to communicate with the book." Rebecca was still looking down at the floor, kicking at the gravel and sand with her foot.

"The Essence…the book…is no longer the book…it's the essence that used to be the book," she said quickly, while continuing to push the gravel and sand around.

"Right, the Essence. I can maybe guide you to connect with the Essence and then you can ask it to transport us back to Shaulmar's house before he encounters the danger." Morghanz lifted Rebecca's chin very slowly and gently and smiled into her eyes for confirmation.

"Oh, ok, yes. I guess I'll try." She gave Morghanz a huge smile. "We should prepare the ceremony as before, just in case it can help the connection."

"That's a great idea, Rebecca. I think this is going to work. Let's get started." They both gathered what they needed to conduct the ceremony from the items transported from above. It was going to take time setting up but they were all intent on finding a way.

CHAPTER 20

BASTIAN ADJUSTED HIS HUGE BLACK LEATHER CLOAK around his shoulders as they walked to the limousine outside his prestigious apartment building.

"Brother, where would you like me to be?" Drandos had learned a few things within the past few days—the most important thing was to wait for Bastian to tell him what to do, and never to assume anything. Draco Bastian disliked having any of his minions think for themselves and that restriction included his brother.

"You, brother, will stay at my side and you will guard me with your life. This is the price you must be prepared to pay if you wish to inherit the power and knowledge of the dark force of the universe from me."

"Yes Master." Drandos hoped his brother was preoccupied enough not to sense the deception in his heart. "I will spare no one. I will forfeit my own life to protect you Lord."

That seemed to have appeased the Dark Angel somewhat and so no more was said. They both climbed into the limousine and then it sped away down the causeway towards the outskirts of the city. Bastian was a very cautious and dark wizard who prided himself on seeing every possible outcome related to an event. This one was no different. He had consulted the darkest forces in line with his own black heart and soul. He saw every possible outcome and prepared for every eventuality that might prevent him from capturing the prize. He wanted the soul of Rebecca Sullivan, not only for the personal reasons that spawned the hatred in his heart, but because according to prophecy she was the key to future treasures beyond any that had gone before since the birth of the universe. The limousine moved through the city as silently as the darkness itself. Inside, Bastian had included his brother, but he also saw the potential for a conflict during the task ahead; therefore, he had his minions escorting them to the rendezvous as well. The black Cadillac seated eight passengers, however, it was designed for regular people, not the giants that occupied the back row and second row of the seats. Each minion occupied more than normal space, leaving the premier seat for Bastian, and the smaller pull-down pedestal seat for Drandos. This made Drandos feel even more inferior than he did during the time he spent with the older apprentices of the Sacred Dark Order.

"How will we be able to locate the soul, brother?" Drandos wanted his brother to think he was 100 percent behind the move to capture the soul of the Prophesied One.

"Do not be concerned about details that are beyond your grasp, brother. The location is already known through the ingenuity of the master who stands before you." Bastian sat facing them, surrounded by the plush black and purple velvet and leather interior of the vehicle. All those around him felt his presence. He was truly a powerful being in his own right. The Dark One placed his hands on his knees so the Ring of Dread could be seen clearly on his hand. Drandos could not keep his eyes off of the ring. There was something about it that pulled him and held his stare.

"Brother, that ring you wear, does it have power of its own?" The young apprentice was trying the patients of the Dark One and the others were made to feel just as uncomfortable. They knew Bastian's anger lived barely below the surface and it didn't take much prodding to release it from its restraints.

"Drandos, tell me the name of the ring that comforts itself by dwelling on my hand?" He was playing with his brother, and Drandos knew it, as did the others. The young apprentice thought very deliberately before answering.

"Anyone who embraces the forces of evil, in this plane of existence, knows the name of the most famous and most powerful ring on earth." His voice trailed off with definite signs of relief. The others joined him in the most audible collective sigh of relief. "It is the Ring of Dread, the most feared of all the ancient artifacts created." Drandos was really pleased with the way he stood strong in the face of his brothers questioning.

"Correct, my young novice. So—can you also tell us what dark entities this *Ring—this incredible wonder of the ancient sorcerers,* has dominion over?" He twisted the ring around slowly on his finger while he watched the rain hammer the window outside. Bastian knew the sum of all knowledge his younger brother was exposed to while studying at the school of the dark arts. He wanted his brother to learn about the dark arts, but he also wanted to make him look small and insignificant in the process.

"No master, I have no knowledge of such things." Drandos's head sank. He looked at the plush carpeting on the floor of the limousine while trying to avoid all the eyes that were upon him. He desperately wanted to be back on Orban. He even wished he were back in school which was better than being made to look like a fool for his brother's amusement.

"Well brother, the price of gaining knowledge of such Sacred Dark Arts is service." Bastian's eyes shone like quicksilver. "Your service is to me—I will have you pay dearly for my knowledge, young apprentice." The Dark Angel laughed and looked out the window once more. He loved the connection to what he felt was chaos, that he got from the rain and hail that was now coming down hard against the window. "We will soon be in battle little one. There you will witness the power, the real power of the arts you wish to learn. Not some training exercise with your friends on Orban created by those who pollute the minds such as yours with schoolboy tricks and childish magic."

His power was building within. Drandos could feel him drawing it from the dark clouds outside, around and above them, that sourced through the torrential miserable rain. Drandos said nothing. All his thoughts were focused on how to get through the ordeal and then figure out a way to return to Orban.

"One more thing before this day begins," Bastian turned to face them once more, "Rebecca Sullivan is mine to take. No one touches her but me. If you value your miserable existence here, you will make that your mantra." He turned to the darkness and the rain, drinking in the energy, as if it were a sweet summer's morn.

***

The feeling was one of being squished between two slabs of marble and stretched by horse-drawn chariots. There was wave upon wave of squishing then stretching...squishing then stretching. The Rhostos were used to it. In fact, they enjoyed it—they enjoyed the sensations, but the only other passenger was not having a great time.

"Ooh...I feel so sick," Alison, groaned. "How much longer is this going to take? It's not like we're going to the moon or anything," she cried out loud.

"Maintain your equilibrium. If they sense you're having trouble, they will follow the imbalance in the propulsion waves, and they will locate you." The warrior spoke while touching the crystal control on his arm.

"What do you mean...they?" Alison was annoyed. She hadn't been forewarned about the potential dangers of travelling through the space between dimensions.

"Do not concern yourself. The only thing you must ensure is that you maintain equilibrium and harmony. Any unorthodox movement triggers alarms with beings within the space," he said quietly almost muffled.

"What you are telling me is that I am not supposed to be traveling in this space. Am I traveling through this space illegally?" she was using a demanding tone that did not sit well with the Rhostos warrior.

"You would do well to remain still and not speak so loudly. The vibration of your voice will surely attract beings that also inhabit this space. Such beings thrive on destroying illeg...uh...unfamiliar travelers within the space." The Rhostos warrior had inadvertently let the truth slip. Practitioners of the dark arts were not looked at with kindness within the space—in fact, you might say they were hunted by entities that resided here. The reason this space exists is because of the conflict between the dark and light forces within the universe. If light were the only power that flourished within the universe, the entities of this space could travel freely throughout, just as other beings do. Since the darkness fractured the harmony of the universe, the space between dimensions was created, and those who vibrated with neither the light nor the darkness were forced to exist between them.

"So, how long must I suffer this indignity of illegal travel through potentially deadly terrain?" Alison could not help noticing how the Rhostos warrior was so adept at this navigation, through what seemed to her, to be extremely deadly terrain. Her admiration of the Rhostos warrior grew in silence with every maneuver he made to avoid potentially catastrophic situations. Even though Alison had ulterior motives for gaining the trust of the Rhostos, she couldn't gain control over the growing feelings within her for the seasoned warrior.

"We are almost at the end of our journey—you must remain patient. When we are within distance of the exit portal, I will inform you, and I will have more instructions that must be followed to the letter for your own protection." The Rhostos was facing forward with Alison behind him—both were encased in the crystal energy that was the vehicle that carried them through the space. They traveled at the speed of light, and the only thing preventing them from being annihilated was the field of energy protecting them, provided by the smoky quartz crystal.

Alison was aware of the Rhostos's energy and she began to realize that it wasn't as unpleasant as she'd first thought. Was it possible for a sorceress of the dark arts to form a relationship with a Rhostos warrior, she couldn't help but wonder?

"We are close to the exit," he said slowly, "you must do exactly as I say—no more no less—do you understand?" He did look back at her this time.

"Yes! Just be clear in your instruction. I do not want to end up as part of whatever inanimate object appears should you get it wrong, Rhostos." Alison was quite calm, but emphatic, as she struggled to stare into his large dark-brown eyes.

"To begin with, there will be a flash of yellow sodium light as we begin to reduce speed, then you must breathe in unison with me so as to avoid detection by the sensors. Can you conjure some magic to help with the situation?" The warrior hoped with all his heart that she could manifest the magic from the etheric, or he thought they were doomed for sure. He wasn't about to share that piece of information with Alison until she had answered him.

"Rhostos—I am a practitioner of the dark arts, what do you think that means? What is it you wish for me to manifest from the ethers?" she was quite put out by the lack of understanding by the warrior of what the sorceress was capable of."

"Well, initially—you must pull energy from outside of the crystal barrier, and at the very moment I tell you, you must direct that power at the one who waits for us beyond the exit." The warrior stared at her so she would know exactly what he meant. He also made sure he read her iris for confirmation of the compliance or intended compliance of his request.

"Rhostos, the one who waits for us presumably, is your apprentice—am I correct?" Alison looked for the indication that showed her the assumption she'd made was correct.

"You are correct, Allison Warrior."

"So, if I direct my energy into that place, your apprentice will not survive—trust me." Alison wanted the Rhostos warrior to understand exactly what she was saying and what was about to happen.

"Yes—and I am counting on your abilities to conjure such an absolute power. I am trusting you to do what you say you can." The warrior meant business and Alison knew that now.

"You wish your apprentice dead. I am curious as to why you want him out of the way?" she was attempting to appear calm to the warrior, but inside of her head, she was thinking many things, sometimes all at once.

"We must do it now—or it will be too late. Can you do it now?" he said with a strong calm voice. Alison closed her eyes and raised her hands, one palm facing ahead and one facing up. Within the limited confines of the protective crystal force field, she whispered what appeared to the Rhostos to be nonsensical gibberish. Almost immediately, a powerful surge of energy left her body from the solar plexus and from the center of her hands. A flash of purple energy pierced the protective force field around them and sped off out of sight. "Thank you. I will be in your debt once more." He closed his eyes and bowed his head lightly, slightly toward her, in appreciation.

"You do realize warrior, when we arrive, your apprentice will be dead." Alison watched for the reaction in his face.

"Yes—as you have already said. There is something more...." The Rhostos faced her. "Allison Warrior, prepare to be strong in your body when we arrive—there will be a powerful recoil when we stop. There are approximately three minutes before we arrive." The warrior fumbled with his wrist control as he continued pushing a few more diamond-shaped crystals that obviously controlled the travel through the space between dimensions. Alison turned her head to watch what was happening outside the protective energy field. The light turned from yellow to blue, then to the beautiful indigo haze, as they slowed. When she could make out physical objects, the energy field around them was a blend of purple surrounded with gold. The sorceress protected herself by surrounding her body with her own power. She had already experienced enough physical pain from the Dark Angel to last a lifetime. So, she was not about to allow the Rhostos to do the same to her with his contraption. Then, they came to an abrupt stop and the exit portal appeared. Alison was thrown around a little, but after she had steadied herself, she made it a point to complain.

"What kind of a landing was that? Are you positive you've travelled that way before," she snapped sarcastically, "because it sure didn't feel like it." She straightened herself up as she looked at the warrior. Even though Alison was from a different dimension and planetary societal structure that didn't put much emphasis on anything besides making money, she was still a woman—she fixed her hair before she exiting the portal.

"Don't you ever give it a rest? The Rhostos are not the most powerful beings of the universe. We don't own the most recent high-speed travel technology. What do you expect, Allison Warrior? The plush ride of your master, Draco Bastian?" He meant that to sting as much as it did. He was annoyed by the fact that her comments rang true. The lack of financial clout and technological advancement of the Rhostos was a strong source of anger and disappointment for him. However, he was more pissed off at the fact that she was a follower of the Dark Angel, by choice. Once it was established that their journey had been successfully completed, the energy field disappeared and all molecular stability returned to normal. Alison stepped onto the earth first while the Rhostos warrior completed the necessary protocol demands of inter-dimensional travel through space.

"Well, I guess he will think again the next time he incarnates to...wherever." Alison went over to the place where the energy burst had scorched the earth and hit its mark. "Pity he wasn't facing the other way—he must have seen it coming for a fraction of a second. The look on his face actually shows he was trying to figure out what the big bright light was, poor fool." She kicked what was left of the corpse, and it fell to the ground, collapsing into four or five small smoldering pieces—the stench of burning Rhostos warrior made her gag.

"Leave him! He is in a better place. He was useful for the beginning of the plan but he just didn't have the ability to run beside me when the most important aspects were to be attempted." The Rhostos warrior pointed his index finger at the remains of his apprentice, and with one jolt of electrical current, he destroyed the remains. No one would be the wiser, and certainly no blame would fall at the feet of the Rhostos warrior, after he reported the apprentice had died fighting for the honor of Orban. Alison turned to the warrior.

"What plan are you talking about, Rhostos? Once again, I remind you to remember your debt to me, Warrior. There is no way I am ending up like your faithful apprentice—be sure of that, Rhostos!" She tried to sound as tough and as menacing as she could.

"You are not my target, nor my enemy, Allison Warrior. On the contrary, we have a destiny together. I am convinced of that. You must have sensed it too—yes? Please do not attempt any deception of the Rhostos—it is not possible. The Rhostos always know the truth—sometimes we wish it was not so, but it is both our gift and our curse." The warrior moved away, seemingly uninterested, if she chose to lie or not. Alison felt sorry for the warrior, which was something that didn't happen very often, for her. The last time she'd felt sorry for someone, was when she'd had Rebecca in her room at the hostel, and she'd witnessed how helpless she was. It would have been so easy for her to capture the soul at that moment, but she chose to wait, which now she realized she paid dearly for when the Dark Angel made her suffer through so much pain.

"What do we do now, Warrior?" she said as he was walking away from her.

"Quiet. I'm thinking." The Rhostos had no idea of what the wrath of a woman could do to a being even as powerful as himself, especially a woman who was a practitioner of the Sacred Dark Arts of the ancient order and who had been so badly hurt by the Dark Angel.

"You would do well to tread carefully with me, Rhostos. I owe you nothing, but you owe me everything. Remember that." There was only silence from the huge being. The only indication that he was present was the slow movement, in and out, of the great appendages on his back.

"The soul we seek is here, but there are others close by, wishing to take her also." He held up his arm, and felt the air with his left hand, as if he were reading the energy. "The one you call the Dark One, Draco Bastian. He is close by and he wants her. He is willing and able to do what is needed to claim her. He truly is powerful. The darkness flows through his soul." The Rhostos spoke with calmness and there was a hint of a healthy respect for the one who caused his race such destruction. That annoyed Alison so much and she didn't try to hide the fact.

"So the Rhostos warrior admires the Dark One?" she moved in front of him so she could look into his eyes. "You have no idea what he is going to do to us, especially to a Rhostos warrior. If we engage him in battle, he will make you look about as powerful as your apprentice." Alison thought that surely would hit home with the huge being, maybe even sting a little, and make him reveal some Rhostos emotion. With a little luck, she thought it might trigger some Rhostos anger that would give her so much joy to see. The sorceress wanted the warrior to express some deep pain, similar to the pain she was forced to express through her own experiences, at different times in her life. The Rhostos warrior only continued to read the energy with his eyes closed.

"There is much darkness accumulating around the soul. We must go there now if we are to succeed." He had dismissed all that she had said which infuriated her even more.

"Where are we?" Alison stepped around in the moonlight. They seemed to be in a park-like setting. There was a strong smell of evergreen sap from the spruce and cedar trees. It took awhile for her physical senses to adjust to the effects of the travel, but she did recognize the moonlight and the wonderful intoxicating aroma of all the trees around her. She wandered around in between the trees while she attempted to figure out where she was.

"Come this way," she heard the Rhostos hiss to her from behind one of the thick bushes, "there is a way to get to the soul. I have tuned into the signature left by the one they are calling Morghanz." He beckoned to her impatiently with his long slender finger.

"She is one of the travelers who was assigned to the soul to teach and guide her," Alison remarked as she continued to wander through the trees. "I felt her power when I was close to the soul, and I would warn the Rhostos, that such power is not to be underestimated. This traveler has knowledge and wisdom gained from many encounters with the dark forces over many years." She inhaled the beautiful aromas and spoke as a matter-of-fact, as if she was an authority on the accomplishments of such power. The Rhostos warrior made no attempt to engage her in any banter or discussion on the subject. It was apparent that the witch practitioner of the dark arts had not realized that the Rhostos were not interested in expending their energies on things that were not going to yield something in return. He had accepted her information and saw no reason to add to it.

"You seem to be in excellent health, Allison Warrior. The healing was good, yes? You seem to bound around in the moonlight between the trees with the energy of a much younger being." He was commenting on how irritable she seemed to be at the lack of control she levied over him. She hated that about him.

"Why don't you just show us the way to the soul and get this over with so that we can conclude our business and go our separate ways, Rhostos!" She was a very sensitive being which was highly unusual for a practitioner of her ability. Normally, the followers of darkness were psychopathic personalities, devoid of conscience or feelings of empathy for others—they certainly did not easily succumb to being hurt by what others said or did. The Rhostos only continued to play with his wristband, obviously tuning it, to guide them to Rebecca.

"There is a substantial power vortex running through the building that houses the soul. It will not be easy to breach the fortress."

"What fortress? The place the soul hides in is but the humble home of two insignificant travellers of the Sacred Order of Light. This will not be a difficult undertaking, unless the Rhostos has developed a fear of the travelers and their ways, or maybe the warrior fears something else? Maybe the Dark Angel conjures the terror of the darkness and sends such visions of death and pain to the feeble mind of the Rhostos? What can it be?" Alison was enjoying toying with the warrior. She could see that the last comment she'd made was at last hitting a nerve.

"You have much to learn about the power of the Rhostos and I will be happy to destroy the dark being as a way of showing the Allison Warrior such power." He was now heating up and walking through the trees in the direction of the town.

CHAPTER 21

THE DARK LIMOUSINE MOVED QUIETLY THROUGH THE residential area. The energy of the vehicle was heavy and black like the coffins of Draco Bastian's ancestral crypt.

"The signature of the soul will be known to me soon. The poison on the traveller will have done its job by now. Drive toward the dark entities signal and there we will find our newest recruit for the Gates of Souls." He laughed in anticipation of seeing the torment on the face of Rebecca Sullivan when she learned of the truth about her mother's supposed death.

"Master, there is a signal coming from the area about three miles ahead of us." The huge man spoke with the voice of a child who is trying not to anger his parent.

"Drive to it and make sure we are not seen before we are meant to—understand?"

"Yes, Master." The driver quickened the pace of the vehicle.

"Turn left at the next junction." The driver obeyed. Bastian sat back in the plush rear compartment of the luxury sedan, sipping a very expensive Scotch. "Brother, do you know what it feels like to taste the nectar of the soul as it cries out to God for help? It relies on hope and faith that their god will magically appear, or send an angel to save them, while I sample the energy that keeps them alive." He was explaining this feeling to his brother, knowing full well he had never known how to do this—he had never even known this to be possible.

"No, Master." Drandos shuffled his position nervously on the leather seat across from his brother. The signal coming from the dark entity, that had infected the traveller, was becoming stronger.

"Master, the entity is not far ahead now—around the next bend, we shall see the building that keeps it, and the soul, of the one you seek." The voice came from the most courageous of men in the employ of the Dark One. The car turned through the hairpin bend in the road, and as it straightened and came to the road ahead, there was complete silence in the vehicle. The driver slowed considerably, and with both hands on the steering wheel, he turned to the figure next to him.

"What should we do?" he said in a frightened whisper. The other man only sat rigidly in his seat, staring straight ahead, not moving, and not uttering a word, just staring at the building at the end of the road.

"Why are we not moving faster?" the third man asked from the rear of the vehicle. He maneuvered his position as discreetly as possible, so as not to annoy the Dark One. He poked his head through the blacked-out privacy window that separated the two front seats from the rest of the vehicle. "If you wish to remain in good favor, you will drive faster." The man looked through the windshield as he spoke—he saw what they saw and immediately fell silent. After what was an uncomfortable period of silence, he spoke again. "Pull over to the side of the road as soon as you can and make sure we are not conspicuous." He closed the dividing window and turned to face his master. Bastian held a crystal whiskey glass in the palm of his hand and waved the finger of his free hand above the glass in a small circular motion. As he did so, the contents in the glass moved in unison.

The Dark One eyeballed the man across from him, and slowly spoke, all the while stirring the drink in his hand. "What do you wish to tell me?"

"Master, a place that hides the soul is ahead of us, about one mile." He took a deep breath.

"And?" Bastian looked out of the side window waiting for him to muster the courage to relate the news that was obviously not going to please him.

"Master, it is a holy place. We cannot enter without being harmed." He realized what he had said, and at the same moment, Bastian snapped his head around again. "Master, of course I would lay myself in harms way for you but we need to be able to claim the soul." He hoped the Dark Angel would find his daring a likeable feature and let him live.

"What holy place is there in such a small residential area of this suburb? Are we not the bearers of the Age of Darkness? Do we not summon the powers of the dark side of the universe?" Bastian looked across at his young apprentice and smiled. "Drandos! Go and see what it is these cowards hide from."

Drandos unlocked the door and slowly swung it open. The moonlight caught him by surprise—the silver rays of reflected light forced him to shield his eyes for a brief moment. He walked a few hundred feet towards the end of the road, periodically looking into the few old houses along the way, to see if he was seen. The air was chilled, making him pull his cloak close around him more tightly. As he walked slowly, he could barely stop his desire to look behind him—he wondered what comments his brother was making about him to the others. His confidence was diminishing with every moment of time he spent with his brother, and his anger grew into to a rage, that festered inside him.

As he got closer to the structure, he was able to perceive the vortex of power well before he could make out the actual building. Drandos knew the power of the dark force of the universe was strong—he had witnessed such strength many times during his initiation and training. However, this was the first time he had personally experienced the power of the light. In this moment, he was absolutely sure the perceptions of the students at his training facility on Orban—regarding the power of the light—were dead wrong—dead wrong indeed. He continued down the street as best he could, staying close to the hedgerows to avoid being seen. He was close enough, now, to make out exactly what kind of holy structure it was. He stopped in his tracks, then turned into the driveway of a large home with a thatched roof and limited lighting. He was able to see enough, to crouch beside the stonewall that edged the entrance to the house, and the acreage it was sitting on.

He saw something that looked like two shadows moving toward the structure, but he couldn't make out exactly what they were. He was sure his brother was not pleased with how long it was taking for him to get back to the car with the information he wanted. Drandos peered through the shrubs and trees, as best he could, to determine the exact nature of the structure. He ignored the two shadows for the moment as he concentrated on the details of the building. He could see the building outline—it was very large and had maybe two or three towers at the front, and one more in the middle, toward the back of the structure. Drandos felt that the power vortex that ran through the building was located at the third tower, near the middle, and towards the back of it. Drandos moved closer still. He navigated his way through the brush and trees along the stonewall that marked the property boundary. He was able to remain hidden, by staying close to the shadow of the wall and avoiding the light of the moon, until he reached the building.

There was a break in the wall, and he crouched down again to get a better view of what he was looking at. He could see clearly now as he peered through the opening. He saw what he knew must be a cathedral of some kind—it was not something he wanted to get too close to. All his trainings advised that practitioners of the Sacred Dark Arts vibrated with a frequency that didn't mesh well with the light of the higher vibrations. If he were to walk through the front door of the cathedral, he would surely not survive for very long. He would be obliterated like a moth being drawn to a bug zapper on a warm summer's evening. The moving shadows were still around the outside perimeter of the sacred ground—they seemed to be searching for a way in. Dodging the rays of the moon so as not to be seen, he followed the shadowy figures with his eyes. The larger of them, who was not careful enough to avoid being hit by the moonlight, had a back that didn't appear normal—it had too much bulk attached to it.

Drandos had seen enough. He decided to retrace his steps back to the others. The night was gaining on him as he pushed his way through the bramble bushes, ground feeders, and trees. He fell a couple of times, as he unsuccessfully, stepped over branches and debris. He cursed his cloak continually, as the brush often tangled it, and the bramble often snagged it. Eventually, he emerged from the driveway. There was not much activity in the area. The homes were upscale and the grounds were considerable—the sidewalks were not lighted very well. The owners valued their privacy more than the safety of walking in a well-lit property—in fact, none of the residents ventured out without their cars. He stayed close to the dark stonewall to avoid being seen, and pulled his cloak tighter to him for more cover of darkness.

Drandos hurried back to the vehicle, looking back down the street periodically, to see if the shadows were still active back at the building. All he could see was moving shadows, that were interrupted by things crossing over them that could have been graveyard animals or other things that crawled about after dark. Drandos made it back to the car. He was dreading the reception he knew he was going to get from his brother. So, he decided to be strong and stand in his power, and just give out any information he had found, regardless of whatever response came his way. As Drandos approached the vehicle, the rear window slowly opened, and the young apprentice moved closer to it.

"Master, the building is as they say, a holy sanctuary. I don't think we can go in." As the words fell from his mouth, Drandos realized he had forgotten to show strength and conviction. Bastian left him waiting outside of the car for his next instructions. Drandos really had formed a deep dislike for his brother that bordered on an obsession to crush his spirit. It even looked sometimes as if Bastian felt some jealousy towards his brother, Drandos did show raw potential and Bastian perceived that as a genuine threat.

"Sanctuary indeed, brother." He swiveled on the plush chair to face his young sibling, menacingly. "Do you really think those travelers could prevent the Angel of Darkness from entering a sanctuary?" He scoffed loudly enough for all inside the car to enjoy the moment. "Get inside the car and wait for me to speak to you again, obviously you are too inexperienced, to be trusted further." Bastian continued to show his obvious contempt for his brother, by slamming the car door, catching Drandos finger in the process, and making the young apprentice wince in pain. "An acute awareness of danger is one of the most prized possessions of every true dark wizard, brother. You must hone your skills to sense the smallest of threats, especially when it involves your pinkies." They all chuckled at the apprentice and a couple of the minions even shook their heads in disgust. How Drandos wished he could return to Orban, to be rid of this constant ridicule and embarrassment.

"That was not funny! I will show you all one day. You will tremble when you hear my name." Drandos tried to sound aggressive, but the way he was holding his hand cradled in his other arm, made them laugh all the more—his brother was stone faced.

"Nurse your wound dear brother. The men will take over from here on." Bastian pulled his cloak around his shoulders and slowly lifted the black leather hood over his head. "Let us go, and be sure to follow my every word, if you value your life." With that, he pushed the door of the luxury car open with his boot—it swung open fully without any effort. Bastian's men left the vehicle and walked up the street toward the structure, Drandos waited until they were a few hundred feet ahead before he left the car and followed. He wasn't about to let them think he was a useless trainee, not when there was such an important event about to take place, where he could make his mark as a real practitioner of the dark arts—even great wizard, he dared to think. He moved in behind the others, carefull not to be detected he spoke to himself as he crept close to the wall. They would see what kind of power he could wield, he thought. The experience on Orban, where he'd captured the soul of a healer, helped strengthen his resolve to make an impact in battling the travelers. Drandos was determined to show his brother how powerful he could be to take the soul of the Prophesied One would be proof of his power, and make him a legend in the Sacred Order of Dark Arts. This would surely force his brother to respect and recognize him as a powerful wizard—all these words he whispered to himself as he followed the others toward the sanctuary.

Bastian led the way—he walked towards the cathedral without any attempts to disguise the fact that he was heading for the driveway that led directly to the sacred structure. The others hugged the bushes, trees, and other barriers, while Drandos quickened his step, and before he was aware of it, he was within 20 yards of the others. The moonlight sprayed the road and brush—it seemed to have painted them silver grey. Bastian had reached the entrance to the driveway. He stopped, and turning to the others, he beckoned with his hand for them to come closer.

"Do you not feel the energy?" They looked at each other in confusion.

"Of course we can feel the energy, Master, we're trained in the ways of the dark order."

"If you are trained as you say, then tell me what you feel?" The Dark Angel closed his eyes and lifted his face slowly upward. He held his left hand in front of him, as if he smelled the beautiful aroma of a delicate rose or the bouquet of a fine wine.

"There is the high vibration of the power of the forces of light in the universe here." The most outspoken of them said with confidence.

"Is that the extent of what you feel?" Bastian had not moved. He still basked in whatever energy he was tuning into.

"Yes, Master," they said in unison, "we sense the power of the light." They were confident after all that they were standing outside the gates of a cathedral, a holy sanctuary, that promised them terrible misery should they dare cross over the boundary and into the high vibration of the sacred territory.

"Then what do you suggest we do to capture the soul that resides beyond those walls?" The Dark Angel held out his arm as straight as an arrow and pointed a finger toward the structure. The most assured of his minions spoke again with a smile on his face, gratified in the fact that he'd beat the others to the answer he thought his master wanted to hear.

"We will wait till the soul leaves the sacred ground, and then take her. She will be no match for me master."

"I dare say you could very well overpower a simple teenage girl." Bastian was bored with the game he was playing. "You!" He pointed to one of the accomplices hanging back behind the others. "I almost missed you there hiding at the back." He was a small man, smaller than the others, and he preferred that one of the others should take the limelight. He was not interested in any glory for himself—he always found that glory hunting brought with it a large helping of pain, for him self anyway. The risk of incurring the wrath of the Dark One, who was known for destroying any one for any reason, was far too high for this little man.

"Yes, Master. Sorry, Master. I didn't mean to hide...I'm just small," he sighed in silence. He had a bad feeling.

"Come forward. I have a task for you and you'd best not fail me." Bastian turned back to face the driveway to the building. The smaller man shuffled his way to the front, and stood half a step back from his master, and to the side. "I want you to walk onto the sacred grounds, up the driveway, and to the doors of the sacred cathedral." The Dark One kept his gaze on the cathedral. "Go! Now!" he hissed. The man jumped forward and walked towards the gateway that led up the driveway to the wooden doors of the building. He tried to evaluate which would be the most painful, the high vibration of the vortex of light that the sacred building stood on or the wrath of his master. The poor soul continued toward the entrance to the gravel driveway. He fully expected to be fried by the surge of power coming from the sacred ground. He stopped at the gateway, and turned his head enough to catch a glimpse of the Dark One, hoping that he would rescind his order. The only thing he saw, and felt, was the long finger of his master poking him in the back with his energy, prodding him to move forward. The minion entertained the idea of fighting for his life for a brief moment. After his moment of insanity, he remembered witnessing how the Dark Angel destroyed his enemies, and decided his choice of how to die was at least in his own hands now. The small man took the first steps onto the driveway, fully expecting to be blown way into the next world.

"Ah…as I suspected," Bastian spoke to no one in particular. The traveler, the one they call Shaulmar, has formidable power and knowledge." He pulled his black leather cloak around him, protecting himself from the chill in the night air. The others followed close behind—they were confused to say the least, to see their colleague was still standing after taking a step inside the sacred ground.

"How can this be?" The small man wandered further along the driveway talking aloud, totally bewildered. "I must be more powerful than even I thought I was. I have surrounded myself with the power of darkness that cannot be penetrated by the light. I am truly worthy of dark master status now." The little man spun around, pulling his short brown tunic with him. Bastian arrived and instantly put a dent in the little man's joy.

"That must be it! You must have gained enough power from the dark world that it has protected you from the power of the light. You truly are blessed by the ancient ones my friend and I bow to your power." Bastian's minion was indeed beside himself with happiness at his good fortune. "The energy you summoned from the dark side of the universe is not easily harnessed. For you to control such power, in such a way as to insulate your body from the forces of light, is truly a sight to behold. Show me again how you did it my friend, so I may learn something more from a truly great practitioner of the dark arts." Bastian stood in front of the man, unmoving, with a cold and stoic expression across his face.

Drandos was close enough now that he saw and heard what was happening. He knew his brother well enough now to know he was up to no good.

"Now," Bastian said, "show me how you conjured the power of the darkness and allowed it to flow through you freely—indeed how you sought to control it and manipulate it—how you commanded that it protect you from the vortex of light that flows through this powerful sacred ground." The Dark One waited, as did the others, wondering why their master was wasting time with this nonsense when there were enemies close by. The little man was still smiling with his chest puffed out and his chin raised he held both arms above his head and cried out…

"Forces of darkness, I command thee to come forth and flow through me and protect me, as you have just done, against the powers of this place." He had a serious expression on his face to convince the onlookers of his deliberate and powerful dark magical abilities. Even though he himself had no clue as to why, or how, he was able to protect himself against certain annihilation from the powers of the light.

"Are you protected at this time, my friend?" Bastian asked with a tone of awe and envy that was indicative of the darkness.

"I am protected by the powers of the darkest forces of the universe. I can feel the power within and around me." The little man had totally convinced himself of what he was saying. It must be true, the others thought, because he stands on sacred ground that is deadly to practitioners of the dark arts.

"Then let me try my humble magic on you so I can learn how a great sorcerer insulates his mind and body with the blessings of the dark forces." Bastian held a fake smile on his face. He twisted his body and cocked his head to one side, pleadingly. The little man drew his brown cloak about himself.

"Please, do your magic. I will show you all how to absorb the energy to make me even more powerful." The poor soul believed every word that came out of his mouth. Slowly, Bastian straightened up and assumed his normal stance. Drandos knew what was coming—he remembered the spear his brother had conjured up out of nothing when he was torturing the soul at his penthouse, when Drandos had arrived on earth not so long ago. A ball of silver energy appeared in Bastian's left hand, and the more he passed his right hand over it, the larger and more powerful it grew. When it had reached the size of a silver grapefruit, slivers of dirty yellow energy ran through it, enhancing the orb. The energy escaped the sphere, and then returned to reconnect at another point on its surface, rather like solar flares from our own sun. Finally, Bastian held up his left hand, with the sphere spinning ferociously a few inches above it, within the boundaries of his palm.

"Well, I'm afraid this is the best I can do. I hope you will not think too badly of me." Before the minion could respond verbally, the sphere left its position and hit its target with such force and venom, that the impact spread the remains of the minion all over the driveway and up to the doors of the Cathedral. "Pity, he had a promising future." The Dark One moved calmly through the entrance and towards the building.

"How could this be?" The others whispered as they followed behind, not giving a second thought about the colleague and compatriot they'd just lost.

"The traveler has manifested this building in order to stall our progress concerning the capture of the soul that is, Rebecca Sullivan. Let this be a very important learning experience for the rest of you. If you wish to become a powerful force within the Sacred Dark order, and more importantly, if you wish to be a member of my elite group, do not make the same mistake he made. Always tune your senses to any changes in energy from one moment to the next, make it second nature, do it without thinking because it could cost you your life." Bastian turned to face them. "We must make our way around the perimeter of the building—presumably the traveler would have anticipated much of what we must do. I want all of you to connect with any energy that does not vibrate to what you are familiar with. Any slight vibration could be of importance, so do not let me down." They knew all too well what was meant by his words. Bastian gave them instructions to move through the grounds in the Zorgan formation, the strongest battle configuration known to them, while he watched over the events from another position.

"When the job is done, and the soul captured, all those who are fortunate enough to survive will be richly rewarded. Fail me and you will not be released from the pain of the fires of hell on Orban for eons. That is my *seal* on this." He turned and disappeared into the shadows. Not even the intense light of the moon could cast a beam on him.

CHAPTER 22

THE MOON WAS AT ITS ZENITH—THE SLIVERS OF MOONlight struck Shaulmar's cloak as he stepped from the bookstore into the alley. He knew there was very little time for him to get to the house. There was only one way Shaulmar knew what would get him there instantly—unfortunately, he also knew he could be destroyed in the process, which was a risk he was prepared to take at this point in time. The great wizard needed to be far enough away from the source of the power, the vortex of light, so as not to be hit with a surge that would be deadly. He quickly found a safe and secluded spot down the far end of the alley, and once there, he pulled the blue stone from his pouch. As he held it in his palm, the healing power of his own soul touched it with his signature. The stone recognized his soul signature, and came to life, lifting off his palm and coming to rest in front of him. Shaulmar was saddened by what he must do, but the beautiful blue stone shone brightly as it was fed by the rays of the moon, shining between and through the clouds. He closed his eyes and spread his arms out to his sides as far as he could, exposing his heart chakra to the blue stone that was directly in front of his chest. It hovered for a moment, then all at once it opened like an egg that had been cracked all over its shell, then it shot toward him, exploding on impact with his heart. There was nothing left behind but the residue of an energy that sparkled in the night, then disappeared like the red embers of a fire that were held on the gusts of summer night breeze until they faded out of sight. Shaulmar was gone.

★★★

Rebecca held Morghanz in her arms—there was a strong bond between them that could only have been fostered many life times before.

"I love you Morghanz. You have given me a lot in the short time we've known each other." Her eyes welled up with tears of love and appreciation for someone who had been good and kind to her. Rebecca had not experienced many instances of such a high level of genuine kindness, in her life, so far.

"Rebecca, I must tell you something before Joaquim gets back."

"What is it?" she loosened her hold on her friend and moved back slightly. Rebecca didn't have a good feeling about what Morghanz was going to say.

"There are extremely low energies around the house above us. I have been sensing them ever since the black entity was removed. I don't get a sense that Shaulmar is there yet, but I do know there are more than one group of beings above us searching this place." Morghanz spoke in a soft, low voice, but stared intensely into Rebecca's eyes as a way of making her understand how serious the situation was. Rebecca turned away from her and walked slowly over to where markings were etched into the ancient cavern wall.

"What do we do? We are safe down here, right? These things can't get us if we stay down here, right Morghanz?" she was looking down at the floor, moving some red gravel stones around with her foot. Morghanz quickly went to her—she put her hand on Rebecca's shoulder and spoke gently to her.

"We cannot stay down here forever, Rebecca. There is danger all around us. Those beings above us are after only one thing, *you*, your *special* soul." She wanted to bring Rebecca back from the denial she was hiding in, and into the reality of the circumstances surrounding them. After a few moments, Rebecca's fear and anger erupted from inside her.

"This is all shit! There is no such thing as ghosts or the devil, and as for taking souls, well that's just...silly crap!" Rebecca had totally lost control. She was heading for the edge of a psychological cliff and was about to plunge herself over the top. Morghanz had to do something and fast.

"We don't have time for this Rebecca, you have to pull yourself together. Think!" She moved towards her slowly. "Think about what has gone on in your life recently. The attacks by the person called Alison, the psychic invasions you experienced by what you call ghosts." Rebecca was looking at her friend by this time and was no longer, childishly, pushing the gravel around. Morghanz continued, "What about the book transporting you down here to the cavern that no one knows of except us." She was trying to make Rebecca relive those experiences, hoping it would bring her back into focus. "The everyday world you hate, Rebecca, you hate for a reason…and that was because your soul was telling you it wasn't real…it was only an illusion…try to remember." By this time, Morghanz had a hold of Rebecca by her shoulders, forcing her to look into her eyes—but Rebecca just started to sob, uncontrollably. "Look Rebecca! I know it is difficult, but you have to hold on," she held her close in her arms and gently kissed the top of her head. Morghanz did not know what else to do to make Rebecca come back. She kissed her again and hugged her closely. She knew the young girl was in so much pain and full of fear. Morghanz felt the tears start to come—they filled her eyes too. The sorceress nuzzled into Rebecca's neck and let the tears fall down her cheeks, then down her neck, wetting her dark hair that was pulled into a ponytail. How could the universe possibly put so much on the shoulders of one, as gentle a soul, as Rebecca, Morghanz thought.

As she wiped a tear from Rebecca's neck, she realized the answer was staring her in the face—it was the only way and had been the only way all along. "Rebecca, Rebecca," she said softly, sniffling at the same time, "your neck! That is your destiny. That is what the sacred prophecy is all about. I mean…your neck is the answer." Morghanz wasn't making any sense, so she took a breath to collect her thoughts. Rebecca looked up at her.

"Morghanz, what are you talking about? What prophecy?" she wiped her eyes and face with her sleeve as she spoke. By now, her eyes were as red as the cavern wall and her face was a little messy and tear-stained.

"It all makes sense now." Morghanz looked up at the cavern ceiling while putting her hands together. "Thank you. I am sorry I lost my trust and faith for a moment. I knew the universe wouldn't let us fall." She turned to Rebecca. "You and I have to go back up above. Can you connect with the book, or the Essence, and take us back up to the house?" Morghanz was full of energy.

"What do you have in mind?" Rebecca used her sleeve to dry her eyes and cheeks some more.

"The prophecy had been handed down, eons ago, by the ancients. I know Shaulmar didn't want to tell you about them, because he believed that to talk about it, made them self-fulfilling." Morghanz prepared the space near the vortex of light while she continued to explain, "the book chose you and transformed its form to become that tattoo on your neck and back. The Dark Angel swore he would make sure the Prophesied One, or soul, would not live long enough to see the balance of souls return to this universe." Morghanz looked up only a couple of times—she was desperately trying to set up a ceremonial altar with the crystals she had with her for the Essence to link them back to the house for transportation.

"So you're saying I am that prophesied soul?" Rebecca had one hand on the cavern wall and the other tenderly fingering her skull and neck where the tattoo began. "What did the prophecy say about this soul?"

"Don't ask me about that, Rebecca. It is not for me to say." Morghanz wasn't about to explain what was written about the soul by the ancient ones. She didn't want Rebecca freaked out any more than she already was.

"You won't tell me! But I am expected to know what to do?" she was annoyed and hurt at the same time.

"You are guided by the Essence now and your soul will tell you what is the right thing to do," Morghanz held her hand against her heart as she spoke. "You must release all fear, and most importantly, you must embrace your future and destiny." She spoke the truth and Rebecca knew it—she felt it inside. As her friend spoke the words, the vibration impacted Rebecca's aura and she saw a purple haze all around Morghanz's head. Because of these things, Rebecca felt like she was telling the truth. She didn't hear the word truth, nor was it printed in neon letters above her friend's head. The way she knew was difficult to describe, it was a combination of feeling the vibration of the words as they struck her heart, and seeing the color. When Rebecca saw the color purple it meant purity and power to her, or wisdom, that could only come with truth.

"I guess I should try to connect with the book then?" Rebecca wasn't at all sure she could—she didn't remember how it had happened the last time, so how could she initiate it this time, she wondered. She sat on a big red boulder with her head in her hands, thinking how she could have ever come to be in such a stupid state.

"Okay, Rebecca, I have done the best I can to replicate the ceremonial occasion—the only things we don't have are a candle and incense."

"That's okay, we can call Joaquim back and use the torch that he made." She pointed down the passageway where they could still hear him talking to himself as he worked to find materials to sustain the torch.

"No…no," Morghanz whispered, "we must leave him here." She was deadly serious.

"Why?" Rebecca felt panic in her heart at the thought of harm coming to her young friend. "If we leave him, he will be scared, and I won't do that to him. I won't desert him." Rebecca was also deadly serious.

"Do you want to see him die?" That was a little bit below the belt, but Morghanz had to get her point across. Rebecca could be just as stubborn as Morghanz, and insist that Joaquim go with them.

"Die! What do you mean? Don't say that okay? Joaquim is just a kid and he shouldn't even be involved in this shit. How can you even say that to me?" Rebecca was angry, but she also knew that Morghanz was telling her this for some good reason.

"Yes I agree—and I don't want to see him hurt either. If he comes with us there is a definite possibility that he will die." She was telling Rebecca, the reality of the situation that made her cry with anger, then basically have a temper tantrum that released a lot of her inner anguish that she'd been carrying around for some time. Being the gentle, compassionate, and caring person for others all of her life, had taken its toll. Most of those on the receiving end of Rebecca's affections and considerations, were just takers from life, and that was always difficult for Rebecca to stomach. She could never understand how one person could intentionally hurt another. She sat back down on the red boulder, hung her head, and breathed heavily.

"So, Morghanz, we leave Joaquim here and tell him *what*?" she was still angry, but not at Morghanz, just at the truth she'd told her.

"Well, it's simple really, we just tell him it is very important that he remain down here in the cavern so he can search the labyrinth for our escape route. We tell him that we are to go up to the house to let Shaulmar know where we are and to help him escape the dark invaders." She raised one corner of her mouth as if to say, unfortunately, men are easily fooled when courage and fearlessness are asked of them. "Joaquim will embrace the responsibility readily. He has a good soul." Morghanz leaned her head to one side, letting Rebecca know there was no other way.

"Well, that really *sucks*!" Rebecca bent her head down, almost to her knees, and wrapped her arms around it, as if she just wanted to hide from everything. Morghanz had made her point—now she just wanted to take Rebecca's pain away—but that was impossible, all she could do was be close to her and maybe console her in some small insignificant way. As she put her hand on her shoulder, and then her head, she asked herself could she live the life destined to be Rebecca's. She was not sure she could, even with all the incarnations Morghanz had experienced, that had provided her with opportunities to accumulate knowledge and wisdom, and to develop the ability to give and receive love unconditionally—she still was not sure she could embark on the path her friend was about to take. Morghanz gently pulled Rebecca's head into her stomach. She wanted to protect her and tell her everything was going to be okay, but she wasn't sure herself.

"It's okay, Rebecca. We must trust in the wisdom of the Creator, and have faith that we walk the path that is chosen for us. As long as we stay on the right path, no matter what happens, we will have fulfilled our destiny." By this time, Morghanz had both hands on either side of Rebecca's face—she braved a smile to try to inject a little love and higher energy into the situation. "If we are going to do this Rebecca, we must do it now, because Joaquim will be back at any moment." Rebecca had lifted her head from Morghanz's embrace and resigned herself to the task of getting them both out of the Templars' cavern and back into the house.

"Okay Morghanz, do you have any ideas about how I can connect with the book again because I don't remember much about how it comes to me." Rebecca was genuinely serious—she had lost consciousness every time the book had connected with her and when she had channeled the Essence, thus far. However, there was one exception, it was when the Essence revealed itself as the green misty light.

"Let me think for a minute. There must be a trigger that allows you to connect to the book." Morghanz paced up and down for a few moments. "I think I may have an idea as to how you can connect." She thought some more and then turned back to her friend. "We must think of what the book, or essence, is here for and why it is with you, bound forever. I will try to recall what the prophecy foretells." Again Morghanz paced up and down.

"Morghanz! Think faster! If Joaquim comes back, I won't have the strength to leave him here alone. We must leave him a note and be gone before he returns, please!" Rebecca was imploring her to quickly remember what the prophecy said about the connection to the book.

"Wait! I think I remember. I think it goes something like…the soul that has chosen to be eternally bound to the Book of Secrets will know the secrets of the book by joining the heart and mind. When heart and mind are brought into alignment, the Essence will be summoned, and there will take place a connection." Morghanz twirled her hand as she spoke the words, "It was not something I was included in when Shaulmar ask the Sacred High Council to send me down to assist with your protection. I did, however, read some things on the prophecy some years ago, and I might add, not many others thought the prophecy to be real." Morghanz shrugged her shoulders.

"So, what do you think now?" Rebecca subconsciously rubbed the tattoo on her neck at the back.

"Well, obviously it's real, and I feel honored to be part of the beginnings of your journey, Rebecca." She meant every word, something Rebecca understood clearly.

"What am I supposed to do according to this so-called prophecy?" she mulled around again, frustrated, not knowing what the future held for her.

"I honestly don't know. It wasn't the kind of thing that was talked about in open circles. Mostly, it was kept under wraps by the Sacred High Council and passed down through the eons as each council changed. Shaulmar was only one of the few respected wizards trusted with its secrets, and, even he took an oath never to speak of it outside the council." Morghanz took Rebecca's hand and led her to the table where she once lay sick, as the tentacles of the black entity did its work. "You must connect with the Essence now—it is time for us to begin this ceremony." She gave her the best reassuring smile that she could while resting a loving hand on Rebecca's shoulder.

"Okay, okay," Rebecca lay on the table, feeling a little anxious, but determined. "All I have to do is bring my heart and my mind into alignment, right?"

"Yes. Remember, it is just like when we used to practice mindfulness meditation. Focus on your breath, and then transfer that mindfulness to your heart, as you visualize your beautiful pink or green heart chakra, then hold that focus, and allow the feelings of calm, peace, and love to merge with any thoughts that enter your mind." Morghanz was confident her protégé could make the connection.

"Then what? Then what? What do I do then? Do I ask the Essence to come or what...what do I say?" Rebecca had her eyes closed and was lying down, almost hyperventilating.

"Just follow my instructions—the rest will take care of itself." Morghanz tried to sound as calm as she could but she knew Rebecca would pick up on her uncertainty.

"Don't worry, Morghanz, if I am truly the Prophesied One, I'm sure the Essence is just as willing to be with me as I am with it." She made simple but logical sense, even if there was a definite hint of sarcasm and an inherent lack of trust and faith in her voice. The young girl began to breathe deeply, trying desperately to relax with every exhalation, as one thought after another careened through her mind, furiously. She wondered whether the Essence was real, for sure, and if it would re-emerge from her again. Rebecca thought about what they would find if they were able to get back up to the house, then her thoughts ran to Joaquim, and what would happen to him if they left. Anxiety and worry entered the fray.

"Rebecca, slow down your breathing and think of your heart, what it feels like, and the many times it sang when you helped someone out of kindness and love." Morghanz could sense she was struggling to reach the state where she could make the connection with the Essence. Finally Rebecca was breathing slower—her inhales were long and slow, and her exhales were similar. "Now, feel the gentle strong beat of your heart; focus on that until it is all you hear." Morghanz was beginning to get a hold on her young friend and was starting to guide her to the place where she could connect with the Essence.

Rebecca looked calm and peaceful, still breathing slowly in a steady and rhythmic fashion, as she lay on the table. "The place you are now is only halfway to the connection to the Essence, Rebecca. Now, you need to send love from the heart chakra to the crown chakra at the top of the head. Visualize a rainbow-colored cord of light that begins from your heart area…traveling up to the top of your head…and connecting with the crown chakra." She did as she was asked, she was feeling as light as a feather, her arms were laying on the table, but she could hardly feel them touching it. She wondered if this was what she had heard on TV as being an out-of-body experience, but she recognized her mind was wandering, and brought it gently back to the picture in her head of the beautiful rainbow. "If you feel okay, and you think you are ready, you can ask that the Essence make a connection with you." Morghanz was worried for her friend, and she did not have a plan in mind to help her, if things went wrong. Trust and faith were the only things she had to rely on, she told herself. Morghanz became very scared as she watched her friend lying motionless, for what seemed to be the longest time—she was about to forget the whole thing, and move to the table and wake her, when Rebecca's eyes opened.

"Morghanz, we have not met previously, however, Rebecca thinks of you many times during her waking hours." The Essence had made the connection and was speaking through Rebecca once more.

"You are the Essence that was once the Book of Secrets?" Morghanz was startled it was the only thing that she could think to say.

"That is correct." Rebecca stared at her friend but there was nothing behind the girl's eyes.

"Can you tell me, is Rebecca okay?" Morghanz realized how silly the question was after it had left her lips. Of course, Rebecca was going to be okay—the Essence had chosen her to bind with—she was in safe hands.

"Yes, my friend, she is in safe hands." The Essence wanted her to know that her thoughts were known as they formed.

"We have to get back up to the house. There is danger forming and we have to get back to our friend." Morghanz felt a little odd speaking to Rebecca when she was actually not there.

"Yes, I have actually known about the danger for some time." Rebecca sat up, swung her legs off the table and reached out a hand to Morghanz. "Please—sit with me." The Essence was truly a beautiful being, and the energy coming from Rebecca, was angelic in nature. Morghanz moved closer. "There have been some changes to the house we've come from. The wizard, Shaulmar, has transformed the house into a structure designed to discourage the Dark Ones from entering."

"My God, we have to help him." Morghanz shuddered.

"We can go back up there, but Morghanz you will not know the place, so be aware, and stay hidden. I will remain with Rebecca always, and protect her as best I can, but she has not fully accepted the binding yet. When she has developed belief and trust that our souls are bound, then she will be ready to fulfill her destiny that was prophesied long ago."

"You must take us back up there, and when you do, you must bring Rebecca back to consciousness. Shaulmar may be in trouble." Morghanz had Rebecca by both hands at this point. She began to feel desperate when she heard Shaulmar was in danger because she loved him so much. "I couldn't bear to lose him again." Rebecca lay back down on the table and adjusted her body for comfort.

"Rebecca will return soon," the Essence said, "then she must call on me to take you back—this is how the binding is to progress."

"What do you mean progress?" Morghanz became anxious again. "Why can't you just transport us as usual? There is danger up there and we need to help Shaulmar, quickly."

"The condition that exists between bound souls is that of progression, through learning and accumulation of knowledge, in order for the evolution of the soul to take place. This begins with Rebecca learning to call upon the powers of the light to assist her. It is her right as the bound soul, and is required for the activation of the sacred law, that wields the power within the prophecy.

"How will she know what to do?" Morghanz was terrified that Rebecca could fail and Shaulmar would be lost forever.

"Trust and faith Morghanz—that is part of *your* learning experience this time around, I am being told." The Essence laid Rebecca down on the table and said no more. After a few moments, Rebecca opened her eyes once more, swallowed hard, and breathed again. The change in her vocal cords made her throat a little sore and dry.

"Ahem, ahem, did everything go okay?" Rebecca rubbed her throat and looked around at the cavern walls. "We are still in the cavern!" She started freaking out. "Why are we still here? Did the Essence speak…or did I just blackout? Oh God…" She was on the verge of having an anxiety attack. Morghanz reached for her quickly.

"It's okay Rebecca, the Essence spoke, so everything is okay," she held her close and kissed the top of her head once more.

"But…but…why are we still here and not in the house then? Something must have gone wrong." She sniffled in Morghanz's cloak.

"Nothing has gone wrong. There is only one thing that is different," Morghanz paused.

"What! What thing?" Rebecca looked at her, very puzzled.

"The Essence said *you* must take us up to the house. You are to connect with the Essence. This means you have progressed, and all I know is, those are the rules attached to this whole binding process." She gave Rebecca a half-smile and half-grimace expression.

"How am I supposed to do that? Did the Essence give instructions on how I can take us up to the house, because I have no clue how to do such a thing?" Rebecca sat up and swung her legs over the edge of the table, she was completely serious, she had no idea how to initiate something like that. Morghanz fell silent for a moment. "Morghanz, what are you thinking? I know when you're having an idea about something. I've known you long enough to know that at least. What are you considering?" Morghanz just slowly walked across the passageway, stroking the amulet on her wrist, as she always did when she was processing information, sometimes glancing over at Rebecca.

"I think you must begin by believing in what is happening, and that you are special. The Essence mentioned that it is your right as a bound soul to call out for assistance from the light." Morghanz was struggling to piece together all the information for Rebecca.

"Call out to the light? What light? I don't know the light, except outside, its light." She was really confused now. She rubbed her eyes and sniffed a couple of times.

"I know, Rebecca, but I thought about it, and it hit me—the power of the light is right here—it's the vortex. It runs directly through the center of the house—it's what keeps the house from being discovered. It's the protection that Shaulmar put around us." Morghanz held up her arms, indicating the vortexes proximity. "The Essence was letting you know what to use to activate your power." Rebecca was silent. She was trying to put her friends words into thoughts she could understand. "You have to start believing Rebecca. Please, embrace your destiny. The reason you incarnated here was to fulfill your destiny and experience the evolution of the soul as was prophesied many eons ago."

"Okay…okay. I remember Shaulmar telling me about the vortex when we were first transported down here. He said it came from the universe, and that it flowed through the earth, and back out to join with the universe again, so the power was actually limitless." Rebecca spaced out for a moment then turned to face her friend. "I…I think I can do this Morghanz. All I have to do is believe like you said, and like Shaulmar said, and then I can do this. You are wizards and travellers, so I will draw upon the energy of your experiences, because I truly believe you guys when you tell me all the things you've done and the places you have travelled to. So, there is no reason that I cannot be part of all that." She fell silent for a moment and Morghanz began to smile. "Those people who are out to kill me must believe me to be the Prophesied One also." The young girl was looking down at the red soil, pushing it around with her shoe, as she spoke. "So, if they believe it, then it must be so, and I will draw power from their belief also." Rebecca was growing in confidence, and the more she thought about it, the more she realized that she was very smart and capable of becoming who she really was.

"That's it, Rebecca! Reason and intelligence are the tools of the wizard, and wisdom and knowledge are the strength. You're going to make a fine sorceress." Morghanz smiled excitedly. "Right, let's get back up to the house, or whatever it is that is manifested but first, we must let Joaquim know where we are and what he must do. I will write a message on the cavern wall so he will see it when he returns. Rebecca, you must get us up to the house as soon as you can." Morghanz picked up a very dark stone and began writing a message on the wall. Rebecca moved towards the passageway where she remembered Shaulmar had told her about the vortex of light, and had showed her exactly where it flowed, and how to connect with it. She put her hand up in front of her, palm facing out, and slowly moved towards the center of the passageway. When she felt the energy intensify, and when she could feel the strength and power of the vortex, she stopped. It felt like pushing her hand against a solid beam of energy of some kind.

"Morghanz, I've found the vortex of light. I can feel a tingle in my spine. It wants to transport us back up to the house I can feel it. I didn't even have to call upon its power." Rebecca was so happy and her belief in the whole wizard-prophecy thing grew with each passing moment. Morghanz ran to where she stood.

"The vortex must have recognized your soul signature and your intent to be of service." She stood next to Rebecca and reached for her hand.

"Just to be sure that you don't go alone," said Morghanz. Rebecca looked at her friend and gave her hand a gentle but strong squeeze. "I can feel the energy connecting to my chest and forehead. Wow! That's a weird feeling."

"Get used to it Rebecca—that is the connection or alignment of heart and mind. Once they are in balance and harmony you can do anything—trust me."

"Morghanz, you're shaking." Rebecca turned to her and reassured her. "Morghanz, I do believe, now, more than ever. Please don't worry. We will find Shaulmar." Suddenly there was a surge of energy that was very powerful.

"Rebecca! Your neck…it's turning green…it's the tattoo…the Essence is connecting also with the vortex."

"Yes, yes. I can feel it tapping into the vortex. I think it wants me to initiate the transportation of us up to the house," Rebecca said excitedly. "I…create the thought, make the intention, and… and send my energy there. The Essence is talking to me, Morghanz. I know how to do this now. It seems so simple."

"When you are pure of heart, and are in harmony with the universe, then that is how it is supposed to be according to the teachings of the sacred order. Those qualities have to be in place before any initiation into the sacred order can be accepted. Rebecca, your abilities are innate—it usually takes years of practice before someone can do what you're doing right now. I'm so proud of you." Morghanz stood ready for the transformation to take place. Rebecca closed her eyes and created the thought of what she wanted to happen, and then basically, wished for it to be so. As soon as the thought was complete, there was an immediate power surge that surrounded them both.

The walls and floor of the cavern became somewhat obscured as the energy swirled faster and faster around them. Rebecca gripped Morghanz's hand harder and harder, moments passed and then they became energy…light. They were in their *light bodies* and were able to communicate and see each other as they travelled. Rebecca sent the thought to Morghanz that she didn't remember this when she was transported the first time with Shaulmar. She heard Morghanz's thoughts too—she told her that this was similar to the way they travelled through the portals to other dimensions, and other worlds, or from just one place to the next. They both watched the colors flash by them as they travelled inside the swirling energy. The next thing they knew, they were slowing down and they felt themselves become so much heavier as they reunited with their physical bodies. Rebecca commented on the heaviness she felt as they slowed and left their light bodies. Morghanz warned her that when they stopped they would be back in the house, and the Essence through Rebecca's channeling, had cautioned them to be very careful when they arrived there.

"Rebecca, the Essence told me the house was no longer the same—its structure has been changed by Shaulmar for the protection of us all. This was to stall the dark ones from entering, and when we leave the protection of the vortex, we must find a place to hide right away until we get our bearings. The swirling energy that transported them from the cavern had slowed enough where they could just make out where they were going to be when it stopped. It looked like a stone room with what looked like an altar, but they couldn't identify it quite yet. Suddenly they were standing there without any protection, in the middle of a small stone room.

"Quick, Rebecca, get behind the altar." Morghanz pulled on her hand and they both crouched behind a table, with the golden silk cloth draped over the altar, covering them as they huddled behind it.

"Wow! This is a church," she whispered, "are we in the right place? Morghanz, maybe I screwed up and sent us to the other end of the planet." Rebecca had a very worried look on her face.

"No, it's okay. This is the place where the house stood. Tune into the vibration beneath us and you will recognize it then." Morghanz was right. Rebecca felt the energy as soon as she thought about it. "Your tattoo is back to its original state. The Essence must have become dormant again."

"Yeah…it must have because I don't feel it any more." She closed her eyes for a moment. "No, I don't hear it speaking to me either. It must've gone to sleep…or whatever it does when it becomes silent." Rebecca felt kind of sad. The Essence was no longer active, she felt more assured when it was with her and she could feel its presence.

"I guess you miss the connection with the Essence. After all, you are bound souls, Rebecca."

"Yeah, but it is kind of creepy when you think about it though." They both remained hidden, listening for any evidence of others in the church. Morghanz turned to Rebecca and put her finger on her own lips. "Don't make a sound. I think there is some one or some energy close by." Morghanz slowly slipped a clear quartz crystal from her pouch—it was programmed to amplify energy, her energy, just in case she needed to blast someone.

CHAPTER 23

THE NIGHT WAS SLOWLY GIVING WAY TO THE DAWN, THERE were still shadows moving through the moonlight but they were very dim. The moon was slowly disappearing into the new dawn sky. A point of light could be seen streaking across between the clouds, it passed through the walls of the cathedral—it could have been mistaken for a ray of sunlight as the sun approached the horizon. Shaulmar had arrived. The master wizard had travelled through time and space to help his friends against the forces of darkness. When the energy of the portal exit allowed the opening of the window, Shaulmar manifested from his light body to his physical body in order to enter the physical plane. Quickly, he lifted from his knees to his feet and slipped behind one of the stone pillars inside the cathedral. He was still dazed and waiting for the energy to reconfigure so as to vibrate correctly in the third dimension, he grounded his energy into the earth while he leaned against the pillar. Shaulmar knew he was taking a huge risk manifesting the sacred space of the cathedral around a vortex of light, and to do it while his friends were not aware was even more of a risk. However, he was not going to stand by and remain at the Great Hall of the Sacred High Council waiting to hear of Rebecca's capture from some committee meeting, or another soul claimed by the dark forces discussion. As he drew all his energy back into his physical body, he noticed his clear quartz crystal glowing like crazy. This meant only one thing; dark entities were close by and were close enough to attack. He wanted to find his friends before the others did, he took in a deep breath and then closed his eyes so he could tune into the energies that were in the ancient cathedral.

After a while he detected the vibration of Morghanz, and determined that it came from the other end of the building, in a small chapel on a lower level, in the wing of St John. He also detected strong vibrational energies around the peripheral of the sacred grounds, and he knew there was little time left before all intentions were clear. There were stone pillars, rooms on either side of the structure, and at the center was a huge space full of pews and other religious paraphernalia. Shaulmar needed to get from one end of the cathedral to the opposite end, in hopes of meeting up with Morghanz and Rebecca. He didn't like being separated from them, especially with the inevitable attack from Bastian and other forces of evil he had detected on the outside of the structure, being so near. His crystal had not stopped glowing, which told him that soon he would be forced to protect his friends or die trying. How could he navigate the huge structure he had called forth, that he'd used all his power and strength of mind to create, he wondered. A pathway would need to be found to give the wizard enough protection and stealth for him to move through the structure without detection. He stood behind one of the huge supporting stone pillars at the end of the cathedral. The pillar held up one end of an incredible wooden beam that ran down the center of the huge hall like the spine in some enormous prehistoric animal. The wizard looked up, and wandered if it might be more prudent to travel to his friends by way of the huge supporting beam, from above. He looked around to make sure he was alone, then he reached into his cloak pulling out a red bag with a substance hidden inside—it tasted like raw ginger root with a hint of Darjeeling tea. As he chewed the substance, the juices ran down his throat, and when he had finished and swallowed the mixture, he whispered an incantation that began with "the Sacred Power of the Light…." Before too much longer he had elevated to the height of the beam and was atop it, sixty feet off the ground, walking steadily to the other end of the Cathedral.

***

"When do you think we should get out from under this alter table and leave this room to find out if there is anyone in this place? Obviously the connection I made with the vortex, and I might add, with the guidance of the Essence, has resulted in a huge mistake because I think we have been transported to a place other than Shaulmar's house." Rebecca was tired of hiding and wanted to get out of the smelly, little room.

"Okay…but I think we should be very, very, careful—don't forget what the Essence said." Morghanz paused for a moment. "Oh, sorry, you don't know what was said.

Let me tell you," Morghanz looked at Rebecca and whispered, "the Essence said the place would be changed into something that could dissuade the forces of darkness from entering, and this looks to me like a church or a cathedral, don't you think?" she said, poking her head beneath the altar tapestry that reached down to the floor and was providing cover for them both.

"It does." Rebecca sniffled. "So we should not be afraid to come from beneath this smelly altar because we are in a sacred space, right?" she had a point, something that Morghanz could not really dispute.

"All right, let me go first then, but let's check our crystals to see if they indicate any danger that may be close." Both of them fumbled for the respective amulets and neither one of them were glowing. "Okay, I will go outside the chapel and see what is there." Morghanz was certain there was nothing outside, because she'd sent her energy outside the room earlier and sensed nothing. She pushed the tapestry away from the altar and emerged from beneath very cautiously. Almost immediately, Rebecca came from beneath the altar also, not waiting for the all clear from her friend. She crawled on her hands and knees to avoid touching the ancient tapestry—to her sensitive nose it smelt like an old musty curtain that had hung in the same window untouched for at least a hundred years.

"Ugh! That smells awful. I think I'm going to throw up," she hissed.

"Don't breathe in again until you reach the door. The spores within the tapestry material are extremely old, you may be allergic to them." Morghanz stepped into the hallway beside the great open area of the cathedral that was full of pews, with cushions on the stone floor at every seat.

"Wow, if this is the old house, how could it have changed into such a huge cathedral? This must be the size of a football field," Rebecca said, forgetting they were trying to stay out of sight, as she walked between the seats into the open area to look at the huge ceiling that hung above them that was cradled by the enormous stone walls and pillars on all sides.

"This is more like a fortress," Morghanz said quietly. "This is the work of only one wizard that I know." She frantically looked around, while pulling Rebecca back, almost causing her to stumble. "Just in case I am wrong, we must remain out of sight for now." She dragged Rebecca backwards gently enough, so as to prevent her from tripping and falling, but strong enough that she was forced to go with her behind a pillar closest to the chapel. "We should navigate a pathway to the other side of the church, just in case we are being tracked by dark forces who may already know of our position. It is always best to keep moving—making it more difficult for them." They both made themselves as small as possible, without restricting their ability to move through the cathedral easily. Rebecca always remained a little behind her friend, it was an unspoken agreement between them, that Morghanz was the protector and Rebecca the protected.

The stained glass windows above the holy altar at the end of the huge congregational area, collected light from outside, and dispersed it throughout the sacred place. The sun was high enough now that shards of sunlight entered and fell all about the stone flooring and sculptures that were positioned beautifully along the hallways. The windows on the east side of the cathedral were also letting in the morning light that was helping Morghanz and Rebecca see more clearly, but they were also able to be seen by others more easily, which was not such a great thing. "It's getting too light in here Rebecca, we have to find a place to hide again until Shaulmar can get to us."

"No need for that my dears." Shaulmar whispered from the rafters directly above them. "I am here now, but we do need to find a secure place inside this manifestation to confer and develop a strategy. The darkness is upon us, make no mistake dear ones." He spoke urgently and floated down beside them where they were standing.

"Oh, thank God you're safe! I was very concerned Shaulmar. We didn't know if we were going to be able to reach you after we were transported back down to the Templars' cavern." Morghanz hugged him—her feelings were never to be denied her ever again, she'd decided.

"Shaulmar, we are scared to death...well I am," the sorceress said. "Things have happened and the bad guys are apparently very close to us here."

Rebecca was also very happy the great wizard was there with them. Just being in his presence she was able to feel safer and not be in fear of danger so much she thought, as she laid her head on his chest and threw her arms around them both. Shaulmar looked around cautiously—even though an ancient stonewall, and huge pillars concealed them—he could still sense the dark forces were ever so close.

"Please," he whispered, "come—we need to find a crypt within the cathedral so we can hide and make plans." He moved away from them and toward the old stone wing of the structure, hidden by an enormous oak and iron doorway. As soon as Shaulmar reached the door, he held up a hand immediately—the door creaked open and he ushered them inside where they encountered an ancient stone stairway leading down the damp passageway to the royal crypt of the ancestors of the sacred order.

"Where are we, Shaulmar?" Rebecca asked, wondering how it was possible for him to move through this immense structure as if he had lived here for years.

"We are where we have always been." He pushed on a couple of stone statues at a certain point and the wall behind them produced a small opening—it was a doorway to yet another room. "What you are experiencing and seeing with your own eyes has always been here. I forced it to manifest on the physical plane. In actuality, this cathedral has been here for many millennia. It was built by a culture that resonated with the light of the universe. They were actually the ones responsible for providing the place where the vortex of light was able to anchor the light of the universe on earth." He was still working to find the location of the royal crypt of the ancestors as he spoke.

"How could human beings manage to provide anything that could be of any possible help, to something with such immense and obvious power, as the vortex of light?" Rebecca was trying desperately to understand, and at the same time, was totally blown away that she had even asked the question.

"There are many wonders to the universe that Shaulmar and I have experienced. The one common thread that links them all to the realm of possibility is very simple and beautiful in nature." Morghanz paused for effect.

"Come on Morghanz, don't let me suffer through the agony of ignorance." Rebecca had certainly grown in stature and maturity, which was reflected by her willingness to engage in such an *out-there* discussion of possibilities.

"Well, what I was referring to is the simplicity and beauty of trust and faith that can be attained through belief and prayer. The people whom Shaulmar was referring to prayed continuously, day and night, in the total belief that they, with the help of the powers of the universe, could be the channels for the vortex of light to be anchored into the earth for eternity." Morghanz was feeling good about being able to inform Rebecca about the history of the ancient ones, and the light of the universe, as it pertained to the Earth and its evolution.

"So, if I cultivate trust and faith that I am protected and guided on my destined path by the powers of the universe, and if I develop belief in such things, then I will create the possibility for soul growth and evolution?"

"No, not possibility, probability, of soul growth and evolution." Morghanz corrected her thinking and directed her to a most important distinction. Rebecca fell silent while she attempted to grasp and process the information and *concept* that had been presented to her. At least it took her mind from the fear of the danger ahead that they were facing. Meanwhile, Shaulmar continued trying to locate the royal crypt. Once he was able to activate a certain combination of locks, and through the use of various hidden icons around the cold stone room, he would be able to find them a safe room for a while. At least that was his idea, because he knew danger was getting closer by the minute. Finally, he located the lock—it was a carving, a stone carving, of Archangel Michael at one end of a sarcophagus, beside the furthest wall, and beyond the stone stairway. He reached into the nook that held the sculpting, and tried to pull down on the spear in the hands of the Archangel, as he plunged it simultaneously into the heart of one of the devil's minions. This was not happening as easily as he'd wanted, his hand was too big, and he was having a hard time getting his thick fingers around the shaft of the spear. Rebecca noticed he was struggling, so she looked around to tell Morghanz about it, but she was at the other end of the room surveying an escape route should they need one. Rebecca couldn't watch the gentle wizard struggle any longer so she slowly walked over to where Shaulmar was kneeling. His body language expressed his frustration at not being able to activate the locking mechanism.

"Shaulmar." He stopped moving and turned his head towards the sound of her voice. He tried to place a fake smile of calm on his face to hide his frustration. Rebecca spoke quite loudly. "It's okay Shaulmar, let me help." He had a blank look on his face. "Well, it's not like I'm forcing you to ask for directions now is it?" she snickered again, and again quite loudly, she was enjoying this. Rebecca gently pushed him away from the hole in the wall. "Now," she said, "what do I do?" Rebecca was always good at putting people at ease in this way, she had done this as far back as she could remember.

"Okay, if you could just place one hand inside the opening and feel around for the iconic sculpting of Archangel Michael holding his spear, then gently put your fingers around the spear between his hand and where the spear enters the body of the evil minion he has his foot on. When you have accomplished that, then all that is needed, is that you pull the spear toward you—then the secret doorway into the sacred royal crypt should reveal itself. I think it would be over there were Morghanz is standing." Rebecca gently moved Shaulmar aside from the space in front of the hole in the wall were Saint Michael was concealed and knelt beside the opening.

"So, I just reach in and pull on the spear like you said, then a door to the royal crypt will magically appear over there—where you said it would be?" she looked at the stonewall at the far end of the room, and as she did, she realized that she was more nervous than she had anticipated—anything could be inside that hole.

"That's right, pull the spear toward you and we will be able to enter into the sacred crypt." Rebecca reached inside the opening, slowly and carefully, and began to feel for Saint Michael's spear. Her hand touched something really soft and web-like and that immediately made her recoil back out of the opening.

"Oh God! That felt horrible! There is a huge spider in there or something furry." She sat three feet away from the sarcophagus, leaning back on her hands, and looking as white as a ghost.

"Rebecca, there are no spiders. I will clean up the hole for you. Then you can try again, okay?" Shaulmar put his hand in opening as far as it would go and pulled out all of the debris, cobwebs, bits of stone and gravel, and bone. "It is clear now, Rebecca. Please, hurry and open the doorway. I can sense the darkness is getting closer." He motioned for her to try again.

"Okay, okay, don't rush me. I don't care what you say, Shaulmar, there was a furry *something* in there." She had a look on her face that let him know that she would be happy to shove his head up the full length of *said* hole to prove it. Slowly, Rebecca moved back to the opening at the end of the sarcophagus and knelt close to it. The floor was made up of ancient stone pieces that knitted together with a laser-like precision that made it more comfortable to sit down or kneel on. However, she still winced a couple of times as she maneuvered into the position that allowed her the longest reach possible once she put her arm back in the opening again.

"When you put your hand around the spear, Rebecca, just gently ease it backward towards yourself…it should move easily without any resistance." He stood over her with his hands inside the sleeves of his cloak.

"No resistance, huh." She remarked sarcastically while making a few odd looking facial expressions as she fumbled around inside the opening. The young girl grimaced a couple of times as her hand touched something soft and hairy. Using all her willpower and trust and faith she avoided yanking her arm from the opening once more. She had always felt a certain amount of fear when putting her arms or legs into places that concealed them. Fear of the unknown had always frightened her but in this situation she figured it was more fearful to remain in that little room than whatever brushed by her hand. Her fingers finally brushed against something hard and cold, she had finally touched the sculpting of the saint. "Shaulmar, I think I found it," she cast her eyes up to the wizard which was all she could do while having her cheek pressed against the opening at the stone sarcophagi. This was the result of her arms being much shorter than his, something she had not considered before offering her help. "Here goes." Rebecca gave a gentle tug on the spear of Saint Michael.

"Rebecca, are you okay?" Shaulmar asked immediately.

"I...I think so. I'm just a little stressed out right now but I moved the spear. You were right it came easily toward me, did the doorway open?" she spoke as she carefully pulled her arm out of the opening. It was at that very moment she felt the most searing pain in her back that she had ever experienced in her life before. "Oh my Lord, what is happening to me? God, the pain is so intense I..." She fell forward onto the stone floor and collapsed in a state of unconscious. Morghanz and Shaulmar rushed to her, but almost immediately the Essence left Rebecca's body and manifested as the beautiful green mist that hovered above her. Shaulmar put his hands out to his side and stopped Morghanz from going any closer.

"It's okay Shaulmar, this is the...was the book. It is the Essence that is bound to Rebecca's soul, we are in no danger."

"But what about Rebecca? What happens now?" He asked with a trace of anxiety in his voice, he had come to love Rebecca as his own daughter and to see her that way was very painful for him. They both picked Rebecca up off the cold stone floor and sat her against the wall. Morghanz put her cloak under her for comfort. Rebecca was in and out of consciousness, but seemed to be okay although, she was in quite a lot of pain.

"Morghanz, can you—can you help with the pain, it feels like something is burning into my skin." She said half conscious and half coherent.

"Yes dear, just hold on I have something in my pouch that should help. Where does it feel like it is burning you?" Morghanz fumbled around in the leather pouch. At that point Shaulmar was satisfied that Rebecca was okay and turned his attention to the energy that had moved away from them and continued to float and hover nearby.

"Can you communicate with me Essence?" He tried to make contact with the green mist. Morghanz held the Salve in her hand and brushed Rebecca's hair from her face then asked once more.

"Tell me where you feel the burning Rebecca."

"Ah, on my back, near my left shoulder Morghanz." It was difficult for her to talk, because the pain was too much, she held her breath periodically to help her with the pain, and slowly exhaled which seemed to help. Morghanz gently move to her right side while still allowing her friend to rest against the wall for support. Rebecca's left side of her back and shoulder became exposed as soon as Morghanz loosened her top to access her skin. She then realized why there was so much pain.

"Rebecca, just relax and breathe in deeply and slowly. Do you remember the meditation and yoga exercises we practiced?"

"Yeah—yes I think so." She whispered.

"Well just focus on that and try to remember how we did the exercises. Inhale what ever you think of as being love, and exhale any anxiety and negativity that is held in your body okay?"

"Uh… Okay I will try." She was in terrible pain but she slowly began to inhale gently which brought her peace and seemed to eventually soothe her and took her mind off the pain somewhat. Morghanz gently rubbed the salve on her shoulder and without letting Rebecca see what she was doing she beckoned for Shaulmar to come over to where they were, she needed him to witness what she saw.

"What is it?" He whispered in her ear.

"Look!" Morghanz pulled back Rebecca's shirt revealing the source of her pain. Shaulmar said nothing for a while he just stood starring in amazement at the manifestation on Rebecca's shoulder. After a few moments he put a hand gently on Morghanz's shoulder and walked back to the Essence.

"You must speak with me, it is important. I insist" he was deadly serious and the Essence was not about to engage the Wizard in any kind of altercation or confrontation. Shaulmar's reputation for having the power of the universe at his side was known throughout time, space, and worlds beyond dimensions. The beautiful green energy hummed as it moved toward him, closer and closer, as if to test the waters. Neither one of them had encountered the other before now. They moved to the opposite end of the stonewalled room for privacy, Shaulmar did not move an inch he only focused his energy and grounded it into the earth ready for anything. The Essence sensed this and decided to remain at a safe distance.

Well—are you going to reveal to me what happened to your bound soul? Shaulmar thought. He realized two things, the first thing was, if they were to commune he didn't want Rebecca to hear anything that was going to distress her any more than she already was. The second being the best way to accomplish the first thing was by communicating with thought energy only. He waited for the response, holding his arms by his sides ready to protect himself and the others if it became necessary.

"I am no threat to you—or the others wizard. The thought enters Shaulmar's mind as clearly as if the words were spoken in the physical realm. The energy spun as if it were excited and had something wonderful to share with the wizard.

"So—if you are no threat to me, or the others, and you have bound your essence or soul with the soul of Rebecca, then what happened to her after she pulled on the spear of St Michael to open our escape route?" Shaulmar was beginning to show impatience that was not something that was common, or usual for him.

"There are many things you do not understand wizard. The prophecy that you are privileged to be part of and have waited for like many others through many incarnations, is the truth, and part of that truth is to play your part. What happened to the soul was part of the prophecy, the icon of the great master St Michael was imprinted on her and joined with us as an energy bonding. The tattoo on her shoulder is the proof of the soul as being the Prophesied One. The Archangel is linked to us through the tattoo that touches her physical brain at the pineal gland that is the jewel in the crown. Then out to her spinal functions by my bonding to her soul by the great power vortex of light that lives through this position of earth. The Essence buzzed and spun a couple of times.

So, the searing pain she was forced to endure is part of the prophecy. Shaulmar past the thought to the Essence, but he was unable to send any feelings of anger or dissatisfaction to the Essence through this mode of communication.

The pain is what the soul needs to evolve, it is the catalyst for soul growth, and was agreed to before the soul incarnated into this earth life. The green mist shone and spun rapidly, until it changed into a violet color, then it slowed back down and regained the green vibration once more. Shaulmar bent his head to think, he wanted to trust the being in front of him, but even with all his knowledge and experience, he still found the wonders of the universe difficult to understand.

So, what happens now? That was all that he could think of to send to the Essence at that moment, he didn't have any choice but to accept and trust that the Essence was telling the truth.

As is part of the universal plan, this soul you refer to as Rebecca, has gained the energy of the Master Archangel. The prophecy is being fulfilled at this time, and that part was an aspect of the process during which the prophesied soul would gain in stature with the addition of the sacred union with the connection made to the icon. Now, the soul will begin to realize and accept, as according to the sacred prophecy, a higher and more divine purpose to life on Earth. Shaulmar could do no more so once again he asked the being what was to happen next. Danger was all about them and he was unsure as how they would escape the Angel of Darkness and his plan to capture the soul of Rebecca Sullivan.

Tell me what we must do to escape, you are the Essence, the soul bound to Rebecca, you must help us to keep her safe. He was as insistent as he could be to a being that did not appear to reveal any emotional affect. Suddenly, the Essence spun rapidly again, and this time there was a high-pitched buzz that filled the air. The green mist became orange in color and the buzz was hard to take. It was obvious now to the wizard, that the Essence had become annoyed, at being asked for so much information. There are rules that must be followed sorcerer, and in addition, there are stated authorizations known only to the Sacred High Council regarding the revealing of future actions to be taken concerning such an important event. The sacred prophesy must be allowed to manifest or come to pass, naturally, according to the universal laws governing time and space. The sphere elevated rapidly, stopping only to prevent a collision with the ceiling.

You know the laws concerning the unfolding of events prophesied by any culture, especially one as old as the inhabitants of this dimension. To reveal what is to come would jeopardize the outcome of the souls evolution. I don't need to remind a wizard, especially one as knowledgeable as you, Shaulmar of the Ancients, of the consequences of such actions. The Essence had returned once more to its normal state, a beautiful green mist that oozed healing and love, effortlessly. Shaulmar was angry because he knew that the *being* hovering in front of him was absolutely correct, and that he would have to figure out what to do, without the help of the Essence. He walked calmly back to where Morghanz was tending to Rebecca.

"How is she?" He whispered into Morghanz's ear.

"I…I am okay Shaulmar. Please try to get us out of here. Don't worry about me." Rebecca had spoken before Morghanz could react to Shaulmar's question. He smiled at her and stroked her head. He looked at Morghanz and read the expression on her face that told him she didn't have a clue about her condition. Rebecca seemed weak and favored her shoulder where the tattoo of the Archangel Michael remained.

"Morghanz can you help me with this stone?" Shaulmar needed desperately to confer with Morghanz as to what they could do, in private, since the door had not been activated when the spear was pulled.

"I will be there in the moment." She put more salve on Rebecca's wound and wrapped some cloth from her tunic on it to keep it as clean as possible. She kissed Rebecca on the top of her head and stood up. Rebecca lay against the wall with her eyes closed.

"Shaulmar, I have no idea of how to activate the door in the stone wall leading to the sacred royal crypt, you must find a way to open it. I couldn't bear it if Draco Bastian found her, and did to her, what he did to the rest of her family." Morghanz had never felt as helpless as she felt at that moment.

"Morghanz, you must keep your voice down, if Rebecca here's what you are saying it will only cause more pain." He pulled her closer to him.

"Yes, you're right." She turned her head toward the young girl to make sure she was not heard. Rebecca was still resting against the wall with her eyes closed. "Sorry." She turned back to Shaulmar.

"We have to come up with a way to open the entrance to the crypt, other than Saint Michael's spear. I think we should use an incantation spell with your ceremonial herbs and crystals to call upon the power of the light to open it. If it is the will of the Source of creation then we will be successful or there will be another way given to us." Shaulmar always had strong, unwavering faith in destiny and in the power of the light within the universe.

"If we are not successful, then Rebecca will be trapped with us down here, Shaulmar. I am not going to let that happen I will give up my own life for her." Morghanz was never more serious than she was at that moment.

"Don't worry—have faith my love. I will not let the powers of darkness take her, trust me, trust that Morghanz." Morghanz saw something in his eyes that told her he would also give up his life for Rebecca. "So, enough of this fear we must raise our energy. Our vibration must be of the highest for this to work Morghanz, as you well know. Would you combine a mixture of the sacred herbs to entice the magic within the crystals so we can open the secret door?" He knew that if there was a sorceress powerful enough to generate the kind of incantation he needed, it was Morghanz.

"How are we going to set up the energy exchange? The link to the vortex of light must be configured also." She was extremely adept at conjuring the correct atmospheric conditions that make the perfect environment for magic to take place successfully.

"Yes, you're right Morghanz, I didn't think of that. I have to calm my anxiety and fear surrounding the situation and place my trust in the universe. I must trust that I am a powerful enough wizard to provide us with an entrance into the crypt." They both worked together, away from Rebecca, in order that she may have peace to rest and heal. What they failed to pay attention to was the green mist and what was transpiring between it and Rebecca. The Essence was attempting to commune with the soul that was forever bound to it. The Essence hovered directly in front of Rebecca and slowly projected a thin, rose pink energy from its center. A thin chord of light reached the heart chakra of the Prophesied One, and as soon as it entered the spinning wheel of light in front of her heart, she moaned softly. The connection was made between them, only this time it was different. Their communication could now take place without the need for the Essence to speak through Rebecca's physical mechanism. They were able to speak with each other through the heart-to-heart connection provided by the thin cord of light. This was now their means for connection and communication—it was to be that way for all eternity. The rose pink colored light was now anchored within the heart of Rebecca, linking her soul signature with that of the Essence. After a few minutes, the chord returned to the Essence and it spun humming through the air, it was almost singing as it spun faster and faster, as if it had made the final adjustments to the binding process between it and Rebecca. The colors of the rainbow were reflected throughout the mist as it moved. The light caressed the walls made of stone and the marble sarcophagus in the center of the room, gently illuminating them.

"Shaulmar! Look!" Morghanz turned towards the Essence and they both watched until the light show was over. "What do you think it's doing?" she asked him, while remaining focused on the green mist floating around the other side of the room.

"I don't know—it seems to be happy about something, maybe you should go to Rebecca and see if there has been any improvement in her condition."

"Yes, okay—just try to come up with a magic strong enough to open the door, or we are all doomed." She gave him the best hopeful look of encouragement that she could.

"Don't worry we are not going to be deserted by the power of the light, trust me." He was calm and very assured now that he was focusing on finding a solution to their situation.

"I will try to increase the healing power of the mixture I gave to Rebecca so she won't suffer from much more pain." Morghanz walked back to where Rebecca was. She decided to walk on the opposite side of the marble sarcophagus opposite where the Essence was hovering—she still didn't quite know how she felt towards the being yet. As Morghanz moved closer to Rebecca, the Essence also advanced towards her, and when she was halfway across the room, the Essence moved into her path at great speed.

"Shaulmar…." Morghanz called instinctively to Shaulmar, using a strong voice but not screaming, so as to disturb Rebecca. By this time the Essence was humming and turning into a rose pink color. Shaulmar rushed to her side.

"What is it?" she pointed to the Essence.

"Why are you preventing Morghanz from reaching Rebecca? She needs our help." He tried to sound calm and rational, while he was mentally preparing to protect them from what looked like a hostile move by the Essence. The Essence was the color of a red mist at this point, and it only spun occasionally—it remained between them and its bound soul.

"I do not want Rebecca to die, Shaulmar!" she murmured into his ear, "do something, Wizard!" Morghanz meant every word she hissed into his ear and he knew it.

"Essence, will you speak freely?" Shaulmar was acting from what his intuition told him—he felt it better to use his physical voice to communicate this time with the Essence, and it seemed to work.

"Yes, please speak freely, my friend." The Essence had reciprocated and spoken with the voice of an angel. Morghanz was just about ready to tear into the being floating near Rebecca, when she felt Shaulmar squeeze her hand.

"So, Essence, please tell us why you stand between us and Rebecca when she is in need of assistance?" He was using large amounts of willpower and restraint trying to reason with the Essence, knowing Rebecca might be dying as they spoke. The red mist spun quickly again in a position directly in front of the bound soul.

"Your assistance is not necessary at this time. In actuality, the assistance you planned to administer to Rebecca was deemed by us to be of an inferior nature." The magical mist hovered back and forth, as if to let them know it was in full control of the safety of its soul mate.

"Ooh, what happened? I feel like I've been asleep forever." Rebecca had regained consciousness and was attempting to stand.

"Rebecca, are you okay? How is the pain in your shoulder?" Morghanz wanted to go to her. She desperately tried to go to her but the Essence didn't move away from the path leading to Rebecca.

"Essence, let us pass, or I will have no recourse but to pass without your permission." Shaulmar was most deadly serious as shown by the display of power in the visible projection of his purple aura. The mist spun once, recognized its bound soul was no longer in danger, the healing was complete, and it moved aside to let them pass without any confrontation.

"Thank you," Morghanz said as she passed the green mist. "I don't understand how you could even think for one second that we could have harmed Rebecca. You and I are going to clash if this happens again." She meant what she said and was giving notice to the Essence.

"It's okay, Morghanz." Rebecca was healing fast with every passing moment. She was now standing on her own and caressing the shoulder that gave her so much pain. "The Essence was only doing what it thought best for both of us," she smiled and walked towards them, and as soon as she passed by the green magical mist, it rose above the girl and entered her head at the base of her skull, disappearing into her body. Her tattoo glowed with a golden hue before returning to the dark blue of the original tattoo.

"Rebecca, do you know what is occurring? Do you know what's happening to you?" Shaulmar marveled at what he saw, but was unsure if Rebecca was consciously aware and willing to accept the obvious transitions that she was experiencing.

"Yes, I do know my friend, more than you know. Please, let me put both your minds at ease. I understand now what is real and what is illusion. All my life, I have allowed myself to be put in situations that were not for my highest good and now I understand why. What is happening to me now, is the most wonderful and exciting and natural event that I have ever experienced, and I know it is something that I have agreed to experience. Shaulmar, Morghanz, I know you're not quite sure of the motives of the Essence, but let me remove any doubts from your minds—the Essence comes only from love. The Essence has my best and highest interests at heart. It tells me we will experience things together that will allow each aspect of us to grow and evolve through knowledge, wisdom, and above all, love." She was stunning in the changes she had gone through.

"The Essence returned to you through the tattoo on your back, and now, did you know you have another tattoo on your shoulder of the very icon you touched while trying to open the door of the crypt." Shaulmar was curious as to the awareness of his friend, concerning the events that have occurred, while she was seemingly in an altered state of consciousness.

"Yes, I am aware of the tattoo of the great Master and Archangel. The Essence has made me aware of the dangers that manifest above us. We have need of an exit from this place." Rebecca was much more powerful now than she was before, which concerned her two friends.

"Rebecca, how do you feel now?" Morghanz wanted to connect with her friend, to satisfy her own mind that she was not being forced or manipulated into the experience.

"I feel good…really. Please, do not be concerned, you would be the one I would come to if I needed to talk about anything, or if there were anything I was unhappy about." She gave her a smile that Morghanz indeed recognized as being that of her friend, Rebecca.

Shaulmar moved closer to the stonewall containing the secret doorway to the ancient crypt. "I am currently formulating a magic incantation, and with the help of Morghanz's herbal concoction, we may be able to override the protective spell that prevents the opening of the doorway without the use of the Archangel spear." Shaulmar was very confident indeed that his formula and plan would work. However, Rebecca had other plans, and without even speaking a single word, she walked over to the wall and placed her hand on one specific stone. As soon as her hand felt the stone, the Saint Michael tattoo on her shoulder glowed yellow-gold then its essence blazed through her body, her hand, and onto the stone, opening the secret doorway to the sacred royal crypt. Rebecca stood back and beckoned for Morghanz and Shaulmar to step through the doorway into the secret crypt of the ancients.

CHAPTER 24

THEY HAD TRAVELLED THROUGH THE PARKLAND TO arrive at the Cathedral. Alison was not very amused by the fact that she had to follow the Rhostos around the grounds of the sacred structure.

"Why can't we go through those big doors at the entrance, and just claim Rebecca Sullivan's soul, then leave?" she was really irritated, not so much as having to go along with someone else's ideas as well as her own, Alison was more irritated by her inability to get the Rhostos warrior to express any emotions.

"There are dark powers close at hand, and I would rather avoid unnecessary confrontation with the one who destroyed so many of my race, until that becomes necessary." The Rhostos was talking very softly, "I will pick the time and place for the destruction of that darkest of beings."

Flowing throughout the warrior's words was a sense of calmness and clarity. The Rhostos were known throughout the universe to be a ruthless and powerful adversary, but they were also known for their desire for peace and harmony. Such a dichotomy resided within the energy, it was not something that could be consciously controlled, and so explains the apparent lack of emotion. They were clinical in their actions and logical in their thinking. Alison wanted to capture Rebecca's soul, and she wanted the adoration that would accompany the capture of the soul prophesied to do so much on earth. She dreamt of being the one who denied the Dark Angel the one thing he desired most, the soul of the Prophesied One.

"Rhostos Warrior, I want that soul," Alison blurted out as a result of the images she had cultivated in her mind. "We must find her and take her. You must think of something!" she demanded. "If you want the power and many rewards the Dark Ones would bestow on you, then you must think of something, fast." She insisted. Alison could see better now that the sun was moving in and out through the trees. She kicked a lump of moss angrily across the open pathway the warrior was walking on—he turned his head slightly.

"You must contain your outbursts, or I fear we will not get close enough to even enter the structure, let alone capture one of the most protected souls of the universe." The warrior was correct and she had to concede the fact.

"Okay...okay!" She looked the other way. She was unable to handle the fact that she was humbled. "Sorry, but just do something, will you?" The Rhostos was doing something—Alison just hadn't realized that.

"We must walk through this doorway." He nodded in the direction of the enormous cathedral stone wall that probably stood 60 feet high, and judging by the age of the structure, many feet thick.

"What do you mean, doorway?" she looked at the huge wall and turned to the left then to the right, "I don't see any doorway," she hissed, and faced the warrior with a look of a teenager having a meltdown.

"The Rhostos are not subject to the laws of the earth plane, so we are able to access space that opens up periodically within this dimension."

"What are you saying? Are you saying somewhere along this wall, there is an opening? A portal?" she was very skeptical at the claims of the Rhostos's. The warrior said nothing he only stepped aside and walked along the wall to the end, then stopped abruptly. He retraced his steps and surveyed the wall at various places and fumbled with his wristband again. She then saw him push his hand, up to his elbow, into the stonewall.

"Warrior Alison, this is where we will enter the structure." He motioned to her to follow him.

"You may be able to move through stone walls, but what makes you think I am stupid enough to try?" she stood back from the wall a few feet and waited to be convinced that it was safe for her to follow him.

"When we travel through the space between dimensions, you are protected by my energy and thought intention. Without such, your physical appearance would have returned to the earth, and you would have reverted to your energetic light body. The same principle applies with moving through pockets of varied frequencies that are attached to the earth plane. This pocket," the warrior put his hand into the stone wall again, "has a variable frequency that I can manipulate and hold, or stabilize, enough for us to move through unharmed." He looked at her, waiting for her reaction—he still had his arm in the wall.

"How do you stabilize the pockets of energy long enough to take me through as well as yourself?" she was still not sure.

"My wristband is a calibrator of energy, it can tune the frequency of the pocket of energy within the wall to its own, and thus hold that frequency for a determined amount of time before it is degraded to the point of death for us both." The Rhostos warrior was quite open about the procedure.

"Normally…two full minutes, but I can configure the wristband to extend the time an extra 30 seconds for emergencies." He was quite confident that they both had enough time to pass through the structure, unharmed. "If you do not come with me, you will not capture the soul, and I don't have enough power without you to get the job done." The warrior pulled his arm from the wall, the two minutes were just about up.

"I was wondering whether you were going to remember to remove your arm. I was curious to see if the wall would encase your arm if you were too preoccupied with our conversation to remember to pull it away." She half laughed as she explained her thoughts to the warrior. The Rhostos warrior said nothing—his response was predictable.

"I never allow my wristband to stabilize a pocket of energy unless it is programmed to alert me 20 seconds before it degrades." He had a look as stony and cold as the wall he had pulled his arm from. "Sorry to spoil your fun, but we are business partners, and you're not going to capture the soul without me, and vice versa." Alison had the grin thoroughly wiped from her face. She walked up and down the alley beside the cathedral for a few minutes. She was deciding whether capturing the soul of Rebecca Sullivan was worth the risk of being trapped for eternity as part of the ancient stone wall, being materialized and dematerialized at various times for millennia to come. "We must decide soon, the pocket will not remain in this place for much longer. I don't know if I could locate another that would allow us to enter the structure, undetected." The Rhostos warrior was becoming weary of her personality traits and unstable moods. She stood beside the great stonewall and picked up a pebble that was smooth all over, then she turned towards the Rhostos.

"I will make the journey with you and trust you know what you are doing. I will keep this pebble with me to remind me that if we end up inside this cathedral and I still have the pebble, I will know it really happened." Alison needed some kind of psychological bridge that allowed her to put her life in the hands of the Rhostos warrior.

"Okay, Allison Warrior, now come close to me, and I will prepare the pocket for our transport." He held up his huge arm, and twisted various parts of his wristband. Alison put the pebble in her left hand, and held his hand with the other. "It is almost time, the frequency will lock in a few moments then you must be ready to embrace the doorway." The warrior tightened his grip on her hand and braced himself. She could feel the muscles in his arm strain. There was a muffled hum as the wristband matched the frequency of the pocket of energy within the wall. The warrior surged forward, pulling Alison with him. She didn't even have the chance to move her legs before his momentum pulled her forward. They were inside the pocket of energy within the stonewall before she knew what had happened.

★★★

Bastian surveyed the structure from every angle, assessing the power within and around it that sustained the illusion of the huge cathedral. The ring on his hand glowed red with agitation, and alerted him to the power of the light that coursed through the building.

"I know...I know my loyal friend." Draco Bastian looked down lovingly at the blood red entity on his hand. "The power of the light is strong here, do not be concerned, I will not let anything happen to you here." The Dark Angel caressed the Ring of Dread as if it were some dark creature to be held and comforted from the light. "Together, we will take the soul and share in the power revealed by the prophecy of the ancients." He put his hand back beneath his leather cloak where the Talisman was safe. Drandos remained out of sight for fear of any more ridicule from the others. Ever since they'd witnessed the Dark One's dislike for him, the minions had assumed permission to treat the apprentice with the same disrespect. He was not about to allow them the opportunity to spew their poison on him again.

"I am going to survey things from above, I want you 4 men..." Bastian turned to Drandos, "as well as you brother—to cover every inch of these grounds, and then report to me if you find a weakness in the energy source used by the travellers. If he can manifest this structure, and maintain its form, then we must not underestimate his power or his knowledge of the realm of magic." Bastian, who was at least 10 feet off the ground by the end of the directives, left his minions and his brother behind, as he headed for the upper levels of the cathedral. The daylight was stronger now and most of the area surrounding the sacred structure could be easily seen. Drandos watched his brother walk across the roof and disappear behind the stone sculpting of a hideous gargoyle. It disturbed him to feel such strong emotions of disgust at certain symbols of the dark forces, such as gargoyles, but they didn't feel right to him and they actually irritated his energy.

"Drandos! Drandos! Get over here and help us find any weakness in the power source that keeps this area stable." The elder of the four minions hated that Bastian had a brother. He was counting on becoming a close ally to the Dark One, but what he didn't know was that Drandos didn't want any part of the family business."

"Okay, I will be there in a moment I have to check something out on the other side first. I think I may have found what we are looking for." He was lying. There was nothing on the other side of the grounds that he wanted to see, he just wanted to stay away from everyone until this nightmare was over, and he could return to Orban where he felt safe.

The others continued to search for the source of the power that kept the manifestation of the structure strong and stable. Drandos watched them move off in the Kogan fighting formation and he was able to see the energy connection between them. When they disappeared behind the back of the cathedral, he returned to the place where they'd begun, so he would not be seen later. He sat beneath the evergreen that grew next to the enormous stonewall that separated the property from the next house. He kept warm by maneuvering his body into the path of the rays of the morning sun. Drandos was beginning to realize how much he hated his elder brother, and he was not about to help him capture the soul that was prophesied by the ancients. This decision led to other epiphany flashes. Why would I not want to capture her soul, especially one who was at the center of the prophecy, he thought. This bothered him as much as hearing voices in the head would bother a human, causing them to question themselves and their sanity. These thoughts made him question who he thought he was. He was supposed to be a practitioner of the dark arts, or at least one, who wanted to practice the ancient arts of darkness. Now, all he wanted to do was to escape his present situation, and that desire made him realize he was not a being harboring an incurable dark soul. Drandos was still processing his thoughts when parts of the two wooden doors at the entrance to the cathedral flew past him, smashing against the wall, shattering into tiny pieces.

"What the hell!" He was barely able to avoid being hit by the debris, as he ran and dove in the alcove next to the buttresses connected to the great stonewall that pushed against the building, keeping it in place. Drandos picked himself up off of the ground and emerged from the alcove. There, at the entrance, stood his elder brother, his leather cloak blowing in the wind. He had destroyed the doors after entering the building from the roof.

"Dammit! Where are you? You bunch of incompetent wannabes." Bastian had zero tolerance for anyone or anything. He stood as if he had just conquered Everest and was waiting for the peasants to hail him as the greatest being on the planet. His minions arrived just as he reached up to the sky intending to draw upon the dark powers that surrounded him.

"Master, we heard your call and came as quickly as we could."

"Did you accomplish what I asked of you?" the Dark One said very slowly and deliberately, something they all knew was never a good sign.

"There is no weakness in the power source supplying the manifestation, Master." He stepped back a couple of paces, anticipating a burst of energy, or a bolt of lightning, that might sting more than a little. Instead, the Dark Angel just spun around and re-entered the church.

"Come with me and stay sharp!" The Dark One was a little concerned but he couldn't let them know it. He had travelled through every corner of the structure from the roof and rafters down to the sacred pews but found no indication of the travellers or the soul, Rebecca Sullivan. His minions followed him like well-trained animals into the cathedral about ten feet behind him. When they were all inside the huge sacred space, they stopped and stood like the many stone sculptures around them, waiting for direction, and not wanting to put a foot wrong. The Dark One did not even turn to face them—he just flipped out his left arm, waving it in the direction of the far wall, where there was many chapels and alcoves. Then he flipped out his right arm, waving it in the direction of the opposite wall. Both times he did this, his minions scurried off like quicksilver in the specified directions.

"Do not miss anything, look for any trace of them, and use every sense you possess—fail and you will possess nothing—understand?" There was no answer, none of them dared to answer. Two men in black coats headed to the aisles on the far left side, and Drandos led the search with the others, on the right-hand side of the aisle.

"Do not anger me. I will not stand for any more abuse." Drandos spoke the words loud enough for the others to hear but there was no response. "Do you understand?" He turned to face them but there was no one near him. Drandos slipped into the nearest alcove to figure things out. He had no idea why he was alone, why they had ditched him. They were there one minute and gone the next. Not even his brother could make the two huge men disappear like that without any indication or trace of what had taken place, he thought.

***

Shaulmar led Rebecca into the ancient crypt first, then Morghanz, and as she passed him, he tugged on her sleeve. Morghanz turned her head and saw his lips mouth something. He wanted her to speak to him without the Essence or Rebecca knowing.

"Rebecca, could you find the exit to the crypt? I think it must be somewhere over by the far wall, the one covered with symbols." It was the only thing Morghanz could think of to give her and Shaulmar the opportunity to speak without Rebecca or the Essence knowing. "What is it you want to tell me, Shaulmar?" Morghanz whispered. She looked back a couple of times to be sure Rebecca was all right. "What can be so important that you can't even tell Rebecca?" she was more than a little annoyed at him.

"I am going to see who is above us. There is danger, and what feels like powerful dark entities, in the cathedral's main hall. I'm sure they are looking for us." As he spoke, she couldn't help but notice that the one she loved so much stood like a column of Italian marble chiseled by a master sculptor. Morghanz turned to look at Rebecca again and then turned back to look at Shaulmar. Morghanz softened as she spoke.

"Shaulmar, if you go up into the main hall and the Dark One is there with his power, his minions, and the Ring of Dread, how long do you think an ancient wizard of the ways of the light will last? Especially, when you no longer have the Archangel Ring?" Morghanz was using reason and logic, but inside she was full of fear for him. She had loved Shaulmar for many lifetimes, but this time she wanted his child. She wanted to experience bringing their child into the physical plane. Of course, she had never told him this, even though they have been partners for many lifetimes, partners in light fighting the darkness. The great wizard knew she was saying these things out of fear. Shaulmar loved her with everything he possessed, but he also knew what he must do—he was driven to be of service to the light.

"I have to do what is meant for me to do, Morghanz." His heart reached out to her. He slowly lifted his hand towards her face, and as it gently cradled her cheek he whispered to her. "My destiny is to face the Dark One, and I know intuitively, that is why I've incarnated on earth at this time. The very moment I stepped into his energy at the hotel restaurant, I knew." Shaulmar was about to kiss Morghanz goodbye when he heard Rebecca calling—they moved over to her at the wall of symbols. "What did you find?" he asked Rebecca before he realized something had occurred to him.

"I am being drawn to the stone symbols on the wall. I heard the voice of the Essence tell me one of these symbols is to be used by you Shaulmar, against the forces of darkness." Rebecca was letting him know that she was aware of his conversation with Morghanz. "There is a sacred amulet that resides behind one of these symbols that can take the place of the one that was taken from you, by those you held in high esteem eons ago, but who have diminished in your eyes." Shaulmar hung his head. He felt uncomfortable that he'd tried to deceive his friend, and what made it worse, was that she did not judge him for that.

"Rebecca, I am so sorry that I had a conversation with Morghanz with the intention to keep the contents from you, when you are actually the one who is in such danger. I promise to let you know everything I plan to do from this moment on." He bowed his head low in a sign of respect for her and to show how humble he felt.

"That is not necessary my friend. I am aware of much more than you can imagine because of the energies that work with me now. Please do not feel badly—you have been the protector of me and my soul for some time now, and I want you to continue and protect me if you wish." Rebecca had surely changed from the girl to the woman in a relatively short time span. Morghanz had tears welling up in her eyes, and was about to say something, when Rebecca suddenly turned to her. "I love you dearly too, Morghanz. You have given me the tools that will help me retain physical health, making me physically stronger, and with the belief in myself as one with everything, when I need it the most." She pulled Morghanz to her and held her in silence for a few moments—they exchanged love on a high vibration that was like the sun coming up over the mountains of the Himalayas in summertime. "What plans do you have, Shaulmar?" Rebecca looked at him. He noticed her eyes, they were no longer the gentle hazel-green color they were—they had changed and become a beautiful sky blue. A gentle strength and determination flowed from them, like stars spiraling through the universe. Shaulmar reached inside his cloak and pulled from it a golden locket. Morghanz moved to him quickly, and with her back to Rebecca, she faced him.

"Are you sure this is a good idea? You don't know what she will do," she whispered. Rebecca stood just a few yards from them and waited. She knew the love between them was strong and ancient.

"My dear friends, I am not the same Rebecca that had to be saved from the streets of New York. I am becoming the *one* I am meant to be. The tattoo of the Essence shimmered in a simmering glow on her back. The tattoo had evolved to cover her spine from its base to her skull, then it moved across her shoulders and up her neck to the hindbrain where it disappeared into her skull—then it connected directly to her pineal gland at the exact geometric center of her head. "Please do not worry about me so much, together we can survive these times of darkness and uncertainty." She sounded as though she were channeling the Essence of the Book of Secrets. However, Shaulmar and Morghanz both knew it was Rebecca, she was talking to them through her heart, it was unmistakable.

"I have something that you will want, and when you have it, you ask me for the reason why I have it to give to you?" This is what had occurred to the great and compassionate wizard of the ancients. Shaulmar reached past Morghanz and held the golden locket up for Rebecca to see. Rebecca was motionless for a few moments then she slowly reached for it taking it gently from his fingers.

"Shaulmar, this locket belonged to my mother. Where did you get it? The authorities, the police, told my grandmother it was stolen when...the thing...happened." she didn't have any words to describe what was done to her mum because her grandmother only called it the thing that happened. Morghanz put her arm around her to comfort her as best she could.

"Rebecca, the reason I gave you the locket is because I feel you are ready to hear the truth about your mother. I also think that we are all in terrible danger here, so my intuition is talking to me, letting me know that it is the right thing to do for you." There was softness in his voice—it was obvious to them both that he was feeling the worst might come for them all. There were traces of hopelessness in the words that he spoke.

"Shaulmar, do you think we are going to be okay?" Morghanz wanted, almost demanding but not quite, to know the reality about their chances of surviving the darkness that existed above them. He knew what she was asking, he turned to her with sadness in his eyes then he pulled her to him and kissed her lips softly.

"My dearest love, I will call on all the power I know, all the ancient ones I can reach, and call upon all their knowledge and wisdom to keep us safe, and bring us safely through this darkness that is upon us." Morghanz lowered her head slightly away from his gaze—she knew what was coming next. "The only power that knows for certain if we are to survive, is the same power that brought us all together, the same power that drew this danger to us. Destiny is a thought created by the power of the universe, no matter what choices we are presented with, and which choices we decide on, the outcome is the one that is pre-destined." The great wizard didn't make the answer sound very comforting to either of them.

"Please, Shaulmar, tell me what my mother died from?" Rebecca was desperate to know. Her heart ached to know.

"We don't have much time for this, Shaulmar." Morghanz explained softly. "I can sense the heaviness of the forces of darkness getting nearer." She almost pleaded with her eyes for him to keep this secret from Rebecca. She knew it would cause her so much pain. Shaulmar stood back from them both for a moment, thinking. Finally, he spoke.

"Keep the locket for now Rebecca. I promise we will sit, and I will tell you everything I know of your mother's history. For now we must survive, so I need you to tell me again what the Essence has told you about the wall of symbols." He put his faith in her hands, hoping she could do as he asked. Morghanz stood close to him and gently held his hand in hers.

"Dearest Rebecca, we must do our best to survive, and when the time is right, you will know everything...okay?" Rebecca's eyes glistened with the moisture building up behind their lids. It was difficult to stay focused and clearheaded with all the sadness and pain she was experiencing at that moment. The girl remained silent and turned away from them.

"Shaulmar, I must know about my mother. I must know the truth about her, but for now, I will do as you ask." She lowered her head against the wall of symbols, and fell silent again. Morghanz comforted her as best she could under the circumstances.

"Rebecca, Shaulmar will make sure we are safe, you can be sure of it." She tried to sound as confident as she could, but Rebecca knew the reality was that the situation was dire. Even Shaulmar, with all his wisdom and strength, could not disguise the hopelessness in his voice and words.

"It's okay, I know you and Shaulmar will do everything in your power to prevent the Dark Angel, Draco Bastian from capturing my soul." Rebecca was saddened, not because of the danger she was in, but because she knew Shaulmar would tell her about her mother's hell. The young girl wasn't sure she could handle hearing what was done to her mother, and the suffering she was forced to endure. The only good thing was that her mom was dead and there was no more harm that could be done to her.

Rebecca turned slowly and spoke. "Shaulmar, I have to focus for a moment to connect with the Essence. It has gotten easier the more I do it, so it should not take long. I will ask what symbol holds the amulet for you." She leaned against the wall again, allowing her back and shoulders to loosen and move gently and freely to awaken the Essence. Morghanz and Shaulmar watched as the connection formed between the two bound souls.

"I hope the Essence does not tell her about her mother before we can get her out of this danger." Morghanz whispered in Shaulmar's ear.

"Yes, I can only hope so too. I think the Essence will recognize the danger in doing so. If Rebecca reacts in any way that may bring more danger to her, such a reaction will probably be known by the Essence. In doing so, it will ensure that such things are kept from her." He made sense she thought.

"The Essence is telling me there is an object behind the 65th symbol, counting from the left, beginning at the north end of the wall." Rebecca inhaled strongly as if she were doing the yoga exercises that she and Morghanz had practiced together. Shaulmar was busy trying to open the front of the stone, on the wall, that turned out to be not as easy as he'd thought. He was having extreme difficulty finding a way to gain access to the amulet. Rebecca came up behind him and put a kind hand on his shoulder.

"Shaulmar, I am being told that you are to use magic to open the symbol stone, the magic that is in your heart. He stepped back from the stone, rubbing his hands together to remove the dirt and dust from the wall. He then closed his eyes and took a slow, deep breath. The Essence told Rebecca to wait with Morghanz across the room. The wizard stood quietly for a few moments, breathing slowly and deliberately, as he drew in the power of the light of the universe. He began calling on all his knowledge and wisdom as a master wizard practitioner of the ways of the light. The only way he knew how to access the energy of the heart was to open his seven sacred chakras to the universe using the sacred breath of life.

The breath that we inhale that keeps us alive is also the key to connecting to our energy body, and the seven wheels of light. The great wizard pondered the dangers they were in while he was in the process of opening himself up to the power of the light. This gave him the insight and vision of what to do regarding the situation they found themselves in. When he reached the point of connection with his energy body, the sacred symbol was revealed to him. The symbol was the amulet he was to use to fight the Dark Ones. In his mind's eye, he saw a knotted Celtic cross that was made of silver—when he consciously embraced the vision, the stone he was standing in front of opened. The front of the stone piece, where the energy of the ancient wizard remained, revealed the amulet inside—it was sitting on a piece of petrified oak with its holy chain draped over it. Shaulmar opened his eyes and saw the beautifully crafted piece and reached for it. As soon as his hand was near, the amulet vibrated and sung, for it knew the one who could call forth the magic living within it was nearby. The amulet was stored there for eons by the ancient ones who also practiced the art of the sacred white light. The silver chain wrapped itself around Shaulmar's hand, eagerly, vibrating and singing like the songs of the crystal bowls of the practitioners that existed long before him.

"I must say a prayer of thanks to the ancestors, to the ancient ones who have left their energy in these symbols for times like these, times when they are asked to come to the aid of those in need." Shaulmar gently put the amulet around his neck and let the cross fall to his chest, directly in front of his heart. Before he began the prayer he reached into his cloak and lifted the knotted silver cross to his lips and kissed it lovingly. "May the power of the light of the universe flow through this amulet, and recharge my energy, so that I may be of service and protect those in need on this day." He kissed the amulet once more and knelt in front of the stone that had hidden it for so long. After the stone returned to its original state encasing the petrified oak once more behind the wall of symbols, the stone wall, once again, appeared to have been untouched for eons. "What I do this day is in service to the highest good of all involved. I will not bring harm or danger to any being that I meet, unless it is predestined and is for the highest good of all concerned. I trust in the power of the light of the universe and lay down my life in service to all beings who are in need." He stood slowly, and threw his hood back off of his head. He tucked the amulet beneath his tunic and let it fall against his bare skin once more.

"Shaulmar, what happens now? How are we going to keep Rebecca safe from Draco Bastian and his minions?" Morghanz did not sound fearful, but they knew she was not feeling very confident about their safety, either.

"I will go to meet them, and you two must stay here, hidden in the secret crypt until my return." He sounded sure it was the right thing to do.

"I'm sorry, I cannot let you go alone. There are many entities wanting to harm us, and I am being told the best thing for all of us would be to try to escape to the portal to the Templar's cavern below, where we left Joaquim." Rebecca walked towards them both and put an arm around each of them. "I know we are in terrible danger but you must trust in the Essence—it is looking out for me and for all of us. If we engage those who wish us dead, I cannot be sure we will survive, so please try to get us to the cavern of the Templars?" she moved close to both of them as she spoke. "You have been so good to me. Please trust what I am being told." She turned back and stood away from them. She seemed a lot taller somehow, Morghanz thought.

"Rebecca, we are all going to be okay. Thought is the first stage of manifestation in the physical plane—we must believe and trust that our destiny does not include us perishing in this place." The sorceress of light sounded strong and self-assured. It was a different feeling than the one sensed within her earlier, Rebecca thought. Shaulmar looked around the crypt, slowly asking himself, and thus his ancient brethren, if there was anything he needed to know before leading the others through the sacred portal and down to the cavern, and hopefully, into safe passage and out of danger. He automatically rested his hand over the amulet beneath his cloak—there was nothing, no sound, no visualization or intuitive sense, at all. The great wizard was disturbed by this lack of response—usually there was an indicator of some kind to let him know one way or the other. He let it go, and put it down to his being in the enclosed marble and stone room of the ancient ones' place of peaceful sleep.

"We must leave now, Rebecca, there is a way out that is not the same way as we came in. This will give us a little better chance of not being seen—if you can use the power of the Essence to open it, we can get going." Shaulmar pointed to the opposite wall of the one where they had originally come through. "I believe it is to the right and lower than where the other door is." He looked at her with some confusion, because she had not said anything. "Can you open the portal, Rebecca?" There was only silence. "Are you okay, Rebecca? Are you okay?" Morghanz moved to her quickly, fearing she had slipped into the altered state once more.

"I…I'm okay," she said. "The Essence comes and goes in my mind, at will, and sometimes it takes me by surprise. I am learning to recognize when the entity wants to speak with me, without it having to send me into the altered state of consciousness. It is going to take time and practice to control the feelings." She looked dazed as she turned to Shaulmar. "I was told that you could open the portal exit, Shaulmar, since you now have the amulet that originated from the crypt." She closed her eyes and began to sway precariously. Morghanz caught her in time.

"Shaulmar, you have to do something," she pleaded, but there was also anger in the way she hissed at him. He helped her set Rebecca back against the crypt and he used her cloak as the headrest for her. "Why is this happening to her, Shaulmar? How can we get her out of here, safely, if she keeps passing out all the time?"

"Please, Morghanz, emotions are the means to drain you of the energy you need for this task. You know that if we don't keep a clear head, we may falter." He was always the one to speak the truth no matter what situation he found himself in. Morghanz always respected that part of him. However, she had never been so attached to a being in her charge before, and with Rebecca, she just couldn't detach and let things happen to her without feeling the emotional upheaval attached to it. Morghanz reached into her pouch again, pulling out the herbal mixture she had learned to keep ready in case of such emergency situations, as this one, but she was getting low and there was no way to create a raw mix until she could access her garden again.

"Shaulmar, when you called on the power of the vortex to manifest the sacred place, were you able to keep the exit portal in the Templars cavern in the same position?" He looked at her uneasily.

"Unfortunately, no. I wasn't able to keep the energy stable enough to do that." At that moment, he was beginning to feel a little inadequate as a great wizard. All through his time as a sorcerer and wizard, he'd never had any problems with energy, until recently. Shaulmar was considered by many to be one of the most powerful wizards alive, so when he failed to stabilize the energy field, then doubts began to filter through his consciousness and into his mind.

"That energy surge must have been so powerful. I doubt anyone could have done more than you did to actually manifest an ancient sacred cathedral from the etheric plane into the physical one. Such a feat is no trivial thing, Shaulmar." Morghanz always knew when he was dealing with doubts and negative self-talk, after all, he was in the physical and human frailties came with the territory. She attended to Rebecca while Shaulmar figured out how to use the amulet to locate the exit portal of the crypt.

"Morghanz," he whispered, as he looked around the stones and marble wall. "I really love you and I have done for centuries, you know." Morghanz had her back to him and was gently pouring the herb tincture into the mouth and throat of her friend.

"Yes," she said. "I have always known that, my love." She held Rebecca's head forward a little to allow the liquid to run down her throat and into her stomach. "I think you've known that I have always felt the same towards you, haven't you?" she continued to work on Rebecca. Shaulmar had found a place on the wall where he sensed the energy was different, so he stopped. The tingling in his hand was stronger as he passed it over one particular piece of marble embedded in the stone.

"I think I have found the exit," he said with confidence. "I will have it open soon, my love. He reached under his tunic for the amulet.

"Rebecca is gaining consciousness, slowly, she will be able to move in a few moments, Shaulmar."

"Good, if I can just figure out how the amulet works, we can get out of here." He began to fumble with the chain and woven cross of silver. He passed his hand over the stone containing the marble piece again just to be sure he had found the right place. There were certain principles involved in the magic used in amulets, crystals, sacred icons, and the like. He needed to trigger the energy of the sacred symbol, and then he could access the magic and thus activate the portal. He held the cross in his left hand, and placed the palm of his right hand over the marble inset in the stonewall. The ingot glistened, as if it had been turned on by some invisible switch on the wall, he recognized the energy almost immediately. "Sporack! My old friend," he said softly. Shaulmar remembered the ancient one with fondness—they had worked together in the early days on Orban.

As soon as Shaulmar recalled the memory of his friend, the amulet began to vibrate and became warm in his hand. He closed his eyes to tune into his friends energy, thus triggering the signature within the object. He was shown the mountains of the northern plains of Orban where the ancient wizard had experienced his first incarnation as a traveller. There was such peace and tranquility being sent through the silver cross to him, to his heart chakra that indicated to Shaulmar that his friend was with him across time and dimensions. He was about to ask for the way to access the magic, when the Celtic Trinity Knot of silver was shown to him. This, he realized, was the key to unlocking the magic of the cross, and his way to open the portal exit from the sacred royal crypt. Without any hesitation, he stretched out the index finger of his right hand and began to trace the outline of the trinity on the marble ingot.

To access the portal, Shaulmar knew the tracing must be perfectly executed. There must be no break, nor lifting of his finger from the stone, at any time during the process. Once the tracing was complete, the wizard would be able to use the portal opening to lead them out of the crypt. He felt the power of the vortex flow through his hand and finger as he outlined the trinity symbol. As his finger made the last turn of the third knot, and made the connection with the beginning of the first knot, the portal revealed itself. The stone and marble opened up enough so they could pass through—they could see the swirling energy of the portal quickening within its boundary. The opening was shaped like the opening of an ancient cave, rounded at the top, and cascading down, narrowing to the floor on each side, making the outline of a heart-like symbol.

"We must leave now, Morghanz. I will help Rebecca to her feet, but there is only enough room to pass through the portal in single file." Shaulmar was again not sounding as calm and together as he normally did. Morghanz hesitated—she felt something was not right, something was telling her not to go through the portal yet. As soon as the portal senses the energy of the user, it activates and is revealed, on the other side of the crypt wall. The portal pulsates at a specific frequency that allows the physical aspect of the stone and marble to take on different attributes, thus enabling the travellers to pass through. Passing through a pulsating portal to another dimension, or just to pass through a stone wall feels the same, like walking through a soft rain shower, only the user does not get wet.

"Wait! Shaulmar! There is someone on the other side of the wall. I can sense them. There are more than one now, maybe three energies." She fell silent for a moment. "Whoever passed by was not of a high vibration, or of the light, the darkness follows them wherever they go." She was so thankful for being a sensitive, and a sorceress, capable of detecting followers of the dark arts.

"Is the corridor clear, Morghanz? I don't know how long the portal can remain active." He was concerned he wouldn't be able to reactivate the portal again. There was no guarantee the magic could be used more than one time.

"Okay, it's clear now," she whispered, as if there was a chance that the Dark Ones might hear her speak.

"I will go first, and if you could help Rebecca through...?" He was never going to let either one of them be the first to face any possible danger while he was around. What ever was on the other side of that wall, he would face first. Rebecca was semiconscious at this point and the tattoo on her neck and spine shimmered slightly. Morghanz helped her to her feet and put an arm around her waist while pulling her left arm up around her shoulder, so she could steady her. As they all made their way to the portal, Shaulmar looked back at them with a degree of concern in his eyes.

"When I am through the portal, send Rebecca through...and try to give her a little push before she disappears...that way the momentum will carry her through should she lose consciousness during the process." He felt so helpless, but he realized he had no choice, for their safety, he needed to go first. The wizard closed his cloak and pulled his hood up over his head—there was protection programmed within the fibers of his clothing. He turned to the two women. "Everything will be all right, I promise." Then he moved through the portal, disappearing from view. Morghanz helped Rebecca to the wall, and as the energy of the portal pulsed and swirled within its boundary, she let go of her friend, and with a hand at the center of her back, she gently pushed her through the doorway. Morghanz had no idea what was waiting on the other side of the wall—all she knew for certain was that the light of the universe flowed through herself and her two friends. The sorceress stepped into the pulsating portal, and no sooner had she done so, then she felt a pull on her arm. There she was, travelling through the space between dimensions at the speed of light. The only thing she could think was what could have happened to Rebecca and Shaulmar.

CHAPTER 25

ALISON DID NOT APPRECIATE BEING FORCED TO FOLLOW the Rhostos through the walls of the cathedral—she felt like there was nothing firm around her and she had the constant awareness of walking through a waterfall.

"How long are you going to drag me around like this?" she was angry and incredibly annoyed.

"Do not be so impatient…all will be revealed in the next few moments." The warrior seemed to be preoccupied as he spoke.

"I know I cannot see you, but it seems like you are doing something other than navigating through this labyrinth of stone and rock." She was not just making conversation. She demanded answers. She wanted to know what he was doing? She could no more function without control of her environment as function without oxygen. She needed her control back, or she would begin to revolt against the relationship, that had been created between the two beings. Just as she was about to continue with her badgering of the Rhostos warrior, she found herself being restrained by a force that was in front of her and pushing on her. The energy around her was also changing it—became more sluggish and heavy in nature. "We're slowing down? Is this the end of the joyride now?" she was not very courteous to the Rhostos…or anyone else come to think of it.

"Yes, we are about to stop travelling. I advise the Alison being to hold onto the back of me for stability." The Warrior was kind enough to move closer to her. Alison placed one hand on his back and braced herself on his waist with the other.

"You sure know how to show a woman a good time." Her sarcasm masked the obvious anger she held towards him. As Alison hung on to the back of his cloak, with a grip of death, she noticed something odd about his physical appearance. Although, she had been close enough to the Rhostos before, to know how he was put together physically, there was definitely something different about him. So, she had the idea to try, very delicately to feel around, while he was busy navigating through the energy field about them…to notice. However, when she felt a large bulge under his leather wing, he moved away from her, giving her the opportunity to stop the search. "Sorry, just getting a bit jittery about this travelling business. I apologize if my movement was inappropriate." She quelled the nervousness of the situation effectively. Suddenly, they stopped travelling and, she found herself in a room that looked like a private chapel, the tapestries on the walls looked as ancient as the mountains. "Ugh-travelling like this makes me tremble and shake inside. How do you manage to continually get around that way?" The question was rhetorical. She was so irritated with the whole business of partnering up with the Rhostos warrior.

"I do not share your opinion about the method of travel we are using." He was facing away from her and was preoccupied with something he had inside one of his leather appendages.

"What are you doing, Rhostos? We have to find Rebecca Sullivan before Draco Bastian does." The dark witch was not pleased at having to wait to be given permission to do anything. Just because the Rhostos had a method of finding the target, and she didn't, was no reason for him to assume control and full authority over everything they did, she thought. Yet, she couldn't say anything because the truth was that he was her only chance of successfully capturing the soul of Rebecca Sullivan, the heart of the sacred ancient prophecy. The warrior continued to fumble with something, and she couldn't see past his huge frame, to identify what it was. Suddenly, she saw. "What the hell is that?" she couldn't believe her eyes.

"This was something I was able to seize during our ride through the stone walls. It was passing through a portal as we raced along the ancient stonewall of the secret rooms on the other side of the cathedral. This, my dear friend Allison Warrior, is one of the travellers." He unhooked his bat like wings and revealed his bundle, tied up with some sort of black-leather rope. Morghanz opened her eyes but could not move at all. The Rhostos and Alison had passed by the exit portal of the sacred royal crypt at the exact same moment that Morghanz was passing through it.

"What do you intend to do with it?" Alison asked.

"I do not know, but the opportunity presented itself, and the Rhostos do not waste opportunities." He had no idea what to do with Morghanz. She was not a soul that was so precious to them, but she was a traveller, a sorceress, a practitioner of the ways of the light."

"We can use her if we need to later, but for now, we must be sure she is securely restrained." Alison reached into the pouch that was wrapped around her waist, and pulled from it a dark-cloudy crystal that was long and thin and had small faceted crystals protruding from one end of it. "This should do it." She smiled as she caressed the crystal. She moved closer to Morghanz, while simultaneously passing her hand back and forth across the crystal in a figure eight formation that represented Infinity.

"Take the light and return to darkness…let the energy filter through…let the Dark Ones come to bind her…and allow those ones to remain true."

Alison had used an incantation to program the crystal to act as a portal for the darker powers of the universe to flow to the place where they were located. Morghanz could not disguise the fear in her eyes—she felt the power that was calling the darkness to her. Suddenly, the room was full of a grey fog that quickly accumulated around Morghanz, gathering speed as it travelled and swirled around her. The energy was alive; it was the darkness, manifested as the keeper. It engulfed the white sorceress and bound her, imprisoning her in a silver-grey fog. The leather ties the Rhostos put on her fell to the floor. Morghanz could not see six inches in any direction. The force of the darkness caused her pain when she came in contact with it—it was like a rabid animal wanting to claim its victim. "There, we do not need to be concerned about this one, she will not be going anywhere, she will be in that exact spot when we return." Alison was pleased with her ability to call the power of the darkness for the Rhostos to see. She was always able to do this, she'd had this ability ever since she could remember, it was innate and it was a natural thing that flowed around and through her. It was time he saw what she could do, she thought. She could tell he was impressed, even if he was trying his best to conceal it.

"That will be acceptable to the Rhostos," he said as he turned away, "we will need to hone our senses a little more to find the soul we seek. This one," he flung out an arm in the direction of the silver-grey fog, "was not easy to take, and if the soul we are seeking is more powerful, then we will need to combine our strength and skill as well as cunning, to succeed." He busily tucked his wings into their receptacles behind and beside him. Alison turned to look back at the fog, making sure the dark crystal was hovering in place, and that the portal was still open to receive the supply of dark energy flowing into it.

"Don't worry, how difficult could it be to capture her right out from under Draco Bastian." She laughed as she turned to follow the Rhostos warrior.

"I am picking up the soul signature now." They had stepped into the corridor outside the room that was holding Morghanz. "It is on the other side of the cathedral structure—we must go through the Great Hall to the other side. So...we must be alert, Allison Warrior, because I am sensing powerful energies in various positions within the structure. We must go in this direction." The Rhostos warrior moved quickly for his size—he moved very slightly from side-to-side, something that was imperceptible to the untrained eye, but something that increased his strength and power when in battle. Alison watched as the warrior led the way. She had plans forming of her own that didn't include her sharing any prize with the Rhostos warrior. It was clear to her that he considered his power and ability superior to hers, and that suited her plan just fine for the moment. The dark sorceress caught up to him and was close enough to speak, softly, to him.

"Do you know where we our going?"

"Yes. There is another corridor ahead that should lead to the stairway that will take us around the building, unseen." He was confident of his own words.

"How could you possibly know all this? You haven't been here before, have you?" she was actually astounded that the Rhostos would know how to navigate so precisely without prior knowledge.

"As you have asked, I will tell you. The Rhostos can do such things because I am here, and also, above."

"I don't understand." She looked at him, as if he were just making stuff up, as if she thought him crazy. "Explain how you can be here and above."

"We do not have time for this. Here is the stairway." The warrior looked over to her and pointed. "If we go down here, there will be a walkway around the perimeter of the building. It should provide good cover for us as we move closer to the soul."

"You first! I am not sure about this whole situation and when my little voice speaks to me inside my head, I usually ignore it, but right now it is screaming at me to slow down and think. So, that is what I am going to do." She looked around for somewhere to sit—out of the way. She remembered an alcove that they had passed by earlier and went back to find it. When she found it, she waited, to see if the warrior would follow her. If he took too long to show up, she planned to wait until the battle, over who would snare the soul of Rebecca Sullivan was complete, then she would attempt to steal it from the victor. As she sat and thought, the Rhostos stood nearby, trying to decide if he should go it alone and attempt to capture the prize, or force his partner to honor their agreement. He entered the alcove.

"I don't think either one of us could accomplish our goal alone, so I must insist you honor our agreement." His tone was strong and definitive.

"What if I decide to cancel our agreement, Rhostos Warrior?" she was right, all he could do was kill her, he thought. The warrior said nothing—he just sat on the stone floor cross-legged, and leaning against the wall.

***

The sounds echoed around the dark stonewalls, marble pillars, and ancient wooden beams of the great cathedral's main hall.

"What do you sense my little brother?" Bastian came up from behind him, silently.

"Oh! You scared the hell out of me," he hissed then hung his head after he realized whom he'd hissed at.

"Yes, I'm sure I did." Bastian's cloak hung on him like the skin of royalty.

"Master, I have not been able to find anything that resembles traces of the travellers or Rebecca Sullivan." He avoided the searching eyes of his brother.

"Is there anything else you want to tell me?" The Dark One knew everything so it was pointless to try and deceive him.

"Yes, the others are missing." Drandos' voice contained traces of defeat and helplessness.

"Why does that not surprise me, brother?" Bastian walked ahead of him and suddenly turned to face him, his black cloak whistled as he moved. "Drandos, when this is done, you and I are going to have a discussion about your future here with me. The reason you think your partners are missing is simply because they thought of you as a danger to them. They would rather risk death from an encounter with the travellers, than trust that you could stand with them and protect them as they could protect you." The darkness flowed from his every breath and spoken word. Bastian could not help himself—he loved to bask in the misery of others, especially when he was the source of their misery. Drandos was in darkness and pain, he knew there was no love in the life he had chosen, and the people in his environment knew only hatred. The young apprentice realized his naiveté, hearing his brother's words, and made a promise to himself that he would escape from the hell he was in.

"What is it you wish from me, brother?" Drandos was almost at the point of despair and desperately tried to disguise the fact. He stared at the stone slabs that made up the floor of the cathedral.

"There are two others, practitioners of the ways of the darkness, who walk through this site. They hunt for the same soul that we do. I am charging you with the task of finding them, and when you do—correction—if you do, I want you to do your very best to kill them. If that task is beyond you, then I want you to stay with them as long as they are here. I want to know their movements at all times. Do you think that is within your abilities as an apprentice, brother?" He knew it was and so did Drandos—pain and suffering continued to be his destiny, he thought. Bastian disappeared, enveloped in a cocoon of red—grey energy, leaving Drandos to the task of finding Alison and the Rhostos warrior.

"How the hell am I supposed to find these ones, let alone try to kill them?" Drandos walked slowly between the rows of pews in the Great Hall, talking outloud to him self. He was totally unaware of the development of a separation growing within his unconscious mind. His inner voice was growing stronger and more powerful with every day that passed. Every demeaning act that his brother subjected him to added energy to the force that made the split within his being. He found himself developing a rapport with the voice in his head. "I am his brother—what gives him the right to do all the crappy things he does to me?" The rhetorical questions flowed from his mind as he found the small hallway on the other side of the grand hall. He was not paying much attention to the adjoining small rooms off the corridors as he ambled passed them. Drandos continued with the inner dialogue that consumed his mind and consciousness.

He made his way down toward the south end of the cathedral—he could barely make out the end where the huge stonewall, housing the magnificent stained glass windows, was located. "Those idiotic minions working for my brother disrespect me so much. One day, I will make them pay. They will suffer as they made me suffer, and my brother will finally see how powerful the dark force flows through my mind and body." His ramblings and preoccupation were removing all, and any protection, he had learned through his training with the sacred teachers of the dark arts. The distraction could be dangerous, even fatal if he allowed it to continue, but there was no one there to snap him back into reality. Soon Drandos was oblivious to all things happening around him—he was at the point of functioning on autopilot, and that was not something he had been warned about or trained to avoid. There was a disturbance in the energy ahead of him, blocking his path, but he was too busily embroiled in the inner conflict to notice. With his head down, and his continual ramblings concerning his brother, taking his attention fully, he walked head-on into the energy. The impact immediately subdued him, he felt like he had fallen into a web of energy that had paralyzed his nervous system. The shock brought him back to the present moment, but it was too late, he could do nothing.

Drandos struggled as best he could but it was futile. He tried to send thoughts to his brother to raise the alarm, but the web prevented anything leaving or entering the energy field.

"So, what do you think about the Rhostos warrior now, Queen of the darkness?" He flexed his wings, knowing that he had accomplished something that dwarfed the grey fog that Alison had imprisoned the traveller with.

"Not bad." She moved closer. "How does something like this remain in place? I mean—where does it get its power source?" she slowly reached out a hand and caressed the ripples of energy in front of her. "It feels like...sound. When I touch it, I can hear sounds." She snickered loudly and childishly.

"The Rhostos have many talents and they are exclusive to us. If I told you all my secrets, I would be doing myself a grave disservice, because you're not a Rhostos warrior. I cannot trust anyone who is not a Rhostos warrior." The warrior had a stone-cold look in his eyes. He watched as she examined the energy, amazed at how it moved and yet seemed to remain stationary, simultaneously. The apprentice held inside the web of energy was unable to move—only his eyes were able to follow her as she made her way around him.

"What do you have in mind for this one?" Alison wanted to know everything. "And who is this one? Do you know him?" she wanted to be part of the warrior, part of his clan. Alison wanted so desperately to be Rhostos. This was a profound epiphany that caused her to lose her breath—she was scared to death at what she was thinking, but at the same time she was extremely excited at the prospect of becoming a Rhostos warrior. All these thoughts raced through her mind as she watched him investigate the prisoner that was caught in his web.

"I have never met this one." The warrior inspected the web. "Maybe we can get the information we require from him?" He continued to survey his captive, paying little attention to what Alison had said. "This one is strong." The Rhostos closed his eyes and stood closer to the energy holding Drandos captive. "His lineage is ancient."

"How can you tell that from where you stand?" she was so envious of his power. The first thought that entered her mind was that he must be a phony, he must be faking somehow, making all this up just so he could look good. The Rhostos moved around to the opposite side of the energy field, his hands were out in front slightly, as he was obviously connecting with the energy. The Rhostos had the innate ability to permeate energy fields without danger to themselves. It was something that evolution had provided to them due to their necessity of travelling in the space between dimensions. "This one is a threat—he has high potential. There was also another connected to this one." The warrior inhaled deeply and slowly, as if he were analyzing every molecule of air for clues to the origin of the captive. "I sense much fear and sadness with this being." He opened his eyes and looked straight at Drandos. The Rhostos had finally connected to his soul signature and felt deep sadness and despair.

"Well, what do you have to share with me?" she was extremely irritated at the whole thing. "Just get the information you require and dispose of this thing." She was adamant to the point of taking the matter into her own hands and destroying the prisoner with her own power and knowledge of the dark arts. The warrior flexed his wings slightly, just enough to stay her intentions. The movement of air produced by his wings was enough to indicate to Alison that she had best be careful of her position in the partnership. "All right." She turned away from him. "Do as you wish, but let me warn the Rhostos warrior we cannot take chances with these kinds of things, if we do not dispose of this one, he will always be a threat." She tried her best to conceal the fact that she knew the prisoner was the Dark One's brother. Alison always found that knowledge was sometimes just as powerful as the energy she used to destroy things. She decided she would wait for the right moment to tell the Rhostos that he had captured the brother of the Dark Angel, or she may never need to tell him at all. If she could convince the warrior to kill him, it would be more efficient for her plans. "You must destroy this enemy of the Rhostos." She was as emphatic as she dared to be. The Rhostos only continued to eye the prisoner inside the energy field—his hand was touching the pulsating power source holding the captive being.

"There is something more." He didn't remove his gaze from the prisoner. Drandos looked back at him, still rigid, unable to move except for his eyes. "Why do you conceal this one's identity from the Rhostos?" He turned to Alison—there was anger in his eyes.

"What do you mean?" she tried her best to sound appalled at his accusation. "How dare you say that to me! To assume that I would deliberately lie to you—well that's too disrespectful to me to even answer." She tried to think of a way out, some kind of manipulation that would allow her to avoid the pain and embarrassment of having to own up to a lie that would put her at his mercy, because she did still need him, after all, to capture the prize.

"The Allison Warrior has not been honest with the Rhostos. If you know of this one, do not deny it. I know you have seen him before—it is reflected in him." The Rhostos knew this because he had accessed Drandos's memory through his neural pathways, and had unlocked the memory cortex of the brain, to reveal his identity. As he did so, he uncovered the memory where he saw the one known to him as Allison Warrior. "You are not as you are now, I see. The healing you received from the Rhostos warrior was beneficial to you, don't you agree?"

"Obviously!" she blurted out, almost in tears. The warrior was witnessing the torture that she had suffered at the hands of the Dark Angel, through the eyes of his brother, Drandos. "So, I am humiliated once more." Alison turned away from him. "Do you enjoy watching my pain, Rhostos?" Her voice betrayed her discomfort. She had tried every day to disconnect from those horrible memories and to have them displayed for the Rhostos to witness was incredibly unnerving for her. Alison was tired of everything, her life in general, and her inability to succeed at anything. She had her back to him, trying to dry her eyes with her sleeve. Suddenly, she felt a huge energy surge behind her; she spun quickly, blinking, so she could see clearly. There, in the middle of the hallway, she witnessed the most beautiful and horrific sight ever to penetrate her eyes. The Rhostos was standing in front of the energy field with his head bent and his arms down by his sides. As he stood, motionless, the energy holding Drandos slowly changed from grey to silver, and quickened the frequency of the ripples it created as it flowed around the captive. She could see Drandos's physical appearance starting to change. It was obvious that hc was in great pain. She stared into his eyes and recognized the degree of suffering he was experiencing, just as his brother had made her suffer.

Drandos was screaming on the inside, the intensity of his pain was reflected in his eyes. For one moment she did feel bad for him, then she rationalized that he deserved everything he was getting, because he was the one who'd boldly urged his brother to kill her or let her go, just so he could go to dinner. All through her ordeal, at the hands of Bastian, the words spoken by his brother gave Alison the impetus she needed to survive the terror of that day. The dark sorceress swore that she would destroy Drandos one day, and that mantra remained with her to this day, as a burning flame in the middle of her head—and now she could savor his demise. The Rhostos lowered to one knee as if collapsing under an immense weight. The energy field began to rotate slowly around Drandos who continued to show signs of physical change. Alison watched intently, looking into the energy field to find the eyes of Drandos, then down to the Rhostos warrior to see what was happening. The young apprentice had closed his eyes at this point—the silver energy was rotating much faster now. The Rhostos warrior stood up, and with his arms outstretched, he caused the energy to spin so fast that it shone brighter and appeared seamless. The Rhostos revealed his huge leather like wings and swung them high above him, while simultaneously a beautiful indigo light shone from within his heart—the intense beam collided with the silver prison. At that exact point in time, the energy and Drandos transformed into a long thin whirlpool of energy and light and disappeared into space. The Warrior sunk over to the wall of the hallway to stabilize himself.

"Wow! What was that?" Alison was in awe of the huge warrior—she couldn't believe what she'd seen. The Rhostos remained silent, recuperating from the drain of energy needed for him to complete the process. "Are you okay? That was amazing! It must have required an incredible amount of power to pull that off?" The warrior continued to remain silent. Alison looked to where Drandos had been, but was no longer. "Now, that is an incredible method of destroying someone. He was forced to endure intense pain. I could see it in his eyes." She was applauding the Rhostos as if he had done something very wonderful. Finally the warrior lifted his head.

"You seem to like to watch other beings suffer. This, however, is not the Rhostos way." He pushed his large frame against the stonewall, which helped him to stand, while he continued his recuperation from the ordeal. "I am Rhostos. We do not kill unless our life is at an end."

"Then what happened to the unfortunate soul who just disappeared before our eyes if he is not dead?" she was letting him know in no uncertain terms that she believed that the Rhostos had just killed Drandos, and was lying about it.

"That one was sent through an unknown portal, and as soon as I activated the opening, the captive was released from the energy field, and transported through it, to an unspecified and totally random destination within our universe. This is how the Rhostos deal with any threats that arise." The Warrior was explicit, and strong in his conviction. "Now, we must move on. There are many threats within this place. If we are to succeed in capturing the soul of Rebecca Sullivan, we must move quickly." He pulled in his wings and covered them with his cloak.

"Wait a minute! I have never heard of this before, and I have access to much knowledge within my order," she challenged him once more.

"The Rhostos are underestimated because we live in the space between dimensions. Many make the mistake of thinking Rhostos are weak or inferior, because of where we reside, and how we travel. Few can match the power and magic the Rhostos wield. "Please, Allison Warrior, do not fall into that group. I have come to enjoy your companionship." The Rhostos warrior looked Alison squarely in the eyes and immediately read her iris.

"Don't do that!" she complained. "How would you like it if I was able to know your innermost thoughts without your permission?" she was angry and her claws were out again.

"Please, forgive me, it is habit only. Forgive the Rhostos. I will try to change that concerning you, Allison Warrior." The Rhostos was sincere. She could tell. The sorceress returned to her own space and huffed a little, feeling somewhat satisfied, but still feeling a bit irritated at his abilities.

"So, what happened to the one you sent through the portal gate? Do you know where he was sent? What part of the universe did the unfortunate end up in?" she didn't look at him at all.

"I do not know. I do not care. That does not concern me at all, because the being wanted to harm the Rhostos, so he got what he deserved." The warrior tucked his cloak in and covered his appendages. They were hidden from view with surprising stealth and efficiency. "Now we must leave, follow me, please," he spoke sternly. She moved quickly to his side, to let him know they were equal in partnership, and that she would accept no less.

CHAPTER 26

THE PORTAL IN THE COLD, STONEWALL HAD CLOSED BEfore Shaulmar could do anything. "Morghanz!" he yelled, as the stones solidified and his fist collided with them. Rebecca was still only semiconscious, and was leaning against the pillar of the room they had entered, after they'd moved through the portal.

"What...what happened to Morghanz?" she whispered. Her eyes were closed and she was holding her head in the palm of her hand—her breathing was erratic and she looked like she was sick... or worse.

"I don't know!" he looked scared. She could hear it in his voice. "She was right behind you! But she did not get through the exit portal." He pushed his head against the wall where the portal gate used to be.

"Don't worry, Shaulmar, she can't be far away. Maybe she is still inside the crypt. I will ask the Essence to open the portal again just as soon as the room stops spinning." She spoke with her eyes closed. Shaulmar leaned against the wall as if he had lost the most precious thing in his life. Rebecca tried to pull herself together as she stood against the marble pillar, and then looked around, to see where they might be. At the far end of the room there was a small chapel behind wrought iron railings and a gate made of the same wrought iron. "Shaulmar." She watched him in so much pain slumped against the stonewall. "Shaulmar, please help me." The wizard pulled his cloak over his shoulders, and tried as best that he could, to conceal the fact that he was wiping away tears.

"Yes, Rebecca. I will be there in a moment." His heart was breaking into a thousand pieces. He couldn't face life if his love, Morghanz, was gone. The great wizard knew he was still responsible for Rebecca's safety and he tried to summon enough strength to carry on through the pain. "What is it?" he spoke softly.

"This chapel." She held onto the iron bars as she peered into the small room. "It may be significant." She turned to him.

"What do you mean, Rebecca? Significant in what way?" He was not seeing what she saw.

"Shaulmar, I think we can find Morghanz. This chapel has the exact same energy signature as Morghanz's soul signature, so this chapel must've been her room in the house, before you transformed it." She smiled. Shaulmar looked into the chapel once more—this time he closed his eyes and connected to the energy. In his mind's eye he saw images of crystals, various colored candles, and other items that he was familiar with.

"Yes, you are right. This is Morghanz's old room."

"I need to get into this chapel and get the Essence to connect with Morghanz and find out where she is." Rebecca sounded as if she had been infused with new energy. "The iron gates here have been fused together—how the hell are we going to get into this damn Chapel?" she grabbed the gates and shook them violently.

"Rebecca, do not concern yourself with such trivial things as iron gates. Stand back behind the pillar—cover yourself." With a wave of one of his hands, there was a powerful flash of bright electric-blue light, and then smoke filled the air. The gates to the chapel sprung open with a clang. "Okay, Rebecca, you can go in now. I will wait here and watch for danger." Shaulmar stretched out his arm for her to go in. She moved past him very slowly, her head was still pounding from her previous connection with the Essence. As she got close to him, he touched her on the arm. "Rebecca, Morghanz is my only love, please help her." She saw the pleading in his eyes, and she smiled and rubbed his back, as she went in through the gates.

"Don't worry, Shaulmar, I love her to. Her words brought immense satisfaction to the wizard. He thanked her with all his heart and paid her the respect of an ancient Persian wizard. He touched his forehead with one hand and his heart with the other, and at the same time, he bowed his head. Rebecca slowly stepped into the cave-like room, looking in all directions, deliberately. She was making sure she was alone before beginning to call upon the Essence, making the soul connection once more. There were a few artifacts at one end of the chapel and a figure of one of the saints, amongst, what looked to her, like a tomb outside an Egyptian pyramid. She thought it strange that such a thing should be in a chapel room of the cathedral, but she was too preoccupied with making sure she was alone, to enquire further. Rebecca turned to the other corner of the room and noticed more objects of interest. A rather large structure in the corner was almost tall enough to touch the ceiling. Rebecca moved toward it, thinking it would serve as a hiding place, while she connected with the Essence. Shaulmar had taken a position behind a pillar in the hallway.

At this point, Rebecca was feeling very tired and her heart was beating faster now, as she leaned against the large object, using her arm to steady herself. She took three or four large breaths to regain some composure and strength. The process of connecting with the Essence required a large amount of energy and mental focus. She found that relaxing her body, then her mind, served to conserve some of that energy, and not resisting when the process began, was the key to the whole process. Shaulmar stood hidden behind a large stone pillar, vigilant in his desire to keep his friend from harm. Protecting Rebecca at all costs was his only thought, now, that he might have lost his love, Morghanz, forever. The great wizard swore to himself that he would find the ones who took Morghanz from him and make them pay. His thoughts were strong, but the soul of the great wizard quelled the hatred and his desire to exact revenge. He hung his head, resting it against the great pillar, allowing it to take the weight of his sadness.

Tears of pain rolled down his face, falling onto the stone and down to the base, eventually creating a puddle between the cracks under his feet on the stone-slab floor. A quiet voice whispered gently to him as the sorrow filled his heart. He felt a gentle urging around him, as if there were old friends, all about him. He lifted his head away from the pillar, and brought the sleeve of his hooded cloak across his face, to dry his tears. Looking around the hall, making sure he was alone, he rested his body against the stone column, and then he tried to sense the energy that was providing comfort to him. Suddenly, he knew who was with him—there was no mistaking the pungent aroma of lavender that seemed to fill the air all about him. Shaulmar allowed the pain in his heart to subside, and a slight smile appeared on his face, as he sniffled back the mucus that was draining from his nose. He bathed in the intoxicating smell. "Sporack," he whispered, "old friend—you comfort me once more." Shaulmar smiled again and the sparkle returned to his dark-blue eyes.

Rebecca had attained a calmness, enough to relax, while she sat on a small stone altar behind a large structure that kept her hidden. She wanted to find her friend because she couldn't bear if anything happened to her—it was something she just could not handle. As the thoughts built in her head—as they formed and were created, they began to grow. Rebecca's emotions shifted, from feeling vulnerable and weak, to feeling anger and injustice. The more she conjured images of her friend, the more energy flowed through her. She began to feel stronger—she could sense the revitalizing energy from the vortex coursing through her, it came from deep inside her and from all around her. Thoughts filled her with injustice, and anger about the fact that some other beings had taken her friend, against her will. The rational mind kicked in, but what she was feeling, did not make sense at all.

Rebecca knew she had been feeling very low, her energy was so depleted, as if she was drained mentally and physically, and that all she wanted to do was lay down and sleep through all eternity. Now all those feelings had disappeared—she was feeling like she could take on the world, she was feeling so strong inside, and so filled with energy…but she knew it were not her. So she took a breath, and slowly inhaled, to prepare to search for the source of the energy that filled her. After a few moments, it became obvious that it was the Essence that was making her feel revitalized and strong. The Essence had risen from its dormant state and connected with her once more. It had activated without Rebecca calling upon it—this was very strange—with the soul of Rebecca bound to the essence of the book, essentially the *soul* of the Book of Secrets, there was no need for Rebecca to ask the book to connect, it was already connected, and could feel everything she felt.

When she stood straight, there was a prickling feeling at the base of the skull where her head met her neck. She knew this was the onset of her tattoo becoming active again. Thanks to the Essence, she was about to experience more pain, as the tattoo came to life.

This was really becoming a pain in more ways than one, she thought. She wanted it to be over before it began. She read the signs as the Essence became visible. The green mist oozed from her back, over her shoulders, and collected gently, softly, in front of her. It was very beautiful, she thought. She still had difficulty veiwing the Essence, the beautiful and glowing green mist appear from her body in this way. Rebecca knew what was coming next, the tattoo would begin to glow and a searing pain would tear at her back for a couple of minutes, and then subside. The young girl hated this part of the process; she sent thoughts to the Essence as it skimmed ahead of her, waiting for the tattoo to conclude the manifestation. She pleaded with it to find a less painful and intrusive way to come forth from her; however there was no response, just the onset of pain. After it was done, the Essence spoke to her as it glowed slightly.

"My friend. I am sorry to have come forth without making it clear to you first. I will try to let you know before I manifest in the future." Rebecca grunted, as she felt the remnants of the painful episode subside.

"Well, that might help a little. I wonder if you could feel my pain since we are bound? Tell me, do you feel everything I feel, except my pain?" she was irritated to say the least.

"Since it is the Essence that calls forth the book from within you, and the tattoo is the portal for the Essence to manifest in the physical, I am the pain you feel. So, in answer to your question, no...I do not feel your pain." There was an exhalation of exasperation from Rebecca as the pain finally disappeared.

"You can manifest without my permission, now, that is something new." She sat down on the altar again, prepared to have the Essence locate Morghanz.

"This is correct. We are bound by the thinnest of threads." The Essence spun quickly for a few moments, and as it did, Rebecca saw a silver cord emanate from the central, or what she assumed to be the heart area, of the green mist.

"What is that?" Rebecca stiffened as the silver lining slowly made its way to her.

"Do not be afraid. The cord of life belongs to you too." She was a little freaked out.

"What exactly do you mean that it belongs to me too?" she said nervously, backing up off the stone altar and coming to rest pressed up against the wrought-iron railing that surrounded the small room. Suddenly, without warning, the chord shot to the center of her chest. She gasped as if a silver lance had skewered her.

"Rebecca, do not be afraid. This has been part of you from the moment we were bound." The Essence spoke with a degree of nonchalance that really pissed her off—something she would have expressed more gratifyingly if she could just catch her breath. The silver cord disappeared, and she was able to return to normalcy, somewhat. "You may feel some discomfort from time to time, Rebecca. This is only because of your human physiology, your human form. Because of your physical body, the cord can seem rather bothersome when it reveals itself—this is due to the difference in vibration. Rebecca had recovered her breath at this point, but thought it was redundant or useless to get angry, besides, she knew the Essence would not be affected by emotion. She composed herself, and focused on having the Essence locate Morghanz, although she didn't really want to hear anything bad that may have happened to her friend. Rebecca lifted her head and looked up at the swirling, vibrating mist.

"I need your help. I want to know what happened to my friend Morghanz. Can you find her?" she spoke with a soft, gentle, voice that contained a hint of hopelessness as she looked on expectantly. The Essence spun slowly, as if thinking, or even trying to decide whether to do as she had been asked. "Please, you are our only hope. If you have the ability to find Morghanz, please do so." There was only an eerie silence as if the Essence was somewhere else. Suddenly, it shone excitedly.

"I think I can find her! I must connect with her soul signature." Rebecca was hopeful again.

"We are in the same place her bedroom was when this place was not the cathedral, but a house. Maybe that can help?" Rebecca was becoming more excited by the moment, and happy, the more she thought of them finding Morghanz again.

"That will be enough for me to locate Morghanz. Do not worry Rebecca. You and I will find Morghanz, that I promise," the Essence assured her. Rebecca let out a sigh of relief, reinvigorated by the anticipation that the Essence was powerful enough to make a difference.

"I will do what I am able. Just let me know what to do," she said calmly. The mist spun, then fell silent once more. The room glistened from the green energy being thrown off, as the Essence quickened, creating a swirl of green-silver light that travelled up and down the vision that hung in the space near her. Rebecca was pleased that she saw the process unfolding as before. She was absolutely convinced that once the Essence stopped spinning, she would know where her friend was—that was exactly how the Essence worked. Suddenly, there was a loud crack as if something had gone wrong. Rebecca's heart was in her throat, she held her breath—there was a flash of green-silver light that filled the small chapel. Her eyes slammed shut, when she opened them again, the Essence was gone. All that remained was the smell of burnt air, with electric-blue light. Shaulmar rushed through the iron gates. He was filled with fear as he thought the worst. If Rebecca was harmed, he felt he would not be able to deal with it. He couldn't lose both of them—that was not something he could deal with. When he arrived at the object at the far end of the chapel, he rushed around to the back of it, hoping she was still there.

"Rebecca! Rebecca!" He was breathing heavily. "What happened? Are you okay?" The wizard stammered a little, composing himself, only when he saw she was unharmed.

"I'm okay, Shaulmar. I don't know what happened, it was there one moment, and then gone the next. That sound, the crack, oh, I hope nothing happened to the Essence, Shaulmar." She threw her arms around his neck with such force that it took his breath away.

"I'm here, it's okay, I'm here," he heard his voice saying the words but he couldn't stop the thought that haunted him. How could he comfort and protect her, when he failed to do the exact same thing for Morghanz, his love, his heart, his life. Rebecca sobbed into his neck as her tears fell once more.

"When will it end, Shaulmar?" she was beginning to fall apart and he knew it.

"Nothing ever ends my dear one. The only thing we can count on is self. You are in the midst of incredible changes, Rebecca, embrace them all, for they summon you to your destiny." The wizard knew of what he spoke. Rebecca clung to his shoulders in a desperate attempt to disappear into his cloak. All she wanted was to see the end to this horrible nightmare.

"Shaulmar, I will do what is expected of me." She slowly released her grip on his neck and shoulders and pulled away, averting her eyes from his, because she didn't like being seen in this state by her friend.

"Now," said Shaulmar, "we must think of how we can escape this place, and when we are clear, we can make plans for the future. Until then, we must stay strong, and above all, trust that the universe is guiding us." The wizard looked away, to make it easier on her, and to allow her the opportunity to pull her self together, unnoticed. He turned around and walked slowly to the entrance to the chapel. He lifted his arms and opened his hands while reaching for the iron bars of the gate. He stared into space, his fingers wrapped around the bars, tightening with every moment. He knew the anger deep inside him was getting stronger—the signs were there for him to see plainly. After a few moments, his fingers were white, through lack of blood circulating through them—the pressure he exerted on the iron bars was enough to bend them slightly. If he concentrated hard enough he could have ripped the doors from its hinges—he had done it before.

"Shaulmar!" Rebecca's voice broke his trance. "Do you know what we must do next?" she spoke with such gentleness that it almost broke his heart. He tried to sound as positive as he could.

"Now…let's think this through Rebecca. The cathedral is my creation—we need to escape from it." He began to pace up and down the chapel, shuffling his grey ankle-length boots as he moved and kicking the dust up as he went. "I must recreate a way out, an exit, that we can use." He scratched his chin as he walked back and forth, his long hooded cloak dragged on the floor behind him as he walked. "There must be an incantation to create an escape," he muttered. Meanwhile, Rebecca just sat on the small stone altar watching him walk slowly back and forth in front of the tall object she had first hid behind. As she watched the great wizard pacing back and forth, it dawned on her that sometimes he disappeared briefly, as he passed in front of the object and then reappeared. Suddenly, she sat bolt upright.

"That's it! That's it Shaulmar!" She jumped off the altar and hurried to him. "The Essence—the Essence hasn't disappeared because of anything done to it, it has created the opening for us," she explained. "The obelisk you have been pacing back and forth in front of is the portal out of here. The Essence has transformed the object into an exit portal, that is why I saw you disappear as you passed in front of it, and then reappear on the other side." Shaulmar looked very puzzled. "Don't you see? The Essence is changing too, it searched for Morghanz's soul signature in the hopes of finding her, but it connected with her sacred altar instead, which is now the large obelisk you created when you manifested the cathedral and created a portal." She was jumping up and down, pointing out the object. "That is what you have been pacing in front of." She smiled excitedly, waiting patiently for Shaulmar to come to the same conclusion. He suddenly snapped his fingers.

"You're right, Rebecca! You're right. This is where she had her alter if I remember correctly." He looked at the object and turned to scan the rest of the chapel then turned back to the object. "Yes, this is exactly where she had placed the altar when she first came to earth, to my house, to work with me." Rebecca stood next to him, trying to see what he was seeing.

"So, what do we do now?" she whispered, looking at him, then at the object, then back at him. Shaulmar thought for a moment. The sleeves of his cloak hung low as he rested his hand on his arms.

"Well, if the Essence has connected with Morghanz through the object, and that provides us with the escape from here, then we must first find Morghanz before we can attempt to use the portal, for two very good reasons. The first being that the object belongs to Morghanz and her energy would activate it, so it would be prudent for us to have her use it first, and secondly, I fear for her safety, not only from those who have her, but from the portal itself." The Wizard stared at the tall, beige stone object.

"What do you mean? Are you saying the Essence might want to harm us?" Rebecca moved away from him, not wanting to hear that the book would do something like that. Shaulmar calmly put a friendly hand on her arm before she got too far away.

"No, dear one, only that we must be cautious. The Essence is changing like you said, and we must trust that it is learning about the changes in power and abilities. We also must be alert to the possibility that the Essence may take some time to bring those things under control." His words made sense and Rebecca knew it. She relaxed and gave him a slight smile, letting him know that she was okay with it, for now. Shaulmar watched as his friend moved closer to the object, he knew she was daring to sense the one bound to her. "Do you feel it yet?" he asked, knowing that she would turn to him surprised.

"No...and how did you know I was trying?"

"Well, I am a wizard after all, that is what we do," he laughed. He was trying to neutralize some of the tension in Rebecca or transform it into something positive.

"So, what do we do now?" Rebecca wanted to do something—she hated just waiting and doing nothing to help her friend. She also wanted desperately to trust in Shaulmar, he was an ancient wizard, and must have been in desperate situations before, she thought. "Shall I touch the stone obelisk and try to sense the Essence?" she spoke in a voice that urged him to say yes, even though she wasn't very sure if she could do such a thing, and even if she could, would it be the same or not? One scary thought after another. Would it ever end? No sooner did she quell the rising fear inside her, resulting from one thought, when another would take its place. She put her hands to her ears. "Enough!" she yelled.

"Rebecca, those thoughts are not yours, fear is attached to them—they are attracted by the desperation in your heart for your friend," he spoke gently to her. Do you remember when Morghanz told you to go inside yourself, and summon the energy from down deep inside, to quell your fears?" she nodded slowly and she sat with her arms wrapped around her middle. "You must call on the words she spoke," Shaulmar reminded her, "and have them assist you now in your time of need. Morghanz taught you well. Please honor her with your strength and power of the mind and heart." He was right; the words he spoke touched her heart and soul immediately. Rebecca slowed her breathing as she was instructed; she slowly brought her hands from her middle to her sides.

"Thank you, Shaulmar. I had forgotten what Morghanz gave to me." She felt calmer now.

"Rebecca, you can try to sense the Essence but promise me you will stop if you feel danger, please." He loved her as his own child.

"I promise," she reassured him. He could only watch as Rebecca exhaled, forcibly, and walked closer to the stone object. Her heart began to beat faster and she could feel the heat of nervousness and anxiety rising up from her stomach. "No..." she said to herself, "believe. Morghanz, help me." She spoke the words as a whisper as she got closer.

In her mind, she recalled her time with her teacher, Morghanz, and replayed the words of her friend as she walked the last few feet towards the stone obelisk. As she did, the vibration was strong, she could feel it all around her, she stopped just an arms length away from it. Shaulmar moved to the side, about 10 feet away—he could see the energy around the tall obelisk, and his friend was totally engulfed in it. She held up her arms in front of it, palms facing away from her, as if she were resting them against something solid, even though she was still about a foot away from the object. Shaulmar saw the waves of energy wash over her like honey falling from the honeycomb. He hoped with all his heart that if it became too dangerous she would pull herself safely away in time...or...would she be able to pull away at all? he wondered. Shaulmar was becoming very anxious. Rebecca had been in the circle of energy for at least five minutes, without moving. The great wizard was beginning to fear for her safety and decided to prepare his strongest incantation for an assault on the object. Thankfully, she began to move backwards out of the energy. She lowered her hands, and when she left the circle, she turned and walked forward towards him.

"Rebecca, are you alright?" He reached for her as she neared him.

"Yes, I'm fine."

"What happened?" He was eager to know if she had connected with the Essence.

"Well…that was very weird." She sat on the small altar again just staring at the floor.

"What was weird?" He didn't know how to react. He wasn't sure if she was really okay, and wondered if he should reassert his questions. He wondered if she thought she was okay, but really wasn't, he couldn't tell. Shaulmar was not used to, and definitely hated, feeling uncertain.

"Did you see all the stuff? The colors and waves of light and things?" she was lifting her arm, and stroking the air as if she were reaching for something that he couldn't see. Shaulmar followed her hand in the air and tried to see what she was reaching for.

"I don't see anything, Rebecca." His frustration was showing itself in this voice. She snapped out of it when she realized he couldn't see what she saw.

"Sorry, Shaulmar, I will tell you everything in a moment. I just need to come back to this place." She had been somewhere that only she could describe.

"Okay…do you need anything…anything at all?" He wanted her to tell him everything so they could figure out what to do next.

"N…no. I'm good. The Essence had connected to the obelisk, it activated the portal, but I don't know where it is now." She was coping with her connection with the Essence much better now that she hadn't slipped into unconsciousness, at all. Also, she wasn't feeling drained of energy, now, as she had with the previous connections. However, she was confused as to why she had no idea where the Essence was or how to locate it.

"That's great, we can find Morghanz, and get out of here, right?" Shaulmar watched as she just sat on the stone altar, eyes closed, taking a breath, and slowly reorienting herself. "The Essence does know where Morghanz is…doesn't it?" By this point, he was only whispering—his voice was loaded with hope. Rebecca looked up at him to explain as best she could, without letting her emotions interfere.

"Morghanz is in the cathedral, but the Essence says she was taken by two beings, not of the light." Shaulmar said nothing. Rebecca paused to allow him to speak, but he just stared at the ground and said nothing. "One of them is a sorceress, a practitioner of the darkness, and the other is what the Essence called, a Rhostos warrior." She fixed her eyes on him while she spoke, and the only response she saw, was a sudden clenching of his fist.

"Rhostos warrior, are you sure?" Shaulmar spoke slowly but his voice was full of anger.

"That was the name I heard in my head when I connected with the Essence. Who is the Rhostos, Shaulmar? Is Morghanz going to be okay? Can we go get her?" Rebecca fired questions at him but Shaulmar was no longer there—he had left and was staring at the floor again, only this time he had slumped to the floor, and was sitting in the dirt with his back against an old wooden chest against the wall. "Shaulmar, we must find her, the Essence said she was not far from here. One floor up and along the corridor." She began to get anxious, if Shaulmar gave up, how was she supposed to continue on alone to survive. It was not good. He was heartbroken. Morghanz was being held by the Rhostos. This meant to him that he was probably never going to see her again and that was more than he could handle. "Shaulmar! Please, help me to find her." Rebecca was now sounding despondent. She knelt down in front of him, placed her hands on his knees, and tried to make him speak to her.

It was useless—the wizard could not break away from the pain he felt at the thought of never been able to see or hear from his love, Morghanz, again. Shaulmar couldn't bear not been able to smell her scent again, or touch her hand, or caress her hair. Rebecca thought everything was at an end. She would be helpless in the face of the ones trying to take her, she thought. She turned from him and shuffled over to the stone altar and sat down again, feeling utterly dejected. "I don't want to die a horrible death," she muttered under her breath as if there was no one else in the room with her. "I don't even know what a soul is, but I don't want it taken from me." She began to sob again, the quartz crystal she carried glowed dimly, and it only shone when the dark forces were close by. This frightened her to death. "Shaulmar, they're coming for me." She was terrified at this point. Shaulmar looked up, he was so torn between losing the love of his life and the sight of his terrified friend. He seemed rooted to the floor. He couldn't muster enough energy to forget about his Morghanz and help Rebecca. His heart was in pieces. How could he fight the ones who came for her when all he wanted to do was die, himself?

★★★

Down the long cathedral corridor, the echoed cries of grieving souls could be heard. Bastian moved quickly, gathering his minions to him.

"Follow me, and move quickly," he hissed as he passed each of them. At the end of the corridor, they gathered inside one of the ancient burial chambers and stood on stone slabs that made up the floor. They were the lids of ancient tombs that housed the dead warriors of the ancient order of the Templar priests. "We are close to our prize." The Dark One swung his cloak, as he paced in front of them. "When we…" He stopped walking, suddenly, and quickly he scanned the group. "Where is my brother?" No one answered. They just looked at one another bemused by his words. "Well—which of you were with him?" Bastian eyeballed one of them partially hidden by the others. "You!" He pointed to Arengra.

"Master." The figure pushed his way forward. "I saw him across from me near the south exit of the Great Hall, I looked away and when I looked back I could no longer see him. He was there one minute and then the next he was gone." The man looked to the others for corroboration, but they offered nothing, he lowered his head to avoid being eyeballed by the Dark Angel, directly. Draco Bastian knew there must be more. He closed his eyes—he lifted his head as he inhaled through his nose, as if seeking an odor of information. As he inhaled deeply, his black leather cloak that seemed to be part of him, spread slowly, outwardly, expanding as if it had a life of its own. He was sending out his thoughts trying to locate the soul signature of his brother but there was nothing. Bastian struggled to connect again but once more there was nothing. He knew that even if his brother were dead, there would still be remnants of his signature for some time, before there would be no sign of him at all. Definitely, not enough time had passed to be no sign of him…at all…if he'd been killed.

"My brother is no longer on this earth plane." His words were met with confusion. His minions did not care too much for Drandos, but that was not the concern, it was the fact that he was not in this dimension that worried them. The Dark One paced back and forth again, thinking, searching. "The Rhostos are here," he said finally. His followers muttered anxiously amongst themselves for a few moments. Bastian allowed them to digest his words, knowing full well that if the Rhostos were there, then they had better prepare for the fight of their lives. "Now, hear me!" Bastian spoke like death, cold and dark. "I will destroy any one of you who runs from this fight. You will do well to look on the Rhostos as the only way to stay alive—kill them or face me." They knew he spoke the truth. They would rather face the devil than the Dark Angel. One of them stepped forward.

"Master, I will follow you into the dimensions of death." He knelt down, bowing his head low, hoping the Dark One would accept his allegiance quickly. Bastian did not even cast an eye on him—his gaze remained on the others. They all knelt where they stood, repeating the words, collectively.

"I will be watching from a place nearby, do not disappoint me." His voice cut them like the frozen wind that carves the landscape. "Hunt them down. Do not separate. Remain as one. This place is an illusion created by the traveller—his power comes from the vortex of light that is anchored here and is helping to sustain this cathedral. When we have destroyed the one who protects the prophesied soul, only then, will we take the soul and destroy, forever, the travellers. He revealed the Ring of Dread to them, and as he did, the blood-red rays pierced their eyes, forcing each one to cover them, desperately.

"Yes, Master," each one of them spoke. Bastian disappeared before any of them could focus again.

CHAPTER 27

THE DENSE, NOW BLACK FOG, ONLY ALLOWED ENOUGH oxygen through to keep Morghanz alive, barely alive. She kept her eyes closed tight for fear of the darkness. She never did have a tolerance for it. That was something no one knew about her. Whenever she summoned enough energy and courage to send out thoughts to Shaulmar and Rebecca, they were never able to penetrate the fog, they just rebounded right back at her and resounded loudly within her mind. She was ready to give up at this point. The prison of darkness had worn her down. She was already weak from the ordeal with the dark entities invasion of her body. If she died, she thought, she would be able to move over to the realm of spirit where she could, at least, watch over her loved ones. It was time, she thought. Morghanz did not want to suffer the horrible undignified and painful death that she assumed waited for her when the ones who imprisoned her returned. Even worse, what if they didn't return—she would be left to rot inside the black suffocating fog for eternity. Morghanz couldn't take it any more. She decided to throw her body against the dark energy, hoping it would kill her...quickly. She might need to do it more than once, she thought, so she prayed for the strength to accomplish her wish. In her mind, she said goodbye to her loved ones, and in her heart, she kissed Shaulmar for the last time. She was ready now. She kept her eyes closed because she didn't want to see the darkness when it took her. Her breath quickened, and moments later, she slammed against the fog. She was like a beautiful firefly colliding with an electric force field. The pain was like nothing she had ever experienced before, it seared through every nerve, muscle, and bone in her body.

Morghanz wanted to die, but it was not to be, she still lived and she knew she needed to repeat the process. She was weak now. She knew she would need to force her will on her mind with every bit of strength she could gather. Every thought in her head said, stop, but her will was strong—once more, the sorceress of the light commanded, that's all it would take, then it would all be over. She talked to the resistance within her, she knew what needed to be done, and she was resolute. Nothing, not anything was going to prevent her from going home. She was tired. Morghanz took a deep breath, as deep as she could; she mustered up all her strength, all her resolve. She must do it now—or never. All at once, she inhaled again then took control of her being. Morghanz mentally took hold of her energy, and anything else that could possibly prevent her from destroying herself, and threw everything, that was *she*, against the darkness. It was done…for a split second in time…for a microcosmic moment in time and space…it was done. Then she felt herself collide with the hard cold stone-floor of the small room. The very next thing she remembered was hearing someone call her name.

"Morghanz! Morghanz! Wake up! Don't die!" She opened her eyes, then closed them again, trying to adjust and sharpen her vision to focus on who it was calling her name.

"Am I dead?" she couldn't quite see who knelt over her.

"No…no…don't think so. I really don't think you are dead, but then again, I've never seen a dead person…so I could be wrong."

"Joaquim?" she recognized the young boy's voice.

"Yes, yes it's me, Joaquim." He was glad to see she was not dead. Morghanz tried to explain what had happened but she was too confused.

"I was in…in thick fog…I…I thought I was dead. I tried to kill myself." She was angry at the thought that she'd tried to commit suicide.

"It's okay. You're okay now, I think." Joaquim helped her to her feet and found a place where she could sit and rest.

"How…how did you find me? Why wasn't I killed when I slammed against the darkness?" Morghanz held her head. "I don't understand," she moaned.

"I was looking for a way out of the cavern. I wanted to find you and Rebecca to protect you." He fell silent. The boy realized he had failed. "I'm sorry, Morghanz, I wanted to protect you both." She lifted her head, looking over at him.

"You did protect me, Joaquim, I was held captive by the Dark One and you set me free." She smiled at him. "How did you prevent me from being killed?"

"I don't know. I was in the cavern, walking through the passageways. I thought I was lost, so I decided to sit down on a rock. I was about to give up. I sat there, wondering what to do, when I saw something scurry behind me that freaked me out. I jumped up, and slipped, and fell against the wall, and before I knew it I found myself in a secret passageway. I realized it might be possible to find you guys. My hope grew and I began to search again…I just kept walking until I saw an opening high on the side of the cave. I climbed up to it, and squeezed into it, pushing a big boulder out of my way. That's when I found myself in this room, when I stood up, it was so dark I had to light this candle," he pointed to the gold candlestick on the floor. "When it brightened up the room, I saw the big black cloud and the dark crystal floating in front of it. I just knew this was something bad. When it turned toward me, I was so scared. I didn't know what to do. Suddenly, I just swung. I always do that, swing first, and ask questions later. That's when you appeared, right after I smashed the thing to pieces." Joaquim was so proud of himself as he looked at the smashed crystal on the stone floor.

"Thank you, Joaquim, you saved my life. I will never forget that."

"That's okay. I'm glad I could help." He didn't know what else to say. He'd never saved someone's life before. Well…not in real life anyway. He looked around and then turned back to Morghanz. "So, where are Rebecca and Shaulmar?" The young boy had no clue as to what was really going on. "Where are we anyway?" Joaquim looked around the chapel again, trying to figure out where he was. He thought there was a sense of familiarity about the room he was in, but his rational mind kept telling him he couldn't possibly have been in that room before. Morghanz was standing now, and had gained some sort of conscious awareness of the situation.

"Joaquim, I think we have to leave this place." Her voice was slow and soft like she was functioning in slow motion. "We had better go now." She tried to instill a sense of urgency within him.

"Okay, are you sure you can walk okay? We could rest for a bit, the crystal is dead, or smashed, and there are no more around." He cast his gaze all around the room as if to say there's no danger here, and I could protect you, if there was. Morghanz said nothing. She only took in a deep breath to stabilize her mind and body with oxygenating blood. She had no energy left to discuss the situation, or the danger, that she knew was waiting nearby for them.

"Could you pick up what is left of the smashed crystal for me... we may need the pieces later." Her voice was getting stronger. She forced the blood through her lungs to be replenished. She needed to get the both of them away from this place and down to where she thought Shaulmar and Rebecca were waiting. "Hurry, sweet boy, we must find our friends."

"Almost done, Morghanz," he said, as he picked up the last shards of the crystal. Joaquim put his arm under his friend's arm, and around her waist, being careful not to cause her any more discomfort, as he helped her to the doorway.

"Joaquim, you're going to have to listen to me closely. What I am going to tell you is very serious and very real." She kept her gaze on the path ahead of her, and on her legs, as she was getting used to being mobile again.

"What is it? It can't be any worse than having to walk around in those caverns with the smelly critters running around my feet and flying into my hair, can it?" He paused to digest his imaginative thoughts as they flooded into his mind. She looked up to see where they were.

"We must stop here...around that pillar...for cover," she whispered tenderly to him, as she leaned against the backside of the pillar that shaded them from the side of the passageway leading to the other end of the cathedral. "We're in big trouble. I mean big trouble," she impressed upon the young boy with measurable seriousness of the danger that awaited them. "You saved my life, and for that you will gain much, young warrior. Shaulmar is below us trying to keep Rebecca safe from harm, and at the same time, he is trying to stay alive." She was looking at Joaquim as best she could, and trying with all her heart, to bring his young mind into the reality that she knew was all around them. "Do you understand what

I'm saying, Joaquim?" Morghanz hoped she wouldn't need to give details of every possibility that might lie ahead of them, as she spoke. He stood before her his mouth a little agape, and then suddenly, he reached forward and gently touched her hand.

"Morghanz, do you not know my heart, not know my soul?" He held her hand like a man would, like Shaulmar would.

"What do you mean?" she was a little stunned by the young boy's actions.

"I will never let anything happen to you." Joaquim knelt beside her. "We are going to find the others and find a way out of here."

"Okay, you're right." Morghanz didn't understand how he could be so tuned into the situation and she didn't question it. "So, I think we should try to get below without being seen. If I remember rightly, there is a stairway at the end of this passageway, leading to the level where the ancient crypt is." She held out her hand for Joaquin to grab. "Joaquim, help me to my feet. We will try to make it to the stairway."

"Okay, we can slip beside the pillars without being seen. We will make it, Morghanz, I promise." He was sincere and determined to bring the four of them back together. He was no longer the funny little boy. This time he was going to have to become the strong resourceful man. He knew how to manage stressful situations, having spent the majority of his young life navigating the streets of New York. He guided Morghanz down the passageway, carefully, being mindful that silence didn't necessarily mean they were safe. "Can you sense anything, Morghanz? Can you tell if we are close to the stairway?" He hissed his request so she could make out what he was saying, but quiet enough as to remain unseen, undetected.

"The way is dark, Joaquim, I am still very weak. The black fog depleted my energy and I will need to stop to refocus my thoughts." Morghanz was weaker than she was telling him. Joaquim went ahead of her and found an alcove between two huge pillars, halfway down the huge passageway that was dimly lit.

"We can rest here, and you can tune your thoughts to find Shaulmar and Rebecca, okay?" He held her arm as she came close to the hidden space. Morghanz grasped his shoulder as she stepped into the alcove. This space had the aroma of roses and jasmine flowers even though there were no flowers visible.

"I must still my mind in order to bring them to me. Please remain at the entrance. There may be danger close by us. After I send out my thoughts, they can be seen as a beacon to the dark ones," she urged him to do her bidding.

"Why would they find us just because you send out thoughts, Morghanz?" He was really confused. There was no way they could be found. He was really good at hiding things, he thought.

"You may find all this difficult to understand, Joaquim, and there is precious little time for me to explain. However, I will say this, we have energy and we are energy, and because of that, we have a signature. Everyone has a particular energy signature, we as travellers know it as the soul signature." Morghanz found a stone jutting out of the wall that contained a candelabrum—she placed it on the floor and sat on the stone and prepared herself in order that she could enter an altered state once more.

"Okay Morghanz. I will keep an eye out but I still don't understand." He moved past her to the alcove entrance, and stepped between the two pillars, taking up the position where he could see in both directions, up and down the passageway. There was only the dim light of the early morning that entered the small window, nearest the ceiling, in the cold stonewall of the passageway. He moved from one pillar to the next, in one direction in the corridor, and then the other direction, to be sure there were no dark ones around to hurt them. Morghanz closed her eyes, placed her hands together, and chanted softly. The energy in the alcove was neutral, so it neither hindered nor enhanced her attempts to connect with her loved ones. Even though the alcove energy did not offer any assistance to her as she tried to connect, her own energy was more than enough, as she chanted softly and sent her awareness to her heart center where she knew she could recall her love, Shaulmar, with ease.

She became more and more centered and balanced. Even in the face of all the darkness around her, she was able to sense the beauty and harmony of the universal power that supplied the vortex that was anchored at this sacred site. Morghanz's heart responded by quickening to the name of her love, Shaulmar. His was an ancient name, and was created by followers of the light, eons before. When she added the name to the chant, the vibration of the sound quickened the energy around her, and gave it strength and power. The power was strong enough to send it through objects and find the corresponding vibration to the soul signature of the one who bore the name. Morghanz steadied her physical body and anchored herself to the earth through visualization. The sorceress conjured images of her legs becoming entwined with the roots of an ancient oak tree that sent them deep into the earth. Once she was comfortable that she was safely anchored to the earth, she strengthened her chant, thus increasing the magnitude of the vibration to seek out her true love. Joaquim remained vigilant, he still thought of this as an adventure, to a degree, even though he did know there was real danger close by. He still could not shake the feeling of excitement and challenge in defeating the dark ones. He made a promise to himself, to be there to fight alongside Shaulmar when the time came.

★★★

The Rhostos was careful to sense the energies of the building he moved through. If anything should change, then he wanted to know beforehand, not after the fact. Alison, however, was not concerned with such things—she was only interested in where Draco Bastian was and if he had acquired Rebecca's soul yet.

"Where are we? Are we anywhere close to the prize or are you as lost as I am?" she was impatient, and the Rhostos was the only being close to her, to share that with.

"Do not hesitate to do as I say, when I tell you, your life may depend on it. Your life depends greatly on my ability and my honesty." The Rhostos warrior sounded deadly serious and that kept her silent for a while. They made their way through the structure very carefully and often disappeared into alcoves, small rooms, or anything that could prevent them from being seen. The Rhostos was still unsure as to the intentions of his partner, but he was not going to sacrifice all he wanted for himself and his kind, because of a partnership with a sorceress, a practitioner of the black arts. "We will come to the main hall soon, and when we do, you must trust me and do only as I say." The warrior looked at her for confirmation.

"Okay." She was cautious—also, her voice was telling her not to make any smartarse remarks. He was a strange being, but she was being drawn closer to him every minute they spent together. The hallway was dark and the daylight was not yet strong enough to illuminate the great cathedral. The two beings had to cross the ancient hall to reach the stairway, leading to Shaulmar and Rebecca. The warrior stopped, suddenly, holding out his arm to prevent Alison from passing him.

"The ones we seek are close, but I sense dark forces close by too." The Rhostos tipped his head back, pointing his nose in the air, as if to smell the air around them and above them.

"What are you doing? Are the Rhostos practitioners from the animal kingdom also?" Alison was feeling disgusted at being part of this kind of thing. She could hold back no longer and decided to let him know. "I have been silent long enough, Rhostos. I want to go across that hall," she pointed across the hallway to the doorway leading into the ancient gathering place, "and walk across the podium to the other side, and go down the stairway to locate Rebecca Sullivan, and take her soul and leave—understand?" The warrior turned to her, unmoved.

"The Allison Warrior is forgetting all she has learned about the Rhostos…so soon." His slow deep voice and gaze were threatening. "The Rhostos are not fond of ridicule, and if the Allison Warrior wants to do what she says, then the Rhostos would be happy to wait for her return." He was deadly serious again. She was furious at his lack of emotion. She was not accustomed to taking a backseat to anyone. However, she did know when to heed the wisdom of her inner voices that she recognized as her logic and reason—her mind whispered the rational words in her ear to wait, and she listened.

"Okay, Rhostos Warrior," she droned out the words as if she had just been busted for something. She held her hands in the air while turning away from him. "You got me, we will wait and play it your way, but let me offer you this," she turned sprightly looking the warrior square in the face from about three meters away, "when the trouble begins, as I think it will, you, the great Rhostos Warrior had better make sure you keep me safe, because if you don't, I will kill you at the first opportunity." Her tone was cold as was the look in her eyes.

"We will see, Allison Warrior…we will see." The Rhostos warrior only continued to survey the situation, waiting for the right moment to move into the Great Hall. Alison was fuming inside, she made all the gestures and all her words were perfect, but the effect she looked for never materialized. It was clear to her that one of two things was occurring, either the Rhostos could not be killed, or he was really dumb. She didn't quite know which one was closer to the truth, but she would know in time, she thought. Alison stood with him near the entrance to the main cathedral hall, waiting for him to give the go-ahead, but as she stood behind him, she could not halt her desire to inch closer to his huge muscular frame and to take in the leathery odor that seeped from him. She gave herself a mental slap, and abruptly stopped herself from almost falling into the back of him. She reached up and jammed her hand into a crevice on the wall just behind his shoulder and held her breath till the momentum subsided. "Is there something the Allison Warrior wishes to say?" His voice was deliberate and dark.

"No…no of course not. If I wanted to say something I would. If I want to do anything I will do it, and anything else I want to do as well, okay?" she was backpedaling really fast this time, and she heard her own voice saying as much, she hated how she sounded. The Rhostos remained silent, just watching for the right moment. She hated that he did this to her, making her feel those feelings, when she didn't even like him. She tried to convince herself it was his doing, maybe he was sending some kind of energy that was tricking her magically or something. Above where the Rhostos was standing, was what looked to her, like an orb of some kind that caught her eye, as she stood behind the huge warrior. Alison looked at it closely—it seemed to be orange in color and roughly about the size of a small egg. She watched it for a moment or two, trying to decide whether to tell the Rhostos or not, when it just disappeared as quickly as it had first appeared. Alison questioned her sanity for a moment, insisting that she'd imagined it, or that it was just a reflection of the early morning sun—she was still pissed at the Rhostos so she said nothing. After all, she thought, if it was there at all, it didn't stay, so she left the whole thing alone and let it slip from her mind. As she returned to him, waiting, she felt a nagging feeling in the back of her mind. Her voice of reason was tapping on the inside of her skull with a bony finger, at first, then when it was being ignored, it started to tap with a big stick, then a hammer, until she recognized it and paid some attention to it. All of a sudden, she went icy cold all down her back from skull to waist.

"Rhostos! I think we have had a visitor," she said slowly.

"I know, the orb that moves above us." He was remarkable.

"What do we do now?" she hissed.

"We move…now!" The warrior turned to her with his hand open and in front of her, beckoning for her to place her hand in his, once more.

"Oh no…not again." She hated this more than anything else she hated about him.

"Deep breath, Allison Warrior." Sound and color merged before her very eyes, once more, then the light pierced through every cell…until there was nothing but calm.

★★★

Shaulmar lurched up as violently as if he had been struck in the back with an arrow, or spear, or something heavy. Rebecca was at the opposite end of the chapel, sitting with her back to the object that was transformed by the Essence, with her head between her knees and her hands clasped together, holding her head down between them. She was waiting for the Dark Angel to come and take her, it might not be so bad as long as it was quick—she would even become one of them, anything was better than being dead, she thought. She lifted her head from her knees when she heard Shaulmar moan.

"Shaulmar, are you okay?" she came running to him. Rebecca skidded to a halt when she saw him, his body was contorted and he seemed to be in excruciating pain. "What happened? What can I do to help, Shaulmar?" she moved about him, not knowing what to do. She didn't dare touch him in case she caused him more pain. Shaulmar continued to writhe about on the stone floor, moaning, and periodically gasping for air as he pressed his chest.

"Rebecca! She is here!" It was all he would continue to say.

"Who? Shaulmar, who's here?" she decided to just sit next to him and wait until he could tell her what to do. Rebecca covered him with his cloak and comforted him as best she could.

"She is calling to me…Morghanz is calling to me." The wizard was helpless to do anything. He was in so much pain.

"Morghanz, she is alive?" Rebecca felt joy for the first time in what seemed a long time.

"Yes. I can feel her energy trying to connect with me…but something is interfering…the pain…it is increasing." He was suffering with pain that was coming from the darkness.

"How can this be, Shaulmar?"

"The darkness is powerful it…ugh…it…argh…can do many things…ugh." The dark force was attacking him.

"What shall I do, Shaulmar?" she knelt by his side.

"You must find her…and warn her. Rebecca, you must find Morghanz and warn her." The wizard was crumpled on the floor at this point.

"What about you? What about you? What should I do? What should I warn her about? I don't understand, Shaulmar, how can she be in danger? You are the one being attacked.

"They will find her through our connection…ugh."

"Do you mean that they can find her because she's trying to connect with you?"

"Yes…they will follow the energy linking us and they will kill her. You must go and find her—warn her! I will be okay, Rebecca. Go now! Please!" He curled up into the fetal position and said no more. Rebecca stood up. She didn't want to leave him, but she wanted to warn Morghanz, also.

"Shaulmar, I will go and find Morghanz. I will come back soon." She turned to leave.

"No, no Rebecca…argh…go to the Great Hall and I will come to you." The wizard was as emphatic as he could be in his condition.

"Okay. I hope you can make it Shaulmar, we are not going to leave you, so you had better make it to the Great Hall or we're all dead." She wanted, desperately, to motivate her friend, and that was the only thing she could think of to say, that would do the job. The irony was that she knew the words she spoke were true, and they would be no match for the dark forces, if they were as deadly as all the stories she'd been told. Rebecca left the chapel and could still hear Shaulmar's faint moans and groans of pain as she left. She looked back once more to say goodbye in her heart—she saw the cloak of the great wizard crawling across the floor to disappear behind the stone object. Rebecca lowered her head and hurried away, leaving the chapel behind. The cathedral passageways were a little brighter because of the morning sun reflecting through the huge stained-glass windows. She moved quietly down the passageway, ever cautious of the dangers that lurked at every turn. The one thing that she remembered was that Shaulmar was indeed a great wizard, supposedly, there were stories written about him, and the proof was in the great cathedral he created for them to hide. Rebecca had faith that he would join them soon, that is, if she could do her part and find Morghanz to warn her of the impending attack coming her way.

Rebecca was still not one hundred percent sure that she would find Morghanz, after all she had been taken by something. What if Shaulmar was wrong about her still being alive and trying to connect with him, she thought, he could have been delirious with all the pain. Rebecca slowed down when she realized she might be on a wild goose chase. Should she trust Shaulmar's sanity and continue to look for her friend, or should she look for an exit, and depart this nightmare. After all, she hadn't asked for any of this, she thought, so why should she continue to be part of it. By this time, she had come to a stop, and leaned against one of the many stone pillars that held the huge structure in place. Just when her own dark side began to surface, she felt a sharp twinge in her chest, and automatically, her hand went to that location and caressed the pain. She saw an image in her mind that could have been her memory, or it could have been the love energy that flowed through her, but she thought she saw her mother.

The image was carrying a tiny bundle of life in her arms. Rebecca knew immediately what she must do. There was purpose in her stride, now she knew her mother had come to her in her time of darkness. She was reminded who she was, who the soul was that her mother had given life to. Rebecca knew she had come to her because it had been a long time since she had thought of her. She moved down the corridor towards the stairwell, trying to remain calm and focused, just as Morghanz had taught her to do. She realized how important it was for her own wellbeing to breathe slowly and steadily. Rebecca passed great paintings on the walls, and religious carvings and sculptures between the pillars, as she made her way.

The Essence nudged Rebecca's consciousness, telling her that Morghanz was located one level above her. She wanted to jump up and down—Morghanz was alive! Rebecca created an image in her head as to where she thought Morghanz might likely be. She reached the end of the corridor, where she saw the ancient stairwell, made of the most beautiful beige and brown stone. Cautiously, she climbed up the steps, one at a time, and leaned against the curved wall as she took each step, so she could see as far ahead of her as possible. The stairwell was spiral in shape, and this gave Rebecca a secure feeling, because she would be able to hear anyone above or below her as she moved up. Eventually, she reached the next level. Her heart was pounding at the prospect of walking out of the stairwell, and into the passageway, of which she knew nothing about, and even less of what she might expect to encounter when she got there. The only thing that was on her mind, except for the total infusion of deadly fear that was now constant, was finding her friend and leaving that place.

Rebecca was now at the entrance to the next passageway. She pushed her shoulders and head against the inner wall to become composed—to calm her mind as well as her body before continuing. The teenager took a deep breath, closed her eyes, and said the following words repeatedly, 'strength and courage come to me—s-trength and courage come to me—' She counted to five with every inhalation and every exhalation, repeating the mantra inside her head. Finally, she knew it was time to face whatever she might encounter, so she took one last deep breath, leaned around the corner of the stairwell, and peeked down the passageway. Left first, then she turned her head in the opposite direction, and let out a breath. She could see no sign of danger, so she eased herself into the passageway. She headed, slowly, in the opposite direction to where she remembered leaving Shaulmar as he was struggling with the dark forces. She moved down the passageway, staying close to the wall that ran in behind the main pillars that held the bulk of the structure in place. She could feel the heaviness of the darkness as she continued down the huge arched passageway. A sudden impulse came over her, urging her to quicken her steps, as if she felt the energy of her friend calling to her from deep inside the darkness. Her heart quickened. She wanted to help Morghanz. She passed two marble pillars on the left, and a huge hanging tapestry that ran between them, halfway to the ceiling. She was almost at a trot when she felt something like a dull thud hit her leg, she went down quickly, unable to steady herself or regain her balance.

Then the pain began, it was a sharp pain at first, then a dull ache that spread across her thigh, pulsing with every heartbeat. There was no sound, only a dim light that she could see reflected off the marble pillar, as she squinted with pain. Her survival instinct kicked in and made her survey her surroundings for possible avenues of escape from whatever it was that was attacking her. The young girl looked instinctively for any items of weaponry that might be found close by she could use to survive. She wondered what it was that had hit her, then her eyes caught sight of the orange glow that was floating in front of the pillar—then amidst all the adrenaline coursing through her veins, she realized she had seen that orange light before.

The orb that she remembered seeing earlier, that was observing her and Shaulmar, was the same color as what seemed to be attacking her now. Suddenly, the orb drifted down from the rafters of the arched ceiling, revealing itself to her, knowing that it had hit its mark. The object was only about three inches in diameter, but it was highly charged, and it seemed to be very powerful. It spun as it danced closer to her, moving in a zigzag pattern. Rebecca was in pain, and there was nothing around her to help her to defend herself. She supposed this was going to be the way that she would finally die. How uneventful, she thought, to die this way in a dimly lit hallway of an old stinky church, where no one would know that she had even died. Such silly notions to go through the mind at this time, so close to death, she thought to herself—as she tried to overcome the pain she felt by using the mind-over-matter thing that Morghanz had introduced her to. However, it wasn't working, the pain intensified, spreading upwards into her abdomen where she felt her solar plexus, her power center, vibrating furiously. The orb descended slowly towards her, spinning as it examined its prey—it observed the full spectrum of pain it was subjecting Rebecca to, from sharp precise surgical knife-like jabs to escalating blunt trauma thumps that sent pulsating pains throughout her body. Rebecca tried to pull her body into the nearby alcove behind the pillars. It took all the strength she had. It was surprising to her just how difficult it was to move when she had no more use of her legs. It was just like pulling a dead weight. The orb continued to observe and follow her, rotating one way and then the next, as it did so.

"Damn you!" Rebecca yelled at the spinning object as the pain progressed into her other leg. The orb just hovered above her body about three feet away. She was only able to pull her deadweight as far as the pillar before she had run out of energy, before she just sank into the stone floor. "I hate you...you bastard!" she screamed. She didn't care who else heard her in that moment, as the pain was so intense, it was the only thing that occupied her mind. She was crying as she lay on the floor, and the orb circled her, she only wanted the pain to stop. As the orb move the length of her body, the pain seemed to increase—there was obviously some kind of dark force responsible. "Why? Why are you...doing this to...ugh... me?" she lay helpless against the old wall. She could feel the coldness of the ancient stone on her back and shoulders; even through the intense pain was experiencing, the icy coldness penetrated through to her bones.

"You are the one prophesied to come to earth through the strength of the universe. Your soul is valuable to us." The orange orb moved sideways, and up to the height of the figure depicted in the tapestry, on the wall behind her. "We were made aware of the event of your incarnation, as were others within this universe, but only after you had experienced your 16th year of existence in this dimension—as set forth by the conditions of the creator." The orb spun, descending as it did so, coming within a foot of Rebecca's head.

"I…I know nothing…ugh…of what you say…of any such nonsense…argh…what prophecy?" Rebecca attempted to engage the object with conversation while she tried to come up with a survival strategy. "I…I am…argh…just a…girl," she said, while trying to pull her body further up the wall for stability.

"I must take you with me, Rebecca Sullivan, but first I must free your precious soul from the heaviness of your physical body. I am sure you will thank me for that." The orb backed away from her. "However, I'm not so sure you will thank me for what we have in store for your soul, when you are placed at the center of our world." The orb glowed an orange-red that slowly intensified as it spoke.

"Who are you?" she insisted. "Don't you know I have people looking for me and they will not let you do anything to me…." She couldn't think fast enough to talk her way out of the situation. Rebecca didn't believe for one moment that Shaulmar or Morghanz would really let her die. She leaned her head back against the tapestry and took in a large breath. "I am not the one you're looking for," her voice was calm and soft, "I don't know anything about a stupid prophecy." By this time, her eyes were closed completely shut and her head was still resting against the worn tapestry that hung on the wall behind her. "Please, I am in so much pain, could you just stop the pain, I beg you?"

"Well, I suppose you pose no threat, and you certainly don't seem to be very powerful. So, in answer to your question, yes, I will take away the pain." The orb slowed and changed color from the orange-red to a bright green. Soon afterwards, Rebecca felt the muscles in her legs start to relax as the sensation of a small electrical charge shot through her calves and thighs; at the same time, the searing pain began to subside.

"Ooh, thank you. That's much better." She sat up much higher, and rubbed the sides of her legs, as if she had just come inside from the freezing cold of winter. Gradually, the feeling came back to her legs, and as the orb settled down again, just two feet in front of her, she focused her eyes upon it. The orb was silent. Rebecca was also quiet. "What happens now?" she didn't have much choice but to accept what must be her destiny at this time.

"You must surrender your soul to me, willingly. It will be the best thing for you. If you resist by putting up a fight, the more you struggle, the more painful and longer the process will take, and the outcome will be the same anyway you choose, it is inevitable." The orb spun again, slowly this time—small shards of electrical energy emanated from it.

"How do I surrender?" Rebecca said calmly, "Do I just close my eyes, like this, and wait for it to happen? Or do you zap me with something that will get it over with, quickly?" she had all but given up as she waited for the response from the orb.

"Well, seeing as how you are so interested, I will initiate the process in a few moments, and you will be free of that physical body before you realize what has occurred." The object spun once more, growing in size as it moved, and the electrical energy coming from it also got stronger.

"I think I will keep my eyes closed, if you don't mind? It will be less frightening for me." Rebecca straightened up against the wall, pushing back with her feet against the floor—her knees were bent and her head was resting on them. Her hands were clasped behind her head—she was just waiting now with her eyes tightly shut. All that Rebecca could do was interpret the sounds coming to her from what she assumed was the orb, and what she thought it was about to do to her, to claim her soul. One thought entered her mind that had been nibbling at her throughout this whole ordeal—why hadn't the Essence come to her aid? Her rational mind told her that if she was about to die, then surely the Essence was about to die also.

"Be still now. I am almost ready to begin. The ceremony must be performed before the final stage of the soul collection can be initiated. Once the ceremony is complete, the collection begins automatically." The orb was stationary, six feet in front of Rebecca. The electrical energy crackled as it leapt from one charged pole of the orb to the other. Like a solar flare that jumps from the surface of the sun, and then returns at another position in the opposite direction, making a beautiful arc of light that dazzles the eyes. Rebecca remained still, but all she could think of was why help hadn't arrived. All her experiences so far with the Book of Secrets and the Essence seemed to be lies—the power within the magic she had seen was all a joke, all phony, and totally fake.

She was to die, and that was simply that, nothing more. She had been drawn into Shaulmar's stories of magic and the universe, but ultimately he was unable to prevent her death at the hands of the darkness. The darkness had plagued her all her life, from her earliest memories, where she saw figures move through the walls of her room as the moon cast its shadows. Where were all her friends, why hadn't Shaulmar, or Morghanz, or the Essence for that matter, come to save her. The orb spoke to her once more. "If you surrender to the process willingly there will be minimal pain for you, Rebecca Sullivan." The spinning object became three times its normal size at this point, and was ready to begin the process of extracting Rebecca's soul. "I do not mean to be disrespectful but you're not what I expected to be doing battle with." The orb was gathering energy and momentum as it spoke. The air immediately around the orb was visible—it became dense due to the lower and heavier vibration of the dark power that was drawing energy into itself. Rebecca slowly lifted her head from her knees—she was feeling the prickly sensation of the static electricity as it struck all around her.

"What do you mean when you say you didn't expect to be doing battle with someone like me?"

"Well, when I was chosen for the task of bringing the soul of the Prophesied One back with me, let's just say, I didn't think it would be so…easy. In fact, I'm a little disappointed in not having the opportunity to show my master what I can do in battle situations." Rebecca began to feel a sense of relief as the orb spoke, she didn't understand why, necessarily, because the last thing she was feeling was relief.

"I am just a young girl. What did you expect from someone as young and as inexperienced as me? If I were a sorceress, a witch if you like, maybe you would have been given the opportunity to show your master of what you are capable." She became increasingly aware of an uneasiness growing and rising from deep inside of her. The words of the orb, and the attitude it displayed towards her, began to resonate with something very deep within her being.

"Maybe, but we will never know because I am almost ready to begin the ceremonial chant that will indicate the onset of the soul claiming process."

"Not that it matters, now, but who is the one that you call master? I am curious, because there is more than just yourself, after the same prize." There was no response. The orb only remained in its position in front of Rebecca as it continued to create a vortex of energy around itself.

"Before I begin, I must thank you for making this so easy. I realize you're just a girl and that there must be some mistake about you being the Prophesied One." Rebecca looked up at the orb. "I feel sorry for you…I really do. After I take your Soul back to my master, I will be known as the one, who changed the prophecy of the universe." It was excited by the idea of becoming a legend. Rebecca squirmed a little as she felt the static electricity growing in strength—this was the beginning of the process that would eventually kill her, she thought.

"I thought you said this was not going to be painful?"

"It is not painful. I am assured by the master of the process, that it is completely painless, if the soul to be taken is given freely." Rebecca thought for a moment, and then she was hit by another burst of static electricity from the sphere.

"I am being hit by the static electricity coming from you. If you tell me once more that the procedure is painless, I will scream. I will be forced to resist this stupid soul claiming crap and splatter you all over that wall." She had no clue where these words were coming from. She looked as puzzled as ever. Before one more moment had passed, Rebecca was standing upright and facing the sphere. At that point, it had begun the ceremonial chant of death. First came the deep low vibrational toning to set the frequency required for the orb to connect with the soul signature of the victim being taken.

"In the name of the holy one, I invoke the authorized toning given to me by my master." The orb spun wildly and scattered light and energy as it did so. "Do not move. I must connect to the points of light that house your soul." Streams of orange and yellow lights headed for Rebecca, striking her head and chest.

"This...is not...how I'm going to die! You are not powerful enough to make that happen," she spoke, but it was not the young girl who was doing the talking. "I am here by order of the universe and karma called upon by the human unconscious mind—that is the divine purpose for my being here. *You*...will not prevent what has been set in motion by the one who gives us all purpose for being." By this time, Rebecca was standing straight and strong, the energy coming from the orb was shifting.

The intention of the orb was for the soul inside of Rebecca, to be called forth from her physical body through the mental, energetic, and etheric bodies. As the colored lights coming from the sphere resonated at different frequencies, it had the power to permeate the auric field of the victim. It then locked onto the soul energy through the specific soul signature frequency, and extracted it from the body with ease, thus capturing the Essence of the being. A thin green ray, embedded in the orange beams that enveloped Rebecca, shot from the center of the rotating orb. Its target was the center of her heart where the connection between the physical and soul bodies resided. As soon as it struck her, her arms were thrown out to the sides, she lurched her head and shoulders backwards as if being forced back by some invisible energy. She was lifted off the floor and the center of her chest was pulled towards the orb.

"Come forth! Come from your prison, soul of light." The orb thrust the green light deep into Rebecca's heart looking for her soul, her essence. She was a foot off the ground by this time—her eyes were the color of ice. The orb came to a complete stop in midair at this point.

"Ugh, help me, Morghanz." The stifled words and voice of the young girl seeped from her body.

"Do not struggle—we are almost there. All that is required, now is the final incantation and you will be free from that pathetic vehicle that is your prison." The orb glowed and pulsed as the beams of light held Rebecca. "Essence...Essence...come to your master." The sound coming from the orb resonated with the beams of light causing them to move. They seem to flow like water, like waves across the sea. "Release the soul of Rebecca Sullivan…come from her heart and join your new Master." The colored lights illuminated the hallway of the cathedral while the moans coming from Rebecca grew louder.

"Argh…ne…never…never…." Something snapped inside the girl. She opened her mouth and yelled, "I will never be separated…never!" She fell quiet while the orb continued its work in silence. Still, the orange and small green beams of light continued to pulse and flow from it to Rebecca's heart. The orb spun wildly, beams still connected to Rebecca vibrated faster and faster, shaking as they moved back and forth from the orb to the center of the heart.

"Come now!" The voice came from the orb, sounding a little annoyed and a little confused, "come to your master. I command you!" The small sphere became bigger and changed color from orange to electric blue, "I command you in the name of the Master. Separate! Come forth!" The body of Rebecca remained still, only, her face looked contorted and grimaced, as the lights tried desperately to take her soul from her. What happened next was only the mere smallest exertion of energy that manifested between them. Rebecca's heart was beating strongly—the orb strained to extract her soul from deep within her. The orb stuttered, struggling to spin, as if it were pulling the very earth from underneath them. "What is happening? What are you doing? This cannot be…" Rebecca slowly raised her head, looking directly into the sphere.

"You presume to act above the one who was given life by the creator…you presume too much." The voice was familiar to her—she felt warmth flooding into her chest, flowing up to her head, and down to her feet. The teenager knew who spoke from her.

"Stop! Stop! This cannot happen. The Master is all-powerful." The orb struggled to maintain the beams of light that continued to connect with Rebecca. Her voice grew more menacing by the second, but it was not her voice, the all to familiar mist had emerged from behind her once more. The tattoo of Saint Michael etched into her shoulder came to life, shining brightly. The Essence was once more joined with its soul mate, and it was not about to allow the intruder another opportunity to harm Rebecca.

"There are many ancient stories that will unfold while the great prophecy is fulfilled, and when the story is passed on from generation to generation for eons to come—becoming itself an ancient story of prophecy and adventure—there will be no mention of an orb of such insignificance."

Rebecca was nowhere to be heard, the Essence had deliberately allowed her to feel her way through the danger, through the experience. This was done in order for the young soul to learn as quickly as possible, for the Essence knew what might be coming. Now the Essence had ushered Rebecca to safety, to the place shrouded in light and love, to the archangel realm.

"Argh…stop! Stop! The energy is getting out of control. I…I cannot hold it, please!" The energy within the orb was feeling pain, the like of which, it had never felt before.

"I…am…the Essence! I am the twin flame of the Prophesied One. The attempt you made to capture this bound soul was a mistake, one that you will not live long enough to regret." The Essence moved through the air, the green mist flowing like a great green ocean towards the sphere.

"Please! Help me! I was only doing what was commanded of me! You must believe me…please!" The Essence came closer, all the time redirecting the beams of light to the orb, and they were intensified so much that the exterior of the sphere began to vibrate so ferociously, that cracks began to appear and became visible through the orange skin.

"I must admit, if Rebecca were still here and not safely hidden away, I doubt that she would allow me to do what I am about to do to you." The orb was now contained within the sea of green energy. "Wherever you come from is of no concern, and the great powerful Master you speak of, has no power here. Unfortunately, you are about to leave this dimension without the knowledge you seek. Do you wish to leave any record of who you were, before I send you on your way?" The Essence was not in the habit of destroying anything, and it was, especially, not used to the cruelty, fear, and terror it projected onto the orb. However, there was information required regarding who exactly was behind the attack, and if possible, its degree of strength, ascertained. The Essence had to be clever enough to extract the information—it could help them escape Bastian and his dark lords down the road if needed.

"Please, do not destroy me I beg you," the orb continued.

"Why did you come for the prophesied soul? Who sent you here?" The Essence increased the energy to the orb, its pain threshold was not nearly enough to withstand the increase, and the Essence knew it. It was just enough to force the orb to disclose the needed information but not enough to fracture it beyond repair. "Answer…or Die!"

"I was sent…sent through the matrix of darkness by…by the… argh…the *Master Xin.*" The sphere was in terrible pain. The Essence didn't really want to hurt it any more, so the mist returned to the soul of Rebecca. The orb, on being released, fell the five feet to the floor—it was damaged but not destroyed.

"Here…I will leave you. Tell your master—Xin, the soul he desires is protected by a force he could never overcome—nor ever hope to. At this point, the Essence brought Rebecca back into her body. Although, she had spent her time enveloped within the bliss of the angelic realms, she was still a little shaky and out of it, thus, the Essence remained in control as they moved away from the orb, and headed down the corridor in the direction of the Great Hall where they hoped to find Morghanz.

CHAPTER 28

BASTIAN'S DARK LORDS MOVED THROUGH THE CATHEDRAL quickly, and efficiently, each one alert to any sign of the Rhostos or the travellers. They could navigate the hallways with surprising ease, considering their size—added to that, with various weapons and heavy layers of protective clothing, the members of Bastian's group of mercenaries were quite a threat to anyone.

"Make your way to the Great Hall and kill anything that you find along the way." Bastian curled the cloak around his body and shot like an arrow towards the highest point in the cathedral. The group of minions knew how to fight, they were no strangers to battle, that is what they were cloned to do. They were each created with abnormally large lung and heart capacities that could supply enough pressure to pump blood around two human bodies. The engineered physique was similar to that of a small bear, it had a low center of gravity that made it very stable in a fight, making it difficult for anyone to knock it off balance. As this militia moved around the hallways toward the Great Hall, one of them snagged an arm on a metal stand that held a large stone sculpture. The stone object crushed the chest of the unfortunate minion directly behind him, this caused him to collapse to the floor and lose consciousness the others scattered, causing more noise and mayhem.

"Stop! Stop everyone! Stand perfectly still!" The largest of the group took control. "You and you check on him, and if he cannot move, kill him!" The two minions pushed the stone away from the body—one knelt close to him for a moment and then stood up.

"He is unconscious." The other said nothing. He calmly moved closer to the body on the floor, and took out a large knife, lifting it high above him. He spun around, letting the full weight of the weapon find its own path to the chest of the soldier, caving in the sternum and the left side of the rib cage that protects the heart.

"He will not slow us down anymore." The two fighters moved back into position, and the group moved on. There were only three left as they made their way to the stone staircase at the end of the corridor.

Bastian's soldiers reached the top of the staircase, and moving quietly, they entered the corridor adjacent to the Great Hall of the cathedral where they remained in wait for the Rhostos and the travellers.

***

The air was very thin as they moved between dimensions, and Alison was beginning to feel the strain of the experience on both her mind and body.

"I don't feel so great, Rhostos, my strength is being drained with all this traveling."

"Don't worry, Allison Warrior, we will stop soon. I can sense a stairway ahead. It is a spiral stone staircase that leads to the Great Hall. The soul we seek is close now. I can feel it." The Rhostos touched his wristband again and they began to decelerate, allowing the density of the third dimension to claim them once more. The two beings manifested again in the physical realm, where they found themselves surrounded by a circular stone and mortar room, that was approximately twenty feet in diameter, and seemed to rise up to the cone-shaped roof, that was approximately thirty five feet above them.

"Where are we, Rhostos? All I see is stone and tile, stone walls surrounding me, and old worn-out stone tiles beneath my feet, and I do not see Rebecca Sullivan." Alison was angry and tired of being sucked through the space between dimensions.

"We are not in the Great Hall, that is where the one we seek will be, soon. There are many dangers in this place, Allison Warrior, and we need to be focused and diligent and acutely aware at all times, or we will lose our lives here." The warrior knew what he was saying would drag her back to reality. He moved around the walls, trying to determine if they could get to the main hallway, by avoiding the spiral stone staircase that opened at one side of the room. "Make sure the stairwell is clear while I search for another way to get to the Great Hall." The Rhostos continued to feel the stones with his hands, looking for something that indicated a hidden doorway or even a portal, and gave no more attention to the dark priestess.

"Fine! If I come across Draco Bastian or any dark ones that are close by, I will be sure to run back as fast as I can to warn you, okay?" she was getting angrier and angrier as she walked across the circular room towards the stairwell. She stood at the foot of the stone staircase listening for any sounds that indicated others were close by. Alison was at the end of her rope, the only thing she wanted to do was to find Rebecca, and take her through the dimensions to the home of the Rhostos. Once there, she would kill the warrior and capture Rebecca's soul for herself. This would allow her unlimited power and wealth according to the prophecy handed down through eons of time through the Sacred Dark Order. There was so much riding on her getting the soul, there was so much to lose should she fail, something that Alison would never allow her mind to fully contemplate. She flung the cape around her body, trying to stave off the chill of the morning air that was coming down from the Great Hall of the cathedral, via the spiral staircase.

The Rhostos stood silent, looking up at the tiled roof beyond the top of the huge stonewall that he faced. He was motionless—his leather outer appendages slowly became taut.

"You know if I have to stand here any long…" Alison was about to finish her sentence but she found the thud, and ensuing numbing pain, threw her into immediate shock as she pummeled against the stone floor—blood was spurting from her shoulder where the axe made contact. The leader of Bastian's men appeared from the stairwell and headed for his axe, two more followed him, both ready to fight. Alison remained unconscious, with the wound near her neck releasing a pool of blood while she lay there, motionless. The three men stood in formation facing the Rhostos, they meant to kill, and looked like they could do it.

"You are the travellers," one of them spoke in a deep tone. The Rhostos only turned his gaze to the bundle on the floor for a second or two, enough to make an assessment.

"Yes…a traveller…of sorts." He was calm in the face of such heavy odds. The men revealed blades from beneath their sheathed garments, and held them in each hand, ready to kill.

"We are sent by the Dark Lord who says you must be destroyed. There can never be anyone other than Draco Bastian to take the soul of the Prophesied One." The largest of the three men took one step forward. "You are…"

The Rhostos's physique quivered for a nanosecond—the minion lost an arm. The Rhostos warrior moved between and beyond the attackers, using the energy of the vortex that sustained the cathedral. The two remaining assassins spontaneously turned, and lunging at each other they became entwined—interlinked, but it was an attack formation that was deadly when executed the correct way. The Rhostos was twenty feet away, with his arms at his side, his leather cloak fully extended, and his appendages projected outwards.

"You need not die here. You are warriors as am I. There is no dishonor in your leaving this place. Go home and know you have fought well. Take your dead with you." The Rhostos meant every word—he had dismembered their leader and cleaved his head from the rest of him. The entwined minions listened to his words—then they attacked. Without hesitation, the Rhostos brought his wings together—the noise was so deafening that the attackers could no longer remain in formation. They reached up to cover their ears to stop the searing pain. The force of the Rhostos's movement, and the speed of his actions, tore through the two remaining minions. Limbs and blood scattered around the stone-tiled floor.

At the finish, the Rhostos brought his appendages back into place and focused his attention on the bloody heap in the corner. The warrior knelt at the side of Alison—she was still cold. He touched her brow with his large hand, pushing her hair back off of her face.

"Allison Warrior, please come back to me?" she lay motionless—the huge frame of the Rhostos warrior shrouded the dark sorceress, she was still alive but just barely. Alison had lost a lot of blood. The Rhostos fumbled with his shroud and eventually pulled a small pouch from it. He leaned forward and put one hand beneath Alison's wounded shoulder, pouring the contents of the pouch directly onto the wound. Almost immediately, the wound was engulfed in a green light, that remained for a couple of seconds, then it seemed to dim and disappear into the wound on the shoulder of the dark witch.

"Argh…ugh…ugh." She lurched forward into the arms of the Rhostos, coughing and spluttering blood, from her nose and mouth.

"Welcome back, Allison Warrior." He helped her to the wall where she leaned against it, still only half conscious, and unable to move her shoulder.

"What…what happened? I…I don't feel good." Her head was foggy but she knew the warrior, something that brought her comfort. The Rhostos said no more, he just reached into his pouch again, and gave her something to drink. "Oh, that tastes awful." She opened her mouth to spit it out but he clasped his huge hand over her face until she swallowed the brown substance. "Ugh…argh, you bastard." She could say no more because she'd lost consciousness again. The Rhostos took the cloaks from two of the dead men—folding one into a pillow he put it beneath Alison's head, he put the other one over her body while the medications worked on her. Then he dragged the dead men to the far side of the stone room where they would represent less of a distraction.

★★★

The walls of the corridor could be seen clearly, now that the light escaped from the Great Hall and began falling into the hallways on either side. Morghanz didn't want to move anywhere she was so tired.

"Morghanz, we must look for Shaulmar and Rebecca or we may never get out of here," Joaquim whispered. He had to make her realize they needed to keep searching or they were dead.

"Okay Joaquim, let's continue down the corridor, but we must stay hidden. We must find them before it's too late." She put her back against the beautifully carved stone pillar, and with the help of the boy, she was standing again and ready to continue. They were close to the Great Hall now. With no warning, she grabbed the boy's wrist, making him stop dead in his tracks. She ushered them both into a nearby corner that was shrouded in darkness.

"What is it?" he whispered. His gaze went from the hallway ahead of them and back to the sorceress.

"There is a low vibrational energy ahead of us. I don't know how much of a danger it is to us but we should stay here, and stay hidden, until whatever it is passes us by." Morghanz was still very weak and not up to a fight with the darkness, not for a while, anyway. Joaquim was scared inside, but he daren't let her see that, because it might make her feel even worse to think that she had to take care of him rather than the other way around.

"Don't worry. I am ready. They will not harm you.

"Thank you, Joaquim. I don't know what I would have done without you." He just rested his hand on her shoulder and watched for any movement down the hallway. He was beginning to doubt his friend's ability, when he saw something move from around the corner, and into the hallway.

"Quiet! Quiet Morghanz! Someone comes," he hissed. His young heart was in his mouth, beating faster with every breath. They both retreated into the shadows and waited. The figure coming down the hallway filled the space with darkness, even as the light entering through the overhead openings of the Great Hall were usually illuminated, the hallways were dulled and absorbed by the figure causing an unnatural dimming of the passageway. Draco Bastian had finally descended into the corridor, and was heading for the entrance to the Great Hall, bent on taking Rebecca Sullivan's soul no matter what stood before him. As he moved, ripples of energy were thrown off him, that were powerful enough to bend the surrounding energy of the earth—as the sun and moon moved oceans, such was his power. Bastian meant to take her.

They pushed their bodies harder into the cold stonewall as he passed by. They held their breath. Joaquim squeezed his eyelids shut tight so nothing could enter, he was so afraid. Morghanz closed her eyes while taking the boy's hand in hers softly, she asked the beams of light to protect them as the Dark One passed. The air felt muggy—it felt as if they were being zapped of all their life force energies. A few moments passed and all was well—they were not detected. Bastian looked like he was gearing up to kill, and because of that, his focus was elsewhere. He was not even aware of Morghanz and the young boy—he was only focused on finding Rebecca Sullivan.

Finally the two of them inhaled. Joaquim almost passed out through lack of air and Morghanz just remained stationary against the alcove wall.

"Oh...my God." Joaquim let out a sigh. He whispered with total relief, "Who the hell was that?" The impact of the encounter sent him sliding down the wall to the floor.

"That, my young friend, was the Dark One, Draco Bastian." Morghanz spoke in a gentle whisper, not believing their luck at not being detected—simultaneously, she was desperately trying to decide what to do next. "Be sure to embed that experience on your memory, Joaquim. Keep the impact of that feeling alive, and it will keep you alive, longer than anything else you could count on."

"What do we do? How can we possibly fight against something like that?" He was becoming louder. Morghanz looked at him with total disbelief.

"Quiet! Unless you want to ask him yourself when he comes back," she hissed. There was another silence, and Joaquim slumped to the floor of the alcove once more, and leaned his head back against one of the wall coverings. "We can only follow him to the Great Hall and let destiny play out." She spoke as if she knew it was futile to do anything else.

"Oh God—that guy will definitely kill us." Joaquim spoke the words while he looked up at the roof that seemed so far away. The matter of fact way the words came out, made him feel like he was back in New York City, about the time he had been caught shoplifting. The store cop held him in the storeroom until the real cops came with the social workers. It was lucky the guy forgot there was a window to the alley. Joaquim wished for a window right now. With all his might, he screwed his eyes tight shut—his face resembled someone who had just seen something really disgusting.

"Joaquim! What are you doing?" she was still in a little pain from the ordeal in the grey fog.

"Nothing." He quickly returned to normal. "Morghanz, what are we going to do…really?" The boy was losing his nerve after seeing what real evil was, not the fantasy he always saw in his imagination, when he was the hero conquering the evil warlord. Morghanz leaned against the pillar, trying to regain some clear-headedness before she answered.

"It seems Bastian is on his way to claim Rebecca and he plans to do it in the Great Hall. For this to be successful, Rebecca must be there or heading there too. He will wait for her and then take her. We must go and warn her, or stop him, before she is lost forever." The two followed the shadow down the hallway…staying well back. "Joaquim, I don't know what is going to happen when we get to the Great Hall, but I am sure of one thing," she turned to him and put her hand on his arm, "there is more than this dimension in the universe and we are never alone."

"What do you mean?" he said.

"Draco Bastian is one of the strongest and most dangerous of all the dark powers. There are not many who could defeat him, if any. He has spent centuries in many dimensions steadily increasing his powers. I have no idea what is destined for us in this place, but I do know that our universe is where the prophecy has been declared to manifest. All that is manifest here is orchestrated by higher intelligences than we can know." She was very weak and it showed in her face and body language.

"What do we do then? Are you telling me that I am going to die here?" The boy was silent. He didn't want her to answer.

"All I can say…is that you must empty your mind of all thoughts of fear and dread. Allow yourself to connect with that which is bigger than the here and now, the present moment." Nothing more was said.

"Okay now, stay close, and we will make our way to the Great Hall." Morghanz began to walk in the direction of the huge wooden doors leading to the Great Hall. The boy took to her side, while they stayed close to the inner wall of the hallway and the row of marble pillars, for cover.

They continued down the hallway between the pillars, passing beautiful tapestries, wooden carvings, and ancient icons that seemed to embrace them as they passed.

"I think these things are watching us." Joaquim pointed to the icons as he helped her move between the pillars.

"They are not watching us, they are sending love and healing to us." Morghanz concentrated on her legs while she walked, not taking the time to look up. She knew if she were to be of any help in getting them out of the building alive, she needed to return to optimum health.

"Joaquim, I must stop at that dark place up ahead," She pointed to the shadows. "I am going to do something important and I do not want you to be afraid or concerned. Joaquim looked around.

"What do you mean?" He had no clue as to what she was about to do.

"Just help me into the shadows and I will explain." She limped into the dark recesses of a huge stone room and sat on an old oak bench that was placed against one of the walls where a large painting of a beautiful landscape hung. Morghanz leaned against it and closed her eyes. She felt very weak. She didn't know how to tell the young soul, that what she was about to do, was for the best and highest good of her friends and loved ones.

"What is it Morghanz? Have you thought of a plan? I knew you would come up with something to get us out of this mess." He sat next to her, smiling, full of renewed excitement and expectation.

"Yes. I have a plan my friend." The white sorcerers let her head fall forward while she reached into her hooded robe.

***

Shaulmar crouched in the corner covering his head with the hood of his cloak. He was deep in sadness and unable to conjure the strength or energy to move. The only thing he focused all his energies and concentrative abilities on, was shielding himself from his love, Morghanz, who was desperately trying to connect with him.

It took everything he had to keep her location from the darkness that was trying to locate her—the pain was immense.

"Where are you my friends? I cannot hold on much longer." Shaulmar pulled his knees to his chest to ease the painful energy that pulsed through him whenever Morghanz's image or energy entered into his consciousness. His eyes were closed tightly in an attempt to numb his brain from the pain. He thought of his friends at the council and wished they were close—he knew they would help him out of this nightmare. The wizard released his eyes for a brief moment to rest them, and then closed them to the pain once more. Suddenly, he realized he had seen something in the corner of his field of vision that didn't register until he had closed his eyes again. A new event forced his mind to enquire, and this was a good respite from the pain, and more effective than anything he had attempted so far.

The wizard released his grip on his eyelids once more, just enough to peek through them, the conscious intention of such an easy task for the mind to perform was more than enough of a distraction from the invading dark energy. He was looking for the same flash of light he had seen before. With his face scrunched up, and his eyes open just enough to let in a little light, he searched around using his peripheral vision. Shaulmar was able to block the pain while looking about him. The more he searched and found nothing, the more disappointed he became, so much so, his resistance to the attack of darkness diminished rapidly.

"Where are you? I know you are there. I trust my senses. I will never doubt them, no matter what is happening." The wizard whispered to himself furiously as the pain grew and his resistance fell. Just as he was about to succumb to the pain, he saw it again. Instantly the wizard became infused with energy. "Please! Please! Help me get out of this room." He held his knees, pulling them into his chest, making it difficult for him to breathe. "I cannot connect with you. I am helpless. You must get me free from this room." With his head buried in his knees, he pleaded. The wizard thought he was truly going to die. Suddenly, he felt a tingling in his chest that was barely perceptible but it brought focus to his pain-filled mind. The wizard's hand slowly loosened its grip and moved up to his chest where he laid it flat on his cloak—he was able to feel warmth coming from the center of his chest to the center of his palm. He noticed a slight decrease in the pain, the dark powers felt less intense than they were before, and the warmth that connected with him was steadily increasing. The talisman around his neck had activated. The Celtic knot was receiving light energy from his old friend, who was pushing the dark forces back from the great wizard, allowing him to gain the strength he needed to break free from his bonds—enough to escape from the room. He crawled to the doorway at the end of the wall and pulled himself up by grasping onto the wrought iron railings and gate. The darkness wasn't about to let him go that easily. The Dark Angel wanted Morghanz's location in order to get closer to Rebecca. The light poured through the talisman and through the wizard, his hand was pure white light. As it shone through him, he was able to pull himself through the gateway and into the hallway towards the stairwell, where Rebecca had gone before him. He fell against the wall, resting his head back against it, and with one hand he reached into his tunic and felt for the amulet.

"Thank you…old friend." His hand stroked the silver with gentle loving care. "We will meet again somewhere my friend where I can thank you properly." The wizard made his way to the stairs and cautiously walked the steps, leaning against the round stairwell as he looked about him, just as Rebecca had done before him. He knew the dangers that awaited him. He had been in situations such as this many times. With each step he took, he grew stronger while the talisman continued to glow, a white silver. The wizard embraced the energy of the vortex that was providing the life-giving force that was pouring through him. He wanted desperately to find his friends and stop the dark wizard from taking Rebecca's soul. He was the architect of the 4th dimensional cathedral that had been manifested in the physical 3rd dimension, so he knew he had the element of surprise over any of the others in the sacred space. This advantage had to be used to its fullest effect if he was ever to overcome the dangers that were facing them. The wizard tossed around some ideas as he moved to the main floor, where he slowly lowered his body close to the ground, to avoid being detected. Shaulmar looked around the many pillars that held the stairwell in place that led to the main floor. There was no movement down the corridor, as far as he could see, in either direction.

At this point, he was feeling more or less normal, completely removed from the attack by the dark forces in the bowels of the sacred building. Shaulmar was the architect of the cathedral and knew that the power source that sustained it ran through its center deep into the earth and far out into the universe. Even though he'd made the connection to the source, using divine magic handed down through the ages by great magi that had gone before him, their allegiance to him was not guaranteed. He was well aware that such things were determined by the divine destiny of predetermined events that were known only at higher planes of existence. He wanted to find his friends, but he also wanted to stand in front of Draco Bastian once more. Shaulmar had been a wizard for many centuries, he was aware of the differences in strength and potency of power that existed between the dark forces and the light. He knelt on one knee at the top of the stairwell, out of sight of anyone in the main hallways, and spoke in a whisper with his head bowed.

"Lord of all creation, please flow through me this day. I must place myself in harm's way so that your prophecies may be fulfilled—this I do willingly." The great wizard stood up, pulled his hood over his silver hair, and walked slowly and deliberately down the hallway toward the entrance to the Great Hall, not knowing who or what he would be facing. He moved down the main hallway with stealth, his thoughts never settling on one thing. He had the feeling he was about to breach a significant episode in his life, with no idea of the outcome.

The hallway was quite immense, with huge pillars supporting the magnificent cathedral roof and tapestries that hung on the walls high above the wizard's head. Many fine pieces of ancient artifacts were displayed along the entire hallway. Shaulmar moved between the pillars and the dark alcoves. The gateway to the Great Hall was close now, the wizard's pulse quickened with every step. At last, he reached the large stone pillar that stood beside the huge oak and iron gates. There was only silence, he brushed past the pillar and rested a hand on the gate, closing his eyes as he did so.

"Magi, tell me who is beyond these gates?" Shaulmar asked from his heart as he concentrated and became still. The great wizard's will was strong and the energy he connected with felt very heavy and very powerful—Shaulmar recognized it as the one he had faced in the restaurant back in New York City. There was no other way for Shaulmar to do this; he had to know if his love Morghanz was alive, and if Rebecca was okay. The wizard pushed open the gate and slipped silently inside.

Shaulmar was able to observe the inside of the Great Hall without being seen, it was immense. It seemed to the great wizard that the structure he had created to protect himself and his friends that was supported by the vortex of light anchored at its center had somehow evolved. He concluded that the vortex had magnified and intensified the energies, not only his higher intentions that had manifested as the cathedral, but it seemed it had embraced and enhanced the heavier energies brought in by the dark ones as well. This was possible, he realized, because the universal energy that supported the light was also in harmony with its polar opposite, the darkness. The wizard of the light had to be cautious because the dark ones could also call on the vortex now. The Great Hall was lit with the morning light, and Shaulmar had no idea what he would find, as he moved around the great columns and sculptures that filled the sacred space. The only thing on Shaulmar's mind was to find his love, Morghanz. He didn't care how much dark energy there was waiting for him; he could feel his own soul energy building in anticipation of the inevitable confrontation that he knew waited for him. He paused for a moment, and then stood against one of the large oak doors that hid a room off the walkway beside the center area of the Great Hall. Shaulmar tightened his stomach muscles. His power center was telling him there was danger close by. Immediately, he closed his eyes and relaxed his entire body, letting his arms fall to the sides, and slowly allowing his consciousness to leave his physical body and guiding it upward toward the ceiling.

The great wizard's energy body moved effortlessly, higher and higher, all the while he was consciously aware of the chord of light connecting him to his physical body below. He had raised his awareness to the highest point in the Great Hall, and began to survey all that he could, while the light shone through the stained glass windows at both ends and both sides of the huge area. His attention was focused, and he desperately needed to become aware or connect to his love and his friends. They all needed him, and his soul knew it, his conscious awareness diligently scanned the Great Hall below for the faintest sign of anything living or moving. There was nothing he could see or connect to. His heart cried out for her. The energy echoed silently around the empty hall. His *light-body* slowly sank from where it was. Shaulmar's consciousness stirred because of a disturbance that registered on him as he descended. He stopped and instinctively felt for his connection to his physical body below, it seemed to be intact and undisturbed so he moved to the shadows above a large statue of one of the saints close to him. He looked more closely to where he felt the energy that had alerted him—it was near the huge circular mandala above the main altar at one end of the Great Hall. Draco Bastian hovered in front of the large mandala—only his silhouette could be seen, the light had not found him yet. Shaulmar's consciousness returned to his physical body and slowly he came to life again. He intended to step from the doorway and into the light of the Great Hall, but he became aware of an energy searching through his meridian lines around all the major nodes and points of his body, so the wizard remained hidden.

The Dark Angel glided to the floor of the raised altar in all his dark majesty knowing this time was to be, both, the end times and the beginning times—he felt it clearly. Shaulmar sensed the energy of the Dark One had increased in power, significantly, since they'd last met—he was sure this was solely due to Bastian calling on the power of the universal vortex of light that sustained the cathedral. What was he to do, he thought, the great wizard closed his eyes, but this time he was filled with sadness, his heart was in pieces. His love, Morghanz, was nowhere close and he didn't know where she was or if she was okay. He was also experiencing intense fear for his own life, even though he was a wizard of the light, and had experienced many encounters with the dark side on many incarnations through the universal cycle of death and rebirth.

The fear of death remained a constant in the physical realm regarding personal harm, trauma, or such things as the events leading up to any stressful and harmful death, like a confrontation with Draco Bastian, for one. Shaulmar remained stationary. The force that filled his mind began to grip his consciousness—it was only a tightening that he felt around his heart that brought him back to the room. He was a practitioner of the ways of the light, and with that awareness, he pushed away the fear and opened his eyes taking a deep peaceful breath—he knew what had to be done. He stepped from the shadows. He didn't know if Bastian had seen him in his light body but he didn't care. All he wanted was to find his friends and get them to safety, and to this end, he was now prepared to put his own life on the line. No sooner had the great wizard revealed himself, than he heard the low vibration of the voice coming from the direction of the sacred altar below the large mandala where Draco Bastian stood.

"Traveler, you will not survive this day, we both know this, yes?" Shaulmar was about to reply when he felt the force of energy impact his chest. Instinctively, he spun around to lessen the momentum of the attack, and as he did, he used both palms to absorb the low vibrations, transmuting them, and sending them harmlessly into the ethers. The great wizard was surprised how much the impact of the energy had stung him, leaving multiple welts on his chest around his heart chakra, he could feel them rising quickly. "That was only the teaser, Wizard, this day will not belong to you. No doubt you are becoming aware of my powers as being much greater than yours, thanks to the power of the vortex that I have been able to gain access to through the sacred dark force that I breathe." Draco Bastian was enjoying every second of the exchange. "I am in two minds, Traveller. I wonder if you could advise me?" The Dark Angel walked around the sacred altar, slowly and deliberately. "Shall I stab you now?" he said, while dragging his scabbard knife across the wooden table of offerings in front of the circular mandala that created a deep gouge in its wake. "Or maybe…I ought to wait and play for a while, so that miss Sullivan can see what real power can do?" He looked at the wizard, eyes blood red and his mouth agape, revealing a blackened tongue. Shaulmar remained silent. Many thoughts bombarded his mind. He was overwhelmed with his situation.

"Bastian…if that is your name," Shaulmar offered the only mask he had to keep the Dark One from knowing his fear, "you would do well to heed my words and leave this place. Your black heart cannot survive in a holy and sacred place such as this for much longer, especially, when I summon those who would take you to a place from which you would not return." The wizard was biding time. He was trying to figure out what he could possibly do next.

The only thing he struggled with was what to do, if in fact, Rebecca was on her way to the Great Hall as Bastian had claimed.

"Do not concern yourself with my wellbeing, Bedouin. It would serve you well to plan your own escape...if you can...ha hah." The Dark One seemed to know more than he was letting on, and Shaulmar knew it. The great wizard had to come forth to show the Dark Angel that he was not afraid, and to show power and confidence, even if felt it was a lie.

"Laughter from someone in your position of vulnerability indicates false courage, does it not?" Shaulmar made the point of eyeballing Bastian in order to contain his focus, and to keep him from the possibility of seeing Rebecca and the others enter the Great Hall. It was becoming more and more inevitable that Shaulmar would reach the point of no return with the Dark Angel and that he might lose his life as a result—but he knew in his heart if that was the case, it was his destined path, then he would do his best to take the Dark One with him. There was only sixty feet between them now. Shaulmar had made himself fully visible to the Dark Angel, and continued to move slowly towards him, staying focused eyeball-to-eyeball, making sure that he took Bastian's full attention.

"Do not think you can prevent me from taking her soul, Wizard!" Bastian moved slowly back and forth on the platform, his leather cloak scraping the wooden floor as he did so. "I shall render you helpless so that you can witness her capture." Shaulmar only continued to edge closer along the main isle that ran between the rows of oak and brass pews. The Great Hall encompassed the majority of the building—this area of the hall was cut in half by a platform that held the sacred pulpit and numerous sculptures of various holy icons and ancient religious figures. The great wizard began to move between the pews to his right, while he continued to keep track of the dark sorcerer, as he addressed him from the platform at one end of the cathedral. Shaulmar was not sure what was going to occur between him and the dark lord or whether he was ever going to prevent the soul of Rebecca from being taken. The only thing he knew for certain was that he would do whatever he could to prevent any harm coming to his loved ones, with his last breath if necessary.

"As I advised you at our last meeting, I am authorized by sacred high powers, greater than even you can dream up, to banish you from this reality if necessary." Shaulmar stood strong, as if he actually believed what he was saying. Draco Bastian was silent as he stood facing the white sorcerer, who stood in the aisle approximately forty feet away from him, between the rows of oak and brass pews. Without warning, a flash of blue energy hit Shaulmar in the chest. The bolt of lightning sent the great wizard sprawling backwards at great speed. He collided with one of the stone pillars that held the huge ceiling aloft.

"Argh..." Shaulmar almost lost consciousness. He was bewildered as to why he hadn't seen the hit coming. As he struggled to regain his awareness, and his ability to protect himself, another flash of light hit him in the stomach area near the solar plexus. He knew something was wrong. His energy was cloudy and his strength was wavering fast. He should have been able to defend himself against Bastian's attacks. He knew he should have, he thought, as he lay on the stone floor trying to get his bearings and some degree of strength back. He also realized he must move away from the source of the attack or he was probably going to die.

The Dark One floated off the front of the platform and onto the floor by the first row of pews. His cloak of darkness seemed to follow him—it billowed behind him like an obedient Rottweiler with the energy of the dark force flowing through it. Bastian paused for a moment, looking at the crumpled heap on the stone floor that was the white wizard, as if he had become cautious of him. Maybe you try to trick me with your feigning and display of weakness Shaulmar of the Ancients, he thought.

"Why do you not defend yourself, huh? Why do you not fight? Sending me to hell with the strength and power of the light...oh Great Wizard," he muttered out loud. Slowly, the Dark Angel moved closer, rising higher as he moved, making sure he was above the tops of the oak and brass benches that were between them. "You do not fool me, Bedouin. If you persist in this nonsense, I will destroy you where you lay." The dark sorcerer was ten feet above the pews at that point—he was assessing the heap on the floor covered in the purple and beige cloak. Shaulmar was still groggy. He was searching for the reason why he was unable to muster much of anything of his power. He knew he had to answer the Dark One or he would surely perish.

"It is true. You are very powerful, Draco Bastian. However," Shaulmar's voice was shaky but he mustered enough strength and control to project his energy into it enough to shroud the fact, "you are mistaken if you perceive yourself to be powerful enough to destroy me!" The wizard struggled within his mind to find a solution to his obvious dilemma. The force of the attack had hurt Shaulmar quite badly, not only had the energy cracked a couple of his ribs, but it had ripped a hole in his auric field about the size of a fist. Bastian wanted to finish him, but he was unable to connect with the wizard, to make sure he was not faking him out. He hovered about fifteen feet away, moving slowly one way then the other, trying to search for an indicator as to the real state of the wizard. Finally, the suspense was too much. The sorcerer flung open his cloak, revealing his large hands that were glowing blood red.

"Enough of this! Prepare to be blasted into the next realm oh great and powerful Wizard." The Dark One commanded the darkness to come forth and join with the energy of the vortex of light that was anchored into the earth. He intended to destroy Shaulmar as fiercely as he could. He didn't want to leave any doubt as to the strength of his power. The Great Hall filled with energy that rippled the air like a shockwave after a nuclear explosion and met with the energy of the Dark One at his solar plexus. Once it had connected with the energy of the Dark Angel, it travelled through his body to exit through the palms of his hands, where it was aimed at the wizard. Shaulmar watched the shockwave travel through the air. He pushed his energy as best he could toward the wave to try to disrupt or distort it. The great wizard felt incredible pain as he tried to send his energy towards the oncoming shockwave through his connection with the vortex of light. Shaulmar's pain intensified to the point where he had to stop. He fell back against the pillar and gasped for air. Sensing that his life was about to end, Shaulmar took a deep breath, closed his eyes, and focused his will on releasing his consciousness so it could leave his body thus terminating his life force.

Shaulmar heard the crackling and burning of the air as the huge high voltage energy travelled through it and so he braced himself for the impact. There was nothing—no sound, no pain, only a muffled cry, and a noise of something heavy crashing through the pews to hit the ground. The wizard steadied himself, and opened his eyes just in time to see Morghanz collapse to the floor after she had blasted the Dark Angel. Luckily, Joaquim was behind her to break her fall with his body as they both smashed to the floor. Shaulmar breathed in hard, as the adrenaline surged through his body with such force, that he was on his feet and dragging his injured body towards them quickly. Joaquim held Morghanz in his arms with his head buried in her neck—his cries were amplified by the Great Hall's acoustics, so much so, that it sounded like the hounds of hell were loose.

All that Shaulmar could do was call her name with everything he had in his being, while dragging himself sixty feet across the floor, to where she lay. At the same time, he was scouring all directions for the darkness. The dark sorcerer was nowhere to be seen. Shaulmar scanned all over the great hall as he moved closer to his love. The great wizard was only twenty feet from her. His hands gripped the tops of the oak pews so ferociously as he propelled himself towards her that they cracked, dripping blood onto the hardened old oak. He saw the silhouette of Draco Bastian high in the rafters. The shadow figure became larger, and moved slowly, changing its shape as it moved closer. Shaulmar knew what was about to happen. His heart raced up to his throat and he moved every part of his body that was willing, with every ounce of energy and strength that he could muster, to get to Morghanz but he knew he was too far away to stop it.

The air in the Great Hall crackled and burned once more as the molecules were heated to the intensity of the burning sun—a large flash of orange-yellow light illuminated the Dark One as it left his hands, destined for the being crumpled in the arms of the boy. A small object bent over the white sorceress preventing the energy from hitting its mark. Rebecca was in tears at the sight of her friend, and teacher, in the throes of death. The deadly orange-yellow bolt was rendered helpless, before it was able to impact the girl's body, by the activation of the Archangel icon tattoo that was embedded in the shoulder of the Prophesied One.

Rebecca felt like she'd been kicked by a mule, and before she was able to recover, the Dark Angel descended, quickly, as he realized his target was missed. He was not going to miss a second time—he made a direct path towards Morghanz. The archangel energy belonged to Saint Michael, but only the energy of the image was manifested, not the original force and power of the Archangel himself. This meant that she would not be safe unless the Essence came forth to protect her. Rebecca sent a thought to the bound soul asking for help, though that was not necessary, as the green mist had already manifested while the girl was in mid-thought. The Essence formed a sphere once more and positioned itself between Rebecca and the force of darkness that was heading for her. The girl had managed to regain her senses and made a dash for the nearest pew, diving headfirst, as she slid underneath the bench.

"Shaulmar, help us!" she yelled at the top of her lungs.

The wizard moved as fast as he could—he was close to Morghanz and Joaquim when the great wizard yelled,

"Joaquim, help me get Morghanz to the pews…to Rebecca…for safety."

The darkness that was Draco Bastian met the Essence midway between the rafters of the Great Hall and an enormous golden organ that was suspended above the main altar. The orb grew to two feet in diameter and shone like a silver bullet—indigo energy spun slowly around its circumference as it hovered in mid air waiting for the Dark One to engage it.

"You will not harm us," the Essence glowed as the voice spoke.

"So you are the Essence that has chosen *this* one for your soul mate." Bastian hovered six feet away from the silver sphere. "You must be so disappointed to find that after all the eons of searching and scouring this dark planet, that you had chosen the soul destined to be in *my* power, under *my* control." The Essence only continued to spin, saying nothing. "I will destroy you and claim the soul I need. There is no power greater than mine when combined with the vortex which supports this impressive structure." The dark figure hovered a few feet away from the Essence, and was preparing an incantation in his mind, that would create enough energy to strike at the heart of the Book of Secrets.

"The darkness is only a small aspect of the totality that is the universal energy force. You are but a tiny fraction of the darkness. With all my knowledge and wisdom, gained and earned through eons of incarnations into this place, I doubt that your power is enough to destroy the Essence that is the Book of Secrets." At this point, the Essence reverted back to the green mist in anticipation of what was being prepared by the Dark One. At ground level, there was commotion and confusion amidst the others. As all these things were in progress a disturbance in the immediate vicinity became apparent. A portal was generated that opened fully, and through it emerged the Rhostos Warrior, with Alison holding tight to the leather belt around his middle.

CHAPTER 29

OOH—I REALLY *HATE* THIS SHIT!" ALISON HAD LET GO OF her ride and was in the process of throwing up against the nearest pillar. The Rhostos took flight as soon as he saw the dark figure above the golden organ, his dark leather wings opening fully on the way, and beating the air with such ferocity that it was only a mere millisecond of time that elapsed before the Dark Angel was caught in the force of the object that carried both beings high into the rafters and out of sight.

The Essence quickly returned to the soul it was bound to. Rebecca was still as, she came to realize Morghanz was dead or dying. Shaulmar held his love in his arms with tears streaming down his face.

"Oh God…God, please! Please! Don't take her, please!" Joaquim was sitting against the wall, with his arms pulling his knees into his chest so fiercely, that it became difficult for him to breathe.

"Joaquim…it's okay…don't be sad." Rebecca touched the boy on his hand, as she passed him, on her way to her friend and teacher. Rebecca knelt at Morghanz's side and rested her hand on Shaulmar's hand that held his beloved so tightly. "My dear friend… I love you so much." With tears in her eyes, Rebecca kissed Morghanz's forehead. "Please don't die…I don't think I could lose another one so dear to me." She kissed her again and looked into her face.

"Sweet Rebecca," the white sorceress turned to her and spoke softly, as she was nestled in the arms of the great wizard. "There is something that you have the right to know, something that you must know, it is knowledge that will ignite a great fire inside of you." Morghanz coughed and gasped for air, the pressure of the earth's pull was even too much for her at this point. "Your mother is alive!" Morghanz was glad she had revealed this at last. It had weighed heavily on her for years, ever since she had fought with the great high council regarding their secret dealings with various entities in the universe. Rebecca was speechless, her mouth dropped and a thousand thoughts raced through her mind, as did many memories of the few years that she'd spent with her mother. Shaulmar held Morghanz in his arms and wept with his head buried in Morghanz's beautiful hair.

"Morghanz, tell me where she is. I must find her. I must go to her. Please…tell me how I can find my mother?" The young girl pleaded with her. She feared her mother was in terrible pain, and being tormented, in some horrible torturous way. Rebecca's heart was breaking at the thought of her mother sitting in some dark place, thinking she was alone, with no one to care about her or to help her. The white sorceress beckoned for her friend to come close. Rebecca leaned in toward her and their cheeks were almost touching as Morghanz whispered in her ear. Rebecca pulled away suddenly. "Oh God…No!" she cried fearfully and with utter disbelief. Immediately Morghanz's body went limp.

"No! No! My Morghanz." The wizard tightened his grip and pulled her to him. He couldn't prevent his heart breaking in two—it was not the only thing within him that snapped.

★★★

Alison rested her back against the stone pillar, recovering from the arduous method of travel she'd had to endure with the Rhostos warrior. She arched her back and rolled her head against the pillar, forcing her face upward, towards the rafters of the huge cathedral. With her eyes closed, she drew in a large breath to calm her mind, as she readied her tongue for the verbal attack she had prepared for him. He'd once more forced her to suffer through the ordeal of travel through the space between dimensions. She relaxed and returned to the present moment as she prepared herself for the retaliation.

"Where are you, Rhostos?" she turned her head to locate the huge being. "There is something I wish to yell at you." She had no idea where he was. The Rhostos had taken flight so quickly, when they'd exited the portal, that she was unaware that he had even left.

There were faint moans and mumblings halfway down the Great Hall, on the opposite side, to where Alison was positioned. She was scared inside—it was the first time in her life that she'd felt so vulnerable. She wanted to be with the Rhostos, and was very uneasy at being left alone, without the huge creature at her side. Without thinking, she moved cautiously towards the noise, assuming the Rhostos was the cause of the commotion.

She pulled her dark cape around her and continued down the dimly lit hallway, under the huge stained-glass windows, and through the multicolored shards of morning light that illuminated her hair, her cape, and her features with rainbow silhouettes for brief instances. The noise became louder and more audible, but she still could not make out who or what was making the sounds. The sorceress was still a little groggy from the travelling, and because of this, she needed to rest as she prepared to throw up again. So, she scurried between the pillars and towards the shadows that covered the walls. With one hand on her belly, and the other leaning up against the wall where she rested her head, she waited for the eruptions to begin again. "Oh…I hate you, Rhostos!" She felt the pressure building. "Even worse than this…I think I love you," her voice trailed off as the retching took over.

★★★

The Essence returned to the icon tattooed on the back of the bound soul, making the host wince a little, but Rebecca was too drained and preoccupied to give the usual rant of displeasure.

"Sis, what did Morghanz say to you before she…uh…you know…left?" The boy was afraid of death but didn't know why. He had been afraid of death for as long as he could remember but could never tell anyone. He didn't like the uncomfortable silence—it was the very reason why he spoke, which was a good thing, because Shaulmar was in a very destructive place emotionally at that point and needed to be brought back to the present.

"I think I might know what she said." The wizard lifted his head, gently, from his beloved Morghanz and he began to explain…Rebecca just sat against the old oak pews, still numb from the revelation about her mother. "Morghanz…my love…my heart and soul…my friend." He paused a moment. The pain of losing her was more than he could bear. "She told Rebecca that the abomination that is, Draco Bastian, captured her mother's soul many years ago." The wizard let his head fall back into the nest he'd made in Morghanz's hair and he fell silent once more. Joaquim went over to Rebecca, and with one hand on her lap and the other gently caressing her back, he whispered to her softly.

"Sis, is what Shaulmar just said the truth?" He continued to slowly rub her back. She sniffed a couple of times and turned to the boy, tears filled her eyes again, and with her chin and lips trembling uncontrollably, she uttered,

"Yes…the one known as the Dark Angel captured my mom's soul, thinking she was the one named in the ancient prophecy." She let out a burst of loud sobs and moans. "Now, I have got to try to find her. I cannot bear that she is suffering alone in some dark place."

"I know how we can find your mom, Rebecca." Shaulmar had laid Morghanz's body to rest on pillows he had pulled from the prayer pews, and as he spoke, he arranged her cape over top of her. "A captured soul, of a practitioner of the dark arts, is typically held in a place that does not conform to the laws of this realm. Such a place may be accessible, if the being who captured her is still using her as a source of energy, and her soul signature, as a guide to the real soul named in the prophecy." He eventually walked towards them and away from his love. Rebecca felt something, a vibration of energy around her neck—she put her hand to her chest.

"There is someone here, someone dark. My crystal is warning of a dark force nearby, Shaulmar."

"Come…don't fear. We will hide again and wait." She saw a change in the way he spoke and in the way he looked at her.

"What about Morghanz? We can't leave her here for them to find and do whatever they want with her." Joaquim was not going to allow that.

"It's okay. Morghanz is no longer here. She is with the Light of the Universe. Nothing can harm her now. He shepherded the two into a hiding place, nearby, where they could monitor whatever dark force might appear before them. "We will still need to escape from here. We are not yet safe."

Alison appeared from the corridor. Her black cape was pulled around her body—the hood covered most of her face. She stopped near a wrought-iron candelabrum that rose up from the floor—nine feet—it had twelve white candles at the head. She moved through the pews to the other side of the Great Hall, not realizing, she was being watched. Joaquim looked at Rebecca.

"Sis, wasn't she the one that you met before?" Rebecca didn't even bother to look up—she was overtaken by thoughts of her mother's plight. Rebecca wanted and needed to find her mother so she could be with her again.

"Shaulmar, you have to help me find my mother. You have to get us out of here." The great wizard said nothing. He only continued to observe the dark sorceress in the distance. He watched steadfastly, never taking his eyes off the sinister figure. He slowly moved along the oak and brass pews, making sure to remain hidden, as he stalked the movements of Alison as if he were a cougar stalking its prey.

"Sis! Shaulmar is acting weird. I've never seen him like this." The boy turned to her. "Rebecca!" he hissed, "you must do something—otherwise we will end up like Morghanz." He was desperate, and that was the only thing that brought her back to the present, back to the cathedral and the obvious danger that faced them all.

"Okay, I will try to talk to him, but you must understand that when Morghanz died a part of Shaulmar died too." Rebecca pulled her body up from the floor and slowly raised her head above the oak benches to see what Shaulmar was doing. She saw the wizard scurrying down one of the rows of pews towards the shadowy figure that was about twenty rows ahead of him. It was too late for her to speak with him but what she saw was very disturbing. Shaulmar had pulled his cape around him and covered his head with the large hood. It was obvious to her that he intended to kill the dark shady figure, and if Joaquim was right, then it meant that the great wizard was about to destroy Alison.

Rebecca knew that Alison was a rotten person, and a lonely soul, but not one deserving of the wrath of the wizard. The pain and suffering coursing through the veins of the great wizard was meant for Draco Bastian, no one else. She knew deep in her heart that she had to stop him from taking this devastating step, making this dreadful mistake.

Alison moved carefully around the pillars and the many large sculptures, quickly surveying the area, looking for anything to indicate that the Rhostos, or anyone else, might have been there or might be close by.

"Where the hell are you Rhostos?" she whispered out loud, hoping that he was hiding close by and was about to send one of his large hands from behind a pillar, or alcove, and yank her to him. She would be really pissed off, but extremely relieved. Nothing happened—something that made her even more scared. This had never occurred before she knew the Rhostos would not abandon her if he had a choice. Alison knew this to be true and that realization brought her an enormous amount of fear and dread—it meant that she was *truly* alone. Worse than this, Alison felt the trembling, and then a quickening of the vibration within her. A sharp heat pierced her breast, and she knew immediately, the crystal around her neck was warning her of danger. Alison backed up to the darkened stonewall as she tried to hide in its shadows. She was vigilantly scanning the Great Hall for the encroaching danger, and at the same time, she was wishing the Rhostos were beside her once again.

She was not as powerful as other sorcerers in the universe, and that made it very difficult for her to be recognized as a practitioner of the dark force, that she wields. It was clear to her that she might finally be close to the end of her life, and with the crystal glowing red and vibrating off her chest on the chain around her neck, she was left with little doubt. The sorceress stood as tall as she could, next to an iron gate in the dark shadows of the stonewall, behind a small wooden carving of the apostle, Saint Peter. She pulled her cape around her as best she could—she waited. The only defenses she had were her incantations, any potions she might be able to conjure, and any energy she could direct through the crystal. Alison thought that whatever danger was lurking, it would not wait for her to concoct anything, before attacking. She felt incredibly lost and abandoned a feeling that had eluded her until she'd met the Rhostos warrior.

***

Rebecca moved as quickly as she could, after the wizard, without being seen. She had no idea where the Dark One, Draco Bastian, was and wasn't about to give him a second chance at taking her. It was quite dark at that end of the cathedral, even though some morning light entered through the stained-glass windows, along the walls, and at the opposite end of the Great Hall. Light had not yet reached the part of the cathedral where Rebecca and the others were hiding. Rebecca continued to travel along the rows of benches, trying to keep the dark figure of her friend in sight, but it was getting difficult, as the light lessened the further she moved downward. Finally, she noticed the figure of Shaulmar had stopped, so she hurried to get to him before he did something he would regret. As the girl came upon the place where she had seen Shaulmar stop, there was no sign of anyone. The young soul looked around, baffled. She was sure she'd maintained a perfect reference point to the exact place where she'd seen him stop.

Rebecca looked around but all she saw was a small altar, an iron gate, and a sculpting of what she thought might be a depiction of another saint. She walked around, being sure to stay hidden as best she could. Periodically, she crouched down in the shadows to listen for anything—anything at all. It was too bizarre she thought. How could anyone just disappear? She sat in the shadows and replayed the last few minutes again in her mind, trying to reassure herself that she had watched Shaulmar all the way to that very place. As she processed the information, it occurred to her that she was forgetting that Shaulmar was, and still is, a great and powerful wizard. His power had seemed to be weak at that moment, but she had an idea. To locate him, all she had to do was—a noise interrupted her—she took in a deep breath and held it. As she pushed her back against the beautiful woven tapestry that hung on the ancient stone wall behind her, not knowing what she would be seeing next, Rebecca fumbled for her crystal, wondering why had she not been forewarned.

"Sis—Sis" Joaquim hissed again. Rebecca appeared from the shadows.

"Jeez, don't do that!" she hissed back, softly. She bent at the waist letting her hands rest on her thighs. "You freaked me out Joaquim!"

"Sorry," he whispered, as he let his hand fall gently onto her back as she calmed herself and breathed easier. "What happened to Shaulmar? I couldn't bear to wait were Morghanz was—left, it was too creepy," he explained before Rebecca could ask. He knew he sounded like he was afraid of ghosts or something, but he didn't care any more what people thought, it was just too damn creepy for him.

"I don't know what happened to Shaulmar or Alison. I was about to ask the Essence to find them, when I heard a noise, and thought I was done for." She looked at him with piercing eyes.

"Sorry Sis—again—really, I'm sorry. I know you—I know how scary this place is getting and I didn't want to frighten you, honestly." The boy was genuinely sorry that he'd freaked her out again.

"Okay, Joaquim. I forgive you." Rebecca had calmed enough now. Her breathing had returned to normal and her pulse had slowed. "This might take a few minutes to bring the Essence forward, and to get it to locate Shaulmar, but it is the only way I can think of right now." She sat on one of the old oak benches and began to take up the meditation position that Morghanz had showed her months before. She thought it might be an effective way to bring forth the Essence. Joaquim moved about and was just about touching everything in the area, candles, the beautifully crafted golden-colored rope that hung from the tapestry, and the armor that stood on an iron frame close to the gate. He grabbed the chain holding the heavy iron ball on the mace connected to the suit of armor—the medieval weapon made a loud clang that resonated through the air and made him panic a little.

"Sorry—sorry! I'll try to be more careful, Sis." Rebecca looked him with frustration in her eyes and lifting her arms almost to her shoulders.

"We are not yet safe, Joaquim. You heard what Shaulmar said. We have to get out of here. Please, no more noise, okay?"

"Okay—okay." He held up his hands and lowered his head apologetically. "No more noise, I promise."

Rebecca closed her eyes once more and made the clear intention for her mind to call forth her soul mate. Joaquim was kind of relieved that his disturbance was forgiven. He couldn't bear to be chastised by Rebecca because he thought so highly of her. The boy rested against the wrought-iron gate and promised himself he would be more mature, or at the very least more careful, so that Rebecca would see him as someone she could trust. Without warning, the gate swung wide open, allowing the boy to tumble backwards down the first set of stone steps. He was lucky there were only four steps, with a woven carpet running down the center of each one, cushioning his fall somewhat.

"Argh! Ouch! Shit!" He tumbled and rolled until he came to a stop with his legs tangled, and his face planted, squarely into an old clay pot on the next stone landing. Rebecca rushed over to him.

"What happened? Are you okay, Joaquim?" she hurried down the steps to her friend.

"Yeah, I'm okay." He wasn't hurt, only embarrassed again. She knelt by his side and made sure he was okay. "Where are we?" he asked, looking around and rubbing his head.

"I don't know but we should continue down the stairs. I think this is the only place they could have gone to." She thought Shaulmar must have come to his senses by now.

***

The wizard forced Alison back into the room…using his formidable powers. He had taken every form of defense that she had, and destroyed them, while she watched.

"You think these baubles are a match for my power?" The wizard had crushed her crystals. "Do you think these will protect you from me! You're going to pay for taking my Morghanz from me. You are going to pay with your life—and with your soul." He was lost in the pain and grief that had taken possession of his mind. Shaulmar had lost touch with the ways of the white wizard, and the sacred order, that he'd pledged his life to be in service to. What he was doing now would undo all of his soul progression up to this point and through this incarnation. His higher being was aware of this fact, but the strength of the pain and loss he was experiencing, prevented him from stopping himself.

"I didn't kill the one you love. I wasn't even here!" Alison yelled at him. She was crouched in the corner behind the large obelisk that Rebecca had previously hid behind and the Essence had opened as a portal.

"That is of no concern to me. I know you are in league with those ones and that is enough for me. When I dispose of you, I will find Draco Bastian, and destroy him too. Then, every practitioner of the dark arts in this universe will also be hunted down by me and destroyed, until there are none left alive, or I die in the process."

Shaulmar had now fallen fully into the abyss of grief and loss. Even the love he had for the universe, and all within it, was obscured by the darkness now. The wizard threw back his cloak and sent his arms up towards the heavens. He prepared himself to call upon the vortex of light to join with his energy and bring destruction to the dark sorceress.

"I invoke the power of the universe—the dark void must be destroyed, it cannot be allowed to grow without being challenged."

The wizard closed his eyes and used his energy body and all his magic all his knowledge of the ways of the light, to a focused point within his mind. He concentrated on his intension and intertwined that with the vortex of light. The light flowed through him, he glowed, and the vortex amplified the power he was generating. The wizard brought down his arms and sent a wave of light towards the large stone object that protected Alison. The obelisk, enveloped by the light, rose off the ground about six inches. Alison stepped back and watched, as the object moved sideways, slamming into the opposite wall.

"I did not kill your friend. You don't have the right to do this. There are rules! You have sworn an oath to do no harm to the innocent!" she screamed. Shaulmar only stared at her and produced an amulet from inside his cloak.

"This amulet belonged to my love and my friend, Morghanz. It has a facsimile of her soul signature embedded within its energy matrix, because of this—wherever she is— she will share in the destruction of the dark force that runs through you. The darkness permeates every cell of your physical body. I can feel its desire to spread and contaminate everything it comes in contact with." He held the amulet in his hand, letting the silver chain fall through his fingers. "I cannot allow this *darkness* to move freely through the universe, taking and destroying young souls with such impunity."

The great wizard pushed up the sleeves of his cloak to the elbows. "I do not take pleasure in the destruction you are about to face. I only take pleasure in knowing that it prevents you from destroying any more young souls. Those who have incarnated in this realm to evolve and progress through the light of the creator must be protected. Shaulmar lowered his head and looked at the amulet in his hand. "I feel great joy in the knowledge that I will deprive the darkness of this realm any power you would add to it." The words stopped, and the great wizard looked at the frightened sorceress, backed up against the wall.

"You are not allowed to do this to me. For a practitioner of the ways of the Sacred Order of Light to execute any being that possesses no threat to them has to be sanctioned by your Sacred High Council." Alison's voice trembled as she tried to impose the rules on the great wizard. Shaulmar was immovable, his grief matured; it nurtured a deep hatred of the beings that embraced and cultivated the dark forces. He was falling into the trap of low vibrational thinking. The only image that was constant in his mind was the fact that the darkness had taken his beloved Morghanz from him, his heart was in pieces, and his mind was fractured.

"You are correct in what you say regarding the boundaries and rules of a practitioner of the light, however, there is one flaw in your assertion." The great wizard wrapped the silver chain around the wrist of the hand that it nestled in. He then reached into the leather pouch on his belt inside the cloak. It revealed a large blue crystal that fit into his palm like a gun would in the hand of a skilled marksman. "When you say a member of the sacred white order cannot take the life of any being without the authorization of the high council, you are correct. However, the person you are addressing is no longer a member of that brotherhood." Shaulmar raised his head slowly looking at the sorceress eye to eye; he was drained of all humanity.

"*Please*—do not do this, I am not that person any more. I was shown the power of love, there is someone I wish to spend the rest of my days with, and who I wish to experience life here with."

The sorceress spoke from her heart; she had been forced to negotiate for her life before. This time it was different; she was negotiating from love not fear.

"I wish to experience family, I want to bring souls into this world through family and show them life in ways other than the ones that were shown to me."

Alison was expressing real emotion, something she hadn't ever done before. Shaulmar just continue to prepare the power of the sacred light.

"I am in love with the Rhostos warrior, I must find him. Please wizard do not do this—you know love, you know of what I speak." She was cornered, and she knew it. All she wanted was to see the Rhostos burst into the room and take her in his huge arms where he would protect her and transport her into the space between dimensions where they could live, love, and travel together. The amulet and crystal held by Shaulmar connected with the energy of the vortex of light. The power surged through Shaulmar's energy centers until he glowed. The surge of power would come from the merging of his sixth energy center, the crystal he held, and the amulet as the focal point, only then would the target be destroyed forever. The dark sorceress watched the energy intensify, she couldn't believe after all she been through that this was going to be it. After finally falling in love she was never going to see the Rhostos warrior ever again. Alison sank to the floor covering every part of her with her dark cloak; she didn't want to see the end coming for her.

"I hate you wizard," she spoke calmly and gently. "You are blinded by your loss and your pain has made you no different than the darkness." She fell silent. The wizard only kept his eyes closed allowing the energy to build through him. The dimly lit room became bright as the power of the vortex singed the air all around the great and powerful wizard.

CHAPTER 30

REBECCA AND JOAQUIM STUMBLED AROUND THE SMALL passageways deep below the Great Hall, they had no idea where Shaulmar had gone and whether he had found Alison or not.

"Sis, we had better hurry and find him, I don't think he is acting as his normal self—if you know what I mean?" The boy came down the next set of stairs two at a time, but his feet clipped the second bottom step causing him to stumble and collide with the wall at the landing.

"Joaquim, be careful, I don't think an injury is going to help us right now." Rebecca skillfully navigated the stairwell like a young gazelle moving through the open fields of the Serengeti. "Listen for anything when we turn the corner and enter the hallway, it looks familiar to me but I cannot be sure. I think this is where we began when we decided to look for you guys earlier." Rebecca sensed something not good, but without the Essence she couldn't make out what. The two friends moved into the darkened hallway and stayed close to each other.

"There is something down here Sis. I thought I saw a flash of light." He had noticed the light flash against the wall at the end of the hallway, and then it disappeared. "We must get down to the end quickly before he does something—something really bad!"

Joaquim ran down the hallway before Rebecca could say anything. She knew he was right, but it was not safe to remain in the open like that because they didn't have a clue about who or what were close by. Joaquim headed for where he saw the light flash, he meant to get there to save the day, or so he thought. He had always fantasized about being a hero to someone—it didn't matter much to him who, but now, especially since he had met Rebecca, the young lad wanted it to be for her. Another flash of blue white light bounced off the wall in the corridor, Joaquim saw where it was coming from and hurled himself through the doorway of the chapel.

"Shaulmar! Stop! Stop!" Joaquim saw the great wizard glowing with the blue white light. The wizard's arms were stretched wide with a beam of light coming from each hand as well as his chest. The powerful beams of light met in the space in front of him where they joined to form a sphere of pulsing energy that looked like it was about to explode. No sooner than the words left the boy's lips, he felt an excruciating pain in his chest and head that made him shake violently as he was being slammed against the wall and floor in the corner of the room. Blood spurted from his head and mouth, moments later Rebecca entered and before anything else could transpire she lost consciousness.

"Great and powerful wizard," the calm strong voice called from across the room, "the source does not wish you to destroy this being." Alison shivered with the fear and anticipation of her death, as she remained huddled on the floor.

"Do not pretend to me that you know what the source of all, wishes. You are only a record of what has been not what is to be." Shaulmar snapped at the being speaking through the young girl. The powerful sorcerer held the energy that was collecting at the spinning sphere in front of him. The only measure left for the great white wizard was to join the sphere with the light from the energy center in the middle of his forehead, and then the process would be complete. The dark sorceress would be dispatched from this physical realm to a place only she will know as her soul experiences it.

"Shaulmar, the only thing left is for you to call upon your soul body, your consciousness, and make the clear intention that you destroy the being before you." Rebecca's physical body move toward the sobbing sorceress at the far end of the room, "if you do what you intend, there will be many consequences for you that will affect many lifetimes past and future, wizard of the light." The Essence was now halfway to Alison, and it was clear that the soul of the Book of Secrets meant to stand between the wizard and the sorceress.

"Do not interfere with my business I will not be responsible for you if you persist. This one must be destroyed as well as many of them as I can find, so they all can suffer her fate. The darkness must not be allowed to upset the balance of souls in the universe, and I pledge my own being to this end." Shaulmar's voice increased in power and the intensity of the light energy coming from him through the vortex responded accordingly.

"Great wizard you are filled with hatred because of the loss you have suffered. Morghanz is not in pain, she lives with the ones who love and care for her like you once did. She has been able to move into a higher vibrational dimension because of the way she lived in this reality. She expressed love and compassion throughout her life of service, and as a result the love vibration resonates strongly with her." The Essence had placed Rebecca between the spiral of energy and its target. "Do not relinquish your power to the lower vibrations of hate and vengeance, there is no need good friend." Rebecca was fully connected with her bound soul once more, she spoke with the Essence and they were one. At this point there was a clear beam of light coming from Shaulmar's forehead and was now connected to the spinning orb of energy. The intention was created.

"It is too late for this nonsense, remove yourself or you will suffer the fate of this one." The wizard took a deep breath and lifted his arm slightly. He was ready nothing was going to stop this. The air cracked and the great wizard moaned as the power moved through his energy bodies. "Argh…argh." Shaulmar lurched back and moved his right leg back behind him to brace himself against the force of the surging light. The blue white light pulsed from the spiraling sphere of energy, burning the air as it was released.

The instant the energy was set in motion from the orb, a profound response was triggered from the being that was the bound soul. Nothing continued—all movement ceased, everything that was, no longer continued. The pain and suffering that had manifested as dark hatred through Shaulmar, and sent from the great wizard to destroy the dark sorceress was made null. Rebecca had levitated a foot off the stone floor, her arms spread wide inside a cocoon of purple gold energy that enveloped her. The Essence had emerged from the brain stem of its host and rose two feet above and behind her, shining and sending out a vibration that sounded like a high-pitched tone that pierced the air around them.

"Come forth! You cannot hide any longer. We know what you do! We know how you operate. "The voice was strong and powerful coming from the young girl, it was strange to see such an energy flowing through such an unimposing figure. Shaulmar did nothing, the power channeled through him from the vortex of light was no longer connected, and the spiraling energy in front of him had vanished. The great wizard had remained in the position he took when he was initially about to destroy the sorceress. The only difference was his arms had changed position; they had fallen to his sides and gone limp. "Come forth! Reveal yourself." Rebecca spoke once more as the Essence sang again spinning as an orb beside its bound soul. There was no movement from Alison, the dark heap on the ground next to the stone obelisk remained unrecognizable as a person, and Joaquim lay where he fell, unconscious and hurt.

"Shaulmar—the great and ancient wizard at your service, ha, ha, hah." The voice came from the wizard. Shaulmar threw back his head as he laughed, with his hands resting on his hips. Almost immediately the laughter stopped and an expression of excruciating pain appeared on the face of the wizard. Shaulmar's frame hit the floor as if it had been dropped from a great height, and his soul had been torn from him on the way down.

A dark shadow was left standing behind the body of Shaulmar, the being moved slowly away from it and stood near the entrance way. The Shadow-being was completely covered in a protective, dark shell that seemed to be hiding what was beneath. Only blood, red eyes were visible behind the mask to confirm the being had form, or was of the physical realm.

"Leave this place—you're not welcome here." Rebecca spoke with authority and power indicating changes had in fact taken place inside the reality of the souls bound together for eternity. It was obvious that the next stage of the evolution of the bound souls was in progress. Rebecca must have provided something new, something that was activated inside her when she entered that room. When the threat of danger was sensed it triggered whatever evolution of the souls was agreed upon with the source. Even something as powerful as the Essence, was not enough on its own to stop time in order to cancel the threat coming from within Shaulmar. The Shadow-being said nothing, its darkness only moved like waves of crude oil on the ocean after a disaster at sea. "What is it you want?" The Essence pulsed next to Rebecca as she spoke, the shadow moved slightly and as it did so the icon of St Michael shone bright on the shoulder of the girl.

"The soul of the Prophesied One!" Came the reply. The voice vibrated slowly as if it were speaking the words while assessing every possible avenue that could lead to taking the soul of Rebecca.

"The one you speak of is bound and cannot be taken. It is protected, you must leave—your task cannot be completed." The vibration of the voice coming through the mechanism of the girl had been raised significantly.

"And what protects this soul?" The darkness began to vibrate slowly.

"The ancient Book of Secrets protects this one." The Essence glowed as Rebecca sent the words to the darkness.

"I doubt very much if such a protector has the power or the knowledge necessary to prevent the darkness from taking whatever it desires, especially the darkness such as I."

The shadow being had doubled in size, filling the corner of the room closest to the entrance and was absorbing all the light that entered the room from the stairway, it was truly powerful. Rebecca was aware of what was happening but she felt as if she was surrounded by a strong and powerful protection. She knew the Essence of the Book of Secrets was bound to her, but this felt different. It was as if her higher consciousness had merged with her physical consciousness.

Essence—something is different, what has happened? She sent the thought to the bound-soul.

I do not know exactly, the progress of bound-souls is not information that is made available to me at this time. Even in the knowledge of the Book of Secrets there isn't any reference to this evolution. The telepathic connection between them had also changed, becoming much stronger. We would be wise to remain consciously connected, if this threat is as powerful as it seems, or as it claims. I don't know how the protection works; I only have trust and faith that our binding was destined by the highest. Therefore, it seems to me that our destruction is to be prevented, in the early stages that is. The telepathic conversation continued.

"My God! Is that what you are basing my protection on?" Rebecca hissed out loud.

You must attempt to remain conscious throughout this experience, it will help us to progress and help me to better protect you. The Essence sent the last thought through the heart of the girl.

The shadow-figure shifted its form, and without warning the darkness filled the room removing any light, preventing Rebecca from seeing anything at all. Almost immediately, the Archangel-icon on Rebecca's shoulder shone like a Sun tearing through the darkness to reveal the Shadow-being manifesting close by. The Essence spun away from its host swirling and sending a barrage of light and sound toward it, hurling the dark entity backward, slamming it into the wall and ceiling. Blood red energy made its way toward the girl activating a burst of light from the Archangel that met it six feet in front of her causing her to fall into the black cloak bundle on the floor. Rebecca felt dizzy she had hit her head during the fall, and was lucky that Alison had been between her and the wall.

She pushed against the floor with one hand to get to her feet, she had to get back and connect with the Essence. The young girl had remembered what it said about remaining conscious during the experience this time. Just as she tried to get up, something was pushed into her hand; she looked down and saw that Alison had given her the dark Crystal she used for protection. The sorceress slid the cloak from her face and looked Rebecca in the eyes.

"If you get within three feet of the assassin, and can place the crystal at its feet, you will destroy it." She half smiled as if attempting to let Rebecca know that the dark force no longer flowed through her. Rebecca grasped the crystal fully and turned away from the sorceress, while Alison covered her face again. The Essence held the assassin at bay but it took all the power it was able to channel from the source to do it. What it needed was the bound soul of Rebecca to reconnect with it to help. The girl ran towards the Essence the crystal buzzing strongly in her hand, it hurt her energy so much that she wanted to let go of it. She daren't drop it for fear the Shadow-being would be powerful enough to capture her soul, something that still held a huge fear for her.

The darkness bombarded the swirling green mist with a barrage of dark red energy. The Essence was able to absorb it and responded with the sound and light energy of the vortex that cut through the darkness. Rebecca connected again with the Essence through the tattoo etched on her shoulder leading directly to her brain stem. The green mist returned to its silver sphere manifestation and continued to fight the dark entity. Rebecca knew that at this time it was normal for the Essence to take full control of the situation and extinguish the threat. However, that was not the case this time and it was becoming obvious that the Essence was only holding its own in the battle. She watched the darkness as it moved and absorbed the barrage of light and sound from the silver sphere. She tried to discern the center of the entity where the heart of the Shadow-being would be and where she would need to go. The dark energy flowed like the light would flow; it astounded and confused Rebecca to see the likeness of the darkness to the light. She had to do something soon and she knew it, it was becoming a losing battle for the Essence, and if that were so then Rebecca was also finished.

The girl moved slowly with her back against the wall and as she did so she noticed the darkness pulsing at the far end of the wall. This is where she intuitively felt was the place where the being was, were the center or heart of the darkness lay, she took a chance and picked her moment. Just as the battle was intense enough, where the darkness bombarded the Essence and the Essence was forced to focus on staying alive, Rebecca threw herself into the fray. The young girl ran as fast as she could with the dark crystal vibrating heavily in her hand, toward the pulsing, dark energy. Rebecca dove to the floor when she was within a few feet of it, and slid across the dark entity leaving the crystal behind as she moved through. The darkness filled her mind as she moved through it for a Nano-second, she felt like her consciousness was being absorbed and her mind strangled. Then all was light within her mind again as she slammed against a wooden door on the other side of the darkness. As soon as the crystal was in place, the black cloak at the other end of the room was thrown to the floor from the sorceress, as she sprang to life. Alison began to recite a secret dark incantation, her eyes were focused, and her hands came together like *lightning* as if in prayer. She was all of five foot six inches and stood in the dimly lit room between the great wizard and the hurt boy. There was a ripple of power in the air as her connection was made with the vortex within the sacred building. Simultaneously, as the black crystal lay vibrating on the floor beneath the darkness, a third connection was made between them. All this happened within a fraction of a second and the triad was complete.

The Shadow-being was preparing to deliver a major blow to the Essence to destroy the connection between it and Rebecca. Once the Essence was destroyed then Rebecca was completely vulnerable, that was how it intended to capture her soul. As soon as Alison completed the words of the incantation, the energy connection with the dark crystal was complete. The crystal activated and exploded with a vibration of sound energy that was deafening. The Essence saw the crystal rise off the floor and as it did a net of yellow energy was immediately sent out catching the Shadow-being with a web of sticky, electrically charged goo. The yellow substance was extremely toxic and the darkness was devoured little by little until only the consciousness that was the Shadow-being remained.

Alison was still standing in the same place with her arms straight out ahead of her, palms outward as if she were pushing something ahead of her, her face contorted and her eyes remained shut tightly. The Essence returned to Rebecca and together they moved away from the darkness.

Essence, what is going on? What is she doing? Rebecca sent the thought to the bound soul.

The Essence responded. I think she is destroying it by transformation of one state to another. The energetic net continued to tightened around what was left of the darkness and persisted to shrink while the yellow goo held the darkness as a magnet would hold a piece of iron. The transformation seemed to be slow and it appeared to inflict severe pain and torturous agony on the dark entity. Eventually, the lines dug into its energy. The darkness was forcibly compressed into a space that was eventually going to disappear into nothingness. Rebecca couldn't bear to watch any longer she turned to the dark sorceress and witnessed her power as she held on to the connection with the vortex of light and the dark crystal. Holding firm, Alison watched as the darkness eventually diminished, and disappeared in a flash of yellow light. It left its impression on the wall as if it were stained with death forever. Once the deed was done, Alison collapsed to the floor exhausted, Rebecca ran to Joaquim who was still unconscious from the blast of energy that came from the dark-shadow when he entered the room.

"Joaquim are you okay?" she stroked his hair. The boy had stopped bleeding from his wounds now, but he didn't look too good. Rebecca kept one eye on Alison, at this point she wasn't sure what she was up to. The sorceress sat up wedged between the wall and the floor, and watched Rebecca. She pulled her cloak around her again with the hood covering her head and much of her face once more. Alison saw Rebecca clean the blood from Joaquim's face and head with such gentleness that it forced tears from her eyes. The only thing on her mind at that moment, the only thing that mattered to her was finding the Rhostos, and hoping he was still alive.

As she continued to observe the Prophesied One taking care of her friend, she imagined how she would feel if she were to care for the warrior. It was too much for her to handle the fact that she had felt the power of love through her time and experience with the Rhostos. Now she might have lost him forever, and that was beginning to feel more and more painful than anything Draco Bastian had made her feel. Alison was not used to feeling weak and vulnerable; the dark sorceress watched as Rebecca struggled to move the unconscious boy to a safer place by the wall, where he would be more comfortable should he wake. She went over to help her, something else that was completely foreign to her.

"Rebecca—let me help." The sorceress grabbed both of the boy's legs and lifted without saying another word.

"What are you doing Alison? What do you want?" Rebecca spoke as they carried the boy over to the wall near were Shaulmar had fallen.

"Don't worry, I am no longer the person you think I am." She looked Rebecca in the face, but there wasn't the usual horrible energy, Rebecca could see clearly there was a change in her.

"Then who are you Alison? Because the Alison I knew had done some really horrible things to me and my friends."

Alison placed the black cloak around her body, the room was not warm at all and the air was chilled and damp.

"I know it's difficult to believe, but that was who I was, I was a lost soul. I no longer enjoy the pain and suffering of others as I once did."

"Why did you help us destroy that being? I mean—you are part of all that so it makes me think you are trying to pull a fast one." Rebecca experienced too much to trust the dark sorceress.

A muffled groan came from the great wizard; Rebecca rushed to him.

"Shaulmar, Shaulmar you're back." She was really happy.

"Ooh, that really hurt! What happened?" The wizard sat up holding his head.

"Oh, Shaulmar, I'm really relieved that you're okay. I don't think I could have continued alone." Rebecca hugged him for a long time. Alison was trying to stay out of harms way, she didn't want the wizard to confront her. The sorceress knew what had happened to him, and how the shadow being was able to possess the great wizard. She also knew that as soon as he realized she was there, he would automatically assume she had some part in the whole thing. So, the sorceress stepped away from them and stood silently waiting, she was certain she was not going back to the darkness. Going back to the darkness was not possible after her heart had been touched by her love for the Rhostos, something she hated but loved at the same time, she was really confused.

"I remember now Rebecca," Shaulmar was reminded with sadness by the memory of the passing of his Morghanz. "The darkness came in all around me and filled my heart with such pain and grief. It was when I was weakened by the death of my love, but that was not the only reason I was possessed by the shadows." Shaulmar was standing now.

"What do you mean Shaulmar?" The girl asked.

"There is something more happening here Rebecca." The wizard pointed a finger in the direction of the dark sorceress who had by now made her way back to the shadows in the corner. "That one knows what."

"He is right—I know how he was made weaker, and a good idea as to why." Alison had once again pulled her cloak about her, and her hood covered most of her head. Only glimpses of her face could be recognized, and she had no idea what the wizard would do nor did she know if Rebecca would unleash the Essence for protection.

"Shaulmar, would you please look after Joaquim? I think he desperately needs your attention." Rebecca made eye contact with Shaulmar knowing he would see she wanted to deal with the situation with Alison on our own terms. Shaulmar thought for a moment, and then moved away from them both. He knew Rebecca had to learn to navigate her way through delicate, and dangerous situations in times to come. So this, he thought, was a good opportunity for her to begin developing all the skills she may need to survive.

"Okay, I will take care of the boy." He headed for Joaquim. As the wizard moved toward the lifeless body of his young friend, Alison slowly pushed back her hood revealing more of her face.

"I'm sorry for what happened to her, I am." She genuinely wanted the wizard to know that was how she really felt, but Shaulmar only continued to the boy.

"Alison, we need to talk. I know you claim to reject the darkness and those things that have drawn you to do the things that you do as a practicing dark sorceress. However, I need to be given more information than that if you're to avoid any conflict with us. I may only be able to stop Shaulmar from taking matters into his own hands for so long, you know what I mean—right?" Rebecca spoke softly she never saw the need for heightened emotions during confrontations—it was something her gran instilled in her.

"What do you want to know?" Alison seemed detached from the situation as if she were numb.

"First of all, what did you mean when you said you knew what happened to Shaulmar, and second who was that shadow-being?" Rebecca waited for the answers, but as she did so a thought occurred to her. If Alison was lying and still aligned with the dark forces, then surely her crystal would activate because of the danger in the immediate area. As it was, Rebecca's crystal was still in her pouch but it was silent.

"The Shadow-being was able to move into the mind and energy of the wizard because he allowed the death of the one he loved to shatter his heart center. This trauma opened it to possession by the dark force. In addition, I witnessed the entity had entered the heart center behind your wizard, which is very unusual. That led me to believe that Shaulmar's power of protection was compromised by an external force rather than the darkness." She spoke with an assertive tone almost with a note of irritation.

"So what do you hope to accomplish now, Alison? There is no way we can go back to being friends, not in this lifetime anyway." Rebecca could feel a sense of personal power in her words, such words she would have been too meek to express before.

"There's nothing I want from you any more Rebecca. I know there was a time when I was intending to take your soul as a way to become powerful and respected amongst the dark ones, but that no longer lives inside me. All I want is to find the Rhostos; I have no idea if he is still alive. The only thing I know is we arrived, then he was nowhere to be seen." Alison was saddened at the thought of never ever seeing him again.

"I am sorry you have lost him—the pain never stops in situations like this, I lost my mom when I was young, as you know, and still carry the pain everyday. I don't know what we can do…?" Before she could finish what she was saying she felt the familiarity of the prickling sensation on her neck and shoulders, she knew fully what was coming.

"Oh, that still hurts." She bent forward and Alison moved back instinctively, a few moments passed and the green mist had manifest behind and above Rebecca.

"So that is how it's done?" Alison seemed amazed to witness the magic of the light of the universe. The Essence gathered around its bound soul in a protective way, Rebecca closed her eyes for a moment.

"Alison, the ancient Book of Secrets wants you to know something." The mist swirled higher and closer to the sorceress as she spoke. "The one you have lost—the warrior known as the Rhostos, is still alive, or was when the Essence saw were they went." She opened her eyes knowing that Alison had heard what she had said. However, Rebecca immediately dismissed it as being of no use because the Rhostos and the Dark Angel had been transported to another dimension. The girl assumed that Alison would probably have no way to find the warrior, so more than likely, she would have preferred not to know that he was still alive, and would rather think of him as lost to her forever. However, Rebecca was totally astounded at Alison's response.

"So where is he? How can I go to him?" The sorceress's heart quickened at the thought of being with the Rhostos again.

"I don't know if it's possible to go to him," Rebecca tried not to look directly at her, she hated letting people down after they have been given a morsel of hope.

"What do you mean?" Alison's eyes filled up once more, Rebecca could see she was not the person she had first met, that was very obvious for all to see.

"I don't know how to say this, the Essence said they were grappling with each other, and amid exchanges of flashes of energy and blows to each other, the Dark Angel seemed to be getting stronger and also seemed to be gaining the upper hand as he accessed the vortex that supports this sacred place. The Rhostos, according to the Essence, was losing ground, but the Essence witnessed the Rhostos touch his wristband as he grasped onto the throat of the Dark Angel just before they both disappeared." Rebecca waited for Alison to speak. The sorceress looked like she was struck down, her jaw dropped as she processed the information.

"He took the Dark Angel through the space between dimensions," she had a half smile on her face, "he took him to his domain and away from the source of power that was helping him, the vortex of light."

"Yes, I guess that's what he did." Rebecca agreed, but did not really understand a word of what the Rhostos had accomplished. The young girl did feel somewhat pleased about the fact that Alison managed to avoid feeling such heart breaking loss. Even though, her own loss was so fresh and she was, after all, only human, it would have been comforting to know that Alison was not going to side skip the pain that accompanies such trauma.

"Thank you Rebecca, I will always be indebted to you for giving me this hope that I might find the Rhostos once more." The dark sorceress was sincere, that was clear to Rebecca and made her feel good, which only made her think of our own sadness regarding her mother. The young girl couldn't allow thoughts of what her mother must be suffering through in some dark place that may never be known to her. She could not stop the emotion rising through her body that came from deep inside her, and the pain she felt about losing her mother only to find that she is captive somewhere in the darkness.

The great wizard was unaware of the pain Rebecca was experiencing; he was preoccupied with bringing the boy back to consciousness. The blow Joaquim sustained after hitting the wall, when the shadow being sent him flying across the room had caused him to be concussed. Shaulmar needed to use a powerful incantation, through the power of the vortex energy, to connect with the boy's higher self and ask that Joaquim return to this reality before any permanent damage was done.

Alison stood, and not knowing how to console Rebecca as the young girl covered her head in her hands, she decided to go over to where the wizard was attending to Joaquim.

"Rebecca needs your help. I don't know how to help her so, let me help the boy while you help Rebecca—please?" she urged the wizard hoping he would do as she asked, she showed him her crystal.

"If you hurt this boy I will *kill* you—be sure of your intentions because I make no shallow threat, I make only promises to you." Shaulmar spoke with such coldness it assured her that he had no problem in doing as he said. The wizard went to Rebecca and sat close to her. "We must be strong dear one, there are things to be done." He put his hand on her back stroking it gently. Rebecca allowed the tears to run down her cheeks she had no desire or the energy to stop them.

"I feel like I have lost my mother a second time Shaulmar." Her voice was full of deep pain, not the pain of a child who has lost her toy, but the pain only felt as an old soul was suffering.

"I know I am supposed to have answers for you, and I am given the precious task of guiding you through difficult times, but I was never prepared to lose Morghanz. I have no idea of what to tell you Rebecca, I have no clue how to find your mother, nor do I have the faintest idea as to why my power has deserted me. I'm sorry my dearest friend—I'm so sorry." The wizard hung his head and fell into the same dark, emotional abyss as the young girl.

"I know how to find her." Alison was working on the boy but she also couldn't avoid listening to Rebecca and the great wizard simultaneously. Rebecca was silent for a moment, she tried to process the words but instinctively she didn't want to trust Alison, but the words ignited hopefulness in her that she couldn't stop.

"What do you mean?" she got up and walked over to Alison wanting to believe her words, but not wanting to be tricked again either. Alison took her attention back to the boy she passed her hand across the crystal and placed it on his chest, almost immediately he stirred.

"Sis—are you—are you okay?" Joaquim's first words betrayed his real feelings for Rebecca, as he became conscious. Shaulmar and Rebecca gathered round him, they were so glad he was awake.

"Thank you." Shaulmar found himself addressing the dark sorceress, that same dark figure that imprisoned his love in a black cocoon of death. Of course, if he knew this there would be no amount of restraint that would keep him from destroying her where she stood. Alison was never going to admit to what she had done to Morghanz, to the great wizard.

The Essence was high above them at this point, spinning, observing, and staying close to its bound soul. When Rebecca was satisfied that Joaquim was okay, she wanted Alison to explain what she had said about being able to locate her mother.

"So how about it Alison? What did you mean when you said you could find my mother?"

"I didn't say I could find her, but if Draco Bastian captured her soul there is only one place she could possibly be." Alison didn't hold out much hope of Rebecca been able to get to her mother.

"Where?" Rebecca really didn't want to know the answer, because it could only be some horrible, dark, and nightmarish place somewhere in the universe.

"Let me just say this," she looked right at her—right to her heart, "there is a huge difference in me telling you where she is, and you being able to actually go there. If you still want to know I will tell you."

"Yes! Of course I want to know! *Where* is it?" Rebecca's heart sank because she knew Alison was probably right but she still wanted to know even if it meant she wouldn't be able to go there.

"The Dark One sends every captured soul to a place that resides in a dimension that belongs to the darkness and all dark forces of the universe. It is known to us as the gates of souls." The sorceress peered through the opening in her hooded cloak, her eyes searched for Rebecca's face for anything that indicated she was willing to make the attempt, or at least show signs of interest.

The sorceress had other motives for trying to entice the Prophesied One into a pact that would involve a journey together. Shaulmar looked sullen as he sat across from the boy, the wizard found himself staring at Joaquim and as he did so he imagined he was travelling back in time to a place where he was once happy. The great wizard's thoughts were filled with wonderful, recreations of events from his young life. The memories took him away from the sadness of the present, as he sat his eyes seemed to glaze over, and his face was devoid of emotion; he was gone.

"What have you got in mind Alison? I *know* you, do not forget that, and if you want to help me find my mother, then I think there may be other reasons, so *talk*!" Rebecca had grown up really fast in the last few weeks, in light of all that has happened. She was no longer the easy mark that had been her weakness in the eyes of the ones who knew who she was.

"What do you mean?" Alison continued to read Rebecca's stare, as she placed the crystal back inside its home and place of concealment in her cloak.

"Do not mistake me for the girl who you once tried to kill—you would be unhappy at the result."

Alison decided it was time to offer some more information to the bound soul in order to keep her occupied. As she spun her lies once more, she pushed her hood back off of her face and head, she was going to find the warrior no matter what she had to do, or whom ever she had to use.

"I realized how much I miss judged you-you have to believe me." Alison poured her syrupy voice onto Rebecca knowing that the compassion that flows through the girl would be too much for her to contain.

"Okay, I understand people change, but if you think you can con me again, I will not be responsible for what happens to you, is that clear?" Rebecca knew she could not harm anyone, however, she could not promise the same thing about the Essence. Just at that moment Joaquim tried to stand, he hated being inactive and made the most awful noise when he fell to the ground again. Rebecca turned quickly on hearing the commotion.

"Joaquim are you okay? You must not try to stand before you can sit brother." He felt good after hearing the concern in her voice, although he didn't expect to hear her call him brother for the first time. However, it did make him feel warm inside and made him realize that he did, in fact, finally have a family.

"Okay Sis," he said in a subdued voice as he pulled himself back on to the slab of marble where the dark sorceress had treated him.

There was silence around the room as each waited for the other to ask the next obvious question, a question that no one wanted, nor dared to let loose in the air.

"Well, are we going on this journey?" The wizard had returned. "We had better make a decision one way or the other before other dark entities arrive or Draco Bastian returns and all hell breaks."

Rebecca turned sharply to face him. "Do you mean it Shaul-mar?" The girl wanted so much to find her mom, "I *need* that so much." She choked back the rising emotions. "I don't have any idea how we can do it, but that is what I want most."

"I don't know either," he turned to the dark sorceress, "however, there is someone who does know." Alison became quite uncomfortable at that point. She wanted to string Rebecca along but not with the others in tow.

"Erm—I uh…"

"What troubles you sorceress? Do you have the way to the so called gate of souls or do you lie once more?" He moved slowly, and deliberately toward her.

"Well, uh—yes—yes of course." She stammered. Shaulmar grunted and moved back to where Rebecca stood.

"So, where do we begin?" Rebecca looked right through the dark witch.

Alison paused for a brief moment.

"It is not so much where as when." The sorceress was thinking fast while simultaneously projecting calm, deliberation. "The only path to the gate of souls is through time and dimensions." That was the end of her offering; she knew she had them now.

Rebecca turned away from her and faced Shaulmar. "What do you think? She looked at him hopefully.

"What I think is we have much to do before we travel, and the initial requirement is that we all leave this place before it collapses, I don't have the energy or desire to sustain this *creation*." He was tired of it; he didn't want to be reminded of his loss.

"We must take some things with us, some supplies and personal things." Rebecca stuttered a little as she struggled to get the words out for what she really wanted to ask. "I—I need to find Robbie and huh—see how he feels about huh—me and if he could come with us." She said pleading with him softly. After thinking and shuffling about, Shaulmar gave her a warm smile and nodded his head then spoke.

"I will collapse this sacred manifestation to its original creation. We must gather what we can use on the way through then we can be on our way before we are found". The wizard gathered his things as he spoke. "There are many beings in the universe, and I have the feeling that by now they are all aware of the arrival of the Prophesied One." His words felt heavy and ominous.

Rebecca didn't see the need to ask Joaquim, besides he was still more or less out of it, so she turned back to the dark sorceress.

"We must begin the journey. Are you sure you can handle it?" The girl knew that the sorceress understood what she was being asked.

"Yes, I can." She said calmly.

"Then let's get moving." Rebecca picked up the pouch she took from Morghanz and tying it around her waist she moved towards the stairwell. She suddenly turned sharply to them and spoke to the wizard. "Shaulmar, what are we going to do if the darkness is waiting for us outside?"

"Don't worry we will think of something if that happens." He had no clue what they would do.

All four of them headed back up the stairwell and into the corridor leading to the huge grand Hall. The wizard waved his hands in front of what was left of the main cathedral doors, as they swung open the travellers moved through the entrance way. When they were outside Shaulmar asked that they all move away to a safe distance. The great wizard took a breath and closing his eyes he punched the air with one hand while grasping his dark, smoky crystal tightly in the other holding it out in front of him.

"Crashing down to earth you must come, I don't need you further. The time has come for us to disappear as smoke in the wind."

He slowly brought his arms back to his sides and in turning to them he cried tears of pain unstoppable for the next few minutes. Shaulmar had said his final goodbye to his love, his soul mate, Morghanz.

Made in the USA
Charleston, SC
23 December 2016